Books by Tim Powers

LAST
CALL

TIM POWERS

AVON BOOKS
An Imprint of HarperCollinsPublishers

AVON BOOKS
An Imprint of HarperCollins*Publishers*
10 East 53rd Street
New York, New York 10022-5299

Copyright © 1992 by Tim Powers
ISBN-13: 978-0-380-71557-2
ISBN-10: 0-380-71557-0
www.avonbooks.com

First HarperPerennial paperback printing: December 1996
First Avon Books paperback printing: October 1993
First William Morrow hardcover printing: April 1992

Avon Trademark Reg. U.S. Pat. Off. and in Other Countries, Marca Registrada, Hecho en U.S.A.
HarperCollins® is a registered trademark of HarperCollins Publishers Inc.

Printed in the U.S.A.

10 9 8 7 6 5 4 3 2

For Gloria Batsford

With heartfelt thanks for more than a decade's worth of help and advice and great dinners and sociable friendship; may we all have many decades more.

And with thanks, too, to Chris and Theresa Arena, Mike Autrey, Beth Bailey, Louigi Baker, Jim Blaylock, Lou and Myrna Donato, Don Ellison, Mike Gaddy, Russ Galen, Keith Holmberg, Don Johnson, Mike Kelley, Dorothea Kenney, Dana Kunkel, Scott Landre, Jeff Levin, Mark Lipinski, Joe Machuga, Tim McNamara, Steve and Tammie Malk, Dennis Meyer, Phil Pace, Richard Powers, Serena Powers, Randal Robb, Betty Schlossberg, Ed Silberstang, Carlton Smith, Ed and Pat Thomas, and Marv and Carol and Rex Torrez.

PROLOGUE

1948: A CASTLE IN THE WASTELAND

In March of 1951, testifying before the Kefauver Senate Crime Investigating Committee, Virginia Hill stated that Siegel had told her the Flamingo Hotel was "upside down"—though she was able to cast no light on what he might have meant by that statement.

—COLIN LEPOVRE, *Siegel Agonistes*

And upside down in air were towers
Tolling reminiscent bells, that kept the hours
And voices singing out of empty cisterns and
    exhausted wells.

—T. S. ELIOT, *The Waste Land*

Son, I have seen the good ship sail
Keel upward, and mast downward, in the heavens,
And solid turrets topsy-turvy in air. . . .

—ALFRED, LORD TENNYSON, *Idylls of the King*

CHAPTER 1

"I'll Still Have You, Sonny Boy"

Georges Leon held his little boy's hand too tightly and stared up from under his hatbrim at the unnaturally dark noon sky.

He knew that out over the desert, visible to any motorists along the lonelier stretches of Boulder Highway, the rain would be twisting in tall, ragged funnels under the clouds; already some flooding had probably crept across the two lanes of Highway 91, islanding the Flamingo Hotel outside town. And on the other side of the earth, under his feet, was the full moon.

The Moon and the Fool, he thought desperately. Not good— but I can't stop now.

A dog was barking a block or two away, in one of these alleys or parking lots. In spite of himself, Leon thought about the dog that appeared on the Fool card in the Tarot deck and the dogs that in Greek mythology accompanied Artemis, the goddess of the moon. And of course, the picture on the Moon card generally showed rain falling. He wished he were allowed to get drunk.

"We'd better be heading for home, Scotty," he told the boy, keeping the urgency out of his voice only with some effort. Get this done, he thought.

Palm fronds rattled overhead and threw big drops down onto the pavement.

"Home?" protested Scotty. "No, you *said*—"

Guilt made Leon gruff. "You got a fancy breakfast and lunch, and you've got a pocketful of punched chips and flattened pennies." They took a few more steps along the puddled pavement toward Center Street, where they'd be turning right toward the bungalow. The wet street smelled like dry white wine. "I'll tell you what, though," he said, despising himself

3

for making an empty promise, "tonight after dinner this storm will have cleared up, and we can drive out of town with the telescope and look at the stars."

The boy sighed. "Okay," he said, trotting along to keep up with his father, his free hand rattling the defaced chips and pennies in his pocket. "But it's gonna be a full moon. That'll wash everything else out, won't it?"

God, shut up, Leon thought. "No," he said, as though the universe might be listening and might do what he said. "No, it won't change a *thing*."

Leon had wanted an excuse to stop by the Flamingo Hotel, seven miles outside of town on 91, so he had taken Scott there for breakfast.

The Flamingo was a wide three-story hotel with a fourth-floor penthouse, incongruously green against the tan desert that surrounded it. Palm trees had been trucked in to stand around the building, and this morning the sun had been glaring down from a clear sky, giving the vivid green lawn a look of defiance.

Leon had let a valet park the car, and he and Scott had walked hand in hand along the strip of pavement to the front steps that led up to the casino door.

Below the steps on the left side, behind a bush, Leon had long ago punched a hole in the stucco and scratched some symbols around it; this morning he crouched at the foot of the steps to tie his shoe, and he took a package from his coat pocket and leaned forward and pitched it into the hole.

"Another thing that might hurt you, Daddy?" Scott asked in a whisper. The boy was peering over his shoulder at the crude rayed suns and stick figures that grooved the stucco and flaked the green paint.

Leon stood up. He stared down at his son, wondering why he had ever confided this to the boy. Not that it mattered now.

"Right, Scotto," he said. "And what is it?"

"Our secret."

"Right again. You hungry?"

"As a bedbug." This had somehow become one of their bits of standard dialogue.

"Let's go."

* * *

The desert sun had been shining in through the windows, glittering off the little copper skillets the fried eggs and kippered herrings were served in. The breakfast had been "on the house," even though they weren't guests, because Leon was known to have been a business associate of Ben Siegel, the founder. Already the waitresses felt free to refer openly to the man as "Bugsy" Siegel.

That had been the first thing that had made Leon uneasy, eating at the expense of that particular dead man.

Scotty had had a good time, though, sipping a cherry-topped Coca-Cola from an Old Fashioned glass and squinting around the room with a worldly air.

"This is your place now, huh, Dad?" he'd said as they were leaving through the circular room that was the casino. Cards were turning over crisply, and dice were rolling with a muffled rattle across the green felt, but Leon didn't look at any of the random suits and numbers that were defining the moment.

None of the dealers or croupiers seemed to have heard the boy. "You don't—" Leon began.

"I know," Scotty had said in quick shame, "you don't talk about important stuff in front of the cards."

They left through the door that faced the 91, and had to wait for the car to be brought around from the other side— the side where the one window on the penthouse level made the building look like a one-eyed face gazing out across the desert.

The Emperor card, Leon thought now as he tugged Scotty along the rain-darkened Center Street sidewalk; why am I not getting any signs from *it?* The old man in profile, sitting on a throne with his legs crossed because of some injury. That *has* been my card for a year now. I can prove it by Richard, my oldest son—and soon enough I'll be able to prove it by Scotty here.

Against his will he wondered what sort of person Scotty would have grown up to be if this weren't going to happen. The boy would be twenty-one in 1964; was there a little girl in the world somewhere now who would, otherwise, one day meet him and marry him? Would she now find somebody else?

What sort of man would Scotty have grown up to be? Fat, thin, honest, crooked? Would he have inherited his father's talent for mathematics?

Leon glanced down at the boy, and wondered what Scotty found so interesting in the rain-drabbed details of this street—the lurid red and blue hieroglyphs of neon in tiny round bar windows, the wet awnings flapping in the rainy breeze, cars looming like submarines through the filtered gray light. . . .

He remembered Scotty batting at the branches of a rosebush during a brightly sunlit walk around the grounds of the Flamingo a few months ago and piping out, "Look, Daddy! Those leaves are the same color as the city of Oz!" Leon had seen that the bush's leaves were instead a dusted dark green, almost black, and for a few moments he had worried about Scotty's color perception—and then he had crouched beside the boy, head to head, and seen that the underside of each leaf was bright emerald, hidden to any passerby of more than four feet in height.

Since then Leon had paid particular attention to his son's observations. Often they were funny, like the time he pointed out that the pile of mashed potatoes on his plate looked just like Wallace Beery; but once in a while, as had happened at lunch today, he found them obscurely frightening.

After breakfast, while the sun had still been shining and these rain clouds were just billowy sails dwarfing the Spring Mountains in the west, the two of them had driven the new Buick to the Las Vegas Club downtown, where Leon held an eight-dollar-a-day job as a Blackjack dealer.

He had cashed his paycheck and taken fifty cents of it in pennies, and had got the pit boss to let Scotty have a stack of the old worn chips that the casino defaced by die-punching a hole through the centers, and then they had walked to the tracks west of the Union Pacific Depot, and Leon had shown his son how to lay pennies on the tracks so that the Los Angeles-bound trains would flatten them.

For the next hour or so they ran up to lay the bright coins on the hot steel rails, scrambled back to a safe distance to wait for a train, and then, after the spaceship-looking train had come rushing out of the station and howled past and begun to diminish in the west, tiptoed out to the track where the giant had passed and tried to find the featureless copper ovals. They were too hot to hold at first, and Leon would juggle them into his upended hat on the sand to cool off. Eventually he had said that it was time for lunch. The clouds were bigger in the west now.

They drove around, and found a new casino called the Moulin Rouge in the colored neighborhood west of the 91. Leon had not even heard that such a place was being built, and he didn't like colored people, but Scotty had been hungry and Leon had been impatient, so they had gone in. After Scotty had been told that his flattened pennies wouldn't spin the wheels of the slot machines, they went to the restaurant and ordered plates of what turned out to be a surprisingly good lobster stew.

After Scotty had eaten as much as he could of his, he shoved the sauce out to the rim of the plate; through the mess at the center peeked the harlequin figure that was apparently the Moulin Rouge's trademark.

The boy had stared at the white face for a moment, then looked up at his father and said, "The Joker."

Georges Leon had shown no expression as he followed his son's gaze to the face on the plate. The androgynous harlequin figure did resemble the standard Joker in a deck of cards, and of course he knew that the Joker was the only member of the Major Arcana figures to survive the truncation of the seventy-eight-card Tarot deck to the modern fifty-three-card playing card deck.

In previous centuries the figure had been called the Fool, and was portrayed dancing on a cliff edge, holding a stick and pursued by a dog, but the Joker and the Fool were unarguably the same Person.

A piece of lobster obscured one of the grinning figure's eyes.

"A one-eyed Joker," Scotty had added cheerfully.

Leon had hastily paid the bill and dragged his son out into the rainstorm that had swept into town while they'd been eating. They'd driven back as far as the Las Vegas Club, and then, feeling conspicuous in the big car, Leon had insisted on leaving it there and putting on their hats and walking the few blocks back through the dwindling rain to the bungalow on Bridger Avenue that was their home.

*   *   *

Scott's eighteen-year-old brother, Richard, was on the roof, scanning the nearby streets and housefronts when they walked up, and he didn't glance down when they unlocked the front door and went inside.

Leon's wife was standing in the kitchen doorway, and the smile on her thin, worn face seemed forced. "You two are home early."

Georges Leon walked past her and sat down at the kitchen table. He drummed his fingers on the Formica surface—his fingertips seemed to vibrate, as if he'd been drinking too much coffee. "It started raining," he said. "Could you get me a Coke?" He stared at his drumming hand, noting the gray hairs on the knuckles.

Donna obediently opened the refrigerator and took out a bottle and levered off the cap in the opener on the wall.

Perhaps encouraged by the drumming, or trying to dispel the tension that seemed to cramp the air in the room, Scotty ran over to where his father sat.

"Sonny Boy," Scotty said.

Georges Leon looked at his son and considered simply not doing this thing that he had planned.

For nearly twenty years Leon had worked toward the position he now held, and during all that time he had managed to see people as no more a part of himself than the numbers and statistics that he had used to get there. Only today, with this boy, had he begun to suspect the existence of cracks in his resolve.

He should have suspected the cracks earlier.

The boat trips on Lake Mead had been strategy, for instance, but he could see now that he had enjoyed the boy's enthusiasm for baiting hooks and rowing; and sharing some of his hard-learned advice about cards and dice had become, as he should have noticed, more a father sharing his skills with his son than mere cold precautions.

Donna clanked the bottle down in front of him, and he took a thoughtful sip of Coke.

Then, imitating the voice of the singer they'd seen in the lounge at the Las Vegas Club one night, he said, "'Climb up on my knee, Sonny Boy.'"

Scotty complied happily.

"*'When there are gray skies . . .'*" Leon sang.

"'What don't you mind in the least?'" recited Scotty.

"*'I don't mind the gray skies . . .'*"

"'What do I do to them?'"

"*'You make them blue . . .'*"

"'What's my name?'"

"*'Sonny Boy.'*"

"'What will friends do to you?'"

Leon wondered what friends that was supposed to refer to. He paused before singing the next line.

He could stop. Move back to the coast, go into hiding from the jacks, who would surely come looking for him; live out the remainder of his life—twenty-one more years, if he got the standard threescore and ten—as a normal man. His other son, Richard, might even still recover.

"'What will friends do to you?'" Scotty repeated.

Leon looked at the boy and realized with a dull despair that he had come, in the last five years, to love him. The lyrics seemed for a moment to hold a promise—maybe Scotty *could* make these gray skies blue. Had the Fool been holding out a last-chance offer of that?

It could have been.

But . . .

But it didn't matter. It was too late. Leon had come vastly too far, pursuing the thing whose dim shape and potential he had begun to discover in his statistical calculations all the way back in his twenties in Paris. Too many people had died; too much of himself had been invested in this. In order to change now, he would have to start all over again, old and undefended and with the deck stacked against him.

"'Friends may forsake me,'" he said, speaking the line rather than singing it. *Let them all forsake me,* he thought. *I'll still have you, Sonny Boy.*

He stood up and hoisted the boy easily onto his shoulders. "Enough of the song, Scott. You still got your money?" The boy rattled the worthless chips and pennies in his pocket. "Then let's go into the den."

"What for?" asked Donna, her hands hooked into the back pockets of her jeans.

"Man stuff," Leon told her. "Right, Scotto?"

Scott swayed happily on his father's shoulders. "Right!"

Leon crossed the room, pretended to be about to ram the boy's head into the door lintel, then at the last moment did a deep knee bend and stepped through. He did the same trick at the door to the den—provoking wild giggles from Scotty—and then lifted him down and plopped him into the leather chair that was Daddy's chair. The lamp flame flickered with the wind of it, throwing freakish shadows across the spines of the books that haphazardly filled the floor-to-ceiling shelves.

Scotty's blue eyes were wide, and Leon knew the boy was surprised to be allowed, for the first time, to sit in the chair with the cup and lance head and crown hanging on wires overhead.

"This is the *King's* chair," the boy whispered.

"That's right." Leon swallowed, and his voice was steadier when he went on: "And anybody who sits in it . . . *becomes* the King. Let's play a game of cards." He unlocked the desk and took from it a handful of gold coins and a polished wooden box the size of a Bible.

He dropped the coins onto the carpet. "Pot's not right."

Scotty dug the holed chips and flattened pennies out of his pocket and tossed them onto the floor in front of the chair. He grinned uncertainly at his father. "Pot's right."

Defaced currency against gold, Leon thought. The pot is indeed right.

Crouching in front of the boy now, Leon opened the box and spilled into his hands a deck of oversize cards. He spread them out on the carpet, covering their bets, and waved at them. "Look," he said softly. A smell like incense and hot metal filled the room.

Leon looked at the boy's face rather than at the Tarot cards. He remembered the night he had first seen a deck of this version, the suppressed Lombardy Zeroth version, in a candle-lit attic in Marseilles in 1925; and he remembered how profoundly disturbing the enigmatic pictures had been, and how his head had seemed to be full of voices, and how afterward he had forced himself not to sleep for nearly a week.

The boy's eyes narrowed, and he was breathing deeply and slowly. Awful wisdom seemed to be subtly aging the planes of his young face, and Leon tried to guess, from the changing set of his mouth, which card was under his gaze at which moment: the Fool, in this version without his characteristic dog, standing on a jigsaw-edged cliff with an expression of malevolent idiocy; Death, also standing at the wavy cliff edge, looking more like a vertically split mummy than a skeleton, and carrying a bizarrely reminiscent-of-Cupid bow; Judgment, with the King calling up naked people from a tomb; the various face cards of Cups, Wands, Swords, and Coins . . . and all with repugnantly innocent-seeming patterns of branches or flower vines or ivy in the foreground somewhere . . . and all done in the vividest golds and reds and oceanic blues. . . .

Tears glistened in Scotty's eyes. Leon had blinked away his own before gathering in the deck and beginning to shuffle.

The boy's mind was opened now, and unconnected.

"Now," said Leon huskily, "you're going to choose eight c—"

"No," interrupted Donna from the doorway.

Leon looked up angrily, then relaxed his face into wooden impassivity when he saw the little gun she held with both fists.

Two barrels, big bore, .45 probably. A derringer.

In the instant Leon had seen the gun, there had been a faint booming overhead as Richard had scrambled across the tiles on the roof, but now there was no sound from up there.

"Not him too," Donna said. She was breathing fast, and the skin was tight over her cheekbones, and her lips were white. "This is loaded with .410 bird-shot shells. I *know*, I figured it out, what you did to Richard, okay? I figure that it's too late there for him." She took a deep breath and let it out. "But you can't have Scotty too."

Check and a big raise, Leon told himself. You were too involved in your own cinch hand to watch the eyes of all the other players.

He spread his hands as if in alarmed acknowledgment of defeat . . . and then in one smooth motion he sprang sideways and swept the boy out of the chair and stood up, holding Scotty as a shield in front of his face and chest. And a devastating raise back at you, he thought. "And the kid," he said confidently. "To you."

"Call," she said, and lowered the stubby barrel and fired.

CHAPTER 2

No Smell of Roses

The blue-flaring blast deafened and dazzled her, but she saw the man and the boy fall violently forward, and the boy collided with her knees and knocked her backward against the bookcase. One of her numbed hands still clutched the little gun, and with the other she snatched Scotty up by his collar.

Leon had been hunched on his hands and knees on the blood-dappled carpet, but now he reared back, the cards a fan in his fist. His face was a colorless mask of effort, but when he spoke, it was loud.

"Look."

She looked, and he flung the cards at her.

Several hissed past her face and clattered into the book-spines behind her, but through her collar-clutching hand she felt Scotty shudder.

Then she had turned and was blundering down the hall, shouting words that she hoped conveyed the fact that she still had one shot left in the gun. By the kitchen door she snatched the car keys off the hook, and she was trying to think, trying to remember whether her Chevrolet had gas in the tank, when she heard Scotty's whimpering.

She looked down—and the ringing in her ears seemed to increase when she realized that the card attached edge-on to the boy's face was actually embedded in his right eye.

In the stretched-out second in which nothing else moved, her numbed hand tucked the gun into her pocket, reached down, and, with two fingers, tugged the card free and dropped it. It slapped the floor, face down on the linoleum.

She wrestled the door open and dragged the shock-stiffened little boy out across the chilly gravel yard to the car; she unlocked the driver's side door, muscled him in and then got in herself, pushing him along the seat. She twisted the key in the ignition at the same moment that she stomped the accelerator and yanked the wheel sideways.

The car started, and she slammed it into gear. She snapped the headlights on as the back end was whipping across the gravel, and when the gate to the road came around into the glare, she spun the wheel back to straighten the car out and then they had punched through and were on the street, having only caved in the driver's side against one of the gate's uprights.

"Okay, Scotty," she was mumbling inaudibly, "we're gonna get you help, kid, hang on. . . ."

Where? she thought. Boulder, it's got to be Boulder. There's the old Six Companies Hospital out there. Anything in town here is too close, to easy for Georges to find.

She turned right onto Fremont.

"He *is* rich," she said, blinking but keeping her eyes on the lights of traffic amid the casino neon that made a glittering rainbow of the wet street. "I was thinking of you, I swear—Christ, he *liked* you, I know he did! Richard's gone, it was too late for Richard, and I never thought he'd decide he needed more than one."

She swerved around a slow-moving station wagon, and Scotty whimpered. His head was against the far doorjamb, and he was bracing himself against the handle with one hand and covering his ruined eye with the other.

"Sorry. Boulder in fifteen minutes, I promise you, as soon as we get clear of all this. He does have loads of money, though. He only works at the Club to keep in touch with the cards—and the *waves*, he says—keep in touch with the waves, as though he's living out on the coast, trying to track the tides or something."

"There are tides here, too," the boy said quietly as the car's motion rocked him on the seat. "And the cards *are* how you track 'em."

His mother glanced at him for the first time since turning south on Fremont. Jesus, she thought, you and he *were* very damn close, weren't you? Your daddy shared a lot with you. How could he then want to erase you? Erase *you*, not your little body, of course. Your *body* was supposed to wind up crouched on the roof with Richard's, I guess—one of you watching west, the other east, so Georges can sit in his den and have a sort of three-hundred-and-sixty-degree motion-picture stereopticon.

Ahead of the Chevrolet a Packard convertible with two people in it pulled out of Seventh Street onto Fremont. "Shit," Donna muttered absently. She took her foot off the accelerator and let the engine wind down—until she glanced in the rearview mirror and was immediately certain that the pair of headlights behind her had been there for the last several blocks, matching her every lane change. There were two people in it, too.

Her stomach was suddenly empty and cold, and she closed her throat against a despairing monotone wail.

That's Bailey and somebody in the Packard, she thought, and behind us could be any pair of a dozen of the guys that work for him, commit crimes for him, worship him. There're probably cars on 91 too, east and west, to stop me if I was going to run for L.A. or Salt Lake City.

The Chevrolet was still slowing, so she gave it enough gas to stay ahead of the car behind—and then at Ninth Street she banged the gearshift into second and pushed the accelerator to the floor and threw the car into a screaming, drifting right turn. People shouted at her from the sidewalk as she fought the wheel; then the tires had taken hold and she was racing south down Ninth. She groped at the dashboard and turned off the headlights.

"I really think you'd be better off dead," she said in a shrill whisper that Scotty could not possibly have heard over the roar of the engine, "but let's see if that's all there is."

The lights of a Texaco station were looming up ahead. A glance in the rearview mirror showed her that for the moment she had lost the following car, so she hit the brakes—saw that she was going too fast to turn into the station lot—and came to a smoking, fishtailing stop at the curb just past it. Scotty had slammed into the dashboard and tumbled to the floor.

She wrenched her bent door open and jumped out, scuffling on the wet asphalt to catch her balance. The gun was in her hand, but a truck towing a boat on a trailer had pulled out of the station and was for the moment blocking her view. It ponderously turned right—it was going to pass her.

Already keening for her doomed child, she dropped the gun, leaned into the car and dragged Scotty's limp body out by the ankles. She caught only a glimpse of the bloody mask that was his face before she grabbed his belt and his collar and, with a last desperate effort that seemed to tear every tendon in her back and shoulders and legs, flung him as high up into the air as she could, as the boat behind the truck trundled past.

The boy hung in midair for a moment, his arms and legs moving weakly in the white light, and then he was gone, had fallen inside or onto the deck, was perhaps going to roll all the way across and fall off onto the street on the other side.

She let the follow-through of the throw slam her back around against the Chevrolet, and she controlled her subsequent tumble only enough so that it left her on the driver's seat. Almost without her volition, her right hand reached out and started the car.

The boat was receding steadily away. She didn't see a little body on the road.

Headlights had appeared behind her, from the direction of Fremont. She dragged her legs inside, pulled the door closed, and made a screeching first-gear U-turn, aiming her car straight at the oncoming headlights, and shifted up into second gear as soon as she could.

The headlights swerved away out of her focus, and behind her she heard squealing brakes and a sound like a very heavy door being slammed, but she didn't look back. At Fremont she downshifted and turned right, once again gunning toward Boulder, twenty-five miles away.

The knob of the stick shift was cool in her hand as she shifted up through third to fourth.

She was peaceful now, almost happy. Everything had been spent, and any moments that remained were gravy, a bonus. She rolled down the window and took deep breaths of the cool desert air.

The Chevrolet was racing out past Las Vegas Boulevard now, and all that lay ahead of her was desert . . . and, beyond any hope of reaching, the mountains and the dam and the lake.

Behind her she could see headlights approaching fast—the Packard, certainly.

That snowy Christmas in New York in 1929, she thought as the desert highway hissed by under her wheels. I was twenty-one, and Georges was thirty, a handsome, brilliant young Frenchman, fresh from the École Polytechnique and the Bourbaki Club, and he had somehow known enough about international finance to get *rich* when the Depression struck. And he wanted to have children.

How could I possibly have resisted?

She remembered glimpsing the bloody, exploded ruin the load of .410 shot had made of his groin, only a few minutes ago.

The speedometer needle was lying against the pin above 120.

Some anonymous cinder-block building was approaching fast on her right.

God, Georges, she thought as she bracketed it between her headlights, *how miserable we managed to make each other.*

Leon hung up the telephone and slumped back in the king's chair. Blood puddled hot around his buttocks and made his pants legs a clinging weight.

Okay, he was thinking monotonously, *okay, this is bad, this is very bad, but you haven't lost everything.*

He had called Abrams last. The man had sworn he'd be here within four minutes, with a couple of others who would be able to carry Leon to the car for the drive to the Southern Nevada Hospital, five miles west on Charleston Boulevard. Leon had for a moment considered calling for a ride to the hospital first, but a glance at his groin had left him no choice but to believe that his genitals were destroyed—and therefore it had been more crucial to recover Scotty, the last son he would ever beget.

You haven't lost everything.

His entire lower belly felt loose—hot and wet and broken—and now that he had hung up the telephone he had two free hands with which to clutch himself, hold himself in.

It's not everything, he told himself. *You* won't die of a mere shotgun wound, your blood is in Lake Mead and you're in Las Vegas and the Flamingo's still standing, out there on Highway 91 in the rain. You haven't lost everything.*

The Moon and the Fool. He blinked away sweat and looked at the cards scattered on the floor around the bookcases and the doorway, and he thought about the card that had left the room, wedged—the thought made him numb—wedged in Scotty's eye.

My reign is not over.

He crossed his legs; it seemed to help against the pain.

He rolled his head back and sniffed, but there was no smell of roses in the room. He was getting dizzy and weak, but at least there was no smell of roses.

His face had been inches from a flourishing rose bush, he remembered dreamily, on the night he had killed Ben Siegel. The branches and twigs had been curled and coiled across the trellis like a diagram of veins or lightning or river deltas.

Leon had stalked Siegel for nearly ten years before killing him.

The East Coast gangster lords had seemed to sense the kind of kingship that nobody had yet taken in the United States. Joseph Doto had assumed the name Joe Adonis and took pains to maintain a youthful appearance, and Abner "Longy" Zwillman had shot a rival named Leo Kaplus in the testicles rather than through the heart, and in 1938 Tony Cornero had established a gambling ship that stayed outside the three-mile limit off the coast of Santa Monica; Cornero named the ship the *Rex*, Latin for "king," and Siegel had owned fifteen percent of it. Eventually the attorney general had organized a massive bust, and slot machines, Roulette wheels, dice tables, and Blackjack tables—with all their numbers that had so passionately concerned so many gamblers—were thrown into the nullifying sea.

One night a few weeks before the bust, Leon had taken one of the little motorboats, the water taxis, out to the ship, and he had walked over as much of the deck as the public was allowed access to; from one vantage point he was able to see a man way back on the stern holding a fishing pole out over the dark water below. Leon had asked a steward who the solitary nocturnal fisherman was, and the steward had explained that it was one of the owners, a Mr. Benjamin Siegel.

One of Leon's heels slid forward now on the blood-soaked carpet, and the first pains seized his abdomen like wires tightening, and he gritted his teeth and moaned.

The longer Abrams took getting here, the more horrible the jolting drive to the hospital would be. *Where the hell are you, Abrams?*

When the pain subsided a little, he thought for just one moment about the card that was not in the room. Then he pushed his thoughts back to his past victory, his taking of the western throne.

Leon had moved west from New York to Los Angeles in 1938, bringing with him his thirty-year-old wife and his eight-year-old son, Richard; and he soon learned that Siegel had preceded him in that westward pilgrimage. After the disquieting visit to the *Rex*, Leon joined the Hillcrest Country Club in Beverly Hills, and it was there that he finally met the man.

And though Siegel had been only thirty-two, he had fairly radiated the power. Like Joe Adonis, he was anxious to keep fit and young-looking, as the king would have to be, but Siegel had seemed to know that more than shed blood and virility and posing would be necessary.

They had met in the bar, and the man who introduced them noted that they were the only two people in the room who were drinking plain soda water.

The remark had seemed to focus Siegel's attention on Leon. "George, was it?" he asked, his half-closed eyes qualifying his smile. His brown hair was oiled and combed back from his high forehead.

"Close enough," Leon said.

"You ever play cards, George?" Siegel's Brooklyn accent made "cards" sound like "cods."

"Of course," Leon had said, lowering his head over his glass so that the quickened pulse in his throat wouldn't show. "Would you be up for a game of Poker sometime?"

Siegel had stared at him then for several seconds. "No, I don't think so," he said finally. "It only bores me when Jacks keep calling my Kings."

"Maybe I'll have the Kings."

Siegel laughed. "Not if I'm the dealer—and I always am."

Leon had tried to pay for the drinks, but Siegel waved him off, telling him with a wink that his money was no good.

*   *   *

Flattened pennies and holed chips, Leon thought now.

Leon had kept track of the man.

In the summer of that year Siegel had organized a treasure-hunting expedition to Cocos Island, several hundred miles off the west coast of Costa Rica; by November he was back and denying reports that he had found there a life-size gold statue, supposedly of the Virgin.

But Leon obtained a photograph of the statue from a drunken old man called Bill Bowbeer, who had provided the original treasure map; the picture was blurred and stained, but Leon could see that the metallic figure wore a crown in the shape of a crescent moon embracing a sun disk—much more like the Egyptian goddess Isis than the Christian Mary.

Shortly after that Siegel went to Italy with the countess who had funded the treasure hunt, and a few weeks later Leon had got a letter from an associate in Milan.

One of the fifty-nine card fragments was missing from the Sforza Castle playing card collection; the informant had not known enough about the collection to be able to say which one.

Leon had bought a ticket on the next plane to Milan.

The Sforza cards had been discovered in the long-dry medieval cisterns of Sforza Castle during a renovation at the turn of the century. They had been a roughly stratified mix of eleven different incomplete decks, the top scattering of which were recent enough to have the French suits of Hearts, Clubs, Diamonds, and Spades; but the lowest were from a Tarot deck painted in 1499, and Leon was certain that the missing card would be one of these. He had catalogued them in detail in 1927, and so he was probably the only person who would be able to determine which was absent.

When he got to Milan, he found that the missing card was indeed from that oldest deck. It was the Tower card. Looking it up in the notes he'd made eleven years earlier, Leon knew that it was a nearly whole card depicting a tower being struck by lightning, with two human figures caught frozen in mid-fall along with some pieces of broken masonry.

For the next eight years Leon had been unable to guess why Siegel would have wanted that particular card.

The knocking at the front door came only seconds before Leon heard someone come in through the kitchen door, which Donna had evidently left open.

"Georges?" called a voice he recognized as that of Guillen. "Where are you?"

Leon, too weak to answer audibly, sat back and concentrated on breathing and waited for them to find him. He heard Guillen unlock the front door and let Abrams in, and then he heard them padding nervously through the living room.

At last Abrams cautiously peeked into the den. "Jesus, Georges!" he shouted, rushing to where Leon was slumped in the chair. "Jesus, they—they shot you good. But don't worry, the doctors will pull you through. Guillen! Get the guys in here damn quick!"

A few moments later half a dozen men were carrying Leon through the hall to the kitchen, with Abrams holding the door and calling tense directions. As they shuffled into the kitchen, Abrams bent to pick up the card that lay face-down on the floor.

"No," Leon rasped. "Leave it there."

Abrams drove fast, but managed to avoid any bad bumps or jolting turns. The pain was back, though, and to his humiliation Leon couldn't help letting some of it out in explosive grunts. His groin-clutching hands were slick with blood, and when once he hiked himself up to peer down at himself, his hands looked black, with glittering multicolored highlights from the passing neon.

I haven't lost everything, he reminded himself feverishly. Siegel did, but I haven't.

Leon had taken up fishing himself in 1939, out at the end of the Santa Monica Pier on moonless nights, catching big, deformed nocturnal sunfish and eating them raw right there on the weathered planking; and he grew unheard-of giant, weirdly lobed squashes in the garden of his little house at Venice Beach and burned the biggest and glossiest of them at various dams and reservoirs in Los Angeles and San Bernardino and Orange counties; and he played Poker in a hundred private games and got a reputation as a spectacularly loose, eccentric player; and he penciled a garageful of maps and graphs and charts, marking in new dots on the basis of his reading of newspapers from all over the world and his observations of the weather; and like Siegel, he had begun cultivating friendships among the wealthy aristocracy of Beverly Hills. *Pluto was also the god of wealth,* he had told himself.

And very shortly Leon had begun to see results: Siegel's position had begun to falter. He was twice arrested for the murder of a New York hoodlum named Harry Greenbaum, and in April of '41 he was arrested for having harbored the gangster Louis "Lepke" Buchalter.

Siegel proved to be able to evade these charges, but he must have been able, like a defensive king in a game of chess, to tell that he was under attack.

But before Leon could decisively topple his rival, the Japanese bombing of Pearl Harbor propelled the United States into World War II, and the frail patterns and abstract figures Leon had been coaxing from his graphs were hidden behind the purposeful directing of industry and society and the economy toward the war effort. His patterns were like ghost voices in static lost when the tuner brought in a clear signal; a few factors, such as the weather, continued to show the spontaneous subtle randomnesses that he needed, but for four years he simply worked at maintaining his seat in the game, like a Poker player folding hand after hand and hoping that the antes wouldn't eat up his bankroll.

Eventually President Truman returned from the 1945 Potsdam Conference—feverishly playing Poker with reporters, night and day, during the week-long voyage home—and by the time Truman got back to Washington he had come to the decision to drop the atomic bomb on Japan. The spotter plane for the bomb-carrying *Enola Gay* was named the *Straight Flush*.

With the war ended, Leon was able to renew his aggression.

And in 1946, again like a beleaguered chess king, Siegel had sensed the attacks, and castled.

Most people in the gambling business thought Siegel was a megalomaniac to build a grossly expensive luxury hotel and casino in the desert seven miles south of Las Vegas—but Leon, to his alarm, saw the purpose behind the castle.

Gambling had been legalized in Nevada in 1931, the same year that work was begun on Hoover Dam, and by 1935 the dam was completed, and Lake Mead, the largest man-made body of water in the world, had filled the deep valleys behind it. The level of the lake rose and fell according to schedules, reflecting the upstream supply and the downstream demand. The Flamingo, as Siegel named his hotel, was a castle in the wasteland with a lot of tamed water nearby.

And the Flamingo was almost insanely grand, with transplanted palms and thick marble walls and expensive paneling and a gigantic pool and an individual sewer line for each of its ninety-two rooms—but Leon understood that it was a totem of its founder, and therefore had to be as physically perfect as the founder.

Leon now knew why Siegel had stolen the Tower card: Based on the Tower of Babel, it symbolized foolishly prideful ambition, but it was not only a warning against such a potentially bankrupt course but also a means to it. And if it were reversed, displayed upside-down, it was somewhat qualified; the doomful aspects of it were a little more remote.

Reversed, it could permit a King to build an intimidating castle, and keep it.

And to absolutely cement his identification with the building, and cement, too, his status as the modern avatar of Dionysus and Tammuz and Attis and Osiris and the Fisher King and every other god and king who died in the winter and was reborn in the spring, Siegel had opened the hotel on the day after Christmas. It closed—"died"—two weeks later and then reopened on March 27.

Close enough to Christmas, Good Friday, and Easter.

Sagebrush-scented air cooled Leon's damp face when they opened the back of the station wagon.

"Okay, carefully now, he's been shot, and he's lost a lot of blood. Guillen, you get in the back seat and push as we pull."

Doctors in white coats were scurrying around the wheeled cart they slid him onto, but before they could move him in through the emergency room doors, Leon reached out and grabbed Abrams's sleeve. "Do you know if they've found Scotty yet?" Wherever the boy was, he was still psychically opened, still unlinked.

"No, Georges," Abrams said nervously, "but I wouldn't have heard—I left the house the minute I got your call."

"Find out," Leon said as one of the doctors broke his weak grip and began to push the gurney away, "and let me know! Find him!"

That I, too, may go and worship, he thought bitterly.

Southwest on Highway 91 the truck with the boat behind it rumbled across the desert landscape toward distant Los Angeles, the glow of the headlights superfluous under the full moon.

CHAPTER 3

Good Night. Sleep Peacefully . . .

A month later Leon sat in the passenger seat of Abrams's car as they drove—much more slowly now—through sunlit streets away from the hospital. The foothills were a dry tan color, and sprinklers threw glittering spirals of water across the artificially green lawns.

Leon was bandaged up like a diapered baby. The doctors had removed his prostate gland and two feet of his large and small intestines, and his genitals had been a shredded mess that had virtually come away from the body when the doctors scissored his pants off.

But I haven't lost everything, he told himself for the thousandth time. Siegel did, but I haven't. Even though I no longer have quite all the guts I used to.

"Holler if I jiggle you," said Abrams.

"You're driving fine," Leon said.

In his role as Fisher King, the supernatural king of the land

and its fertility, Ben Siegel had among other things cultivated a rose garden on the grounds of the Flamingo. Roses were a potent symbol of the transitory nature of life, and Siegel had thought that by keeping a tamed plot of them he could thus symbolically tame death. The flowers had eventually become routine to him, not requiring the kind of psychic attention of which, as the Fisher King, he was capable.

Leon had heard that they had bloomed wildly in June of 1947 before he had killed Siegel, throwing their red petals out across the poolside walkway and even thrusting up sprouts through the cracks between the concrete blocks.

Still living in Los Angeles, Leon had been whittling away at Siegel's remaining vulnerabilities, the aspects of his life that had not been withdrawn behind the walls of the castle in the desert.

These vulnerabilities were two: the Trans-America wire service and the woman Siegel had secretly married in the fall of '46.

Bookmaking couldn't go on without a wire service to communicate race results instantly across the country, and Siegel, as a representative of the Capone Mob, had introduced Trans-America to the American west as a rival to the previous monopoly, James Regan's Chicago-based Continental Press Service.

Trans-America had prospered, and Siegel had made a lot of money . . . until Georges Leon had visited Chicago in June of '46 and killed James Regan. The Capone Mob had quickly assumed Continental from Regan's people, and then Trans-America was superfluous. The Capone Mob expected Siegel to transfer all his clients to Continental and then fold Trans-America, but Leon managed to see to it that the order was delivered in the most arrogant terms possible. As Leon had hoped, Siegel refused to abandon his wire service, and instead told the board of directors of the Combination that they would have to buy it from him for two million dollars.

The Flamingo was already under construction, and Siegel was bucking the still-effective wartime building restrictions and material priorities. Leon had known that Siegel needed the income from Trans-America.

And Leon had managed to meet Virginia Hill, who still

frequently visited Los Angeles, where she maintained a mansion in Beverly Hills. She was ostensibly Siegel's girl friend, but Leon had seen the ring she wore, and had seen how dogs howled when she was around them, and had noticed that she stayed out at parties all night when the full moon hung in the sky, and he had guessed that she was secretly Siegel's wife.

Leon had forced himself not to let show the excitement he had felt at the possibility; like a player who tilts up the corners of his cards and sees a pat Straight Flush, he had changed nothing in his day-to-day behavior.

But if he was right about Virginia Hill, he had caught Siegel in a strategic error.

A girl friend would have been of little value, present or absent, but if the King had been foolish and sentimental enough to split his power by voluntarily taking a wife and could then be *deprived* of that corresponding part of his power—if she could be separated from him by water, a lot of it—he'd be seriously weakened.

And so Leon had conveyed to Virginia Hill the idea that Lucky Luciano intended to have Siegel killed—which was true—and that she might be able to prevent it by appealing to Luciano in person in Paris.

Hill had flown to Paris in early June of 1947.

Leon had cashed in some real estate and some favors and some threats, and arranged matters so that the Trans-America wire service showed serious problems in its books and personnel.

And late on the night of June 13 Siegel had flown from Las Vegas to Los Angeles to investigate the wire service's apparent problems.

Siegel's private plane touched down on the runway at Glendale airport at two in the morning on June 14.

Georges Leon couldn't act until the twentieth, so for several days he parked at the curb across the street from Virginia Hill's house on North Linden Drive in Beverly Hills and watched the place. As Leon had hoped, Siegel was staying in town, sleeping at Virginia Hill's mansion.

On the afternoon of the twentieth, Leon drove through the hot, palm-shaded streets of Los Angeles to a drugstore telephone booth to deliver the required final challenge.

Siegel answered the phone. "Hello?"

"Hi, Ben. Get a chance to do much fishing out there in the desert?"

After a pause, "Oh," Siegel said impatiently, "it's you."

"Right. I've just got to tell you—you know I have to—that I'm going to assume the Flamingo."

"You son of a bitch," said Siegel in a sort of tired rage. "Over my dead body you will! You haven't got the guts."

Leon had chuckled and hung up.

That night Leon knew the stars were working for him, for Siegel and three friends drove to a seaside restaurant called Jack's at the Beach. Leon followed them, and when they were leaving and thanking the manager, Leon gave a waiter ten dollars to hand Siegel a copy of the morning's *Los Angeles Times* with a note paper-clipped to it that read, *"Good night. Sleep peacefully with the Jack's compliments."* Siegel took the newspaper without glancing at it.

An hour later Leon parked his car by the curb in front of Virginia Hill's Spanish-style mansion. He switched off the engine, and it ticked and clicked like a beetle in the shadows of the dark street.

For a while he just sat in the driver's seat and watched the spotlighted, pillared house, and what he thought about more than anything else was what it had so far been like to live in only one body, to experience only what one person could live; and he tried to imagine being vitally connected to the eternal and terribly potent figures that secretly animated and drove humanity, the figures that the psychologist Carl Jung had called archetypes and that primitive peoples, in fear, had called gods.

It was impossible simply to imagine it—so he got out of the car and carried the .30–30 carbine up the sloping lawn to the rose-covered lattice that blocked the view of the living room from the street. Crickets in the shrubbery were making enough noise to cover the *snap-clank* of the first round being chambered.

The barrel of the rifle rested comfortably in one of the squares formed by the lattice, and for several minutes Leon just crouched on the seat of a wooden bench and swiveled the gunsight back and forth and gauged the layout.

Beyond the intimidatingly close glass of the living room

window, Siegel was sitting on a flower-patterned couch, reading the sports page of the very newspaper Leon had passed on to him; next to him another man was dozing with his arms crossed. The furniture of the room was rococo, all cupids and marble and statuary lamps. A little figure of Bacchus, the god of wine, stood on a grand piano, and on the wall hung a painting of a nude woman holding a wineglass.

As the window disintegrated into glittering spray, the first two shots shattered the statue and punched through the painting; Ben Siegel had started to get up, and the next two bullets tore apart his face; Leon fired the last five shots of the clip blindly, but he had the impression that at least two more had hit Siegel. The noise of the shots racketed up and down the street, but Leon had been able to hear the clinks of the ejected shells bouncing off the wooden bench he was crouched on.

Then he had run back to the car and had tossed the rifle into the back seat and had started the engine, and as he drove fast out of the neighborhood he had exulted in being able to regard what he had just done from the vantage points of twenty-two new, crystalline personalities.

It was June 20—in pre-Christian times the first day of the month-long celebration of the death of Tammuz, the Babylonian fertility god, who had reigned in a desert region where the summer sun imposed a sort of hot winter's death on the growing cycle.

There would be a new King reigning at the end of the celebration on July 20.

And out in the bleak heart of the Mojave Desert that night a sandstorm raged around the Flamingo Hotel and stripped the paint from the bodies of all the exposed cars, right down to the bare metal, and permanently frosted the windshields.

Later Leon learned that four of his nine bullets had hit his quarry, and that Siegel's right eye had been blown cleanly out of his head and into the next room.

Back home in his bungalow now, Georges Leon hobbled from room to room on crutches and watched the sleepy, hot street through the two eyes of Richard on the roof. He listened to the radio and read the newspapers and penciled marks on his charts and avoided going into the kitchen, where the dropped card still lay on the linoleum.

He had at first heard that Scotty had died with Donna in the car crash, then that the police investigation had failed to find a child's skeleton in the burned-out shell of the wrecked Chevrolet; Abrams had talked to Bailey and the other men, and he was able to figure out where Donna had got the boy out of the car, but by that time it had been hopeless to try to track any other cars that might have been driving around Ninth Street on that evening.

Advertisements and radio appeals and a police missing person report all had failed to get the boy back. And in the course of his searches and tracings, Leon had come across the disquieting fact that there was no casino called the Moulin Rouge anywhere in Las Vegas.

Frenziedly he took up hobbies—stamp and coin collecting, buying items and staring at the faces and denominations and trying to read the meanings of them. He slept only when exhaustion knocked him down, and paid no attention to the ringing of the telephone.

For hours he sat painfully on the floor of the den, inventing a new form of Poker; for he now needed another way to become a parent.

Finally one night he could ignore the issue no longer, and at midnight he crawled out of the bedroom on his hands and knees and crouched on the kitchen floor with a cigarette lighter.

The card still lay where Donna had dropped it after pulling it out of Scotty's sliced eye. For a long time in the darkness Leon sat with his trembling fingers on it.

At last he turned it over, and he ignored the wind whispering around the bungalow as he spun the flint wheel of his lighter and looked.

The card was, as he had feared, the profile figure of the Page of Cups, the equivalent in modern terms of the Jack of Hearts. A one-eyed Jack.

The wind rattling the flimsy screens was from out of the west, sighing across the Mojave Desert from Death Valley and beyond. For at least an hour Georges Leon crouched on the floor and stared in that direction, knowing that it was from that quarter of the compass that his adversary, the one-eyed jack, would one day come.

BOOK ONE

The People in Doom Town

You know, my Friends, how long since in my House
For a new Marriage I did make Carouse:
Divorced old barren Reason from my Bed,
And took the Daughter of the Vine to Spouse.
> —*The Rubáiyát of Omar Khayyám*,
> EDWARD J. FITZGERALD translation

                "Stetson!
"You who were with me in the ships at Mylae!
"That corpse you planted last year in your garden,
"Has it begun to sprout? Will it bloom this year?"
> —T. S. ELIOT, *The Waste Land*

I watched her fly away for Vegas,
I waved the plane out of sight,
Then I tried to drive home without stopping at a bar,
    but I
Didn't make it, quite.
And sitting with those blue-jeaned shadows there, that
    had
Been there all night,
I found myself shivering over my chilly drink,
Half dead of fright.
> —WILLIAM ASHBLESS

CHAPTER 4

A Real Clear Flash

Crane recoiled out of sleep, instantly grateful that the sun was shining outside.

His heart thudded in his chest like a pile driver breaking up old pavement. He knew he'd been dreaming about the game on the lake again, and that something in the real world had awakened him.

The nights were still chilly in March, and though the sun was now well up—it must have been nine or ten o'clock, at least—the can of Budweiser on the floor beside his bed was still cool. Crane popped the tab and drank half of it in one continuous series of gulps, then absently wiped a trickle of beer from the gray stubble on his chin.

The can had left a pale ring on the hardwood floor. Susan never criticized his drinking, but she didn't seem to like it in the bedroom; she'd pick up the can as casually as if it were a magazine or an ashtray and carry it out to the living room. After he noticed the habit, he had purposely set his Budweiser on the bedside table a few times, but her patient persistence had made him feel mean, and now he did it only accidentally.

The doorbell bonged, and he assumed that it had rung a few moments before, too. He levered himself up out of his side of the queen-size bed and pulled on a pair of jeans and a flannel shirt, then plodded out into the living room. Still buttoning his shirt, he opened the door; he never bothered to look through the peep-hole anymore.

His next-door neighbor Arky Mavranos was standing on the porch. "Ahoy, Pogo!" Mavranos said, waving two cans of Coors. "What *seeems* to be the *problem*?"

All this was Mavranos's standard greeting, so Crane didn't reply but just stepped outside, sat down in one of the porch chairs and accepted a beer from him. "Ah," Crane recited dutifully as he popped the cold can open and held the foaming thing to his ear, "the sound of breakfast cooking."

"Breakfast?" said Mavranos, grinning through his unkempt brown mustache. "Noon's gone—this is lunch."

Crane squinted out past the porch rail at the tower of the Fidelity Federal Savings building, silhouetted against the gray sky half a mile north on Main Street, but he couldn't focus on the flashing letters and numbers on its rooftop sign. The Norm's parking lot had enough cars in it to indicate the lunch crowd, though, and the daytime crows had replaced morning's wild parrots on the telephone lines. Mavranos was probably right.

"I brought your mail," Mavranos added, pulling a couple of envelopes out of his back pocket and dropping them onto the battered table.

Crane glanced at them. One was the long gray Bank of America envelope with the waxed paper address window— probably his statement. It was never current; if he wanted to know how much he still had in his savings account, he could just look at the slip that was spit out of the Versatel machine when it gave him his card back next time. He tossed the unopened envelope into the plastic trash can.

The other envelope was addressed in Susan's mother's handwriting.

He tossed it away even faster.

"Just junk!" he said with a broad grin, draining the beer and getting up. He opened the door and went inside, and a few moments later was back in the chair with the half can of Budweiser that he had, in spite of himself, again left on the bedroom floor.

"Wife off shopping?" asked Arky.

Off shopping, Crane thought.

Susan loved those discount stores that were as big as airplane hangars. She always came home from them with bags of things like shark-shaped plastic clips to hold your beach towel down, and comical ceramic dogs, and spring-loaded devices you screwed onto your instant coffee jar that would, when you worked a lever on top, dispense a precise teaspoonful of powdered coffee. Her purchases had become a sort of joke among the neighbors.

Crane took a deep breath and then drained the Budweiser. This looked like being another serious drinking day. "Yeah," he answered, exhaling. "Potting soil, tomato cages . . . Spring's on us, gotta get stuff in the ground."

"*She* was up early."

Crane lowered his chin and stared at his neighbor expressionlessly. After a pause he said, "Oh?"

"Sure was. I saw her out here watering the plants before the sun was even up."

Crane got dizzily to his feet and looked at the dirt in the nearest flower pot. It did look damp; .had he watered the plants himself, yesterday or the day before? He couldn't remember.

"Back in a sec," he said evenly.

He went into the house again, and walked quickly down the hall to the kitchen. The kitchen was uncomfortably warm, as it had been for thirteen weeks now; but he didn't look at the oven—just opened the refrigerator and took out a cold can of Budweiser.

His heart was pounding again. Whom had Archimedes seen on the porch? Susan, as Crane could admit if he had a fresh beer in his hand and the alcohol was beginning to blunt his thoughts, was dead. She had died of a sudden heart attack— *fibrillation*—thirteen weeks ago.

She had been dead before the hastily summoned paramedics had even come sirening and flashing and squealing up to the curb out front. The medics had clomped into the house with their metal suitcases and their smells of rubber and disinfectants and after-shave and car exhaust, and they had used some kind of electric paddles to try to shock her heart into working again, but it had been too late.

After they had taken her body away, he had noticed her cup of coffee, still hot, on the table in front of the couch she'd died on—and he had numbly realized that he would not be able to bear it if the coffee were eventually to cool off, if it were to wind up as passively tepid as some careless guest's forgotten half can of soda pop.

He had carefully carried the cup down the hall to the kitchen and put it in the stove and turned the broiler on low. And he had told the concerned neighbors that Susan had fainted, and later in the day he had explained that she was back, but resting.

She had covered for *him* often enough, calling his boss and saying he had the flu when all he really had was a touch of "inebriadiation sickness," as he had called hangovers.

In the ninety-one days since her death, he had been making excuses—"She's visiting her mother," "She's in the tub," "She's asleep," "Her boss called her in to work early today"—to explain each instance of her absence. He had been drinking instead of going to work for a while, and so by mid-afternoon or so he often half believed the excuses himself, and when he left the house, he'd often find himself pausing before he locked the front door behind him, unthinkingly waiting for her to catch up, imagining her fumbling with her purse or giving her hair a couple of final brush strokes.

He had not looked in the stove, for he knew he wouldn't be able to stand the sight of the cup cooked dry.

This was only his third beer for today, and it was already after noon, so he took a deep gulp.

Whom had Archimedes seen? "Before the sun was even up"—Crane had been asleep then, dreaming again about that long-ago game on the lake. Had the dream conjured up some frail ghost of Susan?

Or could the house itself generate some replica of her?

At this moment, as he stood swaying in the middle of the kitchen, it didn't strike him as completely impossible—or at least not *inconceivable*. Her personality was certainly imprinted on every room. Crane's foster father had quitclaimed the house to him in 1969, ten years before Susan had moved in, but neither the young Crane nor his foster father before that had seen a table as anything more than a thing to stack stuff on, nor any sort of sturdy chair as being preferable to another; pictures on the walls had just been snapshots or pages scissored from art books, thumbtacked to the drywall.

Now there were curtains and carpets and unmottled walls and refinished bookcases that didn't look as though they'd been bought in thrift stores—though in fact most of them had been.

He sniffed the warm kitchen air, which still seemed to carry the scent of coffee. "Susan?" he whispered.

There was a faint rustling from down the hall, probably in the bedroom.

He jumped and lost his footing and sat down heavily on the floor, and cold beer splashed out onto the tiles. "Nothing," he said softly, not daring to believe that he was talking to anyone besides himself. "I'm cleaning it up." He bent forward and wiped up the foamy drops with his flannel-sleeved forearm.

He knew ghosts were impossible—but lately a lot of impossible things had seemed to happen to him.

On a rainy midnight recently he had been sitting in his chair in the living-room corner—he could never sleep on rainy nights—and he'd been absently staring across the room at the dead philodendron hanging limp over the rim of its pot; and suddenly he had lost all sense of depth and scale—or, more precisely, he had seen that distance and size were illusions. Behind the apparent diversities that distinguished plant tendrils from things like river deltas and veins and electric arcs, there were, dimly perceptible in the fog of true randomness, shapes that stood constant, shapes that made up the invisible and impalpable skeleton of the universe.

He had been holding a glass of scotch, and he took a deep gulp—and the whisky seemed to become a whirlpool in him, sucking him down into some kind of well that was no more physical than the abstractable *shape* of the philodendron had been; and then the scope widened and his individuality was gone, and he knew, because knowing was part of being in this place, that this was the level everyone shared, the very deep and broad pool—the common water table—that extended beneath all the individual wells that were human minds.

There were universal, animating *shapes* down here, too, far away in the deepest regions—vast figures as eternal-but-alive as Satan entombed in the ice in Dante's *Inferno*, and they were ritualistically changing their relationships to one another, like planets moving around the sun, in a dance that had been old long before the early hominids had found things to fear in the patterns of stars and the moon in the night sky.

And then Crane was nothing but a wave of horror rushing away, toward the comfort of close boundaries, up toward the bright, active glow that was consciousness.

And somehow when he surfaced, he had found himself in a blue-lit restaurant, a forkful of fettucine Alfredo halfway to his mouth. Smells of garlic and wine rode the coldly air-conditioned breeze, and someone was languidly playing "The Way We Were" on a piano. Something was wrong with the set of his body—he looked down and saw that he had female breasts.

He felt his mouth open and say, in an old woman's voice, "Wow, one of them's ripe—I'm getting a real clear flash from him."

I came up through the wrong well, he thought, and forced himself away, back down into the blackness—and when he was once more aware of his surroundings, he was in his own living room again, with the rain thumping against the dark window and scotch spilled all down his shirt.

And only a few days ago he had been sitting on the front porch with Mavranos, and Arky had waved his beer can at all the Hondas and Toyotas driving busily up Main Street. "Suits," Arky had said, "going to offices. Ain't you glad we don't have to wake up to alarm clocks and scoot off to shuffle papers all day?"

Crane had nodded drunkenly. "*Dei bene fecerunt inopis me pusilli,*" he had said, "*quodque fecerunt animi.*"

Mavranos had stared at him. "What *seeems* to be the *problem*?"

"Hmm?"

"What did you say, just then?"

"Uh . . . I said, 'The gods did well when they made me lacking in ideas and in spirit.'"

"I didn't know you spoke Latin. That was Latin, wasn't it?"

Crane had taken a deep sip of beer to quell a moment of panic. "Oh. Sure. A little. You know, Catholic schools and all."

Actually he had never been a Catholic, and knew no Latin beyond legal terms picked up from mystery novels. And what he'd said didn't sound like any part of the Catholic Mass he'd ever heard about.

Sitting on the kitchen floor now, he put the beer down and wondered if he was simply going insane—and if it made any difference.

He thought about going into the bedroom.

What if there's some form of her in there, lying on the bed?

The thought both frightened and excited him. Not yet, he decided—that might be like opening an oven door before a soufflé is done. The house probably needs time to exude all of her accumulated essence. Fossils need time to form.

He struggled wearily to his feet and brushed the gray hair back from his forehead. And if it's not *quite* her, he thought, I won't mind. Just so it's close enough to fool a drunk.

On the oven-hot sidewalk of Las Vegas Boulevard, just across the highway from the fountains and broad colonnade of Caesars Palace, Betsy Reculver paused and sniffed the desert air. The wrinkles in her cheeks and temples deepened as she narrowed her eyes.

The very old man walking beside her kept hobbling along, and she reached out and caught his sleeve. "Halt your ass a sec, Doctor," she said loudly. Several brightly dressed tourist women stared at her as they walked rapidly past.

The old man who was known as Doctor Leaky had apparently not heard. For a couple of seconds he tried to continue walking, then seemed to grasp the fact that he was being impeded by something. His bald, spotty head slowly turned around on his corded neck, and his eyes widened as if in vast astonishment when he saw that Betsy had taken hold of his sleeve.

"Hah?" he said hoarsely. "Hah?" He was wearing an expensive gray suit, but somehow he always tugged the pants up too high. Right now the silver belt buckle was up around his solar plexus. And of course he could never manage to lift his slack lower jaw and close his mouth.

"Can't you smell it anymore, you worthless old jug? *Sniff.*" She inhaled deeply.

"It's them!" exclaimed Doctor Leaky in his shrill, birdy voice.

She looked at him hopefully, but he was pointing at several life-size painted statues of men in togas under the Caesars Palace sign across the street. A tourist had wedged a Bic lighter into the outstretched hand of one of them and was having his picture taken leaning close to it with a cigarette in his mouth.

"No, it's not them." Betsy shook her head. "Come on."

A few steps further up the sidewalk, when they were passing the west-facing Mississippi-showboat facade of the Holiday Casino, Doctor Leaky again became excited. "It's them!" he squeaked, pointing.

Statues in nineteenth-century dress stood on the deck of the boatlike structure, and in the fenced-off lagoon between the sidewalk and the building floated a moored raft with two Huck Finn-like statues on it. A red sign on the coping read: DANGEROUS CHEMICALS—KEEP OUT OF WATER.

"You moron," Betsy said.

Doctor Leaky giggled. Betsy noticed that a dark stain was spreading across the crotch of his suit pants.

"Oh, fine," she said. "God, why do I even keep you around?" In the middle of the sidewalk crowd she raised her hand, and a gray Jaguar XJ–6 pulled up and double-parked in the street.

She led the old man over the curb and across the pavement to the rear door. The driver, an obese bald man in a woolen Armani suit, had got out and was holding the door open. "My corpse pissed its pants, Vaughan," she told the fat man. "I guess we're going home."

"Okay, Betsy." The fat man took Doctor Leaky's forearm impersonally.

"It's them!" Doctor Leaky piped again.

Betsy sniffed the air again. The resonance was still on the hot breeze. "Who, Doctor?" she asked with weary patience and still a little hope.

"The people in Doom Town—the lady in the car, and the lady in the shelter in the basement, and all the rest of them. Those kids."

She realized that he was talking about the simulated town that had been built in the desert near Yucca Flats when the government had been testing the atom bomb in the early fifties, and false suns had seemed to rise instantly in the night sky beyond the Horseshoe Club and the Golden Nugget. To make it all more realistic, the Army had put mannequins in the houses and in the cars at the test site. Betsy could remember having gone out and looked at the fake city, which had been known to the locals as Doom Town.

"No, Doctor, get in the car, it's not them. Those were all fake people."

Doctor Leaky laboriously lifted one foot into the car. "I *know* that," he said, nodding with ponderous dignity. "The *problem* is that they weren't a realistic enough. . . ."

"Unlike the plaster boys in front of Caesars, sure. Get in the car."

"As an *offering*, a *sacrifice*, they weren't realistic enough," the old man quavered. "The cards weren't fooled."

Vaughan leaned forward to help Doctor Leaky get the rest of the way into the car. For a moment Betsy could see the SIG 9-millimeter semi-automatic pistol Vaughan wore in a shoulder holster under his coat.

Before getting into the car herself, she lifted her face into the breeze. Yes, at least one of the fish was grown to nearly keeping size out there. Maybe it was the fellow who had swum up into her mind at the Dunes the other night. I wonder, she thought, who drink is to *him*.

The cycle took twenty years, but they did eventually ripen. Somebody's out there having a bad time right now.

Come Holy Saturday, the day before Easter, there would be another resurrection.

CHAPTER 5

Chasing the White Line

Crane got to his feet and carried a fresh beer out onto the porch. "What?" he said.

"I don't mean to be readin' your mail, Pogo," said Mavranos, "but you're gonna lose your house if you don't pay these people." He was holding out an unfolded sheet of paper with typing and numbers on it. The long gray envelope lay torn open on the table.

"Who's that? The bank?"

"Right. They're talkin' foreclosure." Mavranos was frowning. "You'd better pay 'em. I don't want to take my chances

on a new neighbor who might object to a beery bum living next
door." He leaned forward, and Crane could tell he was serious,
for he used his Christian name. "Scott," Mavranos said clearly,
"this is no joke. Get a lawyer, homestead the place, file chapter
thirteen bankruptcy—but you gotta do *something*."

Scott Crane held the paper up to his good eye and tried to
make sense of it. He couldn't let himself lose the house, not
now that it seemed Susan's ghost was here.

"I guess I've got to get back in business," he mumbled.

Arky blinked at him. "Are you still working at the restaurant?"

"I don't think so. They've called me a few times, but I
haven't been in there . . . in weeks. No, I think that's gone.
I've got to . . . get back into my *old* business."

"Which is what? It better get you a paycheck quick—and a
big one."

"If it works, it does that. I quit doing it . . . eight, nine years
ago. When I, when I married Susan, and started at the Villa.
She never said anything, but I could tell it was time to get into
something else. Yeah, that'll work, that'll work."

"So what *is* it? These people want their money yesterday."

Scott Crane had spilled some beer on his pants, and he
rubbed at it ineffectually. "Oh, I—didn't I ever tell you?—
I used to be a Poker player."

"You should have seen 'em tonight," he had told Susan at
three o'clock one morning as he pulled wads of twenty-dollar
bills from his pants pocket. *"They were all quiet and grouchy,
'cause they didn't have any crank, and they kept looking up,
real wide-eyed, every time they heard a car door slam, 'cause
a friend who drives a tow truck had said he'd bring some by if
he got a call to anywhere near the game. I could bluff 'em out
any time with a five-dollar raise—they were having a terrible
time, asking the guy whose house it was if he was sure he
didn't have any old mirrors to lick, and even thinking about
grinding up some of my NoDoz and snorting that. Finally
their friend did knock on the door and gave 'em a bindle, this
little bitty folded bit of paper with about a quarter teaspoon of
crystal meth in it, and then they were all happy and laughing
and tapping the powder out on a mirror and scraping it into
lines with a razor blade and then snorting it up through a*

little metal tube. Sudden cheer, yukking it up, you know? And suddenly they'd stay with any hand, and call any raise, and not give a damn if they lost. It was great. But then one of 'em's eyes go wide, you know, like this—and he gets up and runs for the bathroom. And a minute later all the rest of 'em are bowleggedying around in the hall like Quasimodo, banging on the bathroom door and cussing the guy in there. It turns out the crank was cut with some kind of baby laxative."

Susan laughed, but was sitting up in bed and frowning as he took off his pants and shirt. "I don't mean to be critical, Scott," she said, "but these people sound like idiots."

"They are idiots, honey," he said, pulling back the covers and getting into his side of the bed. "It's not profitable to play Poker with geniuses." He reached up and turned out the light.

"But these are the people you . . . look for, and hang around with when you've found them," she said quietly in the darkness. "These are the people who you, what, do your life's work with . . . or at least who you do it to, or upon. You know what I'm saying? Aren't there any Poker players you admire?"

"Sure there are—but I'm not good enough to play with them and win, and I've got a living to make. And I admired my foster dad, but since he took off, I haven't found anybody to partner up with."

"It must be weird to look for people dumber than you, and avoid people as smart or smarter."

"Keeps you and me in groceries," he had said shortly.

Crane left Mavranos on the porch and went back inside.

For a couple of hours he managed to lose himself in the recipes and advice columns and personality quizzes in a stack of old issues of *Woman's World* and *Better Homes and Gardens*, and he drank his beers slowly and set his cans down only on coasters. Then he watched television.

When the house had darkened enough so that he had to get up and turn on the lights, he reluctantly made coffee, then went into the bathroom to shave and take a shower. The shades in the living room were down, so a few minutes later he walked right from the shower to the chair by the telephone.

*   *   *

Today was Thursday. That was good; one of the most endur-
ing mid-level red-spot games he had ever instituted had been
an L.A. area Thursday night game. He pulled out the Orange
County and Los Angeles white pages phone books and tried
to remember the names of some of the people who had been
the steadiest players a decade ago.

He found a name: Budge, Ed Budge, still living on Beverly
in Whittier. Must be sixty by now. He dialed the number.

"Hello?"

"Ed, this is Scott Smith. Scarecrow Smith, remember?"

"Jesus, Scarecrow Smith! What have you been doing? How's
Ozzie?"

"I don't know, man, I haven't seen him in twenty years.
I—"

"And he had another kid he used to talk about. What was
her name?"

"Diana. I don't know, I last talked to her in '75 or so,
just briefly on the phone. I dreamed—I mean, I heard she
got married." Crane took a sip of his third consecutive cup
of coffee and wished he would sober up faster.

He remembered the call from Diana. He had been scuba
diving in Morro Bay and had managed to fire his three-barbed
spear into his own ankle, and the telephone had been ringing when he got home from Hoag Memorial Hospital the
next day. She had refused to tell him where she was, or
where Ozzie was, but she had been upset, and relieved to
hear that he was all right. She couldn't have been more than
fifteen then. Three years later he had dreamed of her in a
wedding.

There had been no contact since. Apparently neither of them
had been seriously hurt, physically at least, in the last fifteen
years—or else their psychic link had withered away.

"So," Crane said now, "is the game still going?"

"I don't know, Scott, I quit playing a few years ago. One
day I figured out I was bleeding away ten grand a year in that
damn game."

Crane suppressed a sigh. If Crane had still been the moti-
vating force of the game, Ed would never have quit. Crane
knew how to baby valuable losers along—flatter their winning
plays, never take full advantage of their weaknesses, make the

game seem more social than financial—so that they kept coming back; just as he knew how to repel good, winning players by criticizing their Poker etiquette and refusing to lend them money and trying to upset them, and encouraging the other players to do the same.

"Oh," Crane said. "Well, do you keep in touch with any of the guys?"

"Keep in touch? Outside the *game*? Scott, do you remember the plain old *breakfasts*?"

This time Crane did sigh. Sometimes the game had gone on for eighteen hours or more, and the players had taken a break to eat at some local coffee shop at dawn; and the fractured, desultory table-talk had made it stiflingly clear that none of them had anything in common with one another besides the game.

"Okay, Ed. Have a nice life."

He hung up and looked through the phone books for another name.

This was a solid game, he thought. *It has to be still spinning out there. Old Ozzie taught me how to build 'em to last.*

His foster father had been Oliver Crane. Using the name Ozzie Smith, the old man had been one of the country's respectable mid-level Poker players, from the 1930s through the 1960s. He had never quite been up there with the superstars like Moss and Brunson and "Amarillo Slim" Preston, but he had known them and played with them.

Ozzie had explained to Scott Crane that a good Poker game can have a life of its own, like a slow-motion hurricane, and he had shown him how to start them and vitalize them, all around the country, so that, like reserve bank accounts, they'd be there if you should someday need one of them. "They're like that great red spot on the planet Jupiter," the old man had said. "Just a lot of whirling gas, but always there."

If Ozzie were even still alive, he'd be . . . eighty-two now. Crane had no way of getting in touch with him. Ozzie had made sure of that.

Jube Kelley was in the book, living in Hawthorne now. Crane dialed the number.

"Jube? This is Scott Smith, Scarecrow Smith. Listen, is the game still going?"

"Hey, Scott! The game? Sure, you can't kill a game like that. I only go once in a while now, but they're doing it at

Chick's house now. This is Thursday, right? They'll be there tonight."

"Chick's house. That's on Washington, in Venice?"

"Right," said Sam. "Between the old canals and the Marina Del Rey basins."

Crane was frowning, and he wondered why he was uneasy. . . . He realized that he wasn't looking forward to being that close to, that *surrounded* by, the ocean; and going so far west seemed . . . mildly difficult, like pressing the positive poles of two magnets together. Why couldn't they have moved the game east?

"You still there, Scarecrow?"

"Yeah. What stakes are they playing these days?"

"Ten and twenty, last I heard."

Perfect. "Well, I gotta run, Jube. Thanks."

Crane hung up and walked slowly into the bedroom. The cool evening wind sighed in at the window, and he saw no ghost.

He relaxed and let out an unwittingly held breath, not sure whether he was disappointed or not.

He was still damp from the shower, but he got dressed in a fresh pair of jeans and old sneakers and another flannel shirt. He tucked a lighter and three unopened packs of Marlboros into his pockets and picked up the Versatel card; he could draw three hundred with it, and he had another forty or so on the bookshelf. Not lavish, but he ought to be able to make it do. Play the first hand noticeably loose, then tighten up for a while.

And the car keys are in the living room, he thought as he started out the bedroom door—and then he paused.

If you bring a machine, you'll never need it, Ozzie had always told him. *Like a fire extinguisher in a car. The day you don't bring it is the day you'll need it.*

Not, Crane thought now, *not* in a ten and twenty game at Chick's! He laughed self-consciously and stepped into the hall, then stopped again.

He shrugged and went back to the dresser by the bed. *This isn't the time to ignore the old man's advice,* he thought. He pulled open the top drawer and dug behind the socks and old envelopes full of photographs until he found the blocky stainless steel Smith & Wesson .357 revolver.

What the hell, he thought, at least you're fairly sober.

He flipped out the cylinder. All six chambers were still loaded, and he pushed up the ejection-rod to get one out. 125-grain hollow-point cartridges, as he remembered. He let it fall back in and snapped the gun shut again and tucked it into his belt, hearing the cartridges rattle faintly in the chambers.

When he opened the front door, he paused.

"I might be a little late," he called to the empty house.

He stopped at a nearby 7-Eleven store for hero sandwiches, a couple of twelve-packs of beer, a box of No Doz and a dozen decks of cards, and then he got on the freeway.

Back to chasing the white line, he thought as the lane markings of the 5 Freeway flew past like fireflies under the tires of his old Ford. I can remember a hundred, a thousand nights like this, driving with Ozzie along the 66 and the 20 and the 40, through Arizona and New Mexico and Texas and Oklahoma. Always a game behind us and a game ahead of us.

It had been what Ozzie called a semi-retired life. They traveled and played during the three months of spring, and then lived off their winnings in the Santa Ana house during the other three seasons.

Scott had been five years old when Ozzie had found him, in the back of a boat on a trailer in a Los Angeles parking lot. Apparently he had been a messed-up little kid—one eye split open and dried blood all over his face. Ozzie had talked to him for a few minutes and had then driven him in his old truck to a doctor who owed Ozzie a lot of money.

Old Dr. Malk had fitted up young Scott with his first glass eye. The eyes were still real glass in the forties, and for kids they were round, like big marbles, to fill the orbit and make sure the skull grew correctly. The next day Ozzie had taken the boy home to the house in Santa Ana, and had told the neighbors that Scott was his cousin's illegitimate child and that he was adopting him.

Ozzie had been about forty then, in '48. He had quickly begun teaching Scott all about Poker, but he had never let the boy play with anyone else, and never for real money, until the summer of '59, when Scott was sixteen, and they went off on one of the annual trips together.

"You never play for money at home," Ozzie had said. "You don't want the cards to know where you live."

Scott had become known as Scarecrow Smith, because before about 1980 doctors couldn't effectively attach glass eyes to eye muscles, and so it was more natural-looking for him to turn his whole head to look at something than to have only one eye move to the side; to some players this had made his eyes seem painted on and his neck appear unnaturally loose. And "Scarecrow" had fitted with his adopted father's nickname: whenever Oliver Crane was asked where he lived, he had always just said, "Oz."

In fact, Ozzie had not let anyone in the Poker world know where he lived. He used the name Smith when he played and insisted that Scott do the same, and he always kept his car registered to a post office box.

"You don't want to take a chance on your work following you home," he'd said. To make that even less likely, he had always bought new tires and had his Studebaker tuned up before setting out, and he never went to a game without a full tank of gas. And there was always a twelve-gauge pump shotgun under a blanket on the back seat to supplement the pistol in his belt.

And he had made sure Scott understood when it was that you had to fold out of a game.

That had been the advice Scott had ignored in the game on the lake in '69.

"If the drink in your glass starts to sit at an angle that ain't quite level, or if the cigarette smoke starts to crowd in over the cards and fall there, or if plants in the room suddenly start to wilt, or if the air is suddenly dry and hot in your throat, smelling like sun-hot rock, fold out. You don't know what you might be buying or selling come the showdown."

By the end of the spring of 1969 Ozzie had been sixty or so, and Scott had been twenty-six.

Both of them had been wanting to get back home to Santa Ana—Scott had a girl friend whom he hadn't seen in three months, and Ozzie missed his other foster child, Diana, who was nine years old and staying with a neighbor woman—but they had decided to hit Las Vegas before once again burning on home across the Mojave to southern California.

They had got in on a Five-Stud game that started in the Horseshoe on Fremont Street in the evening, and at dawn they had moved it upstairs to one of the rooms, and in the middle of the afternoon, when all but Ozzie and Scott and a pudgy businessman called Newt had been eliminated, they had declared a sleep-and-food break.

"You know," Newt had said slowly, almost reluctantly, as he finally unknotted his tie, "there's a game on a houseboat on Lake Mead tonight." Newt had lost more than ten thousand dollars.

Ozzie had shaken his head. "I never gamble on water." He tucked a wad of bills into his jacket pocket. He had increased his roll from about twelve to about twenty-four thousand in the past twenty hours. "Even when they had the boats out there in the ocean, three miles off Santa Monica, I never went."

Scott Crane was down. He had had ten thousand when they'd driven into Las Vegas, and he had about seven and a half now, and he knew Ozzie was ready to declare the season finished and start for home.

"What kind of game?" Scott had asked.

"Well, it's odd." Newt stood up and walked to the window. "This guy's name is Ricky Leroy, and ordinarily he's one of the best Poker players in town." The stout young businessman kept his back to them as he talked. "But for the last two or three days he's been playing this game he calls Assumption—weird game with a weird deck, all pictures—and he's losing. And he doesn't seem to mind."

"Assumption," said Ozzie thoughtfully. "Twenty years ago a guy was hosting a game of that out on a boat on Lake Mead. Different guy—George something. He lost a lot, too, I heard."

"My luck's gone here," Newt said, turning around to face them. "I'm going to drive out there tonight. If you want to come, I'll be standing under the million-dollar-display Horseshoe at eight."

"You may as well just go," Ozzie told him. "This was our last game of the season; we're going to sleep twelve hours and then drive home."

Newt had shrugged. "Well, I'll be there just in case."

Back in their own room at the Mint Hotel, Ozzie had at first been unable to believe that Scott wasn't kidding when he said he wanted to go meet Newt and get into the game on the lake.

The old man had kicked off his polished black shoes and lain down on one of the beds, and he was laughing with his eyes closed. "Sure, Scott—on water, *tamed* water, with a guy that always pays for hands, and playing with what obviously is a *Tarot* deck, for God's sake. Shit, you'd win a few signifying hands, and a month later you'd find out you've got cancer and you're getting arrested for crimes you never heard of and you can't get it up anymore. And then one day you'd walk out to the mailbox and find your goddamn *head* in there."

Scott was holding a glass of beer he'd picked up on the way to the elevator, and now he took a long sip of it.

Most Poker players had superstitions, and he had always conformed to Ozzie's, out of respect for the old man, even when it had meant folding a cinch hand just because some cigarette smoke was moving in ways the old man didn't like or someone had kicked the table and the drinks were wobbling.

Ozzie had folded some good hands, too, of course—hundreds, probably, in his forty years of professional play. But Ozzie could *afford* to: He had made a lot of money over the years, and though he rarely played the very-high-stakes games, he was regarded as an equal by the best players in the country.

And right now he had twenty-four thousand dollars rolled up tight in the hollow handles of his shaving brush and shoehorn and coffeepot.

Scott had less than eight thousand, and he was going home to car payments and a girl friend who liked steak and lobster and first-growth Bordeaux wines.

And he had heard that next year Benny Binion, the owner of the Horseshoe, was going to host a World Series of Poker, with all the best Poker players converging there to determine who was the very best. Scott could remember having met old Binion once, at a restaurant called Louigi's on Las Vegas Boulevard. Scott had been only three or four, staying out late with his long-lost real father, but he remembered now that Binion had ordered the house's best steak and had then shaken ketchup onto it.

He was sure he could win this competition . . . if he could come into town with enough money to spread a good-size net.

"I've *got* to go, Oz. My roll's short, and the season's over."

"*Your* roll?" The grin was fading from Ozzie's face as he raised his head to look at Scott. "What you've got in your pocket is a hair less than twenty-five percent of *our* roll, yours and mine and Diana's. We've got thirty-one and a half, and if that ain't lavish to live a year on, I don't—"

"I've got to go, Oz."

Ozzie now wearily forced himself back up onto his feet. His gray hair was disarranged, and he needed a shave. "Scott, it's *on water*. It's *Tarot cards*. You want to play, take our money to any of the hundred games in town here. But you *can't* go play *there*."

You can't go play there, thought Scott, as the beer amplified his own massive fatigue. That's what you say to a kid who wants to ride his tricycle to a park where there might be bad boys.

I'm twenty-six, and I'm a damn good player on my own—not just as *Ozzie's kid*.

The cross-cut wooden grip of his .38 revolver was poking up out of the dirty shirts in the open suitcase on the bed. He pulled the gun free and shoved it into his jacket pocket.

"I'm going," he said, and went to the door and pulled it open and strode rapidly down the hall toward the door to the stairwell.

And he was crying by the time he stepped out of the cool darkness of the casino into the brassy afternoon sunlight, because for at least several floors he had heard Ozzie shuffling in his stocking feet down the stairs behind him, calling and pleading weakly in his frail voice as he forced his exhausted old body to try to catch up with his adopted son.

CHAPTER 6

We're Now Thirteen

"Assumption," Newt said.

He was talking quickly, hunched over the steering wheel of his Cadillac as the hot dark desert swept past on either side. "This guy Leroy won't play it unless there are twelve other people at the table with him. A hundred dollars ante. Everybody's dealt two down cards and one up card, and then there's a round of betting, two hundred a bet, and then one more up card and another round at two hundred."

Scott popped the cap off a fresh bottle of beer. "That's fifty-two cards," he said blurrily. "You're out of cards, except maybe for a Joker."

"Nah, he won't play it with a Joker, and actually there's four more cards left, 'cause there's an extra face card in each suit, the Knight. And the suits are different, they're Sticks and Cups and Coins and Swords. But anyway, no more cards are dealt."

The lights of the bars and brothels of Formyle swept past. The Cadillac was now four miles out of Las Vegas and must, Scott thought, be doing a hundred by now.

"What happens then," Newt went on, "is that each four-card hand in turn goes up for bid. The term is 'the mating.' Say you've got two Kings down and a Three and something up, and you see a hand with a King and a Three showing; well, you'd want to bid on that hand, 'cause if you got it, you'd have a Full Boat in your eight-card hand—or, if one of his down cards turned out to be the case King, you'd find yourself with four Kings, get it? When you put the two hands together, yours and the one you bought, they say that the resulting eight-card hand has been *conceived*, rather than completed or something. With the bidding you usually wind up paying a guy, for his hand, a hundred or so more than what he's got in the pot. A lot of guys never mean to stay for the showdown, they just want to sell their hands at the bid, at the mating. And when it gets down to the last three guys who haven't bought a hand or sold theirs, the competition gets hot 'cause nobody wants to be left out in the cold holding an unsold and unplayable—unconceivable—four-card hand."

Scott nodded, staring out through the dusty windshield at the dim bulk of the McCullough Range denting the dark sky ahead. "So there might be as many as . . . six guys in at the showdown."

"Right. And even if you're out of the hand, you're still watching 'cause you've still got an investment in the hand you sold your four cards into. You're called a parent of the hand, and if it wins, you get ten percent of the pot. That's another reason a lot of guys just want to sell their hands and get out: they can clear a fair profit at the mating and then still have a one-in-six chance of getting a tenth of a pretty sizable pot."

Scott Crane drained his beer and pitched the bottle out the open window into the gathering night. "So have you played it yet?"

"Sure I've played it," said Newt, apparently angry. "Would I bring guys to it if I hadn't played it? And I've played Poker with Leroy a lot."

Scott was suddenly sure that Newt had lost a lot, too, to Leroy, and owed him at least money. For just a moment he considered making Newt pull over to the shoulder and getting out of the car and hitch-hiking back to the Mint.

Lightning made silent jagged patterns over the mountains, like the momentarily incandescing roots of some vast tree that carried the stars as buds.

"And then there's the Assumption option," said Newt as he leaned over the big wheel and tugged it back and forth, sounding as tired as Scott felt. "If you're the absentee parent of the winning hand, you're free to put up an amount of your own money equal to the amount in the pot, and then have the deck shuffled, and cut the cards for the whole thing."

Scott frowned, trying to make his sluggish mind work. "But you'd already be getting a tenth of the pot. Why risk . . . fifty-five percent to win forty-five, on a fifty-fifty chance?"

Scott couldn't tell if Newt sighed or if the whisper was just the tires on the Boulder Highway pavement. "I don't know, man, but Leroy is a sucker for that bet."

There were a lot of cars parked in the Boulder Basin marina lot, and the white houseboat at the dock was big and wide, and lit brightly enough to dim the emerging stars. The moon was dark—a day short of the newest sliver.

Gravel crunched underfoot as they walked from the car toward the lake and the boat, and the wind from up the distant twistings of the Colorado River fluttered Scott's sweat-spiky hair.

A figure who could only be their host stood on the lighted deck. He was a big, tanned man in a white silk suit; by his lined face Scott guessed him to be around forty, but his hair was brown and full with not a thread of gray, and at least in this light it didn't look like a toupee. A big gold sun disk hung on a chain around his neck.

"Here's a young man wanting to play, Mr. Leroy," said Newt as he led Scott up the ramp to the teakwood deck. "Scarecrow Smith, this is Ricky Leroy."

When Leroy smiled at Scott, it was absently, with the politeness of a distracted host, but Scott opened his mouth to ask the man *How've-you-been?*, for he was unthinkingly sure that he had once known him well. Leroy caught Scott's look of recognition and raised one eyebrow curiously.

Scott realized that he couldn't remember where he knew Leroy from, and at the same moment he became aware of the open port beyond the tall white figure. *Never talk about anything important in front of the cards,* he thought. "Uh, beautiful boat you've got," he said lamely.

"Thank you, Mr.—I'm sorry?"

"Smith."

"Mr. Smith. I hope you get a few beautiful boats yourself!"

Newt led Scott across a couple of yards of deck and through the broad double doors. Their steps were suddenly muffled in thick red carpet.

"You know him already?"

"I don't know," Scott mumbled, looking around, ignoring for the moment the crowd of people standing by the bar in the corner or sitting around the long green felt table.

He guessed that a wall or two had been knocked out to make the central lounge so big; the room was at least twenty feet by forty feet, and the dark rosewood paneling gleamed in the yellow light of the many electric lamps hanging on the walls.

Newt was whispering to himself and bouncing a finger this way and that. "Just made it," he said quietly. "We're now thirteen. Grab a seat."

The engines started, and the boat shook.

"I want another beer first."

The boat surged forward as he was walking toward the bar, and he almost sat down on the carpet. The person who caught his arm and steadied him was Ricky Leroy. "Can't have you down yet!" said the big man jovially. "Smith, you said your name was? No relation to Ozzie, I suppose?"

"Actually," Scott said, taking another step forward and leaning on the bar, "yes. He's my dad. A Miller, please," he added to the obese bartender.

"He couldn't make it tonight?"

"Thanks," Scott said, accepting a tall glass from the fat man. "Hmm? Oh, no—he doesn't like to gamble on water."

Leroy chuckled indulgently. "I guess he's old enough to have picked up a lot of superstitions."

When Leroy fanned the deck out face up across the green felt, Scott stopped breathing.

The vivid gold and red and blue images on the oversize cards seemed to intrude forcefully into his brain through the retina of his one eye, and to blow away all the memories and opinions and convictions that were the scaffolding of his adulthood, so that the cards' images could settle into perfect-fit indentations laid down long before.

The smells of hot metal and perfume clogged his nose, and it seemed to him suddenly that it was raining outside, and that someone had just been singing "Sonny Boy." And he remembered for a moment the grinning face of the Joker staring at him, somehow, from out of a plate of lobster stew.

Something in him was now unlocked—not opened yet, but unlocked—and he thought fleetingly of a night nine years earlier, and the infant girl he had held in his arms for eight hours as Ozzie drove them homeward across the Mojave Desert.

*   *   *

He took several deep breaths, then with trembling fingers
lit a cigarette and took a sip of beer.

He looked at the other players around the table. They all
seemed shaken, and one man was holding a handkerchief
across his eyes.

Leroy gathered the cards together, flipped them facedown,
and began shuffling them. "The ante is a hundred dollars,
gentlemen," he said.

Scott drove the old thoughts out of his head and dug into
his pocket.

Assumption was a game that promoted action. Nobody
seemed to want to fold before the mating and thus lose
the chance to sell his four cards or buy another advanta-
geous four.

By the time the first hand's mating came up there were
ninety-one hundred dollars in the pot. That was a fifth again
as much as Scott had walked in with, and he was in for only
seven hundred.

He had a Knight of Cups and a Six of Swords down, and
was showing a Knight of Swords and a Six of Sticks. When
his four-card hand came up for auction, the bidding went up
to eight hundred, but another hand out there was showing a
Knight, and he decided to wait and bid on it. Sail out of this
hand aboard a Full Boat, he thought.

But the man holding the Knight bought a hand before the
bidding came around to him. The man's hand was now "conceived" and no longer for sale.

There were five hands left to be auctioned, but none of them
held any obvious help for Scott, and he wondered if he should
have taken the eight hundred when he'd had the chance.

And then he waited too long, until his was one of only three
unconceived hands.

"I'm willing to sell now," he told the other two players.

They both looked at him and at his two showing cards. "I'll
give you two hundred," said one, a thin man in a cowboy hat.

The other player smiled at the one who'd bid. "I'll give you
three for *yours*."

The man in the cowboy hat seemed to be considering the
offer, and Scott said quickly, "I'll take one."

The old cowboy gave him a hundred-dollar bill in exchange for his hand, and Scott picked up his empty glass and made his way to the bar.

Scott was leaning on the bar and sipping his new beer when Leroy walked up and tossed a stack of bills onto the wet wood next to the beer glass.

"Congratulations!" Leroy said heartily. "You're a parent."

Scott reached forward and fanned the bills. There were ten hundreds and three twenties.

"The pot went up to ten thousand six hundred," said Leroy, "and the old cowboy had a Straight Flush. Not all that uncommon in this game. Do you want to match that and cut the deck for Assumption?"

"Uh, no," Scott said, picking up his beer. "No, thanks, I'll keep this. The next hand's about to start then?"

Leroy waved him forward. "Your throne awaits."

At the mating in the next hand Scott had a Two and a Six down and two Kings showing, and when his hand went up for bid, two players, each of whom showed a King, bid the price of it up to $2,000 before one of them finally dropped out.

Scott pocketed his $2,000 and went back to the bar. He was already ahead by $1,860—his roll was now $9,360— and this had only been the second hand. And he hadn't even won yet!

But it was on the third hand that he really tied on to it.

As Ozzie had taught him, he quickly scanned every one of the other twelve players' up cards and then tried to watch as each of them peeked at his down cards. One man blushed slightly and began breathing a little faster, and another quickly looked away and began riffling his chips.

They both scored, Scott thought.

The first had a Queen showing; he almost certainly had a Queen and an Ace down, since two other Queens and three Kings were exposed on the board. The other man was showing an Ace; he probably had one of the other two Aces down.

Finally Scott looked at his own cards. He had a Six and a Five down and a Seven showing. Unsuited. Hope for a Straight.

He stayed, along with everyone else, through a bet and two raises. There was now ninety-one hundred in the pot.

The room was layered with cigarette smoke, but it seemed to be thicker over the pot.

The second up cards were dealt, but though he watched the players' faces, he wasn't able to glean any readable tells. He looked down at his own—a Six.

The man to his left was white-suited Ricky Leroy, who showed a Six and a Five, and Scott decided to buy Leroy's hand and hope for a Full Boat and not just a low Two Pair.

The round of betting showered another twenty-six hundred-dollar bills into the pot.

Leroy proved willing to let the hand go to Scott for twelve hundred dollars—and when the four cards were flipped to him, all face up as the rules demanded, Scott made sure that he only blinked sluggishly, as if he were too tired and drunk to have focused on them yet.

The four cards were the Six and the Five that had been showing and a Deuce and a Six. Crane now had four Sixes.

With a steady hand he lifted his glass and took a sip. So Leroy's houseboat lists a little, he told himself when he noticed the tilted surface of the beer; so what?

The rest of the mating seemed to take hours, but at last there were six players still in the game with eight cards each, two down and six up. Leroy had walked away to the bar.

"Three Sixes bet," said the man who was dealing.

"Uh," said Scott, peeking again at his down cards, "check."

The man to his left bet two hundred, the next man folded, the next two called, and the last man raised it another two hundred. The stack of bills in the middle of the table looked like a pile of green leaves that some gardener would eventually bag up and haul away.

"That's four hundred to the three Sixes," said the dealer.

"See the four," said Scott, peeling six bills off his roll, "and raise it two."

"A check-raise from the Sixes," noted the dealer.

Everyone folded but the man who had raised. He stared at Scott for a long time. He was showing two Knights and two Tens and two worthless cards. "And two," he said finally.

He thinks that the three Sixes are all I've got, Scott thought, or that at best I've got a low Boat. He's got a high Boat, probably Knights over Tens, and he knows the Aces and Queens and Kings are effectively gone.

"*And* two," Scott said, throwing the bills out onto the table.

The other player didn't move, but a glow seemed to go out of him. "Call," he said, pushing two more hundreds across the felt.

Scott flipped over his two down cards, and the other player bowed his head and tossed his hand into the discards.

"The Four of a Kind beats the Boat," pronounced the dealer.

Scott started to reach out with both arms for the pile of money, but Leroy, who had left the table after selling his hand to Scott, had returned and now stepped forward.

"Maybe not the *house*boat." He grinned, showing big, even white teeth. "There's thirteen thousand six fifty in there, I believe." He took a leather billfold from inside his jacket and carefully separated out of it thirteen one-thousand-dollar bills and six hundreds and a fifty. He leaned forward and pressed them down onto the heaped money.

Hot, dry desert air sighed in through the open portholes, and Scott's throat burned with the smell of hot stone.

"I'm claiming the Assumption," Leroy said.

CHAPTER 7

It's All Yours

Scott sat back, put his hands on the edge of the table and grinned curiously up at this new opponent. Somehow he had forgotten Newt's telling him that Leroy liked this bet.

Scott had sunk $3,050 into this pot, counting the $1,200 he had paid for Leroy's hand. If he lost the cut, it would take him down from the more than $25,000 he had thought he had before Leroy had spoken—about three times what he'd walked aboard with—to less than $12,000. But if he won it, he'd be sitting on nearly $38,000. And at least the odds were in Scott's favor.

The dealer shrugged, gathered in the cards and shuffled them several times, handed them to another player to cut, and then slid the deck, solid as a brick, to the patch of felt in front of Scott.

The cigarette smoke was a narrow, upright funnel in the middle of the table now, like a tiny slow-motion tornado.

Still grinning, Scott slid his fingers halfway down the card-edges and lifted off the top half and showed the exposed card to the company—getting in return some looks of sympathy—and then he looked at it himself.

It was the Three of Cups. There were only four cards in the deck lower than that, the Deuces, and only three that would tie it. Seven cards out of fifty-five. One chance in about eight and a half.

Still holding the card up, Scott finished his beer, proud that his hand didn't shake in this almost certain defeat. He didn't have to tip the glass back very far at all.

He laid the top half back down on the deck and pushed it across to the dealer, who reshuffled and passed it for the cut and then slid it to the place where Leroy had been sitting.

Leroy leaned forward and curled his brown hand down over the cards; for a moment he seemed to be kneading them gently, and Scott was dully sure that the man was cheating, feeling for a crimp or an unshaved edge. Ozzie had taught him long ago that cheaters were to be either used or avoided, but never challenged, especially in a game with strangers.

Then Leroy had raised a segment of the deck, and the exposed card was the Deuce of Sticks.

There were sighs and low whistles from the other players, but Scott's ears were buzzing with the realization that he had won after all.

He reached out and began raking in and stacking the bills, glad of the revolver pressing against his hip-bone under his sweater.

Leroy sat down in the chair beside him. Scott glanced at the man and said, "Thanks."

Leroy's pupils were wider than normal, and the pulse in his neck was fast. "Yeah," he said levelly, shaking his head,

"I don't know when I'm going to learn that that's not a smart bet."

Scott paused in his gathering and stacking. Those are *tells,* he thought; Leroy is *faking* dismay.

"You're taking the money for the hand," Leroy observed.

"Uh . . . yes." Again Scott was aware of the bulk of metal against his hip.

"You sold the hand."

"I guess you could put it that way."

"And I've bought it," Leroy said. "I've *assumed* it." He held out his right hand.

Puzzled, Scott put down some bills and reached across and shook hands with the big brown man in the white suit.

"It's all yours," Scott said.

It's all yours.

Now, twenty-one years later, driving his old Ford Torino north up the dark 5 Freeway toward the 10 and Venice, Scott Crane remembered Ozzie's advice about games in which the smoke and the drink levels behaved strangely: *Fold out. You don't know what you might be buying or selling come the showdown.*

He had not ever seen Ozzie again after the game on the lake.

The old man had checked out of the Mint by the time Scott got back, and after Scott had rented a car and driven west across the desert to Orange County and Santa Ana, he had found the house unoccupied, with an envelope tacked to the front door frame.

It had contained a conformed copy of a quit-claim deed giving the house to Scott.

He had talked to his foster sister Diana on the telephone a few times in the years since, most recently in '75, after spearing his own ankle, but he had not seen her again either. And he had not any idea where she or Ozzie might now be living.

Crane missed Diana even more than he missed old Ozzie.

Crane had been seventeen when he and Ozzie had driven out to Las Vegas to pick up Diana in 1960. The game on the lake had still been nine years in the future.

He and Ozzie had been driving home from a movie—
Psycho, as Scott recalled—and the radio was playing Elvis
Presley's "Are You Lonesome Tonight," when Ozzie had
pulled the Studebaker over to the Harbor Boulevard curb.

"What's the moon look like to you?" Ozzie had asked.

Scott had looked at the old man, wondering if this was a
riddle. "The moon?"

"Look at it."

Scott leaned down over the dashboard to look up at the sky;
and after a few seconds he had opened the door and stepped
out onto the sidewalk to see more clearly.

The spots and gray patches on the moon made it look like
a groaning skull. The bright dot of Venus was very close to
it—about where the moon's collar-bone would be.

He heard dogs howling . . . and though there were no clouds
that he could see, rain began pattering down and making dark
dots on the sidewalk. He got back in the car and pulled the
door closed.

"Well, it looks like a skull," he admitted. He was already
wary of Ozzie's tendency to read portents into mundane occur-
rences, and he hoped the old man wouldn't insist that they go
swimming in the ocean now, or drive to the peak of Mount
Wilson, as he had occasionally done at times like this in
the past.

"A suffering one," Ozzie agreed. "Is there a deck of cards
in the car?"

"It's November!" Scott protested. Ozzie's policy was to
have nothing to do with cards except in the spring.

"Yeah, better not to look through that window anyway,"
the old man mused. "Something might look back at you.
How about silver coins? Uh . . . three of them. With women
on them."

The glove compartment was full of old auto registrations
and broken cigarettes and dollar chips from a dozen casinos,
and among this litter Scott found three silver dollars.

"And there's a roll of Scotch tape in there," Ozzie said.
"Tape pennies onto the tails side of the cartwheels. Copper
is Venus's metal, I heard from a witchy woman one time."

Envying his friends in high school who didn't have fathers
who made them do this kind of thing, Scott found the tape and
attached pennies to the silver dollars.

"And we need a box to put 'em in," Ozzie went on. "There's an unopened box of vanilla wafers in the backseat. Dump the cookies out in the street—not now. Do it when we're crossing Chapman; it'll be better in an intersection, a crossroads." Ozzie clanked the car back into gear and drove forward.

Scott opened the box and dumped the cookies out as the car surged through the intersection, and then he dropped the silver dollars into the box.

"Shake 'em around, like dice," Ozzie said, "and tell me what they say, heads and tails."

Scott shook the box, then had to dig in the glove compartment again for a flashlight. "Uh . . . two tails and a heads," he said, holding the flashlight beside his ear and peering into the box.

"And we're going south," said Ozzie. "I'm going to make some turns. Keep shaking them and reading them and let me know when they come up all heads."

It was when Ozzie turned east onto Westminster Boulevard that Scott looked into the box and saw three heads—three profiles of a woman in silver bas-relief. In spite of himself, he shivered.

"Now they're all heads," he said.

"East it is," said Ozzie, speeding up.

The coins had led them out of the Los Angeles area, through San Bernardino and Victorville, before Scott worked up the nerve to ask Ozzie where they were going. Scott had hoped to spend the evening finishing the Edgar Rice Burroughs book he'd been reading.

"I'm not *certain*," the old man replied tensely, "but it sure looks like Las Vegas."

So much for *The Monster Men*, Scott thought. "Why are we going there?" he asked, keeping most of the impatience out of his voice.

"You saw the moon," Ozzie said.

Scott made himself count to ten slowly before speaking again. "What's going to be different about the moon when we're in Vegas than it was when we were home?"

"Somebody's killing the moon, the goddess; some woman has apparently taken on the—what would the word be—

goddess-hood and somebody's killing her. I think it's too late for her, and I don't know the circumstances, but she's got a child, a little girl. An infant, in fact, to judge by how close Venus was to the moon when we saw it."

Here I am, Scott thought, holding a vanilla wafers box with three crumb-covered silver dollars in it with pennies taped to them, driving to Las Vegas and not reading Edgar Rice Burroughs—because Venus was close to the moon tonight. Venus is probably close to the moon all the *time*.

"Dad," said the seventeen-year-old Scott, "I don't mean to be disrespectful, but—but this is nuts. For *one* thing, there may be a lady being killed in Las Vegas tonight, but you don't know about it from looking at the moon, and if she's got a baby, it's got nothing to do with Venus. I'm sorry, I don't mean to . . . and *even if there was,* what are we supposed to do? How is it the job of two guys in California and not the job of somebody in Vegas?"

Ozzie laughed without looking away from the highway rushing up at them beyond the windshield. "You think your old man's nuts, eh? Well, a lot of people in Vegas would *like* it to be their job, I can tell you. This baby is a daughter of the goddess, and so she's a T-H-R-E-A-T to them, you bet. A *big* threat. She could bounce the King, if she grows up, which . . . *certain persons* . . . would like her not to do. And there's other people who want her to grow up but would want to, what, be her manager, you know? Boss her, use her. Climb into the tower by means of her Rapunzel hair, yes, sir. *Right* into that tower."

Scott sighed and shifted on the seat. "Okay, look, if we *don't* find a baby, will you agree—"

"We'll find her. I found you, didn't I?"

Scott blinked. "Me? Is this how you found me?"

"Yep."

After half a minute of silence Scott said, "You shook coins in a cookie box?"

"Hah! Sarcasm!" Ozzie glanced at him and winked. "You think your old man's nuts, don't you? Hey, I was swimming down in Laguna late one afternoon in '48, and the surf was full of fish. You know how it is when they're bumping into you under the water? And you gotta get out 'cause you know it's gonna attract barracudas? That's how it was, and the sky was full of those cirrus clouds, like they were spelling something out in a language nobody's got a Rosetta stone for. And Saturn was shining in the sky that evening like a match head, and I know that if I'd had a telescope I'd have seen all his moons disappearing behind him, being devoured like the myths say Saturn devoured his children. There's a Goya painting of that, scare the crap out of you."

The signs along the side of the highway were beginning to refer to Barstow, but Scott didn't ask his foster father to stop for dinner.

"So I got me a deck of cards," Ozzie went on, "and I started shuffling and drawing them to see where to go, and it led me straight to Lakewood, where I found you in that boat. And I walked across the parking lot to that boat *slow,* with my hand on my old .45 that I had in those days, because I knew I wasn't the only one who'd be tracking you. There's always some King Herod around. And I drove to Dr. Malk's in a *highly circuitous* fashion."

Scott shook his head, not wanting to believe these weird and morbid things. "So am I the son of some goddess?"

"You're the son of a King, a bad one, an honorary Saturn. I grabbed you for the same reason we're going to grab this little girl tonight—so that you could grow up outside of the net and then *decide* what you want to do, once you're old enough to know the rules of the game."

When they'd got to Las Vegas at about midnight, Ozzie had made Scott shake the box and peek into it continuously as Ozzie steered the car through the brightly lit streets. The flashlight's battery was getting weak when they rounded a corner and saw the whirling red lights of police cars by one of the side entrances of the Stardust.

They parked and joined the crowd on the sidewalk around the police cars. The night air was hot, with a dry wind from the stony mountains to the west.

"Somebody shot some lady," said a man in answer to Ozzie's *What's up?*

"It was that Lady Issit, the one who's been kicking everybody's ass at the Poker tables," another man added. "I heard tell a big fat guy shot her right in the face, two or three shots."

Ozzie had walked away, shaking the coins in the vanilla wafers box. Scott followed him.

"She ditched the baby, or Venus would have been *behind* the moon," Ozzie said. "And the moon's still up and Venus is down, so the kid's still around somewhere, alive."

For an hour, while Scott grew more and more impatient and embarrassed, the two of them walked up and down Las Vegas Boulevard as Ozzie kept shaking the box and looking into it.

And to his own chagrin Scott was not surprised when they heard an infant's sobbing from behind a row of bushes on the south side of the Sands.

"Careful," Ozzie said instantly. The old man's hand was inside his jacket, and Scott knew he was holding the butt of the Smith & Wesson .38.

"Here." Ozzie turned to Scott and passed the gun to him. "Keep it out of sight unless you see somebody coming at me."

It was only a few steps to the bushes, and Ozzie came back with a baby, wrapped in a light-colored blanket, in his arms.

"Back to the car," Ozzie said tensely, "and don't watch us, *look around*."

The baby had stopped crying and was sucking on one of the old man's fingers. Scott walked behind Ozzie, swinging his head from side to side and occasionally walking backward to monitor all 360 degrees. He wasn't doubting his foster father now.

It took only five minutes to get back to the car. Ozzie opened the passenger-side door and took the gun, and then Scott got in and Ozzie handed him the baby—

—and for a moment Scott not only could feel the baby in his arms but could also feel the pale blanket surrounding him, and could feel protective arms sheltering him. Something in his mind or his soul had for years been unconnected, flapping loose in the psychic breezes, and was now finally connected, and Scott was sharing the baby's sensations—and he knew she was sharing his.

In his mind he could feel a personality that consisted of nothing but fright and bewilderment. *You're all right now*, he thought. *We'll take care of you now; we're taking you home*.

The link he shared with the infant was fading, but he did catch a faint surge of relief and hope and gratitude.

Ozzie was behind the wheel, starting the car. "You okay?" he asked, glancing at Scott.

"Uh," Scott said dizzily. The link was gone now, or had receded below the level at which he could sense it, but he was still so shaken by it that he wasn't sure he would not start crying, or laughing, or trembling uncontrollably. "Sure," he managed to say. "I just . . . never held a newborn baby before."

The old man stared at him for another moment before clanking the car into gear and steering out onto the street. "I hadn't thought of that," he said, alternately looking ahead and peering at the rearview mirror. "That's . . . something I hadn't . . . considered." He gave Scott a brief, worried glance. "You going to be okay?"

Ask *her*, Scott thought. "Sure," he said.

On the long drive home Ozzie had alternately driven very fast and very slow, all the while asking Scott what headlights he could see behind them. When they got back to the familiar streets of Santa Ana, the old man wasted a full hour driving around in circles, lights off and lights on, before at last pulling up to the curb in front of the house.

Diana had been passed off as another illegitimate child of Ozzie's cousin's. The nonexistent cousin was getting quite a reputation.

Now Scott Crane parked the Torino in front of Chick Hurzer's bungalow on Washington Street, and after he turned off the engine and lights, he just sat in the dark car for a few minutes. For the first time in thirteen weeks he was thinking about a different loss than the loss of his wife.

Ozzie and Diana and Scott.

They'd been a family, *his* family, in that old house. Scott had fed Diana, had helped teach her to read, had admired the crayon drawings she had brought home from first and second grades. She had done a drawing of him as a Christmas present in 1968. Once she had broken her arm falling off the jungle gym on the playground, and once some neighborhood kid had thrown a rock at her forehead, and she'd got a concussion; both times he had been miles away but had known about it, and had gone looking for her.

I never should have gone to the game on the lake, he thought as he impatiently blinked back tears—and Ozzie never should have left me.

He opened the door and got out. Clear your mind for the cards, he told himself.

CHAPTER 8

Just Back from the Dead

Two hundred and seventy-two miles to the northeast, Vaughan Trumbill and Ricky Leroy sat panting on a couch in the houseboat lounge. The two men stared at the scrawny, wet, naked body of Doctor Leaky, which they'd just dragged out of the bathroom.

Trumbill, whose bulk took up more than a third of the couch, wiped his huge bald head with a silk handkerchief. He had taken off his shirt, and his gross, pear-shaped torso was a coiled rainbow of tattoos. "The bathroom light *and* the fan *and* the water pump," he said, speaking loudly to be heard over the roar of the generator. "I think he died about the same time the battery did."

"Be glad he didn't drown," said Leroy. "You'd have to empty his lungs again, like out at Temple Basin two years ago." He stood up and stretched. "He'll probably be up at around the same time the battery is. I'm already in a cab from the airport. Half hour, say."

The body on the carpet twitched.

"See?" said Leroy, getting to his feet. "He senses me already." He fetched a towel from the bathroom and tossed it over the old man's scarred, featureless pelvis; then he crouched and prodded Doctor Leaky's cheek and brow. "I hope he didn't fall on the same side of his face as last time. They rebuilt his skull with coral."

Trumbill's eyebrows were raised. "Coral? Like—like seashells, coral reefs, sort of coral?"

"Right. I hear they've got some kind of porous ceramic they use now. Nah, the old jug doesn't seem to have any chips floating loose." He stood up.

"I wish you'd stay away long enough sometime for him to die for good."

"It'd take a while; there're some good protections on that body. And—"

"I know, cryogenics and cloning."

"They're getting closer every day . . . and this . . . jug of my own personal DNA is still unbroken."

The naked old body yawned, rubbed its eyes, and sat up. The towel fell away.

"Looking like shit, though," observed Trumbill.

"Welcome back, Doctor," said Leroy wearily.

"They get in all right?" asked Doctor Leaky.

"Everybody's fine, Doctor."

"Good kid," said the naked old man. He peered at the two men on the couch and scratched the white hair on his sunken chest. "One time on the lake—this must have been, oh, 'forty-seven, I hadn't got the Buick yet—or—no, right, 'forty-seven—he got a hook in his finger, and—" He gave each of them a piercing stare. "Do you think he cried?" He waved off any replies they might have had. "Not a bit! Even when I had to push the—the part that, the *barb*, the barb, not even when I pushed it through so I could clip it off. Clip it off." He squeezed imaginary clippers in the air, and then he stared from Trumbill to Leroy. "Didn't . . . even . . . cry."

Leroy was frowning in embarrassment. "Go to your room, you old fool. And put your towel back on. I don't need to be reminded."

Crane got out of the car and carried his plastic 7-Eleven bag across the sidewalk and up the stepping-stones to Chick Hurzer's front door. The lawn and shrubbery looked cared for. That was good; Chick's car dealership must at least be making enough money for him to hire gardeners.

There was garrulous shouting from inside when he rang the doorbell, and then Chick opened the door.

"I'll be goddamned," Chick said, "Scarecrow Smith! Good to have you back; this game needs a good loser."

Crane grinned. He had always avoided being any evening's conspicuous winner. "Got room in your fridge for some beer?"

"Sure, come on in."

In the bright hallway he could see that Chick had had a prosperous decade. He was heavier, his face puffy and threaded with broken veins, and his trademark gold jewelry was bigger and chunkier.

In the living room five men sat around a card table on which a game of Seven-Stud was already in progress.

"Got us a live one here, Chick?" one of them asked.

"Deal me in next hand," Crane said cheerfully.

He leaned against the wall and watched as they finished out the hand. They were playing with cash now—Crane had always insisted on chips, which tended to make the betting more liberal—and they were apparently playing straight Seven-Stud, no High-Low or twists or wild cards, and the betting seemed to be limited and three raises only.

Crane wondered if he'd be able to do anything about all this tonight. He had set up this game a quarter of a century ago, out of the remains of a Tuesday night game that had begun to draw too many genuinely good players to be profitable, and he had fine-tuned it to seem loose and sociable to the good losers while actually producing a steady income for himself.

The hand ended, and one of the men gathered in the pot.

"Sit down, Scott," said Chick. "Guys, this is Scott Smith, known as Scarecrow. This next hand is . . . Five-Draw."

Crane sat down and, after the deal, watched the other players around the table look at their cards. This would be his first hand of Poker in eleven years.

At last, having noted some mannerisms that might, as he got to know the play of these men better, prove to be valuable tells, he curled up the corners of his five cards and looked at his hand.

Doctor Leaky had managed to tie the towel around himself, but halfway to his room he halted and sniffed the night breeze wafting in off the lake through the open porthole.

"There's one," he said.

Trumbill had stood up and started toward the old man, but Leroy waved at him to stop. "Just back from the dead," said Leroy, "he might sense something. What is it, Doctor?"

"On the hook," said Doctor Leaky.

"Oh, hell, you already told us about the hook. Will you—"

"One of 'em's on the hook, just now bit it, cards in his hands, blood in the water. The jacks will smell him. But now he's on the hook, you can smell him, too. You've got to find him before they do, and you've got to put him safe in the fishbowl."

Leroy stared at the old man, who was blinking and gaping around in imbecilic fright as if he expected enemies to swim up out of the depths of the lake. As a matter of fact, there *was* an enemy deep in the lake—the head of one, anyway.

After several seconds Leroy turned to Trumbill. "Maybe you'd better do as he says."

One of the players had asked to be left out of the hand so that he could call his wife, and he stood now at the telephone in the open kitchen, holding the receiver tightly. He could clearly hear the voices of the players around the table behind him.

After a dozen rings a man's voice answered by repeating the number he'd dialed.

"Hi, honey," the player said nervously, "I'm gonna be late, I'm playing *Poker*."

"Hi, sweetie," said the voice in a mock-gay tone. "Poker, eh?" There came the clicking of an electric keyboard. "Got a lot in that list. You got any cross-references? A name?"

"Hey, come on, honey, I can't get mushy; this is the only phone here; these guys can *hear* me."

"Got you. Give me a category or something then, unless you want to listen to about a hundred names."

"That's your dad all over," said the player with a forced laugh. *"Goes fishing all the time but doesn't catch anything."*

"Fishing and poker," said the voice. "To me that sounds like that poker champ in Gardena who goes sports fishing all the time in Acapulco; matter of fact, I've heard he can't catch anything." There were several measured clicks on the keyboard. "I'll know it when I see it . . . here we go, the guy's name is Obstadt, Neal."

"That's it, dear, and it's worth fifty thousand dollars." He glanced toward the game room and added, "The equity in that place, you know, after I added on that guest room and all—"

"And the aluminum siding and all the goddamn painted lawn squirrels, I know." There was more clicking. "There's only one under Obstadt for that kind of money—a poker player, last seen in '80, name of Scott 'Scarecrow' Smith, son of Ozzie Smith, last seen in '69. I see Obstadt has been distributing pictures throughout L.A. and San Diego and Berdoo and Vegas since January of '87. That's your basis?"

"Not really, it's an old picture. Mainly it was the name."

"He's playing as Scarecrow Smith?"

"Right."

"That looks like a score for you, honey. Build: tall . . . medium . . ."

"Uh-huh."

"Medium build. Weight: fat . . . average . . ."

"Okay."

"I hope the clothes are distinctive. Hair: black . . . brown . . . blond . . . gray . . ."

"Yup."

"Jacket—"

"No."

"Saves us time. Shirt: plaid . . ."

"Right. For this weather."

"Gotcha, flannel. Jeans with that?"

"Yeah. And what you'd figure."

"Say if it ain't sneakers. Okay. Is that enough?"

The player turned toward the table and looked at the other men. "It's enough. Listen, hon, you don't have to worry about that. We're at Chick Hurzer's house, on Washington in Venice."

"Was gonna be my next question." *Clickety-clickety click.* "Okay, he's in the book; I don't need the house address. What's your code number?"

"Four-six-double-three-two-oh."

The voice repeated it slowly, saying "zero" instead of "oh." "That's correct?"

"Yeah, that's it."

The player could hear rapid clicking now. "I got you in," the voice said. "Call the payment number a week from now.

If it checks out to be the right guy, you got forty-five thousand bucks coming."

The game went well for Crane. The extra dozen decks of cards encouraged players to call for a new deck after a loss, a good start toward getting some superstition back into the game, and the sandwiches, when he brought them out at midnight, were a good enough diversion to produce a couple of instances of positively idiotic play. And there were a couple of doctors at the table, and doctors always had a lot of money and played loose, staying in with just about every hand; and nobody was completely sober, and Scott was apparently the only one who had any concerns about money, and by the time the game broke up at two in the morning he had won more than two thousand dollars. That was two payments on the mortgage right there, and he could certainly find another game somewhere within the next couple of days.

Chick Hurzer had been a bigger winner and was now drinking scotch. "So where have you been, Scarecrow?" he asked jovially as people were standing up and stretching and one man turned on the television. "You've got time for a drink, don't you?"

"Sure," said Scott, taking a shot glass. "Oh, here and there. Honest work for a few years."

Everybody laughed—one of the players a little tensely.

Obstadt's man had been apologetic on the telephone about its being short notice, but Al Funo had laughed and assured him that it was no inconvenience; and when the man had started to discuss payment, Funo had protested that old friends didn't argue about money.

Sitting in his white Porsche 924 now, waiting for Scott Smith to emerge from this Chick Hurzer person's house, Funo tilted down his rearview mirror and ran a comb through his hair. He liked to make a good impression on everyone he met.

He had removed the Porsche's back window, but with the heater on the car was warm enough, and it idled so quietly and smokelessly that a pedestrian walking past it might not even know the engine was running.

He was looking forward to meeting this Smith character. Funo was a "people person," proud of the number of people he could call his friends.

He watched alertly as half a dozen men ambled out through the front door of Hurzer's house now into the glare of the streetlight, and he was quick to pick out the gray-haired figure in jeans and a plaid flannel shirt. Other people were shaking Smith's hand, and Funo wished he could have joined in the camaraderie of the game.

He got out of his car and began sauntering along the sidewalk, smiling, not minding the waterfront chill in the salty air. Ahead of him the men had separated, heading for their cars.

Smith seemed to be aware of Funo when he was still some yards off along the sidewalk; he had his hand by his belt buckle, as if about to tuck in his loose shirttail. A gun? Funo smiled more broadly.

"Hey, pal," Funo said when he was close enough for an easy, conversational tone to be heard, "have you got a cigarette?"

Smith stared at him for a moment, then said, "Sure," and hooked a pack of Marlboros out of his pocket. "There's only three or four in there," Smith said. "Go ahead and keep the pack."

Funo was touched. Look at the car this guy's driving, he thought, a beat old Torino covered with dust, and he gives me his last cigarettes!

"Hey, thanks, man," he said. "These days it's damn rare to meet someone who's possessed of genuine generosity." He blushed, wondering if the two *gen*'s in his last phrase had made him seem careless in his choice of words. "Here," he said hastily, digging in the pocket of his Nordstrom slacks, "I want you to have my lighter."

"No, I don't need a—"

"Please," Funo said, "I have a hundred of them, and you're the first gen—the first, uh, considerate person I've met in twenty years in this damn town." Actually Funo was only twenty-eight and had moved to Los Angeles five years ago, but he had found that it sometimes helped to lie a little bit when making new friends. He realized he was sweating. *"Please."*

"Sure, man, thanks," said Smith.

Was he uncomfortable about it? "*Two* hundred of them I've got."

"Fine, thanks. Jesus! This is a gold Dunhill! I can't—"

"Don't insult me."

Smith seemed to recoil a little. Had Funo spoken harshly? Well, how could someone spurn a sincerely offered gift?

"Thanks," Smith said. "Thanks a lot. Well—I've got to go. Getting late."

"You're telling me!" Funo said eagerly. "We'll be lucky to be in our beds before dawn, hey?"

"Lucky," Smith agreed, starting toward his pitiful car.

Only when he noticed the Porsche for the third time did Crane remember another piece of Ozzie's advice—*Three-sixty at all times—they can be in front just as easy as behind.*

Driving east on the Santa Monica Freeway in the pre-dawn darkness, the moon long since set and the skyscrapers of downtown Los Angeles standing up off to his left like the smoldering posts of some god's burned-down house, Crane had been seized with the idea of just staying eastbound on this freeway; cruising right on past where it became called the Pomona Freeway, and all the way out past Ontario and Mira Loma to where it joined with the 15 in one of those weird, dusty semi-desert suburbs with names like Norco and Loma Linda, and then straight on up to Las Vegas.

Be in Vegas in time for a late breakfast, he had found himself thinking. *And you've got two grand in your pocket.*

He had known he didn't want to go anywhere besides home, much less to Las Vegas, but still he had had to fight the compulsion and concentrate on turning south onto the Santa Ana Freeway.

And then he had seen the Porsche for the third time.

There were only a few cars on the freeway at this hour, and he'd been able to swoop through the long dark curves with just three fingertips swinging the bottom of the steering wheel, but now he snapped the seat belt across himself and took the wheel firmly in both hands.

The Porsche was ahead of him now, as the two cars drove past the Long Beach Freeway junction. It seemed to Crane that it had been behind him or ahead or flanking for at least ten minutes. If Ozzie had been driving right now, he would have sped up and got in the fast lane and then done a squealing three-lane change to get off at Atlantic, and then taken some long way home.

But Crane was exhausted. "No, Ozzie," he said aloud. "I can't be spooking at every car making the same trip I am." He sighed. "But tell you what, I'll watch him, okay?"

The swooping overhead lights gleamed on the Porsche's body but not on its rear window. Frowning with the effort of focusing, Crane realized that the Porsche didn't *have* a rear window.

Cold night and a well-kept Porsche, he thought, but no back window?

He imagined Ozzie sitting beside him. *Heads up*, the old man would have said. "Right, Ozzie," Crane replied, and peered at the car ahead.

And so he saw the driver twist around and extend his arm out across the back of the seat, and he saw a gleam of metal in the hand.

Crane flung himself sideways across the seat as the windshield imploded with an ear-stunning *bang*. Tiny cubes of windshield glass sprayed across him, and the headwind was a cold, battering gale in the car as he pulled the wheel strongly to the right. He braced his feet and sat up, then just winced and held on.

The Torino hit the shoulder hard, tearing up ice plant as the old shocks clanked shut and the car dug in for an instant and then sprang up with the impetus of its own weight. As soon as the heavy old vehicle slewed to a stop, he shoved the shift lever into reverse and tromped on the accelerator and wove the lumbering machine down off the slope and back along the blessedly empty slow lane to the last off ramp.

Back in drive, he sped down Atlantic Boulevard, squinting in the headwind. After tracing a maze path through the dark streets, he pulled into the parking lot of a closed gas station and turned off the lights. He pulled the revolver out of his belt and watched the street.

His heart was thudding in his chest, and his hands were trembling wildly. There was a half-finished pint of Wild Turkey in the glove compartment, and after a minute or two he fumbled it out and twisted off the cap and took a deep gulp.

Jesus, he thought. It has not ever been closer. It has not ever been closer.

Eventually he put the car back into gear and drove south all the way to Pacific Coast Highway and then took Brookhurst up to Westminster. The car leaned perceptibly to the right now, and he wondered what he had done to the suspension and alignment.

"What *seeems* to be the *problem*?" whispered Archimedes Mavranos.

He sat on Scott Crane's porch in the darkness and listened to his own heart. He had read in an Isaac Asimov article that humans averagely got two billion heartbeats, and he calculated that he had used up only one billion.

It wasn't fair, but fairness was something you had to go get; it wasn't delivered like the mail.

He reached down and took hold of his current can of Coors. He had read that Coors was anti-carcinogenic—it had no nitrosamines, or something—and so he drank it constantly.

God knew why Crane drank Budweiser constantly. Mavranos hadn't heard anything about Budweiser.

Spit in the palm of your hand and then whack it with your other fist, he thought, and watch which way the spit flies. Then you know which way to go.

Mavranos had dropped out of high school when his fiancée had got pregnant, and for nearly twenty years he had made a pretty good living by buying cars from the Huntington Beach police impound yard and fixing them up and selling them for a profit. Only last April had he started studying science and math and myth.

April is the cruellest month, he thought.

Last April he had gone to a doctor because he was getting tired all the time, and had no appetite anymore, and had a lump under his left ear.

"What seems to be the problem?" the doctor had asked cheerfully.

What had turned out to be the problem was lymphoma, cancer of the lymphatic system.

The doctor had explained it to some extent, and Mavranos had done a lot of reading on his own. He had learned about the random nature of cancer cells, and had then studied randomness—and he had begun to discern the patterns that underlay true randomness: the branchings, the repeating patterns, the fat man in the complex plane.

A car turned down Main from Seventeenth, but it wasn't Crane's Torino.

If you were to decide to measure the coastline of California, it would be of little use simply to lay a ruler across a page of an atlas and then determine the length of the roughly ten degrees of longitude it spanned. But it would be of even less value to walk the length of the coastline with a one-inch stick, taking into account every open tide pool and shoe-size peninsula; if you measured *too* finely, in fact, your answer could approach infinity. Every little pool, if you measured finely enough, had a virtually infinite coastline.

You had to approach such things differently.

You had to back off just far enough.

Turbulence in a water pipe or disorder in the signals to the nerves of the heart—or the cellular hysteria called cancer—were effects of randomness. And if you could . . . find the patterns in randomness, maybe you could manipulate them. Change them, restore the order.

Spit in the palm of your hand and whack it, he thought.

And he had found this neighborhood, this house, Scott Crane.

Crane never washed his Torino, and Mavranos had noticed patterns in the dew-streaked dust and the splashing of bird shit on the car body—circles, and straight lines and right angles on a sloping surface, and once a spatter of little wailing faces like that Munch picture—and once, when Crane had been standing on the porch, blearily going through his pocket change for a quarter to buy a newspaper, he had dropped a handful of dimes and quarters and pennies—Mavranos had helped pick them up, and had noticed that every coin had landed heads side up; and any watch Crane wore would run too fast.

And animals died around this house. Mavranos had once noticed dead ants in a line that pointed to a forgotten third of a cheeseburger on the porch, and a neighbor's cat that frequently used to sleep on Crane's roof had died; Mavranos had gone over to the woman's house, ostensibly to commiserate, and had learned that the veterinarian had diagnosed cancer as the cause of death.

And throughout the whole block fruit juices fermented abnormally fast, as though some god of wine visited this Santa Ana street and breathed on the houses, very late at night when he'd be seen by no one but the furtive youths out to steal car stereos and batteries.

Since it was randomness that was out to kill him, Archimedes Mavranos had decided to find out where it lived, find its castle, its perilous chapel.

And so a year ago he had withdrawn five thousand dollars in twenties and put it in his pocket, told his wife and two daughters that he would be back when he had retaken his health, and had walked away down the street. At the corner he had spit in his hand and punched it with his fist, and then started away in the indicated direction.

He had walked for two full days, eating beef jerky he bought in liquor stores and pissing behind bushes and not shaving or changing his clothes or sleeping at all. Eventually he had found himself circling this block, and when he saw a house for rent, he had called the number on the sign out front and given the landlord fifteen hundred dollars in cash. And then he had devoted his efforts to fine-tuning.

He had come to suspect early on that Scott Crane was the major local signpost to the castle of randomness—but only tonight, when Crane had mentioned having been a professional Poker player, had he found any reason to be confident. Gambling was the place where statistics and profound human consequences met most nakedly, after all, and cards, even more than dice or the numbers on a roulette wheel, seemed able to define and perhaps even dictate a player's . . . luck.

Crane's living-room window was open behind the screen, and Mavranos now sensed someone standing inside, behind him. He shifted around in the chair.

"Scott?" came a whisper. "Come to bed."

"It's me, Susan, Arky," said Mavranos, embarrassed. "Scott's still off at his . . . whatever he's doing."

"Oh." Her whisper was weaker. "My eyes aren't very good yet. Don't . . . tell him I spoke to you, okay?"

She added something else, but it was too faint for him to hear.

"I'm sorry?"

He could hear her take a deep breath, like wind sighing through a leafless tree, but when she whispered again, he was only just able to hear it.

"Give him a drink," she said, and added some more words, all he caught of which were the syllables *back us.*

"Sure, Susan," Archimedes said uncomfortably. "You bet."

The next car to turn onto Main was Crane's Ford, and Mavranos stood up, for the windshield was just a white webbed skirt around a gaping hole on the driver's side.

CHAPTER 9

The Only Fat Man I Know About

"I just want to go to bed, man," Crane said. He had brought the pint bottle with him from the car. "Well, okay, one beer to chase this stuff with." He took a cold can and sat down heavily in one of the decrepit porch chairs.

Mavranos had been saying something. "What, now?" said Crane. "A fat man in the desert?"

Mavranos closed his eyes, then started again. "A song about a fat man who drives along the highways that cross the Mojave. The 40, the 15, even the I-27 out by Shoshone. A country-western song is how I've heard it, though I guess there's a rock one, too. This fat man's got a warty bald head, and his car has about a million rearview mirrors on it, like the mods in England used to hang on their scooters."

Scott Crane finished the bottle and put it down carefully on the table. "So the question is, have I heard about him?" He shook his head. "No. I haven't heard about him."

"Well, he's not real. He's a—a *legend*, you know? Like the Flying Dutchman or the Wandering Jew. His car is supposed to break down all the time, because the carburetor's just a wonder of extra hoses and valves and floats and clips and stuff."

Crane frowned and nodded, as if to show that he was understanding all this. "And you say he's green?"

"No, damn it. *No*. He *used* to be green, and just a *big* man, not fat, but that version stopped applying sometime. That image stopped being vital, and you see it now only in things like the Hulk, and the Jolly Green Giant who grows vegetables. Now he's not the Green Knight that Sir Gawain met anymore—because the water's sick and the land's barren, like in Second Kings—now he's real fat, and he's generally black or gray or even metallic. That little round robot Tik-Tok in the Wizard of Oz stories, that's him, a portrait of him." Mavranos looked at his sodden companion and wondered why he was even bothering to explain. "But you haven't heard of him."

"No. The only fat man I know about," said Crane, pausing in mid-sentence to take a long sip of the beer, "is the one that shot the moon in the face in 1960."

"Tell me about that."

Crane hesitated, then shook his head. "I'm kidding, it's just a—a John Prine song."

Some people shouted at each other in the Norm's parking lot, then got into cars; headlights came on, and they drove out onto Main and away into the night.

Mavranos stared at Crane. "Rebar, you said."

"Yeah, rebar. A goddamn iron pole. Fell off a truck. If I hadn't ducked to the side, it would have punched a hole right through my head. I should have got a name off the side of the truck; I could sue 'em."

"And you threw it away."

"Well, I couldn't drive, could I, with it stuck through my car?"

"This fat man," Mavranos went on after a pause, "like I said, he's not real, he's a *symbol*."

"Of course he is," Crane agreed vaguely; "of basketballs, or Saturn, or something."

"Why did you mention Saturn?"

"Jesus, Arky, I don't know. I'm exhausted. I'm drunk. Saturn's round, and so are fat men."

"He's the Mandelbrot man."

"Good. That's good to hear. I was afraid he was the Pillsbury doughboy. I've really got to—"

"Do you know what the Mandelbrot man is? No? I'll tell you." Mavranos took another sip of his own beer to ward away the cancer. "If you draw a cross on a piece of paper and call the crossing-point zero, and you mark one-two-three and so on to the right, and minus one, minus two, and all to the left, and one-times-the-square-root-of-minus-one and then two times that and then three times that upward from zero, and that times minus one, and minus two, and so forth, below the zero point, you wind up with a plane, and any point on it can be defined by two numbers, just like defining a place by latitude and longitude. And then——"

"Arky, what's this got to do with fat men?"

"Well, if you apply a certain equation to as many of the points on the plane as you can, apply it over and over again—you gotta have a powerful computer—some of them go flying off to infinity and some stay finite. And if you color the ones that stay finite black, they form the silhouette of a warty fat man. And if you color-code the other points by how *quickly* they want to go infinite, you find that the fat man is surrounded by all kinds of shapes, boiling off of him, that look like squid tentacles and seahorse-tails and ferns and rib-cages and stuff."

Crane seemed to be about to speak, but Mavranos went on.

"And you don't always need Mandelbrot's equation. The fat man shows up in a lot of *other* functions on the complex plane, as if the shape of him is a—a role that's just waiting for something to come along and assume it. He's a constant figure, along with other lobed and geometrical shapes that look like . . . well, case in point tonight, like Hearts and Clubs and Diamonds and Spades, often as not."

Crane squinted at him for several seconds. "And something about . . . the Wizard of Oz, you said. How'd you learn about all this?"

"It's become a—a hobby of mine, studying weird math."

"And this fat man's name is . . . Mandelbrot?"

"No, no more than Frankenstein's monster was named Frankenstein. The equation was developed by a guy *named* Mandelbrot, Benoit Mandelbrot. A Frenchman. He belonged to a group, a club in Paris, called Bourbaki, but he split from them because he began to *understand* randomness, and it didn't sit well with them. They were real prove-it-by-the-rules boys, and he was finding new rules."

"Bourbaki," said Scott drunkenly. "École Polytechnique and the Bourbaki Club."

Mavranos forced himself to breathe slowly. Mandelbrot had gone to the École Polytechnique. Crane did know something about this, or about something that had to do with this.

"You seem to take it pretty lightly, somebody shooting out your windows," Mavranos said carefully.

"'When there are gray skies,'" Scott sang, "'I don't mind the gray skies—you make them blue, Sonny Boy.'"

Mavranos blinked. "Do you have a son?"

"No, but I'm somebody's son."

Mavranos sensed that this was important, so he spoke casually. "Well, yeah, I suppose so. Whose son are you?"

"My foster father said I was a bad King's son."

As indifferently as he could, Mavranos asked, "Is that why you play Poker?"

Scott took a deep breath and then put on a grin in a way Mavranos could imagine someone putting on armor. "I don't play Poker anymore. Actually I went out for a job tonight. I think I'm going to be a rep for . . . Yoyodyne. They manufacture . . . stuff, locally. Maybe you've heard of them."

"Yeah," said Mavranos, backing down, "I think I have."

"I'd better be heading for bed," Scott said, elbowing himself up out of the chair. "I've got to meet with them again tomorrow."

"Sure. Susan's been wondering where you've been."

Oddly, this seemed to shake Scott. "I bet," he said finally. "See you *mañana.*"

"Okay, Pogo."

After Scott had gone inside, Mavranos sipped his Coors thoughtfully. He's it, all right, he thought. Scott Crane is definitely my connection to the place where math and statistics and randomness border on magic.

And magic is what I need, he thought, fingering the lump under his ear.

Again Scott Crane dreamed of the game on the lake.

And as always, the dream-game progressed just as the real game had happened in 1969 . . . until he won the cut, and was raking in the pile of money.

"You're taking the money for the hand," said Ricky Leroy softly. Already tension was filling the big room, like a subsonic tone that Scott could feel in his teeth and his belly.

"Uh . . . yes."

"You're selling it."

Scott looked around. Something profound was moving or changing somewhere, but the green table and the other players and the paneled walls looked the same. "I guess you could put it that way."

"And I've bought it. I've *assumed* it." Leroy held out his right hand.

Scott reached across and shook hands. "It's all yours."

And then Scott was outside his own body, floating above the table in the whirling smoke; perhaps he had *become* the smoke. The scale of everything was changing: the table below him was an enormous green plain, and the other players were giants, expressionless, all trace of humanity left behind in the tininess of comprehensible distances. The walls were gone, Lake Mead was as vast as the night sky, and three of the dam's intake towers were gone; the remaining tower in the water soared away above and seemed to threaten the moon, which in the dream was full and bright.

There was motion out in the night. A figure was dancing on one of the remote cliffs; it seemed to be as far away as the stars, but with the clear vision of nightmare Scott could see that the person carried a long stick and that a dog was leaping around its ankles. The dancing figure was smiling up into the dark sky, apparently careless of the wavy-edged precipice at its feet.

And though Scott couldn't see him, he knew that there was another giant out there, in the lake, under the black water, and that like Scott he had only one eye.

Seized with vertigo, Scott looked down. His own body, and Leroy's, were looking up at him, their faces broad as clouds and absolutely identical. One of the faces—he couldn't any longer tell which—opened the canyon of its mouth and inhaled, and the smoky wisp that was Scott's consciousness spiraled rapidly down toward the black chasm.

"Scott," Susan was saying. "Scott, you're just dreaming, I'm here. This is me, you're in your own bedroom."

"Oh, Sue," he gasped. He tried to hold her, but she slid away across her side of the mattress.

"Not yet, Scott," she said with a yearning tone in her voice. "Soon, but not quite now. Go have a beer, you'll feel better."

Scott climbed out of bed on his side. He noticed that he had slept in his clothes, and his Poker winnings were still a bulk in his pants pocket. Even his shoes were still on. "Coffee right now," he said. "Go back to sleep."

He blundered down the hall to the dark, stove-warmed kitchen and put a coffee cup full of tap water into the microwave oven and punched full power for two minutes. Then he went to the window and wiped out a clear patch in the condensation.

Main Street was quiet. Only a few cars and trucks murmured past under the streetlights, and the solitary figure walking across the parking lot had an air of virtuous purpose, as if he were going to the early shift at Norm's and not away from the scene of some shabby crime. Dawn was still an hour or so away, but already some birds were cheeping in the big old carob trees along the sidewalk.

Susan's not really in there, he thought dully. She's dead. I know that.

I'm forty-seven.

I never should have lived this long.

It's like sitting in the jungle, changing your bandages and eating canned C-rations or whatever soldiers eat, and watching the skies: *There should have been choppers by now.*

Or like riding a bicycle with your feet wired to the pedals. You can do it, for a very long time, but eventually you start to wonder when somebody's going to come along and stop the bike and clip your feet loose so you can get off.

Am I supposed to just keep on doing this?

He thought he could hear someone breathing softly in the bed.

No good could come of thinking about it.

He thought about the six or eight beers in the refrigerator. He had laid them out on the cold rack before he went to bed, like an artilleryman laying out the shells that would be needed for tomorrow's siege.

The microwave binged softly five times, and he opened its door and took out the cup and stirred a spoonful of instant coffee into the heated water, then cooled it with a dribble of water from the tap.

Back at the window with the coffee, he abruptly remembered singing a snatch of "Sonny Boy" in front of Arky. What else had he done or said? He couldn't remember. He never worried about anything he said or did when sober, but he had not been sober last night. Or any night recently.

He walked to the back door and looked through the window at Mavranos's apartment across the alley. The lights were all out. Arky would probably sleep past noon, as always. God knew how the man made a living.

Scott's .357 revolver was lying on the shelf that held all the cookbooks. He remembered laying it there a couple of hours ago when he had had to bend over to pick up the half-full carton of beers.

Rebar. Arky had noticed the shot-out windshield. And Scott remembered that Ozzie had always registered his car with a P.O. box address, in case someone took down his license plate number.

Scott had stopped bothering with that in '80, when he quit Poker and married Susan. His current registration listed this address.

He put the coffee down.

Suddenly he was certain that the gunman had written down his license plate number and had found the address and was now waiting outside in the Porsche, or in another car, watching this house. Perhaps he had planted a bomb under the foundations. That would be the easiest way.

The death panic of his dream was all at once back on him, and he grabbed the gun, thankful that he had not turned on the kitchen light. He took a few deep breaths—and then slowly, silently, with trembling fingers unhooked the chain and carefully forced the warped old door open.

The night air was cold on his sweaty face and scalp. He quickly scanned the dark yard over the extended barrel of the gun, then with his free hand pressed the door closed behind him and stole down the steps. For several seconds he just stood and breathed through his open mouth, listening; then he picked his way slowly through the unmowed grass toward the loose boards in the fence. Beyond that lay the alley, the secret city capillary that led to a hundred dark and solitary streets.

*   *   *

One of the jacks found him first and killed him, thought Vaughan Trumbill when the Jaguar's headlights swept across the parking lot on Second Street and made a glittering snow-field of the Torino's holed rear window. *Her Easter wardrobe is gonna be slim if this keeps up.*

He drove on past, turning his big head rapidly from side to side to see if the killer or killers might still be nearby, but all the parked cars he could see were empty and dark.

Could be anywhere, he thought, *on a dark porch, on a roof,* but they probably wouldn't hang around.

He drove quickly around the block and then pulled in to the parking lot and stopped next to the Torino.

For several moments he just sat in the idling car. The small trout in the tank on the seat next to him—the *poisson sympathique*—was just bumping around randomly. That might mean that Trumbill's quarry was dead, or that the damned fish was just dizzy from motion.

Trumbill got ponderously out of the car and walked to the driver's side of the Torino—and he allowed himself a sigh of relief when he saw that there was no body in the car, nor even any evidence of blood on the upholstery or the billion-faceted windshield.

They only tried, he thought as he got back into his own car and backed out of the parking lot. He noted the license plate number of the Torino when his headlights were on the car, and after he had parked on the street, he used his car phone to call for the data on the registration. His source promised to call him back in a few minutes.

Then he called for back-up—a clean van and a couple of guys to help.

Finally Trumbill sat back in the leather seat and opened a Ziploc plastic bag full of celery and carrot sticks.

It had been a long drive from Lake Mead. The damned trout had first led him to Las Vegas, and then for half an hour had sent him circling counterclockwise around the Flamingo Hilton—Flamingo Road to Paradise to Sands to the Strip to Flamingo again—but had finally settled down and faced southwest. It had stayed pointed that way while Trumbill drove across the midnight desert on the straight dark line that was I–15 to Baker, and then down to Barstow into, eventually, the maze of Orange County. At that point freeways proved to be too fast for the fish to be reliable, and Trumbill had had to exit and negotiate surface streets, slowly enough so that the trout would have time to shift around in its tank on the seat.

During the drive Trumbill had finished the hastily thrown-together bag of tropical fish and seaweed, and now the carrots and celery were gone. He eyed the leaves of the ginger plant in the lawn beyond the curb.

Not yet, he told himself.

He glanced around at the neighborhood. There was a 1930s-vintage duplex across the street—Spanish style, white stucco and clay tile roofs—and a similar house at the Main Street corner and a couple of featureless new five-story condominiums behind him. The Torino's owner probably lived in one of the little duplex houses, which he or she probably rented.

I need a snack now, he thought.

Trumbill opened the door and walked across the sidewalk to the planter, and as he peeled off a few leaves, he wondered which of the last game's winners this would turn out to be—and why he or she had refrained from playing cards again until this evening.

He got back into the car and closed the door.

There was no mystery about why the person was playing cards now, of course. Several of Betsy's fish had started to play again last year, and Trumbill had managed to find and fetch two of them, and they were now safely sedated in a remote house outside Oatman, down the river near Lake Havasu, where London Bridge had been moved to. The start of the third big series of Assumption games was only a little more than a week away. This person tonight would be very eroded by now, obsessed by memories of the '69 game, drunk and personifying the vice, and all in all getting very *ripe*, as Betsy Reculver would say. The tendency to move east, away from the abhorrent ocean, would soon be an overwhelming compulsion. Well, Trumbill would try to assist in that.

Betsy would want the person, whoever it was, to be protected until after the game, when at last the twenty-one-year-old assumptions could be consummated, when her resurrections could take place.

Git along, little dogie, he thought. *It's all your misfortune and none of my own.*

The telephone buzzed, and he picked it up and wrote down the data the voice gave him: Scott Crane, born 2/28/43, address 106 East Second Street, Santa Ana. That was the old house at the corner.

He turned on the dome light and shuffled through the six manila envelopes. It was probably the young man who had used the name Scott "Scarecrow" Smith in the '69 game.

Trumbill opened the envelope and looked at the photographs of Scott Smith. In the twenty-one-year-old pictures he was a dark-haired, lean-faced young man, often in the company of an old man identified in ink on the margins as Ozzie Smith, evidently Scott's father. Paper-clipped to the photographs was a copy of a bill from the Mint Hotel in Las Vegas; the bill had a Montebello, California, address for both Scott and Ozzie, and someone had written across it *"Phony."*

Montebello was one of those cities that were part of Los Angeles—close enough to Santa Ana. This Smith person had to be the fish Trumbill was looking for. The nearest of the other five lived in Sacramento.

Also in the envelope was a photograph of a pregnant blond woman stepping out of a car; her face, caught turning toward someone out of the scene, was taut and strong.

"Issit," read the note taped to the back of the picture. "Born c. '35. Folded 6/20/60. Daughter, born 6/19(?)/60, believed to be alive—'Diana Smith'—possibly living with Ozzie Smith—address unknown—*urgently FOLD.*

Trumbill looked at the woman's face, absently remembering how the face had changed as he had fired three bullets through it, thirty years ago.

Diana Smith. Trumbill looked at the dark bulk of 106 and wondered if she might be living there, too. That would be all right.

He put the photographs back into the envelope and then pulled out his wallet and looked at his laminated FBI identification tag. It was the most recent version, with the gold band across the top, and nobody would believe that the obese Trumbill was a newly hired agent, but this Crane fellow wasn't likely to know anything about FBI IDs.

Better to leave the car here, he thought, in case any jacks are in the area who might be watching the place. Better to be a pedestrian.

He opened the door, pocketed his wallet, patted the holstered SIG 9-millimeter automatic under his coat, and began ambling in an aimless fashion toward 106.

Crane was breathing fast and shallow as he peered over the hood of one of Mavranos's impound-yard cars. Goddammit, he thought, it's not the guy in the Porsche, but it's got to be somebody *with* him.

Crane was shivering. Shit, he thought miserably.

The sky was graying behind him in the east. Crane had walked around a dozen blocks, and finally the cold and his weariness and the thought of his bed had convinced him that he must have been wrong about the man in the Porsche. It must have been one of those random freeway shootings, he'd told himself; probably I cut him off without knowing it, and he got mad and decided to kill me. . . . A guy that would drive around with no rear window would probably do that kind of thing.

But here was a serious-looking man checking out Crane's car and talking on a cellular telephone and now walking toward his house. This was as true and horribly undeniable as a broken tooth or a hernia. Even if the man was a plainclothes policeman, something was going on, something that Crane didn't want.

He thought about the beers in his refrigerator. He'd been an idiot not to bring them along in a bag.

The fat man must nearly be up to his porch; impulsively Crane sprinted across the street to the parked Jaguar. By the streetlight's glow he could see some manila envelopes on the seat.

He looked at his house. The man was up the steps and onto the porch now, and if he walked up to the door, he wouldn't be able to see the Jaguar.

The man went to the door and disappeared from view.

Crane turned his back to the Jaguar and then drove his elbow hard at the driver's window; it shattered inward with no more noise than a bottle breaking inside a paper bag, and he spun around, leaned in and snatched the envelopes, and then ran back across the street to the dark, recessed door of Mavranos's half of the duplex. He banged on the door with his free fist.

After a few seconds he banged on it again. *Come on, Arky,* he thought. *I'll tell you what seeems to be the problem.*

He could hear footsteps inside the house.

"Let me in, Arky," he said in an urgent, low voice. "It's me, it's Scott!"

He heard a chain slide through its channel and rattlingly fall, and then the door was pulled open and Crane had pushed his way inside. "Close it and lock it and don't turn on the lights," he gasped.

"Okay," Mavranos said. "What're you, delivering mail now?" Mavranos was wearing a shirt and undershorts and socks.

"Jesus, I hope you've got a beer."

"I've got enough for the disciples, too. Let me put my pants on."

CHAPTER 10

Irrigating the Cavity

"Your fat man's out there," Crane said, with false and querulous bravado, after taking a solid slug of Coors in Mavranos's dark living room. The place smelled like an animal's cage. "He was messing with my car, and then he ate the goddamn bushes across the street, and now he's gone to my house. What's his name? Handlebar?"

Crane was on the couch and Mavranos was standing by the window and peeking out through the blinds. "Mandelbrot is the name you're trying to think of. He's the guy that outlined him. All I see is a Jaguar with its window broke."

"I broke it. Fucker ate the bushes."

"What're the envelopes?"

"God, I don't know. I took 'em out of his car. I can't go home."

"Susan still up there?"

"No, she—she went to her mother's house, we had a fight, that's how come I was out walking and saw this guy."

"You can stay here. But we gotta talk."

"Sure, sure, let's talk."

"Is this the fat man that shot the moon in the face?"

Scott Crane exhaled and tried to think clearly. "Great God. I don't know. It might be. I didn't see him, in '60. We got there after." He rubbed his good eye and then drank some more beer. "God, I hope it isn't connected to all that crap. But it probably is. The first night I go play cards. The goddamn cards."

Mavranos was still standing by the window. "You ought to tell me about the cards, Pogo."

"I ought to fucking *know* about the cards, I don't know shit about them; it's like letting a kid play with blasting caps or something."

"Your fat man's coming back."

"He's *your* fat man."

"He just noticed his window; he's looking around. I'm gonna hold the blinds just like they are."

"I've got a gun," said Crane.

"So do I, Pogo, but let's hold our horses. He's getting in the car. He's starting it up. Nice car, no way it's the original Jag engine in that. He's moving off, but my guess is he ain't going far." Mavranos let the blinds fall and turned around. "Nobody'll see a light in the kitchen; bring your envelopes there."

"I'll just leave 'em here. In fact, if I could just go to sleep on this couch—"

"Sleep later, and right now bring them into the kitchen. I *am* in this for my health."

Crane just stared at the note on the back of the photograph of Lady Issit while Mavranos shuffled the photographs from the other envelopes around on the kitchen table and read the notes attached to them.

"So who are these people?" he asked. He looked up, then snapped his fingers at Crane. "Hmm? What's this . . . *category* you're a part of?"

Crane blinked and looked up. "Oh, they're—a couple of 'em I recognize. Poker players. One of them was in a game with me in '69, in a houseboat on Lake Mead. He won a big pot, what in this game is called the Assumption. He—" Crane sighed. "He took money for the hand. So did I. These others were probably at one of the other lake games that week, and I bet they won some Assumptions, too."

Crane looked back at the note on the picture of Lady Issit. For the dozenth time he read, "*Diana Smith—possibly living with Ozzie Smith—address unknown—urgently FOLD.*" He realized that his heart was pounding and his palms were damp. "I've, uh, got to get in touch with somebody," he said.

"You can use the phone."

"I don't know where she is. And I don't know anybody that would."

"I got no Ouija board, Pogo."

Urgently FOLD.

He thought of the awed care with which he had held her during the long drive back from Las Vegas in 1960, and of the portrait she'd done of him, and he tried to remember what each of them had said the last time they'd talked, when she'd called him after he'd put the fishing spear through his ankle. When she'd been fifteen.

He'd dreamed that she got married. He wondered if she had children. She'd be thirty now, so she probably did. Maybe her psychic link was with the children now, and no longer with him.

Mavranos had got up and slouched back into the living room; now Crane heard him say, quietly, "Blue van just pulled up, and three guys got out of it; they're heading for your place."

What's in the pot is gone, Ozzie had always said. *It ain't yours anymore. You might win it, but until you do, you gotta regard it as spent, not chase it.*

"Up on your porch now," Mavranos said.

Of course, when the antes or blinds have been high, so high that it's as much as you're worth to stay in a dozen hands, why then you gotta play looser.

"Lights on in your living room," Arky said. "Kitchen now. Spare bedroom. Real bedroom, too, probably, but I can't see it from here."

And if the antes have been so big that guys are staying just because of it, sometimes you can bet everything you've got and win with a damn poor hand.

Crane turned the photograph over and looked at the pregnant woman. Then he got up and walked into the living room and stood beside Mavranos. Crane watched the silhouettes moving in his house. One was obviously the fat man. He must have met the van somewhere nearby.

"I've got to get in there," he said.

"No way tonight—and these guys'll probably watch the place for a couple of days. What's in there that we can't get somewhere else?"

"The phone."

"Shit, I told you you could use mine."

"It's gotta be that one."

"Yeah? Tell me why." He was still staring out the window.

Crane looked at Mavranos's lean silhouette, the narrowed eyes glinting in reflected streetlight glow. The man looked like a pirate.

Can I trust him? Crane wondered. He's obviously got some sort of stake in this situation, but I'll swear he's a loner, not associated with any of these—these murky thrones and powers and assassins. We've been sociable neighbors for a while, and he always got along with Susan.

And God, it would be wonderful to have an ally.

"Okay," Crane said slowly. "If we both tell the other guy everything we know—I mean, that he knows—himself—about this stuff—"

Mavranos was grinning at him. "You mean we lay our cards on the table."

"That's it." Crane held out his right hand.

Mavranos enveloped it in his own callused, scarred right hand and shook it firmly twice. "Okay."

Eighteen hours later Crane was crawling on his hands and knees across the floor of his own living room toward the telephone, his right eyelid stinging and his cheek saltily wet.

The intruders had turned off the lights when they had left, but the blinds were raised, and the traffic and neon signs and streetlights of Main Street gave the room a flickering twilight glow in the middle of this Friday night.

Ten minutes earlier Mavranos had driven his car up to the curb in front of Crane's house and had got out and walked up to the front door, to attract the attention of anyone who might be watching the place. After knocking and getting no response, he had gone back to his car, leaned in through the open window, and honked the horn three times—two shorts and one long.

Crane had been in the alley behind the house.

At the first of the short blasts Crane pushed his way through his dilapidated back fence; the second honk blared as he was sprinting across his dark, unkempt back lawn, and when the third began, he punched a leather-gloved hand through his bedroom window, brushed the glass splinters away from the bottom edge of the frame, and dived through and scrambled across the bed.

By the time the horn stopped he was standing beside the bed. The air was warm, almost hot; the heater had been running all night and all day and half the night again, and of course the stove was on.

He took off Arky's work glove and tossed it onto the floor.

The bedroom had been ransacked. The blankets and sheets had been torn off the bed, and the mattress had been slashed, and the bureau drawers had been dumped out on the floor.

He walked down the hall to the bathroom, stepping carefully in the darkness and bracing his hands on the walls, for the floor was an obstacle course of scattered magazines and books and clothes. The bathroom was completely dark, and he groped through the litter of boxes and bottles that had been spilled out of the medicine cabinet into the sink.

He hadn't been able to stop yawning, and his palms were damp.

Among the litter in the sink he had come across the rubber bulb and the bottle of saline solution, and he'd shrugged. As long as you're here, he thought.

Working by touch, he poured some of the solution into the coffee mug that was miraculously still on the sink. He reached a finger up to his face and pushed inward on the side of his right eye. With a sort of inner *sploosh* the plastic hemisphere came loose from the Teflon ring that was attached to two of the muscles in his eye socket. The medial rectus, he remembered, and the lateral rectus. He'd had the ring put in in about 1980. Before that he'd had a glass eye, and once a month he'd had to go to the eye man to have it taken out and cleaned. Now it was a task to be done every day at home, like cleaning contact lenses.

He carefully put the artificial eye into the mug and then used the bulb to suck up some of the saline solution and begin squirting it into the cavity of his empty eye socket.

He hadn't done it this morning, so he squirted it out thoroughly. Irrigating the cavity, his doctor always called it.

Finally he couldn't pretend any longer that he hadn't finished. What had he come in here for?

Oh, he thought. Right. Rubbing alcohol and a sterile pad and a roll of sterile gauze bandage. He replaced his artificial eye, yawned again, then began groping through the darkness. He didn't seem able to take a deep breath.

I bet they cut it, he thought now, crawling across the living-room floor and blinking the excess solution out of his eye. *I bet they did.* He was dragging along the bandages and the bottle of rubbing alcohol, wrapped in a shirt from the laundry hamper.

He lifted the telephone down from the table and picked up the receiver and then took a deep breath and let it out slowly when he heard the dial tone. They had not cut the phone line.

Well, he thought.

He replaced the receiver carefully.

He ran trembling fingers through his hair and glanced around.

All his telephone books, he saw, were gone—not only the ragged spiral-bound notebook with inked entries, but the big Pacific Bell white pages and yellow pages, too. I guess people write numbers in those as well, he thought, in the margins and back pages, and maybe draw asterisks by some of the printed ones, like to distinguish one particular Jones from among a column of them. I wonder what sort of calls all my old friends are going to get.

He peeled a couple of yards off the roll of sterile gauze and tucked the long strip under his leg.

He leaned back, and for nearly a minute he looked up through the window glass at the dark, shaggy head of the palm tree out front swaying in the night breeze. He didn't dare raise his head high enough to be seen from outside, but he could crouch here and watch the palm tree. It's outside the hole I'm in, he thought. All it has to do is suck up nutrients and get ready for tomorrow's photosynthesis session, like every other day.

At last he sighed and pulled Arky's Schrade lock-back knife out of his pocket and opened it. Smoke marks mottled the broad four-inch blade, from Arky's having held it over a lit burner on his stove, but Arky had said to use rubbing alcohol, too, if possible.

Crane twisted the cap off the plastic bottle and poured alcohol over both sides of the blade. The stuff reeked sharply, and it chilled his thigh when he shook a couple of liberal splashes of it onto the left leg of his jeans. He was shivering, and his heart was thudding coldly in his hollow chest.

He had to keep reminding himself that he had thought this out a hundred times during these last eighteen hours, and had not been able to see any other way out.

With his right hand he held the knife upright on his left thigh, the point pricking him an inch or two to the outside of where he figured the femur was; his left hand, open, hovered over his head as he gathered his courage.

He was panting, and after a few seconds his nose caught a new depth and mellowness in the alcohol reek. He glanced away from the knife—

—and then stared at the opened bottle of Laphroaig scotch that was standing on the carpet, with a half-full Old Fashioned glass beside it. They had certainly not been there when he had crawled across the floor three or four minutes ago.

"*Scott*," came Susan's voice softly from the shadows beyond the bottle. He looked up, and he thought he could see her. The diffuse, spotty light made camouflage of the patterns on her clothing, and her face was turned away, but he was sure he could see the fall of her black hair and the contour of one shoulder and leg.

"*Don't, Scott*," she said. "*Why* hurt *yourself to get* her *when you can have a* drink *and get* me?"

Crane's face was dewed with chilly sweat. "Is that what you are?" he asked tightly. "Drink? Delirium tremens? Did *I* bring that bottle out? Am I talking to myself here?"

"*Scott, she's not worth this, have a drink and let me—*"

No, he thought, this can't be a hallucination. Arky saw it twice yesterday, this figure, this creature.

"Come into the bedroom. Bring the bottle."

He could hear a chitinous rustling as the vague figure in the corner stood up. Would it go into the bedroom, or would it come toward him?

It's not Susan, he reminded himself nervously. Susan's dead. This thing has nothing to do with Susan, or nearly nothing. At most it's a psychic fossil of her, in her shape and with some of her memories but made of something else.

It was coming toward him. The light climbed the approaching figure—slim legs, hips, breasts. In a moment he would see its face, the face of his dead wife.

As if he were slamming a door against something dreadful, he slammed his hand down with all his strength onto the butt end of the upright knife.

Breath whistled in through his clenched teeth, and the room seemed to ring with a shrill, tinny whine. The pain in his stabbed leg was a scalding blackness, but he was cold, freezing, and the blood had come so fast that the knife hilt standing up from his thigh was slick with it, and his scrabbling hands slipped off the hot, wet wood of the grip. At last he got a good hold on it and pulled, but the muscles inside his leg seemed to be gripping the blade; it took all his strength to tug the thing up and out of himself, and he gagged as he felt, deep in his leg, the edge cutting more flesh as it was dragged free.

He squinted around at the dim room. The thing that had seemed to be Susan was gone.

His hands were heavy and clumsy as he laid the bandage on the cut in his sopping jeans—*Should have took the pants off first,* he thought dizzily—and then dragged up the length of gauze and tied it off around his leg, as tightly as he could, over the bandage.

His heart, which had been racing before he stabbed himself, seemed to have slowed and taken on a metallic clanking, sounding like a weary old man pitching horseshoes. He thought he could smell the kicked-up dry dust.

Shock, he told himself. Lean back, put your feet up on the couch, elevate the wound above the heart.

Try to relax your rib-cage so you can breathe deep and slow.

Go ahead and hold the leg as tight as you like.

The refrigerator's compressor-motor turned on, then after a minute clicked off again. A siren howled by down Main Street, and he listened to it, vaguely hoping that it might stop somewhere nearby. It didn't.

Come on, he thought; *call.*

Blood was seeping out from under the bandage and running up his thigh and soaking the seat of his pants. The rug will be ruined, he thought; Susan will—

Stop it.

He looked at the glass of scotch. He could smell the smoky, welcoming warmth of it, of her—

Stop it.

The ringing of the telephone jolted him awake. How long had it been ringing? He fumbled at it and managed to knock the receiver off.

"Wait!" he croaked, scrabbling at it with blood-sticky hands. "Don't hang up, wait!"

At last he got the fingers of one hand around it and pulled it across the wet rug and lifted its weight to his ear.

"Hello?"

He heard a woman's voice. "Scott! What happened? Are you all right? What happened? I'm calling paramedics if you don't say something!"

"Diana," he said. He took a deep breath and made himself think. "Are you at home?"

"No, Ozzie made me promise—it doesn't matter, what—"

"Good," he said, talking over her. "Listen to me, and don't hang up. I don't need paramedics. God—give me a minute and don't hang up."

"You sound terrible! I can't give you a minute—*just tell me what happened to your leg.*"

"I stabbed myself, I—"

"How badly? Quick!"

"Not too bad, I think, I did it with a sterilized knife and made sure to hit the side away from that big artery—"

"You did it on *purpose*?" She sounded relieved and very angry. "I was at work, and I fell right over! The manager had to use my sign-off number on the register and make one of the box boys drive me home! Now I'm clocked out, and I don't get sick pay till I've been there a year! What was it, a game of Amputation Poker?"

He sighed deeply. "I needed to get in touch with you quickly."

She seemed to be coughing softly. Then: "You *what*? You must be crazy, I can't—"

"*Goddamm it, listen to me!*" he said harshly. "I may pass out here, and I probably won't be able to get to this phone again. You and Ozzie—and me—somebody wants to kill us all, and they've got the resources to find you and him the way they've found me. Is Ozzie still alive?"

She was quiet for a moment. "Yes," she said.

"I need to talk to him. This has to do with that game I played in on Lake Mead in '69. There was something Ozzie knew—"

"Jesus, it's been more than a minute. I'm out of here—stay by the phone—I'm crazy, but I'll call you from another booth."

He managed to juggle the receiver back onto the phone. Then he just lay on the floor and concentrated on breathing. Luckily the room was warm. A deep, throbbing ache was building in his leg behind the steady heat of the pain.

The phone rang, and he grabbed the receiver. "You?" he said.

"Right. Ozzie made me promise not to talk to you on a traceable phone, especially now, twenty years later. Talk."

"The people that killed your mother want to kill you. And me, and Ozzie. Don't know why. Ozzie knows why, or he wouldn't have ditched me. To save us all, I need to talk to him."

She inhaled. "You're doomed, Scott," she said, and there seemed to be tears in her voice. "If you are still Scott. What did I give you for your birthday in '68?"

"A crayon portrait of me."

"Shit!" she sobbed. "I wish you were already gone! No, I don't. Scotty, I love you. Good-bye."

There was a click in his ear, silence, then the dial tone. He gently hung it up, then sat there for a while and stared at the telephone.

He was bleakly sure that he could stab himself again, in the other leg, or in the belly, and she wouldn't call again.

Tears of self-pity mingled with the sweat and saline solution on his face.

Forty-seven-year-old one-eyed gimp, he thought. He laughed through his tears. What made you imagine you could *help* anybody? She's smart to kiss you off. Any person would do the same. Any real person.

His leg seemed to have stopped actively bleeding, though it throbbed with pain, and the section of rug he was lying on was spongy and slick with cooling blood.

Eventually he reached out and picked up the glass of scotch.

For several minutes he just lay there and inhaled its heady fumes. If he was going to drink it, he was going to drink it, so there was no hurry. Anything that might be waiting in the bedroom could continue to wait. He'd probably have to get fairly drunk, anyway, to be fooled. To get the—the suspension of disbelief.

"'And human love needs human meriting,'" he whispered, quoting Thompson's "The Hound of Heaven," which had been one of Susan's favorite poems. "'How hast thou merited—Of all man's clotted clay the dingiest clot?'" He laughed again, chokingly, and took a deep sniff of the smoky fumes. "'Whom wilt thou find to love ignoble thee, Save Me, save only Me?'" The speaker in the poem had been God, but he supposed gods were relative.

He stared into the glass.

The telephone rang, and he didn't move. It rang again, and then he shook his head sharply and poured the liquor over his bandage. He hissed at the new pain as he grabbed the receiver.

"*Ahhh*—you?"

"Right." Diana sniffed. "The only reason I'm doing this is that I think *he* would, if you'd got *him*. Do you remember where he used to take us for—for *bodonuts*, a lot of Sunday mornings?"

"Sure, sure." This is urgent, he told himself; you're back in the fight, pay attention.

"I'll call him and tell him you want to meet him there tomorrow at noon. I've met him there once or twice; it's the only place he'll agree to talk. Okay? He probably won't come at all. And listen, if"—she was crying, and he could hear fright in her voice when she spoke again—"if he does, and you've got bad friends, tell them he doesn't know where I am or how to reach me, will you? Make them believe it, I swear on my children it's the truth."

"Okay, I'll be there." He rubbed his face. "Diana, you have kids? Are you married? How long——"

"Scott, this isn't a social call!"

"Diana, I love you, too. I swear I'll kill myself before I let anybody use me to get at you." He laughed hoarsely. "I'm good at stabbing myself, I discover. God, kid, this is your brother, Scott, please tell me, where are you?"

He could hear her sniffling. "Where I am is, I'm flying in the grass."

The phrase meant nothing to Crane.

Again there was the click of a broken connection.

He rolled over gingerly and then got up on his hands and knees, sweating and cursing and wincing as he involuntarily flexed the torn muscles in his leg.

I can't leave by the front door, he thought. Even the back door is probably being viewed through the cross-hairs of a riflescope, according to Arky.

It's got to be the bedroom window.

And I've got to crawl, at least as far as the hallway, so as not to be seen from outside.

He knew there was no one else in the house . . . no other human. What the hell was the Susan thing? It was real enough for Arky to have seen it—and even spoken to it!—and substantial enough to have carried a bottle and glass into the living room.

The chair in front of him—Susan, the real Susan, had re-upholstered it a couple of summers ago. And she had moved the leaning bookcase against the wall corner so that it stood up straight, and she had painted the floors. Yesterday he had wondered if her imprint was so distinct on the place that it could project a tangible image of her.

Yesterday, somehow, he had not found the notion horrible.

Now he was trembling at the thought of meeting the thing in the hall, perhaps also on its hands and knees, face to fake face.

He imagined the face white, with solid white eyeballs like an old Greek statue. What might it say? Would its smile resemble Susan's remembered smile?

He shivered and blinked tears out of his eyes. Susan, Susan, he thought, why did you die? Why did you leave me here?

How much of *you* is in this thing?

He began crawling toward the dark hallway arch. Ozzie had never taught him or Diana any prayers, so he whispered the words of religious Christmas carols . . . until he found himself reciting the lyrics of "Sonny Boy," and he closed his throat.

In the hall he stood up, putting his weight on his good leg. Through the open bedroom door he could see the gray rectangle that was the broken-out window, past the dark bulk of the bed, and he made himself walk forward, into the room.

The door of the closet was open, and she was in there, crouched on the pile of clothes that had been yanked off of the hangers.

"Leaving me to go off with your friends," she whispered.

He didn't look at her. "You're—" he began, then stopped, unable to say "*dead*." He knelt on the bed and crawled toward the window. "You're not her," he said unsteadily.

"I'm becoming her. Soon I'll be her." The room was suddenly full of the smell of hot coffee. "I'll fill the cavity."

"I've . . . got to go," he said, clinging to the ordinariness of the phrase.

He carefully swung his cut leg out the window first, then followed it with the other and gripped the sides of the window frame. The night air was cold.

There was a quiet but violent thumping and whining in the closet—apparently she was having some kind of fit. He boosted himself down to the dry grass and limped away across the dark yard toward the gap in the fence.

CHAPTER 11

How Did I Kill Myself?

Crane squinted against the glitter of the morning sun on the rushing freeway pavement.

Rain had been clattering in the roof gutters and hissing in the trees when he and Mavranos had furtively left Mavranos's apartment by the back door, a couple of hours before dawn; but after they'd eaten breakfast in a coffee shop on the other side of town and had walked back out to the parking lot, Mavranos sucking on a toothpick, the sun had been shining in a cleared blue sky, and only the chill of the door handle and the window crank had reminded Crane that it was not yet summer.

They were driving in a station wagon-style truck Mavranos had bought from some impound yard last fall, a big boxy 1972 Suburban with a cracked windshield and oversize tires and an old coat of desert-abraded blue paint. The truck shook and squeaked as it barreled along down the Newport Freeway, but Mavranos drove it easily with one hand on the big steering wheel and the other holding a can of Coors wrapped in what he called a "deceptor"—a rectangle of supple plastic with the Coca-Cola logo printed on it.

In the passenger seat, with his knees up because of the litter of books and socket wrench sets and old clothes on the floorboards, Crane sipped lukewarm coffee from a Styrofoam cup and tried to brace himself against the vehicle's shaking. Mavranos had bandaged his gashed thigh with the easy competence of an old Boy Scout and had assured Crane that it wouldn't fester, but the leg ached and throbbed, and the one time Crane had bumped it against a chair arm the world had gone colorless and he had had to look at the floor and breathe deeply to keep from fainting.

He was wearing a pair of Mavranos's old jeans, rolled up at the ankles like a kid's because they were too long in the legs.

Leaning his hot forehead now against the cold window glass, he realized that it must have been a long time since he had last traveled on this freeway. He remembered broad, irrigated fields of string beans and strawberries stretching away on either side, but now there were "Auto Malls," and gigantic buildings of bronze-colored glass with names like UNiSYS and WANG on them, and clusters of shiny new banks and condominiums and hotels around the double-level marble-and-skylights-and-ferns shopping mall called South Coast Plaza.

It was an Orange County with no orange trees anymore, a region conquered by developers, who had made it sterile even as they had made it fabulously valuable, and the moneyed complacency of the area seemed by definition to exclude people like him and Arky as surely as it had come to exclude the farmers.

"Suits," growled Mavranos after a glance away from the traffic ahead. He paused to sip his beer. "They . . . *replicate*. The freeways are dead stopped half the time, you can't exercise in this air and you can't eat fish you catch in the bay, and nobody who'd speak to you or me can afford a house even though the suits have terraced all the old hills and canyons with the damn things . . . and have you noticed that these people don't *do* anything? They're all *middlemen*—they sell stuff or broker stuff or package stuff or advertise stuff or speculate in stuff."

Crane grinned weakly against the window glass. "*Some* of 'em must do things, Arky."

"I suppose—but any such'll soon be crowded out. The suits I'm talking about are growing, replicating, at the expense of everything else, even the plain old goddamn dirt and water."

A new BMW passed them at high speed on the right.

"Susan's dead," Crane said suddenly. "My wife."

Mavranos turned to stare at him for a moment, and his foot was off the accelerator. "When?" he barked. "How? When did you hear this?"

"It happened thirteen weeks ago. Remember when the paramedics came, and I said she fainted?" Crane finished the coffee and tossed the Styrofoam cup into the back of the truck. "Actually she died. Fibrillation. Heart attack."

"Bull*shit* thirteen weeks, I—"

"That's not her, what you saw and talked to. That's . . . I don't know what it is, some kind of ghost. I'd have told you about it before, but it was only last night that I . . . figured out it must have something to do with this cards stuff."

Mavranos shook his head, frowning fiercely. "Are—are you *sure*? That she's dead? You weren't drunk, maybe, and she left you or something?"

"Arky, I—" Crane spread his hands helplessly. "I'm sure."

"Goddammit." Mavranos was staring straight ahead at the traffic, but he was gulping, and his eyes were bright. "You better tell me about this shit, Pogo."

Crane took the beer can out of Arky's hand and took a deep sip. "She was drinking coffee one morning," he began.

They parked in a big lot just west of the Balboa pier and then walked away from the thunder and spume of the surf to the narrow, tree-shaded lane that was Main Street. Crane's leg ached and throbbed, and several times he called for a pause just to breathe deeply and stand with his weight on his good leg.

Balboa was quiet on this spring morning. Cars hissed past on the wet pavement of Balboa Boulevard, but there were empty parking places along the curbs, and the only people on the sidewalks seemed to be locals heading for the bakery, lured by the smell of hot coffee on the chilly breeze.

"Where'd you used to get these—these godonuts?" asked Mavranos, his hands in the pockets of his tattered khaki jacket.

"Bodonuts," Crane said. "My kid sister made up the word. It's Balboa doughnuts. Not here. Over on the island."

Over on the island. The phrase upset him somehow, and he didn't like the idea that even now there was a lot of water nearby—the channel ahead of them and the ocean behind.

"'Fear death by water,'" said Mavranos.

Crane glanced at him sharply. "What?"

"That's from *The Waste Land*—you know, T. S. Eliot. At the beginning of the poem, when Madame Sosostris is reading the Tarot cards. 'And here is the one-eyed merchant, and this card,/ Which is blank, is something he carries on his back,/ Which I am forbidden to see. I do not find/ The Hanged Man. Fear death by water.'"

Crane stopped walking again, and stared at him. A sea gull was strutting along the sidewalk, and somewhere overhead another one called shrilly.

"You go around reading T. S. Eliot," Crane said.

Mavranos squinted belligerently. "I *study.* I may not have read all your Hemingway and Prowst and H. Salt Fitzgerald, but I find out a lot of stuff, from all sorts of books, that has to do with me finding a cure—and if you can't see that it also has to do with *your* troubles, then—"

"No, no, I do see it. You're going to have to tell me a lot more about *The Waste Land* and about Eliot. It's just that . . . it's rare to run across someone who just pops off with an Eliot quote, just like that."

"You evidently haven't noticed that I'm a rare person, Pogo."

Doing a kind of limping shuffle now, Crane led Mavranos down Main and past the dressy seafood restaurant to the far sidewalk, beyond the railing of which pleasure boats rocked at their moorings on the gray-green swell. The ferry dock was to their left, past the Fun Zone with its arcades and palm-readers and frozen-banana-on-a-stick stands, but even this narrow area had taken on an air of sophistication since the days when he used to come here with Ozzie and Diana.

It used to be all garishly painted shacky plywood buildings, with hippies and drunks slouching along the stained sidewalk, but now there were stairways with brass railings leading up to terrace restaurants with patio umbrellas, and video games flashing in the arcade, and a glossy merry-go-round that played a weirdly swing version of "Ain't We Got Fun."

Crane felt even more out of place here than he had on the freeway.

One ferry was at the dock, its iron gate swung up to let three cars move booming and creaking up the wooden ramp to the pavement; another ferry was receding away, now about halfway across the mile-wide channel. The ferries, with their worn red and white paint and weathered floorboards, seemed to be the only elements of the local scene that might date from Crane's time.

Crane stepped aboard, not liking the shifting of the deck. *Fear death by water,* he thought.

The wide wooden seats were puddled with rain water this morning, so after giving two quarters to the girl in the yellow rubber rain suit with the money changer on her canvas belt, Crane and Mavranos stood braced on the gray-painted tar paper deck as the engine gunned and the boat surged gently out onto the face of the water, and they watched the palm trees and boat masts and low buildings of Balboa Island draw closer.

Mavranos pushed back his ragged black hair and peered over the rail. "Jesus, look at all the fish—bass and mackerel, damn, and that's a sand shark. You could fire a shotgun into the water and kill a dozen of 'em."

Crane looked down into the water at the many vague forms under the surface. "I'll bet Saturn will be bright tonight," he said softly, "with all his moons moving behind him."

They got off the ferry at the island dock and walked east along the broad waterfront walk, between expensive, yardless houses to the left and a short, sloping beach fretted with private docks to the right. Crane was limping along steadily, though his face was sweaty and pale.

Dark clouds were moving in again from the north and west, contrasting vividly with the patches of blue sky. Crane looked up and saw high-circling sea gulls lit white by the slanting sun against a backdrop of black cumulus.

At the southern end of Marine Street a thick pipe protruded from the sand slope and extended a few yards out into the water. DANGER, said a sign above it, END OF STORM DRAIN.

More water, thought Crane, *and dangerous*. "It's to the left here," he said nervously. "There's a market up ahead. Vegetables, bread—that's where we used to get the doughnuts. Old place, been there since the twenties. You wait here."

"I might be able to help."

"You look like Genghis Khan. Trust me, wait here."

"Okay, Pogo, but if the old guy's there, remember everything he says."

"Hey, I'm *sober* today, remember?"

Crane limped away up the street, still in sunlight but walking toward the darkness that was tucked in under the northern clouds. Narrow houses crowded up to the sidewalks; the only people he saw were women kneeling in tiny gardens and men doing incomprehensible work with shrill, hand-held power tools in open garages on this Saturday morning.

The market was called Hershey's Market now, not the Arden's Milk Market Spot as he remembered, and what used to be a drugstore across the street was currently a real estate office; but the shapes of the buildings were the same, and he began trying to walk faster.

"Freeze, Scott."

The remembered voice was still authoritative, and Crane obeyed automatically. Hesitantly he looked to the side and saw a tall, thin figure in the shadow under the awning of the old Village Inn restaurant, twenty feet away across the puddled street.

"Oz?"

"I've got a gun, cocked, hollow-point slugs, pointed straight at my own heart," said the old man tensely. "Who's your friend down by the water?"

"He's a neighbor of mine, he's in the same sort of trouble I'm in. I—"

"What the hell kind of truck is that to drive around in?"

"Truck . . . ? The one we came in? It's his, it's a Suburban; he buys cars from an impound yard—"

"Never mind. What book were you reading when we went to get Diana?"

"Goddamn, Oz, you've got no right to expect me to remember that, but it was *The Monster Men*, by Edgar Rice—"

"Okay, he hasn't had the next game yet. Probably be *this* Easter, though." The old man stepped out of the shadows, leaning on an aluminum ortho cane with a quadripod base. His hair was thin and cottony white over his pink scalp, and he was wearing a baggy dark gray suit with a white shirt and blue tie. His free hand stayed in the right side pocket of his coat as he walked slowly across the wet pavement to Crane. "What do you want from me?"

Tears blurred Crane's eyes. "How about *How've you been?* Christ, I made a mistake, I was a stupid kid; how many kids aren't? Aren't you going to forgive me even now, twenty years later? This thing looks like *killing* me, and you're acting like—"

"You look like hell," the old man said harshly. "You drink way too much, don't you? And now, when it's too late, you're driving around with some bum in a joke truck trying to figure out how to stop the rain. Shit." He let his cane stand by itself and stepped forward and threw his free arm around Crane. "I love you, boy, but you're a dead man," he said muffledly into Crane's collar.

"Christ, Oz, I love you," Crane said, clasping the old man's narrow shoulders. "And even if I am dead, it's good to see you one more time. But listen, *tell me what happened*. How did I kill myself by playing in that—that God damned game?"

Ozzie stood back and again gripped the rubber handle of his standing cane, and Crane could see how the years had withered the once-strong face, extinguished the evidence of all emotions except for anxiety and—maybe still—some of the old humor.

"Assumption," Ozzie said. "That guy, that Ricky Leroy, *assumed* you, put a lien on your body. A sort of *balloon* lien. Shit, son, I read up on this, and asked around, after I lost you to it—and I had known a good deal about the dangers of cards even before, all that stuff you thought was like step-on-a-crack-break-your-mother's-back."

A car was making its way down the narrow street, and Crane and Ozzie stepped up onto the curb.

"You're still yourself now," Ozzie went on, "looking out of your eyes, but after the next game on the lake it'll be *him*, and he'll have everybody else, too, that took money for the assumed hands in that game in 'sixty-nine, that series of games. Leroy'll have you all like a collection of remote, mobile, closed-circuit TV sets. Don't start reading no real long books, son." The old man's eyes were wet as he shook his head. "And don't think it gives me any pleasure to tell you all this."

Crane clenched his fists, feeling the muscles in his palms with his tingling fingertips. "There's—isn't there anything I can *do*? Is it just *over*? Can't I go . . . I don't know, *kill* this guy?"

Ozzie shook his head sadly. "Let's go walk back to where your friend is. No, you can't kill him. You could kill one of the bodies he's in, or a couple even, but he'll have at least one stashed somewhere that you couldn't even hear of, much less get to. And besides, he's already started killing you, loosening your soul for the eviction. Dionysus has got his hand on your throat in the form of drink, and any family or pets you may have are going to start dying of the randomness illnesses: cancers, heart irregularities—"

Heart irregularities, Crane thought.

Heart irregularities.

He kept walking. "That would be . . . caused by me?" he said as evenly as he could.

Ozzie gave him a piercing look. "Shit, I'm sorry, that was damn thoughtless of me. Of course, it already has happened, hasn't it? Who?"

"My wife. She—" He was sitting on the curb suddenly. "Heart attack." His body felt hollowed out, and his hands moved vaguely in front of him as though he were groping in darkness for something he didn't know the shape of.

One of the randomness illnesses, he heard Ozzie's voice say in his memory. And then he heard his own voice: *Caused by me?*

"Get up, Scott." Ozzie reached down with his free hand and shook Crane's shoulder, and Crane got slowly to his feet, not even wincing when his bad leg took his weight. "It's—really, it's no more your fault than if you'd been driving and got in a crash, and she died. But your hippie friend might be smart to . . . continue his friendship with you over the phone," Ozzie said.

Crane was blinking around. Nothing had changed—the people who had been walking past the shops further up the street were still walking—but there seemed to be a ringing in the air and a quiver in the pavement, as if some *thing* had just happened.

Caused by me . . .

He and the old man resumed their labored progress down the sidewalk.

"My hippie friend," Crane said absently. He yawned. "It's, what, it's too late for my hippie friend, he's already got cancer. Had it before he ever found me." Crane felt very tired—he hadn't got any sleep last night—but his heart was pounding, and his forehead was cold with nausea.

"I'd hate to see him *eat* through that mustache." Ozzie was staring ahead; Crane followed his gaze and saw Mavranos sitting on a brick planter.

"Yeah, it is a sight," said Crane automatically. He waved, and Mavranos hiked himself off it and slouched forward.

"You say he found you," said Ozzie. "Why was he looking for you?"

It was an effort to speak. "He thinks I'll lead him to the place where randomness lives—" He paused to try and take a deep breath, "—and he'll·be able to trick randomness into undoing his cancer."

Still frowning, Ozzie laughed softly. "That's not bad. Like raising to the limit and then throwing away all five cards for new ones. Stupid and hopeless, but I like the style." The old man's hand was still in the pocket of the windbreaker. "Why don't you go explain to him about my gun, hmm?"

CHAPTER 12

To the Chapel Perilous

All three of them sat on the coping of the brick planter. Ozzie was on the end, a couple of feet away from Crane, and he looked at his watch.

"I can give you boys ten minutes," the old man said, "and then I won't ever see either of you again in this world."

Looking away, the old man reached over and squeezed Crane's hand for a moment.

"After Diana called me last night," Ozzie said, "I got in touch with some friends, and they've been watching the cars that park, and the ferry, and they had you two down for doubtful as soon as you'd got out of your truck. If I don't walk away from you within half an hour of when I first spoke to you, Scott, a couple of them'll walk down here and escort me away. And if I go any farther than this here spot *with* you, they'll kill both of you. And of course, if anyone *else* should authoritatively join us—and even a helicopter would have a time getting in or out of here easy—we're probably all *three* dead instantly."

Mavranos stared past Crane at Ozzie for a moment, then laughed. "I like this old fart, Scott," he drawled.

Crane forced himself to think. "How did that game on the water, the game on Lake Mead, give Ricky Leroy a lien on my body?" he asked quickly.

Ozzie ran his free hand through his sparse white hair. "Fortune-telling by cards works sometimes. But it's *pre*scriptive rather than *de*scriptive. When it's working, if you take money for a hand, you've sold the hand, sold the lucky-in-finances or unlucky-with-girls or whatever the cards may happen to represent. If you *pay* money, you've *bought* it, bought those qualities, bought that luck. And a hand of Poker is a number of qualities. The sum of the five cards may mean that you're rich but impotent, or happy but gonna die young, or any other combination of factors. You buy or sell all five at once, or all seven if it's Seven-Stud. This much I told you years ago."

"Yeah, I—"

"Shut up. That's how you can buy or sell . . . *consequences* with cards; with *bodies* it's trickier. To buy a guy's body, you've got to become his parent first. I don't know how that works; it's got something to do with genes and cards both being quantized things, discrete things, and the fact that it's a random selection of 'em from two sources that defines the resulting individual. There was a hand that was a combination of two people's cards, and that hand defined *you*, and then you took money for it. It was you, it was the makeup of you, as surely as the pattern of your genes is the makeup of you, and you let Ricky Leroy assume it. Have it. Buy your body. He's let you run around with it for twenty years, but after this next game, when he'll buy another lot of idiots, he's gonna take possession of the ripe old ones." The old man had been staring hard at the pavement as he spoke, and now he pressed his lips together firmly.

"And there's nothing I can do even to . . . slow this down?"

Ozzie looked up and exhaled. "Oh, slow it down—sure. Don't drink alcohol. Dionysus isn't a nice guy these days— he's also known as Bacchus, the god of wine—and he's on Leroy's side. A case could probably be made that Leroy *is* Dionysus. Stay by water—on it, if you can—though you're gonna start hating the sight of water like a hydrophobic dog. Don't play cards; he can sense you if you do. But after Easter none of it will have made any difference." He shook his head. "I'm very goddamn sorry, son."

Crane took a deep breath of the chilly sea air. "I'm going to fight it," he said wonderingly, realizing that he meant it. "Fight him."

Ozzie shrugged and nodded. "It's good to have something to occupy your time."

Mavranos leaned forward. "Me ditching my cancer. Is there a chance of it?"

Ozzie smiled gently, and though it deepened his wrinkles, it made him look younger. "Sure. A worthless chance, but no worse than playing the lottery. If you can be in a . . . place, a focus, where a heavy recurrent statistical pattern turns random, or vice versa . . . something like when the pattern of a Craps table changes from hot to cold, if you could be at a sweaty high-stakes game when it shifts . . . it's practically got to be in Las Vegas, you need the odds swarming like flies around you real thick, a lot of games working . . . and they all of them at once shift from in-step to not-in-step, a *phase change,* with you participating, you could come out with your cells not remembering that they wanted to go cancerous."

"Like what Arthur Winfree did with mosquitoes," said Mavranos. Seeing Ozzie's blank look, he explained, "Mosquitoes eat and sleep in a regular cycle, and the—the timing gear is the sunlight coming and going every day. You can shorten or lengthen that cycle, readjust the timing, by keeping 'em indoors and changing the periods of light and dark; and the various possible patterns, if you chart 'em, contain a math thing called a *singularity.* If you hit the mosquitoes with a bright light at precisely the right instant, they lose the cycle, just sleep and fly and stand around with no sense or pattern at all. Another calculated flash will put 'em back into the cycle."

Ozzie stared at Mavranos. "Yes. Very good. That's a better example than my Craps table, though I still think you'll have to try it in Vegas. Freest possible flow of numbers and odds around you, and psychic factors, too, you better believe it. And it'd help to go in with a very conspicuously *ordered* thing or person or something, so that when the rearrangement wave collapsed, there'd be incentive for it all to fall out on the side of order. Like a seed crystal." The old man yawned and shrugged. "I think."

Crane shook himself and dug in his pocket. "And what can we do to save Diana?"

Ozzie was suddenly alert. "What does she need saving from?"

"Look at this," said Crane, passing the old man the photograph of Lady Issit. "I assume 'fold' means 'kill.'"

"Yes, it does," the old man said, reading the note on the back after having glanced at the picture. "She'll be all right, I'm pretty sure. They'd like to use her, some of them, or kill her, but she's not conspicuous—*she* never played any Assumption—and even if they captured you and me right now and shot us up with sodium pentothal, it wouldn't help, because neither of us knows where she is." He handed the photograph back. "No, son, the best thing we can do for her is leave her alone."

Ozzie looked at his watch and got down off the planter. "Time's up." With a sort of unhappy formality the old man held out his right hand, and Crane took it. "Now I'm going to go away and enjoy what's left of my life," Ozzie said, in the awkward tone of someone reciting a memorized speech, "and I suggest you . . . two . . . do the same. As it stands, I look like outliving, uh, the two of you, and I'm honestly sorry about that. Scott, it's good to have seen you again . . . and I'm glad to hear you were married. Sometimes I wish I'd got married. Archimedes, I wish you luck."

Crane got down, too. "Diana didn't say where she was living, but she said she was . . . what was it?"

"Flying in the grass," said Mavranos.

Ozzie's eyes lost their focus for a moment, and his head lowered slightly. Then he inhaled and exhaled, and he straightened up and pumped his fist three times in the air.

Somewhere up the street a car horn honked twice.

Ozzie gave Crane a tense look. "That means 'please confirm.'" Again he pumped his fist three times overhead.

The car honked again, and now a boat in the channel behind them hooted.

"Okay," Ozzie said, his voice shaky for the first time since Crane had met him, "You've bought an extension on your time. Tell me everything she said."

After Crane had recounted everything he could recall Diana's saying, with Mavranos reminding him of a couple of details he'd mentioned last night while he was getting his leg bandaged, Ozzie leaned against the planter and stared up at the blackening sky. After a minute or so Crane started to speak, but Ozzie waved him to silence.

Finally the old man lowered his head and looked at Crane. "You do want to save her," he said.

"It's . . . nearly all I've got *left* to want," Crane said.

"Then we're going to have to go back to your telephone, and you're going to have to stab yourself again, or something, shove your hand in the garbage disposal if that's what it takes, and when she calls, I'll tell her to get out of where she is. If she stays there, she's had it, she's dead or worse, especially since she's so naïve about all this stuff, the cards and all. I thought she'd be safer that way, but look where the little idiot runs to. But I'll tell her to leave. And I'll tell her how. She'll listen to me. Okay?"

"Put my hand in the garbage disposal."

"Not literally, but whatever it takes. Okay?"

". . . Sure, Oz." Crane tried to put some irony into it, but even in his own ears he sounded sick and scared and eager to please.

Mavranos was grinning. "Before you start making sausage out of yourself, Pogo—before we even go back home—let's call your number. No use even going there, much less chopping you up, if they've cut the lines or got somebody there."

"Good thought," said Crane, wishing he had a drink.

There was a pay telephone back up the street in the entry of the Village Inn, and Ozzie put a quarter in the slot and then tilted the receiver aside as he punched out the remembered number.

After two rings there was an answer. "Yeah," a young man's voice said earnestly, "this is Scott Crane's residence, he's— listen, could you hold a minute?"

"Sure," said Ozzie, nodding grimly at Mavranos.

They heard the clunk of the distant telephone being put down; a dog was barking somewhere in the relayed background, and a car alarm was hooting.

After a few moments the voice came back on. "Yeah, hello?"

"Could I speak to Scott Crane, please?"

"Jesus, Scott was in an accident," the voice said, "he—wait, I can see Jim's car pulling up, he was off visiting Scott at the hospital, Jim's a friend of his, claimed to be his brother to be able to get in to see him, you wanna hang on 'til Jim gets in here? He'll be able to tell you what's what."

"I'm just calling for the *Orange County Register*," Ozzie said, "to see if he wanted to subscribe. Sorry to have disturbed you at a bad time." He pressed down the hang-up lever.

"Wow," said Crane. "They've got a guy in my place."

"Don't talk for a minute," Ozzie said. He walked away from the telephone, staring out the window at the yellow-lit street under the black sky. "I could put an ad in the personals," he said softly. "But I couldn't even hope she'd see it or get it unless I used her name, and I don't dare do that . . . and I don't even know what her last name is now. . . ." He shook his head, frowning and unhappy. "Let's go outside."

Crane and Mavranos followed the old man out onto the Marine Avenue sidewalk and matched his slow pace south, back toward the water. Shingled roofs steamed in the sunlight on the houses along the street, even as rain silently made spots on the pavement.

"I haven't held a hand of cards since that game in the Horseshoe in '69," Ozzie said. "I couldn't take the chance on being recognized, and word getting back to you. I was sixty-one years old, with a car and twenty-four thousand dollars and a nine-year-old foster daughter and no skill, no trade."

Crane had started to say something, and Ozzie waved him to silence. "You already said you're sorry," the old man went on, "and it was a long time ago. Anyway, she and I went somewhere a person can live cheap, and after a while I got a *job*—first time in my life—and Diana went to school. I made some good investments, and for these last . . . say, ten years . . . I've been *comfortable.* I know enough about how things work to get help like I had this morning, and if it's only once in a long while, I can even afford it."

Ozzie laughed. "You know what I do for work now? I make ashtrays and coffee mugs and pots, out of clay. I've got a kiln in my back yard. I sell 'em to these boutique-type shops, the kind of place that's mostly for tourists. I've always signed 'em with a fake name. Anytime the demand for 'em gets serious, I stop making 'em for a year or so, 'til people forget they wanted 'em. One time a local paper wanted to do an article on me; I quit making the damn things for about six years after that. Publicity I don't want."

The rain was coming down more steadily now, and the light was fading.

"You ever been in jail, either of you?" Ozzie asked.

Both men nodded.

"Tell you what I hate, that little toilet with no seat, and you got six guys who gotta use it. And I hate the idea of someday maybe living behind a dumpster, wearing four dirty shirts and three pairs of weird old pants at the same time . . . and the idea of getting seriously beat up, you know, where you can feel stuff breaking inside you and the guys won't stop kicking. And I hate the idea of being in a hospital with catheters and ventilators shoved into me every which way. Bedpans. Bedbaths. Bedsores."

He sighed. "What I like is my house, little old Spanish-style place I live in, all paid off, and my cats and my Louis L'Amour books and my Ballantine scotch and an old Kaywoodie pipe stuffed with Amphora Red cavendish. And I've got all the Benny Goodman and Glenn Miller and Bing Crosby on cassettes."

"That's what you *like*," said Mavranos softly.

"Right," Ozzie agreed, staring ahead at the water. "Diana I love." His wrinkled old face was wet with rain. "But I wonder . . . if I can even *do* anything. Of course, that's my cats and L'Amours and cassettes talking: *There's nothing an eighty-two-year-old man can do about it—so, sad as it is, stay home, with us.*"

"What's 'flying in the grass' mean?" asked Crane uncomfortably.

Ozzie blinked and looked over at him. "Hmm? Oh—it's an old pilots' term for flying very low, crowding the ground, to avoid showing up on radar screens. Scoot in around the hills and barely clear the power lines, and you're just one more bit of the base-fuzz that's the features of the terrain. You can be right under the enemy's nose, but you're keeping such a low profile that he doesn't even see you."

They were back to the storm drain warning sign, and Ozzie led them to the right along the waterfront walk, toward the ferry. Mavranos, evidently impatient with the slow pace of his companions, was walking backward in a zig-zag pattern ahead of them.

"What have you got in the way of travel necessities?" the old man asked. "I don't think it'd be smart to go anywhere near your place."

"Actually," said Crane, touching his pocket, "I've got about two grand on me."

"I've got some bucks, too," said Mavranos, "and Scott's got a .357 in the car, and I've got a .38 Special in the glove compartment, and I gather you've got a gun. A shotgun and ammo we can pick up on the way—and a locking box so we'll be legal when we cross the border."

Ozzie was nodding.

"Border?" repeated Crane. "Where are we going?"

"To where your foster sister is," said Mavranos impatiently, "to the Chapel Perilous in the Waste Land. Las Vegas."

Ozzie was shivering. "Yes. Back to Las Vegas." He began walking faster. "Let's step it up here, gentlemen," he said in a brittle, nearly cheerful tone. "Do you have a heater in your fool truck, Archimedes? I probably forgot to say that being cold is also one of the things I hate."

"Got a heater that'll hard-cook eggs in your shirt pockets," Mavranos assured him. "But I got no air conditioner; that'll be a factor when we're out in the nowhere middle of the Mojave Desert."

They filled the Suburban's gas tank and radiator and checked the tires, and then spent two hundred dollars at the Grant Boys on Newport Boulevard for a Mossberg shotgun and a box of number six shells. The shotgun was a pump-action twelve-gauge with a seventeen-inch barrel and no shoulder stock, just a hard black-plastic pistol-grip, and Crane winced at the thought of all that recoil slamming into the palm of his hand; Ozzie would probably shatter his old wrist if he were ever to shoot it. They also bought a four-foot-long gun-carrying case with an orange plastic finish molded to look like alligator hide; it had a piano-hinge down the long side away from the handle, and when it was opened out flat, the interior was two sheets of gray foam rubber knobbed with patterns of rounded pyramids. Mavranos said it looked like an electron microscope view of atoms in a crystal, and Ozzie said shortly that he had already gathered that Mavranos was smart, and didn't need to be reminded all the time.

Ozzie let the two younger men carry the purchases out to the truck—Scott moving slowly and favoring his bad leg—and then the old man climbed carefully into the back seat and got himself settled before Mavranos started the engine and turned right onto the boulevard.

The interior of the truck was steamy, and Crane cranked down his window to get relief from the smells of motor oil and old socks and crumpled takeout bags from Taco Bell.

Newport Boulevard had just broadened out into the Newport Freeway when Ozzie leaned forward from the back seat and tapped Mavranos on the shoulder. "Take the 405 north there, like you were going to the LAX airport."

Crane looked back over his shoulder at the old man. "I thought we were going to Vegas—straight up the 55 here to the 91 east."

"Do as I said, please, Archimedes," said Ozzie.

Mavranos shrugged and made the long turn northward onto the 405. He took a sip from a fresh can of Coors.

"Uh," said Crane. "Isn't this . . . the *long* way to Las Vegas?"

"You think your old man's nuts," said Ozzie tiredly, rocking on the back seat next to a battered tin Coleman stove. He sighed. "Listen, you wouldn't sail to . . . Catalina, even, would you, without checking reports on the weather and currents and tides? And there's nothing between here and *Catalina* that would particularly love to see you dead, and anyway, it's only twenty-six miles. Well, boy, right now you're aiming to drive more than *two hundred* miles, through all sorts of weather and tides you never even *heard* of, with a lot of bad guys watching for you." He shook his head. "You gotta clock the tides first, boy." He bared his yellow teeth in what might have been a grin. "We gotta check the weather, lick a finger and hold it up in the breeze, so we'll know what kind of rigging to use. We gotta go to Gardena."

Mavranos squinted into the rearview mirror. *"Gardena?"*

"There's legal Poker clubs in Gardena," Crane said, "and in a lot of the other areas of L.A. around there." He shifted around on the front seat. "But you always said not to play in those places."

"Not for money, no," said Ozzie, "paying for your seat and playing with people whose betting habits you don't know. But we're not after money today, are we? And the worst thing about trying to make *money* at these big Poker emporiums, with like fifty or a hundred tables working, is that the fortune-telling effect naturally happens that much more often, and when it starts at one table, a lot of times it'll spread."

"Like a seed crystal again," said Mavranos.

"Right. You'll find the savvy players always have cigarettes burning even if they don't smoke, so they can watch how the smoke behaves—it starts puddling above the middle of the table, they get out—and they'll have some drink, mostly just Coke or water, so they can keep an eye on the level of it, same reason. But I'm gonna *want* to see the . . . tides of fortune. And I'll get into some smoke-puddling games, and if the hands I get apply to us, I'll try to buy us good luck, or sell bad luck to somebody else."

"What do you want us to do?" asked Mavranos.

"You got cigarettes?" Ozzie asked.

"Half carton of desert dogs back there. Camels."

"Well, you two can play if you'll keep cigarettes lit and watch the smoke—and fold out when it acts funny. Now I think of it, Scott, it might be a good idea for you to play some; if they sense you, they'll put you in L.A., which you're not gonna be for much longer. Otherwise be railbirds—watch, have a sandwich, whatever." Ozzie was peering out ahead through the cracked windshield. "North on the 605 here—catch the 5 and take it north, that should take us into the middle of it, and being close to the L.A. River won't hurt, though it's always dry."

Even after twenty-one years Crane knew Ozzie's voice well enough to know that the old man was scared—taking risks he'd avoided even in the days of his prime, jumping out of his comfortable old man's routine with no time at all to prepare, without even spare clothes or personal possessions or books or any idea of where he would wind up sleeping tonight, or the night after—but Crane could sense, too, the disguised excitement.

The old man was chasing the white line again.

CHAPTER 13

Come Back Here on New Year's Day, You See Nothing but Dirt

Al Funo drove slowly past the old Spanish house that was 106 East Second Street. He had put the rear window back into the Porsche, and the heater was keeping him warm in spite of the chilly wind shaking the palm trees.

He drove on past the house, and when he saw the old green Torino with its shot windows in the parking lot beyond the duplexes, he smiled. This was the guy all right.

He had got the address from a friend who could run license plate numbers; it had taken more than twenty-four hours, but Scarecrow Smith—or, as his real name seemed to be, Scott Crane—apparently hadn't gone anywhere.

A blue van with tinted windows was parked on the other side of the street, and as Funo drove slowly past it, he noticed a faint, powdery white mark on the front side of the rear tire; that implied that a meter maid had chalked the vehicle recently, so recently that the driver had moved only a few yards before parking again. Was someone watching Crane's house? Obstadt's man had warned him that this assignment might be contested.

He looked more closely at the other cars parked along the street under the carob tree boughs, and noticed: an old pickup truck, empty; a Honda, empty; and a gray Jaguar, with a fat bald man sitting inside.

Funo turned left onto Bush Street and then right onto Third. He drove for a block and then pulled into a Chevron station that had a pay telephone at the edge of the asphalt apron, out by the self-serve air and water hoses. He got out of his car, got Crane's telephone number from information, and punched it in.

The phone rang twice at the other end, and then a young

122

man's voice said, breathlessly, "Scott Crane's residence, can you hold a minute?"

"Sure, friend," said Funo easily, watching the sweep second-hand of his Rolex. He had at least three minutes before anybody could possibly trace the call, even if they'd managed to get Pacific Bell security to put a trap on the line.

"Sorry," said the voice after only ten seconds. "Scott was in an accident, he's in the hospital."

Nicked him after all, thought Funo. "Jesus," he said in a shocked tone, "what *happened*? I was playing Poker with him Tuesday night!"

"You were? Listen, he keeps asking for two people—he's semi-conscious—two people named Ozzie and Diana. Do you by any chance know who they are?"

"*Sure* I know Ozzie and Diana!" said Funo instantly. "Listen, what hospital is he in? I'll bring them over."

A car alarm in the Norm's parking lot started up, monotonously honking *beep . . . beep . . . beep* as a couple of shabbily dressed men walked hastily away down the sidewalk. Stupid bums, Funo thought.

"It's," said the voice at the other end, "shit . . . I can't remember the name. Jim's the one who knows it, and he's on his way back . . . right now, matter of fact. Why don't you pick up Ozzie and Diana and bring them over to the house? Or just give me their numbers, sure. I—"

"I can't right now," said Funo. "How about if I call back soon, when Jim'll be home?" He spoke loudly, for he could hear the car alarm both directly and, more faintly, over the telephone.

"Could you give me their numbers?" asked the agitated young man. "Where do they live? Diana he 'specially needs to see."

"I don't know exactly, they're friends of friends. When can I call and catch Jim?"

"God, I don't know how long either of us is gonna be able to hang around here. Uh—are you at a number where Jim can get hold of you?"

Funo looked around at the gas station lot. "For the next half hour anyway, sure. Got a pencil?" He read off the number of the pay phone.

"Okay," said the voice on the other end, "got it. We'll get back to you quick."

"Thanks," said Funo. "I really appreciate it. I mean it."

He hung up the phone.

Something was bothering him, and he always paid attention to his hunches. What was it? That noise, the car horn honking on and on . . .

He'd heard it over the telephone as well as directly. Therefore, the young man at the other end had probably heard it both ways, too, and would know that Funo was calling from a nearby outdoor telephone.

Funo quickly folded himself into the Porsche and drove across Third and parked behind a Pioneer Chicken restaurant, then walked inside and sat at a table from which, through the tinted glass, he could watch the gas station. If nothing happened within half an hour, he would drive to another phone and call again.

Within five minutes the gray Jaguar had pulled into the Chevron station, and the fat man hauled his startling bulk out of the driver's seat. He looked at the telephone, and then for several seconds looked around at the nearby cars and pedestrians. After a while he stumped over to the cashier window and talked to whoever was inside.

Funo's heart was thumping, and a twitchy grin bared his teeth. Pretty good, he thought. They could tell I was within earshot to the north. I wonder what they had for south—another car horn, in a different pitch or cadence? A barking dog? A realistic-looking street lunatic chanting about Jesus?

Through the tinted window Funo watched as the fat man got back into the idling Jaguar, and for several minutes just sat there behind the wheel; then the car moved off, turning left onto Third Street, back toward Crane's place.

The Jaguar had a Nevada license plate. Funo wrote down the number.

The Commerce Casino was the first one Crane saw, a gigantic cubical building that from the front looked like some ancient Mediterranean temple, with its arched entrance and gold pillars and expanses of windowless wall, and looked like a prison from around in the back lot, where they had to park. There was even a little guard tower back there. To the south side of the casino a dozen high-tension electrical cables hung from the skeletal silver shoulders of a line of tall towers that marched away to the north and south; on the long, narrow plot of land under the towers, as if nourished by the electromagnetic fields, knee-high pine trees grew in dense rows.

Ozzie stared back at the cables and the trees as he and Crane and Mavranos slowly walked toward the building, and he muttered something about evergreens under hydroelectric power.

Mavranos told him that land under power lines wasn't good for much, and that a lot of such stretches were used as Christmas tree farms. "Come back here on New Year's Day, you see nothing but dirt."

Ozzie nodded, frowning.

The inside of the casino was one vast room; when a person had walked in through one of the several glass doors, street level became just the level of a wide, raised, railed walkway that ran all the way around the acre of playing floor five steps below. Tables and chairs and couches lined the rails, and doors in the high walls opened onto a delicatessen, a bar, a banquet room, a gift shop, and even a hair salon. Mirrored pillars, square in cross-section, rose to the high mirrored ceiling.

Mavranos sat down to have a beer, and Crane and Ozzie split up.

Crane hopped down the nearest set of steps to the playing floor and then limped through the maze of tables.

The games were quick, the house dealers shuffling low to the table and then skimming the cards out across the green felt, the players checking and folding and betting so inconspicuously and rapidly that Crane several times found himself unable to tell whose bet it was, or what the amount. Some of the players had hamburgers—or even full dinners, with mashed potatoes and gravy—on little wheeled wooden carts beside them, and they found a calm second or two now and then in which to bend over the food and shovel some into their mouths without taking their eyes from the table.

Crowds of Asians stood around tables where some game was being played that involved dice in a brass cup as well as cards, and the chips being shoved back and forth in tall stacks were the black hundred-dollar ones. The hasty diners around these tables all seemed to be eating noodles with chopsticks.

Under the frequent loudspeaker announcements—"JT, One and Two-Stud," "DF for the one-three Hold 'Em"—were the constant click and rattle of chips.

Crane gave his initials to the floorman who was working the five- and ten-dollar Five-Card Draw chalkboard, and while he waited for his turn to get a seat at a table, he leaned against the rail and watched the nearest game.

It was as fast as the others he'd watched, with the white plastic disk that indicated the honorary dealer moving around the table at nearly the pace of a plate of food being passed at a Thanksgiving dinner, and he noticed that players had to chant, "Time . . . time . . . time," if they wanted to consider their next actions without risking being passed over.

For the first time since his teens, Crane felt intimidated by the idea of getting into a poker game with strangers. It's like some kind of fast, complicated folk-dance, he thought, that I'm not sure I know all the moves to.

"SC, five-ten Draw," said the floorman into his microphone.

Crane hopped down the steps and waved, and then walked to the indicated seat. The people at his table all seemed to have been there for at least hours, and seemed to have grown old in this room or others like it.

Crane bought a couple of stacks of yellow five-dollar chips and waited for his first hand. The dealer, an expressionless woman in the house uniform, shuffled and whirled out the cards. Crane was the first person dealt to, and he belatedly noticed that the dealer button lay in front of the bearded man to his right. *I'm under the gun,* he thought.

Crane gathered in his cards and curled up the corners— and repressed a smile. In a textbook example of first-timer's luck, he had been dealt a pat Full Boat, Tens over Queens. He passed, and then raised when the bet came around to him after someone else had opened; and when the draw came, he tossed out the two Queens, face up. "I know I can fill this Flush!" he remarked cheerfully.

The irrational move got some raised eyebrows and muttering from the others at the table—but one of the two cards he was now dealt was the last Ten, giving him Four of a Kind. Five people besides him stayed, and two of them were still in for the showdown after three raises. There was complete silence at the table when he showed his hand and swept the stack of yellow and tan chips into his corner.

On the next hand he had a Two, Five, Seven, Nine, and Ten, unsuited. Someone opened, someone else raised, and Crane raised again, and then raised again when the bet came around one more time. At the draw he threw all five of his cards away and asked for five more.

This time a couple of players muttered angrily, as though Crane were making fun of the game.

His new cards were a Seven, Eight, Nine, Ten, and Queen, again unsuited. When the bet came around to him, he shook his head and threw the cards down face up. "Almost caught the Straight that time," he said, frowning thoughtfully.

After this he played tight, staying only with a pair of Aces or better before the draw and only with a very high Two Pair or better after it, and the lunatic image he had established with the first two hands impelled at least one of the other players to call him every time he stayed.

He had won about $350 when, after an hour and a half of play, he glanced at the ashtray and saw the smoke from his current Camel beginning to swirl in toward the center of the table. He looked at his tepid glass of Coke: The level was off, dipping toward the table.

It was before the draw, and he was holding three Hearts, Jack high, and the Joker. He would have liked to stay and try for the Flush, but he put the cards down on the table and pushed them away from him.

He gathered up his chips, tossed four yellow ones to the dealer, and stood up. "Thanks, everybody," he said, and walked away between the tables and up the stairs to where Mavranos sat drinking a Coors at a table by the rail.

"Check out the smoke," Mavranos said after Crane pulled up another chair and sat down.

Crane could see it at the nearest table, where a five- and ten-dollar Hold 'Em game was in progress: A little cloud was gathering over the center of the table.

Mavranos lit up a Camel and puffed, and the smoke drifted

away over the sunken floor of the playing area. "And my beer's crooked," he said.

"Where's Ozzie?"

"He's in that Seven-Card Stud to the right there."

Crane stood up and walked over to the section of brass rail nearest Ozzie's game.

The old man was looking at the cigarette in the tray by his chair, and the dealer had to remind him that it was his bet.

The players were about to be dealt the seventh card, and there were only two staying with Ozzie, for the old man had three Queens showing and the other two hands showed only low pairs.

Ozzie turned his three Queens over and pushed the cards toward the center of the table.

A cocktail waitress walked past Crane, and he was about to wave at her . . . but then he thought of Ozzie's three abandoned Queens. Gotta make sacrifices, he thought. He sighed and turned back to watch the table.

One of the remaining two players had won with a Full Boat, and as the man scooped in the chips, Crane idly wondered what sort of luck the man had sold.

Ozzie stayed in all the hands now, folding only after what Seven-Stud players called Sixth Street, the sixth card dealt. Even at the rail Crane could see that the old man's play was drawing the attention of the other players; at one point Ozzie folded showing a high Two Pair when nothing else at all showed on the board.

Crane drank three Cokes while he watched, and smoked half a pack of Camels. The smoke kept swirling out over the tables, and Ozzie kept folding before the showdown.

And so Crane was surprised when in one hand, finally, Ozzie hesitated at Sixth Street.

The old man was showing a Two of Spades, a Three of Clubs, a Five of Diamonds, and a Nine of Hearts.

One of his opponents showed four Hearts, and another showed Two Pair, black Kings and Tens. The Two Pair bet ten dollars, and the four Hearts raised it ten—strongly representing a Flush, thought Crane.

"Twenty to the Nine," said the dealer to Ozzie.

He looks a hundred years old, thought Crane anxiously as

he stared at his foster father. The old man's eyes were down, looking at his cards.

"Time," said Ozzie, so quietly that Crane could deduce what he said only from the motion of his wrinkled lips. "Time . . . time . . . time . . ."

The smoke was a funnel over the table, and the constant undertone of clicking chips suddenly sounded shriller to Crane, like the whirling of a rattlesnake's tail. The air-conditioned breeze was as dry as the breath of the desert.

Ozzie was shaking his head. "Time!" he said again, loud enough this time now for even Mavranos to hear him and look up from his beer.

Ozzie's lip was curled now in something like defiance or resentment, and he looked up. "And ten," he said clearly, pushing forward three tan chips.

Crane saw the other players look curiously at this old contender, whose best hand could only be Two Pair, Nines and Fives. From their point of view he could only be hoping to fill a Full Boat, and the Kings and Tens looked like being a better one.

The man with the Kings and Tens raised, and so did the man with the probable Flush.

Ozzie pushed more chips out.

He sighed. "Call," he said.

The dealer spun another, face down, to each of the players. The Kings and Tens bet, and the Flush raised.

"Call," said Ozzie clearly, pushing more chips forward.

It was the showdown now, and the players flipped their down cards face up.

The Kings *were* a Full Boat, Kings over Tens, which beat the Heart Flush Crane had expected. Ozzie's hand, which he exposed almost ceremonially, was the showing Two, Three, Five, and Nine, and, down, the Eight of Diamonds, the Ace of Spades, and the Four of Hearts.

Nothing at all. The other players must have thought he'd been trying to fill a Straight—which would have been beaten by either a Flush or a Boat, which the other hands had been, and had looked to be all along.

Ozzie pushed his remaining chips toward the dealer as a tip, then stood up and walked across the burgundy carpet toward the far stairs. Crane looked back to Mavranos and cocked his head after the old man. Mavranos nodded and stood up, bringing his beer with him as they walked around the sunken playing floor.

Ozzie was standing by an awning with PLAYERS CORNER scripted above it in neon. "I'm having a drink or two," he announced. "You," he said to Scott, "are sticking to coffee or Coke or something, right?"

Crane nodded, a little jerkily.

Slowly, but with his bony chin well up, the old man led Crane and Mavranos into the bar and to a tartan-patterned booth against the back wall.

The bar was nearly empty, though a wide oval of parquet in the middle of the floor and a mirrored disco ball turning unilluminated under the ceiling implied times of festivity here in the past. In spite of the Victorian flourishes on the dark wood pillars of the bar and the sporty prints framed on the walls and the heavy use of tartan, the band of mirror under the ceiling and the vertical mirrors that divided the walls every few yards made the walls look like freestanding panels, subject to disassembly at any moment. A wide-screen television was mounted on the wall, showing some news program in black and white with no sound.

"What did you buy, in that last hand?" Crane asked.

"Luck," said Ozzie. "It's not too hard to speed-read the hands, get the gist of them, as they go by, like identifying creatures in an agitated tide pool—but if you're gonna reach in and *grab* one, you've gotta be sure you know exactly what it is. I had to wait for a hand that was—that would further us. That we could—that was acceptable. And it's hard to calculate seven cards and all their interactions when you've got a tableful of gamblers joggling your elbow." He rubbed his face with gnarled, spotty hands. "Took a long time for a—an acceptable hand to show up."

Mavranos slouched low in the seat and peered around at the decor with an air of disapproval. "'Where fishmen lounge at noon,'" he said sarcastically, "'where the walls/ Of Magnus Martyr hold/ Inexplicable splendor of Ionian white and gold.'"

"More Eliot?" asked Crane.

Mavranos nodded. He waved at the nearest cocktail waitress and then turned to Ozzie. "So how's the weather?"

The old man shook his head. "Stormy. A lot of Spades, which is the modern version of the Swords suit in the old Tarot deck. Just about any Spade is bad news, and the Nine's the worst—I saw it a lot. A double Ballantine scotch on the rocks," he added to the cocktail waitress, who was now standing beside the table with her pad ready.

Coke, thought Crane. Soda water—maybe with bitters. Goddammit. V-eight. Seven-Up.

"Hi, darlin'," said Mavranos. "You've got to excuse our friend here—he doesn't *like* pretty girls. I'll have a Coors."

"Maybe he doesn't think I'm pretty," said the waitress.

Crane blinked up at her. She was slim, with dark hair and brown eyes, and she was smiling. "I think you're pretty," he said. "I'll have a soda water with a shake of Angostura."

"There's conviction for you," said Mavranos, grinning behind his unkempt mustache. "Passion."

"He didn't sound like he meant it," agreed the waitress.

"Jesus," said Crane, still distracted by sobriety and Ozzie's talk of bad weather, "you're half my age. Honest, ten years ago you'd have had to beat me off with a stick."

The waitress's eyes were wide. "Beat you off?"

"With a *stick*?" put in Mavranos.

"God," Crane said. "I meant—" But the waitress had walked away.

Ozzie didn't seem to have heard anything after he'd ordered his scotch. "The Hearts suit—that used to be Cups—seems to be allied with Spades, and that's bad. Hearts is supposed to be about family and domestic stuff, marriage and having children, but now it's in the service of—of ruin. The King and Queen of Hearts were showing up interchangeably in the same hands as the worst Spades." He looked at Crane. "Were you playing when the smoke shifted?"

"Yeah."

"You had the Jack of Hearts and the Joker in your hand, I'll bet."

Even though he had decided he believed all this, it made Crane uncomfortable to see evidence for it. "Yeah, I did."

"Those were your cards even in the old days, I remember—the one-eyed Jack and the Fool."

The drinks arrived then, and Ozzie paid the waitress. She left quickly.

Crane stared after her. It bothered him to realize that she was, in fact, pretty, for she held no more attraction for him than did the pattern in the rug. He could imagine her naked, but he couldn't imagine making love to her.

"So," said Mavranos after taking a deep sip of his Coors, "what does all this mean to us?"

Ozzie frowned at him. "Well . . . the Jack of Hearts is in exile, and the Hearts kingdom has sold out to the Swords; if the Jack's going back, he better do it disguised. And every water card I saw was bracketed by Hearts, meaning the water is tamed by the King and Queen. Since we're headed for Las Vegas, that means we should be leery of tamed water, which sounds to me like Lake Mead."

"Fear death by water," Crane said, grinning vaguely at Mavranos.

"And the," Ozzie went on, "the *balance* is way out of kilter, so your cancer cure looks a little less unlikely, Archimedes. It's like the ball's bouncing around crazy in the Roulette wheel, and it might not even fall into a slot but fly right out onto the floor. Anything's possible right now."

The old man turned to Crane. "*Your* situation is *completely* crazy. I told you the King and Queen of Hearts were acting as though they were the same person? As far as I can deduce, that's the person that's after you, and it's your parent, and is male and female at the same time."

"Ahoy," commented Mavranos. "A her*maph*rodeet."

"My real, biological father . . . or even my mother . . . might still be alive," Crane said thoughtfully.

"This almost certainly *is* your biological father," Ozzie said irritably. "The bad King. He must not have recognized you at that damned game; he wouldn't have bothered to become your parent through the cards if he'd known he already was, genetically."

Crane's mouth was open. "How . . . no, how could Ricky Leroy have been my *father*?" He was remembering the older man who had taken him fishing on Lake Mead so many times when he was four and five years old.

"It's a new body," said Mavranos.

"Right," Ozzie agreed. "He can *do* that, don't you listen? And maybe he's had a sex change operation since you saw him."

"Or maybe," Crane said, "he's got both male and female bodies he works out of."

Ozzie frowned. "Yes, of course. I should have thought of that—I hope I'm not too old for this." He sipped his scotch. "And I saw a whole lot of Nines and Tens of Diamonds together, and they mean, in effect, *action now*."

"I'm ready to go," Mavranos said.

Ozzie looked at Mavranos's cigarette—the smoke was rising more or less straight up—and then he held his glass up and stared at it. He hiked around on the seat to look at the television screen, which was now in color. "Don't you guys want lunch?"

"I could do with something," said Crane.

"I think the fortune-telling window has gone by," said Ozzie. "I'm gonna take this drink and go back to that table and kick some ass, now that they all think I'm the poster boy for Alzheimer's disease."

Crane and Mavranos walked around to the little delicatessen in the far corner of the hangar-size room and had roast beef sandwiches while Ozzie went back down to the playing floor.

At one point Crane got up and walked around the perimeter to the men's room. When he came out, one of the pay telephones in front of him was ringing, and he impulsively picked it up.

"Hello?"

There was no answer, but suddenly his heart was beating faster, and he felt dizzy. "Susan . . . ?"

He heard only a click, and after a while the dial tone, but when he finally hung up, he had to admit that, his experience with the cocktail waitress notwithstanding, his sexual responses were working fine.

When Ozzie finally reappeared, taking the steps up from the playing floor slowly and bracing himself on his aluminum cane, he had made back what he'd lost earlier and four hundred dollars besides.

"You guys ready to go?" he asked.

"Truck awaits," said Mavranos, standing up and finishing his beer. "Where to?"

"Some store, like a Target or a K Mart, for supplies," said Ozzie. "And then . . ." He looked around blankly. "On to Las Vegas."

The air was suddenly dry, and as he got up, Crane thought he heard the pay telephone ringing again, over the constant rattling of the chips.

"Let's drive fast," he said.

BOOK TWO

Mistigris

CHAPTER 14

Toward the Terminal Response

Southeast of the Sierra Nevada range, the Mojave Desert stretches across more than a hundred miles of vast, bleak wilderness before finally rising into the rugged peaks that corrugate California's easternmost edge, peaks with names like Devils Playground and the Old Woman Mountains. The desert is bordered in the south by the San Bernardino Mountains, beyond which lie the Coachella and Imperial valleys, broad quilts whose different-colored squares are fields of carrots and lettuce and cantaloupe and date palms. The water for their irrigation travels west in canals that cut horizon-spanning lines of silver through the Sonora Desert from the Colorado River, tamed now by the Hoover and Davis and Parker dams.

But the river can still be rebellious—in 1905 it flooded and broke through the man-made headgates near Yuma, cutting itself a new channel through the farmlands and towns all the way out to a low plain of salt-frosted desert that had been known as the Salton Pan. The Southern Pacific Railroad managed after two years to block the new flow and force the river back into its original channel—but the Salton Pan had become, and remains still, the Salton Sea, a thirty-five-mile body of water that grows so increasingly salty as its water evaporates that red tides frequently stain the betrayed water like blood, and water-skiers have to avoid sargassos of dead, floating corbina fish.

The river has been harnessed to make the Coachella and Imperial valleys bloom, but the Salton Sea, desolate with wind and sand and salt, sits between them like the patient eye of the wasteland.

In Laughlin, Nevada, fifty miles south of Hoover Dam on the Colorado River, a stiff wind from the jagged Dead

Mountains was raising whitecaps on the high, sun-glittering water.

A man in a tuxedo stood on the ferry pier and pulled handfuls of brightly colored casino chips from his pockets and flung them out over the choppy water. Tourists asked him what he was doing, and he replied that he worked for one of the casinos and was disposing of worn chips in the routine way; but he closely watched the patterns the chips took as they flew, and he seemed to be whispering to himself, and when he had scattered the last handful, he stood looking at the water for half an hour before bowing to the river and then walking to a car and driving away, very fast, north.

Fifty miles south of that, at Lake Havasu City, the river flowed high around the massive pilings of London Bridge, the same arching granite structure that until twenty years ago had straddled the Thames. The river's border was green, but the desert was close beyond the bright new hotels and restaurants, and because of the clarity of the air the desiccated mountains seemed nearer than they actually were.

A white-bearded man in a dusty old pickup truck drove over the curb of the parklike area near the bridge; he tromped the accelerator until he was doing about thirty—tourists were yelling and running—and then he yanked the wheel hard to the right, and the old truck spun like a compass needle across the sprinkled grass.

When the vehicle came to a squeaking, rocking halt, it was pointing north. He restarted the stalled engine and drove off in that direction.

And far out in the sagebrush reaches of the desert, in cinder-block houses and trailers and shacks in Kelso and Joshua Tree and Inyokern, isolated people were sniffing the dry air, and then, one by one, slapping their pockets for car keys or searching shelves for bus schedules.

And, in Baker, Dondi Snayheever left his box forever to go find his mother.

Travelers know Baker as just the brief string of gas stations and car repair garages and burgers-and-fries restaurants on I-15 in the middle of the vast desert between Barstow and the California-Nevada border—and in fact, it's not much more.

West of Baker's main street is nothing but a few short, powdery dirt roads and a couple of clusters of old mobile homes behind tall salt-cedar windbreaks, and at the west edge of town—out past the wide grassless yards and the forlorn swing sets and the old barbecues and dressers and half-stripped cars and the occasional satellite dish, all baking in the purely savage sun glaring out of the empty sky—the fenced-in grounds of the ECI minimum-security prison mark the town's west boundary. Beyond the prison's farthest fence is nothing but the desert, stretching away toward the astronomically remote Avawatz Mountains, the flat sand plain studded in the middle distance with huge jagged rocks that look like pieces of a long-ago-shattered planet half-buried in the sand.

A month ago Dondi Snayheever had walked away from his job in an upholstery shop in Barstow. He hadn't been sleeping well, and voices in his head kept saying things in a tone that was urgent but too soft to be understood, and so he had returned to the place he'd grown up in, a big plywood box behind the abandoned house where his father had lived. It was a long mile outside Baker on a dirt road, but somehow every time Snayheever went back, he found empty liquor bottles and used condoms on the carpeted floor of his box. The door couldn't be locked anymore.

It was hot and dim inside the box, and cramped because of the stacks of maps, but his attention was drawn to the oversize playing cards that his father had tacked up on every available section of wall and ceiling.

His father had built the box in 1966, when Dondi had been a year old, and Dondi had spent nearly every hour of his life in the box until 1981, when his father had driven away to Las Vegas, supposedly just for a weekend, and had never come back.

His father had built other boxes for him to stay in when they occasionally went traveling together—one in the woods west of Reno, one in an empty warehouse in Carson City, and one in the desert outside Las Vegas. The Las Vegas box had even had a stained glass window, an inexplicable pietà of the Virgin Mary mourning over the dead body of Christ.

Dondi never knew his mother, though sometimes he would stare at some of his tracings and he'd imagine he could see her.

When Dondi was about twelve, his father had explained to the boy that the plywood structure he lived in was a Skinner box. It was an "environment" engineered to produce a "terminal response."

It was based on his father's understanding of the teachings of a psychologist named Skinner, who had apparently taught pigeons to bowl with little miniature balls and pins. The theory held that desirable qualities in an adult human could be defined, and then a procedure could be set up, a pattern of education that would help shape a child toward the terminal response, the desired state.

Dondi's father had wanted to produce the ultimate Poker player. The attempt had been a failure. His father had wound up making something else.

In previous years the box had been filled with Poker books, and hundreds of decks of cards, and a television that showed nothing but films of real Poker games. His father would come out of the house and crawl into the box and play a hundred hands a day with him, criticizing ("extinguishing") inappropriate play, and rewarding—with bags of M&M's candies—play that could be shaped toward the terminal response.

Now the only things left in the box from those days were the big cards on the walls . . . but Dondi Snayheever stared hard at them, knowing that it would be through them, even more than through the maps, that he would be able to find his mother.

Besides, he already knew what she looked like from studying his tracings.

She was beautiful, like the Queen of Hearts.

"Baker for an early dinner, I nominate," said Crane. "And a full tank of gas, too. After Baker there's nothing but straight lines through lunar landscapes till at least the Nevada border."

"Right," said Ozzie.

"Gotcha," said Mavranos. "Pop me another beer, will you, Pogo?"

Crane hooked up a Coors from the cold water in the ice chest, opened it, and handed it to the driver. Mavranos seemed to drain half of it in one swallow, then tucked the can between his thighs. The windows were open, and the hot wind battered at Crane's ears and had blown his gray hair into a tangle of spikes and curls.

They'd been driving for three hours northeast along I–15. Ever since they'd driven through Victorville, the roadside brush and the shoulder of the highway had been consistently glittering with broken bottles, contrasting with long black strips of retread thrown from truck tires. Mirages and the broken glass gave Crane a spurious sense of being surrounded by water, an illusion strengthened by the boats being towed along on trailers behind many of the other cars they saw and by Ozzie's remark that this all used to be sea bed, and that you could find primeval sea shells out there in the cross sections of broken rock.

Crane had frequently thought about his own first trip across this desert forty-two years ago, when he had crouched for five hours in the scuppers of a boat, under the inert echo sounder, instinctively hiding from the stars in the high black sky.

Now, in spite of the chain-link fence along the side of the highway and the sand and the twisted Joshua pines beyond it, the desert crossing seemed—even more than it had then—to be a journey over water.

And Crane noticed geometry everywhere, straight lines: mirages out on the flat desert, and the long and nearly horizontal slopes that led away from the low mountains and seemed to stretch halfway across the world, and the line of the highway itself. Sometimes the whole, world-spanning horizon was tilted, and he'd find himself leaning with it.

Mavranos's truck was a contrast to the eternal regularity and hugeness of the desert.

The boxy blue vehicle, dusty and plain only this morning, now looked like a truck strayed from the caravan of a modest circus. Ozzie had bought several dozen Cobbs Airflow Activated Deer Warning whistles and glued the little black plastic things all over the hood and roof of the truck, some of them aimed diagonally instead of straight ahead, and some lined up so that the exhaust of one was the intake of the next, "like Newton's prisms"; and he had made Crane and Mavranos cut their fingers to dot bloodstains on each one of a bagful of pennants and banners, all of which he subsequently hung from the antenna and bumpers and luggage rack; and he had glued playing cards onto the walls of the tires, all the way around, and on the fenders, too.

As Ozzie had worked on the wheels, Crane had heard the old man mutter something about diesel and the windshield, but Crane, embarrassed by his foster father's eccentric precautions and by Mavranos's deadpan acceptance of them, didn't want to speak and perhaps provoke some further equipping of the Suburban.

At last they had got moving and had taken the Pomona Freeway out of Los Angeles, and it was only now, after three hours of uninterrupted traveling, that Crane's impatience and unease had relaxed enough to let him think of stopping.

Baker's legendary Bun Boy restaurant proved to have burned down, so after pulling off the highway, they stopped at a diner called the Mad Greek.

It was a little place, blue and white with outside tables and a low white picket fence, and Ozzie sat down at a table in the shade while Crane and Mavranos went inside to order.

The menu was self-consciously Greek, with things like souvlaki plates and Kefte-K-Bobs and Onassis Sandwiches, but they just ordered cheeseburgers. Mavranos got beers for himself and Ozzie, and Crane made do with a cup of some cold drink called Tamarindo.

They didn't talk much as they ate. Mavranos insisted, over Ozzie's snorting derision, that hibernating sea monkeys crawled out of the floors of the dry lakes when the spring rains came, and Crane just sipped his Tamarindo and stared at the two plastic cups of beer and thought about the pay phone he had picked up in the Commerce Casino.

The three of them were about to leave—Ozzie had unhooked his cane from the edge of the table, and Crane had thrown down enough money to cover the dinners and the tip—when a skinny hand darted in and snatched up the ceramic bowl full of wrapped sugar cubes.

The young man who stood by the table had the bowl in one hand and his other hand inside his undersize, slept-in–looking brown corduroy jacket. A sudden spasm of giggling made his teeth seem big, and his eyes were feverishly bright.

For a moment Crane and Ozzie and Mavranos just stared up at him.

"Oh, well, I *guess* I got a gun!" said the intruder, shaking stringy hair off his forehead. "It's the only shape drill-press buttons really *taste* like, did you hear me say that?" He smelled, Crane noticed, like air freshener and old sweat.

Mavranos smiled and spread his hands as if to say *We don't want any trouble*, and Crane saw him brace his feet under the table.

"If a person's mother was the moon," the young man said earnestly, "he could find her by where she—where she—"

Ozzie shook his head sharply at Mavranos, who lowered his hands.

"Where she left her—*her face*! Or the raven's face, the eye of the raven!" The young man put the bowl down and wiped his own face with his sleeve. "Queen of Hearts," he said, more quietly, "and the Jack going to find her." He dragged up a chair from an empty table nearby and sat down. Keeping his right hand under his jacket, with his left he dug a box of blue Bicycle brand playing cards out of his pocket and tossed it onto the table. "We gonna play?"

A waitress inside had been staring out the window at their unsavory visitor; but Ozzie smiled at her and waved, and she seemed satisfied.

Ozzie was facing their visitor again, frowning at him, obviously trying to figure out how this madman might fit into the structure they were dealing with and how it would affect things if they were to play with him.

"What . . . stakes?" asked Ozzie.

"M&M's," the young man said, "against your sugars." He pointed at the bowl he'd snatched up earlier and then pulled two packs of regular M&M's out of his pocket. "Candy. And sugar, too. It's bad for your teeth if you let it." He swatted ineffectually at one of the circling flies. "And flies like it," he added. "The word for 'fly' is *mosca* in Spain." He chuckled and shook his head.

"Uh," said Ozzie, "do you know where the moon . . . 'left her face'?"

"My name's Dondi Snayheever. Yeah, I got some—some maps, in the car. It's very difficult to say, as you would say, maps in the car."

Ozzie nodded. "Let's play for a map or two. We'll fade 'em with cash."

"Letters and lockets and lesson plans, you can't do otherthing but keep them, because they—they—they're the leadages candlewise to the father and mother." He looked hard at Ozzie. "You can't see any of my maps, sir."

"What's the game?" asked Crane cautiously. "That we're going to play here."

Snayheever blinked at him in evident surprise. "Go Fish."

"Of course," said Ozzie. The old man met Crane's eyes and made a sort of *over there* twitch with one white eye-brow.

You want me to go find his car and steal a map or two, thought Crane. Okay. But if I've got to do it, I'm by God going to award myself a prize. That's my ruling.

"I bet the engine's cooled enough for me to pop the cap off the radiator," Crane said, getting to his feet. "I'll go check." He looked at Mavranos. "Keys?"

"Keys?" echoed Snayheever. "Your radiator is inside the car?"

Mavranos had pulled out his key ring and tossed it to Crane. "Locking hood," Mavranos said easily. "Where we come from they'll steal your battery soon as blow their nose."

"Where do you come from?" Snayheever asked.

"Oz," said Ozzie testily, his voice sounding very old and reedy. "Shall we cut for the deal?"

Crane got up and walked out to the asphalt, and as he rounded the bushes toward where the cars were parked, he heard Snayheever say, "No, for this I've got to deal."

He's probably a cheat, Crane thought with a weary grin. We'll wind up with no sugar cubes at all.

Crane wondered how he was supposed to recognize Snayheever's car . . . until he walked past Mavrano's Sub-urban and saw the weird little vehicle parked on the other side of it.

It looked like a 1950s English version of a Volkswagen—it had the same bulbous fenders and arching roof—but the body flared out into a slight skirt around the sides. It was impossible to guess the little vehicle's original color; it seemed to have been dipped in oil decades ago and been driven relentlessly on remote desert roads ever since.

Crane walked forward, feeling as though he were pushing against the hot air and leaving it curling in slow turbulence behind him, like the wake of a ship.

He read the rusty emblem on the front of the car's hood: *Morris*.

Crane peered in through the dusty passenger-side window. The car was a mess: The upholstery was all split, stacks of newspapers filled the back seat, and the glove compartment had no door.

A number of ragged-edged folded maps protruded from the open compartment. The passenger door was not locked; Crane opened it, leaned in and pried free a couple of maps from the center of the pile, and then closed the door and walked over to the Suburban, fumbling with Mavranos's keys.

He got into the truck and stared at Mavrano's ice chest.

"Go fish," he whispered, and then slowly reached out and lifted a can of Coors from the cold water. One won't hurt, he thought. This desert air will dry me out like a dead rat in no time.

He popped the tab. The beer foamed up but didn't run over the rim of the can.

He looked behind him, but there was no one else in the truck.

Tired of alertness, he drained the beer in one long, gulping series of swallows. It stung his throat and brought tears to his eyes, and he could feel his tense muscles relaxing.

The air inside the Suburban was hotter than the air outside, and smelled of spilled beer and old laundry. Crane tossed the can into the back, where it would not stand out. He hid Snayheever's maps under an old nylon windbreaker and then got out, locked the door, and trudged back around the bushes to the table.

Ozzie and Mavranos looked up as Crane walked up; young Snayheever was staring at the cards in his hands and moving his lips silently.

"Should we go?" asked Ozzie.

Meaning, thought Crane, will the nut be able to see that I robbed him, in which case we should be gone before he goes to his car. "No," said Crane, resuming his seat and draining the ice-diluted Tamarindo in his glass, "nothing looks different. Uh . . . it could do with a little more cooling off."

" 'Kay. Here, I gotta hit the men's room. You take my cards, Scott."

Ozzie got laboriously up out of his chair and then hobbled to the nearby rest room door, leaning heavily on his cane.

Crane picked up the old man's cards. "My turn? To Mr. Snayheever? Okay. Uh . . . do you have any Nines?"

Snayheever grinned and jiggled in his chair. "Go fish!"

Mavranos pointed at the undealt stack of cards, and Crane picked up the top card. It was the Jack of Hearts.

"How about—" he began.

"Gotta bet!" Snayheever said excitedly. His dirty hair was down in his eyes.

"Oh. Uh, I'll . . . what's the limit?"

"Two."

Crane grinned lopsidedly and added two more sugar cubes to the pile of M&M's and sugar cubes in the middle of the table. "Have you got any Jacks?" A big semi truck drove by on the highway, gunning its engine and rattling the windows at Crane's back.

"Go fish!" said Snayheever.

Crane took the top card. It was the Ace of Spades, and a second after Crane picked it up Ozzie was somehow standing right behind him. "We're leaving," the old man said tightly. "The game will go unfinished. Throw down your hand."

Crane shrugged and obeyed. When the cards hit the tabletop, the Ace of Spades lay nearly covering two other cards he'd been holding, the Ace and Queen of Hearts.

"We're leaving now," said Ozzie shakily. "This minute."

"Fine!" said Snayheever as his long, trembling fingers gathered in the cards. "Fine! Just go then! I don't need you!"

Mavranos took Ozzie's elbow as they walked away from the table, for the old man was trembling and breathing fast; Crane walked out of the patio backward, watching Snayheever and wondering if the young man really did have a gun—but Snayheever, having apparently forgotten about the three of them, was thoughtfully folding a card around an M&M and a sugar cube. Just before Crane stepped around the bushes into the hot breeze, he saw the young man lift the strange burrito to his mouth and effortfully gnaw a bite out of it.

The breeze was from the reddening west, throwing veils of dust and stinging sand across the parking lot and making the lot and the whole town of Baker seem like the architecture of a temporary outpost, due soon to be abandoned to the elements. Crane watched Ozzie hobble along ahead of him, frail in his wind-fluttering old-man's suit, and for a moment he thought that Ozzie belonged here, a tiny, exhausted figure in a vast, exhausted landscape.

And if they just drove away without the old man, Crane could have as much beer as he wanted. The beer he'd drunk a few minutes ago shifted coldly and pleasantly in his abdomen.

But he forced himself to remember Ozzie as he had been when they'd been father and son—and to remember Diana, and how Ozzie had found her and made her his daughter, Crane's sister—as he helped Mavranos boost the shaking old man up into the rear seat of the car.

When the old man had sat down, Mavranos slammed the door. "Keys?"

Crane dug them out of his pocket and dropped them into Mavranos's palm.

"Think he'll be all right?"

Crane shrugged. "He wants to go."

Mavranos nodded, squinting off at the point where the highway disappeared into the eastern horizon. Then he looked down at his shadow on the asphalt, stretching away for yards in that direction. When he spoke, it was so quietly that Crane could barely hear him over the wind: "' . . . I will show you something different from either/ Your shadow at morning striding behind you/ Or your shadow at evening rising to meet you;/ I will show you fear in a handful of dust.'"

Crane knew he was quoting Eliot again.

Crane climbed into the passenger seat and pulled the door closed as Mavranos started the truck and clanked it into gear. Crane looked back at Ozzie. The old man's head was leaned back against the top of the seat. His eyes were closed, and he was breathing through his mouth.

CHAPTER 15

What Would Your Husband Say to That?

"Cannibal burger," said Al Funo, smiling at the woman. "Very rare, with raw onions." He took a bite of it and nodded in approval.

"I never could eat rare meat," she said. "I always like my steaks very well done."

Funo swallowed and wiped his mouth. "That's probably because you grew up in the Depression," he said. "In those days it didn't pay to eat rare meat. Nowadays they say you can even eat pork rare."

"I did not grow up in the Depression," she said. "How old do you think I am?"

"I like women who are older than myself," Funo said, frowning and nodding. "Ben Franklin felt the same way I do. I say you leave your car here and ride to Vegas with me, in my Porsche. What would your husband say to that?"

She simpered. Evidently she'd forgiven him for the Depression remark. "My God, me pull up to the motel in a Porsche with a . . . sexy young man? It'd be World War Three all over again."

She was eating some kind of big salad. Probably she was worried about her weight. Funo could see that she was a little heavy, but he thought she looked good.

He smiled and winked at her. She blushed.

They were sitting at a table in the Harvey House restaurant in Barstow. Funo had stopped for a hot meal, and he'd noticed this middle-aged woman sitting by herself at one of the tables by the big windows that overlooked the early-evening desert, and he had carried his plate over and asked her if he could join her. He preferred not to eat alone—he enjoyed good talk with good people over good food.

"And what are *you* going to be doing in Vegas?" she asked.

"I'm going to look up a friend of mine," he said. "I think he may be injured."

"A close friend?"

Funo was still smiling. "Let's just say I recently gave him a Dunhill lighter. A *gold* one."

"Oh," she said vaguely.

He took another bite of his cannibal burger and chewed thoughtfully. *He's alive, but you're off this one, Al,* Obstadt's man had told him when he'd called in earlier today. *We'll let the guys in Vegas take it.*

Vegas, eh? Funo had thought. And there were Nevada plates on that gray Jag.

Well, Funo wasn't about to leave his friend to some damn strangers. He had taken one last assignment—one of the ones he called auto-assignments—and then had got right into his Porsche and taken off for Vegas.

That last assignment had been an older woman, like this one. He had followed her to a 7-Eleven store and struck up a conversation with her about Danielle Steel's novels. Funo could converse plausibly about anything, even things he knew nothing about. It was a gift. Out of sight of the checker he had given her an incapacitating electric shock with a black plastic stun gun, and then, after lowering her unconscious body to a sitting position on a stack of newspapers by the video games, he had taken a sharpened ice pick out of his jacket pocket and carefully stabbed her through the heart. He had left unhurriedly.

An auto-assignment.

Funo really did like older women. He wasn't ashamed to admit that his mother had been the finest person he'd ever known, and he was convinced that years of experience, years of *life,* were what made a woman attractive. Younger women, he'd found, tended to be shallow. Al Funo had no time for shallow people.

"I'd better be going," his new friend said, getting to her feet. "Hours yet to Vegas, and Stu will be worried if I'm too late."

"I'll walk you out," said Funo quickly, pushing his own chair back.

"No, really, thank you," she said, picking up her purse.

"I can check your oil and water," he said, standing up. "Out on that desert you don't want to—"

"Honestly, I'm fine."

Was she . . . worried? Suspicious of him? "I'll walk you out," he repeated, perhaps a tad harshly.

She was walking away, her head down. When she paid her bill at the register, the cashier girl looked over at him, not smiling. What had the old bitch said?

Well, that put the kibosh on making *her* an auto-assignment. He didn't need any kind of brouhaha. The thing about auto-assignments—the ones you took on all by yourself, for nothing more than the satisfaction of being important to strangers—was that they had to be done even more carefully than the business assignments because you wouldn't be getting any protection. And of course, you wouldn't be getting paid.

He looked away from the cashier, forcing himself to breathe deeply and relax.

He stared at the painting on the high wall above the kitchen. It was of a covered wagon leaving a little western town, but some trick of perspective made the wagon appear to be as big as a mountain, or else the town a miniature toy. The scale was impossible to judge.

It didn't upset him. Scales, the sizes of things, didn't matter—people were people. There had been the woman in the 7-Eleven earlier today, and soon enough there would be Scott Crane.

Al Funo just wanted to be important to people.

The highway was a straight line in the twilight, a tenuous link between the dark horizon so far ahead and the red horizon so far behind. The old Suburban barreled along steadily, squeaking and rocking but showing a low temperature and a full tank of gas in the green radiance of its gauges. On either side of the highway the desert was pale sand, studded as far out as the eye could see with widely spaced low markers that looked like, but couldn't have been, sprinkler heads.

The ember of Mavranos's Camel glowed as he inhaled, and half an inch of ash fell onto his already gray-dusted jeans. He exhaled, and smoke curled against the inside of the cracked windshield.

"So what's it like," he asked quietly, "Vegas?"

Crane inhaled deeply on his own cigarette. This section of desert was far bleaker and more humbling than the stretch before Baker had been, without even any broken glass along the shoulder, and the small smells and sounds and glows inside the truck were precious.

"I haven't been in twenty years."

"What you remember."

"It's . . . pure," Crane said. "It's self-indulgence with no . . . no marbling."

"Sounds like a lean steak, no marbling."

Crane leaned forward to tap off his ash, but it fell to the floor. He leaned back. "Yeah. Yeah, did you ever read about that chicken heart that scientists took out of a—a chicken, and kept alive? The heart's been alive for like fifty years now, and it's grown to the size of a couch. Las Vegas is self-indulgence with every other part of life trimmed away, and it's grown to a size that's freakish. Not just grown like a city, you know, buildings and suburbs and all, but . . . grown to fill all the space, psychically. And what you get, the result—probably like the chicken heart—is—is *blandness*, with a kind of burnt aftertaste."

"How do they treat you? The casino people."

"Oh, everybody's real cheerful, real helpful. The cops see you walking down the sidewalk with a drink in your hand, they just smile and nod. Everybody's that way around the casinos, which is to say downtown around Fremont Street and out on the Strip. They don't have to say 'screw you' because they already are screwing you, in more ways than you know, and in more orifices than you knew you had."

Mavranos took a gulp from the can of beer that had been catching ashes between his thighs. "Sounds like fun."

For a while Crane watched the monotonous pavement rushing at them and tumbling away under the humming wheels. "It is, actually."

Ozzie had begun wheezing in the back seat, but now he coughed and shifted on the seat and resumed breathing normally.

"Bother you," Mavranos asked Crane quietly, "me drinking beer?"

"Nah. I'm full of that damned tamarind stuff—couldn't think of drinking anything."

"How you think you're gonna do, being on the wagon?"

Crane thought of the beer he'd chugged in Baker. "I don't think it'll be any hassle. It's just a habit I've got into, like coffee in the morning, or parting your hair on the left. I'll probably just replace it with . . . I don't know, Ovaltine, or Bazooka gum, or crossword puzzles." He yawned. His cigarette had burned down to the filter, and he poked it into the ashtray and dug another one out of the pack.

"You don't figure you're an alcoholic."

"I don't know. What's the definition of 'alcoholic'?"

Mavranos shrugged, staring at the highway ahead. "Can't stop."

"Well, look at me. I stopped . . . hours ago, and I'm fine."

"Settles that," said Mavranos, nodding. A big Harley-Davidson full-dress bike roared past them, its wide, light-studded rear end looking like the transom of a receding speedboat; in a few moments it was just a spot of red light in the darkness ahead, and its engine was a distant whine.

Crane hadn't slept for about forty hours, and he was very tired—he was thinking of curling up against the door and napping for a few dozen miles—and Mavranos's truck had a constant background noise of rattles and slidings and clanks and squeaks, so he was sure that the voice he seemed to be hearing from the back was imaginary.

. . . it all anyway, and if they want to borrow it, ask them what happened to the weed whip thing, or our forks, and you remember what Steve said about that plant he had in his front area by the door and they stepped on it . . .

"What are we doing out here?" he asked sleepily.

"We're off to see the Wizard," said Mavranos. In a piping voice he said, "Do you think the Wizard can *cure* my *cancer?*"

"I don't see why not," said Crane in an exhausted soprano. *"We're* going to see him about saving my *foster sister* from getting shot in the *face* like her *mom,* and maybe even to see if I can keep my *real dad* from stealing my *body.*"

"Hey, Pogo," Mavranos said suddenly, holding his right hand out from the steering wheel, "like the Three Musketeers, let's form a partnership—one for all and all for one, you know? Birth to earth?"

Crane shook his hand. He remembered the movie *West Side Story,* too, so he added, "Womb to tomb."

"The thing that'll save me is statistics," said Mavranos, grinning as he put his hand back on the wheel. "I say I'm trying to find its castle, so I'm personifying it, right? I'm looking for the vizard of odds." ·

"That's mighty funny," said Crane. He yawned so widely that tears ran down his cheeks. "I'm crowding fifty years old. How come I'm not . . . what time is it? . . . I guess it's too dark to be playing basketball with a kid of mine. I should be turning the burgers on the hibachi, and . . . Christ, if I had a kid, he could be twenty or thirty. He'd be home playing ball with *his* kid. Well, I should be . . ."

Cooking spaghetti for Susan and me, he thought; she'd be in the spare room playing some Queen tapes, or some of her Styx or Cheap Trick, and I'd be sautéing onions and garlic and bell peppers, taking a swig every now and then from the cold Budweiser on the sill of the open window. There'd be no coffee cup in the stove. . . .

Coffee in the morning, said the faint voice that seemed to come from the back of the truck, *or combing your hair on the left. Ovaltine, Bazooka gum, crossword puzzles. Why do you run me down to your friends all the time?*

Abruptly wide-awake, Crane turned around and looked past Ozzie's sleeping form to the piles of litter in the dimness of the back of the truck. His forehead was cold with a dew of sudden sweat. ·

"What's up?" asked Mavranos. "Hear something?"

Crane forced himself not to breathe fast. "No," he said levelly. "Nothing."

Nothing, echoed the voice. *I'm good enough for a quickie in the truck while your friends are inside, but when they're around I'm nothing.*

Ozzie's head came up. He looked around quickly, frowning and wiping drool from his chin. "Who are you and where are you taking me?" he demanded.

"Oz, it's me, Scott, remember?" Fright made Crane speak too loudly; in a quieter tone he went on, "We're going to Las Vegas to find Diana. She's—what was it?—flying in the grass."

The old man sagged, all his imperiousness gone. "Oh, yeah," he said faintly, and then he shivered and pulled his suit coat more tightly around his narrow shoulders. "Oh, yeah."

"Be across the border into Nevada soon," said Mavranos without taking his eyes off the highway.

Ozzie wiped his eyes and blinked out the window. "I'd like to have seen more of California," he mumbled. In a firmer voice he said, "Over the border we'll be on their turf, *his* turf. Play tight."

Mavranos lifted a fresh can of beer from the ice chest and swirled his hand in the water, bumping a few cans together. "How much longer?"

"To Vegas?" Crane said. "Another hour or so."

Ozzie shifted awkwardly on the seat. "I've heard that there's a casino just over the border now. Dirty Dick's or something. Let's stop there for a bit. I think I'm going to throw up my Baker cheeseburger, and then I should eat something like a— a tuna fish sandwich, maybe, or a bowl of soup." His knobby hands found the rubber grip of his aluminum cane and held it tightly.

"I wouldn't mind a bite myself," said Mavranos. "Something with some onions and salsa."

Ozzie shut his eyes and clenched his jaw.

Are you going to leave me in the car again? Why don't you take me inside with you? You used to love me. You used to—

"What was it," asked Crane loudly, "that you didn't like about the cards I threw down, when I was playing with the nut back there, I think it was the Ace and Queen of Hearts and the Ace of Spades?" The disembodied voice seemed to have stopped, so he let himself stop jabbering.

Both Ozzie and Mavranos were looking at him with expressions of puzzled uneasiness.

"Well," Crane went on in a more normal tone, "you didn't look as though they were good news, Ozzie. I thought of it just now and wanted to ask before I forgot." He knew his hands would shake if he gestured with them, so he clasped them in his lap.

"Oh," said Ozzie. "Huh. Well, it may not have counted for anything, playing for sugar and candy like that. And I didn't notice any funny business with smoke or drink levels."

"I read somewhere voodoo gods like candy," put in Mavranos.

"Or sea monkeys," said Crane impatiently. "But what *was* it?" he asked Ozzie.

The old man rubbed his face. "Well, as I told you, Hearts is the suit of the—the King and Queen. The sun King and the moon Queen, you know. And the Ace of Hearts is the combination of them, like yin and yang. Your father doesn't want any such combination, though, or at least not one that's not contained in himself. And the Queen of Hearts is probably still Diana's card in some sense, since she's the daughter of that Lady Issit, who was the goddess."

Crane remembered the card that had covered the Ace and Queen of Hearts. "And what's the Ace of Spades?" he asked.

Ozzie waved one spotted old hand. "Death."

That reminded Crane of something, but before he could catch the memory, Mavranos was speaking.

"I think this place up ahead here is what you were talking about—Whiskey Pete's it's called," Mavranos said, and a moment later there was the *click-click, click-click* of the turn indicator as he signaled for a lane change, and the sound continued as, moments later, he slanted off the highway onto the exit ramp and began to press the brake pedal.

"How many maps did you get?" Ozzie asked suddenly.

"Maps," echoed Crane without comprehension. It alarmed him that he didn't know what Ozzie was talking about, and he clasped his hands together even tighter.

"From the nut," Mavranos said. "When you went out to his car."

"Oh, right. I don't know—three or four. They're under Arky's windbreaker there."

Whiskey Pete's was a tan-colored, spotlighted and neon-lit castle, with turrets and towers and arches, and crenellations along the tops of the walls as if for the emplacement of only momentarily absent archers. The caricature figure of a gold prospector sat on the highest wall, above the giant CASINO sign, and at the far ends of the lower wall were two figures of Parisian-looking dancing girls. Behind the glowing edifice the hills of the desert were black humps against the purple sky.

"Jesus," said Mavranos as he drove across the vast parking lot toward the spectacle. "It looks like something that aliens would catch people in and then fold up just before dawn and fly back to Mars with."

"Does your dome light work, Archimedes?" asked Ozzie.
"You bet."

"Let's look at these maps right here in the car. I don't like
the idea of looking at them inside that place."

Mavranos parked and turned off the engine and the headlights, then switched on the dome light as Ozzie carefully pulled
the folded maps out from under Mavranos's windbreaker. He
began unfolding the top one.

In the anonymous darkness and swooping headlight glare of
the highway, the dusty little Morris droned right on past the
Whiskey Pete's exit ramp, heading east, toward Las Vegas.

CHAPTER 16

God, There's a Jack!

"Poland?" said Crane, staring at one of the maps. "She couldn't
be flying in the grass in *Poland*, could she? And shit, look at
the caption: 'Partition of Poland, 1939.'" He laid the map over
the back of the front seat so the other two could see it.

"Look, though," said Mavranos, squinting through cigarette
smoke, "he's marked half a dozen routes, from somewhere to
somewhere." With a callused finger he traced one of several
heavy pencil lines that meandered across the map.

"This one's California and Nevada," said Ozzie tensely,
looking at a map he'd just unfolded. "More routes marked."

The old man held it up, and Crane tried to make sense of
the map lines that had been emphasized in heavy pencil.
The Colorado River was traced from about Laughlin down
to Blythe, and then the line moved inland to some town called
Desert Center; the 62 Highway was marked from the Nevada
border west to the 177 junction; one line just followed the
California border from the I–15 to the river, though there was
no road or river along the route, only the imaginary straight
line; and heavy pencil strokes had crossed out two names; in

the glove compartment Crane found a pencil with an eraser and rubbed out the shiny black patches and then just stared, as puzzled as before, at the names "Big Maria Mts." and "Sacramento Mts." revealed underneath.

"It looks like a big round trip," said Crane, "from Riverside to the border, down the length of the border to Blythe, and then back up to the 40 on unpaved roads, and back to Riverside."

"With a lot of side trips," said Ozzie. "Notice the fainter pencil lines along these dirt roads out around the 95."

"Gentlemen," said Mavranos ponderously, "the man was nuts."

But Ozzie was shaking his head doubtfully. "The moon, the Jack and Queen of Hearts . . . He was plugged in somehow. Don't throw these away."

There were two other maps, one of Michigan and one of Italy, both deeply scored with pencil lines.

"I wonder if he'll miss them," said Crane.

"Yeah," said Mavranos unsympathetically, "next time he's in Poland he'll be up Shit Creek without a you-know-what, as my mom used to say. We ready to go inside, or what?"

"You okay for walking?" Crane asked Ozzie as he opened the door and climbed down to the pavement.

"There's nothing wrong with me," said Ozzie peevishly.

Ozzie hurried away in the direction of the men's room, while Crane and Mavranos stood in the entry and blinked around in the glare-punctuated dimness.

Just inside the bank of glass doors, isolated on the red-carpeted floor by a circle of velvet ropes hung from brass poles, was a 1920s-vintage car, its body riddled with big-caliber bullet holes. A nearby sign announced that this was the very car in which Bonnie and Clyde had been shot to death. Welcome to Nevada, Crane thought.

After a few minutes Ozzie came back, white-faced, red-eyed, and leaning on his cane.

"And Ozzie makes three," said Crane, pretending to notice nothing out of the ordinary.

This was the first time he'd been in a Nevada casino in more than fifteen years, but as he led the way through the ranks of clattering slot machines to the restaurant in the back, he felt as though no more than a week had passed since he'd last been in this ubiquitous, rackety hall, doors into which could be found in hundreds of places across the breadth of Nevada. Whether you walked in through a door in Tahoe or Reno or Laughlin, or across a littered pavement in the Glitter Gulch area of downtown Las Vegas or up a polished marble stair on the Strip, it always seemed to be the same big, noisy dark room that you found yourself in. It was carpeted, and it smelled of gin and paper money and tobacco and air conditioning, and a disquieting number of the people at the tables and the slot machines were crippled or deformed or startlingly obese.

Mavranos was blinking around in apparent bewilderment. "Where the hell are all these people when they're not here?" he asked Crane quietly.

"I think they only look like people in this light," said Ozzie with a tired grin. "Before they spun in through the doors at sundown they were dust devils and tumbleweeds and cast-off snakeskins, and their money was warpy bits of busted mirage; and at dawn they'll all leave, and if you were watching, you'd see 'em puff away, back to their real forms."

Crane grinned, reassured to note that Ozzie could still spin his whimsical fantasies, but he noticed that Mavranos only looked more apprehensive.

"He's kidding," Crane said.

Mavranos shrugged irritably. "I know that."

Without speaking, the three of them began filing down the aisles between the slot machines.

In the restaurant Ozzie had a grilled cheese sandwich and a Coors, and Mavranos had a bowl of chili and a Coors, and Crane just had a Coke and ate Mavranos's crackers.

Mavranos had begun to tell Ozzie about the Mandelbrot fat man, and Crane stood up and said he was going to go hit the men's room himself.

He paused on the way to thumb a quarter into one of the slot machines, and after he'd pulled the handle, not even watching the machine's window, twenty quarters were banged one by one into the payout well.

He scooped them out in two handfuls and dumped them into the pockets of his jacket, then touched the machine's handle. "Thanks," he said.

He pretended that the thing said, *You're welcome*. Then he found himself pretending that the thing had said, *Give her one good-bye kiss, at least*.

"I . . . can't," Crane whispered.

Doesn't she deserve at least that? the machine seemed to ask him. *Are you afraid to look her in the face one last time?*

I don't know, Crane thought. I'll have to get back to you on that.

Slowly he limped away from the machine, to the bar, and he dumped a fistful of quarters onto the polished surface.

"A shot of Wild Turkey and two Budweisers, please," he told the bartender. Just one last kiss, he thought. I'm no good to my friends if I'm shaky and forgetful.

The glass screen of a video Poker game was inset flush with the surface of the bar, and Crane dropped a quarter into the slot and pushed the deal button. The images of patterned card backs in the flat glass screen blinked and became face up, and then he was looking at a garbage hand, unsuited and with no Hearts.

At that instant, about forty miles to the east of where Crane stood, five mouths opened and exclaimed, "God, *there's* a Jack!"

The other people on the bus stared at the old man who had shouted. "What'd he say?" one person asked.

"There's a Jack," someone else answered.

"What's he looking at so hard out the window?"

"Trying to find a rest room, I bet—look, he's wet his pants!"

"Jeez, what's he doing running around loose? He's a hundred if he's a day."

Thought fragments flickered like deepwater fish in the mind residue that occupied Doctor Leaky's head, frail sparks of luminescence darting about on unknowable errands in darkness. *Ninety-one, ninety-one, ninety-one*, ran the unspoken, scarcely connected words. *Not a hundred. Born in '99, born in . . . that was a Jack. That was a hell of a Jack, west of here . . . don't smell roses, that's good . . . don't smell nothing . . . well, piss . . .*

Art Hanari finally let himself be coaxed into lying back down on the padded table. The masseur had stopped asking him what he'd meant by the remark about a Jack, and now resumed rubbing a lanolin solution into his taut pectorals and deltoids.

The masseur ignored Hanari's perpetual erection. Curious about it at first, he had looked up Hanari's file, and had found that a "penile implant," a silicone rod, had been surgically inserted into the organ as a drastic cure for primary impotence; it seemed a waste of time, for Hanari saw no women except for a couple of the nurses and physiotherapists, and he showed no interest in them—or in anyone. He nearly never spoke, and he'd had no visitors for at least eight years.

But the masseur had not been surprised to read of the implant operation. Patients at La Maison Dieu could afford anything, and he'd seen much more extravagant cosmetic surgeries.

What had surprised him was Hanari's birth date: 1914. The man was seventy-six . . . but his pale skin was smooth and firm, and his hair appeared to be genuinely dark brown, and his face was that of a placid thirty-year-old.

Finished, the masseur straightened and wiped his hands on a towel. He looked at the man on the table, who had apparently gone back to sleep, and he shook his head. "God, there's a jack-*off*, you mean," he muttered, then turned to the door.

"Twenty to the Sixes," said the dealer patiently. Old Stuart Benet always needed to be reminded. Right now Benet was snorting at an asthma inhaler.

"'At's you, Beanie," said the player to Benet's left.

"Oh!" The fat old man put down the inhaler, lifted the corner of his seventh and last card, and squinted down past his white beard at it.

"Beanie, you just *said* it was a Jack," said another player impatiently. "And if it is, you got Two Pair, and I got somp'n better anyway."

Benet smiled and pushed four orange chips forward.

The remaining players called, and at the showdown Benet proved to have only the pair that was showing in his up cards.

"Hey, Beanie," said the winner as he gathered in the chips, "what happened to that Jack you were shouting about?"

The dealer suppressed a frown as he collected the cards and began to shuffle. Benet was employed as a shill to fill out sparse tables in the Poker room, and even though the casino had hired him as a favor to a valued business associate, he was good at the work—always cheerful, and happy to stay and call and lose money. But shills weren't supposed to bluff or raise, and that *God, there's a Jack* yell had been a kind of bluff.

The dealer made a mental note to ask Miss Reculver to remind Benet of the rules. The old man never seemed to listen to anyone else.

The reference desk at the UNLV library always got busy around six in the evening. The students who worked during the day all seemed to come in at once, always shuffling hesitantly up to the desk and beginning in one of two ways: "Where would I look for . . ." or, even more often, "I have a quick question . . ." Old Richard Leroy would listen patiently to their intricate descriptions of what they wanted and then, almost invariably, either lead them to the business desk or show them where the psych indexes and abstracts were. Right now he was methodically replacing an armful of books to their proper places on the shelves.

A few of the students were still glancing at him warily, but he had forgotten having yelled, and was back in the state his co-workers called "Ricky's ticky-tocky."

And Betsy Reculver, the one who had voluntarily spoken the simultaneously chorused sentence, walked slowly along the broad, brightly lit and always crowded sidewalk in front of the Flamingo Hilton.

For a while she stared up at the procession of stylized flamingos, illuminated by what must have been a million light bulbs, that strutted along in front of mirrored panels above the windows of the new front of the casino. Behind the casino, hidden from the traffic on the Strip, was a long swimming pool, and on the far side of that, dwarfed now by the glass high-rise buildings that were the modern sections of the hotel, stood the original Flamingo building, the place Ben Siegel had built to be his castle in 1946.

Now it was her castle, though the Hilton people would not ever know it.

Some other people knew it, though—the magically savvy would-be usurpers called jacks—and they would like to take it away from her. This new jack, for example, whoever it might be. I've got to gather in my fish, she thought, and avoid the jacks while I do it.

She turned and looked across the street, past the towering gold-lit fountains and pillars of Caesars Palace, past the blue-lit geometrical abstraction of its sixteen hundred hotel rooms, to the still faintly pale western sky.

A jack from the West.

The phrase bothered her, for reasons she didn't want to think about, but in spite of herself, for just a moment she thought of an eye split by a Tarot card, and the bang and devastating punch of a .410 shot shell, and blood-slick hands clutching a ruined groin. And a casino called the Moulin Rouge, which hadn't got around to appearing until 1955. *Sonny Boy,* she thought.

She thrust the memories away, fleetingly resentful that they had followed her from the old body.

It doesn't matter *who* this jack may be, she told herself. Who*ever* it is, I've defeated better men before this, and women, too: Siegel, Lady Issit, and dozens more. I can do it again.

Suddenly in her mind she tasted liquor—and then a flood of cold beer. She was still facing west, and she could tell that the impression was coming from that direction.

And there's one of the fish, she thought with cautious satisfaction. Probably a male one since he's drinking boilermakers. Across the border now, driving into Nevada, onto my turf, following the irresistible impulse to flee the ocean and seek the desert, to abandon everything and make his way *here*—or maybe tied up in the trunk of Trumbill's Jaguar, if it was that particular fish and if we're lucky.

If he's not with Trumbill, I hope that jack out there doesn't find him. I can't afford to be losing my future vehicles, my customized garments—the *selves* I'm going to have to rely on for the next twenty years.

It didn't occur to her that the jack and the fish might be the same person.

She smiled when the walk signal at Flamingo Road turned green just as she reached the curb. And, ignoring the curious stares of the tourists crowding past in their colorful shorts and printed T-shirts and foolish hats, she quoted aloud four lines from Eliot's *The Waste Land*:

> *I Tiresias, though blind, throbbing between two lives,*
> *Old man with wrinkled female breasts, can see*
> *At the violet hour, the evening hour that strives*
> *Homeward, and brings the sailor home from sea. . . .*

She turned her smile on the purple western sky. *Come home,* she thought.

Come home.

Crane drank off the last inch of his second Budweiser and tucked his last quarter into the slot in the bar. He tapped the deal button and watched as his cards appeared. A pair of Twos, a Four, a Queen, and the one-eyed Jack of Hearts.

He pushed the hold buttons under the Twos, then hit the draw button. The other cards blinked away and were replaced by a Four and a King and a Two. Three of a Kind. Three quarters clattered into the well.

He stood up and scooped out the coins. They were warm, almost hot; and for a moment he remembered shiny copper ovals that had been pennies before the L.A. train thundered over them, and he remembered his real father juggling the hot, defaced coins into his hat to cool off.

He limped back onto the gaming floor, and as he was passing the slot machine that had paid for his drinks and the video Poker, he noticed a cellophane-wrapped peppermint in the payout well.

"Thanks," he told the machine as he took the mint and unwrapped it. "One-armed bandit," he said thoughtfully, popping the mint into his mouth, "but on my side, right? One-armed. You're . . . maimed, aren't you, like so many of these people? I'm maimed, too." He touched the surface of his right eye. "Fake, see?"

A man who seemed to have had his entire lower jaw taken out shambled up to the machine and managed to convey a question.

"No, I'm not playing this machine," said Crane. "I was just *conversing* with it."

Come home.

It was time to be moving on, eastward. He walked back to the restaurant, where Mavranos and Ozzie were sitting over their empty plates and still talking about the imaginary fat man.

Ozzie squinted up at Crane with exhausted eyes. "What kept you?"

"That Baker cheeseburger didn't sit right with me either," Crane said cheerfully. "Between us you and I must have grossed out half the guys here tonight."

Ozzie didn't seem to have heard. "From what you remembered of Diana's statements to you on the phone last night, I believe she works at a supermarket, a late-evening shift. When we get to Las Vegas, we can start checking all the markets."

Back on the highway, Ozzie fell asleep in the back seat again, and Mavranos was whistling tunelessly as he frowned at the pavement rushing by under the glow of the headlights.

Crane had stretched out his bad leg and was drifting in and out of a doze, lulled by exhaustion and roused by Arky's occasional random high notes.

He kept promising himself that he would complain soon, and had finally reached the point of keeping himself awake, waiting for the next high note—when Mavranos stopped whistling.

"Speeder behind us," Mavranos said.

Crane hunched himself around and looked out through the dusty back window. A pair of bright headlights was coming up on them quickly.

"How fast are we going?"

"Seventy."

A red light came on above the approaching headlights, making a pink field of the Suburban's back window.

"Wake up the old man," said Mavranos, "and get in the back and unlock the gun case. Do it," he added as Crane opened his mouth to protest.

"But it's *cops!*" Crane protested as he nevertheless scrambled over the top of the front seat, accidentally hitting Ozzie's arm with his knee.

"It looked like a pickup truck before the red light came on," said Mavranos.

Ozzie was awake, blinking forward and to the sides and then twisting his head around to look back. "You're not slowing down," he said.

"I think it's a truck," Mavranos said. "Would people want to stop us bad enough to fake being cops?"

"Sure," said the old man harshly. "I've still got my gun in my pocket. Where's yours?"

"In the box. Got it open?"

"Yeah," quavered Crane, "you want yours?"

"Pass it over subtle."

Crane knelt on the litter of books and clothes to block the view as he passed the gun to Mavranos's upheld hand.

Ozzie was panting. "I think you've got to pull over. If they're not cops, don't get out of the car. And—and if they've got guns . . . I don't know. If they raise the guns, point them at us, I think we've got to kill them. God help us. God help us."

The Suburban shifted when Mavranos hit the brakes, and Crane braced himself as he lifted out the short black shotgun and with trembling fingers tucked five shells into the magazine tube. Then he clicked off the safety and racked the slide back and forward, chambering the first shell, and tucked one more shell into the tube.

He slid the gun under Ozzie's seat, then picked up his .357, loaded it, and shoved it down inside the waist of his jeans and pulled his jacket closed and zipped it an inch.

"They're right behind us," he heard Mavranos say.

Crane had his hand on the shotgun's plastic pistol-grip, and though his breath was fast and his heart was pounding, in his mind he was rehearsing how he would pull the gun out from under the seat and swing the barrel in line and fire it with his trigger hand down by the point of his hip-bone. All six as fast as you can pump them out, he told himself tensely, right through the windows, and then grab the revolver in both hands for accurate aiming. Christ.

The Suburban grated to a stop on the sandy shoulder, and a moment later Crane could hear a car door open and close, and then he could see flashlight beams highlight the dust on the side windows and gleam on Ozzie's scalp.

"Shit," came a voice from outside, "there's only three people in it."

"Two of 'em," said Mavranos softly. "One right here and one hanging back."

There was a rap on the driver's side window, and Crane heard the crank squeak six times, and a moment later he smelled the dry, cooling desert.

"Step out of the car," said the voice outside, clearer now.

"No," said Mavranos.

"We could drag you out, asshole."

Crane could see a corner of Mavranos's grin. "I pity de fool," Mavranos said cheerfully, in a bad imitation of Mr. T.

The man outside laughed shortly. "We've got guns."

Ozzie leaned forward, and his old voice was steady. "You open with checks like that, son, in a no-limit game like this, you might see some powerful raises."

The man stepped back, and a flashlight beam danced across the litter in the back of Mavranos's truck. "Three's it, all right," he called to his companion. "They could maybe be hidin' a dog or a baby somewhere, but there ain't no more adults."

Against the headlights of the pickup truck Crane could see the tall silhouette of the other man, who now walked slowly to Mavranos's truck. Crane saw a sculpted-looking profile and wavy, styled hair.

"No," said the newcomer, "this vehicle no longer seems to be the one that contains a lot of people. The one we want is very close, though." He turned to Mavranos and, in his carefully modulated baritone, asked, "Have you seen a bus, or an RV, or a big van, driving along this highway during the last half hour?"

"I don't know about the last half hour," drawled Mavranos, "but since dark we've probably passed more buses and such than regular cars. Las Vegas, you know," he added, gesturing ahead helpfully.

"I know."

The man turned toward the back of the Suburban and spat on the glass. He turned to his companion. "Would you clean the glass, Max?" he asked.

The other man obediently rubbed at the spot with the sleeve of his nylon jacket, and when the glass was cleaner, he turned the flashlight on Crane's face.

Crane was blinded by the glare, but he could feel the leader staring at him, and he just blinked and tried to keep his face expressionless.

After half a minute the light was gone, and the leader was at Mavranos's opened window. "The man in the back there," the leader said. "What's the matter with him?"

"Oh, shit, you name it," Mavranos said.

"Is he . . . mentally retarded?"

"Clinically," said Mavranos, nodding. It was one of Mavranos's favorite words to give a statement authority. "He's *clinically* mentally retarded. Aren't you, Jizzbo?"

Crane was sweating, and his heart was pounding with real fear, for he could tell that his tension was close to breaking out in hysterical giggling. He bit his tongue very hard.

"You're not helping when you talk to him like that," said Ozzie.

Crane could no longer contain himself—the best he could do was to emit his hysteria as a sort of harsh, choked quacking. He coughed blood from his bitten tongue out through his nose, then snorted and leaned forward, gagging loudly.

"Jesus," said Max.

"Okay," the tall man said. "You can go."

Mavranos rolled the window back up, then put the car into gear and steered back onto the road and stepped on the gas.

He and Ozzie both broke out in wild laughter, and after Crane had blown his nose on one of Mavranos's old shirts, he was laughing, too, rolling around helplessly on the litter and making sure he didn't bump the cocked shotgun and wishing, desperately, that he had a drink.

CHAPTER 17

The Sound of Horns and Motors

When the laughter subsided, Ozzie wiped his eyes and turned around to face Crane. "You didn't drink anything back there at Dirty Dick's, did you?"

"Just the Coke you saw." Crane was glad he was lying in darkness, for Ozzie had always been hard to ·bluff.

The old man nodded and frowned in thought, and it occurred to Crane that in the old days Ozzie would have gone on to ask, *Really?* Crane's apparent maturity, and the obvious importance of what they were trying to do, clearly led the old man to trust him.

"And of course you didn't play cards there."

"Sure didn't," Crane agreed, trying not to think of the video Poker. He sat up and lifted the shotgun back into the gun case.

"Then it's my fault," Ozzie said quietly, "for letting you play in that damned Go Fish game. That's the only other thing that could have alerted them." He closed his eyes and shook his head. "I wonder if I'm really . . . *quick* enough for this. Mentally."

"Jeez, you're fine, man," said Crane hastily. "Those guys probably didn't have anything to do with us; they were looking for a bus or something."

"They were after us all right; the bus business proves that. Which reminds me—pull over as soon as you can, Archimedes, we've got to take down our camouflage."

"I don't like stopping, not with those guys slamming around out here," Mavranos said.

"They'll catch us again if we don't—and then that jack with the hair and the voice will wonder why this vehicle keeps looking like a crowded bus to him. What's wrong with right here?"

"Nothin' we can't adapt to, I'm sure," said Mavranos wearily, turning the wheel toward the shoulder again and tromping the brake.

"Why did we look like a bus?" asked Crane.

"Moving, we're a very busy, agitated wave form," said Ozzie. "Those little plastic deer whistles make a complication of ultrasonic sound waves, all interfering and amplifying and damping each other, and the blood-spotted flags are a lot of organic motion, a lot of pieces of protoplasm, all elbow to elbow with each other, changing their positions all agitatedly. And then the *main* thing is the cards on the wheels, which are whizzing past the cards on the fenders, so you every second get a dozen new combinations of cards. *Configurations.* The card configurations aren't personalities, but of course they're descriptions of personalities, so all in all, at a hasty glance, a psychic would tend to assume that there are a lot of people traveling in one vehicle."

"And when we stopped, it all stopped," Crane said. "The whistles, the flags, the cards on the wheels . . ."

"Right. His bus evaporated, and we were standing there. Happen twice, he'll know we *are* the bus, and that the guy he's after—which is you—is aboard *this* car, this truck."

The truck was stopped, and Mavranos had got out and was tearing cards off the left front tire. The desert breeze unfolded the car's stale interior air and threw it away into the night sky; now the car smelled of cooling stone.

"Why did he think I was retarded?"

"I don't know. I guess you're a blur to him, being one of the King's victims on the one hand and a son of the King's on the other. To a psychic you must look like a nighttime and daytime double exposure. Either way you're somebody an ambitious jack would want to kill."

"Hey," called Mavranos from outside, "you two don't mind if this takes me a little while?"

"I'm coming," Crane called as he opened the right rear door.

"Tell Archimedes to put a tire from one side onto the other side, with the cards still on that tire and fender, so the tire'll be moving diesel now if it was windshield before, or vice versa. And I don't care if they're radials."

"Tire from one side to the other," said Crane, nodding. "Don't care if they're radials."

As he stood under the million distant bright stars in the black sky and broke the little black whistles off the car and tore the spotted flags from the luggage rack, Crane wondered if he would ever dare to drink again, after this near-calamity; and, if not, how he could possibly keep from going crazy or killing himself; and he wondered what the old man meant by diesel and windshield; and he wondered if being the King's son meant that he was a jack himself, with a claim to whatever this mysterious throne in the wasteland was.

An anonymous sedan swept past on the highway, and in the instant that he noticed it he imagined that the woman in the passenger seat, who glanced his way for a moment, had been Susan. Now he stared after the car. The face had been expressionless, but at least had not seemed to be angry.

You did give her a nice kiss, he thought as he remembered the bourbon and beer.

When he and Mavranos had stripped all the camouflage from the Suburban, they got moving again. Mavranos kept the speedometer needle at around seventy, but they didn't catch up to the car in which Crane had possibly seen the ghost of Susan.

After a while they drove past the bright oasis of Nevada Landing, a casino built to look like two ornate east-facing Mississippi riverboats. The mock vessels had risen from the horizon ahead, and soon they sank below the horizon behind, and then the Suburban was driving in darkness again.

Maybe she stopped there, Crane thought, climbed aboard a boat. He looked back, wondering if she'd find him again.

"Two moons," said Mavranos around his cigarette.

Crane blinked and shifted on the rocking seat. "Hmm?" He had nearly been asleep again.

"Doesn't that look like any-second-now moonrise up ahead? But we got the moon behind us."

"The one ahead of us will be Las Vegas."

Mavranos grunted, and Crane knew he was thinking about the castle of randomness.

And, slowly, the ripplingly molten white and blue and orange towers climbed up out of that bright quarter of the horizon and dimmed out the stars.

* * *

They got off I–15 at last at Tropicana Avenue, then turned left onto Las Vegas Boulevard, the Strip. Even down here at the south end it was glaringly lit, with the Tropicana and the Marina and the not-yet-opened Excalibur crowding back the night sky.

"Damn," said Crane, staring out the car window at the Excalibur's gigantic white towers and brightly colored conical roofs. "That looks like the grandest hole in God's own miniature golf course."

"Excalibur," said Mavranos thoughtfully. "Arthurian motif, I guess. I wonder if they've got a restaurant in there called Sir Gawain, or the Green Knight."

Ozzie was staring back at the place. "I read there's going to be an Italian restaurant in there called Lance-A-Lotta Pasta. Restraint and good taste all the way. But yeah, Las Vegas seems to be sort of subconsciously aware of—of what it is. What Siegel made it."

"Ben Siegel made it Arky's perilous chapel?" asked Crane.

"Well," said Ozzie, "I guess he didn't exactly *make* it here; he *invoked* it here. Before Siegel this place was just *ripe* for it."

"Keep on north?" Mavranos asked.

"Yeah," said Crane. "There ought to be a fair number of supermarkets on Charleston; that's the first big east-west street after the Sahara." Which, he thought, is where we found the infant Diana in '60. God knows where we'll find her now. "Left or right—play it by ear."

"And find us a coffee shop sometime," said Ozzie. "Or no, a liquor store, we can get some Cokes and ice and put 'em in this cooler. Diana's shift probably ends at about dawn, and we're gonna need some caffeine to keep our eyes open till then." He yawned. "After that we can find a cheap motel somewhere."

Mavranos glanced at Ozzie in the rearview mirror. "Tonight we hit the grocery stores," he said, "but tomorrow we hit the casinos, right? So I can start trackin' my . . . *phase change*."

"Sure," Ozzie said. "We can show you the ropes." He shifted on the seat and leaned against Mavranos's Coleman stove with his eyes closed. "Wake me up when you find a supermarket."

"Right," said Crane, staring blearily ahead.

After the grandeur of the Tropicana intersection the street dimmed to normal urban radiance until Aladdin's, and then Bally's and the Dunes and the Flamingo raised their towering fields of billions of synchronized light bulbs.

Crane stared at the Flamingo. The entrance doors and broad driveway sat in under a rippling red and gold and orange upsweep of lights that made the place seem to be on fire. He remembered seeing it twenty years ago, when there had only been a modest tower at the north end and a freestanding neon sign out front; and he dimly remembered the long, low structure it had been, set back from the highway by a broad lawn, when he had gone there with his real father in the late forties.

Siegel's place, Crane thought. Later—maybe still—my father's.

Even at midnight Fremont Street's three broad one-way lanes shone in the white glare of the lights that sheathed Binion's Horseshoe, and the tourists getting out of the cab were blinking around and grinning self-consciously. The fare was eleven dollars and some change, and when one of the tourists handed Bernadette Dinh a twenty, she looked at him with no expression and said, "Are we okay?"

As she'd hoped, he took it as meaning something like *Is this downtown enough for you?* and he nodded emphatically. She nodded, too, pocketed the twenty, and unhooked the microphone as though about to call for another fare. Too embarrassed now to ask for his change, the tourist closed the door and joined his companions, who were huddled uncomfortably in the sidewalk limelight.

Stage fright, she thought. They think everybody's looking at them, and they're afraid they don't know the moves and the lines.

Strikers from the culinary and bartenders unions were walking back and forth carrying signs in front of the Horseshoe, and one of them, a young woman with very short hair, had a megaphone.

"*Baaad luck,*" the striker was chanting in an eerie, flat voice. "*Baad luck at the 'Shoe! Come on oouut, losers!*"

God, Dinh thought. Maybe I'd have stage fright, too.

Every Thanksgiving Binion's gave a turkey to each cabdriver, and Dinh, known as Nardie to all the night people of Las Vegas, had always dropped off her downtown fares in front of the place. She wondered if she'd soon have to start unloading them back by the Four Queens.

A couple of police cars were parked across the street in front of the Golden Nugget, but the officers were just leaning against the cars and watching the strikers; the tourists on this Saturday-night-or-Sunday-morning were plentiful, ambling along the sidewalks and drifting from one side of the street to the other, lured by the racket of coins being spat into the payout wells of the slot machines, a rapid-fire *clank-clank-clank* that was always audible behind the car horns and the shouting of drunks and the droning blare of the striker's megaphone. Nardie Dinh decided to wait for another fare right where she was.

Down here between these high-shouldered incandescent buildings she couldn't see the sky—she could hardly make out the traffic signals in the sea of more insistent artificial light—but she knew that it was a just-about-half-moon that hung somewhere out over the desert. Dinh knew she was working at half power—for the next few days she'd still be able to handle pennies without darkening them, to touch ivy and not wither it, wear purple without fading it and linen without blackening it.

But she was vulnerable, too; and would be all week—only able to really *see* through the patterns of the initialed dice at her other job, and able to defend herself only with her wits and her agility and the little ten-ounce Beretta .25 automatic under her shirt in her waistband.

In nine days the moon would be full—and by then she would have beaten both her brother and the reigning King . . . or she would not. If she hadn't, she would probably be dead.

A bearded man in a leather jacket was walking, apparently drunk, toward her cab. She watched him speculatively, thinking of some big losers who had in the past decided that this short, slim young Asian woman would be an easy target for robbery or rape.

But when he opened the rear passenger door and leaned in, he said, hesitantly, "Could you take me to a—a wedding chapel?"

Should have guessed, she thought. "Sure," she said. The man's face was pudgy and uncertain behind the bushy beard, and she knew she didn't need to call in his ID and destination; and he looked prosperous and out of shape—no need to get a ten in advance; he wasn't the runout type.

He got in, and she put the car in gear and pulled out into traffic. The chapels, of course, didn't pay kickbacks on solo fares, so she decided to take him to one of the ones down below Charleston.

She stopped at a red light two blocks up, at Main, in front of the Union Plaza Hotel, and she suppressed a grin, for the hundreds of little white light bulbs over the hotel's broad circular driveway shone in the polish on the unloading cars, making them seem to be luminously decorated for a Fremont Street wedding procession.

Weddings.

Link the yin and yang, she thought, the yoni and the lingam. Other cabdrivers had told her she wasn't the only one getting a disproportionate number of solo fares to the chapels in the last two weeks. All sorts of people wanted to go to the places, and when they got there, they just stood around in the little offices, staring in a lost way at the ELOPED and HITCHED and WED 90 license plates on the walls and reading the laminated Marriage Creed plaques.

It was as if there were a slowly increasing vibration in the sky and the land, something that had to do with a combining of maleness and femaleness, and on some subconscious level these people felt it. No doubt the bar joints and parlor houses out along the 95 and the 93 and the 80 highways were also getting more visitors than usual.

But that thought brought back memories of DuLac's outside Tonopah, and of her brother, and of the room with twenty-two paintings on the walls—and she stomped the accelerator and made a left against the light, speeding down Main to Bridger.

"Jesus," said her fare, "I'm not in a hurry."

"Some of us are," she told him.

Only one side of Snayheever's license plate was screwed down, so it was easy to swing the plate aside and fit the head of the crank through the hole cast in the bumper.

He spread his feet on the pavement and whirled the crank, leaning into it. The engine didn't start, though the back seam of his old corduroy coat, the one he thought of as his James Dean coat, tore a little more. At least he didn't seem to be having any of his involuntary twitches; his tardive dyskinesia was quiet tonight.

Cars were honking behind him, and he knew that meant that the drivers were angry, but the people on the sidewalk seemed to be cheerful. "Lookit the guy with the wind up car!" yelled one. "Careful you don't break the spring!"

"I'd hate to wind up a car," said a woman with him, laughing.

On the second spin the car started. Snayheever got back in, clanked it into first gear, and drove across Sixth Street toward the El Cortez. He had been driving around the downtown area for nearly an hour before he stalled, and he still wasn't having any luck in tracking the place where the moon lived.

But the half-moon was still up, though low in the west, and he watched for clouds and paid attention to the wind and any debris it might carry.

Snayheever knew why he had not ever become a great Poker player. Great Poker players had a number of qualities: knowledge of the chances, stamina and patience, courage and "heart" . . . and, maybe most important of all, the ability to put themselves inside the heads of their opponents, to be able to tell when the opponent was chasing losses, or letting injured ego do the playing, or faking loose or tight play.

Snayheever couldn't put himself into their heads.

The men Snayheever had played with had all seemed to be . . . atoms. That is, indistinguishable from one another, and emitting things—atoms emitted photons, and players emitted . . . passes and checks and bets and raises—without any pattern or system or predictability. Sometimes, Snayheever thought as he drove across Fremont, atoms emitted beta particles, and sometimes players emitted all-in raises or turned up Straight Flushes. All you could do was retreat and lick your wounds.

It was different when he was dealing with *things*—river and highway patterns, and the arrangement of mismatched jigsaw puzzle pieces, and the postures and motions of clouds. He was sure he'd be able to read tea leaves if he were ever faced with a cup of them, and he felt he understood the Greeks—or whoever it had been—who had foretold the future by looking at animal entrails.

Sometimes the people he met seemed like the recorded ladies who spoke to him on the telephone when he needed to know what time it was. But *things* had a *real* voice, albeit a far and faint one, like what comes through a telephone if someone has unscrewed the earpiece and taken out the diaphragm disk.

There was someone *at home* behind the constantly shifting arrangements of things. And who else could his mother be?

He hoped that reincarnation was true, and that after he died as an unconnected human, he might come back as one of the infinity of connected *things*. He thought of what the woman on the sidewalk had said when he'd been cranking the car's motor: *I'd hate to wind up a car*.

You could, he thought now as he turned left to zigzag through the downtown section again, do a lot worse than to wind up a car.

Half a mile southwest of Snayheever, the gray Jaguar was tooling east on Sahara Avenue.

Skinny man waiting to get out.

Vaughan Trumbill's mouth turned down at the pouchy corners as he remembered the remark. The young woman had had something to do with physical fitness; she guided people in exercises, he believed.

In the back seat of the Jaguar the old Doctor Leaky body mumbled something.

Betsy Reculver was sitting back there beside the old man. "I think he said south," she said, her voice scratchy.

"Okay," said Trumbill. He spun the wheel and turned the Jaguar right, from Sahara onto Paradise, east of the Strip. For a while they drove between wide, empty dirt lots under electric lights.

The woman had wanted to get him to join some diet program. Clients, he gathered, were given little bags of dried foods to boil. The idea was to lose weight and not regain it.

I just know *that somewhere inside you is a skinny man waiting to get out.*

She had said it with a laugh, and a crinkling of the eyes, and a hand on his forearm—to show affection, or sympathy, or caring.

Reculver was now sniffing irritably. "I forget what you said. Is that—that Diana person coming here?"

"I have no reason to think so," Trumbill said patiently. "The man on the telephone said he knew her, and I got the impression that she lived locally, there, in southern California. Our people have been monitoring Crane's house since early Friday, and his telephone since Saturday dawn. I'll hear if they've made any progress at locating her, and she'll be killed if we can find her."

Reculver shifted in the back seat, and Trumbill heard the click as she bit one of her nails. "She's still there, then. In California. With the game coming up again I'm real sensitive—I'd have felt her cross the Nevada line like I was passing a kidney stone."

Trumbill nodded, still thinking about the young woman at the party.

He had made himself smile, and had said, *Would you come with me, please?* He had taken her by the arm then and led her out of the lounge to the hall, where a couple of the casino security guards stood. They had recognized him. *These men will see that you get home,* Trumbill had told her. She had gaped at him, taking a moment to realize that he was evicting her from the party, and then she had started to protest; but at Trumbill's nod the guards had taken her out toward the cab stand. Of course she hadn't meant any harm, but Trumbill wasn't going to let even an unknowing idiot thrust that particular card at him.

"That jack, and that fish, are over the line, though," Reculver said. "I felt them both, at nearly the same time. I wonder if the fish is this Crane fella, coming on his own."

"It's possible," said Trumbill stolidly, ready to parry any suggestions that it was his fault that Crane hadn't been captured.

But for a while they drove in silence.

"My nerves are bad tonight," said Reculver, softly from the back seat. She was apparently talking to the old body next to her. "Yes, bad. Stay with me. Speak to me. Why do you never speak. Speak. What are you thinking of? What thinking? What? I never know what you are thinking. Think."

Old Doctor Leaky shifted and giggled. Trumbill couldn't imagine what the two of them got out of this game, this shared reciting of T. S. Eliot poetry.

"I think we are in rats' alley," the old man said in his sexless voice, "Where the dead men lost their bones."

A skinny man trying to get out. Trumbill honked the car horn in a jarring *da-daaaaaa-dat* at an inoffensive Volkswagen.

"Do you know nothing?" Reculver was apparently still reciting, but her voice was genuinely petulant, uneasy. "Do you see nothing? Do you remember nothing?"

Trumbill glanced in the rearview mirror. Doctor Leaky was sitting upright with his hands on his knees, expressionless. "I remember," the old man said, "Those are pearls that were his eyes."

Reculver sighed. "Are you alive, or not?" she asked softly, and Trumbill, not knowing any poems at all, couldn't tell if she was still reciting or just talking . . . nor, if she was talking, to whom. "Is there nothing in your head?"

"And we shall play a game of chess," said the old body, "pressing lidless eyes and waiting for a knock upon the door."

Paradise Road was dark here, south of the neon red-streaked tower of the Landmark, and most of the traffic was south-bound taxis heading for the big casinos and avoiding the Strip traffic.

"I . . . don't sense them now," said Reculver. "They might both of them be in town now, and other fish and jacks, too, and I wouldn't know. Too close, like blades of grass right in front of your binocular lenses. Did you *meet* anyone, Vaughan? Did you make any—any *deals* you haven't *told* me about?"

"No, Betsy," said Trumbill. She had told him what to say to her when she got like this. "Remember what you read about paranoia in elderly women," he said. All of us in this car are just reciting things tonight, he thought. "And about fluid intelligence versus crystallized intelligence. It's like RAM and ROM in computers. Young people got the one; old people got the other. Think about it."

"I can't think. I'm all alone. I have to do everything myself, and—and the Jacks could be anywhere."

On to phase two, thought Trumbill. "Is Hanari awake?"

"Why should he be awake? Do you know what time it is?"

"I think you should step into his head and look around from there."

"What's wrong?" she demanded loudly. "I'm not going into his head! I'm not even going to think about him! Has he had a breakdown? Are you trying to trap me in something like *this*?" She slapped Doctor Leaky, who just giggled and farted loudly.

Trumbill hoped the old lady would last the two weeks until Easter. He rolled down his window. "You're not thinking clearly right now," he said. "You're upset. Anybody would be. And you're tired, from handling everything by yourself. But right now is when you've got to be extra alert, and the Art Hanari body is calm and well rested. And wouldn't it be a relief to be a man again for a little while?"

"Hmmph."

Trumbill turned right onto the dark emptiness of Sands Avenue, driving now between houses and apartments, the Mirage a glowing golden monolith visible over the low buildings ahead. He wondered whether Betsy Reculver had taken his advice or was simply not speaking to him. He sighed.

A skinny man.

Trumbill was sixty years old now, and he didn't want to lose his position. With Reculver he had his garden and his tropical fish and the arrangements for how his body was to be disposed of when he should eventually die. Among strangers none of those things would be assured, especially that most important last item. Isaac Newton would be able to get at him after all, with his damned Second Law of Thermodynamics, and—and *uniformize* him, grind off the serial numbers and scavenge away all the customizations, the extra mirrors and fog lamps and seat covers, as it were. Then there'd be just the equivalent of a stripped frame in a fenced-in lot stacked full of other stripped frames.

All indistinguishable from one another.

Any differences that can be taken away, he thought with a shudder, could never have been real differences to begin with. He flexed his massive forearms, knowing that the tattoos were rippling under the cloth.

The cellular telephone buzzed, and he picked it up. "Hello."

"Vaughan, this is me, in the Hanari. Of course that was all nonsense, all that stuff I was saying. Listen, have I been *bathing* enough?"

It had never quite ceased to startle Trumbill when the boss did the body switch, apparently as effortlessly as someone shifting in a chair so as to look out a different window.

"Bathing," said Trumbill. "Sure."

"Well, watch me. I read that old ladies sometimes forget about cleanliness. Listen, we're not going to find them tonight. Let's head back to the house."

"Back to the house," Trumbill repeated.

Doctor Leaky yawned. "But at my back from time to time I hear," he said, "The sound of horns and motors, which shall bring Sweeney to Mrs. Porter in the spring."

Trumbill heard the Art Hanari body's flat *ha-ha-ha* laugh. Reculver had once told him that laughing that way didn't produce wrinkles. And then the Hanari voice began singing:

> "*O the moon shines bright on Mrs. Porter*
> *And on the daughter*
> *Of Mrs. Porter.*
> *They wash their feet in soda water*
> *And so they oughter*
> *To keep them clean.*"

Trumbill hung up the phone and drove with both chubby hands on the wheel.

The moon had gone down by the time the woman walked out of the bright entrance of the Smith Market on Maryland Parkway, and the sky behind the Muddy Mountains was pale blue. She shuffled tiredly out across the parking lot to a tan Mustang, got in, started it up, and drove out of the lot, turning north on Maryland.

North of Bonanza she passed a dark blue Suburban heading south; she didn't glance at it, and the three men in it were oblivious of her.

But the high walls and the parking lots of the city echoed briefly to a faint, harsh shout, a grating exclamation that coughed out of the plaster throats of the Roman and Egyptian statues in front of Caesars Palace, and the southern belles and ship's officers on the deck of the Holiday Casino, and the Arabs on the stone camels in front of the Sahara, and the miner crouched over a panful of gold-colored light bulbs on the roof of the Western Village souvenir store, and from the plywood necks of the two smiling figures in front of the dealer's school on Charleston, and from the steel crossbeam in the neck of Vegas Vic, the five-story-tall man-shaped structure that towered over the roof of the Pioneer; and the neon-lit paddle wheels on the riverboat facades of the Holiday Casino and the Showboat and the Paddlewheel shivered for a moment in the still air of pre-dawn, shaking dust down into the blue shadows, as if about to begin to move.

CHAPTER 18

Fool's Day

And thirty miles to the southeast, beside the curl of the U.S. 93 Highway just short of the arching crest of Hoover Dam, the two thirty-foot-high Hansen bronzes flexed their upswept wings and shifted slightly on their black diorite bases. The star chart inlaid in the terrazzo pavement at their feet vibrated faintly as it reflected the depths of the dawn sky.

From Lost City Cove and the Little Bitter Wash at the north end of the Overton Arm, through the broad basin named for and dominated by the giant square monolith known as the Temple, and out to the farthest reaches of Grand Wash to the east and Boulder Basin to the west, the vast surface of Lake Mead shivered with a thousand tiny random tides, rousing for a moment sleeping vacationers aboard the countless rented houseboats.

And in the mountainside below the Arizona Spillway, the water in the dam's steel penstocks shook with momentary turbulence, and the technicians in the big control room noted the momentary irregularity in the hydroelectric power through the step-up transformers below the dam, as the blades and stay-vanes of the electric generators hesitated for a moment before resuming normal rotation of the turbines.

On the broad concrete gallery below the dam an engineer felt a tremor and glanced up at the seven-hundred-foot-tall afterbay face of the dam and had to look twice to dispel the illusion that the face was rippled like a natural cliff, and that there was a figure on the wall way up at the top, dancing.

Diana Ryan had changed out of her red Smith Market uniform into a green sweat suit, and now she was sipping a glass of cold Chardonnay and reading the Las Vegas *Review-Journal*. She would try the old man's number again in a little while. It was Sunday morning, and if he was home, there'd be no harm in letting him get a little more sleep.

She heard the master bedroom door open, and then water running in the bathroom, and then Hans shambled into the kitchen, blinking in the sunlight slanting through the window. His beard was pushed up into an odd curl on one side.

"You're up early," she said. Now she wished she had tried the call as soon as she had got home.

"It's later than it looks," Hans said. "Daylight savings is sleep time losings, in the spring." He plugged in the coffee machine and then sat down in the vinyl-covered chair across from her. She had finished with the Metro section of the paper, and he slid it to his side and stared at it.

Diana waited for people-are-bloody-ignorant-apes. He had said he'd be working on his screenplay last night, and the glow of his late-night inspirations had always become resentment by morning.

She could hear Scat and Oliver moving around now, and she finished her wine and stood up to rinse the glass and put it away before they came out.

"Don't tell me how to raise my kids," she said to Hans, who had of course opened his mouth to speak. "And I know you didn't say a word."

Hans knew enough not to roll his eyes, but he sighed softly as he looked back down at the paper.

She crossed to the telephone and punched in the number

again, impatiently brushing long strands of blond hair out of her face with her free hand. While she stood there listening to the distant phone ring, the boys came into the kitchen and hauled out boxes of cereal and a carton of milk.

She turned to look at them. Scat was wearing his Boston Red Sox T-shirt, and Oliver had on the camouflage undershirt that she thought emphasized his belly. Oliver gave her what she thought of as his sarcastic look, and she knew Hans must have rolled his eyes at the boy.

Hans is just not father material, she thought as the repetitive ringing went on in her ear. Where's . . . Mel Gibson, Kevin Costner? Even Homer Simpson.

Hans was shaking his head over some article. "People are bloody ignorant apes," he said. Diana believed it was a line from *Waiting for Godot*.

At last she hung up the phone.

"Grampa still not home?" asked Scat, looking up from his Rice Krispies.

"He's almost certainly just off with your brother," Hans told Diana. "You worry too much."

"Maybe they're gonna come here," said Scat. "Why don't they ever visit?"

"They prob'ly don't like little kids," said Oliver, who, at ten, was a year older than his brother.

"Your grandfather likes little kids," said Diana, going back to her seat. Probably Scott convinced Ozzie to leave, she thought, to move somewhere else. Ozzie'll get the same phone number tranferred to his new place. Probably the people who killed my mother didn't follow Scott and kidnap the two of them. Or hurt them. Or kill them.

"Okay we ride our bikes to Herbert Park?" asked Scat. "That's what everybody calls it," he added to Oliver, who predictably had started to remind him that it was called *Hebert* Park.

"Sure," Hans told the boy, and that annoyed her.

"Yes, you can," she said, hoping her tone made it clear that it was *her* permission that counted.

"I've got to have peace and quiet, get my treatment typed up today," said Hans. "Mike at the Golden Nugget knows a guy who knows Harvey Korman. If he can get him to read it, that's just about a sure fifty K."

Since the boys were in the room, Diana made herself smile and knock the underside of the table.

But after they'd finished their cereal and put the bowls in the sink and gone charging out of the apartment to get on their bikes, she turned to Hans.

"I thought you weren't hanging around with that Mike guy any more."

"Diana," said Hans, leaning forward over the newspaper, "this is *biz*. Harvey Korman!"

"How did you find *out* that he knows somebody who knows somebody? You must have been talking to him."

"I'm a writer. I have to talk to all sorts of people."

Diana was standing at the sink, rinsing the cereal bowls. "He's a dope dealer, Hans," she said, trying to speak in a reasonable tone and not seem to be nagging. "And the one time we went to his place he was all over me like a cheap suit. I'd think you'd . . . resent that."

He was giving her his lordly look now, and it looked particularly foolish with his snagged-up beard. "Writers can't be judgmental," he told her. "Besides, I trust you."

She sighed as she toweled her hands. "Just don't get *into* anything with him." She yawned. "I'm going to bed. I'll see you later."

He was making a show now of being absorbed by the newspaper, and he waved and nodded distractedly.

The sheets were still warm from him, and when she had pulled the covers up to her chin, she blinked around in the dimmed room and wondered if he would come back to bed when he was done with the paper.

She hoped he would and she hoped he wouldn't. In the springtime, around Easter, she was always . . . what? Hornier? That was a word Oliver would use, and if she rebuked him, Hans would say, in his most satirical tone, *To me, sex is something beautiful shared by two people in love.*

Over the buzz of the air conditioner she heard the kitchen chair squeak, and she smiled derisively at herself when she became aware that her heart was beating harder. A minute later, though, she heard the muted *snap-snap-snap* of the electric typewriter, and she rolled over and closed her eyes.

He's better than nothing, she thought. Is that what they all are, just better than nothing? Wally Ryan was a pretty sorry excuse for a husband, bringing home the clap because he had to go screw other women. He told all his friends that I was frigid, but I think any of them could see that he was just intimidated by being *married* to a woman, and having actual children. Women are safely two-dimensional, hardly more than magically animated animals from the pages of *Penthouse*, if you don't have to . . . *live* with one of 'em, deal with her, every day, as a actual 'nother human being.

She wondered how Scott had got along with his wife. Diana was pretty sure it had been the wife's death that had upset him so badly just before New Year's. It had been a strong, deeply personal emotion of loss. She had thought she ought to call him then, but after a week or so she had decided it would be awkward to call so late, and she had let it go. Still, his grief had kept her from sleeping well for a week or so.

Diana had always thought of Scott's wife as *that slut*, though she knew it wasn't fair; after all, she had never met the woman or spoken to her or even seen her.

Diana had tried to rationalize her strong disapproval by telling herself that her foster-brother was a drunken Poker-bum, and that any woman who would marry a man like that wasn't worthy of her brother, who was, after all, a good person at heart; but she knew that her real resentment stemmed from the shock she'd felt on that summer day in her eighteenth year when she'd realized he was in the process of getting married, was actually saying *I do* to some priest somewhere and staring into some woman's eyes.

By that time she hadn't seen him for nine years—but she had always somehow assumed that he would marry *her*. After all, they weren't blood-related.

She could admit now that she had married Wally Ryan a year later just as a kind of revenge on Scott, knowing that he would be aware of her wedding, too.

Wally had been big on fishing and hunting, and he was tanned and had a mustache, but he had been uncertain and blustering and *mean* behind his macho front. So were all the boyfriends she'd had since. She was just a sucker for broad shoulders and squinty, humorous eyes. But by the time of the inevitable breakup she had been sick of every one of them. When she'd learned from the divorce lawyer two years ago that

Wally had died drunk in a car crash, she hadn't felt anything more than a faint sadness that had been mostly pity.

She had told the boys that their father was dead. Scat had cried and demanded to look at old photographs of Wally, but in a day or two his friends and school had distracted him from grieving over the father whom, after all, he hadn't even seen since he'd been six or so. Oliver, though, had seemed oddly satisfied with the news, as though this were what his father had deserved—for abandoning them? Probably, though the divorce had been Diana's doing. And Oliver's schoolwork, good until then, had become mediocre. And he had got fat.

She should marry again, give the boys a real father—not a succession of Hanses.

She shifted to her other side and punched the pillow into a more comfortable shape. She hoped Ozzie was all right. And she hoped Scott's stabbed leg was healing.

Some boys had made a ramp out of a log and a piece of plywood and were riding their bicycles over it—the braver ones yanking up on the handlebars as they flew off the end, so as to go unicycling for a few seconds up on the back wheel after they landed—and Scat watched for a while and then got on his bike and took a couple of jumps over it himself. On the last jump he stood up and really yanked the handlebars and wound up sitting down hard on the dirt and watching his bike go wobbling away upright across the grass. The other boys applauded.

Oliver, meanwhile, had climbed the chain link backstop and now sat up on the saggy top of it, pointing his plastic .45 automatic at each airborne rider in turn.

He was thinking about nicknames. When he and his brother had first moved to North Las Vegas, they had been known as the Boys from Venus, because they had moved into one half of a duplex on Venus Avenue. That hadn't been too bad— there had also been a couple of Boys from Mars, which was the street four blocks north—but while Scott had kept the same individual nickname he'd always had—Scat, which was all right—Oliver had soon become known as Hardy, because he was fat.

That wasn't all right. Even if they were just calling him that because they were scared of him.

Some of the parents were scared of him, or at least didn't like him. He liked to startle grown-ups by springing in front of them and shoving his toy gun in their faces. Since the gun wasn't real, they couldn't really object, especially when he laughed and yelled something like *Pow, you're dead!*

But this Hardy business wasn't any good.

Lately they'd begun calling him Bitin Dog, which was distinctly better. A dog belonging to one of the neighborhood boys had been found dead on the street a month ago, and the animal was generally assumed to have been poisoned. When someone had asked Oliver if he'd poisoned it, he had looked away and said, *Well, it was a bitin' dog.* As he'd hoped, everybody took that to mean that he had done it . . . though, in fact, he had not.

He had seen Scat take the spill jumping the ramp, and for an instant he had been scared—but when Scat had got up, grinning and dusting off the seat of his jeans, Oliver had relaxed.

The chain-link under him squeaked now as he shifted around to a more comfortable position. He wished he had the nerve to go over the ramp himself, but he was too aware of the bones in his arms and legs and the base of his spine. And he *was* heavier. He could do things like climb this backstop, but it didn't get much attention.

What the hell kind of a name was *Oliver* anyway? So what if it *was* his grandfather's name? Probably *he* hadn't liked it much either. And it wasn't like they ever saw the guy. It didn't seem fair that as the oldest *he* had had to get the joke name, while his younger brother got to be named after their uncle. Whom they likewise never saw.

Way up here off the ground he could admit to himself, but only very softly even so, that the name he wished he had been given was . . . *Walter.* He couldn't imagine how that had not happened; his father couldn't have been too ashamed of him *right from birth* to give his firstborn his own name, could he?

Suddenly there was a snap and sag as one of the wires tying the chain-link to the crossbar broke, and Oliver convulsively clawed his fingers into the lattice pattern. His face was dewed with sudden sweat, but as soon as he was sure he wasn't going to fall, he looked toward the ramp. Luckily none of the boys had noticed. The fat-boy-Hardy-breaking-the-backstop jokes would have lasted for weeks. Shakily he tucked his gun into his belt and began inching his way back to the vertical section of the fence.

When he was back on solid ground, he sighed and pulled his damp shirt away from his chest and belly.

School tomorrow, he thought.

He wished something would happen. He wanted to stop living the life of an obviously worthless little kid.

Sometimes he watched the gold and red clouds terraced across the still-blue sky at sunset, and he pretended that he might see a horse-drawn chariot, tiny in the immense distance, racing along the cloud ridges. If he were ever to see such a thing, and if the chariot were to sweep down and land in this field, like for a breather before taking off again for the cloud kingdoms, he knew he would race across the grass and jump aboard.

He played Mario Brothers a lot on the Nintendo set on the TV at home, and as he walked across the grass now, he thought of the invisible bricks that hung unsupported in the air of the Mario world. If a player didn't know about one of them, he would have the little Mario man run right on by, but a savvy player would know to have the little guy jump up at just the right spot—and bump his head on what had looked like empty air a moment before but was now a brick with one of the glowing mushrooms on it. Catch the mushroom and suddenly you were big. And if it was a lily instead of a mushroom, and you caught that, you could spit fireballs.

He jumped now. Nothing. Empty air.

As he drove around on the Strip in the dusty Morris—even as he walked along the morning sidewalks downtown, under the shadow of the Binion's Horseshoe Casino—Snayheever's cheap feathered Indian headdress had not excited much attention. He had bought it for five dollars at the Bonanza souvenir shop at dawn, and had worn it out of the store and not taken it off since, but it was only now, driving the little old Morris slowly through the streets of North Las Vegas, through these little tract-house-and-apartment-complex suburbs west of Nellis Air Force Base, that adults laughed and pointed and honked their car horns, and children shouted and ran madly after the car.

It couldn't be helped. He had to wear feathers today.

Traffic was light this morning. He looked around, noting palm trees throwing long shadows across quiet sidewalks. The residents he saw seemed to be mostly Air Force personnel, and student types who probably went to the Clark County Community College behind him on Cheyenne.

This was his third pass along this section of Cheyenne, and this time he made himself turn right on Civic Center—though he instantly pulled over and put the car into neutral so that he could check his figuring one more time.

He unfolded the AAA map and with a dirty fingernail traced the pencil outline he'd drawn on it.

Yes, there was no mistake, the outline did still look to him like a stylized, angular bird; he thought it was probably a crow or a raven. Usually he traced out patterns that were implicit in the tracks of roads and rivers and boundaries, but this bird pattern was imposed over all such.

The points of the angles were streets with names like Moonlight and Moonmist and Mare. The high point of the bird's tail was a couple of streets called Starlight and Moonlight alongside the 95 out toward the Indian Springs Air Force Base, and the tip of the beak was three streets called Moonglow, Enchanting, and Stargazer at the east edge of town on Lake Mead Boulevard. The diagonal straight line between those two points would contain the point that was the eye of the bird, and sure enough, he had found an intense cluster of streets at the right point, about two thirds down the line toward the tip of the beak—a whole tract with streets named Saturn, Jupiter, Mars, Comet, Sun, and Venus.

That tract was now only a block ahead of him.

Venus was obviously the street his mother would live on.

He tromped the clutch and muscled the car back into gear and started forward again. At Venus he turned left.

Along Venus Avenue he saw a lot of two-story apartments and duplexes. He drove slowly down the center of the right lane, lugging in first gear, squinting in the already hot breeze that was blowing in through the rolled-down windows.

How was he to know which place would be his mother's?

Would there be clues in the kind of plants out front, the paint, the—

The street number. One of the duplexes had four weathered wooden numbers bolted to the street-facing white stucco wall. The numbers were 1515, but Snayheever read them as letters:

ISIS.

Isis, the Egyptian goddess of the moon.

He had found her house—but he drove on past, tromping the little steel gas pedal and grinding the stick shift into second, for he couldn't approach her *today*.

If he made contact on this here particular Sunday, it would be like—like a king bringing along his army to visit another king. Snayheever was too powerful today; he'd be perceived as imperious rather than how he wanted to be perceived, which was . . . as supplicating, as humble. He might, it was true, have to do something a little heavy-handed in order to get her attention, but he wouldn't be so presumptuous as to use . . . *protocol*. And right now the moon was still half a hair on the new side; she'd still be in the weak half of her cycle. And of course she was always weaker in the daytime and only really herself at night. That was why she slept during the day.

Tomorrow night, Monday, the second of April, the moon would be precisely at its half phase. He had discovered that valuable fact only an hour ago, in a newspaper.

He would approach her then.

Crane sat up in the sleeping bag on the motel room floor and tried to shake dream images out of his head.

A rusty lance head and a gold cup. Where had Crane seen them before? Hanging on wires over a chair, long ago, in a—a place that had been home? The memory made his plastic eye ache, and he wasn't sorry that he couldn't trace it. In this last, disjointed fragment of dream the two objects had been set out, with apparent reverence, on a green felt cloth draped over a wooden crate. The light on them was red and blue and golden, as if filtered through stained glass.

Crane's mouth was dry now, though somehow he thought he could taste . . . what, a dry white wine. A Chardonnay?

The air conditioner was roaring, and the room was cold. There was white light beyond the curtains, but Crane had no idea what time it might be. This was Las Vegas, after all; it could be midnight, and the light outside could all be artificial.

He sighed and rubbed his face with trembling hands.

Again.

He had dreamed about the game on the lake again.

And he had been so exhausted this time—having gone forty-eight hours without sleep—that he had not been able to recoil awake when one of the two vast faces below him in the night had opened its canyon of a mouth and sucked him downward like a wisp of smoke.

He felt the inside of the sleeping bag now, and was glad to find that he had not lost control of his bladder during that part of the dream.

He had spiraled down helplessly through the moonlit abyss of the mouth and down the throat into darkness, and then he was deep under the water of the lake.

Things moved far below him, vast figures that he couldn't see, and that had no real form anyway—but the vibrations of them shook images loose in his mind, as earthquakes in succession might wring chords out of a piano and thus remotely express themselves:

. . . he saw his real father, weary and old, dressed in a red ermine robe and a hat like a horizontal figure-8, sitting at a table on the wavy edge of a cliff, and on the table was a round collection of coin stacks, and a knife, and a bloody lump that might have been an eyeball;

. . . and he saw his real father's '47 Buick, as shiny and new as he remembered it, being pulled along the glistening pavement of a rainy street by two harnessed creatures that had the bodies of horses and the heads of men;

. . . and he saw his foster-sister, Diana, crowned with a tiara like a crescent moon embracing a sun disk, dressed in papal-looking robes and attended by dogs that howled at the moon;

. . . and between the leafy arms of an oval wreath he saw himself, naked, frozen in a moment of running with one leg bent, while around the outside of the wreath stood an angel, a bull, a lion, and an eagle; and then the perspective changed and the figure that was himself was upside-down, hanging by the straight leg while gravity folded the other;

. . . and he saw dozens of other figures: Arky Mavranos,

walking away across the desert, carrying a bundle of swords as long as stretcher-poles; old Ozzie standing on a sandy hill and leaning on a single sword; Crane's dead wife, Susan, hanging what seemed to be a basketful of hubcaps on a branch of a dead tree . . .

. . . and he saw a bodiless, winged cherub's head, pierced through and through with two metallic-looking batons.

The cherub's one eye was staring straight into Crane's one eye, and he screamed and tried to run, but his muscles wouldn't work; he couldn't turn away or even close his eyes. There was nearly no light, and he couldn't breathe; he and the cherub head were far underwater, hidden from the sun and the moon and the stars and the figure that danced on the far cliffs, and he moaned in fear that the thing would open its mouth and speak, for he knew he would have to do what it said.

The dream had become trivial and stiflingly repetitious after that. He had seemed to be in a wide, airless, natural underground pool, trying to find a well up which he could swim to the surface, and there were a lot of wells, but every time he made his way kicking and paddling and bubbling up to the surface of one of them, he found that he was in someone's house—a cigarette would be trailing smoke from an ashtray, or fresh clothes would be draped over a chair and the shower would be running—and, alarmed at the thought of being caught in someone else's place, he had, over and over again, submerged himself and let the air out of his lungs and kicked back down into the darkness of the common pool that underlay all the individual wells. Eventually the hopeless repetition had left him awake, staring up at the white plastic smoke-alarm on the flocked motel ceiling.

The last dream house had been the one where the lance head and the cup lay in a pool of color-stained sunlight on green felt. Without even needing to touch them, he had known that they weren't really there, didn't belong there, and were there even in this illusory form only because there was not, today, any place where they belonged.

Now Crane looked at the digital clock on the bedside table. 2:38 P.M. And there was a note on the table, held down against the air conditioner breeze by a Coors can.

He and Ozzie and Mavranos had checked into this motel at

about six-thirty this morning, he recalled now. It was a little ten-unit place somewhere out past the Gold Coast on the wrong side of I–15, he remembered, and a "credit card imprint" had been necessary to get a room. Crane had two Visas in his wallet, one for Scott Crane and one for Susan Iverson-Crane, and Ozzie had made him use Susan's, to avoid being traced by anyone looking up the name *Crane, Scott.*

Crane and Mavranos had let the old man have the bed, and had dragged in a couple of sleeping bags from the Suburban for themselves.

Crane wriggled out of his sleeping bag now and stood up, wincing at the hot pain in his bandaged leg.

Something was wrong. What?

He tried to remember all the events of the last forty-eight hours. Gardena, he thought, and Baker, with that weird kid who played *Go Fish,* and the beer I sneaked in the car . . . Whiskey Pete's, and the beer and bourbon I got on the way to the men's room . . . that pickup truck, the man with the hair and the voice, and his friend Max with the gun . . . the streets around the downtown area, and a dozen goddamn grocery stores, not one of which employed anyone named Diana. . . .

None of it was particularly reassuring, but neither did any of it seem to call for the degree of dread that was speeding his heartbeat and chilling his face. He felt as though he had overlooked something, failed to think of something, and now someone who had depended on him was . . . frightened, alone with bad people, being hurt.

Caused by me.

He picked up the note. It was in ball-point ink on a piece of a grocery bag.

Archy and I have gone to check out a casino or two, it read. *Seemed like you could use more sleep. Be back around four.—Oz.*

Crane looked at the telephone, and after a moment he realized that his open hand was hovering over the instrument. What *is* it? he asked himself uneasily. Do you want to call somebody, or are you waiting for a call?

His mouth was dry, and his heart was pounding.

Outside, a white Porsche pulled into the motel parking lot. Al Funo stepped out of the car and stared around quizzically at the row of windows and doors, each door a different bright color. Poor old Crane, he thought. *This* is where he stays when he's in Vegas?

He tucked his sunglasses up into his styled sandy-colored hair as he walked across the lot toward the office. He knew he was going to have to approach Crane a bit more carefully this time. The bullet through the windshield, or something, had apparently spooked him into some elementary caution, and if Funo hadn't gone to the extra trouble of using a jewelery store's ID number to get the details of Crane's credit file from TRW, he'd never have learned about the Iverson-Crane Visa card.

Bells on strings clanged as he pushed open the office door and stepped into the air-conditioned dimness. The floor was shiny green linoleum, and aside from a standing rack of pamphlets and coupon books for tourists, a green vinyl couch was the only furniture.

Just not any class at all, Funo thought sadly.

When a white-haired woman appeared from the little office in the back, he smiled at her with genuine affection. "Hi, I'd like a room, please—probably just for one night."

As he was filling out the form she handed him, he said, "A friend of mine is supposed to be staying here, too—Crane, Scott Crane? We had to drive out separate; I couldn't get the extra day off work."

"Sure," said the old woman. "Crane. Fortyish guy, with two buddies, one with a mustache and the other real old. They're in six, but they just a little bit ago drove off."

"In his red pickup?"

"No, it was a big blue thing, like a cross between a station wagon and a Jeep." She yawned. "I could put you next to them, in five or seven."

"Hey, that'd be great, thanks. Heh-heh, listen, don't tell them I'm here, okay? I want to surprise them."

She shrugged.

Funo gave her his MasterCard rather than his American Express because he knew she would call it in; that's how he had found Crane after all. This was becoming expensive, in both money spent and work time lost. He wondered if there was some way to make it pay, to get it out of the category of auto-assignment. He thought about the gray Jag,

and the telephone number that he had got with the registration
data on the Jag's Nevada license plate number. That fat man
driving it had been after something. And he had seemed to
have money—but what did he want?

When Funo signed the draft, he noticed the date: 4/1/90.
April Fool's Day.

It upset him. It seemed to mock what he was doing, make
him seem insignificant.

He gazed at the old woman until she looked up, and then
he gave her a wink and his best boyish smile.

She just stared at him, as if he were a stain on the wall, a
stain that might resemble a person if you squinted at it in a
certain way.

He was glad he had already signed the voucher, for his
hands were trembling now.

Mavranos drove out of the multilevel parking structure
behind the Flamingo and steered the big Suburban along
the broad driveway, past the taxi stand and the loading zone
toward the Strip. He took it slow over the wide speed bumps,
but still the car rattled as it crested the lines of raised asphalt,
and the ice shook and swashed in the ice chest. The Strip was
clear either way for a hundred yards when he got to the street,
and he made his left turn as easily as he would have in some
quiet Midwest suburb.

"What are the odds of that?" he asked Ozzie, forcing himself
to squint intently and not smile. "Making a left so easy in front
of the Flamingo?"

"Christ," wailed the old man, "you're looking for big statistical *waves,* okay? If you start watching for, I don't know,
numbers on license plates, or two fat ladies wearing the same
flowered shorts, you're—"

Mavranos laughed. "I'm kidding you, Oz! But I swear a
couple of things back there signified."

They had watched a Craps table at the Flamingo for a while,
had walked across the street to listen for patterns in the ringing
and clattering of the slots at Caesars Palace, and then had
written down a hundred consecutive numbers that came up
on a Roulette wheel at the Mirage. Twice, once crossing the
street west and once east, Mavranos had simultaneously heard
a car horn honk and a dog bark and had looked up to catch

hard sun glare off a windshield, so that for half a minute afterward he'd seen a dark red ball everywhere he looked, and at Caesars, three different strangers had whispered, "Seven," as they shouldered past him. He had eagerly asked Ozzie if he thought these coincidences might mean anything, and the old man had dismissed them all impatiently.

Now, stopped for a red light in the right-turn lane at the Flamingo Road traffic signal, Mavranos dug out of his pocket the penciled list of Roulette numbers and scanned them.

"Light's green," said Ozzie after a few moments.

"How I need a drink . . ." said Mavranos thoughtfully, taking his foot off the brake and turning the wheel but still staring at the list.

"Watch the road!" said Ozzie sharply. "You've got a beer between your knees, as usual, and frankly I think you drink way too much."

"No," said Mavranos, "I mean *pi,* you know *pi?*"

Ozzie was staring at him. "You want a pie? Instead of a drink? What the hell kind of pie? Can't you—"

Mavranos passed the list to the old man, eyed the traffic, and stepped on the gas pedal. "Here. Pi, the ratio of a circle's circumference to its diameter, you know? Radius times pi squared, you've heard that kind of talk. Pi's what they call an irrational number, three and an infinitely long string of numbers after the decimal point. Well, there's a sentence you memorize, a mnemonic thing, to remember the numbers that are pi, out to something like a dozen places. I read it in a Rudy Rucker book. It starts, 'How I need a drink . . . '—that's three, one, four, one, five, get it? Number of letters in each word. But I can't remember the rest of the mnemonic sentence."

They had crossed over I–15. Ozzie squinted through the dusty windshield and pointed. "That's our motel on the right, don't miss the driveway. Archimedes, I really am not following—"

"See where the Roulette numbers were three, one, four, fifteen in the middle there? Look at the paper, I can see where I'm going. What numbers come after that?"

"Uh . . . nine, twenty-six, five, thirty-five, eight . . ."

Mavranos turned into the lot, parked near their room, and turned off the engine.

"Yeah," he said, "I'm pretty sure that's pi. Well now *that's* got to signify, don't it? Goddamn Roulette wheel just spontaneously starts reciting off pi? I wonder what numbers the other tables were listing. The square root of two, I suppose, or the square root of minus one."

Ozzie pulled on the handle and pushed his door open, then stepped carefully down to the hot pavement. "I don't know," he said, frowning, when Mavranos had locked his own door and walked around the car, "I guess so, if those numbers *are* this pi business of yours . . . but it seems to me this isn't the thing you're looking for. This is something else; something else is going on here—"

A sporty-looking young man was taking an overnight bag out of the back seat of a white Porsche in the next parking space. He was studiedly looking away from them, so he didn't notice that Ozzie had stepped forward, and he hit the old man in the shin with his bag when he swung it out of the little car.

"Watch it," said Ozzie irritably.

The young man muttered and hurried to the door of number seven, rattling a key against the lock.

"Goddamn zombies, you got in this town," Ozzie remarked to Mavranos.

Mavranos wondered if their neighbor had heard the remark. A moment later the young man was inside his room and had slammed the door hard.

I guess he did hear it, Mavranos thought.

A wind was blowing southeast from the jagged Virgin Mountains, tossing the yellow brittlebrush flowers on the miles of canyonside and rippling the wide, deep blue waters of Lake Mead. Vacationers were awkwardly bumping the docks with their rented boats at the Mead Resort Circle, and gasoline made a volatile perfume on the breeze and rainbowed the surface of the water around the docks and slips.

Ray-Joe Pogue gunned his jet boat straight out across the water for a hundred yards, away from the waterfront grocery store and bait shop, but the wind-raised waves made the lake choppier out here, and after a few seconds of being slammed up and down on the tuck-and-roll upholstery of the seat, he took his foot off the gas and let the rented jet boat rock in the water under the empty blue sky.

In the sudden relative silence he squinted around at the wide-scattered islands and the far reaches of the Boulder Basin coastline. There were a lot of boats out on this Sunday afternoon, but he didn't imagine he'd have any problem finding a secluded shore where he could sink the head. The metal box had bounced off the seat beside him onto the floor, and he carefully picked it up and put it back and laid the coiled line on top of it.

The head in the metal box.

He had killed several people in his life, and it had never bothered him, and so he was surprised at how much it had hurt him to kill Max. He felt disoriented now, as if he were seriously hungover, and he felt uneasy whenever he looked at the box.

He had met Max in high school—at one time Max had been in love with Nardie, Pogue's Asian half-sister—and he and Max had for years been preparing for this summer, this election year, this once-every-two-decades changing of the king. Max was to have been his . . . who, Merlin, Lancelot, Gawain? But last night, after failing to find the mysterious bus vehicle on I–15, Pogue had ordered Max to pull over and get out of the pickup truck, and had then fired the 12-gauge shotgun into the man's back.

He shuddered now in the harsh sunlight, the wind cold on his face, and he didn't look at the box. He gripped the white plastic gunwale of the jet boat and stared out across the water.

He had had no choice. Ideally he should not have had to perform this old Phoenician Adonis ritual, but there were too many uncertainties right now. Some jack had got past him last night on the highway, and there had been something suspicious about those three guys, the pirate, the old man, and the retard, in that blue Suburban with all the ribbons and crap all over it. And he couldn't get a line on Nardie Dinh; for months now he hadn't picked up any of her dreams. How the hell could she not dream? Was there some drug that suppressed it?

He had to find her, and before Easter. As his half-sister she was the only one who could serve as the moon goddess, his queen. All the fertility gods and kings mated with women who were in some way their sisters—Tammuz and Belili, Osiris and Isis, even King Arthur and Morgan le Fay—and he had thought he had effectively broken her will during the month-long confinement in that parlor house outside Tonopah. The diet regimen he'd had her on, the blood rituals, the room with the twenty-two pictures—he had groomed her perfectly to assume the goddess-hood, and then, when he had thought she was the broken sleepwalker he wanted, she had knifed the house's madam and stolen a car and fled to Las Vegas. And now she wasn't even dreaming anymore.

He squinted across the waves at a rocky little island a couple of miles away, and then looked at his Lake Mead map, folded to show Boulder Basin. Deadman's Island, the place was called. That sounded appropriate.

He turned the wheel, then stepped on the gas. The acceleration pushed him back into the seat, and as he straightened out of the turn, the wind threw the high rooster tail of spray out ahead of him, and heavy drops of water stung his face and knocked his black hair down onto his forehead.

He dug out his comb as he steered one-handed, and he swept the hair back up where it belonged. From now until Easter, physical perfection was going to be absolutely essential.

The man who takes the throne can have no flaws.

He circled the island in a series of jackrabbit starts, and on the far side he found a little rocky beach with no picnickers on it. He got in fairly close and then threw over the cinder-block that was the anchor.

Reluctantly he picked up the box, then climbed over the gunwale and waded ashore through the cold water, holding the box high.

In ancient Alexandria, Phoenicians had enacted the annual death of Tammuz by throwing a papyrus head into the sea, and seven days later the summer current invariably left the head at Byblos, where they'd fish it out and celebrate the god's resurrection. It was during the interval when the head was in the sea that the location and identity and even the existence of the fertility god were in doubt.

These next two weeks, from this April Fool's Day until Easter, would be the tricky period this cycle, and Pogue was determined that it would be his own head—symbolically—that would be taken out of the water on Easter Sunday.

Max's poor severed head was wearing Pogue's Ray-Bans and had one of Pogue's ties knotted around the stump of its neck, and of course Max had shared Pogue's and Nardie's dietary restrictions, eating no red meat nor anything that had been cooked in an iron pan and drinking no alcohol. That was why Pogue had not been able to simply behead some random tourist for this. The head had to be the closest possible representation of Pogue's own.

His hands were shaking. He wanted to open the box and reknot the tie. Max had never learned how to tie one, and Pogue could remember a dozen occasions when Max had brought a tie to him, and Pogue had had to tie it around his own neck and then loosen it and pull it off over his head and give it to his friend.

When I knotted the tie for him this morning at dawn beside Boulder Highway, he thought now, that was the last time I'll ever do that chore for him.

He clenched his teeth and took a deep breath.

Christ, he told himself, never *mind*, get the box in the water and moor the line somewhere where no goddamn drunk tourists will find it during the next two weeks, and get the hell out of here.

He looked around among the rocks and the manzanita bushes for a good spot, and he noticed the flock of swallows out over the lake.

He assumed they were swallows. They had the individual darting flight patterns of those birds, certainly—but something was wrong about their wings. And there were other flocks, he now noticed, lots of them, further away. He shaded his eyes to look at the flying things.

Then his stomach went cold, and sweat sprang out on his forehead.

They were bats.

Bats, he thought dazedly—but bats don't ever come out during the day. What're they, crazy, rabid? *Is something going on?*

He looked away, to see where they might be headed, and he saw that the sky to the south, too, was peppered with the same jiggling dots.

They're coming here. To this little island, from goddamn everywhere.

He scrambled along the little shoreline to a cluster of rocks, and he tossed the gleaming box out over the water; it splashed in while he was tying the end of the line around a half-submerged rock.

And then shadows were whirling around his feet like spots before his eyes. The bats were circling low overhead, silent except for the clatter of their leather wings, and more were coming in from everywhere. The battering wind of their wings disarranged his hair.

He looked up in horror. The furry, toothy little faces flashing past, the bright round eyes were all *staring* at him.

Something was splashing furiously in the water now, and in panic he swung his head toward it.

The lake water was boiling where he had thrown the box in, and then, impossibly, the heavy box bobbed to the surface, spinning and glittering on the turbulence.

The lake is rejecting it, he thought dazedly. Is that a bunch of *fish* doing that, or has the water changed its density to keep from enclosing the head?

The clatter of the bats' wings was louder, closer, and he thought he could smell them, a smell like death.

Just run, he told himself.

They've beaten you here today.

Biting back bewildered sobs, he yanked the box back in to shore with one hand while shielding his face from the bats with the other, and then, with the shiny dripping box dangling from his fist, he blundered back down the beach and splashed out to the boat.

When he had tossed the box onto the seat, climbed in himself and in neutral gear deafeningly gunned the big car engine under the Plexiglas hood behind him, the bats seemed to circle higher; and when he spun the wheel and slammed the shift into gear and goosed the boat out across the water straight away from the island, they didn't follow, but broke away and dispersed across the sky.

He let the engine fall back to idle then, and sat panting and shaking in the suddenly becalmed boat as he watched the creatures scatter away, back to the mountain caves in which, on any sane day, they'd have lingered until sunset.

For the first time since the day in the school library when he had figured out the nature of this mystical western kingship, he wished he could break the regimen and drink—get really, thoroughly drunk.

Eventually he got the boat moving, as slowly as the erratic throttle would allow, back toward the marinas of the Lake Mead Resort. Tears and sweat slicked his classically handsome face.

I killed Max for nothing, he thought dully. The sacrifice was rejected, like Cain's.

How could that have happened? Did I *disqualify* myself by killing Max? No, worse things were done by the old kings. Should I have waited, or done it sooner? Is there *already* a king's head in Lake Mead, and there isn't psychic room for another?

By the time he got back to the rental dock he had shaken off the passion of loss and hopelessness.

I can still become the king, he told himself as he pulsed the engine and nudged the boat in toward the crowded dock. But I've got to find my damned half-sister—I've got to find Nardie Dinh.

The westering sun was intensifying the orange color of the motel curtains as Crane shuffled the flimsy little deck and dealt out onto the bed five cards each to himself and Ozzie and Mavranos. It was too early to start searching the supermarkets again, and Ozzie had forbidden fooling around with real cards, so Mavranos had fetched from the Suburban a kids' Crazy Eights deck he'd got at a Carl's Jr. hamburger restaurant.

Every card had a cheery, stylized picture of an animal on it, and as the game progressed and cards were discarded face up, Mavranos was amused by the selection of colorful, grinning birds and beasts tossed out across the motel bedspread.

"You know why nobody could play cards aboard the Ark, don't you?" he asked.

Crane rolled his eyes, but Ozzie looked up suspiciously. "No," the old man said, "why?"

Mavranos took a sip of beer. "'Cause Noah was sitting on the deck."

Dry summer thunder boomed, out over the McCullough Range to the south.

Oh, come on, thought Crane, it wasn't that funny.

CHAPTER 19

A Skinny Man Trying to Get Out

The micrometer looked like a monkey wrench for some insanely fastidious mechanic, and its gleaming precision seemed out of place amid the chip racks and adding machines and cigarette-burned desks of the cluttered casino office. Nardie Dinh dutifully held the tool up in the fluorescent light and read the number on the round metal sleeve.

"This one's right on, too," she told the frowning floorman as she loosened the ratchet knob at the base and freed the second of the pair of dice he had brought to her.

She held the translucent red cube close to her face and looked at the faint, tiny initials she had scratched into the one-dot face of the cube, and then she flipped it over and found the microscopic moon symbol she had delicately etched on the six-dot face. Both marks were, of course, exactly as she had scratched them in at midnight, when her shift as night manager of the Tiara Casino dice pit had begun.

She put down the red cube and the micrometer and absently wiped her hands. "They're good," she told the floorman shortly. "He's not switching in his own dice."

"How can he be rolling so many snake eyes then? The boxman says he's been rolling them the right way, bouncing them off the table's far wall every time."

Because, Dinh thought, tonight when I put my mark on the dice, I asked the Craps tables if I would succeed in my purpose, and snake eyes means *Yes, if no others are involved*.

"I don't know, Charlie," she said. Her latest coffee was still too hot to drink, so she held up the Styrofoam cup and inhaled the vivifying steam. "Is he betting the proposition two, or the Any Craps?"

Charlie the floorman shook his head. "No, *he's* losing,

playing the Pass Line with dollar chips. But other people are starting to play those bets, and one of 'em could be a partner."

"It's got to be just chance," she told him, "but let's unwrap some fresh dice from the factory and I'll mark them and we can just retire all the dice that are out there now." And this time I won't ask the tables any question, she thought.

Charlie looked disconcerted. "*All* the dice?"

"That last lot might have been funny. I like to err on the side of safety."

He shrugged. "You're the boss."

When he had gone to get the boxes, she stood up from the desk and stretched. She had applied for this job because the Tiara was perhaps the last casino in town that still had the shift managers initial the dice, and she was so closely aligned with the moon that, with her moon mark on the dice, she had several times been able to get answers from the little cubes.

This was the first time the answer had been so evident as to excite attention, though. I suppose, she thought, if I were to ask them anything next week, when the moon is full, every pair of dice in the place would come up identical, over and over again.

She stretched again, lifting her elbows and massaging her narrow shoulders. Four hours since I parked the cab and got out of the uniform, she thought, and I still feel like I'm bent behind a steering wheel. I'll be glad when dawn rolls around and I can get out of here, drive down to placid Henderson.

For a day job, she had found a little insurance office in Henderson that needed a bookkeeper. She was generally at her most lethargic when the sun was up, so the automatic-pilot work of adding numbers was ideal, and in the insurance office, eighteen miles south of Las Vegas, she was not likely to be recognized by any of the people who knew her from her night jobs.

Which was just as well—they'd wonder when she ever slept.

She frowned, remembering how unconsciousness had nearly caught her yesterday.

Yesterday at exactly dawn she had almost fainted in the cashier's cage while she'd been putting away the drop boxes for the next shift manager, and when the blurry dizziness had passed, she had hurried out onto the floor to the nearest table, where a desultory two-dollar Blackjack game was going on.

For a couple of minutes, like the fading figures on a switched-off computer screen, she had seen the Jack and Queen of Hearts showing up more often than they had any statistical right to, and she had known that a powerful Jack and a powerful Queen had just passed very close to each other somewhere out there in the streets of the city.

Dinh was determined that she herself was the one who would be wearing Isis's crown come Easter, and she wondered now what she might have to do to prevent this mysteriously powerful Queen from beating her to it.

She didn't want to kill anyone except her stepbrother.

The sound of a key turning in a lock.

In the moment of waking up, Funo thought his own motel room door had been opened, and he snatched the pistol off the bedside table. Then he realized that he was alone in the room; the sound had come though the earphones he'd been wearing while he slept.

"I bet she moved," came a man's voice, faintly. He must have been facing away from the wall between the two rooms. "I bet when she got Scott's call, it spooked her into just pulling up stakes and moving to Ohio or somewhere."

Funo put down the gun, then sat up and began pulling on his pants, carefully so as not to dislodge the earphones. He looked at the little electric clock—seven in the morning.

"I . . . don't think so," said another man, his amplified voice louder. "I keep getting . . . *impressions* that aren't my own, little whiffs of worry and humor, and tastes, like yesterday I tasted a wine that I hadn't drunk. I have the feeling she's nearby."

"Well, probably one of those stores we hit was the right place, and they lied. Supermarkets probably have a policy against telling strangers the names of their employees. Especially strangers who look like they've been sleeping in their clothes."

"Nah," came the voice of a third man, who sounded much older, "we've met three wrong Dianas, haven't we? We'll find the right one yet. She didn't have the sense to at least work in one of the North Las Vegas places, so she must be in one of the ones down by the Strip. There can't be more than a couple. We'll find her tonight."

Funo zipped up his pants and, leaning as far as he could against the slack of the headphones wire, managed to grab a clean shirt from his bag.

"What if she's changed her name, then, Ozzie?" the first man's voice went on. "I bet she would have, from the things you told her about this town."

"Then we'll probably *see* her," said the old man in the next room. "And yes, I will be able to recognize her, even after a dozen years."

"You don't have to come, Arky," said the second man, who Funo guessed was Scott Crane. "I mean, we can take cabs. You've been looking tired, and cash ain't our problem."

"Me? What the hell do you mean by that? I ain't been tired. Nah, one more night. You guys might get into a fight, and you'd need me. I can track my odds today, and tonight mess with the slots in the market entrances while you guys go in and ask your question."

"One thing for sure," said Ozzie, "tomorrow we spring for a decent breakfast. One more of these dollar-ninety-nine specials is gonna burn its way right out through the front of my shirt. Boys, it's bedtime. You wanna talk, do it outside."

A loud bumping came over the phones now, and Funo realized that at least one of the men in the next room must intend to sleep on the floor. Funo glanced nervously at the wire that disappeared into the hole he'd drilled in the drywall on his side, and he hoped whichever of them it was wouldn't notice the little hole on the other side.

After a few minutes he relaxed. All he could hear now was slow, even breathing.

He took off the earphones and stood up, buckling his belt, then took the telephone into the bathroom and punched in the number that went with the gray Jag.

The phone at the other end rang once, and then a tape-recorded voice recited the number back at him. Right after that came the beep.

"Uh," said Funo, rattled by the rudeness of it, "I know where the people you were looking for Saturday are in California. I mean, you were in California, looking for them. Scott Crane and Ozzie and Diana." He waited, but no one picked up the phone. "I'm going to call this number again in three hours, that's ten o'clock exactly, let's say, and then we can dicker about how much my services would be worth to you."

He hung up. That should do something.

As he went to the closet to select a shirt, he reflected that old Ozzie was right—a good breakfast was important. Maybe there was a Denny's nearby. He could buy a newspaper and sit at the counter and maybe get into a conversation with somebody.

Vaughan Trumbill had cleaned up the breakfast dishes and vacuumed the living room and hall, and now sat at the desk in his room, writing checks in Betsy's big old checkbook. At a quarter to ten he figured up the new balance and inked the number at the bottom of the current page; then he closed the book and put it in the drawer.

He crossed to the aquarium and allowed himself to net up a two-inch-long catfish; he held it carefully just behind the head and bit off the body. Chewing strongly, he lowered his hand into the water and uprooted an Amazon sword-plant, swirled it in the murky water to get the dirt off the roots, and then folded that into his mouth. The catfish head he wrapped in several sheets of Kleenex and tucked into the pocket of his white shirt as he continued to chew his snack.

Live snacks, though of necessity generally skimpy, were always the most satisfying.

The white walls of his room were uncluttered by any pictures, and his window looked out onto a flat expanse of gravel and a high gray cinder-block wall. As always, he stared around at the sterile simplicity before leaving the room, breathing the chilly, odorless air, imprinting it all in his mind—for the rest of Betsy Reculver's house was a clutter of bookcases and overstuffed furniture and framed photographs, and these days she used too much perfume.

LaShane came trotting up to him in the hall, and Trumbill absently patted the big Doberman on its narrow head. Before stepping into the living room, he automatically glanced at the television screens above the doorway to make sure that there was nobody in the back or side yards or the area around the front door.

Betsy Reculver was sitting on the couch in the living room, staring at her hands in her lap, and when he entered the room she glanced at him blankly. "Beany," she said, then went back to staring at her hands.

He nodded and sat down in the only chair in the room she would let him put his weight on. He dug the Kleenex-wrapped catfish head out of his pocket and unobtrusively dropped it into a nearby wastebasket. He didn't like having organic stuff in the wastebasket in his own room, even just for a little while.

He looked around the living room, remembering times when there'd been half a dozen men sitting around waiting for Betsy's orders. Trumbill had found her and started working for her in 1955, when he'd been twenty-six, newly home from having learned the truth about the world in Korea. Some of the men working for her—Abrams, Guillen—had been with her since before 1949, when she'd still been inhabiting the Georges Leon body.

That poor old Georges Leon body, which was now known as Doctor Leaky.

Eventually, during the sixties, when she'd been Ricky Leroy, she'd had to kill all of them.

Every one of them had eventually come to want the throne for himself, the immortality that could be had through assuming a succession of one's own children. Trumbill knew that she . . . he, it, Georges Leon, really . . . had considered killing him, too, before finally realizing the truth—that Trumbill was not interested in any life beyond the life of his own body.

A skinny man trying to get out.

He knew all about the skinny man. He had seen him many times in Korea, the skeleton in the ditch, all the juices leaked or evaporated away, with only the flimsiest leathery remnant of skin to cover the intolerable bones—all the *substance* lost, gone to nourish *other* life: bugs and plants and birds and dogs.

Emptied.

In Korea he had formed the resolution to fill himself, to contain as much of all that other organic life as possible, to bury the skeleton as far below the surface of his skin as he could. And Betsy had sworn that when he eventually died, she would make sure that he was sunk in a block of cement before burial, so that nothing should be lost, ever.

Reculver stood up now and walked to the bookcase and back.

"Whew. I hope he doesn't choke of asthma before he can get to his fresh inhaler," she said irritably. "I didn't let him take one break since that call at seven."

"Any signs?"

"I had Beany in the Seven-Stud game the whole time, so as to see more cards. The goddamn Queen of Hearts kept showing up, so I think this Diana person is *in town* somehow. There'll be other women around, wanting Isis's crown, but she's the one with the advantage of actually being a physical child of the old Queen, that Issit woman you folded in '60. I wish to hell you'd got the baby, too, then."

There was nothing in that for Trumbill, so he just kept looking at her stolidly.

"And the Jack of Hearts showed up way too often, generally with the Four of Hearts."

"What's the Four?"

"It's—sort of an old-bachelor figure. I don't see it as a threat to me, but I wonder who the hell it is."

"Who's this jack, is the question." Trumbill shifted in the chair and wished he had brought another one of his tropical fish out with him. A cichlid would go down well right now. He hated bringing up awkward topics with Betsy lately; he wished she'd wear the Richard body more often, or even haul the Art Hanari one out of mothballs. "It's got to be the jack you sensed last night, doesn't it? That seemed like the big one, the one to worry about."

"It's a jack," she said shortly. "I can handle jacks. I'm the King."

"But—" Oh, Jesus, Trumbill thought, here I go. "But it sounds like it's as—as far outranking the other jacks as this Diana woman is outranking the other wanna-be Queens. Now, Diana has that advantage because she is the actual kid of Issit." Unobtrusively he took a deep breath. "Way back when you were in the Georges Leon body—didn't you have a second kid, besides Richard? A second biological son?"

Her lower lip was pouched out, and there were tears in her eyes when she looked at him. "No. Who told you that?"

"*You* did, Betsy, one time in the sixties when you were in Richard, Ricky Leroy. Remember? I don't mean to . . . hurt your feelings, but if this jack may be that kid, isn't it something you've got to think about?"

"I can't think. I've got to do everything by myself. I—"

Trumbill flexed his massive arms and legs and got out of the chair. "Time," he said when she looked at him in alarm. "Got to get the tape going."

"Time? Oh, that call. Sure, go ahead."

Trumbill had just got the tape recorder going when the phone rang. He picked it up before the answering machine could cut in.

"Yes?" He turned on the speakerphone so that Betsy could hear.

"This is the guy that called before, about Scott Crane, Ozzie, and Diana. I know where they are, I can get to them for you. Are you interested?"

"Yes," said Trumbill. "We'll pay you twenty thousand dollars, half when you tell us and half after we've determined that your information is valid."

"Uh . . . okay. That'll do. Where do you want to meet?"

Trumbill looked over at Betsy. "The Flamingo," she mouthed.

"The Flamingo," said Trumbill. "Two o'clock this afternoon. In the coffee shop, Lindy's Deli. I'll be at the Trumbill table."

He spelled the name and then hung up.

"I'm going with you," Betsy said.

"I don't think—"

"You don't want me to, is that it? Who *is* this guy you're meeting, anyway?"

"You know as much about it all as I do, Betsy." He thought about asking her to step into the Art Hanari body and give him a call, but he suspected that she was too agitated right now to agree to it. "Betsy, I don't mean to upset you, but it might help me to help *you* if I knew the name of the boy, your son who got away in '48."

"I don't remember," she said, and then she stuck her tongue out at him.

Funo arrived early, and walked around the hotel for a while. He picked up a pamphlet and read it on one of the couches by the registration desk and learned that the hotel had been founded by a gangster named Bugsy Siegel.

Ordinarily that would have fascinated him, and he might

have made a mental note to read up on this Siegel character, but right now his nerves were too jangled. He shook another couple of Tic Tac mints out into his palm and popped them into his mouth, wishing he could get rid of the taste of vomit.

He had got talking to a man at breakfast, and the fellow had seemed very nice, very well educated—but then he had started talking in a direction Funo hadn't followed. Funo had bluffed, pretending to understand and agree, until it had dawned on him that the man believed Funo was a homosexual. Funo had excused himself and gone to the men's room, had rid himself in one of the stalls of every bit of the breakfast, and then had simply hurried out of the place and driven away. He'd have to mail the amount of his bill to Denny's. Ten times the amount of his bill. The waitress must think he was some kind of no-account. He'd go back in person, not mail the money, when she was working again, and he'd not only pay the skipped bill but give her some expensive piece of jewelry.

That'll take cash, he thought.

He knew that these people he was going to meet here today would want to handle Scott and Ozzie and Diana themselves; but he could point out that he was a professional, too. The fat man, assuming that's whom he had talked to on the phone, seemed to be in a position of authority here, not hired by Obstadt back in L.A., and he would probably welcome help from a competent workman.

He wondered how Obstadt's "guys in Vegas" were doing at trying to find Crane. He hoped they hadn't found out about the Iverson-Crane Visa card.

The Pacific Time Zone clock over the registration desk said a couple of minutes to two. He stood up and walked toward the escalator that would take him down to Lindy's Deli.

As soon as he stopped by the cash register and could look out across the rows of booths and quaint dark wood tables, Funo recognized the fat man's big old bald head poking up above one of the farther booths.

He grinned and strode over to the booth. The place smelled wonderfully of corned beef and coleslaw.

Trumbill was sitting with a very attractive older woman, and Funo bowed. "Hi, I'm Al Funo. I believe I spoke to . . . you, sir? On the phone earlier. I got your number by tracing the registration on your Jag."

"Sit down," said the fat man coldly. "Where are the people you mentioned?"

Funo winked at the old woman, as if sharing amusement at Trumbill's bad manners. "Aren't you going to introduce me to your lovely companion?"

She nodded, and Trumbill said, "This is Elizabeth Reculver."

That had been the name the car was registered to. "A p-p-pleasure," said Funo, keeping his smile but blushing at this recurrence of the stuttering he thought he had licked as a kid. Hastily he slid into the booth, next to her.

"Where are the people you mentioned?" Trumbill said.

"I know where they are," said Funo, "and that's what's important, because I'm in your employ, as it were. I've done a lot of this kind of work."

Trumbill was frowning at him. "This kind of work." The fat man leaned back and sighed. "The money is for the information, Alvin. After you give us that, you just take the money and go away."

Alvin? Like the chipmunk? And talking to him as if money meant more to him than people! Funo felt his face heating up again. "I d-d-don't—" *Damn it,* he thought. "I'm a professional, and I don't . . . appreciate—"

Reculver leaned forward.

"Don't, Vaughan," she said, looking the fat man straight in the eye. "I think we should listen to what young Al has to say. I think he *could* help us."

Suddenly the situation was clear to Funo. This ridiculous Trumbill person was in *love* with this woman! And resented the fact that she so clearly found Funo attractive.

After a pause, "Okay," said Trumbill, nodding. "Then I guess I should make a call, tell our other guys to put it on hold until they hear different. It looks like we may be doing it your way after all, Mr. Funo." He slid his bulk out of the booth and got to his feet.

Funo could be gracious. "I suspected you'd come to that conclusion, Mr. Trumbill."

Standing up, Trumbill could see the other tables, and he must have liked what he could see, for his nostrils flared and he licked his lips. "Why don't we have lunch while we talk?"

he said. "Order me a Reuben's sandwich. Extra coleslaw and pickles. And a big V-8."

"Lunch sounds good to me," said Funo cheerfully. He was sure he could hold food down now. "Good talk with good people over good food, right?"

"Right," said Trumbill.

Trumbill strode off toward the exit, and Funo turned to Reculver, his heart beating fast. "I understand," he said softly, giving her his boyish smile.

The old woman smiled back at him a little uncertainly. "Understand what?"

"Your . . . feelings. Really."

"Good, I was hoping you did. Vaughan—that's Mr. Trumbill—sometimes he just . . ." She paused, for Funo had slid over next to her and was pressing his thigh against hers. "Uh, I think you should sit over there, back where you were."

Was she teasing him? Of course. The old *hard-to-get* routine! Ordinarily he'd have played along, done the winks and the short-but-intense glances, the witty *double entendres*, but today he needed a little reassurance.

He looked around. At the moment there wasn't anyone who could see them.

He curled his arm across her shoulders, and then with deliberate slowness lowered his mouth onto hers.

Her mouth opened—

—to cough out one harsh syllable of laughter: an awkward, embarrassed laugh, as if she had suddenly found herself in a profoundly distasteful situation and wasn't sure how to get out of it without giving offense, without making her revulsion evident. There had not been any slightest response in her lips or her body.

Funo felt as if he had tried to kiss an old man.

Then he was up and running, and by the time he burst out of one of the north doors onto the bright Strip sidewalk, he was crying.

He was long gone. Reculver walked back to the booth and sat down. In a few moments Trumbill came swinging and stamping back to the table. He looked at Betsy alone in the booth and raised his eyebrows.

"Gone to the head?" he asked.

"No, he—he ran away." She shook her head bewilderedly. "I . . . had him wrong, Vaughan. I thought he was just a, you know, small-time ambitious hood; Moynihan's guys get him out of here quiet, we shoot him up with sodium pentothal or something, and then we bury him in the desert when we've found out what he knows. But he . . . tried to *kiss* me! Sit down, will you? He tried to kiss me, and I guess I didn't react—properly."

Trumbill stared at her. His mouth kinked in a rare, ironic grin. "I guess you wouldn't."

"I wonder if we'll hear from him again."

He sat down. "If we do, you'd better tell him you were . . . on your period, but now you're okay again and you think he's sexy."

"I couldn't possibly do that."

Two men in shorts and flowered shirts hurried up to the table now, panting. "He got clean away, Mrs. Reculver. He was in a cab and gone by the time we got to the sidewalk. We were walking toward here, from by the kitchen, but then he just up and ran out."

"Yeah," said the other man nervously. "You didn't tell us to watch for him to just up and *run out*."

"I know," said Reculver, still distracted. "Get out of here, and next time be quicker."

"I better get back on the phone," said Trumbill, wearily getting up again, "and tell Moynihan we don't need his guys after all. Did you get a chance to order?"

"No. We should be heading back home."

Trumbill pursed his lips but didn't argue. There were the tropical fish at home.

CHAPTER 20

Isis, I Have Your Son

The sky was dark, but the white lights of the wedding chapels jumped and crawled in the cracks in Arky's windshield.

One beer, thought Crane as Arky gunned the old truck south on Las Vegas Boulevard and the full Coors cans bumped around in the ice chest. What conceivable harm could there be in having one beer? In this town people walk down the street with glasses of hard liquor; get a free drink in one casino, and you can take it right outside with you, leave the glass in the next place you go to and get another.

But it wouldn't be just one, he told himself. No matter how emphatically you swore and promised that it would. And if it's possible to save your life here, you've got to not let Dionysus get any better a grip on you than he's already got.

The World Series of Poker was due to start at the end of this month at Binion's Horseshoe, and if this was going to be like 1969, the Assumption games on the lake would take place before that, during Holy Week. Which was next week. Crane didn't have a plan, but if there *was* any way he could elude the death his real father had planned for him, he would have to stay sober.

But, he thought, Ozzie says I'm doomed—and if he's right, why should I die sober?

Okay, he told himself, maybe. But not tonight, okay? Just this one night you can do without a drink, can't you? If we find Diana, you want to be functioning at your best, don't you? Such as your best is.

"Watch for Charleston," said Ozzie from the back seat. "You're going to turn left."

"I know, Oz," said Mavranos wearily.

"Well," said the old man, "I don't want you missing it and then cutting capers in this traffic to get back."

"Cutting capers?" Mavranos said, sneaking a sip of his current beer. "Those fish eggs?"

Crane was laughing.

"What's so funny?" Mavranos demanded. "Oh—you mean those little birds people cook on New Year's. *Capons.*"

"He means clowning around," Crane said.

"Why didn't he say so then. I don't know about cutting capers." He drove moodily for a while. "I know about cutting farts."

Even Ozzie was laughing now.

A neon sign over a liquor store read PHOTO IDS. Crane read it as one word, *photoids.* What would that be, he wondered, things *like* photons? *False* light? *Faux* light, as they'd say? Maybe the whole town was lit with such.

But suddenly Crane's heart was thumping and his palms were chilly. *I should have done something,* he found himself thinking. *I've got to get home.* His hands were on the upholstery of the seat, but for a moment he could feel a telephone; his right hand seemed to be hanging it up.

This isn't me, he realized; these aren't my thoughts and sensations.

"Diana's worried," he said tightly, "scared. Something she heard on the telephone just now. She's going home."

"Here's Charleston," Ozzie said, leaning forward over the seat and pointing.

Mavranos nodded. He angled into the left-turn lane and stopped in the middle of the intersection, waiting for a gap in the oncoming northbound traffic. The only sounds in the car were Crane's panting and the *click-click, click-click* of the turn indicator.

Crane could feel Diana walking quickly, stopping, talking urgently to someone. He stared at the headlights ahead of them moving slowly forward, and he wanted to get out of the car and run east, toward the next place on their list of supermarkets—what was it, Smith's.

"We'd better find her tonight," he said. "I think she's losing her job. If you could catch all the green lights between here and there . . ."

"I *get* it," Mavranos told him.

At last the light turned yellow and Mavranos was able to make the turn. He drove fast to Maryland Parkway and passed it, then turned right, into the expansive parking lot that was streaked and puddled with the white light spilling out from the wide open entrance of Smith's Food and Drug.

Ozzie pushed open his door as soon as Mavranos had parked, but Crane turned around and grabbed the old man's shoulder. "Wait," Crane said. "I feel pavement under my shoes, her shoes. And warmer air. She's outside." The old man nodded and hastily pulled the door shut.

Mavranos started the car and backed out of the space, drawing an angry honk from a Volkswagen.

"Drive around," Ozzie said. "I'll know her." He was peering at a woman walking a child across the asphalt, then looking past her at another woman unlocking a car. "Is this the right place, the right store?"

"I . . . don't know," Crane said.

"She might be at some other store."

"—Yes."

Crane was staring around too, and Mavranos drove the car past the glaringly bright store entrance, past a closed GOLD BUYERS store, then turned right to loop around again.

"Is she still walking?" Mavranos's voice was harsh. "Is she in a car yet?"

Crane reached out with his mind, but couldn't sense anything now. "I don't know. Keep moving."

Lost her job, he thought. If we miss her now, we've missed her for good.

"Worthless windshield," he hissed, rolling down his window and sticking his head out. Everywhere cars seemed to be starting up, driving out of the lot, disappearing up or down the dark street.

"That's—" squeaked Ozzie. "No. Goddammit, my eyes aren't good enough for this! What the hell good am I?"

Crane squinted forward and around and back, trying to make his eyes focus better and still desperately trying to pick up mental impressions.

"Around by the front of the store again?" asked Mavranos.

"Uh," said Ozzie unhappily, "yes. No. Circle out here."

"Been already probably half a dozen women drive away," Mavranos said.

"Do as I say." The old man had already rolled down his window, and now he put his head outside, too. *"Diana!"* he yelled, his parroty old voice not carrying at all. Crane thought of how the old man had, though exhausted, tried to catch up with him in the Mint Hotel stairwell in '69, when Crane had left to play in the Assumption game, and now his eyes blurred with tears.

"Goddammit," Crane whispered, blinking them away. He made himself calm down and look carefully at each person in the lot.

Away from the store, closer to the Jack in the Box restaurant on the Maryland Parkway side of the lot, Crane saw a woman opening the door of a tan Mustang. She tossed back her blond hair and got in. An instant later the car's lights came on, and smoke blew out of the exhaust.

"That's her," he shouted at Mavranos, pointing, "that Mustang."

Mavranos spun the wheel and stepped on the gas, but the Mustang was already in the exit driveway, signaling for a right turn.

"You sensed it, did you?" panted Ozzie, pulling his head in.

"No, I—I recognized her."

"All the way over there? You haven't seen her since she was nine! That's probably not her at all! Arky, go back around—"

"I know it's her," Crane interrupted.

The Mustang had turned right onto the street, and as Mavranos sped to the exit, Crane wondered how sure he really was. *At least I'm sober*, he thought. *If it's a mistake, it's a sober mistake.*

Mavranos had turned right onto Maryland Parkway and accelerated after the Mustang, and in the next several seconds he changed lanes twice. "I think Scott's right," he growled. "She's going like a scalded cat."

"Can you catch up, pull alongside?" asked Ozzie, his breath hot on Crane's neck. "If she saw me, she'd stop, if I waved her over."

"I'll be lucky to keep her in sight." For once Mavranos had both hands on the wheel. His beer can had fallen onto the floor, and rolled against the door with each abrupt lane change. "What do you want me to do if we get a cop behind us with his lights on?"

"Jesus," said Ozzie. "Just keep going."

"Look for my phase-change cancer cure in jail, huh?"

No one answered him. The only sound was the on and off roaring of the engine as Mavranos's foot hopped from the gas to the brake and back.

By the time she pulled to a stop at the curb in front of the white duplex on Venus Avenue, the woman obviously knew she was being followed; she hopped out of the car and took off at a flat-out run toward the front door.

Crane leaned out his open window. "Diana!" he yelled. "It's Scott and Oz!"

She stopped then, stared at him and at Ozzie, who was leaning out of the back window and waving furiously, and then she sprinted back across the grass to the Suburban.

"Do you know where my son is?"

"No," said Crane. "Uh . . . sorry."

Ozzie had his door open and stepped carefully down to the sidewalk, carrying his aluminum cane. "Let's go inside," he said.

A pudgy young man with a scruffy beard was sitting on the worn living-room couch, his eyes closed and his hands waving as if he were conducting a symphony. "If we could all calm down!" he said loudly, on a rising note. "A tad of silence, if you please!"

Everyone did stop talking, and now stared at him. Ozzie was frowning at him angrily, his wrinkled lip quivering with contempt. Crane imagined Ozzie had caught the scent of the young man's cologne.

"Who are *you*?" the old man asked.

"My name is Hans. I'm Diana's life-partner, and I care for Scat as deeply as if he were my own son, but *he's only fifteen minutes late*." He widened his eyes and looked around. "Di, I'm sorry I even called you. I'm certain he'll be returning at any moment."

Crane looked at Diana, then looked away. She had grown into the beautiful woman he had always known she would become, tall and slim and goldenly blond, and there were twenty years of her life that he passionately wanted to know about, and if he and Ozzie were successful here tonight, he would never see her again.

Diana turned to the chubby little boy who was standing by the fireplace. "Oliver, where did you last see him? How did you lose him? Didn't I tell you to take care of your little brother?"

The boy rolled his eyes. "Which question do you want me to answer first?" he asked, nervously defiant. "Okay!" he said quickly when Diana took a step forward. "We rode our bikes to Hebert Park, and I got talking to some . . . older kids. They call me Bitin Dog," he added, glancing toward Mavranos and Crane.

"You ditched him again, didn't you?" said Diana.

"Sheesh! He'll be home in a minute, like Hans says."

"I suppose you've lost your job?" said Hans neutrally.

Diana ignored him and turned on Crane, who flinched. "Does this have anything to do with that stuff you told me on the phone Friday?"

"I—I don't know," Crane said. "So far I don't think so."

"How's your leg?"

"It's okay."

"Ozzie," she said, crossing to the old man and hugging him, "it's good to see you; it's just a bad time."

"I know, honey." Ozzie's spotted old hand patted her back. "Listen, as soon as he comes home, you've got to leave town, understand? Tonight. Pack as little as you can—I'll give you money—and then just go away, to some distant place, ditch your car as soon as you can and go on by bus, and give me a call and we'll figure a way to get more money to you. Western Union would be quick enough; you could have the money and be long gone within ten minutes of calling me. I'm sorry about your life here, but you must have known this wasn't smart, living *here*."

Her face was buried in the old man's shoulder, but Crane saw her nod. "Okay, Ozzie," she said, her voice muffled. "Wally, my husband, insisted on living here, and then after the divorce it just seemed too silly to leave."

"It's still silly," said Hans angrily, standing up. "What are you people talking about? We can't leave Vegas; I've got the screenplay deal with Mike. What have you—you *fellows* been telling her?"

Diana had stood back from the old man, and now Ozzie looked at Hans with widened eyes. "A *screenplay* deal? You know what, I think you'd better stay. You can meet another woman to be life-partners with."

Crane glanced at the little boy, who was calmly scuffing the carpet with the sole of his tennis shoe. The idea of leaving town, leaving these friends who called him Bitin Dog, didn't seem to bother him. Crane wondered what the boy's father, Wally, was like.

Hans bit back a quick response, then said loftily, "I have confidence in myself—something I think some people around here should work on."

Mavranos grinned at him through his unkempt mustache. "I can see you've done real well with it."

Diana waved her hands. "Don't fight. I always knew we didn't belong here, and all I really *own* is the stereo anyway. Oliver, throw some clothes in your sausage bag, underwear and socks and shirts, and your toothbrush and your retainer."

The telephone rang. Hans waved dramatically for silence and turned toward it.

"No," said Mavranos sharply. "Let the lady get it. Scott, you listen in."

Diana looked at Mavranos as if he'd slapped her, but she let Crane walk her to the phone on the kitchen counter.

"Hello?" she said when she'd picked it up.

"Isis," said a nervous young man's voice on the other end, "I have your son."

CHAPTER 21

Old Images Out of the Ruins

"My name's not Isis, you've got a wrong number—"

Mavranos and Ozzie were both nodding at her. *You are Isis,* both of them mouthed.

"You are so Isis," said the caller. He giggled. "I've seen your face, Mother. On the Queen of Hearts card and in the lines on my maps. Otherwise, what would—would—be the pointing go?"

Crane beckoned to Ozzie and Mavranos, and as they hurried to the open kitchen, he wrote with a pencil on the white Formica counter.

NUT IN BAKER, he wrote. *MAPS, GO FISH.*

Maybe we can help in this, he thought excitedly. Maybe we can rescue her son for her. For Diana, I can stay sober.

"Mother, I need to talk to you," said the caller. "I'm at a telephone right now, as you might say, but I'll be going to my Las Vegas box, which doesn't have a phone, which is where your son is, with tape holding him in a chair. It's a Skinner box, like the bowling pigeons. It's out of town on Boulder Highway past Sunset Road, go till you see a gas station on your right that's boarded up, and there's a dirt road that goes behind it. My box is, can't see it from the road, just."

"Is my son all right?"

"Scat, he tells me. His real name is Aristarchus. He's fine, I didn't tape his nose. I won't hurt him if you'll come and talk to me tonight; if you don't, I'll cut his head off and talk to you later." He chuckled. "A man tried to sink a head in Lake Mead yesterday, can you imagine? The lake made the bats chase him away."

"I'll come and talk to you," Diana said hastily. Her phone-clutching hand was against Crane's cheek, and her fingers were cold.

"I know," the caller went on, "exactly how long it takes to drive from your Isis temple, where you are, to the box, so don't talk to police. If police are in our picture, I'll kill Aristarchus. But you won't call them, and we can talk. You're bothered, by this, and that's arctic should be. I don't mean to—to get you bothered, but I had to do something to make sure you'd talk to me. At least I didn't visit you yesterday, right? It was my day yesterday, and that would have been rude, visiting you with my feathers on."

Crane scribbled, HUSBAND. Above it he wrote, BRINGING YOUR.

Diana nodded. "I—I don't—I have to bring my husband. If he can't come, he won't let me see you ever."

There was a long pause, and Crane wondered if he'd ruined everything, if the young man would now simply hang up.

Then, "My father's with you?" said the voice on the phone.

Crane bared his teeth in indecision, then shrugged and nodded.

"Yes."

"Sure. You both leave right now. The clock has begun to tick." There was a distant rattle, then the dial tone.

Diana hung up. "Let's go, Scott," she said.

"Right," said Crane, tense with an excitement that was almost joy, in spite of the evident fear that had bleached and leaned Diana's face. To Mavranos he said, "You guys can follow us, but way back. We're going to take a dirt road by a boarded-up gas station out of town on Boulder Highway, past something called Sunset Road, on the right. I'll have the .357 under my shirt."

"You're crazy," yelled Hans, "I'm calling the police! You *always* call the police with a kidnapping; they're trained—"

Ozzie's lined old face was twisted, as if he faced a painfully bright light. "This guy knew who Scott was, Diana, and he knows who you are: the Queen of Hearts, Isis, her daughter at least. He might just be able to know it, too, if you called the cops. Anyway, the police would make you stay in town for a while. And I really think you'll be killed if you stay. Your sons, too."

"What's this, *supernatural*?" Hans squalled. "*You* think she's Isis, the Egyptian goddess? Give me that phone."

"I'm the parent," Diana said forcefully to him. "It's my decision. I'm going, and the police won't be called. And we've got to go *now*."

Hans was shaking his head and taking deep, whooping breaths. "Okay! Okay! You're the parent, it's your decision. But *I'll* go with you, then, at least. I *am* your husband, practically, and I can certainly speak more effectively than this bum."

At the door Diana turned. "No. You're nothing like a husband."

Ozzie pointed at the fat little boy. "Oliver there should come along with Archimedes and me."

Hans forced a shout of laughter. "*Archimedes?* Have you got Plato out in the car, too? Let him do the talking."

"Wait here," Diana told him. "I'll call you when I know anything."

Ignoring Hans's continuing protests, the five of them hurried out to the cars.

Al Funo's teeth were chattering, and his face was puffy and streaked with tears, but he wiped his eyes on the sleeve of his silk shirt when he saw people hurry out of the duplex down the block.

There's Scott Crane, he thought, with a woman who must be the famous Diana. Mr. Mustache is giving Crane something from the other vehicle, and now Crane and Diana are in the Mustang. And Mr. Mustache and Ozzie and some kid are getting into the other vehicle. What a ridiculous, Jeepy-looking thing!

It sure does scoot, though, he admitted to himself. I doubt that anyone less than a professional driver could have kept up with them the way I did, from that supermarket. I'm glad I noticed that they were chasing the Mustang and not trying to shake me, before I got a chance to pull alongside and shoot them. If I had, I'd never have got a chance to meet Diana.

And she's an attractive woman. I have no problem with that. I'm not one of these guys who feel threatened by attractive women.

He started his engine and patted the wheel. And I can keep up with them this time, too, he thought. This Porsche can outperform anything. You don't find unimportant people driving Porsches.

Diana was driving, her blond hair fluttering in the night wind coming in through the driver's side window. "Nut," she said expressionlessly. "Baker. Maps. Go Fish." She glanced at him. "Who is this guy, and how did he find my son?"

"Well, his name's"—Crane impatiently snapped his fingers twice—"Snayheever, Dondi Snayheever. I think he's crazy. We met him in Baker, and he talks like—like a nut. He's one of the people who've been . . . waked up, motivated, galvanized, by all the stuff that's going on here right now, with the heavy Easter about to come 'round again, the game on the lake probably due to start up again next week, for the first time in twenty-one years. He's not the only one we met, coming across the desert, and they're probably coming in from other directions, too. In Baker he was talking about you—that is, the Queen of Hearts. He had a bunch of maps that he thought would lead him to you. We stole a couple, but I guess one of them did the trick for him."

"*You* didn't lead him to me?"

"No. We just arrived in time to help answer the phone. We've been looking for you in every supermarket in town since Saturday night. Barely found you tonight. I recognized you."

A rushing streetlight highlighted the planes of her face for a moment. "So is this all actually *true*?" she demanded angrily. "All this supernatural shit?"

Crane thought of the thing that seemed to be the ghost of his dead wife. "I think it must be."

"God." She took a deep breath and let it out. "I guess I didn't ever *really* believe all of Ozzie's warnings."

"Don't feel bad. I didn't either."

"What do you *mean*, don't feel *bad*? You sound like that crazy man on the phone: 'I know this must *bother* you.' My son's life is in danger because I didn't do exactly what that old man said."

"Diana, my wife *died* because *I* didn't listen to him. I didn't mean to sound flip."

She glanced at him for a moment. "I know. I'm sorry. I sensed it, when she died. I meant to call you, but I didn't know what to say, and then it was—it seemed too late."

"I would have pretended she was fine. I fooled everybody, even myself eventually."

"So what are we going to do here?"

"Jesus, I don't know. I think he does just want to talk to you, but he might just as likely want to kill you. I don't think he's got anything against your kid—Scat?"

"Nickname for Scott. He's named after you."

He remembered the way she'd written *Scott* on the crayon portrait of him she'd done when she was eight years old—with one bar through the *T*'s, which she had thought was very sporty—and there were tears in his eyes. "Diana, I swear to you we'll get you and your kids out of this."

She didn't answer, just kept her eyes on the cars ahead. She did reach over and squeeze his hand.

It was the first time they'd touched in two decades.

*   *   *

Waiting for a fare in front of the Four Queens on Fremont, Nardie Dinh fainted at the wheel of her cab. She was unconscious for only a moment, fortunately not long enough for any dreams to illuminate her unconscious mind and pinpoint her location for her brother, but her cab had rolled forward and clanked the bumper of the cab ahead.

She opened the car door and stepped dizzily out onto the noisy, crowded, ripplingly lit pavement, hoping that if she fainted again, the pain of the fall might wake her up, and she fumbled a little plastic bottle out of her shirt pocket and chewed up two crosstops, amphetamine tablets.

The driver of the other cab was standing by her front bumper. He had been cursing until he saw that the negligent driver was a pretty young Asian woman, and now he was just gruff.

"Just a minute," she told him. "I'll be back in a minute."

She hurried in through the open doors of the casino and blundered through the chilly tobacco-scented dimness until she found a Blackjack table. The dealer was using a multiple deck, and two of the hands on the red felt table showed a Jack of Hearts next to a Queen of Hearts.

"Shit," she whispered, really frightened for the first time since escaping from DuLac's.

Dondi Snayheever waited in his idling car in the parking lot of the abandoned gas station until there were no headlights very close in either direction, and then he switched off his own lights and drove very slowly off the cracked old concrete and up the dirt road.

His father had bought this land sometime in the early fifties, and might still own it. The old man had said that the place had strong *vibrations*, that it would be a good place for the boy to learn, that the cards would be livelier here.

His father. His father was coming to see him, for the first time in nine years. With his mother!

Snayheever didn't seem to be able to hold on to any one feeling about his father. Over the years since 1981 he had sometimes missed the old man so badly that he had returned to the Baker box, crawled inside, and then just shouted for him until he was hoarse, thinking that he might that way turn back time, so that his father would not have disappeared yet; at other times he wanted to kill him for having left his son to deal with an incomprehensible world all alone.

The little car lurched over the top of the low hill, and he could see his plywood box off to the left among a stand of yucca.

It occurred to him that young Aristarchus here was his brother. Snayheever was treating him a little harshly, for a brother. He'd have to lift the kid up and put a cushion on the chair under him.

Outside town the glow of the Mustang's headlights on the rushing highway ahead of them was the only light besides the faint silvery glow thrown by the half-moon.

I should have got the kids out of town, at least, Diana thought, as soon as I got off the phone with Scott on Friday night. Anything, like Moses' mother putting her baby son in a boat and just letting the river take him, rather than let them stay for this. That's what a good mother would have done. At least Oliver is with his grandfather in the truck a hundred yards back.

"Closed gas station up ahead," said Scott.

"I see it."

She slowed and signaled for a right turn—and then she saw something out of the corner of her eye, and gunned the engine and yanked the wheel around, and the car spun out in the roadside gravel and came to a halt on the shoulder, rocking on the abused shocks, pointing back the way they'd come. The engine was quiet—stalled.

"What is it?" Scott whispered urgently. His hand was under his shirt, on the grip of the revolver.

"A car—" Dust from the spinout swirled outside the windows of the rocking car, but she could see well enough to know that it had been a hallucination. "I must be going crazy. I thought I saw a car leave the road real fast and blow up—right over there." She pointed at a half-demolished cinder-block wall on the south end of the gas station lot.

Crane squinted in the direction she was pointing, and for just an instant he saw a blooming yellow fireball, curdling

black at the edges, rising into the sky, in perfect silence—
then it was gone, leaving nothing but a dark blur in his
vision.

"I saw it too, for a second—" he began. Then he paused,
his mouth still open.

He had seen it through his right eye. The plastic eye.

"What's the matter? What was it?"

"I don't know," he said, opening his door and stepping out
onto the highway pavement. The broken cinder-block wall
at the south end of the lot was weathered and cracked, surrounded by windblown trash, and didn't seem to have been
even approached by anyone for decades.

Diana had got out, too, and was standing on the curb. The
night wind blew the stirred-up dust away across the desert.

Crane looked at her and shrugged. "Maybe it was something that happened here a long time ago, and the Jack and
Queen of Hearts arriving together stirred old images out of
the ruins."

"Well, let's get back in the car, the dirt road is—"

The flat, hard pop of an outdoor gunshot interrupted her, and
Crane heard the whine of a ricochet off the asphalt a dozen
yards to his right.

He hurried around the car, grabbed Diana and pulled her
back to the highway side, and forced her down into a crouch
behind the fender.

"My father first!" came a call from the crest of a low hill
behind the station. "My mother wait in the car, for just a
minute. Everything's fine! Everything's fine!"

Well, I *guess* you got a gun, Crane thought, echoing what
Snayheever had told them in Baker two days ago.

"Okay," Crane whispered. "Ozzie and Arky are parked back
there; you can just see the car with its headlights out, see it?
If you hear another shot, run back and get them. They'll have
some ideas."

"But you're not this guy's father! Won't he see that right
away?"

"It's dark," Crane said, "and he's crazy. If I can get close
to him and he's not actually pointing his gun at your kid, I'll
kill him. I imagine he'll have the gun pointed at me."

"So *you'll* be killed."

"Maybe not. Anyway, I'm dead already, ask Ozzie."

He stood up and limped slowly around the car. Diana had turned off the Mustang's headlights, so the moon was the only light, but its radiance was bright enough to show the dilapidated station and the lot and the dirt road that curled away behind it to the top of the hill.

"Scott."

He looked back. Diana was standing up behind the car, and now she hurried to him and hugged him tightly. "I love you," she said. "Come back safe."

"*Two little lovebirds*," sang Snayheever up on the hill, "*sittin' in a tree, kay-eye-ess-ess-eye-en-gee.*"

"Christ," Diana whispered, "get my son away from that man."

"I will," Crane told her as he started forward again. "Get back behind the car and stay there."

Crane was sweating as he limped up the dusty, hummocky road, and the breeze not only chilled him but seemed to sting, as if he'd rubbed Ben-Gay all over himself. His bad leg stung and ached. Why hadn't he got a beer from Mavranos as well as the gun?

He wondered how much he might happen to resemble Snayheever's father. Would the crazy young man simply shoot him from a distance when he saw that Crane was the wrong man?

Was Snayheever's finger tightening on the trigger right now?

Crane flinched, but kept limping up the hill.

He tried to imagine being shot, in the frail hope that picturing it would enable him to face it and not stop right where he was and turn around and go hopping and sliding and whimpering back down to the car.

A punch like a hammer, and then you're down, he thought, and the place where you've been hit feels numb and hot and loose.

It didn't help. Each second was a hard choice between going on and running back to the precious penumbra of the car body.

If he kills you, he told himself, you'll just be joining Susan. But the only image of Susan that he could conjure up right now was of the thing that had been convulsing in his closet as he had climbed out of his broken bedroom window on Friday night.

You're going to die anyway, he thought desperately, for having stupidly played in that Assumption game. This way you die trying to save Diana's son's life. Purposeful instead of pointless.

But the death by Assumption won't happen *tonight*. If you run away, you can have breakfast tomorrow, a good breakfast with a big Bloody Mary in a nice place, with Ozzie. Would the old man hold it against me that I turned back here?

Yes, thought Crane, despairingly and almost angrily, he would.

He began taking longer strides, snarling at the pain in his stabbed thigh.

"Dad!" called Snayheever.

Crane rocked to a halt and looked up through sweat-stung eyes, but couldn't see him. "Yes, son?"

"You changed. You did the trick they're all excited about; you got the cards to get you a new body!" The young man's laugh was shrill with excitement. "Are *you* a brother of mine now, *too*?"

Crane couldn't apply logic to it, so he just called, "That's right!" and kept limping up the road.

"That *was* a gunshot," said Mavranos, staring ahead through a rubbed-clean spot of the Suburban's windshield.

"Yes," agreed Ozzie, "but Scott walked up the hill openly enough. Is Diana still by the car?"

"Yeah, crouched behind it. How long you want to wait before we drive up?"

"I don't know."

From the back seat came the sneezy puff of a beer can being opened.

Mavranos glanced back, then leaned back over the seat and took the can from young Oliver. "Thanks, kid—but from now on I'm the only one to touch the beers, okay?"

"I drink beer," said Oliver defensively. "Give me a gun— I'm small, I can sneak around and waste this motherfucker."

"Watch your mouth, Oliver," said Ozzie sternly without looking away from the Mustang.

"Call me Bitin Dog." The boy seemed feverishly excited by the night's events. "Really, I got the kid into this, ditching him, and I can get him out."

"Just sit, Oliver," said Mavranos impatiently. "And if you get out of this car, I'll catch you and whup your butt like I would a little kid, okay? Right here beside the road where everybody'll see."

A white sports car had driven past them, and now its brake lights glowed as it pulled in behind the Mustang.

"Who the hell's that?" asked Ozzie.

"Stranger, probably, thinks Diana needs help. I hope she can get rid of him."

"Be ready to get over there fast."

Diana half hoped this new car was police, but when she saw the well-dressed young stranger get out and start walking toward her, she bit her lip and pretended to be looking at the lug nuts on her wheel.

She smiled up at him. "I don't need any help, thank you. My husband left a long time ago, looking for a phone. He should be back with a tow truck in a second."

"You shouldn't be crouched in the road like that, Diana," the stranger said. "A car could easily hit you. And if I know Scott, I'll bet you dollars to doughnuts he's gone off to find a Poker game."

Diana stood up slowly, unable to take a deep breath. This must be a partner of the crazy man up the hill.

"You and I can be friends, can't we?" the young man asked. He was smiling, but his face was puffy and blotchy in the moonlight.

"Sure," she said eagerly. Apparently this man was crazy, too. *Humor these people*, she told herself.

He exhaled as if in relief and put his arm around her shoulders. She forced herself not to recoil, to maintain whatever sort of smile was tensing her cheek muscles.

"Tell me the truth," he said. "Do you find me attractive?"

Oh, God, she thought. "Of course, I do," she said. He didn't move—his head was still cocked down, listening. Apparently what she'd said had not been enough. "I"—she went on helplessly—"I can't imagine any woman *not* finding you attractive." *What are you doing, Scott?* she thought. *Have you got*

Scat? Kill the nut up there and then come down here and kill this one.

The man chuckled. "There are some *weird* women in this town, Diana, I kid you not. Scott can take your car back to town, can't he? What say you and I get in my Porsche and go have dinner? Las Vegas can be a very romantic town"—he squeezed her shoulders—"if you have the maturity, the self-confidence, to let yourself be open to new experiences."

"I thought you . . . people . . . wanted to talk to me, both of you, I mean. What about my son?"

"You have a son? That's good, I like women who've had some experience of life. I—"

"Do you know why I'm here?"

"Car trouble, I assume. Probably something simple, something Scott doesn't have the mechanical aptitude to deal with. After dinner we can—"

Diana squirmed out of his half embrace and backed two steps across the pavement. "You're just some *guy*? You're not *involved* in this?"

"I want to be involved," he said earnestly. "Let me help you. I'm a good man in a crisis—"

Diana was sobbing with fury. "Get the fuck *away* from me, you piece of shit! Haul your worthless little ass back to that jerk-off car and crank it out of here. Go!"

He was backing away. "D-D-Diana, I don't tolerate—"

She opened the Mustang's passenger door and got in and slammed it. "Clear off, queer bait," she said.

He ran back to his car, started it, and then sped past her so closely that she braced herself against the impact of a crash. Then he had narrowly hurtled past, and his white car was just twin red spots dwindling in the rearview mirror.

"I ought to kill you, Dad."

Crane's sweaty face was cold in the hilltop breeze, and he was panting, largely from the effort of having climbed up here to the crest. "You don't know the whole story," he said. He wanted to look back down the hill toward where Diana waited, but he made himself smile confidently into Snayheever's eyes and peripherally focus his attention on the little automatic in the young man's fist.

"Have I seen your body before, this new one?"

"I don't think so," said Crane, grateful that his sweaty hair was down across his forehead, and that he had been out in the parking lot of The Mad Greek during most of Saturday's Go Fish game.

For ten full seconds Snayheever kept the gun pointed at him, while the wind hissed in the sparse, dry brush, and then he turned and pointed it away across the desert. "Let's go to the box. I'm glad you're here, is what the truth is. I need to know more about my mother before I talk to her."

Crane knew he should pull out his own gun and shoot the young man right now—and his hand wavered up toward his flapping shirttail—but then Snayheever had swung the muzzle of his automatic back into line, aimed at Crane's solar plexus.

The moment was gone.

"After you, Dad," said the young man.

Raging inwardly at his own indecisiveness, Crane shrugged and plodded forward.

The box proved to be a low plywood shack. Crane had to stoop to enter. There was a skylight, and inside by filtered moonlight he saw a little boy sitting in a chair. Duct tape gleamed on his mouth, and on his wrists where they were held against the chair's rear legs. The boy's eyes were wide.

Crane looked back at Snayheever, who had come in right behind him. Snayheever had the gun pointed halfway between Scat and Crane.

Not yet, Crane thought. Wait till it's pointed away, or at least fully at me.

Trying to seem relaxed, he looked around at the shack's interior. A box in one corner was covered with a flannely-looking cloth, and, startled by it, he looked up at the skylight. It was stained glass, though now it shone only in a spectrum of grays. He had dreamed of this place yesterday. In the dream there had been a cup and a lance head on the cloth-draped box.

"Yup," said Snayheever, nodding jerkily. "Yesterday I was caretaker. On Holy Saturday you all get to fight over who gets to hold them during the next cycle."

Snayheever was shaking and frowning. Crane mentally rehearsed pulling out the .357 and aiming it and firing it.

"This is your fault, this shaking," Snayheever said. "Tardive dyskinesia, from too much Thorazine they gave me." He pointed the wobbling gun at the boy in the chair. "Mother's here now, and I don't really need any brothers. In my head sometimes my eyes roll up with this, and then Aristarchus would get loose and kill *me*, so not to share the mother."

The boy in the chair was wide-eyed now, humming shrilly behind the tape and tugging his bound wrists against the chair legs.

Crane couldn't shoot Snayheever now, not with the gun pointed at Scat; the shock of a bullet's impact would probably make Snayheever pull the trigger.

The blood was singing in Crane's ears as he opened his mouth and spoke. "Look what I brought," he said softly.

Snayheever swung the gun toward him, and Crane reached up and yanked the .357 out of his belt.

The little automatic went off, and as Crane fired his own gun he felt that hot punch in his side, above the point of his hip-bone; cocking the revolver for another shot, he jumped sideways and knocked the chair over and went to his knees beside it, blocking Scat from any more shots.

His ears were ringing from the blast of the .357, and he'd nearly been blinded by the muzzle flash, but he could see Snayheever groping for the automatic, which was spinning now on a moonlit patch of the floor.

Crane swung the revolver back over his shoulder and then slammed it down, hard, onto the back of Snayheever's head.

The revolver nearly sprained Crane's unbraced wrist when it fired again, and as he tumbled forward across Snayheever's body, he was showered with gleaming shards of broken glass.

Crane sat up, grabbed Snayheever's gun with his left hand, and flung it up through the shot-out skylight. Then he climbed to his feet, bracing himself on the altar box.

Snayheever was apparently unconscious. Crane tucked the hot revolver back into his belt and, shivering violently, dug his hand into his pocket to get out his jackknife.

The Suburban was already parked right behind the Mustang when Crane and the boy crested the top of the hill, and Mavranos was halfway up from the highway side, running in a low crouch with his .38 glinting in his hand. Ozzie was hugging Diana, perhaps holding her back, beside the Mustang.

"It's okay!" Crane yelled hoarsely. He swayed, his right hand pressed against his side. "It's me, with the kid!"

Then Mavranos had sprinted the rest of the way up the hill and was beside him, panting.

"Damn, Pogo," Mavranos gasped, "are you shot?"

"Yes," said Crane through clenched teeth. "Let's get out of here before we deal with it. The nut's back there in a shed, knocked out. I don't think we have to go back and kill him, do you?"

"Nah, nah, let's just get out of here like you say. Diana and her kids can be in Provo or somewhere by dawn. *You* okay, kid?"

Scat just nodded.

"Your mom's down there, go say hi."

The boy peered down the hill, then saw Diana's Mustang and took off at a run.

"Carefully, kid!" Mavranos yelled after him. He bent and pulled Crane's blood-sopping shirt away from his side. "Aw, this ain't so bad, man. Just grooved you, didn't even touch the muscle layer, and the bleeding's no more than what you'd get from a good cut, no arterial spurting. I can bandage this; it's nothing compared to what you did to your leg."

Crane let his shoulders slump. "Good. You do that, when we get away from here." During the hasty, agonizing walk from the box to the hill crest he had been imagining passing out from loss of blood, and then at best waking up in a hospital bed, his body picadored with drains and IV tubes and a colostomy bag.

"Arky," he said weakly, "when we get down there, I'm going to drink one of your beers, very fast, and then another one very slow."

Mavranos laughed. "I'll join you. And if old Ozzie objects, I'll sit on him."

Mavranos had his arm under Crane's shoulders and was taking his weight as they shuffled down the dirt road. Crane could see Diana break away from Ozzie and come running across the gas station lot, past the wrecked cinder-block wall.

"Here comes Diana," Crane said, for the moment too happy to take a deep breath. "I saved her son."

"And got a battle wound," agreed Mavranos. "Maybe I should let *her* patch you up."

Headlights were approaching on the highway from the south, and they slowed as they approached the two vehicles parked on the west shoulder. Crane made his eye focus on it; he hoped it wasn't police.

No, it was just a white sports car, a Porsche.

A white Porsche.

No, he thought even as his heart began pounding, no, you see white Porsches everywhere—hell, there was one parked in the slot next to ours at the motel.

There was one parked in the slot next to ours at the motel.

"Get down!" he yelled at the top of his lungs, ignoring the pain in his side. "Everybody get down on the ground! Oz! Get 'em down!"

He shook off Mavranos's arm and drew the .357 and tried to aim it at the white car, which had stopped on the far shoulder.

Mavranos had pulled his own revolver out of his belt. "What?" he asked sharply. "That white car?"

"Yes!"

Can't shoot, Crane thought. What if it's just some Good Samaritan? And at this range with this two-inch barrel you'd be as likely to hit Ozzie or Diana.

"Everybody get down!" he screamed again.

Nobody was obeying him. Scat was still running down the sloping dirt road, and Diana was still running up to meet him, and Ozzie was hunching along at what must have been his top speed, far behind her. The fat kid had got out of the Suburban and was standing beside it.

A hollow *pop* rang across the highway in the same instant that the Porsche's driver's side window flared with a wink of yellow light.

Halfway down the hill road, Scat dived forward into the dirt and slid for a yard, face down. Then he didn't move.

Diana's scream filled the desert, and almost seemed to drown the roars of Crane's .357 and Mavranos's .38 as they emptied their guns at the receding white car, which didn't even wobble as it gathered speed.

CHAPTER 22

Alligator Blood

Diana was the first to reach Scat—but when she got to where her son lay she paused, then just knelt beside him with her hands half raised.

As Crane hopped and scrambled and sweated down the hill, Mavranos ran on ahead, and Crane saw him look down at the boy and reel back.

When Crane finally made his way down to where the boy lay, he saw why.

Scat's head seemed to have been shot straight through. His right temple was toward the night sky, and it was an exploded bloody ruin—the right eye was far too exposed, and the ear seemed half torn off. The boy was breathing in gasps that sprayed blood out across the moonlit dirt.

Diana looked up at Crane. "Hospital, quick—in the back of the truck. How are we going to carry him?"

Crane's heart was thumping hugely in his chest. "Arky, get a blanket—we can carry him in a blanket."

Mavranos's face was stiff as he stared down at the boy, and Crane remembered that the man had children of his own.

"Arky!" Crane said sharply. "A blanket!"

Mavranos blinked and nodded, and then sprinted down the road toward his truck.

Diana was panting and blinking around. "Who shot him?"

Crane was dreading this. "A guy across the road, in a white Porsche. I think he—"

"Jesus Christ, he was *talking* to me!" Diana was sobbing now, nearly hysterical. "The guy in the white car, when I was waiting down there! I told him to fuck off, and he came back and shot at me!"

"Diana, he—"

"He was aiming at *me*, this is *my* fault!" Her trembling hand hovered over the boy's blood-glittering head, and then tentatively stroked his shoulder. "*I* did this."

The boy's right arm began jerking, and Crane thought the harsh, wet breathing must be just about to stop forever.

"No, Diana," Crane said, knowing that he was buying her sanity at the high price of having her hate him forever. A minute ago, he thought bleakly, I was a hero. She loved me. She still does right now, and will for another second and a half. "Listen to me. No. The man was shooting at me. He shot at me in L.A. last Thursday. I . . . guess he . . . followed us out here."

When she looked up at him, her eyes were wide, with white showing all around the irises. "Yeah," she said softly, "he knew our names, yours and mine." She bared her teeth in a big smile. "Your friends don't aim so good, do they?"

Crane could think of nothing to say, and after a moment she looked back down at her son.

Mavranos came puffing up with a blanket then, and they spread it out on the dirt and began the tense job of gently lifting the boy onto it.

In the emergency room at Desert Springs Hospital on Flamingo Road, the doctors quickly got the boy onto a gurney and rolled him away into the surgery. Crane's wound was bandaged and taped, and then he and Diana filled out forms on the counter of the glassed-in cashier's office.

They were standing side by side, but they didn't speak to each other. When the paper work was done, Diana went to a pay phone to call Hans, and Crane walked over to where Ozzie sat on one of the waiting-room couches.

The old man looked up at him, his eyes hopeless. "The kid's just the first of us," Ozzie said softly. "There's no way she can leave town now. By Easter all of us will be dead."

"S'pose you're right," Crane said numbly. He saw a coffeepot on a table below the muted flicker of a wall-mounted television. "Coffee in the meantime?"

"Sure, black."

When Crane came back with two steaming Styrofoam cups, Diana was sitting beside Ozzie; a magazine lay open on her lap, and she was staring at an article on how to build a backyard barbecue. Crane noticed for the first time that she was still wearing her Smith's uniform, red-striped black pants and a red and white shirt now redder with her son's blood.

"Coffee, Diana?" he ventured. She shook her head, and he sighed and put Ozzie's down on the table.

He had given up trying to talk to her.

On the high-speed drive to the hospital Ozzie had told them how much to tell the police, and Crane, his eyes on the lanes ahead and the cars they were passing, had stammeringly tried to shout back an apology to Diana, who was crouched in the back over her son, but after only a few syllables Ozzie had interrupted: "Son, she doesn't want to hear about it right now."

So now he just sat down and sipped his coffee and waited.

Random chance, Crane thought. It was only the randomest chance that made the bullet hit the kid. I knew there were *people* after us, but why do God's own luck-dictating *dice* seem determined to fuck us up? Susan's fibrillation, Arky's cancer—I'll have to ask Arky about his precious statistics.

Mavranos had taken Oliver away in the Mustang to wait for them by the carousel bar at the Circus Circus. Diana and Ozzie had agreed that nobody had better go back to her apartment. Crane wondered whether she had managed, in her brief phone call, to convince her "life-partner" to leave the place. Crane guessed not.

A couple of other people sat in chairs closer to the hallway—a young man in a sleeveless T-shirt clutched a blood-blotted rag to his forearm, and a woman muttered softly to a crying child on her lap—but the only voices Crane heard were the occasional laconic, coded calls on the public address system.

After a few minutes a police officer in a tan, short-sleeved uniform came in with the doctor who seemed to be in charge, and they stood talking by the cashier's window. The officer was carrying a clipboard, and Crane got to his feet—feeling hot interior tuggings in his leg and his side—and walked closer to them, hoping to hear something reassuring about Scat's condition.

The officer was filling out a hospitalization gunshot report, and Crane heard the doctor tell him that the shot had been long-range, the caliber anywhere from .32 to 9-millimeter; it had shattered the right eye orbit, entered the skull, and then exited beside the ear, outside the temporal lobe; the temporal lobe was injured, it was too early to say how badly, though the "posturing," the pulling in of the arms, was not a good sign; and no, the wound could not have been self-inflicted.

Eventually the officer walked past Crane and spoke to Diana, and then she stood up and followed him away down the carpeted hallway.

Crane walked back to where Ozzie sat. "She'll probably tell him it was some friend of mine that shot Scat."

Ozzie sighed and rubbed his brown-spotted forehead. "No, son. She understands that making it out to be an interstate thing would probably involve the FBI, and that that would just make for more delays in getting her and her kids away."

Crane sat down and sipped his coffee, holding the cup with both hands so that it wouldn't shake. "I wish we *could* let the FBI take it."

"Sure," Ozzie said. "Explain to them that this is all a battle to see who'll become the magical Fisher King, and that the nut found her by consulting cards and maps of Poland. And they'd never agree to the kind of protective custody and witness relocation that she needs."

When Crane finished the coffee, he picked up Diana's magazine and looked at the pictures of the do-it-yourself barbecue. He tried to imagine himself and Ozzie and Diana and the two boys cooking hamburgers, tossing a Frisbee around, ambling inside when it got dark to watch *Big* or something on the VCR—but it was like trying to imagine daily life in ancient Rome.

Diana and the officer came back in and crossed to the couch, and Diana sat down.

The officer looked at Crane. "You're Scott Crane, the other gunshot victim?" He was younger than Crane, with a mustache that might have been invisible in a harsher light, but he was as relaxed as if he talked to mothers of shot children every night.

Crane started to point at his bandaged wound, conspicuous under his torn-open shirt, but his hand was trembling, and he let it fall into his lap. "Yes," he said.

"Could you come with me, please?"

Crane got up again and followed the man to a small room down the hall. The officer pulled the door closed, and Crane looked around. The anonymity of the room—a couch, a couple of chairs, soft light from a lamp beside a telephone on a table—seemed incongruous in a hospital. It occurred to him that he'd be more comfortable talking in a corner of some white hallway, interrupted frequently by hurrying doctors and nurses pushing IV-hung gurneys.

"Can I see some identification, please?"

Crane dug out his wallet and handed the man his California driver's license.

"Do sit down," the officer told him. Crane reluctantly lowered himself into one of the chairs. "This Santa Ana address is current?"

"Yes," Crane said.

The officer wrote down the numbers and handed the card back. "I'm doing the drive-by shooting report," he said. "Why don't you tell me what happened out there?"

Crane told the man exactly what had occurred, starting with Snayheever's phone call—though, as Ozzie had insisted during the high-speed drive to the hospital, he implied that they had driven out from Los Angeles to visit Diana purely for social reasons, and he didn't mention having been shot at in Los Angeles on Thursday, nor having met Snayheever in Baker. He said Snayheever had told him his name tonight. Halfway through the story the officer called in on his hand-held radio to have a police car sent out to where Crane had left Snayheever unconscious and probably shot.

"I think the man who shot her son is staying at our motel," Crane said. "The guy who was in the room next to ours drives a white Porsche, and my foster father called him a zombie the other day, and he seemed to get pissed—and then tonight, out where all this happened, a guy in a white Porsche, probably the same guy, tried to pick up on Diana and she told him to get lost. Rudely. He might have been shooting at her or at the old man."

"Okay." The officer wrote on his clipboard. "The detectives will check that out." He looked at Crane incuriously. "The revolver you shot at the kidnapper with—where is it?"

"In the car, outside."

"Is it yours?"

"Yes."

"Registered to you?"

"Yes."

"Okay. Where will you be staying?"

"God, I don't know. The Circus Circus, I guess."

"Do that, and let us know your room number as soon as you're checked in."

"'Kay."

The man clicked his ball-point pen and tucked it away in his shirt pocket. "For the time being we'll be considering this two possibly-related events. I've got the names and addresses of the other witnesses, and they say they'll be staying at the Circus Circus, too; the detectives will probably be talking to all of you tomorrow."

Crane blinked at him. "That's it?"

"For tonight. Stay here; the doctor will be in soon with the other family members." The officer tucked the clipboard under his arm and left the room, pulling the door shut.

Crane leaned back in the chair and exhaled. That had been easy; he had been afraid that he'd automatically be jailed for shooting at somebody, or at least have the gun confiscated. I guess I look like an innocent person, he thought.

But goddammit, I *am* an innocent person! The only thing I've ever done wrong was play Assumption twenty-one years ago!

He thought of the bourbon and beer at Whiskey Pete's on Saturday night, then thrust the thought away impatiently.

The door opened again, and Ozzie and Diana shuffled in, followed by the young doctor. Crane found himself resenting the man's perfectly combed black hair. Nobody sat down, so Crane stood up and leaned against the wall.

"I'm Dr. Bandholtz," the doctor said. "Of course you all know that the boy has been shot. The bullet broke the ring of bone around the eye, and the bone of the temple back to the ear. It bled a lot, the head is a very vascular area, but there was no serious loss of blood. I think we can save the eye and rebuild the orbit."

"Will there," whispered Diana, "be any brain damage?"

Bandholtz sighed and ran the fingers of one hand through his hair, mussing it up.

"There is probably some brain damage," he said, "but eighty-five percent of the brain is ordinarily never used, and the functions of damaged areas are often assumed by other areas. The problem we'll have is swelling of the brain; that's bad because there's no *room* for it to swell, without cutting off the blood supply. We've got him on steroids to fight that, thirty milligrams of IV Decadron tonight and then four milligrams every six hours after that. Also we're giving him Mannitol, that's a diuretic, to shrink the tissues. Some doctors would use barbiturates to forcibly shut down the brain function during this, but I feel that's still an experimental procedure, and I'm not going to do it."

"When will he regain consciousness?" Diana asked.

"That's difficult to say. In effect, the computer has been turned off while it tries to heal itself. The brain is—is sort of like an ice-cream sundae. The cherry on top is the cortex, the part that makes us human, with thinking and consciousness and all. Under it are the peanuts and chocolate and so on, that govern other functions, and, below that, the ice-cream itself is the maintenance level, the part that handles breathing and heartbeat and so on. The cherry is the first to shut down in a trauma like this—and so far it's the only part that has shut down."

Crane dully supposed that the man had chosen a trivial, happy metaphor to allay some of their shock and worry. He looked at Ozzie and Diana, and considered his own feelings, and decided that it had only made everything even more disorienting.

Diana glanced blankly at Ozzie, then back at the doctor. "Is he in a coma?"

"That is a word that describes this, yes," Bandholtz said, "but he's young, and getting state-of-the-art care. Listen, he won't regain consciousness tonight. You'll want to be alert when you see him tomorrow, so go home now. I can give you a sedative, if you think—"

"No," she said. "I'll be fine. Before we go, I'd like to see him." She glanced toward Crane. "Alone."

"Okay," the doctor said, "very briefly. You understand he's on life support systems—there's what's called a triple lumen catheter inserted under his collar bone to make sure the blood pressure in the lungs doesn't rise, and—"

"I just want to see *him*."

"Right, I'll take you to him. You two gentlemen can go back to the waiting room."

*   *   *

Ozzie sat next to Crane in the truck, Diana in the seat behind
them. Whenever traffic let him, Crane angled his head to see
her in the rearview mirror; she was squinting steadily out the
side window, the passing lights alternately lighting and shading
her profile.

She finally spoke when he had made the right-hand turn onto
the Strip under the red and gold lights of the Barbary Coast.

"Even if they'd somehow agree to fly Scat to an out-of-town
hospital," she said thoughtfully, "he'd be easily traceable—and
I'd go with him, and the bad guys would know I would."

Ozzie took a breath as if to argue, then just exhaled and
nodded. "True."

The Flamingo was a rippling glare of fire-colored light on
their right, but suddenly real orange flames and luminously
billowing smoke flared beyond the traffic ahead of them, and
Crane swore and lifted his foot from the gas pedal.

"It's the volcano out in front of the Mirage," Diana said.
"Every twenty minutes it goes off. The locals are getting used
to it, not that many of these people are locals." She yawned.
Crane knew that kind of yawn—a sign of long-sustained tension, not of boredom. "I have to stay in town," she said, "and
I won't be too hard for them to find, even if I visit the hospital
in disguise. I need an edge. I need some . . . power here, some
weaponry."

"We've got guns," said Crane, "we can help—"

"Maybe I'll want your help, and maybe I won't," she told
him. "And I'll take a gun. But what I mean, what I need is—is
this kind of power." In the rearview mirror Crane saw her wave
at the gigantic casinos around them. "Certain people want me
killed because I'm some kind of a threat to them, I'm the
Queen of Hearts, right? I'm the flesh-and-blood daughter of
my mother, who was somebody they felt they had to kill."

Ozzie started to speak, but she silenced him by tapping his
shoulder with the backs of her fingers. "I want to learn how to
be an *active* threat," she said, "not just a passive one. I want to
be the target that comes alive and starts shooting back. I want
to become this Isis—with whatever powers Isis has, whatever
it is they're afraid of."

They were directly across from the blazing Mirage volcano
now, and Crane glanced to his left at the crowds of people

standing along the railing beyond the sidewalk. His window was rolled down, and he could hear the roar of the flames over the crowd sounds, and even from way over here he thought he could feel the heat.

He considered what Diana had said. This is all yours, Ozzie, he thought. I'm out of my depth here.

For nearly a minute Ozzie just frowned at the traffic ahead.

Then he said thoughtfully, "Christ. Move all-in. You've been getting penalized like a player in a tournament who oversleeps and automatically gets all the antes and blind bets deducted from his absentee buy-in, and those involuntary bets have—have cost you, horribly. Now you're awake, though you're under the gun with a Jack and a Four down and a Queen showing. But they're suited." He shifted around on the front seat. "Could you fish me a beer out of the ice chest there, honey? It's okay," he added to Crane, "the Four of Hearts is allowed to drink. The Jack's still not, though."

After Diana had opened a can for him and handed it across the back of the seat, the old man took a deep sip. "Yeah," he went on. "You've paid the blind, this latest involuntary bet, and now maybe the only thing you can do is move all-in, shove your whole pile of chips out there right now."

The old man's chasing the white line again, thought Crane. Toward a game where they're likely to kill us all.

"They won't expect alligator blood," Ozzie went on, "in somebody who's been playing like such a rock."

Crane remembered the term *alligator blood*—it was how old Johnny Moss had described the toughness of real Poker players. As far as Crane knew, Moss was still winning tournaments at Binion's Horseshoe, and by now Moss must be . . . as old as Ozzie.

"So what are the chips?" Diana asked. "And how do I push them in?"

"Uh . . . you ought to consult the Queen," said Ozzie, "but she's dead. That was your mother." The old man sipped his beer with a hand that he was visibly forcing to be steady. "Her . . . ghost will probably be rousing up lately, with this unholy Holy Week almost on us, and the moon is at the half and filling now, so she and you should be getting more powerful. And there will be other women in town now, trying for the queenhood, but you're the daughter, you're already standing where they want to be. They're wanting to find you and get you out of the picture and then stand there instead. You're the one the real Queen of Hearts would . . . give an audience to."

Crane was stopped at a traffic light next to Caesars Palace, and he stared at the crowds of pedestrians crossing the street toward the torches and imperious statues above the casino's entrance temple.

"So what do I *do*?" Diana asked. "Consult a Ouija board? Take acid and meet her in a hallucination?"

"No, no. I'm pretty sure anything like that would just make you conspicuous, let your rivals know right where you are. And stay away from playing cards or any gambling. In fact, stay away from Scott—he's to the King what you are to the Queen, and when the two of you are together, it probably shines like a road flare."

"No problem," said Diana.

Crane stared ahead through the cracked, neon-streaked windshield and didn't respond, but his lips were pulled back from his clenched teeth. I stabbed my leg, he thought, to be able to warn you about all this, three whole days ago. If you'd run then, Scat would be fine. I walked up that hill. I got the nut to turn his gun away from your son, onto me.

"Water, fresh water," Ozzie was saying now. "It's associated with the moon goddess. I think if you could bathe in the fresh, wild water of this place, and try to . . . *think* to her, your mother, Lady Issit, you might get something."

"Bathe," said Diana doubtfully. "But Ozzie, I bathed in the water of this place just this afternoon, and nothing happened. I've been bathing in this water every day for eight years!"

"No, you haven't. Don't you read the papers? They're having a water war in Nevada these days. *Las vegas* is Spanish for 'the meadows,' it's in an artesian basin, but even in the forties the wells had begun to run dry, sink-holes started to appear, as the water table dropped. It was only in eighty-two that the city got access to Lake Mead water, and now that's not enough, and they're after the water in central Nevada— Railroad Valley, Ely, Pioche. Las Vegas is supposed to take no more from those places than rainfall puts back, but the city has applied for the right to take more, what they call *mining* the aquifers."

Crane thought about his vision of the vast entities deep in the psychic water table. He wondered if it, too, was low around here, depleted by some unimaginable use.

"The bad king," Ozzie went on, "has almost certainly encouraged all this. He doesn't want any wild goddess power under the ground. He wants *tamed* water to serve as the counterweight. Don't you go *near* Lake Mead before talking to your mother."

Construction was going on at the Holiday Casino to the right. Crane frowned at the big neon-lit replica of a riverboat. The massive, balconied structure was facing north now, and he distinctly remembered it as having faced west the last time he'd paid attention to it. Was it revolving?

"Like," Diana said slowly, "a well? Rain?" In the rearview mirror the right side of her face was whitened by the electrically glaring words HOLIDAY CASINO emblazoned across the towering paddle wheel.

Crane thought about how this road had looked when he had driven out here with his real father, so long ago. The Frontier had been a casual ranch-style place, the El Rancho Vegas up ahead had been a little Spanish-looking inn, and the Flamingo had stood in solitary grandeur far away in the darkness to the south.

"Or the ice cubes in drinks that have been sitting around since the forties," he told Diana.

CHAPTER 23

Go Ahead and Shape It into a Pig

The carousel bar at the Circus Circus was on the second level, which was really a wide railed balcony that ran around the entire circumference of the vast casino, so that the banks of clanging slot machines were visible in the darkness below. The casino was, in fact, hollow; overhead, beyond wide-strung nets in the middle distance, acrobats in tight, sequined suits swung across the firmament on trapezes under the remote light-hung ceiling.

The bar itself was slowly rotating, and as Crane followed Diana out onto the moving floor of it, hurrying a little to get through the gate at the same time as she did and not have to wait for the next gate to orbit around, he remembered wondering if the Holiday Casino was slowly turning in place.

Mavranos was sitting at a booth with young Oliver. Diana slid in next to her son and hugged him, and Crane looked away from Oliver's expression of disdain.

"They think he'll make it," she said.

Mavranos raised his eyebrows at Crane, who shrugged helplessly.

"I'm going to take Diana and Oliver to registration and get them a room," said Ozzie, putting his hand on Diana's shoulder. "Let's go, honey."

She stood up, pulling Oliver after her, and followed the old man to the central barstools, where he apparently told her to wait for him.

Ozzie hobbled back to the booth, where Crane had now sat down across from Mavranos. "She doesn't really blame you," Ozzie said quietly. "She loves you, but naturally she loves the kid more, and right now she's not thinking very far."

"Thanks, Ozzie. I love her, too. And you."

The old man nodded. "Check into a room together, and use Arky's name if you can. I'll be in touch with you boys if there's any way you can help."

Ozzie turned and made his way back to where Diana and the boy waited, and together the three of them got off the turning surface and soon disappeared into the surging, chattering crowds.

Mavranos swirled a half-drunk glass of beer. "You still want those two beers?"

Crane shivered. He did want them, the two he'd mentioned back on the hilltop when the world was good, but he wanted about six others first. Why on earth *shouldn't* he get drunk *now*?

Let the pay phones start ringing, he thought. I'll almost certainly never see Diana again now, and Susan—the thing

I'll be able to mistake for Susan, if I'm good and drunk—has probably gotten pretty solid by now.

But Ozzie had said that Diana still loved him, and that he'd call if Crane could be of any help. If he'd been drinking, he would only be bringing Dionysus to her.

But I *can't* be of any help.

The carousel had turned halfway around now. He was facing away from the brightly colored shops of the second level, off across the clanging abyss. "Sure," he said.

Mavranos shrugged and waved at a passing cocktail waitress, and a few moments later two cold bottles of Budweiser stood, frosty and dark, on the table in front of Crane.

Mavranos had ordered another Coors for himself, and took a sip. "How'd it go?" he asked. "I thought you'd be in jail by now."

Crane described his brief interview with the police officer. "I guess it was clearly self-defense," he said in conclusion. "He did tell me to let them know where I'll be staying."

"Huh. Listen, you should have heard young Bitin Dog on the drive here."

"Bitin Dog?" said Crane absently. "Oh, yeah, Oliver. What did he say?"

Mavranos squinted at Crane and wondered how to explain it.

The boy had smelled of beer, and Mavranos had realized that he must have got right into the ice chest as soon as Mavranos had grabbed the .38 and gone sprinting for the dirt road. That seemed an odd urgency, considering that his little brother was in danger over the hill, but Mavranos had felt that this wasn't the time, nor was it his job, to yell at the kid about having sneaked a beer.

But when Mavranos had started Diana's Mustang and turned north on Boulder Highway, watching the lights of his Suburban recede away very fast ahead, the boy had *laughed* softly.

Mavranos had given him a sharp glance. "Something funny happen out here that I missed, Oliver?"

The boy had frowned then. "My name—"

"Bitin Dog, I heard."

Oliver relaxed. "Something funny?" he said. "I don't know. Maybe it's funny that a kid could grow up in one night."

"Who did that? You?"

"Sure. My friends told me that life and death are all in the cards, and if somebody close to you dies, you just shrug and keep playing. I didn't figure they were right, until now."

Mavranos remembered the evening one of his daughters had been arrested in a local record store for shoplifting. She'd been fifteen, and when he went to the store to pick her up, she had been defiant, as if nothing now had remained for her but a life of crime, and she'd better start working on getting the attitude right.

So Mavranos spoke gently now. "You aren't responsible for this. You ditched him tonight when you were playing, okay, that's bad, but this isn't your fault—"

"What's done is done."

Mavranos was getting impatient. "Who are these friends of yours? These the great guys that named you Barfin' Dog?"

"*Your* name is *Archimedes*!" Oliver shot back. "You think that's not a—a shitty name?" He took a few deep breaths, and again the strange calm descended on him. "But yeah, sort of. People were already calling me that, but tonight they made it my club name. It's my *persona*, if you've ever heard that word. They ride around in white El Camino pickups, but they bust off the *El* and the *C* from the logo on the fender, so it says 'amino.' They call themselves the Amino Acids."

"They've all got cars? How old are these kids?"

"They're not kids, they—"

Abruptly the boy had stopped talking, and when Mavranos looked over at him, he had seemed at first to be struggling not to cry. Then his eyes opened and rolled back, and Mavranos thought he'd have to follow Crane to the hospital, for Oliver seemed to be having a fit. A moment later, though, the boy was relaxed and staring sullenly ahead.

"You okay, boy?" Mavranos asked nervously.

"I'm not a boy."

They had not spoken again until Ozzie and Diana and Crane had joined them at the carousel bar.

Mavranos described the conversation to Crane as the bar slowly turned, and he was absently curious about Crane's not having yet touched either of his beers.

"Your sister's got a weird kid," Mavranos concluded. "It was a little boy talking, but it was as if part of him had *dried out*, kissed off childhood and become an adult by default, like I've read they can remove a gland from some kinds of larvae, and they go into a cocoon way before they should, and the adult butterfly that eventually crawls out is stunted and horrible."

Crane was thinking about this Amino Acids club and the "all in the cards" remark, and he decided he ought to get word of this to Ozzie.

Mavranos pointed at Crane's two bottles. "You gonna drink those beers?"

Crane picked one up and sniffed it; then he sighed. "No," he said. "You can have them."

Mavranos picked one up and tilted it to his mouth—then choked and put it down again. Foam was running down his neck into his collar and surging up out of the bottle neck and puddling on the table.

Mavranos coughed, then looked around in embarrassment. "I must have got some cigarette ash in it somehow. Ashes'll make 'em foam up like that."

Crane nodded, but he suspected that Susan was responsible, angered by Crane's rudeness. He had rebuffed her here, asking for the beers and then changing his mind and passing them on to a friend. "Let me buy you a Coors, Arky," he said, forcing himself to sound unconcerned. "I don't think you're going to have any luck with the other one there either."

Getting a room with cash proved to be no problem, and after Mavranos had unlocked the room door, Crane crossed to the telephone. He called the Metro police and was referred to a Detective Frits, who noted the room number.

"Oh, Mr. Crane," Frits added, "a team of officers went out Boulder Highway and found that shed. They say there's blood and broken glass and a chair with cut duct tape on it and a gun out in the sand, but there's nobody there. Car tracks behind the shed indicate he might have driven away in a very small car."

"I saw the car," said Crane quickly. "I forgot to mention it. It's a boxy little thing like a British Volkswagen, called a Morris. Covered with dust, impossible to tell the color."

"Ah. That'll help, thank you."

After Crane had hung up the phone, Mavranos opened the hall door. "I'm going out on the town, Pogo," he said. "You got your key, right?"

"Right. Have fun."

"Night like this," Mavranos said dully, "how could I not?" He left, closing the door behind him and rattling the knob to be sure it had locked.

Crane looked around the room. The carpet and chairs were bright red, and the walls were striped red and pink and blue. He turned off the light.

In the merciful near darkness he got undressed, and crawled into the window-side bed, wondering if he'd be able to sleep. He had become a night person during these last hundred hours or so, but in this town it wasn't supposed to matter.

He did manage to doze, but some hours later he opened his eyes—and tensed, sweat suddenly springing out all over him.

A rat, almost big enough to look like a possum, was clinging to the shade of the lamp across the room. Very slowly, its free paw turning and its head ducking and then coming up again so that the eyes glinted in the light from a slit between the drawn curtains, the rat was eating a big insect, one of those white beetles known as potato bugs or Jerusalem crickets, which the Spanish call *niños de la tierra*, children of the earth. The bug, too, was moving slowly, waving its long, thick, jointed legs in the air. No sound was being made.

Crane just stared, his heart pounding, all judgment suspended.

For perhaps ten minutes he lay, stiff as a statue and hardly breathing, and watched the rat consume the beetle; and then the rat began to stop moving. First its head stopped its slow bobbing, and then the long tail, which had been flexing out in the air, curled around the body and disappeared. The bug was gone, and the rat's forepaws folded and then there was no motion from the lumpy darkness on the lampshade.

Moving as agonizingly slowly as had the animal combatants, Crane reached out and turned on the small bedside lamp next to his head.

In the sudden yellow light he saw that the dark mass on the

lampshade was nothing but his shirt, tossed there carelessly when he had taken off his clothes.

Mavranos, he saw, had not yet returned. Crane got out of bed and walked over to the lamp. For a while he started at the shirt, and then he carefully lifted it away from the lampshade and tossed it into a corner.

Still suspending judgement, he got back into bed, closed his eyes, and waited for sleep to take him.

"I've seen her boyfriend going in and out," Trumbill said patiently, "but so far she hasn't showed."

He was sitting in a chair by the aluminum-frame window, wearing only a pair of baggy white shorts. Aside from the chair, there was nothing inside the stark apartment but a TV table, a telephone, two whirring fans, a Styrofoam ice chest, and the litter of used-up Ban roll-on antiperspirant tubes around the legs of the chair; he was rubbing a new tube over the vividly tattooed skin of his enormous belly.

He had hastily rented this apartment at dawn, and though the landlord had managed to hook up a phone, the air conditioner wasn't working; in spite of the antiperspirants, Trumbill was losing precious moisture.

"I'll keep on them about the air conditioner," said Betsy Reculver, who was standing behind him, "but you've got to stay here. We can't lose *her*, the way you lost Sc—lost Crane, in California." The cheap carpeting did nothing to muffle the quacking echoes of her voice.

Without looking away from the window, Trumbill held out the tube of Ban. "Do my back?"

"Forget it." He could hear the revulsion in her voice.

Trumbill shrugged and resumed rubbing it over his densely illustrated flesh, still looking out through the half-opened curtains at the white duplex across the street.

He wished he were at home doing the chores or raking his gravel garden, or driving the old Leon body somewhere in the air-conditioned Jaguar, but he could see that this had to be done. This was clearly the Diana they'd been trying to find. The police report had linked the Diana who lived at the duplex's address with Scott and Ozzie Crane, and, as Betsy had been quick to notice, the address was Isis on Venus.

"You didn't use it all?" said Betsy.

For a moment he thought she had reconsidered doing his back, but she was standing by the table and had picked up a fist-size blob of the pink Semtex.

"All of it would take out half the street," he told her. "The two golf ball-size ones I stuck in the basement grates will do fine—even with them, I won't be sitting by this window when I do it; I'll be around the corner in the hall."

"It looks like—like marzipan candy."

"Go ahead and shape it into a pig; it can't go off without a blasting cap. You could probably safely *eat* it."

She shivered and put it down. A moment later she said, "I suppose *you* like this decor."

Trumbill spared a glance around at the bare yellow walls and the flocked ceiling. "Painted white, and a lot cooler, it'd be all right."

"What have you got against . . . *livelier* things?"

I love them, Betsy, he thought. I just want them all to be within the boundaries of my skin. "Don't you have to go meet Newt?"

"Not till this afternoon—but very well, I'll leave you alone." He heard her footsteps scuff across the carpet toward the door. "But I'll call you every fifteen minutes or so," she added.

"You don't have to," he said, but she was already out the door and closing it behind her.

That meant she'd be on the phone with him more often than not throughout the day—unless Diana were to show. He sighed and stared at the duplex and reached into the ice chest for one of the strips of raw lamb.

The noon sun through the window glowed hot red in a prism paperweight on Detective Frits's disordered desk, but of course the office was chilly. Crane, perched in a swiveling office chair across from Frits, wished he had worn a jacket. His cup of coffee still steamed on the edge of the desk, but it was nearly gone, and he didn't want to finish it yet.

Crane had told Frits the same story he'd told the Metro officer last night, and now the detective was leafing through a notebook, apparently at random. His curly brown hair was disordered and receding from his high forehead, and when

Crane first shook hands with him he had thought the tall, skinny detective had probably been a rock musician in his not-long-ago youth.

Crane's thoughts were far away from the little office and the gangly detective.

Move all-in.

Crane wasn't sure whether his hallucination last night, the vision of the rat eating the beetle, had been mild delirium tremens or not—but either way, he had decided to stay sober.

This morning, as he and Mavranos had been walking to the Circus Circus coffee shop to get some breakfast, a middle-aged woman had pushed a baby stroller into their path and asked Crane to heal her little boy by touching him. To get rid of her, Crane had sheepishly touched the boy's forehead—whatever was the matter with the child, he didn't improve visibly—but later, over his fried eggs and bacon, it occurred to Crane that she might not simply have been crazy. She might have sensed what sort of . . . crown prince he was.

And it occurred to him that in spite of the fact that he had taken the money for the Assumption hand in '69, Diana might not be the only one who could become the target that shoots back—who, in Ozzie's phrase, could move all-in. Maybe the way to survive was to challenge his real father on the old man's own terms.

Frits had stopped now at one page in his notebook and looked up. "So the three of you just decided to come visit your foster-sister."

Crane blinked and forced himself to pay attention to this. "Right."

"And Mavranos is your next-door neighbor, back in Santa Ana."

"Right. He's got cancer, and he hadn't ever been to Vegas."

"Your foster-father lives where?"

"I don't know," Crane said, shaking his head and smiling apologetically. "We happened to run into him on Balboa Island." He shrugged. "It was all very spur of the moment."

"Most trips here are." Frits sighed and flipped back through his notebook.

Crane nodded and reached for his coffee now with a steady hand, and he didn't let his relief show in his face or his breathing or any visible pulse.

Frits looked up, and from his smile Crane thought he was going to make another remark about spontaneous trips to Las Vegas.

"Why did you yell, 'Everybody down,' when the Porsche stopped?"

"It was obvious to me," said Crane instantly, buying the virtue of an apparently unconsidered reply at the expense of committing himself to a random beginning, "that he wasn't just a Good Samaritan, pulling over to help. There were two vehicles parked on our side, after all, head-to-head like we had jumper cables, and four adults and a couple of kids visible." He had it now. "Clearly we didn't need help. I figured he had to be a partner of the kidnapper, a lookout who'd been watching from a distance and came up fast when Arky drove up in the Suburban and got out with a gun."

"And then, in fact, he did shoot the boy."

"Right," Crane agreed. He remembered what he had told the officer last night, so he added, "But after Diana told us about the Porsche guy trying to pick up on her, and him sounding like the guy Ozzie had called a zombie the day before, it didn't seem like he was a partner of the kidnapper after all." He shook his head. "Might as well have been, the way it worked out."

Frits stared at him. Crane stared back, at first blankly and then with a faint quizzical smile, as he would have at someone taking a long time to fold or call a bluff.

"I could have you arrested," Frits said.

"For what?" Crane asked quickly, not having to fake alarm. "Shooting at the crazy kidnapper? Or after the Porsche?"

"After the Porsche, say." For a moment Frits continued to stare at him. Crane just stared back, a little more wide-eyed than before. "Where do you know Alfred Funo from?" Frits asked.

Crane exhaled. "I suppose that's the name of the guy registered next to us at the motel? I've never heard the name before. How *would* I know him? Does he live in Orange County?"

"L.A. County."

"I've never heard the man's name. I never saw the car before yesterday, unless it passed me on the freeway sometime."

After three more long seconds Frits looked back down at his papers. "You're staying at the Circus Circus?"

"Right. The room's under Mavranos's name."

"Okay." Frits sat back and smiled. "We'll be in touch. Thanks for coming in."

Crane leaned forward with a concerned frown on his face. "Look, maybe this is standard procedure, this . . . threatening attitude, these insinuations, but if you really think I'm *involved* in this thing, I wish you'd just say so, so I could explain whatever it is you've got wrong. I don't—"

Frits had been nodding sympathetically, and now he held up his hand, and Crane stopped talking. "Thanks for coming in," Frits said.

Crane hesitated, then put the coffee cup down on the desk. "Uh . . . thank you." He got up out of the chair and let himself out of the office.

Mavranos was waiting in the truck. "Didn't take long," he said as Crane climbed in and pulled the door closed. "Were Diana and Ozzie in there?"

"No," Crane said, "I guess he talked to them earlier. I wish Ozzie hadn't swooped everybody away before we got a chance to discuss the story a little. 'Happened to meet Ozzie in Balboa and then just dropped everything and drove straight to Vegas!' How did that detective act with you?"

"Like it was a—a formality." The Suburban shook as he started the engine. "Just had me recite it all. Why, did he lean on you?"

"Yeah, some."

"Huh. Well, at least you're still at large."

Mavranos swung the blue truck across the parking lot toward the exit onto the Strip. "Listen, I'm gonna try the Sports Book at Caesars—they've got one airplane-hangar-size room that must have a hundred TV screens on the wall, and the effects of what's on the screens go rippling across the people that're watching, like wind over a wheatfield. I might find a clue there. You want to come along, or should I drop you somewhere?"

"Yeah, you can drop me off—at the next card-reading parlor you see."

Mavranos glanced at him curiously. "I thought Ozzie said you were supposed to stay away from that kind of thing."

Crane rubbed his face, wondering if he looked as exhausted as he felt. "That's if I'm just going to run and hope to hide. If I want to . . . *do* anything, I think I've got to turn and face . . . it. them. whatever it is."

Mavranos sighed and touched the bandanna under his jaw. "'Because there were no graves in Egypt,'" he said quietly, almost to himself, "'hast thou taken us away to die in the wilderness?'"

"Your man Eliot?"

"*Exodus*. Lots of good stuff in the Bible, Pogo."

Crane shook his head. "Ozzie told me not to start any long books."

CHAPTER 24

Fragments of the Book of Thoth

By early afternoon Betsy Reculver had called Trumbill a dozen times, asking if Diana had shown up yet, or if Crane had, and complaining about everything from pains in her joints to the bad card readings she was getting in her solitaire games.

During this latest call, after cautioning him yet again not to let Diana Ryan get away from him, he heard over the phone the bong of her doorbell, followed by LaShane's barking.

"Is that Newt already?" asked Trumbill.

"Let me haul my weary old bones to where I can see the screens." He heard her breathe harder, and the reception on the portable telephone faded as she walked through a doorway.

Trumbill reflected that it would be a relief when the new game was over and done with and the soul of Georges Leon had a batch of fresh bodies to animate, all the ones that had been conceived and paid for in 1969.

The guy must miss his balls, Trumbill thought. Twenty years is a long gestation period if you need the kids, especially when you've got to conceive more before you can get at the original lot.

It's a weird way to be this king, he thought.

Trumbill gathered that in the past the Fisher Kings would just *have* children, not kill their children's minds and steal their bodies—and that such a King would reign over a fertile green land and not a sterile desert—and that he would share his power with a Queen—and that he would deal face-to-face with the vast old entities that were known as Archetypes or gods, not through the formal, at-a-distance mediation of the terrible cards.

He heard Reculver grunt in surprise.

"My God, Vaughan," she said, "it's that guy, Al Funo! And he's a mess—all unshaven and shaky-looking." Over the line Trumbill heard the click of Reculver's intercom. "Yes?"

Then he heard Funo's voice, tinnily filtered to him through two speakers. "Mrs. Reculver, I need to talk to you."

"Make an appointment," said Trumbill. "Figure a place where we can meet him."

"Uh," said Reculver, speaking loudly into the intercom, "we can meet you . . . at Lindy's again, at the Flamingo—"

"I need to talk to you *now*!" came Funo's voice.

"No," said Trumbill instantly.

The intercom clicked off. "Vaughan, he'll leave if I don't talk to him! And he's the only lead we've got to Diana! She won't go back to the apartment you're watching; she's not that stupid; it's a waste of time you sitting there like a damn toad! *I've* got to do *everything*, don't I?"

"Betsy, get into Hanari, will you? This Funo guy is a nut—"

"He's starting to leave—" Trumbill heard a clunk, and realized that she had put the phone down on the table by the front door. Again there was the click of the intercom. "Very well," Trumbill heard her say, "come in then." He heard the snap of the dead bolt being switched back.

In the bare apartment overlooking Venus Avenue, Trumbill had stood up, his multicolored belly swinging in front of the window. *"Get a gun, at least!"* He shouted into the telephone. "Damn you, Betsy, *get a gun!*"

Then over the telephone line he heard LaShane barking, followed by the unmistakable *bam* of a close gunshot. A moment later he heard a second shot. The dog stopped barking.

"Shit," Trumbill muttered, staring impatiently out at the duplex across the street and holding the telephone receiver tight. "Betsy?" he yelled. "Betsy, are you all right? Answer me quick or I'm calling 911!" He knew that if she could hear him, she'd get on the line and order him not to do that.

All he could hear over the phone was the vague background sigh of an open line.

"Betsy!" he shouted again. Outside the window glass the empty street yawned at him. "Betsy, what's happened?"

He threw down the tube of Ban and switched off the two fans so that he could better hear any sounds from Betsy's end of the line.

Finally there was a click as though someone had picked up an extension, and then a young woman's voice said, "Five-five-five three-eight-one-zero, this is the Operator with an emergency interrupt from Richard Leroy at five-five-five three-five-nine-three. Will you release the line?"

"Yes," he said through clenched teeth.

There came another click, and then a man's shrill voice: "Vaughan, this is me, I'm in Richard." Richard was panting. "J-Jesus, he *shot* me!" He paused to cough, and Trumbill was glad he hadn't called from the asthmatic Beany body. "Funo did. I *bled* to death right on the doorstep, no more than ten seconds after he shot me and ran off." For a moment Trumbill just heard him panting; then Richard went on, "*Merde*, Vaughan, the Reculver body's lying half in and half out of the front door over there!"

"Where are you?"

"In Richard here? I don't know, some hallway with a telephone—the college library, I suppose, I only saw it for a second, long enough to get to a phone. I'm seeing only through Beany right now. In Beany I'm hailing a cab in front of the Flamingo; that'll get me home quicker than walking to my car here on campus. Damn, I hope nobody called in a shots-fired report, or notices the poor body!"

"Will old Newt have the sense to drag it in?"

"Newt. Good thought. He might; he's owed me his soul for thirty years; he wouldn't want to be associated with any police stuff. Of course, if he sees it from the street, he might just drive on."

Trumbill sighed heavily. "I think I should stay here."

"Yes, of course, I was babbling when I said Diana wouldn't show up there. Stay there and kill her; I can't have any Queen of Hearts running around while I'm down to three bodies. I'll work through Richard and Beany."

Trumbill knew that the old man wouldn't want to take the Art Hanari body out yet; it was his showpiece, just as the Richard one had been, the last time. He would want to have the Hanari perfectly rested and beautiful to host this series of Assumption games.

Abruptly Richard's voice shouted, "Renaissance Drive, corner of Tropicana and Eastern!" The line went dead.

Trumbill realized that the last shout had been an involuntary echo of old Beany's, hollering directions at a cabdriver out in front of the Flamingo, relayed to Trumbill through Richard at the university library.

Figured curtains were drawn across the windows of the room, and though there were some fluorescent tubes glowing around the bookshelves and display cases along the back wall, a black iron lamp on the big round table cast most of the light after Crane had stepped inside and shut the door behind him.

A slim white-bearded man put a book aside and stood up, and Crane saw that he was wearing a satiny blue robe. He's going hard for the atmosphere at least, thought Crane nervously.

"Can I help you, sir?" the man asked.

"Uh, I hope so," said Crane. "I need to have a card reading done." The chilly air smelled faintly of carpet freshener and incense, and reminded him that his breath probably smelled of onions. Mavranos had insisted on stopping for cheeseburgers, though once they'd arrived, Mavranos had eaten only a few bites of his.

"Very well." If the man smelled the onions, he was at least not remarking on it. "Do sit down at the table here, please. My name is Joshua."

"Scott Crane." Joshua's hand was limp and cold, and after two shakes Crane let go of it.

The old man opened the office door to hang a plastic Do Not Disturb sign on the knob, then resumed his seat on the north side of the table as Crane sat down in the comfortable leather armchair across from him. The glass-topped table was wide enough so that if they'd been playing chess, he'd have had to get half out of his chair to move the farther pieces.

"A standard reading," said the old man, "that is, a Ten-Card Spread with the twenty-two Major Arcana cards, is fifty dollars."

"Is there a—a more thorough reading?"

"Yes, Mr. Crane. I could do a full Seventy-eight Card Horseshoe Spread. That takes a good deal longer, but it is more insightful. I ask a hundred dollars for that."

"Let's go with the Horseshoe." Crane dug a hundred-dollar bill out of his pocket and laid it on the glass. Crane reflected that anyone watching would probably expect the old man to lay down a bill of his own and then deal out a hand of Head-Up Poker, but Joshua's long-white fingers whisked the hundred away.

Joshua was now unfolding a large square of purple silk from around what proved to be a polished wooden box. "Have you had Tarot readings before?"

"I . . . don't think so. Not really. Can't you do the—the procedure with regular playing cards?"

"In a crude way, yes." Joshua smiled as he opened the box and lifted out a deck of oversize cards with plaid-pattern backs. "But it's so imprecise that I wouldn't take money for it or recommend it for any serious questions. The Tarot is the original instrument, of which playing cards are a simplified, truncated form made for games." He wasn't smiling as he looked at Crane and added, "This isn't a game."

"I wouldn't be here if I thought it was." Crane leaned back in the chair, concealing his nervousness. This would be only the third time he'd been exposed to the Tarot deck, and the first time the cards would be speaking to him, responding to a question from him, and he wasn't looking forward to it. "How does it work? I mean, how do the cards . . . *know* about me?"

"I'd be lying if I told you I knew for sure." Joshua had spread the cards out face down across the unfolded silk and was gently scattering them around with both hands. "Some people think it's out-and-out magic, and I've got a foolish little booklet that will tell you that vibration rays from your fingers somehow combine with the oxygen in the room to direct which cards you touch." He had gathered them up into a deck again and tapped the edges flush. "The fact is, they do work."

He steepled his fingers under his chin, leaving the squared-up deck in front of him. "They may be the surviving fragments of the Book of Thoth," Joshua said, "supposedly composed by the god Thoth, handed down fugitively from the earliest Egyptian kingdoms. Iamblichus, the fourth-century Syrian, claimed that the mystery cults of Osiris locked initiates into a room on the walls of which were painted twenty-two powerfully affecting symbolic pictures—and there are twenty-two cards in the Major Arcana, the suitless picture cards that have been dropped from your modern playing deck. Whatever it is that the cards represent, they . . . *resonate*, strongly, with elements in the human psyche, the way a struck tuning fork can make a glass across the room vibrate. *I* think that, in some micro or macro way, there's sentience behind them; they're aware of us."

Then they'll probably recognize me, thought Crane. *Climb up on my knee, Sonny Boy.*

He wiped his palms down the sides of his pants.

"Now," said Joshua, "I want you to empty your mind of everything except the question you've come to ask. This is serious, so take it seriously."

Clear your mind for the cards, Crane thought. He nodded and breathed deeply.

"What is your question?" asked Joshua.

Crane suppressed a hopeless smile, and when he spoke, his voice was level. "How do I take over my father's job?"

Joshua nodded acknowledgment. "Can you shuffle cards?" he asked, pushing the deck toward Crane.

"Yes."

Crane cut the deck and gave the cards seven fast riffle shuffles, instinctively squaring the cards flat against the table so as not to flash a glimpse of the bottom one. He pushed the deck back to Joshua. "Cut?"

"No."

The old man quickly dealt the cards out into two piles, one twice as big as the other; the bigger pile was then dealt out the same way, and then the bigger of these piles was divvied up in the same two for one ratio. . . .

Eventually he had six uneven stacks, and he picked up the westernmost stack and began laying it out on the table in a vertical pattern.

* * *

The first card was the Page of Cups, a picture of a young man in Renaissance-looking clothes standing in front of a stylized ocean and holding a chalice from which a fish head was peeking out.

Crane relaxed with relief and disappointment. The drawing was a nineteenth-century-style line drawing, and was not one of the vividly colored quattrocento paintings that his father had used. Probably nothing will happen with this deck, he thought.

The faint snap the card made as it touched the silk was followed by the patter of raindrops on the window beyond the curtains.

When there are gray skies, thought Crane.

The next card was the Emperor, an old king on a throne, with his legs awkwardly crossed as if because of some injury.

Close thunder shook the window, and from out on the street came the screech and slam of a car accident. The rain was heavier, hissing on the pavement outside.

Joshua looked up, startled, but dealt the third card.

It was the Fool, a young man dancing at the edge of a precipice while a dog snapped at his heels.

The rest of the cards abruptly flew out of Joshua's hand and sprayed at Crane, who ducked as they whistled and clattered past him. One had ticked against the surface of his plastic eye, and for one shocked moment Crane was a little boy again, stunned with injury and unbearable betrayal.

But he forced himself to think, to remember who he was and why he was here.

The cards, he told himself harshly, remember? Don't cry, you're not five years old now. You came to consult the cards.

I guess any Tarot deck will work after all, he thought.

His heart was pounding.

He thought, But I don't like, or understand, the answer.

Crane let out his breath and straightened up, hearing the cards continue to rattle on the carpet behind him. He carefully hiked around in his chair. The cards were shaking back and forth across the carpet as though the building were in the grip of a big earthquake.

Outside, the rain was thrashing down.

Joshua had pushed his own chair back and got to his feet. "Get out of here," he whispered to Crane. His face was white.

"I don't want to know who you are. Just . . . get out of here right now."

Crane was breathing fast, and his hands were nearly clawed with craving for a drink, but he shook his head.

"I," he said carefully, "still need an answer to my question."

The old man made an unhappy, keening sound. "Isn't it obvious I can't help you? My God—" He paused.

Crane was suddenly sure the man had been about to say something like, Even *so-and-so* couldn't help you!

"Who?" Crane demanded. "Who is it that *can*?"

"Go see the Pope, I don't know. I'm calling the police if you don't—"

"You *do* know someone who can handle a no-limit game of this. Tell me who it is."

"I swear to you, I don't, and I'm calling the police—"

"Fine," said Crane, grinning broadly and standing up. "If you don't tell me who it is, I'll come back here—no, I'll find out where you live and go there—and I'll"—What would scare the old man?—"I'll play Solitaire stark naked on your front porch with a deck of these goddamn things, I'll"—he was shouting now—"I'll bring a dozen dead bodies and play Assumption with them, and we'll use Communion hosts as chips. I'll be the goddamn one-eyed Jack and play for my *eye!*"

He reached up to his face and popped out his false eye and held it out toward the old man in a trembling fist.

Joshua had collapsed back into his chair during Crane's outburst and was now crying. For a few moments neither man spoke.

"It doesn't matter anyway," Joshua sobbed finally. "There isn't any way I could dare stay in Las Vegas now, after doing that reading, that partial reading." His blue robe was twisted around his torso, ridiculous and pathetic. "Damn you, and I'll have to get some other job. I can't possibly ever read cards again. They know my *face* now. Why in God's name did you come to *me*?"

"Luck of the draw," said Crane, forcing himself not to care about this old man right now. He popped his false eye back into the socket and walked to the window. "Who is it?"

Joshua sniffed and stood up. "Please, if there's any humanity in you . . . what was your name?"

"Crane, Scott Crane."

"If there's any human compassion in you, Scott, don't tell him who sent you." He wiped his eyes on a baggy sleeve. "I don't know his real name; he's called Spider Joe. He apparently lives in a trailer out on Rancho, the Tonopah Highway. It's on the right side of the road, two hours outside of town: a trailer and some shacks, with a big Two of Spades sign out front."

The cards had stopped spinning on the carpet now, and Joshua knelt and was gingerly picking them up with the silk cloth, being careful not to touch them. "Would you do me one other favor, Scott?" he asked querulously. When Crane nodded, the old man went on, "Take these cards, my cards, out of here with you—and take your hundred-dollar bill back, too. No, I couldn't possibly use it, and even if I burned it, it might call some more psychic attention to me."

Crane had pulled back the curtain to watch the rainy street, and now he shrugged and nodded. "Okay."

Joshua wearily unzipped his blue satin robe and took it off. Under it he was wearing shorts and a Lacoste polo shirt; he looked fit, as though he exercised conscientiously, and Crane was suddenly sure that his real name was something more mundane than Joshua.

"I've heard that you've got to cross his palm with silver," the old man said tiredly. "Get two silver dollars, real silver. He claims it keeps things from seeing him, blinds the eyes of the dead; it's related to the old practice of putting coins on a dead man's eyes." He threw Crane's bill onto the table next to the bundle of cards, and Crane leaned over to pick it all up.

He stuffed the bill and the cards into the pockets of his jacket. "I'll see him today," he said.

"No." Joshua had walked behind a cash register by the bookshelves, and with a series of muted clicks the fluorescent lights began to go out. "He wouldn't do anything while this same sun is up. It's got to be a new day. Everything is too . . . *waked up* today."

Crane saw that tears were still running down the old man's cheeks. "How about a—a *different* hundred-dollar bill?" Crane asked awkwardly.

"I couldn't touch any of your money." The old man was pulling bills out of the cash register and seemed to be shielding them from Crane's very sight. "Could you leave now? Don't you think you've done enough?"

Crane's eye fixed on a shelf displaying "Floral Remedies" and unhappily he wondered what maladies flowers might need remedies for. He nodded, abashed, and started toward the door, but after a couple of steps he paused and then turned around. "Look," he said harshly, "did you think there was no . . . *teeth* to this stuff? I mean, you do this for a living. Did it for a living. Was it all just a tea party for old ladies and college girls? Didn't you *know* there's monsters out there?"

"I certainly do now," the old man said. "And I think you're one of them."

Crane looked around in the dimness at the innocuous paintings and books and jars of herbs. "I sure hope," he said, and he walked out of the spoiled card-reading parlor and into the hammering rain.

Though his day was two days gone, Snayheever was wearing his feathered Indian headdress again. The feathers were drooping in the rain.

He was sitting on the wet grass of the narrow parklike area along the Strip side of the Mirage—in front of him, beyond the railing where even in the rain the dark silhouettes of tourists jostled each other and hefted video cameras, the choppy water of the lagoon stretched to the foot of the volcano—and though the night wind was laden with the smells of car exhaust and damp clothing, he felt as if he were far underwater. When the wind blew the wet feathers across his vision, they looked like fronds and sea fans.

It kept back the pain of his ruined hand. When he had regained consciousness last night, lying on the plywood floor of the Boulder Highway box, he had looked at his right hand and just wept. The bullet had simply blown it apart, and one finger was gone, lost. He had tried to drive the old Morris back to Las Vegas, but it was too difficult to reach across with his left hand to work the stick shift, and anyway, he couldn't see clearly—every approaching pair of headlights was doubled, and two moons hung in the sky. Eventually he abandoned the car on the shoulder and walked back to town.

It had been a long walk. As his vision began to come back into focus, the pain in his exploded hand had grown to a red-hot throbbing, and so he'd forced his mind back down into the blurriness of the fading concussion.

He had felt like a swimmer letting air bubble out of his lungs in order to sink, and he had dimly realized that it was something like his identity, his personality, his will, that he was surrendering, but he had never treasured those things anyway.

And other people had never seemed to him to be really alive, but now they were diminished to angular mobiles jerking in some unimportant wind, all pretense of three dimensions abandoned. He now knew that people had seemed to have physical depth and volume only because they always faced him, and changed the appearance of their surfaces as he moved.

Now that the people weren't a distraction, he was able to see the gods.

Walking down the rainy Strip sidewalk this evening, feeling as though he were swimming and using his clumsily bandaged hand as a flipper, he had seen them, and the irrelevance of apparent size made them seem at one moment to dwarf the tall casinos as they strode past, and at the next to mimic the hood ornaments on passing cars.

In the open entry of the Imperial Palace he had seen the Magician sitting at a green felt table on which were a stack of coins, a cup, and an eyeball; and, on stilt-long legs of which the knees were the thickest part, mummied Death had walked down the center of the street, throwing a faint shudder through the crowds of stick figures; and the Hanged Man had swayed in the darkening sky over the Flamingo, the upside-down face placid as it stared down at Snayheever.

The silhouettes in front of him were growing agitated now, and Snayheever got to his feet. Flames had begun to billow from the top of the volcano.

But suddenly it wasn't the Mirage volcano. It was the Tower, tall and vast and so old that its stones were eroded like a natural outcrop of the earth, and a dazzling bolt of lightning lashed down out of the sky to hammer at the breaking crenellations of its battlements; huge chunks of masonry turned in the air as they fell in slow motion, and a robed figure that could only be the Emperor fell with them.

Snayheever turned and swam away into the relative dimness of the casinos along the Strip.

CHAPTER 25

And You've Saved Yourself for Me

Out over the desert the thunderclouds gathered like vast tall ships, and the hard rain lifted hazes of dust and then filled the stream beds and washes with rushing brown water. The long, curving line of I–15 darkened and soon shone with the headlights that moved along it like slow tracer bullets.

On Fremont Street the wet cars glistened with reflected neon rainbows, and the children who waited for their parents on the carpeted sidewalks huddled in the casino doorways. The hiss of the rain was the dominant sound—it muffled the rattle and rapid-fire clang of the slot machines, and though the strikers in front of Binion's Horseshoe kept on walking back and forth with their signs, the shouting of the young woman picketer was less strident without her electric megaphone.

Inside the casinos there was only the occasional whiff of wet hair to let people know it was raining outside, but at the Blackjack tables face cards were being turned up about half the time, and actively played Roulette tables were hard to find, owing to the number of wheels that had been shut down for testing because they came up with the zero and double zero more often than they should, and a number of elderly slot machine players had to be led out in tears, complaining that the machines were glaring at them.

Traffic was heavy south of Fremont Street—buses and old VW bugs and new Rolls-Royces and a procession of white Chevrolet El Caminos—and there were lines of people in gowns and tuxedoes standing patiently in the white-lit rain outside the wedding chapels. The big casinos to the south, the Sands and Caesars Palace and the Mirage and the Flamingo, were flares of lurid color in the wet night.

On the roof of the towering pink and white edifice that was

the Circus Circus, in among cables and conduits, below the forest of antennas and satellite dishes, Diana clutched her robe to herself and shivered as the rain drummed and rattled around her.

The city, spread out below her in all its palaces and incandescent arteries, seemed as far away as the dark clouds overhead; the distant moon, not even visible now, seemed closer.

She had called the hospital an hour ago, and Dr. Bandholtz had told her that Scat's condition was a little worse.

The boy had already been connected to a catheter that was inserted under his collarbone and somehow threaded through a vein and then through the "right heart" and lodged in the pulmonary artery—it was to make sure the blood pressure in the lungs didn't rise, for the lungs would not be able to absorb oxygen if it did—but now he was breathing through an "endotrachial tube" taped into his mouth. If his breathing didn't stabilize soon, they were going to put him on an IMV, which she gathered was some very serious kind of ventilator.

After getting off the phone with the hospital, she had called her own apartment number.

And she had sighed with relief and frustration when Hans had answered. At least he was still alive.

"Hans," she'd told him, "you've got to get out of there; it's not safe."

"Diana," he had said, "*I* trust the *police.*"

She had waited wearily for him to tell her that if she had let the police handle the kidnapping last night, Scat would not be dying in the hospital. He had told her that when she'd called last night, and she had hung up on him, and she knew she'd do the same if he said it again.

He didn't. "Besides," he said, "your foster-brother shot the guy, right?"

"No, don't you listen? The man who shot Scat is somebody else, and he knows where I live, and he's probably still in town. *Get out of that apartment.*"

"If you're evicting me," Hans said pompously, "I am entitled to at least thirty days' notice."

"These people won't give you thirty *seconds*' notice, you idiot!" She reflected that Hans was guilty of what Ozzie had used to call *felony stupid*. "I'll call the cops and tell them about your dope plants, and—"

"Have you visited Scat today?" he interrupted angrily.

Quietly she said, ". . . No."

"Hmm, somehow I had thought not. Are you going to tonight?"

"I don't know."

"I see. Why don't you consult a Ouija board," he said, his voice quavering with the weight of his sarcasm, "to see if it would be *safe?*"

"*Get out of there!*" she yelled. She had hung up on him then. *If it would be safe.*

Alfred Funo, she thought now as the rain clattered in the puddles around her bare feet. Someday I hope to be able to deal with Mr. Alfred Funo.

Funo had vacated the motel before the police arrived there last night, but his exit seemed to have been hasty, and they had found a couple of 9-millimeter bullets under the bed. Diana was in no doubt that Funo was the man who had shot her son.

And there were others out there: this Snayheever creature, and the fat man in the Jaguar, and, according to Ozzie, dozens of others.

Bathe in the fresh, wild water of this place, Ozzie had told her.

Her wet skirt, shoes, blouse, and underwear were draped over a taut cable on a big air-conditioning unit, and now she opened her robe and let it fall behind her and stood naked in the thrashing rain.

Mother, she thought, looking up at the sky. *Mother, hear your daughter. I need your help.*

A minute passed, during which all that happened was that the rain abated a little and the air got colder. The puddles around her feet were fizzing and bubbling, as if she were bathing in soda water. She shivered and clenched her teeth to keep them from chattering.

What am I doing? she asked herself suddenly. I'll be arrested out here. None of this is true.

She turned toward where her clothes hung in the darkness, then paused.

Ozzie believes it, she thought. You owe him a lot; can't you make yourself believe it, too, just for a few minutes?

And what other chance have you and your children got?

What *do* I believe, anyway? That I'm able to find a man to share my life with? That Scat is okay, really? That Oliver is actually a normal boy? That I am able to have the one thing I need like flowers need sunlight, a family that's something more than a pathetic caricature of a family? What reason have you ever had for believing any of *that*?

I will try believing *this*, she thought as tears trickled into the cold rainwater on her face. I am the daughter of the moon goddess. I *am* that. And I can call her.

Again she looked up into the cloudy sky. The rain suddenly came down even harder than before and stung her face and shoulders and breasts, but now, even when the gusting wind made her step back to keep her balance, she wasn't cold. Her heart was pounding, and her outstretched fingers tingled, and the twenty-nine-story abyss beyond the roof edge, which had made her nervous when she had first forced the roof door and stepped out here, was exhilarating.

For a moment an old, old reflex made her wish her foster-brother Scott could be out here experiencing this with her, but she forced the thought away.

Mother. She tried to throw the thought up into the sky like a spear. *They want to kill* me, *now. Help me fight them.*

Dimly through the rushing dark clouds above her she glimpsed for a moment a crescent glowing in the sky.

The clouds seemed now to be huge wings, or capes, and under the hiss of the rain she thought she could hear music, a chorus of thousands of voices, faint only because of titanic distance.

Another hard gust of wind made a horizontal spray of the rain, and all at once she was sure that she wasn't alone on the rooftop.

She braced herself against the taut cable, for the gust had made the tar-paper surface of the roof seem to sway like the deck of a ship. And then her nostrils flared to the impossible briny smell of the sea, and the booming thunder sounded like tall waves crashing against cliffs.

Salt spray stung her eyes, and when she was able to blink

around again, she saw, numbly and with a violent shiver, that she *was* on a ship—she was leaning on a wooden railing, and the forecastle ladder was a few yards ahead of her across the planks of the deck. Breakers crashed on rocks somewhere out in the darkness.

It happened when I thought of a ship, she told herself frantically. Something really *is* going on here, but it's dressing itself with my imagination.

Again she could see the glowing crescent above her, but now she saw that it wasn't the moon—and it couldn't have been when she'd seen it a few moments ago, for she remembered that the moon was at its half phase tonight. The crescent was on the crown of a tall woman standing up there on the high forecastle deck. The woman was robed, and her face was strong and beautiful but without any trace of humanity in the open eyes.

The chorus was louder now, perhaps on the shore out in the darkness, and the sounds in the sky were clearly the rushing of wings.

When Diana's forehead touched the wet planks of the deck, she realized that she had fallen to her hands and knees.

For she had realized in the deepest, oldest core of her mind that this was the goddess. This was Isis, who in ancient Egypt had restored the murdered and dismembered sun-god Osiris, who was her brother and husband; this was Ishtar, who in Babylonia had rescued Tammuz from the underworld; she was Artemis, twin sister of Apollo, and she was also both Pallas Athena, the goddess of virginity, and Eileithyia, the goddess of childbirth.

To her the Greeks had sacrificed a maiden before sailing to Troy; she had restored life to her son Horus, slain by the bite of a scorpion; and though wild animals were sacred to her, she was the huntress of the gods.

This was Persephone, the maiden of the spring and the lover of Adonis, who had been stolen away to the underworld by the king of the dead.

Then the awe had washed through Diana, or had been broken for her, and again she was aware of herself as a woman named Diana Ryan, resident of a city called Las Vegas.

She stood up, carefully, on the shifting deck.

The woman on the higher deck was looking into her eyes,

and Diana realized that the woman loved her, had loved her as an infant and had continued to love her during these thirty years of their separation.

Mother! Diana thought, and started forward. The deck planks were bumpily slick under her bare soles.

But now there were figures between herself and the ladder, facing her and blocking her way. She squinted through the spray at the nearest one—and, suddenly and completely, she felt the night's cold.

It was Wally Ryan, her ex-husband, who had died in the car crash two years ago. His eyes, under his rain-plastered hair, were placid and blank—but it was clear that he would not let her pass.

Next to him stood Hans, his scanty beard dark with rain. Oh, no, she thought, is he a ghost, too? Did they kill him trying to get me? But I talked to him less than an hour ago!

There were a couple of other figures, too, but she didn't look at their faces.

She looked up at the woman, who seemed to be staring down at her with love and pity.

Diana stepped back. The booming of surf was louder. The half-heard song of the distant chorusing voices had taken on a threatening monotony.

They're not ghosts, she thought. That's not what this is about. Hans isn't dead. These are images of the men who have been my lovers.

The men I've lived with are keeping me from going to my mother.

As she'd been able to do in dreams that had begun to dissolve into wakefulness, Diana tried to will the phantoms away—but they stayed where they were, as apparently solid as the deck and the railing. This was her own imagination, but she wasn't in control.

Why? she thought unhappily. Was I supposed to have stayed a *virgin* all these years?

She squinted up through the rain into the eyes of the goddess, and she tried to believe that the answer was no. For a length of time that might have been no more than a minute, while the figures in front of her didn't move except to sway with the rocking deck, and the rain rattled like chips of clay on the deck all around her, she went on trying to believe that the answer was no.

Eventually she gave up.

Mentally she tried to convey the idea that it wasn't fair, that she was a person living in this world, not some other world.

Then, looking down at her own bare feet on the deck, she tried to remember, for her mother, what each of the circumstances had been.

And she couldn't remember.

Mother, she thought, looking up again in despair, *is there no way for me to reach you?*

And then a concept flashed into her mind, abstract and free of any words or images. As it faded, she tried to hold words up to it to define it for herself—*Token?* she thought; *relic, link, talisman, keepsake?* Something from some time when we were together?

Then it was gone, and all she had left were the remembered words she had tried to fit to it.

Lightning flared out over the lights of the city, and the following boom was thunder, not surf. She was on the roof of the Circus Circus, alone and shivering in the rain.

She stood for several minutes, looking into the sky; then she reluctantly got back into her sopping clothes and shuffled away toward the roof door.

Nardie Dinh had felt it coming, the terribly close approach of the moon, which was not yet her own mother.

Luckily she hadn't had a fare. She had spun the cab's wheel and cut across two wet lanes of the Strip, drawing angry honks from the cars behind her, and stomped the cab to a halt at a red curb by the Hacienda Camperland south of Tropicana Avenue.

Even as she was switching off the engine, she lost consciousness.

And she dreamed. In the dream she was back in the long, high-ceilinged room in the parlor house near Tonopah, and though the twenty-two pictures on the walls seemed to be moving in their frames, she didn't look at them.

The walls boomed and creaked around her, as if all the girls in the little rooms around this one were busy with enormous clients, minotaurs and satyrs instead of mere businessmen and truck drivers. She sat down on the carpeted floor and made herself breathe evenly, quietly; hoping that, even in a dream, her brother's ruling would still apply—that his half-sister was to be a prisoner in the midst of this carnal focus but was not to participate in any way.

The pictures were making sounds now. She could hear faint laughter and screaming and martial music. Their frames were rattling against the plaster walls.

Then there was another rattling, the knob of the door in front of her. With her hands and feet she scuffed herself backward until she was stopped by the wall opposite the door. Above her, she remembered, hung the picture of the Fool.

The door swung open, and her brother stepped into the room.

His black hair was oiled and swept back in a ducktail, but incongruously he wore a floor-length sable robe. In his right hand he carried a tall gold cross with a looped top, the Egyptian ankh.

"Dreaming at last, my sweet little Asian sister," said Ray-Joe Pogue in his affectedly mellifluous voice. His lean face was twisted into a smile, and he walked slowly toward her. The pictures banged violently against the walls as he passed them. "And you've saved yourself for me."

"Not for you," she managed to say, loudly enough to be heard over all the racket. *Wake up,* she told herself urgently. *Push your forehead into the horn ring, open the car door, listen for calls from the dispatcher.*

"And right here in town, eh?" he said. "South of me, down by the Marina and the Tropicana. I'm on my way. You and I have got a lot of lost time to make up for. Without the female half of the magic, I've been running into obstacles. I had to kill Max, and then Lake Mead wouldn't take his head. I think the lake might take it from you, or from the two of us once we've coupled. Shall we go see?"

She stood up slowly, dragging her back against the wall, and even when she felt the shaking edge of the Fool's frame against her shoulders, she kept pushing.

The picture came loose from its nail and fell, and for an instant she saw her brother's mouth drop open in dismay—

and when the picture hit the floor, the sound it made wasn't that of wood hitting carpet.

It was the sound of a car horn, and when she lifted her head from the steering wheel the blaring honk stopped, and she sat back, gasping in the driver's seat of her parked taxicab, and watched the windshield wipers sweep away the hard spattering of the rain. With a trembling hand she reached out and twisted the key in the ignition.

The engine started right up, and she put it in gear and carefully pulled out into the traffic.

Escaped it that time, she thought shakily, but now he knows I'm in town. I'll get on the 15 north right now, and get off somewhere up around Fremont Street.

Her face was chilly with sweat.

If I knew how to pray, she thought, I'd say a prayer for the soul of poor old Max, who once loved me, may he nevertheless burn in hell forever.

In the back seat of his newly bought '71 Dodge, parked on a dark side street, Al Funo stretched out and tried to get comfortable. The previous owners had apparently had a dog that liked to travel in the car but hated to take baths.

He had sold his Porsche to a car dealer on Charleston in order to buy classy gifts for Diana and Scott. The two long black jewelry boxes—two solid gold rope necklaces that had cost him nearly a thousand dollars each—were wrapped up in his jacket on the front seat.

He had *had* to buy gifts for his friends, to clear up any misunderstandings—but he was still angry at the car dealer, who had called the Porsche 924 "just a glorified Volkswagen," and had given Funo only thirty-five hundred dollars for it. This Dodge had cost him a thousand, leaving him at the end of the day with only about five hundred dollars. And he didn't want to use a credit card if he could help it; the police would almost certainly know who he was by now, and if he used a card, he'd be leaving a trail.

He would have to get out of town as soon as possible. In addition to the police, Vaughan Trumbill would be after him . . . and Funo could feel a tension in the air, as if someone were leaning harder and harder against a plate glass window, or as if a fever were rising somewhere, with convulsions and hallucinations. Something was going to happen here, and it would probably involve the fat man and Scott and Diana, and Funo wanted to be safely back in L.A. in one of his alternate identities when it broke.

He rolled over on the narrow seat and tried to ignore the drumming of the rain on the roof. Better get some sleep, he told himself, if you're going to go make up with Diana tomorrow.

CHAPTER 26

Thanks a Million, Diana!

At dawn Diana ordered up a pot of coffee from the Circus Circus's room service. Oliver was still asleep in the bed, but she carried her steaming cup to the phone and dialed the number of Ozzie's room.

"Mph. Hello?" His old voice was scratchy. "Diana?"

"Yes," she said. "I—"

"Where are you calling from? Did you go to the hospital yesterday? I told you to stay away—"

She pressed her lips together. "No, I didn't go. I chickened out. Scat wouldn't have known I was there anyway, of course, but I still feel like—like I'm deserting him. Oz, listen, I"—she laughed uncomfortably—"took a shower in the rain last night, and I believe I saw my mother. I got the idea that I couldn't approach her, couldn't talk to her, because I'm not a virgin."

Oliver was awake now, she noticed. The boy rolled his eyes and mimed gagging himself with his forefinger.

Ozzie said, "Give me a minute." She heard the old man put the phone down, and then faintly she heard water running. After a while he came back on. "I wish you *were* still a virgin," he said grumpily. "The young men you—never mind. Okay, that may be true, I think it might be important that the daughter of the moon be a virgin. But you *are* still her actual biological daughter; there may be some way to . . . symbolically get your virginity back, you know? Was there any hint of hope?"

"Well, there was a thought, right at the end, after I asked her if there was a way for me to reach her. It was an idea, something like 'relic,' or 'link.' Something from when I was with her, back thirty years ago. I've been thinking about this most of the night; and I think if I could get some *thing* that belonged to her, to the Lady Issit, connecting me with her, I could reach her."

"God, I don't know how you'd do that. I suppose if you could find out where she came from or something—"

"Oz, that old baby blanket you brought me home in, when you and Scott came out here in 1960—was that something you had brought with you in the car, or did you find me in it?"

"Yes!" said the old man excitedly. "Yes, you were wrapped up in it, when I found you there behind the bushes! Do you still have it?"

"Well, not on me. But I think I know where it is at home. I'm going to send Oliver to your room. If I don't get killed getting the blanket this morning, I'll have you paged in the— the lobby of the Riviera, that's right across the street, at ten this morning. If I ask for Oliver Crane, you'll know I'm all right; if it's for Ozzie Smith, you'll know they've got me, and I'll want you to take my boy Oliver to the house of a friend of mine in Searchlight. Her name's Helen Sully, she's in the book, I used to work with her. Helen Sully, write it down, okay? She'll be happy to put him up; she's got a lot of kids of her own." Despite her resolve to be cool and businesslike about all this, there were tears on her cheeks and her voice quavered when she went on. "Have Scott do everything he can to protect Scat, even die; it's his fault my boy got shot."

Oliver had sat up in bed, but his expression was one of languid impatience. "I don't want to go somewhere with the old man," he began, but his mother silenced him with a wave.

"No, Diana," Ozzie was saying, his voice shaky, "I'll go, they won't care about me—"

"You wouldn't know where to look for it, Ozzie; it might not be exactly where I think it is. I'll be quick—no, listen to me, I'll pad myself out to look fat and wear a wig or something, and I'll go in a cab, so if somebody's watching the place, they won't be sure it's me"—she was talking loudly over the old man's shrill protests—"and then I'll leave by the back door and hop the fence and walk out on Sun Avenue, catch another cab on Civic Center."

"I'll tear the house up until I find it, Diana," Ozzie shouted, "I—"

"They're after you, too, Oz," she said. "If they're there, they wouldn't give you the time to find it. Ten o'clock, lobby of the Riviera. 'Ozzie Smith' means run for it."

She hung up in the middle of the old man's pleadings.

Ozzie had hung up, too, and immediately punched in 911. As soon as a woman had answered, he had begun talking fast, trying to find the words and delivery that would get police to Diana's house most quickly.

Sitting on the hotel bed now but leaning forward over the telephone cradle, Ozzie held the handset tightly in his lean, brown-spotted hand.

"My name's Oliver Crane," he was saying shrilly, "and her name is Diana, uh, Ryan. I *am* calm. Fifteen fifteen Venus, in North Las Vegas. Her son was kidnapped and shot last night, you'll have records of it. . . . No, I don't know what this guy looks like; his name is Alfred Funo. . . . Your detective said today. . . . *Trust* me, she's in danger! . . . What? . . . Yeah, there'll be her idiot boyfriend there, his name is Hans. . . . No, I don't know his last name . . . six foot, fat, scraggly beard. She'll be coming in a cab. . . . Of course I don't know what company! No, I won't be here; I'm going over there right now. . . . No, I'm going, I have to be there. Listen, try to make it *two* units, okay?"

Ozzie hung up the phone, and he had barely had time to put on his pants and a shirt before there was a knock at his hotel room door.

He hobbled across the room and let the fat little boy in.

"Where's your mother?" Ozzie snapped, stepping out onto the hall carpet to peer up and down the corridor.

Oliver shrugged. "She's gone. She held the elevator until she saw your door open. She'll be in a taxi before you can get your shoes on." He walked to the window and pulled open the drapes.

Ozzie winced at the white desert sunlight. "I'll have my shoes on soon enough, sonny." He glanced instinctively at his portable coffeepot. No time for that, he thought. He hesitated—*No*, he thought, *I'll need it*—then walked quickly to the dressing table and with trembling fingers opened a Ziploc plastic bag and shook a lot of instant coffee into one of the hotel glasses.

"Now listen," he said as he carried the glass into the bathroom, "I'm going to leave you somewhere out in the children's area here." He turned on the hot-water tap in the sink. "And I want you to wait there for me, y'understand?" he shouted over the roar of the faucet. The water heated up quickly, and he ran some into the glass and stirred the foamy brown stuff with the handle of a Circus Circus souvenir toothbrush. "I'll be gone for only an hour or so, I think, but if noon rolls around and I'm still gone, you call the police and tell them everything, and tell them you need to be hidden from the same people that shot your brother."

"Everybody's ditching me," said Oliver.

Ozzie hurried back into the room and sat down on the bed near his shoes. "I'm sorry," he told the boy. "It's just that there's trouble, and we don't want you to get into it." He drained the barely hot double-strength coffee in one fast series of gulps. *"Jesus."* He shook his head. "Oh, and *don't* call these Amino Acids friends of yours, okay? Do you promise?"

The boy shuddered. "I'm grown up. I can decide who I talk to."

"Not in this kettle of fish, kid." Ozzie tossed the empty cup aside and, with an effortful grunt, bent down and picked up his shoes and began levering them onto his bare feet. "This is stuff you don't know about. Trust me, I'm your grandfather, and we're doing this for your mother's safety."

When the boy spoke again, his voice was pitched lower. "Call me Bitin Dog."

Ozzie closed his eyes. I can't go, he thought. If I leave this kid alone, he's going to call his evil friends, sure as I'm sitting here.

Well . . .

Well, so I stay here, and *don't* go over there to Venus Avenue. The cops will be there. What could one old man do for her that the cops couldn't? Especially an old man whose guts are acting up and who wouldn't have had time to properly go to the bathroom.

"Well, Mr. Bitin Dog," he said tiredly, "maybe you've got a point about everybody ditching you. Maybe you and I could . . . just go have breakfast somewhere—"

"Somewhere where they serve beer," the boy interrupted. "You order it, and then I can drink it when they're not looking, okay?"

"No, you can't have any beer. My God, it's not yet eight in the morning." He was still holding the laces of his right shoe, and to his dull surprise he saw that his knobby old fingers were tying them. Socks, he told himself; if you're not going to Venus, you've got time to put on socks.

His fingers finished the knot and moved, apparently of their own volition, to the other shoe.

"Oh, and you're too young for beer anyway," he said. "I was going to say, before you interrupted me, that you and I could go have breakfast somewhere after we go by your mom's house to make sure she's okay." The shoes were tied, and he stood up, feeling frail. The coffee felt like a shovelful of road tar in his stomach. "You ready to go? We want to get there before she does. We'll be hurrying and she won't, and I hope she'll have the sense to make her cabbie circle the block a time or two first, but she's got a head start on us. Come on."

"What if I don't want to go to—" the boy began, but he flinched back and stopped talking when the old man turned a hard glare on him.

"Come on," Ozzie repeated softly.

Oliver stared at him for a moment; then he let his shoulders droop and he was just a little boy again, and he followed his grandfather out of the room.

Hans was justifiably upset.

The police had actually been pointing *drawn revolvers* at him when he had answered their urgent knocking—of all the John Wayne stunts!—but they had holstered them when he answered the door and blinked at them in sleepy astonishment, and now, as he tremblingly made coffee in the little kitchen, Hans was at least grateful that Diana's crazy old foster-father had given them a *description* of him. Evidently if they hadn't recognized him as Diana's reported "boyfriend," they'd have handcuffed him and thrown him on the floor!

He looked over the counter at the two policemen standing on a patch of sunlit carpet by the front window. "You guys want coffee?"

The older cop, Gould, gave him a blank look and shook his head. "No, thank you."

"Huh." Hans watched the glass pot steam up as the hot coffee started to trickle into it. "Completely nuts," he went on, trying not to talk too fast or sound ingratiating. "The old man—and Diana's brother, too—think she's this Egyptian goddess Isis."

"We're not concerned with their religious beliefs, Mr. Ganci."

"Fine." Hans shrugged and nodded virtuously. "I *told* them to go to the police last night."

"So you said."

Officer Gould nodded out the window. "I think Hamilton sees a cab."

Hans walked around the counter and peered with them out through the window. One of the officers standing by the second police car out at the curb was staring intently down the street toward Civic Center Drive. After a few seconds a yellow taxicab pulled up behind the police car, and a moment later a fat woman got out.

Hans was about to tell them that it wasn't Diana, but then he saw the woman's face. He blinked and rubbed his eyes. It *was* Diana, but she had stuffed something into the rear end of her pants and the belly of her shirt, so that she looked both fat and pregnant. "Yeah," he said wonderingly, "that's her."

The policeman outside, Hamilton, apparently, walked up to her as she was paying the driver, and then he was escorting her toward the apartment.

As the cab drove away and Hamilton and Diana hurried up the walk toward the front door, Hans was annoyed to see that Diana *didn't* look annoyed by the officious policemen. Attention from a man in uniform, he thought.

The older officer pushed past Hans and opened the door. Diana and Hamilton walked inside, bringing the fresh smells of lawns and pavement into the musty dimness. Hans wished her foster-father had called to say that police would be coming over; he would have showered.

"As Officer Hamilton probably told you, ma'am," Gould said to Diana, "we got a phone call saying that your life was in danger. It was from an Oliver Crane, who we gather is your foster-father?"

"Your loony dad," put in Hans helpfully.

"Shut up, Hans," Diana said.

"Why don't you go sit down while we talk to her, Mr. Ganci?" said Gould, not very politely.

Ozzie's cab had rounded the Venus corner just in time for him to see the officer walk into the house with the ludicrously padded Diana, and he sighed and relaxed and sat back on the black vinyl seat.

"It looks like your mom's okay," he said over his shoulder to Oliver, who was sitting in the back seat.

"Smells like puke in here," said the boy.

The driver, who looked as though he might have been a boxer years ago, gave the boy an irritated glance in the rearview mirror. "You want me to stop?"

"Uh . . ." Ozzie couldn't take the boy into the house—gunfire or something still might erupt at any moment—but if he left him alone in the cab, he'd probably run away. "No, just park here. I want to see her leave with the cops."

"You got it." The man pulled in to the curb a couple of buildings down from Diana's duplex and put the engine into park.

Hans had watched with interest when Hamilton had gone cautiously through the house to make sure no killers were crouched in any of the rooms, and he had been making mental notes so that he could incorporate a scene like this into his screenplay; there was nothing like firsthand observation.

But when the officer said he'd check out the backyard, Hans could only sit down, as the man walked out the back door and down the two wooden steps, and hope no one was noticing how pale and sweaty he had suddenly become.

The dope plants, he thought with astonished dismay. He'll find the dope plants, and I'll go to jail. I'll claim I don't know anything about them, I thought those were just weeds out there by the fence. Will they think I'm a dealer? Will they find out I'm a friend of Mike's, who really *is* a dope dealer? I read in Hunter Thompson that you get . . . *life in prison!* . . . in Nevada if you're convicted of being a dealer. That can't still be true.

He thought he might wet his pants, right here and now. God, he thought, make him not find them. Please, God! I'll go to church, I'll make the protagonist of the screenplay a Christian, I'll marry Diana, just *let him come back with no news so the world can go on being like it was.*

He was afraid to pick up his cup of coffee. His hands would shake, and these cops would notice; they were trained to see that kind of thing. Instead, he looked around at the apartment; every trivial object suddenly seemed precious and lost, like the bicycles and fishing poles in the backgrounds of old photographs. He looked at Diana and loved her as he had never managed to before.

The back door creaked, and then boots clonked on the linoleum floor. Hans pretended to be studying the calendar over the telephone.

"You're the lady whose son was kidnapped and shot last night, aren't you?" he heard Hamilton say. Diana must have nodded, for the man went on, "And this is your boyfriend? He lives here with you?" There was a pause. "Okay." Hans heard him sigh. "I'm going to come back here in an hour or two, after I've looked up the shape of a certain sort of leaf in a book at the station, right?" There was another pause. *"Right?"*

Hans looked up and realized that the officer was talking to him now. His face was instantly hot. "Right," he said in a small voice.

Gould had been talking on his portable radio, and now he tucked it back into his belt. "Frits says the old man is eighty-two years old and didn't seem real clear about anything, even why he's in town. And the 911 operator said it almost sounded like he'd dreamed up this emergency. I think he's just upset and disoriented about his grandson." He looked at Diana. "I think we can leave. But be careful about things like answering

the door, Mrs. Ryan, and call us if you get any odd phone calls
or visitors."

"I will," Diana said, smiling. She shook hands with the cop.
"Thanks for the help, even if it was a false alarm."

When the police finally left, and the door closed and Hans
heard the engines start up and drive away, he picked up his
coffee mug and threw it against the wall.

Hot coffee splashed all over the kitchen, and ceramic fragments rattled and spun on the floor.

"This is your goddamned family's fault!" he shouted.

Diana had hurried into the bedroom, and he stomped after
her.

"What'll I do with those plants?" he demanded. "Bury them?
I can't carry them out to the trash; they're *waiting* for me
to do something like that!" She had thrown open the chest
in which she kept old things like her high school annuals,
and was tossing dolls and music boxes out onto the floor.
"And they'll be watching me now," he went on, "anytime I
drive down the street! How can I *possibly* go see *Mike*?" He
punched the wall, leaving a dent in the drywall. "Thanks a
million, Diana! I thought you were *gone*!"

She stood up, holding some kind of little old ratty yellow
blanket. "I am now," she said.

The telephone in the kitchen rang.

"Don't answer it!" she said urgently, so he ran back to the
kitchen and triumphantly picked up the receiver.

"Hello?"

She was right behind him, still holding the foolish little
blanket. He was pleased to see that her I've-got-more-
important-things-on-my-mind-than-you look was gone. She
was just scared now. Good.

"You say you want to talk to Diana?" he said, drawing out
the pleasure of this moment.

She was white, shaking her head at him with the most
imploring look he'd ever seen on a human face. "No," she
whispered, "Hans, please!"

For a moment he almost relented, almost said, *No, she
hasn't been home since yesterday; her sister's here if you
want to talk to her*. Diana had suffered enough in this last
twenty-four hours—leaving behind all her possessions, her son
near dead in the hospital . . .

Through her own fault, and in the face of his sound advice. And now his dope plants were as good as gone, and he was a marked man in the eyes of the police.

His smile was crooked with sweet malice. "Su-u-re," he said, "she's right here."

At the first word she had taken off running for the back door, shouting at him to follow her.

He had even put the phone down and taken one step after her before he remembered his pride. I don't need some damned hysterical woman, he told himself. I'm a writer—a creator all by myself.

CHAPTER 27

I Don't Mind the Car, but Could We Go Now?

With a last glance at the duplex across the street Trumbill laid the telephone receiver down on the table, picked up the little radio transmitter, and stood up. He had put on his pants and shirt and shoes when the police had arrived, and now he carried the transmitter around the corner into the hall, away from the glass of the front window.

Diana sprinted between the trash cans and the gas barbecue and pounded across the scruffy grass toward the redwood fence at the back of the lot, and even as she wondered if she was just making a fool of herself, she leaped, caught the splintery tops of the boards, and vaulted over the fence into the next yard.

A startled dog looked up at her, but before it could even bark she had crossed the yard and scrambled over a chain-link gate and dashed down somebody's driveway and was running across the empty expanse of Sun Avenue, the old yellow blanket flailing from her pumping fist.

Ozzie had opened the cab door and swung his feet out onto the curb and had started to stand up—

—when the hard *bam* punched the air and slammed the car door against him, knocking him over onto the curbside grass.

The front of Diana's apartment had exploded out across the street in a million spinning boards and chunks of masonry, and as Ozzie sat, stunned, on the grass, he watched a cloud of dirty smoke mushroom up into the blue sky. All he could hear was the loud ringing in his ears, but he could see pieces of brick and roof tile thudding into the lawn at his right and shattering on the suddenly smoke-fogged sidewalk, and his nose stung with a sharp chemical tang like ozone.

Oliver was out of the back of the cab and running toward the destroyed apartment. The cabdriver was pulling Ozzie to his feet; the man was shouting something, but Ozzie shook him off and started after the boy.

It was like walking in certain frustrating dreams he often had. The effort of dragging one leg, and then the other, through the thick soup of the air was so exhausting that he had to look down at the littered sidewalk to make sure that he was moving forward and not simply flexing and sweating in place.

A two-foot length of metal pipe whacked the pavement in front of him and instantly sprang away to devastate a curbside bush, and he had dimly, distantly heard it ring when it hit. Perhaps he was not permanently deafened. He kept walking, though it was not getting any easier.

The apartment was a hollowed-out shell, with three walls leaning outward and the roof entirely gone. A yard-long jet of flame fluttered where the kitchen had been. The apartment next door looked relatively whole, though there was no glass in any of the windows.

Oliver was standing on the walkway with his arms spread wide, and then he fell to his knees and seemed to be stressfully vomiting or convulsing, and it seemed to Ozzie that the boy was forcing himself to do it—even though the spasms looked to be tearing his ribs apart—the way a person might cut his hand to bloody ribbons just to cut out of the flesh the unbearable foreignness of an intrusive splinter.

A moment later Ozzie blinked and rubbed his eyes, wondering if he had suffered a concussion when the car door hit him, for he seemed to be seeing double—next to the little boy crouched on the walkway, and half overlapping him, was a semi-transparent duplicate image of the boy.

Then, though young Oliver didn't move, the duplicate image stood up, turned away, and stepped into invisibility.

Ozzie was having trouble breathing, and when he breathed out sharply, he realized that his nose was bleeding. There must be blood all down the front of his shirt.

He finally hobbled his way to Oliver, who was kneeling now. Ozzie knelt beside him. The boy's face was red and twisted with violent sobbing, and when Ozzie put his arms around him, he clung to the old man as if he were the only other person in the world.

In the laundry room of the apartment building on the other side of Sun Avenue, Diana braced herself against a washing machine and waited for her breathing and heartbeat to slow down.

She was too stunned by the almighty slam that had shaken the street under her feet to cry, but in her head was nothing but an endlessly repeating wail of *Hans, Hans, Hans* . . .

At last she was able to breathe through her nose, and she straightened up. Mostly because she found herself facing a washing machine, she fished three quarters out of her pocket, laid them in the holes in the machine's handle, and pushed it in.

The machine went on with a clunk, and she could hear water running inside the thing. The still air smelled of bleach and detergent.

Hans, you damned, arrogant, posing fool, she thought—you didn't deserve a whole lot, but you deserved better than this.

She forced herself not to remember the times, in bed but also cooking dinner or out with Scat and Oliver on a holiday, when he had been thoughtful and tender and humorous.

"Was that a bomb?" came a woman's voice behind her.

Diana turned around. A white-haired woman pushing an aluminum walker was angling in through the door, kicking along in front of her a plastic basket full of clothes.

Diana knew she should say something, seem curious. "I don't know," she said. "Uh . . . it sounded like one."

"I wish I could go look. I was shoving this stuff down the breezeway, and *boom*, I see all this shit go flying into the air! Probably it was a dope factory."

"A dope factory."

"PCP," the old woman said. "Could you put my clothes in here? It kills me to bend over."

"Sure." Diana stuffed the yellow blanket into her tight hip pocket, then hauled the clothes out of the basket and dumped them into a washer.

"They need chemicals like ether and stuff to make their PCP, and they gotta cook it. And since they're dopers, they get careless. Boom!" The old woman looked at the other machine, which was spinning its empty drum. "Honey, these machines are for tenants only."

"I just moved in." Diana dug a twenty-dollar bill out of her pocket. "I don't have a car yet. Could I pay somebody here to drive me to work? It's just—just over at the college."

The old woman eyed the bill. "I can drive you, if you can wait for my stuff to get done, and if you don't mind being seen in a beat-up ten-year-old Plymouth."

"I don't mind the car, but could we go now?"

"What about your clothes?"

Diana waved at a wooden shelf on the white wall. "I'm sure the next person to use the machine will just put 'em aside."

"I'm sure." The old woman took the twenty. "Okay, if you'll fish my stuff out again and carry it all back to my apartment for me. I can do mine later, I guess."

"Great," said Diana. Her elbows and knees had begun shaking, and she knew she was going to break down crying very soon, and she didn't want it to happen while she was still anywhere near this tract of unlucky celestial bodies.

Crane was about to leave his room at the Circus Circus when the telephone rang.

He had left a note for Mavranos, who was off somewhere chasing his statistical phase-change, and had tucked the .357 into his belt and zipped up his nylon jacket, and now he paused with his hand on the doorknob and stared at the ringing phone.

Ozzie or Arky, he thought. Even Diana doesn't know we're here. If it's Arky, he'll want me to go help him in some fool way, and I've got to get out to Spider Joe's trailer. Of course, if it's Ozzie, he might have some news about Diana, some way I can help her, some way I can maybe at least fractionally redeem myself with her.

For Diana, he thought as he started back toward the phone, I'll put Spider Joe off for another day.

He picked up the phone. "Hello?"

At first he couldn't tell who it was—only that it was someone sobbing.

"What?" said Crane uneasily. "Speak!"

"It's Ozzie, son," came the old man's voice, choked with tears. "I'm at the police station again, and they want you to come down, too. And Archimedes."

"Why? Quick!"

"She's dead, Scott." The old man sniffed. "Diana's dead. She went back to her apartment to get something, and they blew her up. I was there, I saw it—I would have followed her in, but I had Oliver with me—oh God, what good have I been to either one of you?"

Diana was dead.

All the tension and hope went out of Crane, and when he spoke, it was with the gentle relaxation of total despair. "You've . . . been a good father, Ozzie. Everybody dies, but nobody gets a father better than you've been to both of us. She loved you, and I love you, and we both always knew you loved us." He sighed, and then yawned. "Oz—go home now. Go back to the things you said you liked, your Louis L'Amour novels and your Kaywoodie pipes." Go gentle into that good night, he thought; rest easy with the dying of the light.

The telephone receiver was fatiguingly heavy, but Crane hung it up without a sound.

For a while he sat on the bed, hardly thinking at all. He knew that the police wanted to talk to him and would eventually knock on his door, but he had no impulse either to seek them out or to avoid them.

The telephone was ringing again. He let it ring.

He had read that the weight of the air at sea level was fourteen pounds per square inch. Vaguely he wondered if he would be able to stand up against that, or even keep from falling backward across the bed.

Eventually a smell broke through to him. A morning smell, he knew what it was—hot coffee.

He turned his head toward the bedside table—and then started violently.

A steaming coffee cup stood there beside the clock, a white McDonald's "Good Morning" cup like the ones he and Susan had somehow acquired half a dozen of.

He stood up and left the room.

The police might come looking for him at the carousel bar, so he took the elevator all the way down to the ground floor and walked out the front doors of the Circus Circus, across the broad parking lot to where a giant white stone ape waved at the traffic coursing south on the brightly sunlit expanse of Las Vegas Boulevard. He flagged a cab and asked to be taken to the Flamingo.

When it dropped him off, he walked slowly across the crowded sidewalk and up the steps and through the brass-framed glass doors into the casino, then threaded his way through the sudden carpeted dimness between the slot machines and the Blackjack tables to the bar at the back.

"A shot of Wild Turkey," he told the waitress who eventually strode over to his corner table, "and a Bud chaser. Oh, and could I have a telephone brought over to this table? I'm expecting a call."

The bar was nearly empty at this early morning hour, and was brightly enough lit so that the casino floor beyond the open arch was a darkness full of meaningless clanging and flashing lights.

"Honey, I can bring you a phone, but you better call whoever it is. We got a lot of lines—the odds are bad on you *getting* any call."

Crane just nodded and waved.

He leaned back and looked nervously around at the framed pictures on the walls. My dad's place, he thought. I wonder if he still comes back here, if he still has a hidey-hole for things that might hurt him. If so, it might be anywhere. It couldn't be in the *same* place, that hole in the stucco under the front steps; those steps are gone, along with the Champagne Tower and Siegel's rose garden and the front lawn. Maybe he does still come back—maybe he'll come back here sometime in this very body of mine, once he's taken it.

Crane thought about his father, who had taken him as a little boy on fishing trips out on Lake Mead, and had taught him about the tides of cards; and who had then hurt Crane, and gone out of his life forever.

The shot and the beer arrived with the telephone, and after Crane paid the waitress, he just stared for a while at the three objects on the dark tabletop.

So much for the target that shoots back, he thought. So much for moving all-in. I'm about to step out of cover empty-handed; fold after calling all but the last terrible raise.

What was it Ozzie said?

They blew her up.

I suppose, Crane thought, that the reason I didn't feel her death through our old psychic link was that she didn't feel it either. Instantaneous destruction—what's to convey?

He lifted the shot glass and stared at the amber whiskey. I could just not do this, he thought; I could put this glass down and get a cab to the police station. Call the raise, and keep on living.

For what?

I didn't share her pain, because there wasn't any. But maybe I'm sharing her death.

He drained the shot glass in one long sip, feeling the rich, good burn of the stuff warm his throat and his stomach. Then he drank half of the icy Budweiser and sat back in the canvas chair, blinking and blank-eyed and waiting.

The telephone in front of him rang, and he lifted the receiver to his ear.

"Hi, Susan," he said. He inhaled, glanced indifferently around the bar for some delaying factor and found none, and exhaled. "Can you forgive me?"

And in the lobby and casino and restaurants of the Riviera, over the babble of the guests and the gamblers and the ceaseless rattling of chips, the disembodied public-address voice called, *"Paging Oliver Crane; paging Oliver Crane,"* for a while, and then gave up on that and went on to other announcements and summonings.

BOOK THREE

The Play of the Hands

But there was heard among the holy hymns
A voice as of the waters, for she dwells
Down in a deep; calm, whatsoever storms
May shake the world, and when the surface rolls,
Hath power to walk the waters like our Lord.
—ALFRED, LORD TENNYSON, *Idylls of the King*

All in a hot and copper sky,
The bloody Sun, at noon,
Right up above the mast did stand,
No bigger than the Moon.
—SAMUEL TAYLOR COLERIDGE,
The Rime of the Ancient Mariner

NANO: Now prithee, sweet soul, in all thy variation
Which body would'st thou choose, to keep up thy
    station?
ANDROGYNO: Troth, this I am in: even here would I tarry.
NANO: 'Cause here the delight of each sex thou canst
    vary?
ANDROGYNO: Alas, those pleasures be stale and forsaken.
—BEN JONSON, *Volpone*

Hopes die, and their tombs are for token
That the grief as the joy of them ends
Ere time that breaks all men has broken
The faith between friends.
—ALGERNON CHARLES SWINBURNE,
Dedication

CHAPTER 28

Bedtime at Last

Though he hadn't been to Las Vegas for twenty years before this trip, Ozzie knew this sort of off-the-Strip bar. In the early evening it would have been full of husky construction workers downing their after-work beers. Now the clientele was stage hands and theater people, and cold white wine was the most commonly poured drink. After midnight the prostitutes would drift in for whatever it was that they favored.

For Ozzie this was the eye of the storm, the period of calm between the first fight and the last.

Ozzie peeled open the pack of Chesterfields he'd bought from the cigarette machine in the corner and shook one out. He had quit smoking in 1966, but he had never quite forgotten the sometimes profound satisfaction of lighting up and hauling smoke deep into his lungs.

The bartender tossed a book of matches onto the bar beside Ozzie's mug of beer.

Ozzie gave him a tired smile. "Thanks." He struck a match and puffed the cigarette alight.

Before he put them away, he took a last look at the other choices.

A message in the personals column of the *Sun* or the *Review-Journal*, he thought. No, Scott won't be reading papers.

And maybe, he thought then, I've done enough by leaving the message at the Circus Circus desk: *I've left young Oliver with a woman named Helen Sully in Searchlight. She's in the book. Diana's dying wish was that you take care of her two sons. It's what you can do—do it. Love, Ozzie.*

But Scott might not go back to the Circus Circus.

Ozzie sipped the cold beer and frowned, remembering how the fat little boy had begged him to stay with him.

"You're not too old to be our dad," Oliver had said tearfully as Ozzie had driven Diana's Mustang south on the 95 this afternoon, toward Searchlight. "Scat and I need a dad." The boy had still been subdued and trembling, all the arrogance knocked out of him by the explosion of his home, the death of his mother.

"I'm going to try to get you a dad, Oliver," Ozzie had said. "Sorry—do you mind me calling you Oliver?"

"It's *your* name," the boy had said, "I don't mind it. Don't ever call me . . . that other name, that I used to want. That was the—I don't even know. I broke that off and chased it away."

The Sully woman lived in a big ranch-style house just outside the city limits of Searchlight. She had worked with Diana at a pizza parlor four years ago, and had liked her and kept up the friendship, and she had six boys of her own; she cheerfully agreed to take care of either or both of Diana's boys until their uncle would get around to showing up.

I broke that off and chased it away.

Ozzie now took a deep drag on the cigarette, and he didn't cough. His lungs remembered smoke, had evidently wondered what had become of it. And the kid wasn't speaking figuratively, he thought as he sipped some more of the beer. I *saw* the Bitin Dog personality walk away, in front of that blown-up apartment.

No, Scott might not get the message at the hotel, and an ad in the paper won't work. He finished the beer and stubbed out the cigarette in an ashtray.

He caught the bartender's eye. "Have you got a deck of cards around?" Ozzie asked.

"Think so." The bartender dug around among the litter by the cash register, then tossed a box onto the bar in front of Ozzie. There was a color photo of a smiling naked woman on the front of the box, and when Ozzie opened it and tipped the worn cards out, he saw that the backs of the cards were all the same picture.

"Hot stuff," he said dryly.

"You bet. You know any card tricks?"

"No." Ozzie wondered why he had not ever learned to do anything with the cards besides make a cautious living. "I was always too scared of them," he said. He looked up at the bartender, noticing that though the man was middle-aged and his apron was tight over an ample belly, he was younger than Scott, and incalculably younger than Ozzie himself. No time to spare, he thought. "Can I buy these from you?" he asked, tapping the sad, worn deck.

The bartender's look of puzzlement became half-concealed contempt. "You can keep 'em, Gramps," he said, turning away and staring at the television set on a shelf up under the ceiling.

Ozzie smiled sourly to himself. He thinks I'm going to go back to some hotel room and . . . and *turn* some card tricks, he thought, with this pathetic, repetitive paper harem. Oh well. One bartender's opinion of me is a pretty small factor in all this.

But he could feel that he was reddening, and he touched the carefully tied knot of his tie self-consciously.

North, he remembered, was to his left. He shuffled the deck quickly seven times, then laid out four cards in a cross. The Jack of Hearts was the card at the north end of the cross.

North it is, he thought, levering himself up off the barstool with his aluminum cane and then digging in his pocket for money to pay for the beer. As always, he left a precisely calculated fifteen percent tip.

Crane shifted in his chair and watched the bet go around the green felt table.

He was in the cardroom of Binion's Horseshoe, right next to the doorway that had been opened in the wall when the Horseshoe had taken over the Mint next door. From the paneled cardroom walls looked down framed photographs of members of the Poker Hall of Fame—Wild Bill Hickock, Johnny Moss, Doyle Brunson—and as Crane sipped his newest bourbon on the rocks, he wondered what the old masters thought of his playing.

He had opened under the gun—the first player to the dealer's left—with three Jacks. Tonight, no matter where he played, he couldn't seem to get any bad hands—and now three other players were calling his fifty-dollar bet. That was good; he'd draw two to his Jacks, and the other players would probably figure he was so drunk that he might well be drawing to a pair and a kicker—or even to a three Flush, or nothing but dreams—instead of high Trips.

It was true that he was drunk. The field of his vision seemed to be shifting up all the time, like a television with bad vertical control, so that he constantly had to be bringing his gaze *down* to focus on anything.

And whenever he looked at his cards, he had to close his false right eye, or else through it would see his hand as consisting of Tarot cards. Not his real father's lethal deck, thank God, nor even the one that poor Joshua had tried to read for him, but a deck he had dreamed of—the deck in which the Two of Batons was a cherub's head speared through by two metal rods.

"Cards?" said the house dealer loudly.

Crane realized that the man was talking to him, and was probably saying it for the second time. Crane raised two fingers and tossed out the Four and Nine of Hearts. The cards he got in exchange were the Nine and Two of Spades, no help.

The two players to his left just rapped the table; they were standing pat, at least pretending to have unimprovable hands.

And, Crane thought sadly, they had both been playing tight all along, not staying with low Two Pairs or trying for gut-shot Straights or three Flushes and apparently never bluffing. They probably *did* have pat hands. Certainly at least one of them did.

So much for three Jacks.

He checked instead of betting, and when one of them did bet, and the other one raised, and the "cold" raise came around to him, he slid two of his Jacks under his chips and threw the other three cards away. When he would be asked to show his openers, he would show the pair, which was the minimum a player could have in order to open; and opening with just a pair of Jacks under the gun was a foolish move. Seeming to have done it would confirm him in the eyes of the other players as a money-careless drunk.

He had been playing Poker all over town for about sixteen hours, starting in the Flamingo's cardroom right after the first phone call from the ghost of Susan. She had called several times since, ringing pay phones he had happened to be standing near; her voice was hoarse, and she didn't talk for any longer than it took for her to tell him that she forgave him and loved him. He knew she'd be waiting for him in the bed of whatever motel room he would eventually wind up in, but like a nervous bridegroom on his wedding night, he wanted just a couple more drinks before . . . retiring.

Twice among a thousand snatches of desultory conversation, once at the Sands and once from a cabdriver who had asked him what line of work he was in, he had heard of a series of Poker games that was to be played on a Lake Mead houseboat next week, starting Wednesday night and continuing through Good Friday.

He tried not to think about that now.

He reached for his drink, then hesitated and glanced to his right—but of course there was *not* a woman standing there. All day he had been catching these glimpses out of the corner of his false eye. Somehow it didn't worry him that he was able to *see* through the painted plastic hemisphere; somehow he had always known that his father could give back what his father had taken away.

Fifty feet away Richard Leroy and Vaughan Trumbill stood watching the Poker game over the tops of two video Poker slot machines; the Horseshoe was crowded, even this late on a Wednesday night, and to maintain their places, the two men kept feeding quarters into the machines and inattentively pushing the buttons.

"Beany's going to need more buy-in money," said Trumbill, staring impassively at the game.

"Hmm?" said Richard, following the fat man's gaze. "Oh, right." His face went blank, and at the Poker table a white-haired little man with an asthma inhaler on the table beside him pulled a billfold from his jacket pocket and separated out twenty hundred-dollar bills; he tossed them across the green felt to the dealer, who slid several stacks of green-colored chips across to him.

A moment later animation returned to Leroy's face. "There," he said. "Hey, did you see our fish open with Jacks under the gun? He must be ready to just fall out of the tree, he's so ripe."

"He *showed* two Jacks, Betsy," Trumbill said. "Sorry, I mean Richard. He might have folded Two Pair or even Trips. I'm not convinced he's as cut free as you think."

In the Betsy Reculver body the old man might have gone into a snit, but now in the Richard one he just laughed. "The way he's been soaking himself in alcohol today? He's as cut free as a blood clot traveling up an artery."

Trumbill just shrugged, but he was uneasy, and he didn't like the old man's metaphor. Several men driving cars with Nevada plates had been to the motel Crane had been staying at, asking questions about a Scott "Scarecrow" Smith, and Trumbill was afraid some jack might be on Crane's trail, out to eliminate one of Georges Leon's about-to-be-assumed bodies, his precious fish, and somehow the assassination this morning was bothering him—maybe because explosions generally tore the bodies to bits and flung the bits away to dry on rooftops and tree branches; and Trumbill's stomach was uncomfortably weighted down with LaShane. This afternoon, naked except for the splendor of his thousand tattoos, he had dragged the dead dog out into the backyard and eaten a good half of it raw. Richard had hosed him off afterward.

A young man in a sweat shirt sidled up to Trumbill now and whispered. "One of the cars that was at the motel just parked in the lot by the liquor store around the corner on First. Three guys, flipping coins, angling this way."

Trumbill nodded. "Keep your people on them," he said quietly, and the young man nodded and hurried away.

Richard was looking at him with raised eyebrows.

"We're not the only ones that sensed him playing," Trumbill said. "Three guys, gotta be working for one of the jacks, coming this way. Can you work the fish yet?" Trumbill asked.

"No, not till day before Easter."

"Why don't you try? If we've got to run, it would help if he was cooperating."

Richard hesitated, then nodded and stared hard at Crane.

Crane was lifting his glass to his mouth—and suddenly his arm jerked and the rim of the glass hit him in the nose and bourbon stung his eyes. His mouth sprang open, and he made a loud, prolonged hooting sound.

Then he blinked rapidly, feeling his face reddening with drunken embarrassment, and he carefully lowered the emptied glass to the paper napkin on the green felt.

"Uh," he said to the house dealer, who was staring at him in some surprise, "just waking myself up."

"Maybe it's bedtime," the dealer suggested.

Crane pictured a motel bed, dimly and whitely lit by a streetlight beyond a curtained window, and he imagined a figure in the bed, reaching out white arms for him. "No, not yet. I've still got some money!"

"Sure, le' 'im ply," said the well-dressed businessman, apparently English, who had won the pot Crane had opened. His graying hairline was damp, and his play so far had been very tight, very conservative; Crane guessed he was uncomfortable in a high-stakes game and appreciated having a moronic drunk at the table. The man now grinned nervously at Crane. "Iss a free country, roit?"

Crane nodded carefully. "Sure is."

"Grite country, too, I my sigh," the man went on eagerly, "though you have goat a lot of goons."

The dealer shrugged and began skimming cards across the table to the players. The button that indicated the token dealer was in front of Crane now, so the first card was dealt to the man on Crane's left, the Englishman.

"Got a lot of what?" asked Crane.

"Goons," the man told him. "Goons everywha you look."

The dealer was quick; each of the eight players now had five cards face down in front of him.

Crane nodded, mystified. "I suppose."

"No use," said Richard Leroy, resting his elbows on his slot machine. Absently he thumbed a quarter into the slot and pushed the deal button, and the front of his suit coat flickered with color as the cards appeared on the screen.

"Not unless you want to have him throw a fit," Trumbill agreed.

Crane mopped his chin with his shirt sleeve, and when the cocktail waitress walked by, he waved his empty glass at her.

Twitches and animal noises now, he thought blurrily. Well, at least I'm developing a terrific table image. I just hope I don't vomit or lose control of my bowels or anything.

The Englishman had opened under the gun, in first position, and Crane knew the man must have a pair of Aces at the

very least. None of the other players called the fifty-dollar
opening bet, and when it came around to Crane, he belatedly
remembered to curl up the edges of his cards and peer down
at them with his right eye closed. He had the Kings of Spades
and Clubs and the Deuces of Spades and Diamonds and the
Seven of Hearts. A very nice Two Pair. He let the cards fall
back flat and slid forward one black hundred-dollar chip.

"I raise," he said clearly.

The Englishman called the bet and then asked for one card.
Crane didn't think the man had the nerve to be chasing a Flush
or a Straight against a raise; probably he was drawing to a Two
Pair, which was unlikely to be better than Crane's Kings Up.

Crane considered rapping pat to scare him off, then decided
that the man would assume he was bluffing, or even so drunk
that he saw a Flush where there wasn't one. He decided
instead to toss the Seven and try for the eleven-to-one chance
of getting another King or Two and having a Full Boat.

But when he tugged at the Seven, the Two of Diamonds
came with it, as if the two cards were glued together.

Surprised, he lifted the cards off the table and opened his
right eye. Then he closed his left one.

Viewed through Crane's false eye, the King of Clubs was a
King holding a metal rod and sitting on a lion-carved throne;
the King of Spades was a weird King of Swords—just a
crowned head poking up out of the surface of a body of water
and an arm raised out of the water holding a sword; and the
Two of Clubs was the by-now-familiar Two of Staves—the
severed cherub head transfixed with two metal rods.

All three faces were toward him, and their painted eyes
seemed to be looking into his false one with urgency.

Dully Crane wished this would all end. Where the hell was
his new drink?

But, obediently, he threw the other two cards away, keeping
the Kings and the cherub.

He closed his right eye and opened his real, left eye. All this
squinting and winking, right after the splash of bourbon, was
making his eyes leak tears. "Two," he told the house dealer.
In spite of the tears running down his cheeks, he was perfectly
calm, and his voice was level.

Seen through his good left eye, the three cards he held were
again just the Kings of Spades and Clubs and the Two of

Clubs. Breaking up the Two Pair and keeping a Two for a kicker was not a move any Poker expert would approve, but the two cards the dealer spun to him proved to be the Kings of Hearts and Diamonds. He now had four Kings, almost certainly better than whatever the Englishman had.

His lone opponent now slid four twenty-five-dollar chips into the pot, and Crane raised with eight of his own, and the Englishman reraised, and so did Crane, and they alternated at raising each other's raises—pausing just long enough for Crane to drain his newly arrived drink and ask for another—until Crane's entire stack of twelve hundred and some dollars in chips was tumbled into the pile in the center of the table. There was cash in his pockets, and he wished the rules permitted him to buy more chips during the course of a hand.

He blinked curiously at the Englishman, who almost looked ready to fling a drink into his own face and then hoot. The man was trembling, and his lips were white.

"Well?" he said in a scratchy voice.

Crane laid down his hand, face up. "Four Kings," he said.

The Englishman blinked at him; his whole face had gone white, but he was smiling and shaking his head. Then he lunged forward out of his seat to stare hard at Crane's cards.

His lips moved silently, as if he were counting the Kings—and then he shuddered violently and rolled over backward, knocking over his chair and tumbling to the carpeted floor.

The house dealer stood up and waved, and in seconds two security guards had loped up, taken in the situation, and were crouched over the fallen Englishman.

"Looks like heart," said one of them quickly. "Yeah, finger-nails already dark." He began thumping the Englishman's chest, hard, with a fist while the other guard unholstered his radio and spoke quickly into it.

In spite of what Crane had heard about the single-mindedness of Las Vegas gamblers, a number of people abandoned slot machines or even Poker hands to come over and peer at the man on the floor. As they speculated in whispers about the man's chances, Crane was glad they couldn't know that it was he who had felled the harmless Englishman. Again he cuffed tears out of his eyes. *I could have just thrown all five cards away,* he thought. *But how could I have known? It wasn't my fault. What was he playing for, if he couldn't afford to lose?*

The house dealer leaned forward across the table—the twin tails of his tie dangling under his chin, each with HORSESHOE lettered down it in silver—and with thoughtful deliberation turned over the Englishman's cards.

An Eight and four Queens. The man had certainly suffered a bad beat.

Crane closed his left eye and looked out at his own laid-down cards. The Kings and the speared cherub head were smiling triumphantly now.

"Get somebody over here with some racks for my chips," Crane told the dealer harshly. "I want to cash out."

The dealer gave him a blank look. "Bedtime at last."

When Trumbill saw Crane stand up from the table, he turned and waved to the young man in the sweat shirt, who was mechanically working a slot machine three rows back; the young man nodded and made a hand signal to someone further back.

"I'll take him as soon as we're outside," Trumbill told Leroy. "He's never seen me, and fat men are reassuring."

"If they smile," said Leroy tensely as he watched Crane laying the stacks of his chips into a wooden rack. "Can you smile?" He glanced at Trumbill.

Trumbill's cheeks tensed upward, and his lower lip pouched away from his teeth, and his eyes became glittering slits. "Ho-ho-ho," he said.

"Forget it," said Leroy. Crane had picked up the rack and started weaving through the crowd toward the cashier's cage, and Leroy strode after him, flanked by Trumbill. "Act sad, like you lost your life savings," Leroy said as they elbowed their way through the phalanxes of gamblers. "A sad, fat man is probably good enough."

Ahead of them Crane had lifted the rack onto the cashier counter, and the woman in the cage had slid it inside.

"Jesus, cash again," said Trumbill a few moments later, watching Crane take a roll of bills and fold it and stuff it into his pocket. "With his scores at the Dunes and the Mirage, he must have twenty grand on him."

"You can have it when we've taken him. He's heading for the door—Moynihan's boys will have a van out there at the curb somewhere. Get him into it."

"Right."

*   *   *

"Baaad luck!"

The picketers were still marching up and down the Fremont Street sidewalk, and the short-haired young woman was using her electric megaphone again.

"Baaad luck at the 'Shoe!" droned her flat, amplified voice on the hot air as Crane lurched out into the glaringly lit night of downtown Las Vegas. *"Come on out, losers!"*

I'm coming, thought Crane as he slapped his pockets for his cigarettes; luckily for the environment, I'm sociodegradable. He found a pack of Arky's Camels, fumbled one out, and tucked it between his dry lips. Now did he have a match? Again he slapped his pockets.

His good eye was stinging with smoke and exhaustion, so he let it close and peered around through his plastic eye. The street and the casinos were hallucinatorily exotic viewed through it, impossible Samarkand-scapes of glowing crenellated palaces and broad boulevards peopled with robed Kings and Queens.

He smiled and breathed deeply, feeling the liquor humming in his veins.

Then it all started to change. The metallic *clank-clank-clank* of the slot machines was the fast, hammering background of a savage music that could be played only by an orchestra of honking cars and pavement-clicking heels and drunken shouts.

"Time to go home, looooozers!" quacked the striker in jarring counterpoint.

The people on the sidewalks were moving jerkily; apparently they were unwilling participants in some degradingly mechanical dance.

Suddenly Crane was near panic, and he opened both eyes wide and breathed deeply. He smelled exhaust fumes, and sweat, and the eternal hot desert wind.

He was on Fremont Street, and the people around him were just random tourists, and he was just drunk.

The cigarette still hung from his lower lip, and he thought that if he could get it lit, he would feel better, would sober up a little.

"Need a light?" asked someone next to him.

With a relieved smile Crane turned—then froze at the double exposure with which he found himself face-to-face.

Through his left eye he saw the fat man who had ransacked his apartment, the fat man who had had on the seat of the gray Jaguar the envelope with the URGENTLY FOLD note about Diana, the fat man who had eaten the leaves from the ginger plant across the street from his house in Santa Ana.

And through his right eye Crane saw a man-size black sphere, with a black, warty head and stubby, bristly black arms; away from the boundaries of it, excluded by it, boiled away a Kirlian aura of green tendrils and teal carapaces and green fishtails and red arteries.

Handlebar! thought Crane—no, the Mandelbrot Man—and then Crane was running away, ignoring the blazing pain in his cut leg, blundering through the crowds and hearing only the whimpering in his own head.

Some traffic light must have been green under the blue-white neon suns of the Horsheshoe, for the crowd stretched entirely across Fremont Street, and he found himself on the opposite sidewalk before he had even realized that he had stepped off the curb.

The crowd was sparser to his left, and he ran that way, his shoes flopping on the stained pavement. A street opened to his right and he spun around the corner, nearly losing his footing when his left knee refused to flex, and half hopped and half jogged toward the blue and red beer signs of a liquor store ahead.

This street, disorientingly, was nearly empty; a cab idled at the curb ahead of him, and a solitary man in overalls was trudging along the opposite sidewalk under the high shoulder of a parking garage. Crane ran for the cab . . . but out of the corner of his good eye he saw the man in overalls look alertly toward Fremont Street and then point at Crane.

"Yes!" yelled somebody from behind Crane.

The man in overalls was suddenly facing Crane, crouching and holding his clasped fists toward him.

Bam.

An instant's smear of white light had obscured the man's fists, and concrete chips were hammered out of the wall at Crane's back.

Without thinking, almost as if something else were acting through him, Crane unzipped his jacket and hoisted out the .357; another shot exploded the edge of the curb in front of him, but he raised the revolver in both hands and pointed it at the man across the street and pulled the trigger.

He was deafened and dazzled by the explosion, and the recoil seemed to shatter the bones in his sprained wrist; he stepped back and sat down heavily on the sidewalk.

Two sharp bangs echoed down from Fremont Street. Crane looked in that direction, blinking against the red glare-blot floating in his vision, and he saw the thing that was both the fat man and the black sphere; it was growing in size, waving its misshapen arms as it rushed toward him.

He stood up and cocked the pistol, dreading the thought of what another recoil would do to his wrist. Then out of the corner of his false eye he caught a glimpse of a woman standing beside him, and once again he involuntarily turned to look.

This time she was there: a short Asian woman who looked to be in her mid-twenties; she was wearing a cabdriver's uniform, and she grabbed his arm.

"Shoot 'em from the cab," she said quickly, "as we're driving away. Hurry, get in!"

Crane's thumb lowered the revolver's hammer as he scrambled into the passenger side of the cab; the young woman had already got in behind the wheel, and sudden acceleration pushed Crane hard into the seat as he pulled the door closed.

CHAPTER 29

Mr. Apollo Junior Himself

Crane tucked the revolver back into his belt. Lights out, the cab made a squealing left turn onto Bridger, gunned past the dark courthouse, and caught green lights right across the Strip and into the dark tracts beyond.

"Did I hit that guy," panted Crane as he gripped the armrest and stared ahead at the rushing asphalt, "the one . . . I shot at?"

"No," said the driver. "But the fat man following you did. Two shots, both hits—knocked Mr. Overalls right down. Who was the fat man?"

Crane frowned, drunkenly trying to imagine a reason for the fat man to save him.

He gave up on it. "I don't know, actually," he said. "Who are *you*?"

"Bernardette Dinh," she said. She had turned right on Maryland Parkway and was now driving at a normal speed through a neighborhood of trees and streetlights and old houses.

There were two baseball caps on the seat between them, and she picked one up and with a practiced motion pulled it on from the back of her head so that her long black hair was caught up under it. "Call me Nardie. And put on that other cap."

"What," Crane asked as he put on the hat, "are you, in all this?"

"In a minute. Open the glove box; the thing in there that looks like a mouse skin is a fake mustache, okay? Put it on."

Crane opened the glove box. The mustache looked more like a strip of horsehide, and when he stuck the adhesive side of it onto his unshaven upper lip, the bristles hung down over his mouth. He thought he must look like Mavranos.

He slouched down in the seat so that the cylinder of the .357 wouldn't poke him in the hip-bone.

A lot of guns on Fremont Street tonight, he thought.

The thought raised an echo in his head, and then he was laughing, softly and unhappily, for he realized that that must have been what the doomed Englishman had meant by *a lot of goons*.

"We'll circle the block around the Flamingo windshield," said Nardie, "to make sure they don't sense you."

Crane wiped his eyes on his shirt cuff. "The Flamingo windshield?"

"Circle the place windshieldwise," she said. "The old term is 'widdershins,' means counterclockwise. Opposite of 'diesel,' clockwise."

Crane remembered Ozzie's having used those terms when he'd had him and Arky reverse the tires on the Suburban. So

that's what the old man had been talking about. Useless bullshit. He sighed and sat back in the rattily upholstered seat.

"You reek of liquor," said Nardie, sounding surprised. "*Hard*
liquor! Are you drunk?"

He thought about it. "Soberer than I was in the casino," he
said, "but yes, I'm definitely drunk."

"And the dice still led me to you," she said wonderingly.
"You must be the biological son, all right. Any mere . . .
ambitious contender, like my half brother, would be disquali-
fied forever by just a sip of beer. *I've* never *tasted* alcohol."

"Don't start," said Crane. The streetlights swept past overhead in bright monotony, and he was getting sleepy. "It's not
for amateurs." He saw the lights of Smith Food and Drug
ahead, where Diana had worked, but mercifully Nardie turned
right onto Sahara Avenue.

"I'm not an amateur, buddy," she said, and her voice was
so fierce that he looked over at the lean profile against the
passing lights. "Okay?"

"Okay," he said. "What are you?"

"I'm a contender. Look, I know you just met the front-
runner Queen of Hearts. I . . . *felt* it when you and she touched
for the first time, Monday night. And yet here you are tonight
acting against your better interests—getting drunk, letting Neal
Obstadt's guys nearly kill you."

"She's dead," Crane said remotely. "Somebody killed her,
the Queen of Hearts, this morning."

Nardie Dinh gave him a sharp look. "This *morning*?"

"Early."

She blinked, and then opened her mouth and shut it again.
"Okay," she said. "Okay, she's out of the picture, then, right?
Now look, you're—" She looked over at him. "You *do* know
what's going on, don't you? What you are?"

Crane was slumped down in the seat, and his eyes were
nearly shut. "I'm the bad King's son," he recited. "Hey, could
we stop for a drink somewhere?"

"No. Don't you know that alcohol weakens you, puts you
at the mercy of the King and all the jacks? You've got a
good shot at unseating your father, if you don't blow it."
She rubbed one hand over her face and exhaled. "There's *one*
thing, though, that you *haven't* got."

"A diploma," said Crane dreamily, thinking of *The Wizard of Oz* movie. "A medal. A testimonial."

"A Queen," said Nardie impatiently. "It's like Hold 'Em, okay? You gotta come in with a pair of cards. A King and a Queen, in this case."

Crane remembered that she had said she was a contender. He sat up straighter and looked hard at her with both eyes, though the vision through the false one had nearly dimmed out.

Through the left eye she was certainly a slim Asian young woman, cute in her little uniform in spite of the hard set of her mouth; was there something different about her, viewed through his false eye? A hint of a glow, the shadow of a crescent at the front of her cap?

"Are you, uh . . . volunteering?" he asked, awkwardly.

"With the moon's daughter dead, I'm the best there is," she said. "I've been exposed to the pictures. I've got to assume you know what pictures I mean—"

Crane sighed. Where was a drink? Susan was waiting for him. "Yeah, I know the goddamn pictures." Out the passenger side window he saw a sign—ART'S PLACE, LOUNGE AND RESTAURANT—GRAVEYARD SPECIALS. Those are the only specials this town seems to have, he thought.

"And for years I haven't eaten red meat or anything cooked in an iron pan, and"—she glared at him—"and I'm a virgin."

Jesus. "That's good—your name was what? I'm sorry."

"Nardie Dinh."

"That's good, Nardie. Listen, you seem like a nice girl, so I'm going to give you some really, really good advice, okay? Get out of Las Vegas and forget all this. Go to New York, go to Paris, go far away, and never play cards. You'll only get killed if you get involved with this stuff. My God, you saw a guy get *shot* just a few minutes ago, doesn't that—"

"*Shut*," she said, "*the—fuck—up.*"

Her hands were clenched on the wheel, and her breath was whistling through her flared nostrils. She was half his age, but Crane found himself cringing away from her, his face reddening under her evident rage.

"Osiris!" she spat. "Adonis, Tammuz, Mr. Apollo Junior himself—not just a broken-winded old drunk, but a—a blind, fatuous idiot, too! Christ, you make my brother look good, I swear."

The cab was stopped now, idling in the left-turn lane facing the Strip intersection. "Look," said Crane stiffly, yanking the door lever, "I'll get out here—"

She stomped the gas pedal and lashed the cab out into the Strip traffic, tugging the wheel around to make the left turn in the jiggling glare of oncoming headlights. The opened passenger-side door swung out on its hinges, and Crane braced himself with his feet and his left hand on the dashboard to keep from tumbling right out onto the rushing pavement; horns honked and tires screeched, and Crane heard at least one bang behind them as she straightened the wheel and sped down the fortunately open southbound lanes.

Crane relaxed a little, and when the head wind blew the opened door back in line, he grabbed the handle and pulled it closed so hard that the handle broke off in his hand.

A car's a lethal weapon, he thought, and I don't want to die any soberer than I have to. Humor this lunatic.

"What I meant—" he began, in a grotesquely light, conversational tone, but she interrupted him.

"Oh, no," she said in a mock-bright voice, "do let me finish my thought, dear." She was driving fast, passing other cars as the hideous pink and white giant clown in front of the Circus Circus swept by on Crane's side. "Let's see. First off, I'm not a girl, okay? I don't think I ever was. And I'm not *nice*—I knifed an old woman in a house near Tonopah on New Year's Eve, and I *really hope* that my brother is the only one I'm going to have to kill between now and Easter. But I won't hesitate to. . . . If your Queen of Hearts wasn't dead, I wouldn't have hesitated to kill her, if she'd got in my way." She seemed to have talked away her anger, and now she shook her head almost bewilderedly. "If I was a *nice girl,* I couldn't save your life."

Crane had relaxed back into the seat again and was consciously having to flex his eyelid muscles to keep them open. "I don't think you can anyway, Nardie," he said. "My father's got his hooks into me pretty deep. I don't think there's been any hope for me since '69, when I played Assumption on his houseboat."

Nardie made an abrupt right turn into the parking lot of Caesars Palace, sped up the driveway, and parked in the line at the cabstand.

She shifted around on the seat to face him. Her eyes were wide. "*You* played *Assumption*?"

Crane nodded heavily. "And . . . *won,* so to speak. I took money for my conceived hand."

"But . . . no, why would he *do* that? You were *already* his son."

"He didn't know that. *I* didn't know that."

"How the hell did you wind *up* there, on his boat? Were you *drawn* to it or something?"

He shrugged. "I don't know. I was a professional Poker player, like my foster-father. It was a Poker game."

"Get out of the car."

Crane held up the broken-off handle. "You'll have to let me out."

In a moment she had opened her door and run around the front bumper and had pulled open his door.

He got out and stood up and stretched in the hot, dry air.

"Some good advice?" said Nardie, looking up at him with an unreadable stare.

Crane smiled. "I guess it is your turn."

"No offense, but I really think the best thing you can do, at this point, is kill yourself."

"I'll take it under advisement."

She walked back around to the open driver's-side door and got in. As the car was shifted into gear, Crane noticed a sticker on the rear bumper: ONE NUCLEAR FAMILY CAN RUIN YOUR WHOLE DAY.

After she had driven away, he stared for a while across Las Vegas Boulevard at the enormous surging neon pyre that was the Flamingo.

When it began to loom larger in his sight, he realized that he was walking toward it. They'll have a room available on a Wednesday night, he thought.

CHAPTER 30

Work Up to Playing with Trash

Susan had, of course, been waiting for him—hungrily. He had quickly got out of his clothes and crawled into bed with her, and they had made desperate love for hours.

Crane hadn't even been aware of the point when his consciousness had finally been pounded away into the oblivion of sleep—there had been a full bottle of Wild Turkey bourbon in the hotel room, and he had pulled his mouth free from Susan's hot wetness whenever she began to deflate under him, and he had each time taken yet another slug from the bottle to restore her sweaty, demanding solidity—but when he woke up, hours later, it was with an almost audible crash.

He was lying naked on the carpet in a patch of sunlight, and for several minutes he didn't move at all beyond working his lungs; the abused machinery of his strength was entirely occupied with trying to hold back the pains that were drawn tight through his body and seemed to have stitched him to the floor. His head and groin were the unthinkably stained, dried-out husks of run-over animals by the side of some savage highway.

Eventually one thought made its way through his mind like a man climbing through the roofless, wreckage-choked hallway of a bombed-out house: *If that was sex, I am ready to gladly embrace Death.*

From where he lay he could see the Wild Turkey bottle, empty and lying on its side on the rug. He realized dully that he was completely blind in his false eye again.

For a while he had no further thoughts. He climbed up onto his knees—noting dizzily that the disarranged bed, though stained with blood and bourbon, was empty—and then got all the way up onto his feet. He swayed perilously as he tottered to the uncurtained window.

He must have been on about the tenth floor. Below him was a big swimming pool in the shape of an oval with its ends dented in, and framing the pool on the east side like a parenthesis was the scabrous roof of a building he recognized at once, despite seeing it from above for the first time.

It was the original three- and four-story Flamingo building, dwarfed and diminished by the mirror-glass high-rise towers that now surrounded it on three sides and hid it from the Strip, and he was obscurely depressed to see that concrete, and pink chaise lounges with tanned bodies on them, covered the spot where Ben Siegel's rose garden had stood.

He lurched away from the window and shakily picked up his pants. If thine eye offendeth thee, pluck it out, he thought; and if thine alertness offendeth thee, go out and find something to drown it with.

There was a liquor store on Flamingo Road just behind the hotel's multi-story parking structure, and after walking up and down its narrow aisles for a while, he fumbled a hundred-dollar bill loose from one of the wads in his pocket and paid for two six-packs of Budweiser and—it seemed important—a cheap leather Jughead-style crown-cap with silver-painted plastic animals hung all over it and LAS VEGAS printed in gold across the front. The clerk had no trouble making change for a hundred.

Crane put the cap on his head and tucked the bagged six-packs under his arm and started walking back toward the Flamingo. After a few steps in the hot sun he dug one of the cans out of the paper bag and popped it open. Legal to drink on the street in this town, he told himself.

He took a sip of the cold, foamy stuff and smiled as it cooled the overheated machinery of him. *And malt does more than Milton can*, he thought, quoting A. E. Housman, *To justify God's ways to man*.

He was walking more slowly now, enjoying the dry sun-heat of the morning on his face, and he began to sing:

*"Makin' breakfast of a . . . pop-pop-pop-pop-pop-pop . . .
   six-pack,
I fought the dri-ink and the . . . drink won,
I fought the dri-ink and the . . . drink won."*

He laughed, took another deep sip, and started another song:

"I'm back on the sauce *again,*
Gonna take up . . . that old True Cross again
Gonna welcome that loss *again,*
Remembering nothing, woe woe, remembering nothing."

Half a dozen men were sitting in a circle next to a Dumpster behind the liquor store, and Crane turned his wavering steps toward them.

When he approached to within a few yards of the Dumpster, they looked up warily, and he saw that they were playing some card game. Five of the men were in their twenties or thirties, but the sixth looked as if he were about a hundred years old; he was wearing a lime green polyester leisure suit, and his bony hands and bald head were stippled with brown spots.

One of the younger men gave Crane an unfriendly look. "You got a problem, Sluggo?"

Crane grinned, remembering that he had left his gun up in his room somewhere. "A problem?" he said. "Yeah, I got a problem. I got a bunch of beer here, and I can't find anybody who'll drink it with me."

The man relaxed and smiled, though he was still frowning. "Around here we help out strangers. Sit down."

Crane sat down on the asphalt with his back against the hot metal of the Dumpster. They were playing Lowball Poker, in which the worst hand wins, for quarters—though when a raise came around, he saw that the very old man was betting with the brown ovals of flattened pennies.

"Doctor Leaky gets to play with junk 'cause he buys the liquor," explained the one who had challenged Crane; his name seemed to be Wiz-Ding. "If you keep up the good work, maybe you can work up to playing with trash, too."

Crane managed to find a couple of dollars' worth of quarters in his pockets, and he played a few hands, but, like yesterday, he kept getting pat high Trips and Full Boats, which were loser hands in Lowball.

"You guys play here a lot?" asked Crane after a while.

The ancient man called Doctor Leaky answered him. "I been playing back here forever," he said. "I used to play around the trash cans behind the Flamingo—there were . . . bungalow-type buildings back there, then—with Frank Sinatra and Ava Gardner." He chuckled absently. "That girl had a mouth on her; I never heard such language."

Wiz-Ding was sucking on a short dog, a bottle of cheap fortified wine, between slugs of beer, and he was steadily losing quarters.

He gave Crane a baleful look. "Since you sat down, I pair up every time I draw even one card."

Even with the beer starting to hit him, Crane knew it was time to leave. "*I* been getting hands that make me wish we were playing High Draw," he said placatingly, "and now you guys've taken all my quarters." He put his hands flat on the asphalt to lever himself up. "I'll come back after I've cashed in my IRA."

Wiz-Ding hit Crane while he was off-balance, and he fell over sideways with his feet waving in the air, disoriented by the hot pain in his left eye socket. When he managed to roll over and struggle up to his feet, two of the others had grabbed Wiz-Ding and were holding him back.

"Take off," one of them told Crane.

Doctor Leaky was goggling around uncomprehendingly. "His *eye*?" he mumbled. "What happened to his *eye*?"

Crane picked up his cap and put it back on his head and stood up. He knew better than to make any parting remarks or to try to retrieve the remaining beers. He just nodded and turned back toward the liquor store.

Another and another cup to drown, he thought, quoting Omar Khayyám this time, *the memory of this impertinence*.

But after he had gone inside and made his way to the beer cooler and carried two more six-packs to the counter, the clerk looked at Crane's swelling left eye and shook his head.

Crane sighed and walked out empty-handed onto the hot Flamingo Road sidewalk.

When he saw the blue Camaro convertible idling at the curb, he remembered that he had been expecting it. Behind the wheel Susan looked entirely solid; her lean, pale face reflected the sunlight as creditably as anyone's would, and her smile was radiant.

After a ten-second pause he shambled over and opened the passenger-side door. There was a freshly popped can of Budweiser standing up on the front seat, and he let that decide for him.

This is legal too, he thought as he lifted the can to his lips and sat down and pulled the door closed with his free hand. Just so the driver doesn't have any.

"What happened to your *eye*, darling?" asked Susan as she pulled out into traffic and got into the left-turn lane.

"Somebody named Wiz-Ding," he said. His left eye was swollen nearly shut, but luckily he found that he could again see through his false eye. So far things looked normal through it—the blue sky, the red facade of the Barbary Coast Casino to his right, the tall Dunes sign ahead with the rippling of its lights still faintly visible even in the hard daylight.

"*That* guy." She laughed, and Crane realized that whatever this woman-shaped thing was, it was intimate with all suicidal drinkers.

The thought made him jealous.

"Not pink elephants for *him*," she said. "What do you think would be appropriate?"

Crane's body still felt as though it had been worked over with baseball bats. "How about one of those big white beetles? *Niños de la tierra*?"

She laughed again as she made the left turn onto the Strip. "You can't still be mad at me about that. A woman scorned, you know? I'd been holding the DTs back from you, and then you asked for me, and I came, and you changed your mind and offered me to your friend." She turned her silvery eyes on him for a moment. "I could have given you much worse than a rat and a bug on the other side of the room."

Crane imagined having a few of the big, thick-legged children of the earth in the bed with him, for example, and he shuddered in the hot sun. "Bygones," he said with an airy wave. "Where are we going?"

"Your memory is nearly gone," noted Susan approvingly. "We're going for a walk in the desert. Visit a ruined chapel that will be there for us. Very spiritually beneficial, help you get ready to . . . *become* the King."

Or vice versa, thought Crane distantly. Help the King get ready to become me. The can in his hand was empty.

"We'll stop at a liquor store for provisions," said Susan, who of course had noted the problem. She giggled. "You know, when I told you to buy a *hat*, I think I meant something more. . . ."

Crane cocked a lordly eyebrow at her. "You have some . . . *criticism* of my choice in gentlemen's headwear?"

"I guess it's a *blackish* canary," she conceded.

Her sentence rocked him, even through the tranquilizing alcohol haze. It was a line from one of the books he and Susan—the real, dead Susan—had loved, Hope Mirlees's *Lud in the Mist:* the book's protagonist, reproved for absentmindedly putting on canary yellow clothing while in mourning, had protested weakly that it was a *blackish* canary.

Was this thing driving the car the real Susan, in some sense? And if she meant to imply that he should be in mourning, was it supposed to be for Diana? Or the dead Susan? Himself, conceivably?

South of the Aladdin, in sight of the garish multicolored towers of the Excalibur, she pulled in to the parking lot of a little liquor store; the 1950s-style sign above the door read LIQUOR HEAVEN.

"I'll wait out here," she said when she had switched off the engine.

Crane nodded and got out of the car. He blinked at the place's glass door, thinking that he had just glimpsed a bent little boy walking in—but the door was motionless, and might not have been opened for hours, or days. He shrugged and stepped forward.

The place was dim inside, after the brightness of the desert sun, and for him the shelves seemed to be full of canned vegetables with faded labels. Under a high shelf that was crowded with dusty ceramic Elvis collector decanters huddled the register and counter and, not visible at first glance, an ancient woman with a star tattooed right onto her face, from ear to ear and chin to forehead.

He nodded to her and walked to the back of the store. There didn't seem to be anyone else in the place.

There was a cooler in the back wall, but on the shelves inside were nothing but short dogs—twelve-ounce bottles of fortified wines like Thunderbird and Gallo white port and Night Train. *Oh, well,* he thought with a smile as he studied them—*any port in a storm.*

Posters were taped on the inside of the glass, advertising a wine called Bitin Dog. "Just Say *Woof!*" advised the ads.

The brand name reminded him of something—something that one hurt boy could apparently manage to lose, and another hurt boy could pick up and find comforting—but he could see no profit in chasing down any memories at this point. He opened the door, took two bottles by the neck in each hand, and started back toward the register.

Ozzie had driven Diana's tan Mustang right past the liquor store lot when the Camaro turned in to park, but he had seen the gray Jaguar stop at the Strip curb behind him, and he realized dully that it must be *the* fat man driving it. He had been forlornly hoping, while he followed the Camaro from the liquor store by the Flamingo, that it was just another Las Vegas Jaguar.

He drove Diana's car into the parking lot of a travel agency and turned it around, to be ready to drive out again when the other two cars got moving.

The old deck of cards with the naked women on the backs was scattered across the passenger side of the seat. It depressed him to look at them, even though they had eventually led him to Scott, and he gathered them up, tamped them square, and put them in his breast pocket.

Dirty cards in my pocket, he thought. He felt his chin and wished he had found an opportunity at least to shave.

Through the dusty windshield he stared at the baking highway and the dry weed lot beyond it. In *Las Vegas,* he thought—where the spiritual water table is as exhausted as the literal one, where the suicide rate is the highest in the world, where this Strip area is called Paradise not because of any Eden-like qualities but just because there was once a club here called the Pair O' Dice.

This isn't the place I'd have chosen. But I can't say I didn't know what was . . . *in the cards.* I bought this hand on Sunday morning, when I stayed to that showdown at the two- and four-dollar Seven-Stud table in the Commerce Casino back in L.A.

The Two of Spades had signified departure, saying good-bye to loved ones; the Three of Clubs had been a second marriage for one or both of those loved ones; the Five of Diamonds had been a wedding present, promising prosperity and happiness in that marriage or those marriages; the Nine of Hearts, the "wish card," was another wedding present, happy fulfillment of ambitions.

Those had been for Scott and Diana. The three cards that had been face down were what he had had to buy for himself in order to try to buy lives for them. The Four of Hearts was the "old bachelor" card, to identify himself; the Eight of Diamonds was an old person traveling far from home; and of course, the Ace of Spades was, simply, Death.

A whiff of Diana's perfume drifted past his nostrils now as he shifted on the seat.

Time, he thought. *Time . . . time . . . time.*

But he patted his coat pocket and was bleakly reassured to feel the bulky weight of his little .22 revolver, loaded with hollow-point magnums.

You've had three days, he told himself. That's enough time.

CHAPTER 31

Did You Meet Your Father at the Train Station?

South of town Susan turned onto the I-15. The red cones of road construction narrowed the highway to one lane for a while, but traffic was light enough so that she didn't ever have to slow below forty miles an hour, and when the construction was behind them, she sped up to a steady seventy or eighty. Out on the face of the desert the little widely separated houses or ranches seemed to Crane to look defensive, like forts.

South of Las Vegas, with the towers and streets left behind, the landscape broadened out; the vast plain around them was not perfectly flat but swept up at the distant edges to meet the mountains. Crane imagined that a car way out there without its emergency brake on would roll right back down to this highway—though from here he wouldn't even be able to see that car.

The breeze that fluttered his gray hair was hot, and in the roofless car the sun was a weight on his arms and legs, so he unscrewed the cap from one of the chilly bottles of Bitin Dog and took a long sip.

The dark wine, much harsher than beer, seemed to generate inside him a fire to repel the desert heat. It woke him up, too, stripped away the foggy blanket of inattention, but he found to his satisfaction that he no longer needed the blanket; he was indifferent now to Diana's death and the problems of Ozzie and Arky. This, he thought, finally, is real, cold adulthood, with not even a scrap of any need for a father.

"You want some of this?" he asked Susan, holding the bottle toward her.

"I *am* it, darling," she said without taking her eyes off the road. "How are you feeling?"

Crane took a moment to think of an honest answer. "Disattached," he said.

"That's good."

Some kind of wrecked old stone structure was visible now beside the highway ahead, on the right, and Crane leaned forward as he felt the convertible's brake drums take hold.

Crane peered at the place that was apparently their destination. Mirages made it hard to judge the outlines of the structure: Its broken gray stone walls seemed at one instant to stretch far back from the highway, and in the next instant looked like nothing but the narrow remains of an abandoned church.

Through the razory optimism of the morning's drunkenness he felt a flicker of uneasy reluctance. "Who," he asked carefully, "are we going to meet here?"

"'Did you meet your father at the train station?'" Susan said in a quacking voice, quoting a joke his real, dead wife had once told him. "'No, I've known him for years!'"

She swung the wheel and pulled off onto the gravelly shoulder. When she turned off the engine, the silence crowded right up to the car, then receded for the faint hiss of the wind in the sparse brush around the uneven stone walls.

As he got out of the car, carrying his bagged bottles and the one he was working on, Crane noticed that a gray Jaguar had pulled off a hundred yards behind them; and a moment later a tan Mustang drove on past, swirling up a faint wake of dust.

He knew he could remember both cars if he cared to, but he didn't care to. He was edgily confident that he had left his emotions behind, with the cast-off shell of his youth.

Susan had taken three steps out into the sand away from the highway, toward the doorway that held up a weathered stone lintel like a segment of Stonehenge. She looked back at him. "Let's walk."

He tipped up the open bottle for another slug of cold Bitin Dog. "Why not?"

The doorway led into a round, roofless area that was floored now only by rippling bone-colored sand. Dead cacti stood like randomly placed crucifixes across the uneven expanse. Crane blinked and rubbed his plastic eye, but he could not estimate the distance to the far wall.

Susan took the bag and held his freed hand. As the two of them plodded over the sand, her hand in his eventually became dry and pebble-knuckled; he drank some of the wine to restore her suppleness, and then before long had to do it again.

The sun was a chunk of magnesium burning whitely in the dome of the sky. Crane could feel its dry heat diminishing him.

The very stones underfoot seemed frailed by rot, honeycombed by some internal erosion; and he saw scuttling snakes and scorpions that were inorganic, made of jewels and polished stones; and dry shells of birds whirled past overhead, making sounds like glass breaking.

He knew that if he could open his swollen-shut left eye he would be seeing a different landscape than the one his false eye was showing him.

When he had first stepped out of the car, he had seen spots of green, and white and red and orange flowers, brought out by Tuesday night's rain—but after he had entered the ruined chapel and walked awhile across this vast floor, he could see only stone and sand and the brown-dried cacti, which, he saw when he and Susan passed the first of them, were split open to show hardened lacy cores like the marrows of dry bones.

His own hands had begun to dry out and crack, so he dropped his now-empty bottle and took another one from the bag Susan was carrying and twisted the top off it, and he sucked at it more frequently than he had at the last one, for he was drinking to maintain both of them now. Astringent sweat stung his forehead under the brim of his Jughead cap.

The wind was singing in the uneven ridges of the broken walls, a monotonous chorus that seemed to Crane to issue from the dry throat of the idiot desert itself, all message lost in a profound, malignant senility.

Ozzie had turned the Mustang around on the shoulder and driven back northward, back toward the desolated building—which he knew had no sane business being here—and he slowed the car and angled over toward the east edge of the highway after he had seen the fat man and a white-haired man walk through the stone doorway into the vast ruin. A third man, younger and wearing a tan security guard uniform, had also got out of the gray Jaguar, but he stood now on the shoulder, watching Ozzie park on the opposite side.

Ozzie noted the holster on the young man's belt. Well, he thought as he switched off the Mustang's engine, I'm armed, too. I'll just have to deal with this fellow, and not let myself forget who he works for.

He buttoned his coat with trembling fingers, then opened the door to the desert heat and began the task of angling his aluminum cane out from the passenger side of the seat.

Behind him he could hear the security guard's street shoes knocking on the pavement of the highway, coming closer. Ignoring the horrified, despairing wail in his head, Ozzie slipped his hand into his suit coat pocket.

During his long life he had four times had to hold a gun on a man, and even that had each time made him tremble with nausea. He had never actually shot anyone.

The man had called something to him.

Ozzie looked over his shoulder at the young security guard, who was right behind him now. "What?"

The guard's brown hand was on the checked wooden grip of the holstered .38 revolver. "I said get the fuck away from the car." He drew the gun and pointed it at Ozzie's knees. "You're not wearing feathers, so you must be the real old guy. Your name's, uh, Doctor Leaky?"

Call it, Ozzie thought. "That's right, sonny."

"Okay, Mr. Leroy said you might show up. You're to stay outside. I'm instructed to kill you if you try to follow them in, and I will."

"Can I sit in the Jag and run the air?"

The young man was still pointing the gun in the direction of Ozzie's knees and staring hard into his face. For a too-brief moment he glanced across the highway at the Jaguar. "I guess so."

"Could you get my cane out of the car? I can't bend over so good."

The man stared at Ozzie in exasperation, clearly wondering if he was worth the trouble of frisking. "Oh, hell," he said finally, and holstered his gun and stepped toward the Mustang.

God forgive me, Ozzie thought. Don't forget who he works for; he's a soldier in their army. He stood back from the open car door.

When the guard leaned in, Ozzie pulled the little .22 from his coat pocket and reached in and touched the muzzle to the curly hair at the back of the man's head.

And feeling his soul wither in his breast, he squeezed the trigger.

The man dived forward across the seat, and his legs flexed and then stood straight out of the car for a moment as he thrashed and huffed and grunted inside; after a moment he went limp, and through tear-blurred eyes Ozzie looked up and down the empty highway.

The bang, muffled inside the car, had hardly been more than a loud snap, and Ozzie knew the wind had carried it away unheard.

He thought about folding the dead man's legs in under the steering wheel. And then he thought about retrieving his cane from under the body.

At last he just leaned in over the man's broad back, resolutely looking at the holster and not at the blood, hooked out the revolver, and turned away to limp, unaided, across the highway and into the perilous chapel in the wasteland.

CHAPTER 32

Get In Close

Like the floor of the ruined Colosseum, the surface across which Crane and Susan walked was hatched with trenches, as if corridors in some vast cellar had collapsed long ago. Walking in the trenches kept the wind-blown sand out of their eyes, though it did nothing to protect them from the weight of the sun.

Every time the two of them climbed a sand slope back up to floor level, Crane could see that the far wall had drawn a little closer.

The wound in his thigh, which had been healing, had begun to bleed again, making a black, shiny spot on his jeans.

At last he climbed up and saw only flat sand between himself and the wall, and he could see an ancient architectural gap in it, blocked now by a tumbleweed.

Crane turned to look back and see if he could gauge how far they'd come, but a thing hanging on one of the nearest cacti made him jump and swear.

It was a dried human body, hung upside down. One ankle was tied to the top of the cactus, and the other leg, though obviously as stiff as driftwood now, had once bent at the knee under gravity and was now bent that way forever. Desiccation had given the face an expression of composure.

And then the eyes opened, their whites glaring against the brown leather of the face, and Crane screamed and scrambled back away from the autistic malice that shone in the bright black pupils.

From behind, Susan touched Crane's arm. "You remember him. Come on and meet the others."

Numbly Crane let her turn him toward the doorway.

The tumbleweed that blocked it was as big as a stove, and

even as he focused his eye on it, the round dry bush exploded into twigs; a flat, hollow boom shook the super-heated air, and Crane realized that somebody had fired a shotgun at the tumbleweed.

He stopped walking and stared at the blown-open bush.

When he heard the two harsh, metallic lisps of the shotgun being re-chambered, he turned around.

A few yards behind him the fat man was stepping carefully over the uneven ground, wearing a business suit and carrying a shotgun slung under his arm, pointed at the ground. Crane was vaguely glad that the fat man wasn't appearing as the warty sphere today. A few steps further back was another man, on whom Crane couldn't get his false eye to focus. Apparently they had been pacing Crane and Susan in one of the parallel trenches.

Susan's bony fingers were still on Crane's arm. "Come on," she said. "Meet *me*."

Crane let her push him through the broken stone doorway. He took a few steps out across the floor of the next wide, roofless expanse of sand, and then he turned and looked back at her.

His head was suddenly singing with shock, but he just stepped back.

Susan had apparently taken off all her clothes since the last time he had focused his eye on her. If he had noticed it, he would have warned her about what would happen, what *had* in fact happened—she had dried out completely, and her nakedness was horrible now.

She was a skeleton covered tight with thin, sun-shrunken leather; her breasts were empty flaps, and her groin was a hole torn open in a sawdust-stuffed doll; her eyes and mouth were pulled so wide open that she couldn't shut them, and steam was wafting out of the holes as her tongue and eyeballs withered away.

But she was smiling, and with a bony brown foot she kicked a big puffball loose from its mooring in the sand, and then she strode long-legged to another and kicked it loose, too.

There were a lot of the ball things poking up out of the sand, he noticed now, and when he made his eye focus on them, he saw that they were the blinking, grimacing heads of people buried up to their necks in the desert. There were arms sticking up, too, holding fanned-out playing cards.

Susan was bounding lightly from place to place, waving her long, thin brown arms over her head like a monkey, pausing before each next leap only long enough to kick another head loose from the stem of its neck.

The senile chorus of the wind in the broken stones was louder here, and Crane was suddenly desperate for a drink.

The bottle he was carrying only had an inch of warming wine sloshing in it, and he tipped it up to his lips—then choked and lowered his head and filled the bottle with vomited blood. He threw it away, and the blood that sprayed from the neck dried to dust in mid-air.

And Susan had gone prancing away across the desert with the other two bottles. Perhaps she would slow down for him.

Through the rheumy eyes of Richard Leroy, Georges Leon watched Crane go stumbling away after the capering figure of Death, and Leroy's mouth smiled with Leon's satisfaction.

There was no problem here. He had accompanied Trumbill on this particular initiation only because there had been something about Scott Crane that had murkily upset him when he had been in the Betsy Reculver body.

He sighed to think of Reculver, whose body Trumbill had buried—intact, as Leon had insisted—in the backyard of the house on Renaissance Drive.

Betsy Reculver had been nineteen when he first saw her—at the first game on the lake, in 1949. She had had a long-legged, coltish grace then, with her brown bangs falling over her eyes as she squinted at her cards, grinning mischievously every time she raised; and when he had cut the deck for the Assumption and won her body, he had been sourly aware of his scarred and featureless crotch, and had wished for a moment that he could have made her his literal Queen rather than one of his honorary children.

And it had been right here, twenty years later in 1969, in this magically conjured ruined chapel, that he had last seen the person who she had been.

Of course, by that time drink and bad dreams had long since pounded the elfin charm out of her, but at thirty-nine she had still been a strikingly good-looking woman. And she had held her chin up as she had followed Dionysus-and-Death, which

Leon recalled had taken for her the form of her father, out into the broken chapel of the barren land.

It was generally the image of a family member that they projected onto the destroying face of Dionysus. With Crane, for a while lately, it had seemed to be a wizened fragment of a little boy, but now, at the end, here, it had again been the image of his dead wife—until it had cast off all images and stood naked and undeniable before him.

But, true to form, he was still chasing it.

Leon looked back the way they'd come, at the jagged walls that hid the highway. He couldn't sense any human personalities out there, not even the security guard. Perhaps the man was asleep and not dreaming.

He wondered if his original body, ninety-one years old now, was going to follow them out here. Leon knew he should keep better track of the damned old thing, which, if nothing else, was the reservoir of Leon's original DNA. If the cloning of human bodies should one day become a reality, that old, senile jug of blood could be used to make another copy of his real body, complete with genitalia, and Leon could assume *it* in a game and be back where he'd been before that disastrous shotgun blast in 1948.

Leon spat into the sand at his feet and watched the spit sizzle. But Doctor Leaky was such a humiliating caricature. And Leon had made sure that samples of the blood were preserved in any number of blood banks throughout the world.

Let the old son of a bitch walk out in front of a bus some day, Leon thought. I won't be responsible; in no sense will I have killed anything that could be called me.

Leon looked at Trumbill, sweating beside him and chewing up another celery stick. The fat man was digging snacks out of his pockets more quickly now that the figure of Death was undisguised.

"I'll follow along with him through one more of the Major Arcana," Leon said.

Trumbill nodded, his mouth full and working, and the two of them started forward again.

Ozzie had been hunching along slowly outside the broken wall, panting and blinking sweat out of his eyes and grinding his teeth with the shoulder ache of constantly holding five playing cards up in front of him—face out, so that every time he glanced up, he was staring at five images of the naked woman's smiling face on the backs of the cards. He kept being reminded of Macduff's soldiers in *Macbeth*, sneaking up on Dunsinane Castle and holding up clusters of branches as disguise.

Every hundred feet or so he had paused and walked wind-shield, in a tight counterclockwise circle, as he flexed his cramping fingers and then fumbled through the cards and selected another five for fresh cover. Always he had selected five that were full of contradictions, like impotence and promiscuity, or infancy and senility, or hysteria and cunning; such combinations constituted null sets that indicated no human mind behind them, and at the same time were somehow portraits of this place, and so served as a kind of psychic camouflage.

The massive gray stones of the wall were rippled and eroded as if by centuries of harsh weather, but he could sometimes see figures that had at one time or another been etched so deeply that they were still visible in the harsh sunlight as faint scratches. He saw angular suns and moons, and writing that looked like bus route maps, all long lines with cross-hatchings at different angles, and at one place a crude picture of fish attacking the underbelly of a stag.

And some of the stones were cold when he braced himself against them, and some were dark as if in shadow though the cobalt sky was cloudless, and two were wet with water that tasted like salty brine on Ozzie's fingertip. This ruined cathedral, or whatever it was, was clearly not entirely in *this* place—perhaps not even entirely in any one time.

He'd been careful never to *shuffle* the cards; God knew what forceful old portraits the deck would assume, or what attention it would bring.

Whenever the wall was broken down low enough to see over, he peeked carefully. Crane and the woman he was walking with had taken so long climbing into and out of the long, interrupted trench that he had been able to keep up with them even at this halting pace, and of course the fat man and his white-haired companion were only pacing Crane.

The four figures inside had hesitated in front of the second doorway, and Ozzie had been able to crouch and watch them over a belt-high section of the wall. The fat man had fired his shotgun, and Ozzie had been standing up straight in an instant, sighting down the gleaming stainless steel barrel of the guard's .38 at the center of the fat man's back, before he realized that the shot had been aimed at a tumbleweed.

He had lowered the hammer shakily. It would have been too long a shot, and the white-haired man would have dived for cover and begun firing back at him, and it was only the white-haired man that Ozzie really *wanted*, anyway.

That would be the body that Crane's real father, who had probably arranged Diana's death, was currently occupying. There was even a chance, just a chance, that it was the only body that the old psychic cannibal had left.

It's time, Ozzie thought, to quit all this tiptoeing around and get in close.

But *can* I shoot another person from behind, with no warning?

Shooting the security guard in the back of the head had been, and still was, too enormous and appalling a thing for him to encompass, like staring straight into the noon sun.

Find out when you get there, he told himself.

He tucked the revolver into his belt and, awkwardly and painfully, climbed over the cold, wet wall in the hot sun.

Crane had stumbled only a dozen yards after his terrible bride when his wounded thigh seized up on him, and he thudded heavily to the hot sand. Ants like curled copper shavings crawled busily over the backs of his hands.

Footsteps crunched behind him, and he looked back. The fat man and his indistinct companion stood now on the sand just a few steps this side of the last doorway. Seen through Crane's false eye, the face of the companion was a bright, flickering blur, as if in some sense he were whirling very fast.

And now there was a third old man, standing in the half shadow of the broken doorway behind the other two, and after a moment Crane recognized him—it was his foster father, Ozzie. Ozzie was carrying a net bag with three gold cups in it, and he was holding out a fourth cup in his right hand.

Crane was only impatient, certain that his old foster-father couldn't have anything important to say or do here, but he closed his right eye and reached up to pry open his swollen-shut left eye.

Now he saw that Ozzie was holding a big steel revolver, pointing it steadily at the backs of the two other old men. He seemed to be hesitating; then,

"Freeze," Ozzie said loudly.

The two men spun toward the sudden voice, and even as they began to scramble and the fat man grabbed the barrel of the shotgun to raise it, Ozzie's gun boomed twice.

Blood sprayed across Crane as the fat man's indistinct-faced companion nodded violently and then rebounded over backward and hit the sand with his shoulders and the blown-out back of his head—and the fat man staggered.

But he managed to raise the shotgun and fire it.

Ozzie's white shirt exploded in a red spray as the buckshot punched him off his feet.

All of Crane's dry maturity was blown away in the hard explosion of that shot, and his mouth was open in a wordless scream of denial as he started forward.

The fat man spun awkwardly, wincing as he pulled the shotgun's slide back and shoved it forward again, the gun's machinery silent in the shocked, ringing air.

The barrel was pointed at Crane's knee, and he skidded to a halt.

The fat man's face was pale as milk, and bright blood was spilling over his right eyebrow and down his neck from the gash Ozzie's bullet had torn across his temple over his ear. He was slowly saying something, but Crane's ears weren't working. Then the fat man stared at the corpse of his companion.

Crane felt hollowed and stricken, as if the blast of shot had hit *him* in the chest; he couldn't look at Ozzie, so for a moment he just followed the fat man's gaze.

The blurringly fast changes in the holed face were slowing down, and Crane could see the face from moment to moment as that of an old man with a crown, and of a vital, tanned, dark-haired man, and of a little boy. The dark-haired man was of course the Ricky Leroy who had hosted the Assumption game on the lake in '69 . . . but it was when he recognized the little-boy face that Crane fell to his knees with shock.

It was the face of his nearly forgotten older brother, Richard, who had been the infant Scott's playmate in the days before the older brother lost all personality and took up his position as lookout on the roof of the Bridger Avenue bungalow.

The shifting faces were replacing each other more and more slowly, and finally it was the old man who lay on the stony ground, the crown no longer visible.

Crane braced himself in the sand with one hand and hesitantly touched the blood-spattered white hair with the other, but this had been a corpse for a long time, since at least 1949.

At last Crane lifted his head and began crawling on his hands and knees to where Ozzie lay sprawled and bloody and motionless on the gravelly dirt.

Peripherally he was aware that the fat man had bent to pick up the revolver and was now plodding slowly away, back through the doorway toward where the highway and the parked Jaguar waited; and then Crane noticed the figure that was now crouched over Ozzie's body.

It was the dried-out Susan, her starvation smile turned on Crane like a bright light through a poisoned fish tank. Her mad leaping had shredded the leathery skin from her, and now she was a sexless skeleton draped only with the most tenuous shreds of organic stuff.

Crane realized that this was no longer drink, Dionysus. This was indifferent Death. This was nobody's ally.

And it had taken Ozzie. Crane couldn't look at the old man's devastated chest; he stared instead at the old, wrinkled hands that had held and discarded and drawn so many cards and now held nothing at all.

Death slowly reached out and touched Ozzie's forehead with a skeletal finger—and Ozzie's body collapsed into gray dust, leaving only the crumpled, pitiful old-man's-suit, and an instant later a hot gust of wind blinded Crane with sand and whirled the clothing and the dust away, over the ruined walls and across the desert's miles-wide face.

The sudden wind had rolled Crane over onto his back, and after it had gone scouring away toward the mountains, he sat up and blinked sand out of his eyes. The animated skeleton was gone, and except for the corpse of Richard Leroy, Crane was alone in the desolate ruins.

The sun was hot on his head; his ludicrous cap had been blown away. He got laboriously to his feet and looked around at the broken walls.

You think your old man's nuts, don't you? he remembered Ozzie saying, on that night in 1960 when they had driven out here to find Diana; and he remembered Ozzie scuffling desperately after him down the stairwell of the Mint Hotel, crying and pleading, when Crane had left to play on the lake in 1969; and he remembered how fragile and dapper the old man had looked on Sunday morning—only four days ago!— when he and Arky had met him on Balboa Island.

Go back to your Louis L'Amour novels and your Kaywoodie pipes, Crane had told him yesterday. But the old man had not, after all, been willing to go gentle into that good night, to roll with the dying of the light.

Was Crane willing to, now?

He looked at some dark spots spattered on the stone wall. They were probably Ozzie's blood.

No, not now. He started limping back toward the highway.

CHAPTER 33

I've Got a Present for Scott, Too

Diana strode along the railed second-floor cement walkway in the gold light of early evening, looking at the numbers on the apartment doors she passed. There was a pool in the courtyard below, and the air smelled of chlorine.

She had alternately dozed and worried for most of the day on a grassy hill at Clark County Community College, using the balled-up old baby blanket as a pillow. Often in the past she had thought it would be nice to get some time away from Scat and Oliver, but now that she had it she could hardly make herself think of anything but them. Had Ozzie got Oliver to Helen Sully's house in Searchlight? Diana had called Helen's number, but there was no answer there. Had Funo or somebody followed Ozzie and killed him and her son? Had some player in this terrible mess gone to the hospital and killed Scat since her last call?

Ever since the explosion she had been insisting to herself that the boys were safer away from her—but the very sight of bright sunlight on green trees made her nauseous with guilt, and she simply couldn't permit herself to think about Scat waking up alone in the hospital, or dying alone in the hospital, or about Oliver alone among strangers and supposing that she was dead.

She stopped in front of apartment 27 now, and she made herself breathe deeply and remember her purpose. She had been here only once before, at night, and didn't remember the layout very well, but according to the mailbox downstairs this was Michael Stikeleather's place.

She knocked, and after a few moments she saw the light through the peep-hole darken; then she heard the chain rattle out of its channel and the door was pulled open.

Aging surfer boy, she thought when Mike grinned at her in pleased surprise, *in the middle of the desert.*

Stikeleather was wearing sky blue slacks and a white shirt open halfway down to show his curly blond chest hair. The shirt was untucked—to conceal a potbelly, she assumed.

"I know who it is!" he said happily, holding up one hand. "It's . . ." His face suddenly fell as he visibly remembered, and he frowned responsibly. "You're Hans's girl friend. I was sorry to read about that. He was good people, Hans was. Hey, come on in."

Diana walked into the living room, which was lit by modern-istic track lights. Aluminum-framed pastels of pretty women and tigers hung on the tan walls, and a black, glass-doored stereo stood in the far corner by a low tan couch.

"Your name was . . . ?" said Mike.

"Doreen," Diana told him.

"Right, right, Doreen. Dor*eeen.* Can I get you a drink?"

"Sure, anything cold."

Mike winked and nodded and stepped into the fluorescent-lit kitchen alcove. Diana could hear him open the freezer and bang an ice tray against a counter. "Do you feel able to talk about it?" he called.

Diana sat down on the couch. "Sure," she said loudly. Six copies of *Penthouse* magazine were fanned out on the glass-topped coffee table.

Mike walked back into the room with two tall glasses. "Seven and Seven," he said, handing one to her and joining her on the couch. "In the papers the police said it was a bomb."

Diana took a long sip of the drink. "I don't think so," she said. "He was trying to make PCP in the back room, had a lot of . . . ether and stuff. I think he blew himself up with it."

Mike's arm was lying along the back of the couch behind her shoulders, and now he patted her head. "Ah, that's a goddamn shame. I guess the police figure a bomb is better for the tourist business than a dope factory, hah?" He laughed, then remembered to frown. "Shit, angel dust—he should have told me, I could have got him all he wanted."

"He always said you were reliable." Diana made herself look into Mike's blue eyes. "He said if I ever needed help, I should come to you."

Clearly this was going the way Mike had hoped it would. His hand was kneading the point of her shoulder now, and his round, tanned face was closer to hers. His breath smelled sharply of Binaca; he must have had one of the little bottles stashed in the kitchen.

"I understand, Doreen. You need a place to stay?"

She stared down into her drink. "That, yeah—and I want somebody to go to his funeral with me tomorrow morning."

Specifically a dope dealer, she thought, if things work out the way I hope they will.

"You got it," he said softly.

He might have been about to kiss her, but she smiled and leaned back, away from him. "And can I use your phone to call my kid? He's staying with a friend; it's here in Nevada, a local call."

"Oh, sure, Doreen, phone's on the kitchen counter there."

Diana stood up and crossed to the telephone. As she punched in Helen Sully's number, she noted that Stikeleather didn't leave the room.

The line rang six times, and her heart had begun to thud heavily in her chest when finally there was a click and she heard Helen's voice say, "Hello?"

Diana exhaled sharply, and she leaned her weight against the counter. "Helen," she said, "it's . . . me. Is Ollie with you?"

"Jesus!" exclaimed Helen at the other end. "Diana? Oliver and that old guy told us you were dead! Is this Diana? God, I—"

"Yes, it's me. That was a mistake. Obviously, right? Listen, is Ollie there? Can I talk to him?"

"Sure, honey, maybe you can get him to say two words or look somebody in the eye. How long are we gonna have—I mean, when are you—"

"Easter, I'll have picked him up by Easter—" Or else I'll be dead, Diana thought. And what will become of my boys if I'm dead? Ah, Christ. "Helen, I can't tell you how much I appreciate this—I owe you—"

"Oh hell, Diana, a week and a half, what's one more kid around the house? I—yeah, it's your mom—"

There was a clatter at the other end of the line, and then Oliver was gasping into the phone: "Mom? Is it you, Mom?"

"Yes, Ollie, it's me, darling, I'm okay. I'm fine."

"I saw the house blow up!"

"You *did*? God, I'm sorry about that, you must have thought—never mind, I'm *absolutely unhurt*. Okay? And I'll be—"

"Mom, I'm sorry!"

"For what, you didn't—"

"For getting Scat killed and for getting the house blown up, I—"

"You didn't do either one! Honey, they were like lightning hitting people, *you* didn't do it! And Scat's gonna be fine, the doctors say—" She pretended to be coughing as she fought back sobs. "Scat's going to be out of there in no time, really, good as new. And I'll be picking you up on Easter or before, week and a half at worst." She covered the mouthpiece and took a couple of deep breaths. "So—how is it at Helen's? The food all right?" She instantly regretted the words, remembering how she had tried to restrict his diet, even when he had only wanted an apple or some pickles.

"Well, we haven't actually *eaten* anything yet. I guess we're gonna have hot dogs for dinner. How soon can you come and get me? You—you know what, Mom?"

"I—what, Ollie?"

"Uh . . . actually, I love you. I just wanted to say."

Diana's heart seemed to stop. He had never said that to her before; perhaps she had never said it to him either. "God, I love you, too, Oliver. I'll come and get you—"

She looked across the carpeted room at Mike Stikeleather.

"I'll come and get you," she said, "as soon as I get a thing or two done here, okay?"

Both Oliver and Stikeleather said, "Okay."

Vacuum cleaners hummed between the tables, and men in uniforms were moving up and down the rows between the slot machines, turning keys in keyholes in the sides of the machines and dumping the change into plastic buckets while bored security guards looked on.

Archimedes Mavranos leaned on the padded edge of a Craps table and wished he hadn't thought about eating the fish in his pocket.

An hour ago he had decided that the sun must be nearly up in the real world outside, and he had made himself go to the coffee shop of whatever casino this was and force down some scrambled eggs and toast, but he had got dizzy and had to run to the bathroom and vomit it all back up. The cashier had been waiting for him outside the men's room door for her money.

But he was still hungry somehow, and a moment ago, after wondering if the goldfish in the water-filled Baggie in his pocket could still be alive, he had momentarily considered eating it.

He forced down his nausea and stared at his bet. There were two black hundred-dollar chips on the Pass Line now, instead of the one he had put there, and three now stood outside the line where he had taken the free odds. His bet had won while he hadn't been paying attention, and the dice were rolling again, so he was now involuntarily letting the Pass bet ride. He pulled in the three chips outside the line, ready to put a couple back again as soon as the shooter got a point.

The dealer moved the white disk to the four at the top of the green felt layout. This was the sixth consecutive time the current shooter had got four as his point, and the boxman, a dour old fellow in a string tie that seemed to be choking him, made a show of picking up the dice and examining them closely.

Mavranos remembered to put two black chips outside the Pass Line for the free odds, and a moment later the shooter rolled another four.

The boxman was staring coldly at Mavranos now, clearly wondering if he was a partner in some sort of cheating here. Mavranos couldn't blame him; what must the odds be against making a hard point like four six times in a row? Especially with a sick-looking bum following the run with black chips and letting the last bet ride?

Mavranos had made nearly two thousand dollars just off this one shooter, who had only been betting his own luck with orange ten-dollar chips; but Mavranos was dizzy and sick, and he couldn't help touching the handkerchief tied around his neck, feeling the lump under his ear. It was definitely bigger now than when he and Scott and the old man had driven out from California. He was losing weight, losing his very substance; no wonder eating even the goldfish had fleetingly seemed like a good idea.

And he was seeing strange things in gambling, but nothing that he could get a useful handle on.

He wondered how Scott and Ozzie and Diana were doing with their own hopeless quests, and he wondered if the boy in the hospital was getting better. Mavranos shuddered at the memory of the boy's head torn open by the bullet.

For a moment he felt bad about having moved out of the Circus Circus without leaving them any way to get in touch with him.

He shook his head. Let them *hire* a chauffeur. Mavranos had problems of his own.

He scooped up his chips in both hands and walked away from the table. No use attracting attention. At some casino tonight—last night, if it was daytime outside—he had won so much at the Blackjack table, raising and lowering his bets to try to conform to the almost reggae pattern of the slot machine bells, that the personnel had assumed he was an accomplished card counter, and two men had demanded to see his ID and then told him that if he ever came into that casino again, he'd be arrested for trespassing.

He frowned worriedly now as he dumped his pile of chips onto the counter of the cashier cage; he couldn't remember which casino that had been. He might go back there by accident. . . .

"Jesus," said someone behind him. Mavranos turned around and saw a man staring at him with amused contempt. "What's the matter, sport, your luck was running too good to duck to the men's room?"

Mavranos followed the man's gaze downward and saw that the left leg of his faded jeans was dark with wetness. For one horrified moment he thought that the man must be right, that in his exhaustion he had wet his pants without noticing it. Then he remembered the fish, and his trembling hand darted into the pocket of his denim jacket.

The Baggie was limp; he must have popped it with his elbow when he was carrying the chips to the cage. The goldfish, which he had been carrying around as a "seed crystal" because he had read that they never died of natural causes, was certainly dead or dying now.

He hadn't slept for twenty-four hours, and somehow the thought of the little goldfish dying in his pocket struck him as unbearably sad; so did the idea that his daughters' father was standing in a casino at dawn seeming to have wet his pants.

Tears were blurring his vision, and he was breathing unevenly as he pushed out through the front doors into the oven heat of the morning.

The passenger-side door of Mike Stikeleather's Nissan truck had a rearview mirror bolted to it, and after the brief and sparsely attended funeral service had broken up and they had walked back out to the parking lot, Diana had twisted the mirror so that she could watch the traffic behind—and she was tensely pleased now to see that the white Dodge was following them.

Last night Mike had taken her to an Italian restaurant near the Flamingo, and when they got back to his apartment, he had tried to kiss her. She had fended him off, but with a wistful smile, saying that it was too soon after Hans's death; Mike had taken that pretty well, and had let her sleep on his water bed alone, while he took the couch—albeit with a just-for-this-first-night manner.

At the first light of dawn, listening carefully to Mike's snores from the living room, she had got up and searched his bedroom, and in the closet she had found a briefcase. She had memorized its position, how it leaned against a pair of ski boots, and had then taken it out and opened it. The white powder in a well-filled Ziploc bag had had the numbing taste of cocaine, and the bundles of twenty-dollar bills added up to more than twenty thousand dollars. She had put it all back the way it had been and got back into bed. Later, while making coffee, she had managed to slide a stout steak knife into her purse, though it was no part of her plan to have to use it.

So far so good.

And at the funeral a few hours later she had said a thankful prayer to her mother, for one of the mourners was Alfred Funo himself.

She had hoped he would show up there. It was the only way she could think of for him to find her, and it would fit in with his weirdly sociable approach to assassination.

And there he had been, standing behind Hans's parents under the canvas pavilion on the grass, smiling sadly at her across the shiny fiberglass casket. She had smiled back at him and nodded and winked, helpless to imagine how he could suppose she wanted to see him, but understanding from his answering wink that he did suppose it.

The car he had got into afterward was a far cry from the Porsche he had been driving when she'd seen him Monday night—the Porsche from which he had shot Scat—but he was at least managing to stay behind Mike's Nissan.

When Mike pulled in to the curb in front of his apartment building, the white Dodge parked a hundred feet behind them.

Diana got out of the truck and waited for Mike by the front bumper. "Don't turn around," she said quietly, "but a friend of Hans's followed us back from the funeral. I think he wants to talk to me."

Mike frowned worriedly but didn't look around. "Followed us here? I don't like that . . . ."

"I don't either. He's a dealer himself, and Hans never trusted him. Listen, let me have the keys, and I'll follow him when he leaves."

"*Follow* him? Why? I've got to get to work—"

"I just want to make sure he leaves the area. I'll be back in ten minutes at the most."

"Well, okay." Mike began sliding a key off his ring. "For you, Doreen," he added with a smile.

She pocketed the key and blew him a kiss and then started walking back toward the white Dodge.

Walk upstairs, Mike, she thought as the soles of her shoes knocked slowly along the sunny sidewalk and her purse swung at her side. Don't spook this guy by hanging around and watching.

She didn't look back, but apparently Mike had not done anything to alarm Funo. When she walked up to his car, he reached across and unlocked the passenger-side door.

She opened it and sat down on the seat, leaving the door open.

Funo was smiling at her, but he looked pale and exhausted. His white shirt and tan slacks looked new, though, and his laced-up white Reeboks shone, she thought, like the bellies of albino lobsters.

"My mystery man," Diana said.

"Hey, Diana," he said earnestly, "I'm sorry we got off on the wrong foot the other night. I didn't realize you were worried about your *children*."

She forced her shy smile to stay in place—but how could this man *say* that to her? After *shooting* one of her children?

"The doctors say the boy is going to be fine," she said, wondering if Funo might have called the hospital and found out that that was not true. She thought it probably wouldn't matter; she sensed that this was some kind of tea party charade, in which statements were only expected to be pleasant.

"Hey, that's great," he said. He snapped his fingers. "I've got something for you."

She tensed, ready to snatch the steak knife out of her purse, but what he pulled out from under the seat was a long black jewelry box.

When she opened it and saw the gold chain on the red velvet inside, she knew enough to show only pleasure, not astonishment.

"It's *beautiful*," she said, making her voice soft and breathy. "You shouldn't have—my God, I don't even know your name."

"Al Funo. I've got a present for Scott, too. Will you tell him?"

I'll tell him when I meet him in hell one day, she thought. "Of course. I know he'll want to thank you."

"I already gave him a gold Dunhill lighter," Funo said.

She nodded, yearning for the normal daytime street outside the car windows and wondering how long she could continue to do this fantasy dialogue correctly. "I'm sure he's grateful to have such a generous friend," she ventured.

"Oh," said Funo off-handedly, "I do what I can. My Porsche's in the shop; this is a loaner."

"Ah." She nodded. "Can we take you out to dinner some time?"

"That'd be fun," he said seriously.

"Do you—is there a number we can reach you at?"

He grinned and winked at her. "I'll find you."

The audience seemed to be over. "Okay," she said cautiously, shifting her weight onto her right foot, which was on the curb. "We'll wait to hear from you."

He started the car. "Rightie-o."

She ducked out of the car and stood up on the curb. He reached across and pulled the door shut, and then he was driving away.

Diana made herself walk slowly back toward the Nissan truck until the Dodge turned right at the corner; then she ran to it.

Traffic was light on Bonanza Road this morning, and she had to keep the truck well behind the Dodge in order to let other cars get between them; twice she feared she had lost him, but then well ahead of her she saw the Dodge turn right into a Marie Callender's parking lot. She drove on past, then looped back, taking her time, and drove into the lot herself.

The Dodge was parked, empty, in front of a windowless section of the restaurant.

Perfect.

She paused only long enough to memorize the license number, and then drove out of the lot again and sped back toward Mike's apartment.

Mike was pacing in the kitchen when she opened the apartment door. "Well," he said impatiently, "where did he go?"

"I don't know, he drove away down Bonanza. Listen, I got his license number, 'cause when I talked to him, he asked if you were Hans's friend Mike, and he knows you're a dealer. I guess Hans must have told him."

"Hans *told* him that? Hans is lucky he's dead." Diana thought Mike looked both angry and ready to cry. "I don't *need* this kind of bullshit!"

Diana crossed to where he stood and patted his spray-stiffened blond hair. "He doesn't know your last name," she told him, "and he doesn't know which apartment is yours."

"Still, I should tell my—the guy I—oh, hell, he'd make me move out of here."

"You've got to be getting to work." She smiled at him. "Tonight I'll see if I can't . . . *distract* you from your worries."

Mike brightened at that. "You're on," he said. "Gimme my key."

She handed it over, and after he had left and she heard his truck start up and drive away, she went to the telephone and called for a cab.

Then she hurried into the bedroom, looped a wire coat hanger around her wrist, and hauled out the briefcase. The bundles of cash she stuffed into her purse, and the Baggie of cocaine she emptied into the toilet, which she patiently flushed three times.

The toilet tank was hissingly refilling when she carried the empty briefcase out onto the walkway and locked the door behind her.

The Dodge was still parked in the Marie Callender's lot. She was glad Funo wasn't a man to rush through breakfast.

Now, she thought after she had paid the cab, you've got to work on sheer nerve for a few minutes.

Forcing herself not to hurry, she strolled over to Funo's car, pulling the coat hanger off her wrist and untwisting the double helix of its neck. She straightened it out and bent the loop into a sharper angle, and when she got to the car, she worked the loop in between the driver's side window and the window frame.

Her hands were shaking, but on the other side of the glass the loop was steady, and she managed on the first try to get it around the knob of the interior door lock button. She pulled upward, and the button came up with a muffled clank.

She looked around nervously, but no one was watching her, and Funo was not leaving the restaurant yet.

She opened the door and slid the emptied briefcase under the seat.

After she had relocked the door, she stepped around to the front of the car and popped the hood release. The hood squeaked when she raised it, but she made herself reach out calmly to the oil filler cap on the manifold of the slant-six engine and twist it off. Then she dug a handful of change out of her purse and tipped it all into the filler hole, hearing the dimes and quarters and pennies clatter among the valve springs within.

A moment later she had replaced the filler cap and lowered the hood and was walking away across the parking lot, breathing more easily as each step took her further away from the doomed man's car.

She had saved a quarter with which to call another cab.

CHAPTER 34

Ray-Joe Active

The ducks in the pond turned out to like cheese even more than they had liked the bread, and soon the entirety of Nardie Dinh's meager lunch had gone into the pond.

She sat back in the shade of a cottonwood tree and looked past the duck pond, across the grassy hills of the park toward the office building where she worked during the day. Soon her lunch hour would be over, and she'd be walking back there, without having eaten anything.

Again.

She hadn't eaten anything at all since a salad early Wednesday evening, nearly forty-eight hours ago, just before going to rescue Scott Crane from Neal Obstadt's assassins.

And of course she hadn't slept—except, briefly, twice during this last week—since the beginning of the year.

She had celebrated Tet in Las Vegas, among the clang and honk and neon of the Fremont Street and Strip casinos, instead of the flower markets and firecrackers and tea-and-candied-fruit booths of remembered Hanoi, and the festive people all around her had been in cars rather than on bicycles, but in both places there had been the same sense of festivity in the shadow of disaster. Sunk into the sidewalks of Hanoi, every forty feet, had been little round air-raid shelters to climb into when the American planes were thirty kilometers away and alarm two sounded, and in Las Vegas she had her amphetamines to gulp whenever her wakefulness-spells began to weaken.

She was fasting just because the sight of any food, and particularly the prospect of putting it into her mouth and chewing it up and swallowing it and assimilating it, now revolted her; it wasn't a consciously adopted measure, as the wakefulness was; but she was uncomfortably aware of a mythological parallel. In an English translation of the thirteenth-century French *Morte Artu*, the Maid of Astolat, who became the Lady of Shalott in the Tennyson poem, offers herself to Lancelot and then, when he refuses her, kills herself by refusing to eat or sleep. Her body is put in a barge and rowed down the Thames.

On Wednesday night she had offered herself to Scott Crane, and they had more or less refused each other. Could this involuntary starvation be a consequence of that?

With a sudden splashing and clatter of wings, the ducks all took to the air. Startled, she looked up at them in alarm to see which way they would fly, but they just scattered away into the empty blue sky in all directions, and in a few seconds she was alone beside the choppy water.

She stood up lithely. He's here, she thought, realizing that her heart was pounding and her mouth was dry. Ray-Joe Pogue is here somewhere. He found me, way out here in Henderson.

Her gaze darted around the green hills visible from where she stood, but there was no one in sight.

I should run, she thought, but in which direction? And if he sees me, he'll be able to outrun me, weakened as I am from hunger.

I should run, I should run, I should run! I'm wasting seconds!

The sky seemed to be bulging down at her, and she was afraid that just the sight of her half brother—tall and slim and pale, dressed like Elvis Presley, another King who was not allowed to be dead, striding over the crest of one of these hills—would rob her of the ability even to move at all.

Her back was against the rough bark of the cottonwood tree, and abruptly she turned around and hugged it—she had not realized that she meant to climb it until she found that she had shinnied several yards up the gray trunk, probably ruining her wool jacket and skirt.

The tree's foliage was a dense mass of round yellow-green leaves, and she hoped that if she could get up onto one of the nearly vertical branches, she would be hidden. Hot, fast breath abraded her throat, and rainbow sparkles swam in her vision, but she didn't faint, though she was afraid that even picturing any face card right now would land her back on the grass, unconscious and ready for him.

She got her scraped hands into the crotch of the lowest branch, and then she swung a leg up, tearing out the seam of her skirt, and got her ankle in beside her left hand, and with an effort that wrung a groan out of her she pulled herself up into the tight saddle. She didn't rest until she had stood up and braced her back against the trunk and her feet high up against the branch, and then she held still and worked savagely on slowing her harsh panting.

At last, though she still had to breathe through her mouth, she was breathing silently. She could hear the whisper of traffic on McEvoy Street, sounding to her now like nothing so much as suitcases dragging around the coping of a luggage carousel at an airport, and the leaves that surrounded her rattled faintly like a lot of very distant castanets. Through a wedge of space between the leaves she could see the yellow square of a Kraft Slice rocking gently on the surface of the pond.

She tried to believe that she had been mistaken, that he wasn't here, but she couldn't. And when she heard feet swishing through the long green grass, she only closed her eyes for a moment.

"Bernardette," he said softly below her, and she had to bite her lip to keep from answering, from shouting at him the way a child in a hide-and-seek game might yell to end the terrible suspense when It was so close.

"No ham," he said now. His words had been clear, she hadn't misunderstood him, but the nonsensical statement made her want even more strongly than before to cry out. Surely he knew where she was hiding, and was only torturing her!

"Cheese," he said. "And bread. That's good, you're still staying away from the meat, that's my girl. Still hanging in there as Mrs. Porter's daughter."

Nardie remembered Ray-Joe telling her once about a very old song that still survived today—though in the current version "Persephone" had been phonetically debased to "Mrs. Porter."

She looked down—and felt her earring fall out of her pierced earlobe. In the same instant she pressed her elbow against the tree trunk, catching the little ball of gold awkwardly between the trunk and the fabric of her jacket. She could feel it pressing into the flesh above the point of her elbow, and, almost objectively, she wondered how long it would be before the muscles of her arm would begin to shake.

"Then up he rose, and donned his clothes," he said happily,
"And dupped the chamber door;
Let in the maid, that out a maid
Never departed more."

He was reciting some of Ophelia's insane singing from *Hamlet*. He had read the play to her frequently during her imprisonment in the shabby parlor house called DuLac's. In her head, rather than aloud, she recited a following couplet:

Young men will do 't, if they come to 't;
By cock, they are to blame.

She wondered if she would even be able to try to fight him off, if he were to see her up here.

He laughed. "Ray-Joe active!" he said to himself in a pep-talk tone. "Ray-Joe Free Vegas!"

Nardie Dinh could see him now, below her, his duck-tail haircut gleaming over the big rhinestone-studded collar of his white leather jacket. He was holding an air pistol, and she knew what kind of dart it was loaded with, a syringe-tipped tranquilizer dart with the CAP-CHURE charge like the one that had brought her down on that December morning in the Tonopah desert, the bright red fletching of the tailpiece standing out like an eccentric decoration on the sleeve of her blouse.

Her arm, the same arm that had taken the dart, had now started to shake. Soon it would lose its awkward grip on the earring, and the earring would fall. Looking down, she estimated that it would land by his left foot. He would hear it, look down and see it, and then look up.

"I wonder if you can hear me, somehow," he said quietly, "in your head. I wonder if you'll come back here to this tree, if I wait. We both know you *want* to. You met him Wednesday night, didn't you? The King's son, the prince, the genetic Jack of Hearts. And you became trackable. And I'm pretty sure you wouldn't be trackable if you'd screwed him. What does that tell you?"

That I'm saving myself for you? she thought. *Is that what you imagine?*

Her shoulder was aching powerfully. *Am* I saving myself for him? she wondered. Has all this—stabbing Madame DuLac, running to Las Vegas, using the powers he gave me to avoid sleeping—been nothing but a show of defiance, a gesture, a sop to my self-respect before allowing myself to sink into the secure zombie-Queen role he has planned for me? Maybe I was afraid that Scott Crane *could* still defeat his father, and I just seized a plausible excuse to run away from him.

Maybe I do want to give in to Ray-Joe Pogue.

No, she thought. No, not even if it's true. Even if I've been living a pretense for the last three months, I hereby declare the pretense real.

She forced her elbow even harder against the tree, wishing she could press the earring right into her flesh.

A noise had risen from the traffic background—someone was driving a car nearby.

Below her she saw Pogue look sharply across the park, and she realized that the car must be driving right over the grass. Then she realized that it was more than one car.

"Shit," Pogue said softly. He took a quick step away from the tree, and then she could only hear him walking quickly away through the grass. She raised her arm and let the earring fall, wondering, even as she did it, if she was doing it too soon, if she had *meant* to do it too soon.

She could hear car tires tearing up the grass, and she turned around, away from the pond, and pushed aside a cluster of leaves. For an instant she glimpsed a white car flash across the grass; it had been one of those sort of pickup trucks, what were they called? El Caminos. Then she saw another one, identical to the first. Had they followed Pogue here?

She didn't hear any shooting or yelling . . . and then after several minutes she heard police sirens approaching. The sound of the cars on the grass diminished away in some direction.

When she heard the unmistakable sound of a police car engine approach and then stop and shift out of gear and begin to idle and heard the loopy sounds of a close police radio, she relaxed and began to climb down.

When those cars started tearing across the grass, she mentally rehearsed, I just went straight up the tree, Officer. Bernardette Dinh, sir, I work for the insurance office right over there.

Got lucky this time.

Diana saw Mike's truck pull up and park on the twilit street, and she reflected that she wouldn't have to fake being scared. She only hoped that she was guessing correctly about what he would do.

Hours ago she had eased the sliding glass pane out of the apartment's living-room window, and then she had gone into his bedroom and dumped out all the drawers and dragged all the boxes out of the closet and dumped them, too. She wished she had noticed a brand of cigarettes that Funo smoked so that she could have lit one and stomped it out on the tan rug.

The apartment door was open, and she could hear Mike's heavy tread approaching along the second-floor walkway.

And here he was, smiling and patting his sprayed hair and reeking of Binaca even across two yards of evening air.

"What's the matter, darlin'?" he asked, giving her what she thought of as a there-there-baby-doll look.

"The place was burglarized today while I was at the store," she said tensely.

Mike's smile was gone, though his mouth was still open.

"I didn't know if you'd want to call the cops," Diana went on, "so I've just been waiting here. *I* can't see that anything's gone, but maybe you can. They hit the bedroom pretty hard."

"Jesus," he said in a whispered wail as he started for the bedroom doorway, "you goddamn bitch, the bedroom, Jesus, make it not be true, make it not be true."

She followed him and watched him shuffle straight to the closet. He stared at the unobstructed ski boots and then peered around at the floor.

"Jesus," he was saying absently, "I'm dead, I'm dead. This was your friend that did this, Hans's friend, that stuff *didn't belong to me*, you're going to have to tell Flores that it was your fault—no. No, I can't say I let you stay here, a woman who—who led another dealer here. God damn you, you've got to get out of here and never come back, take any shit you brought with you." His face when he turned toward her was so pale and scraped with fear that she stepped back. "That license plate number," he said urgently, "I'll kill you right now if you don't remember that license!"

She recited it to him. "A white Dodge," she added, "roughly 1970 model. His name's Al Funo, F-U-N-O." Remembering to stay in character, she gave him a heartbroken look and said, "I'm sorry, Mike. *Can't* I stay here? I was hoping—"

He was walking slowly toward the telephone. "Go find a pimp; you're out of my life."

Diana had already shoved the little yellow blanket into her purse, and on the way out of the apartment she picked up the purse and slung it over her shoulder.

As she walked down the cement stairs toward the sidewalk and the street, she thought of Scat about to spend his fifth night in the hospital, wired to ventilators and catheters, and she hoped that what she had done would succeed in avenging the boy.

Just as the croupier had said, the little white plastic ball lay in the green double zero slot on the Roulette wheel. The man now reached out with a rake and slid the last of the blue chips off the mystical periodic table of the layout.

Archimedes Mavranos had now lost all the money he had won during his three days of gambling. It had taken him even less time to lose it than it had taken to win it. He reached into his coat pocket, and the croupier looked at him expectantly, apparently thinking he was going to buy more chips, but Mavranos was only palpating the plastic Baggie.

The water was still cool; this current goldfish was probably still alive.

But Mavranos had not found the sort of phase-change that he hoped might slap the insurgent cells of his lymphatic system back into line.

He had found other things: the old women who played as obsessively as he did and who wore gardening gloves as they pulled the slot machine handles to fertilize a cold and stingy soil; he had seen players dazed by predawn winning who tipped the dealers nothing after hours of play and thousands of dollars won, or who absently toked cocktail waitresses hundreds for a glass of soda water; he had seen players so obese or deformed that their mere presence would elicit involuntary shouts of wonder in any town but this one, in which the facts of action made physical appearance genuinely irrelevant; and players who with no surprise had "got broke," as the phrase was locally, and were scrambling to raise another stake, which they knew in advance, which they almost *placidly* knew in advance, would soon be lost—one of these players had confided to Mavranos that the next best thing to gambling and winning was gambling.

In all of it he still seemed to see, sometimes, the outlines of his own salvation. Or he tried to believe that he did.

He reminded himself of Arthur Winfree, who had broken the circadian rhythm of a cageful of mosquitoes with a precisely timed burst of light, so that they slept and buzzed in no time pattern at all, and could be restored to their usual up-at-dusk, down-at-dawn pattern only with another flash. Winfree had apparently found the vulnerable point, the geometrical *singularity*, by studying the *shape* of the data on mosquitoes rather than the actual numbers that made up that shape.

People in Las Vegas had the shocked, out-of-step patterns of Winfree's mosquitoes. There were of course no clocks or windows in the casinos, and the man next to you at lunch might be an insomniac who had sneaked down from his room for a "midnight" snack. Mavranos wondered if one of the night-time atomic bomb tests in the 1950s had happened to throw its bright flash across the city at an instant that was a singularity.

He managed a sour smile at the thought that his best hope for a cancer cure might be the nearby detonation of another atomic bomb.

The wheel was spinning again. Roulette was the only casino game in which chips had no fixed denomination, and each player was simply given a different color; Mavranos moved away from the table so that somebody else could play with the blue chips.

He still had about fifty dollars in cash out in the truck, folded into one of crazy Dondi Snayheever's maps, and—and he didn't know what he would do with it. He could try again to eat something, though that was beginning to seem like a pointless, humiliating exercise, or he could use it as a buy-in for some game. What hadn't he tried? Keno . . . the Wheel of Fortune . . .

When he pushed his way out against the spring-resistance of the glass doors, he saw that it was night—God knew what the hour was—and that he had been in the Sahara Casino.

As he plodded dizzily along the walk toward the parking lot, he tried to figure out what it was that he really wanted, and he saw himself working on some old car in the garage, with his wife stirring something on the stove inside, and his two girls sitting on the living-room couch he had reupholstered, watching television. If I use the fifty dollars for gas, he thought, I could be there tomorrow morning, and have . . . a month or so, maybe, of that life.

Before I got so sick that I had to go into the hospital.

He had health insurance, a policy that cost a hard couple of hundred a month and stated that he had to pay the first two thousand dollars of medical costs in any one year—after that the company paid 80 percent or something—but even if dying were to cost nothing, he would still be leaving Wendy and the girls with just a couple of IRAs and no income. Wendy would have to get a job as a waitress again somewhere.

He paused in the white glow of an overhead light, and he looked at his hands. They were scarred and callused from years of gripping tool handles, and some of the scars on the knuckles were from youthful collisions with jawbones and cheekbones. He used to be able to get things done with these hands.

He shoved them in his pockets and resumed walking.

CHAPTER 35

The Partition of Poland—1939

Mavranos paused when he was a few yards away from his parked truck. In the dim parking lot shadows he could see a figure hunched over the hood.

What the hell's this, he thought nervously, a thief? There's two guns in there, as well as my remaining money. But why's he leaning on the hood? Maybe it's just a drunk, pausing here to puke on my truck.

"Move it, buddy," he said loudly. "I'm driving the truck out of here."

The figure looked up. "Arky, you gotta help me."

Though the voice was weak, Mavranos recognized it. This was Scott Crane.

Mavranos walked around to the driver's side, unlocked the door, and swung it open. The dome light lit Crane's face through the windshield in dim chiaroscuro, and Mavranos flinched at the black eye and the hollow cheeks and the stringy hair.

"Ahoy, Pogo," Mavranos said softly. "What . . . *seeeems* to be the problem?"

Mavranos got in and reached across to open the passenger side door. "Come in and tell me about it," he called.

Crane shambled around the door and climbed up onto the seat, then laid his head back with his eyes closed and just breathed for a while through his open mouth. His breath smelled like a cat box.

Mavranos lit a Camel. "Who hit you?"

"Some drunk bum." Crane opened his eyes and sat up. "I hope Susan gives him a lot of big bugs."

Mavranos felt the ready tears of exhaustion rise hot in his eyes. His friend—his closest friend, these days, these bad days—was broken. Clearly Crane was not succeeding in freeing himself from his troubles.

But neither am I, Mavranos thought. I've got to go home while I still can; I've got to spend what time I have left with my family. I can't waste any of that time trying to help a doomed man, even if he is—was—my friend.

Womb to tomb, he found himself thinking. Birth to earth. Shut up.

"Ozzie's dead," Crane was saying now. "The fat man shot him. Ozzie died saving me; he knocked me loose from them for a little while, at least. He saved my life, gave it back to me."

"I can't—" Mavranos began, but Crane interrupted him.

"He always used to put . . . a *banana* in my lunch bag, when I was in grade school," Crane said, his face twisted into what might have been a smile. "Who wants a mushy old warm banana at noon, you know? But I couldn't bear to throw it out—I always ate it—because—he had gone to the *trouble*—see?—to put it in there. And now he's gone to the trouble—Jesus, it's killed him—to give me my life."

"Scott," Mavranos said tightly, "I'm not—"

"And then I got a note he'd left for me, saying I should take care of Diana's kids. Diana's dead, too, they blew her up, but her kids are still alive." He exhaled, and Mavranos rolled down the window. "We've got to save them."

Mavranos shook his head unhappily and squeezed Crane's shoulder. Very little of this was making any sense to him—bugs and bananas and whatnot—and he was afraid most of it was hallucinatory nonsense. "You go save them, Pogo," he said softly. "I'm too sick to be any use, and I've got a wife and kids who ought to see me before I die."

"You can—" Crane took a deep breath. "You can pull a trigger. You can see well enough to drive in day glare. When it gets light, I've got to go see a guy who lives in a trailer outside town. I tried to make it yesterday, but I"—he laughed—"*but I got so damn depressed.* I had the DTs real bad, sat and cried in Diana's car most of the day, in a parking lot. Bugs were crawling out of holes in my face—imagine that! But now I've got some food in me, and I think I'm all right."

You can still *eat,* at least, thought Mavranos angrily. "Then go," he said harshly. "Where's her car now?"

"Parked down the row here. I've driven through every casino lot in town, looking for this here truck. The Circus Circus said you'd checked out with no messages or anything."

"I don't *owe* you any messages, none of you. Goddammit, Scott, I've got my own life, what little is left of it. What the hell do you imagine I could *do*? Who is it you want me to— to pull a trigger on, anyway?"

"Oh, I don't know . . . me, maybe." Crane was blinking around, and he picked up Snayheever's maps. "If I become Bitin Dog again, for instance. At least I can make sure that my real father doesn't have *this* body to fuck people over with."

A car rushed by fast, and the reflection of its red taillights flashed through the cracks in the Suburban's windshield like the streak of a tossed-out cigarette butt.

"You want *me* to make sure of it, you mean," Mavranos said, "and probably go die in the Clark County Jail instead of with my family. I'm really sorry, man, but—"

He paused. Crane had unfolded a map of California, and, ignoring the twenty-dollar bill that fell out of it, was staring once again at the lines Snayheever had drawn on the state's uneven eastern boundary.

"These aren't route lines," Crane said absently. "They're *out*lines. See? Lake Havasu, where the original London Bridge is now, is the bridge of the nose, and Blythe is the chin, and the 10 highway is the jaw-line. And I can recognize the portrait now—it's Diana." There was no expression on his face, but tears were running down his cheeks.

In spite of himself, Mavranos peered at the map. The pencil lines *were* a woman's face in profile, he could see now, turned away and with the visible eye closed. He supposed it might be a portrait of that Diana woman.

Crane unfolded the map of "The Partition of Poland— 1939," and this time Mavranos could see that the heavy pencil lines traced a fat, robed person of indeterminate sex daintily dancing with a goat-legged devil. Bleakly he imagined that this, too, might have to do with Crane's problems.

"I can't help you, Scott," he said. "I don't even have any extra money. I can drop you off somewhere right now, if it's on the way out of town, south."

Crane seemed to be calm, and Mavranos hoped he would ask to be driven to the Flamingo or somewhere, so that Mavranos could seem to be doing him at least some last, paltry favor.

"Not now," said Crane quietly. "When the sun's up. And I'll want to try for a couple of hours of sleep."

Mavranos shook his head, squinting and baring his teeth and trying not to remember the many afternoons he'd spent drinking beer on Crane's front porch.

Womb to tomb. Birth to earth.

He made himself say, "No. I'm leaving now."

Crane nodded and pushed the door open. "I'll wait for you—dawn, in the parking lot of the Troy and Cress Wedding Chapel." He stepped down to the pavement. "Oh, here," he added, digging in the pocket of his jeans. He tossed a thick roll of twenty-dollar bills onto the seat. "If you're short."

"Don't!" Mavranos called, his voice tight. "I won't be there. You can't—you *can't ask* this of me!"

Crane didn't answer, and Mavranos watched the lean figure of his friend disappear into the darkness. After a while he heard a car start and drive away.

Mavranos slapped his pocket for change, then got out of the truck and began plodding back toward the casino. He needed to hear his wife's voice right away.

There was a bank of pay phones off the Sahara's lobby; one of the phones was just ringing steadily, and he fumbled a quarter into the slot of the one farthest from the noise and punched in his home number.

Through the tinny diaphragm he heard Wendy's voice, blurry with sleep. "Hello?" she said. "Arky?"

"Yeah, Wendy, it's me, sorry to call you at this hour—"

"Thank God, we've been so worried—"

"Listen, Wendy, I can't talk long, but I'm coming home." He covered his free ear and mentally damned whoever was making the other phone ring for so long.

"Did you . . ."

"No. No, I'm still sick, but I want to . . . *be* with you and the girls." To be and not to be, he thought bitterly.

There was a long pause during which he helplessly counted the rings of the phone at the far end of the row, and then he heard Wendy say, "I understand, honey. The girls will want to see you. One way or another, they have a father they can be proud of."

"I should be back before lunchtime. I love you, Wendy."

He could hear the tears in her voice when she said, "I love *you*, Arky."

He hung up the telephone and started toward the door, but he stopped irritably in front of the still-ringing phone and picked up the receiver. *"What?"* he yelled into it.

The harsh laughter of a woman grated in his ear. "*I love* you, *Arky,*" the woman said. "Tell Scott I said I love *him*, will you?"

Mavranos was shaking, but he spoke softly. "Good-bye, Susan." He hung up that phone, too, and walked out of the casino.

Back in the truck he started the engine—and then just sat there in the dark cab, staring at the money Crane had tossed onto the seat.

A father they can be proud of, he thought. What does that mean? It *should* mean a father who doesn't *abandon* them. *A father they can be proud of.* What's wrong with just a father they can *love* for a few weeks? What the hell is so terrible about that?

Wendy had said, *I love* you, *Arky.* Well, who did she mean by that? *Who* was it that she loved? The man who had proudly gone off to find his health and who kept faith with his friends? They wore that guy out, honey, he doesn't exist anymore.

He picked up the money and put it in his pocket, knowing he and Wendy would be needing it.

Goddammit, he thought, can you really prefer a dead man that you can be proud of to a—a broken man you can at least *hug?*

Can't we just pretend I never *met* Scott Crane?

At dawn the broad lanes of the Strip were a little less crowded—mostly with Cadillacs heading back to hotels after a night of heavy gambling, beat station wagons out for the forty-nine-cent breakfasts—and Crane was glad to park the Mustang in the Troy and Cress lot and walk away from it. The police might well be watching for the car, and though they shouldn't have any particular reason to hold him, he vividly remembered Lieutenant Frits's telling him that he could be thrown in jail.

Crane walked quietly past the closed multicolor doors of
the honeymoon motel units. A frail smile kinked his face as
he passed them. Have nice lives, you newlyweds, he thought.
Put those HITCHED license plates on your cars, treasure those
photos and videos, take home the Marriage Creed plaques and
put them up on the walls of your bright new homes.

At the curb he leaned against a light post and stared up and
down the Strip, looking for the blue truck. The dry air was still,
poised between the chill of the night and the furnace heat of
the coming day. His hands weren't trembling, and he liked the
idea of stopping for breakfast on the way out to Spider Joe's
trailer, but he was afraid that Mavranos, if he showed up at
all, wouldn't want to eat. Last night he didn't look as if he'd
been eating much lately.

Mavranos might be driving through Barstow right now,
heading back toward the tangle of the Orange County freeways. Crane hoped not.

The top of Vegas World across the street glowed yellow
with the first sunlight, and looking back toward the east, Crane
could see the tower of the Landmark Hotel silhouetted against
the glare of the coming sun.

He looked up and down the broad street. No blue truck.

He sighed, suddenly feeling a lot older as he turned back
toward the Troy and Cress parking lot. Take the car? he
wondered. How long could Frits hold me for? I could call
a taxi, but would the driver wait outside Spider Joe's trailer?
Probably not, if things started flying around like they did at
poor Joshua's card-reading parlor on Wednesday.

He got into Diana's car and started the engine. Find a
car dealership and just buy yourself one, he thought. You've
certainly got the cash.

But he didn't put it into gear yet. He looked around at
the interior of the car, at Diana's country-and-western cassettes and an old hairbrush and a pack of Chesterfields on
the console. Did Diana smoke them? Chesterfields had been
Ozzie's brand, before he quit. Had the old man bought a pack,
suspecting that it didn't matter anymore?

A shotgun blast, out in the desert—and then dust scattered
across the sterile sand. Crane leaned his head against the rim of
the steering wheel and, in the midst of the anonymous sleeping
newlyweds, he finally cried for the killed foster-father who

had found him so long ago and taken him in and made him his son.

After a while he became aware of the muttering racket of a big, badly muffled engine behind him, drowning the steady burr of the Mustang's V-8.

He looked up at the rearview mirror and smiled through his tears to see the blue bulk of the Suburban, with Mavranos's lean face glowering at him from behind the wheel.

He switched off the engine and got out of the car, and Mavranos opened the truck's passenger side door.

"That was eight hundred bucks you gave me last night," Mavranos said belligerently as Crane climbed in and pulled the door closed. "You got a lot more?"

"Yeah, Arky, I got"—Crane sniffed and wiped his eyes—"I don't know, twenty or thirty thousand, I think." He slapped his jacket pocket. "What I gave you was just my twenties. I can't lose lately, except at Lowball."

"Okay." Mavranos drove forward and then clanked the shift into reverse. "For helping you out here, I want all of it except for what we need for expenses. My family's gonna need it."

"Sure." Crane shrugged. "When we get a couple of hours free, I'll make a lot more for you."

Mavranos backed into a parking space and then shifted back to drive and spun the wheel to head out of the parking lot. "We likely to get killed on this errand today?"

Crane frowned. "Not *likely* to, I don't think. As soon as I mess with the cards, the fat man will know where I am, but we ought to be long gone by the time he'd get there, even if he's not in a hospital—and anyway, he apparently works for my father. *He* wants to keep me *alive*." He looked over his shoulder at the piled junk in the back of the truck. "You still got your .38 and the shotgun?"

"Yeah."

"I hope we do run into the fat man."

"Great. Well listen, before we drive out there, I want to stop by a Western Union, and send Wendy a big bundle."

"Oh, sure, man." Crane glanced at him. "Have you, uh, talked to her?"

"Yeah, last night—and I called her again just before I left to come here," Mavranos said. "Told her I wasn't gonna . . . quit, on anything I shouldn't quit on. She understood."

His tired face was expressionless. "I believe she's proud of me."

"Well," said Crane, mystified, "that's good. Hey, take it quiet past these rooms; it's all newlyweds sleeping off their wedding night champagne."

Then he just winced and closed his eyes, for Mavranos swore harshly and leaned on the horn all the way out onto the street.

CHAPTER 36

Some Kind of Catholic Priest?

"That's the place," Crane said two hours later, leaning forward and pointing at the big rusty Two of Spades sign rippling in the heat waves ahead.

"Shit," said Mavranos. He tipped up his current can of Coors, and when it was empty, he tossed it over his shoulder into the back of the truck. "I thought you said you have a lot of money."

Crane had to agree that the trailer-and-shacks structure standing alone by the side of the desert highway didn't look affluent. "I don't think this guy's in it for the bucks," he said. He held out his palm with two shiny silver dollars on it. "This was all I was told to bring."

"Huh."

The two of them had hardly spoken during the drive out from town. Crane had spent most of the drive watching the traffic behind them, but he had not seen any gray Jaguar. Perhaps the fat man had died of a concussion from his gunshot wound, or couldn't track him when he was . . . avoiding Susan.

Mavranos slowed the truck now and signaled for a turn off the highway, and Crane peered at the odd little settlement that was their destination. A big old house trailer—shored up

with wooden frameworks and patched and haphazardly painted
several faded shades of green—seemed to be the original core
of it, but a lot of corrugated iron-roofed sheds had been added
onto the back, and there seemed to be pens and chicken coops
attached to the side. Two pickup trucks from about 1957 sat
in rusty ruin in the unpaved yard between the trailer and
the highway, with a newer-looking Volkswagen van behind
them. The whole place had clearly been baked and warped by
decades of merciless sun.

"*Chez* Spider Joe," said Crane with false cheer.

"That guy was hosin' you," Mavranos said as he slowed
almost to a halt and turned onto the dirt yard. "The one who
told you about this place." The truck shook, and the tires made
popping and grinding sounds as they revolved. "*Hosin'* you."

At last he switched the engine off, and Crane waited until the
worst of the kicked-up dust had blown away and then levered
the door open. The breeze was hot, but it cooled the sweat on
his face.

Aside from the ticking of the engine and the slow *chuff-chuff*
of their steps as he and Mavranos plodded toward the front
porch, the only sound was the rackety whir of an air conditioner. Crane could feel attention being paid to them, and he
realized that he had been feeling it for the last mile or so.

He stepped up and rapped on the screen door, beyond which
yawned the dimness of some unlit room with a couch and a
table visible in it.

"Hello?" he called nervously. "Uh . . . anybody home?"

He could see the blue-jeaned legs of someone sitting at a
chair inside now, but a fast scraping sound from around the
western corner of the trailer made him look in that direction.

And then from out of the trailer's shadow strode a thing
that for one heart-freezing moment seemed to Crane to be a
giant walking spider.

He and Mavranos both jumped down off the porch, but when
Crane peered more closely at the figure that was now stopped
in front of them, he saw that it was a man, with dozens of
long metal antennas sprouting and bobbing from his belt, all
the way around; they were all bent into different arcs, some
brushing against the side of the trailer and some tracing lines
in the dirt.

"Jesus!" said Mavranos, his hand on his chest. "Curb feelers! What are you, Mister, worried about scraping your fancy hubcaps when you park your skateboard?"

Crane had seen that the man's gray-bearded head was tilted back toward the sky, and that he was wearing sunglasses. "Take it easy, Arky," Crane said quietly, catching Mavranos's arm, "I think he's blind."

"*Blind?*" Mavranos yelled, obviously still angry at having been scared. "You had me drive you all the way out here to consult a *blind* card reader?"

Crane remembered the other person inside. "I don't think this is the guy," he said. "Excuse me, sir," he went on more loudly, his own heart still pounding from the fright of the man's sudden, bug-leggedy appearance, "we're—"

"I'm Spider Joe," the man said, talking loudly over Mavranos's building laughter. "And I am blind."

Above the unkempt beard the man's face was sun-darkened and deeply furrowed, and his dirty overalls gave him the look of a down-and-out car mechanic.

"I," said Crane helplessly, "was told that you could . . . uh, read Tarot cards."

Mavranos was shaking with laughter now, bent over and holding his knees. "*Hosin'* you, Pogo!" he choked.

"I do read Tarot cards," the man said calmly, "when I feel I have to. Come inside."

Joshua *did* know *something* about all this card stuff, Crane reminded himself as he shrugged and stepped forward, and his fright that day *was* genuine. "Come on, Arky," he said.

Spider Joe waved one lean arm toward the door. "I'll follow you."

Mavranos was still snickering, though it sounded a little forced now as he and Crane stepped back up onto the porch and pulled open the screen door. The place smelled like old book paper and cumin seed.

The person sitting in the chair was a little old woman who smiled and bobbed her head at them, and she nodded toward a couch against the far wall. Crane and Mavranos shuffled around a low wooden table to it, Crane wobbling as he felt the carpeted floor sag under them, and they sat down.

Spider Joe's silhouette appeared in the doorway, and, with a loud scraping and scratching and flexing of the stiff wires, he forced his way inside. Crane saw that the faded wallpaper of the little room was scored and torn, and the couch cover was burry with snags, and the shelves were all hung up high to be out of the way of Spider Joe's antennas.

"Booger," said Spider Joe.

Crane stared at him.

"Maybe," Spider Joe went on, "you could fix some coffee for these two fellas."

The old woman nodded, got up, and, still smiling, hurried out of the room. Crane realized that her name must be Booger; and, in spite of everything, he didn't dare glance at Mavranos for fear that they'd both succumb to nervous hysteria and fall off the couch laughing.

"Uh," he said, forcing his voice to stay level, "Mr. . . . ?"

"Spider Joe's what I'm called," said the gray-bearded man, standing in the middle of the room with his arms folded. "Why, did you want to write me a check? I don't take checks. I hope you brought two silver dollars."

"Sure, I just—"

"She and I used to have different names. We ditched them a long time ago. These names we have now are only what the people in Indian Springs call us, when we go there to shop."

"Funny sort of names," observed Mavranos.

"They're a humiliation," said Spider Joe. He seemed to be just stating a fact, not complaining.

"I was wondering," Crane pressed on, "if you're blind, how you read cards."

"Nobody who *isn't* blind should ever read Tarot cards," said Spider Joe. "A surgeon doesn't use a scalpel with two blades on it, one for the handle, does he? Shit."

He turned noisily and reached one brown hand up to a shelf. A number of wooden boxes were ranked on it like books, and he ran his fingers over the facing edges of them and selected one.

He sat down cross-legged in front of the table, his antennas bobbing and twanging as they snagged the nap of the worn carpet, and set the box on the table.

"This is the deck I mostly use," he said, lifting off the lid and unfolding the cloth that wrapped the cards. "There is some danger involved in using any Tarot deck, and this is a particularly potent configuration. But I can sense that you fellas are already pretty much fucked, so what the hell."

Crane glanced around at the room, noting the food stains on the carpet and the stack of battered issues of *Woman's World* on a far table, and he remembered Joshua's tastefully mood-conducive parlor. Maybe, Crane thought, if you've got the real high-octane stuff, you don't need to dress it up.

The blind man spilled the cards out of the box face down and put the box aside. With a practiced one-two sweep of his hands he flopped the cards face up and spread them.

Crane relaxed when he saw that it was not the deck his real father had used. But even in this dim light Crane recognized the morbid, fleshy style of the finely crosshatched engravings.

"I've seen this deck," he said. "Or parts of it."

Spider Joe sat back, and two of his antennas sprang loose from the carpet and waved in the air. "Really? Where?"

"Well—" Crane laughed uneasily. Most recently in a Five-Draw game at the Horseshoe, he thought. "The Two of Cups is a cherub's face with two metal rods stuck through it, right?"

Spider Joe exhaled sharply. "Are you a . . . some kind of Catholic priest?"

Mavranos attempted a laugh, but stopped quickly.

"No," Crane said. "If I'm anything, I'm a Poker player. We're dealing with weird crap here, so I'll tell you the truth—I've only hallucinated these cards, and seen them in dreams."

"What you're talking about," said Spider Joe thoughtfully, "is a variation of the Sola Busca deck, one that even *I've* barely heard about. I've never *seen* it; the only known example is supposed to be in a locked vault in the Vatican. Not even qualified scholars can get permission to see it, and it's only known of at all because of a letter from one Paulinus da Castelletto, written in 1512."

With a clanking of cups and spoons, the old woman known as Booger came back into the room carrying a tray. She crouched and carefully set it down on the carpet next to the table.

"Milk or sugar?" asked Spider Joe.

"Black," said Mavranos, and Crane nodded, and Booger handed steaming cups to them; she then stirred three sugar cubes into each of the other two cups and handed one to Spider Joe.

"My deck here," said Spider Joe, "is just the *standard* Sola Busca deck. Sorry. But it'll do. It's a reproduction of a set owned by a Milanese family called Sola Busca—the name means 'the only hunting party,' by the way—which set they permitted to be photographed in 1934. That family and those cards have since disappeared."

Mavranos sipped his coffee and leaned forward, reaching out to touch the margin of one of the cards. "They're marked!" he said. "Brailled, I guess I should say."

Crane looked down at the cards and noticed that each of them had at least one hole poked through the margin of it somewhere, as if they had been tacked up again and again, in all sorts of positions on a succession of walls.

"Yeah, that's how I read them," Spider Joe said. "But also it's a kind of safety measure, that every card in any heavy Tarot deck have at least one tack hole in it. All the serious decks from the fifteenth and sixteenth centuries have tack-holes in the cards."

"Ahoy," said Mavranos, "that sounds like stakes through a vampire's heart, or silver bullets for a werewolf."

Spider Joe smiled for the first time. "I like that. Yeah, I suppose it works like that, but only in the—the head of the beholder. If there's nobody, no human being, *looking* at these things, they're just rectangles of cardboard. It's what they become when they enter your head through your eyes that's potent, and a few tack holes are enough of a topographical violation to step-down their power. It's like the smog equipment on modern car engines." He rocked where he sat, and his antennas bobbed in the air. "Both of you touch the silver dollars to your eyes now, and then pass 'em across."

Crane lifted the two coins to his eyes, and let the silver edge of the right one tap against the plastic surface of his false eye just for luck. He handed them to Mavranos, who touched them to his own closed eyes and then clicked them down onto the Formica surface of the table.

Spider Joe found them and tucked them behind the lenses of his sunglasses. He squared up the deck of cards and pushed them across to Crane face down. "Shuffle."

Crane did, seven times, though each time it was hard to slide the cards into a block, with the edges of the holes sticking up and catching on the card edges.

Spider Joe reached out and felt for the deck, then pulled it to his side of the table. "What's your name?"

"Scott Crane."

"And what, exactly, is your question?"

Crane spread his hands wearily, then realized that his host couldn't see the gesture. "How do I take over my father's job?" he said.

Spider Joe swiveled his head back and forth as though he were looking around the shabby living room of his trailer. "Uh, you *do* know you're in some trouble, right? Having to do with a game you must have played on Lake Mead twenty years ago?" He grinned, exposing uneven yellow teeth. "I mean, *that's* your question? Something about your *dad*?"

Crane grinned pointlessly back. "Yep."

Booger hummed something in the back of her throat, and Crane guessed belatedly that she was a mute.

"Look," said Spider Joe, his voice angry, "I'm here to help you. I'm not here to do anything else. I think you're probably a dead man, an evicted man, but *there might be something you can do*. Ask the cards about that, not about some damn job."

"He's my father," said Crane. "I want his job. See what the cards say."

"Check it out," Mavranos said to Spider Joe, "deal the cards. If everybody's not happy with what you get, we'll go back to town for another two bucks."

For several seconds Spider Joe just rocked on the carpet, his haggard brown face expressionless. "Okay," he said, and picked up the deck.

CHAPTER 37

A Dead Guy Who You Don't Know Who He Is

The first card flipped out face up onto the table was the Page of Cups, an engraving of a young man in Renaissance costume gazing at a lamp on a pedestal.

Crane found that he was bracing himself on the shabby couch in the dim trailer living room—for rain, or for the sound of cars crashing out on the highway, or for the cards all to jump into his face. But though the sunlight slanting in through the venetian blinds seemed to have taken on a glassy quality, like light through clear gelatin, and the *thwick* of the card slapping the tabletop had been particularly liquid and distinct, the only physical change in the room was the buzzing, looping intrusion of a couple of houseflies from the kitchen.

The next card was a picture of a man in armor in front of a globe cut into three sections; the title was NABVCHODENASOR, presumably an attempt to spell *Neb-uchadnezzar*.

Crane noted that these cards didn't show any tendency to fly around in any psychic breeze, and irrationally he remembered Spider Joe's saying that it was a heavy deck.

More flies had come into the room, and they were all buzzing around the cards as if the pictures were aromatic food.

Spider Joe's fingers traced the puncture-holes in the margins of the two cards, and he grunted sharply, and then he opened his mouth and began to speak.

"Hagioplasty one-two-three," he said harshly, the words seeming to be coughed out resentfully like blood clots, *"gumby gumby, pudding and pineal, and Bob's your uncle and the moon's my mother. I could press charges but larges and barges and rivers and fishers, he's fishing all the time there, it's how you say pescador."*

The nonsense words had been echoing loudly in Crane's head, and then he thought they were forming there first and only being repeated by Spider Joe. A stricture seemed to be loosening from around his brain, and he was aware of an invitation to set his thoughts free, like birds, questing out in all directions. It seemed important that the blind man shut up, not say all this in front of the flies.

All sorts of things were important. He knew that he ought to be outside, reading what the clouds would be trying to convey to him.

Beside him Mavranos was leaning forward on the couch, his mouth open. The flies were buzzing loudly—there must have been a hundred of them whirling around in the space over the table now—and Crane wondered if Mavranos meant to eat them and thus learn what they knew. Flies probably knew a lot. The old woman had stood up and was dancing slowly and awkwardly on the carpet, her arms extended, coffee spilling out of the cup she was still holding.

"The father," Spider Joe was saying, *"playing Lowball for trash, after the one-eyed Jack."*

"No," choked Mavranos. With a trembling hand he struck the two cards off the table, and then he stood up and knocked the rest of the deck out of Spider Joe's hand. "No," he repeated loudly, "I *don't* want this."

Spider Joe abruptly sagged on the floor, silent, his jaw slack now as the insane jabbering fit let go of him, and only his arched antennas seemed to be holding him upright. The flies dispersed out across the room.

"You don't want it either," Mavranos told Crane shakily.

Crane took a deep breath and herded his thoughts back together. "No," he agreed in a whisper, waving flies away from his eye.

Spider Joe's mouth shut with a click, and he stood up lithely, the stiff wires waving among the randomly circling flies. "None of us do," he said. He pulled the silver dollars out from behind the lenses of his sunglasses and tossed them onto the table. "Let's go outside. One of you bring Booger."

The old woman had stopped dancing, and Mavranos caught her elbow and led her after Spider Joe, who blundered twangingly out the door and down the wooden steps. Crane followed them outside, being careful not to glance at the cards on the carpet.

Crane squinted against the sun glare on the desert and the highway, and the sudden heat was a weight on his head, but the broad, flat landscape was a relief after the claustrophobic trailer.

Spider Joe strode out across the yard until his antennas scraped against the fender of the nearest pickup truck, and then he turned around and walked halfway back.

"I'm still a channel for them," he said. "And they sometimes take possession of me like that, like the voodoo loas do to those Haitians. It's never been the Fool before."

Or Dondi Snayheever, I bet, thought Crane.

"Your father's job," Spider Joe went on. He shook his head. "You should have told me who you are. I think I would have done this over the phone, or through the mail."

"I'm not—" Crane began.

"Shut up." Mavranos and Booger had sat down on the steps, leaving Crane and Spider Joe standing facing each other. "Booger and I used to work for your father." He rubbed his face. "I don't *ever* talk about this, so listen. I was a miniaturist painter, trained in Italy since I was a kid to be one of the painters of the heaviest Tarot deck, the absolute goddamn hydrogen bomb of Tarot decks—the one known as the Lombardy Zeroth deck."

He pointed at Crane. "You've seen one of mine, when you played Assumption." He shook his head, and the hot breeze twitched at his gray beard. "There's never more than a couple of guys in the world who can paint it, and even if you're young and of sound mind and body, it takes a good year to paint a set. Or a bad year. And then you need a long vacation. Pretty well name your own price, believe me."

He walked in a quick counterclockwise circle, as, it seemed to Crane, a Catholic might cross himself.

"Booger," Spider Joe went on, "was a remora fish, doing errands for him in exchange for the elegantest sort of high life Vegas could provide, which even in the forties and fifties could be pretty elegant. There was a woman who was a threat to him, in 1960—Booger got close to her, became her friend, and . . . *talked* her into meeting her at the Sahara one night. Then Booger stayed away, and Vaughan Trumbill showed up instead, and he killed the woman. Her newborn baby daughter got away, but Booger had set it up for the baby to die, too."

Involuntarily Crane glanced at the old woman. Her face was expressionless.

"I made him a deck," said Spider Joe, "he had to have it for the spring of '69. He used it. And then one day Booger and I were having a meeting with him." Spider Joe's fists were clenched, but he kept his voice even. "He was in one of the bodies he had just assumed after the game, a woman called Betsy, and while we were listening to him, she—he'd only been in the body for like a day or two—she *came back up to the surface* for a few seconds, the Betsy woman did, and it was *her* looking out of the eyes."

Again Crane looked back at Booger. Her face still showed no emotion, but there were tears now on her wrinkled cheeks.

"She was crying," said Spider Joe softly, "and begging us to—to *hold her up*, to do something to keep her from sinking away forever back down into the dark pool where the Archetypes move and individual minds just dissolve, way down in the depths." He took a deep breath and let it out. "And then it was just him again. She was gone, back down into the darkness, and we—we found that we knew more about Death than we had before. Booger and I took our orders and walked out and walked right away from the world—away from our cars and houses and gourmet food and fine clothes, even our names—and never went back. Booger bit out her tongue, and I cut out my eyes."

Crane heard Mavranos mutter, "Jesus!" behind him.

For a couple of seconds Crane just didn't believe it. Then he stared at Spider Joe's deeply furrowed cheeks, and remembered the psychic trauma of viewing the Lombardy Zeroth cards—and he tried to imagine the horror of learning, firsthand, that dead people don't always just go away to oblivion but can come back, suffering, to confront you; and he thought that it might, after all, be true that this woman would choose to make herself mute rather than ever again be able to arrange a death with her lies, or that this man would make himself blind rather than ever again be able to paint another of those decks.

Spider Joe shrugged. "Your father's job," he said again. "Your father has almost got you, I have to tell you that. He's already had you perform a human sacrifice, and—"

"When?" Crane shook his head. "I've never killed anybody!"

Except Susan, he thought. One of the random illnesses. Caused by me. And did I kill Diana, too?

"You may not have known you were doing it," Spider Joe said, almost kindly, "but he handed you the knife, sonny, and you used it. Even in that brief reading it was as clear in your character profile as a birthmark. As I say, you might not have been aware. It would have been sometime this last week—certainly at night, and probably involving playing cards, and probably the victim was from someplace separated from here by untamed water—from over the sea."

"Aah, God," Crane wailed softly. "The Englishman." A lot of goons in this country, the man had said. He was right, Crane thought now. A lot of goons that don't even know they're goons. He blinked rapidly and forced away the memory of the man's weak, cheerful face.

"Your father's job," Spider Joe was saying yet again. "He *is* your father, so theoretically you *could* take it. I don't know how. You need to consult an old King."

"Who?"

"I don't know."

"Where would I find him?"

"I don't know. A cemetery, probably—old Kings are nearly always dead Kings."

"But how do I—"

"That's it," Spider Joe said. "The reading is over. Get out of here. I *probably* should kill you—I could—and I certainly will if you ever come back here again."

The sparse, dry brush along the highway shoulder hissed in the breeze.

Mavranos had stood up and was walking toward the Suburban. "You have a nice day, too," he drawled. "Come on, Scott."

Crane blinked and shook his head, then found that he was plodding after his friend.

"Oh, there was one more thing," called Spider Joe.

Crane halted and turned.

"You met your father the other day—his old, discarded body, anyway. When the Fool was in possession of me, I saw it. The body was playing Lowball Poker, for trash." He turned back toward the trailer and walked toward Booger, his antennas cutting lines in the dirt.

"Well," said Mavranos as he straightened the wheel and tromped on the accelerator, "that clears it all up, hah?" His window was rolled down, and as the gathering head wind began to toss his black hair around, he tilted up a new can of Coors and had a long sip. "All you gotta do is go ask some dead guy some questions. A dead guy who you don't know who he is or where he's buried. Shit, we could have this wrapped up by dinnertime."

Crane was squinting out at the scattered low bushes and broken rocks that became a blur in the middle distance, fading out to the hard edge of the distant horizon against the blue sky.

"I thought he looked a hundred," he said quietly. "Actually he'd be . . . ninety-one this year. What was it they were calling him? Not Colonel Bleep. Doctor Leaky."

Mavranos gave him an uneasy smile. "Who's this? Your dead King?"

"In a way. No, my real father's body. It's senile now, and I guess he doesn't use it anymore, lets it wander around on its own. I remember him . . . taking me boating on Lake Mead, showing me how to bait hooks, and on my last day with him, when I was five, he took me to the Flamingo for breakfast and to the Moulin Rouge for lunch. It burned down in the sixties, I think."

He shook his head and wished he could have one of Mavranos's beers. A really cold beer, he thought, drunk fast and then uncoiling icily in your stomach . . . no. Not now that there was something to be done.

"He blinded my right eye, that evening. Threw a deck of those Lombardy Zeroth cards at me, and the edge of one split the eye. No wonder the Bitin Dog personality fit me—a broken-off piece of a hurt and abandoned little boy, cauterized to feel nothing."

"Pogo, I'm really willing to *try* to believe you're not crazy, but you gotta help me a little, you know?"

Crane wasn't listening to Mavranos. "Actually, I think if I'd known *then*, two days ago, who that was, that decrepit old man, I'd have . . . I don't know, wanted to hug him, maybe, or even ask him to forgive me for doing whatever it was I did to make him mad at me. I think I still loved him, I think the bit of me that's still a five-year-old kid did." He shook one of Mavranos's Camels out of a pack and struck a match, cupping the flame against the wind. "But that was before he had his fat man kill Ozzie." He blew out the match and tucked it into the ashtray. "Now I think I'd like to cave in his blinking old head with a tire iron."

Mavranos was clearly bewildered by all this, but he nodded. "That's the spirit."

Crane resumed watching the highway in both directions for the gray Jaguar.

He paid no attention to the big tan Winnebago RV with a bicycle-laden luggage rack on top and a GOOD SAM CLUB sticker on the back window. They passed it, and then it just chugged laboriously along in their dusty wake, never quite receding out of sight.

They stopped at a Burger King for lunch, and Crane ate two cheeseburgers while Mavranos managed to drink most of a vanilla shake. Crane thought Mavranos seemed to be having trouble swallowing.

They got a room for cash in a little motel on Maryland Parkway, and while Mavranos slept, in preparation for going to a pet store for a goldfish and then setting out on yet another night of chasing his statistical phase-change, Crane bought a succession of Cokes from the machine in the motel office, and for two hours he paced around the pool, staring into the water and trying to figure out where he might find a dead King.

When Arky came reeling back to the room at midnight, Crane was sitting up in the sleeping bag on the floor, doodling on a pad.

"Lights out, Pogo," said Mavranos, his voice harsh with exhaustion, as he fell fully clothed across the bed.

Crane got up and turned out the light and got back into the sleeping bag, but for a long time he lay awake and stared at the ceiling in the darkness.

The moon was two days short of being full, and as Georges Leon carefully hung up the telephone, it irritated him that out here east of Paradise the moonlight shone in through the window of the big Winnebago more strongly than any artificial lights did. He didn't like natural light, especially moonlight.

He wasn't going to let himself get angry at the things Moynihan had said on the phone, or the kind of money Moynihan had demanded.

He could hear Trumbill clunking around in the little bathtub, and even with the air conditioner turned all the way up the chilled air smelled of celery and blood and liver and olive oil. Leon would wait for Trumbill to come out; he didn't want to go in there and see the gross, tattooed naked body kneeling on the floor, the head and arms buried and rooting away in the appalling salad that the man had flung together in the tub.

Leon was in the bandy-legged old Benet body now—he'd have to make sure no one went on calling it Beany—and he dreaded trying to give harsh orders, convey authority, with it. The face was too round and red, the cheeks and eyes were too deeply etched with the fatuous grin Leon had let the thing assume when he had left it to its automatic-pilot job as a Poker shill at several casinos. He looked like Mickey Rooney. Even the voice, as he had helplessly noticed on the phone just now, kept trying to be squeaky.

Of course the beautiful Art Hanari body still rested in physical perfection in a bed at La Maison Dieu, but he did very much want to debut that body Wednesday night, at the first of the Holy Week games on the lake.

Well, that was only four days away. He could work out of Benet for that long.

And then on Holy Saturday he could begin assuming the bodies he had defined and paid for in 1969.

High damn time. This had been a long twenty-one years. It would be good to get into some fresh hosts. That Scott Crane looked all right—Leon glanced out the window to make sure Crane's motel room was still dark—and several of the ones Trumbill had already captured and sedated looked damn good. People took better care of themselves these days.

He could hear water running now, and Trumbill grunting as he toweled himself off. The RV rocked a little on its shocks.

A few minutes later Vaughan Trumbill came stumping into the narrow room, his voluminous pants cuffs billowing around his bare blue and red feet, buttoning a sail-like shirt around his enormous belly. The bandage above his ear had begun to blot red again. The man's blood pressure must be like the penstocks in Hoover Dam, Leon thought.

"They coming?" Trumbill asked.

"Not until tomorrow, he said. And it's got to be away from crowds, and all he'd agree to do was haul away an unconscious body. I don't think his guys will even be armed."

The bandage wobbled as Trumbill's eyebrows went up.

"Moynihan doesn't know me," Leon went on, keeping his voice level. "I said I was Betsy Reculver's business partner, and he said I should have *her* call him, or at least Richard Leroy. I told Moynihan he should ask you about it all, and he just said he heard you'd been shot. How's your arm and leg?"

Trumbill rolled his massive left shoulder. "Just feels strained now, like I've been digging ditches. Not numbed anymore. And I've been eating stuff to restore all the lost blood." He glanced out the window at the dark motel room. "I hate head wounds."

"You were lucky. Richard and the guard both took it square." Leon touched the forehead he had now. "Twice in a week I've been shot right out of a body."

Trumbill turned away from the window and stared at him impassively. "A drag, right?"

Leon grinned, then stopped when he remembered how the expression looked on this clown face. "At dawn I'll call the garage," he said "and have them send the Camaro over here. This thing can follow, but it can't chase."

"'Kay. And I've got the tranky gun loaded up."

Leon sat down and shifted the chair to face the window. "I'll take the first shift watching," he said. "I'll get you up at"—he glanced at the clock on the plywood wall paneling—"four."

"'Kay." Trumbill shuffled sideways into the back of the RV, where the bunk was. "Bathroom might be a little high by morning."

"As soon as we've got Crane in a cage, we'll sell this thing as is."

The sun was up and the air was already hot when Crane, still disheveled from sleep, walked back from the motel office and kicked the room door. When Mavranos opened it, blinking in the daylight, Crane handed him one of the cold cans of Coke.

"They don't have coffee," Crane said, stepping inside and closing the door. "This'll do; it's caffeine at least."

"Christ." Mavranos popped the top, took a sip, and shuddered.

Crane leaned against the battered dressing table. "Listen, Arky," he said, "did you ever do any scuba diving?"

"I was a city boy."

"Damn. Well, you can wait in the boat."

"That's what I'll do, all right. I'll wait in the boat. Your dead King's underwater somewhere?"

"I think he's in Lake Mead," said Crane. "I think his head is, anyway."

Mavranos took another sip of the Coke, then put it down and stalked outside. Crane heard the truck door clunk, and when Mavranos came back in, he was carrying a dripping Coors can.

"I *did* see the flies buzzing around the cards," Mavranos said slowly, after he'd taken a deep sip, "and I heard that guy Snayheever's words coming out of Buggy Joe's mouth. And those things *were* weird. And I'm willing to admit that there's a *lot* of weird shit going on. But how the hell are you going to have a conversation with a cut-off head, underwater?" He laughed, though not happily. "And with a scuba gadget in your mouth?"

"Oh," said Crane, slapping the air carelessly with the back of his hand, "as to *that*—I don't know."

Mavranos sighed and sat down on the bed. "Why do you think he's in the lake?" he asked quietly.

"When Snayheever was on the phone to Diana, he said somebody tried to sink a head in Lake Mead." Crane was pacing up and down the room now, talking rapidly. "Snayheever's aware of a lot of this stuff, even if he is nuts, so maybe sinking severed heads in the lake is something people involved in this kind of shit *do*. And he made it sound like the lake didn't take it and that it was foolish of the guy to have even tried, like the lake already *has* a head in it, see? And couldn't hold another, not that kind anyway. Tamed water Lake Mead is, remember Ozzie saying that? Maybe it tames any stuff *in* it, too, so that'd be a good place to put an old King's head, if you're the new King and want to keep an old one down. And I *don't* think it was my real father, the current King, who had me . . . shit, *kill* some poor Englishman at a Poker table at the Horseshoe. I think it was the king in the lake that did it, that made me do it, I think it was *him* that was grinning at me out of the Two of Wands card, with his head cut off and two metal rods through his head."

Crane grinned wildly at Mavranos. "You with me so far?"

"You poor fucked-up son of a bitch."

"And along with the severed-head Two of Wands, I had a strange King of Swords; it was an arm, with the hand holding a sword, poking up out of a body of water, like a weapon was being offered by somebody below the surface."

Mavranos just looked puzzled and irritated—and terribly tired. "And . . . ?"

"And when I've dreamed about playing Assumption on Lake Mead, I see the Fool dancing on a cliff edge, but I also see—sense, really—a giant deep in the lake, and even though I can't see him, I know that he has only one eye."

"Orpheus, in Greek myths—they cut his head off, and it kept talking for a while, making prophecies and such stuff." Mavranos stood up. "Okay, okay. You've done scuba diving before?"

"Oh, sure. Last time I went, I shot a spear through my ankle." He was smiling when he said it, but a moment later he winced, remembering that fifteen-year-old Diana had called him then, as soon as he'd got home from the hospital.

"May as well go right now, I guess," Mavranos said. "I'm getting nowhere with my mystimatical cure."

Crane opened the door. "'Maybe what you're waitin' for'll be twitchin' at the dance tonight!'" he said, quoting something Riff had said to Tony in *West Side Story*.

Mavranos smiled sourly as he slapped his jacket pocket for his keys. "You remember it killed Riff and Tony."

When he drove the Camaro under the 93 overpass, Vaughan Trumbill picked up the cellular telephone and punched redial.

Even with the seat levered all the way back, his belly kept getting brushed by the steering wheel, and the car still smelled of Betsy Reculver's flowery old-lady's perfume.

"Yeah, Vaughan," came Benet's squeaky voice over the phone.

"Bets—, uh, Benet—"

"From here on in just call me Georges."

Trumbill realized that he never had called him that, in any of the man's bodies. When Trumbill had first started to work for him, he was already in the Richard Leroy.

"Okay, Georges. They're heading out Fremont. Either they're going back to where that kid got shot, or they're going right on out Boulder Highway to the lake."

"Where the kid got shot." For some reason Georges's voice, even coming out of the Benet vocal cords, sounded stony. "Yeah, I remember that place. Some damned woman destroyed a nice Chevrolet of mine right there." For a moment the phone Trumbill held to his ear was silent, and all he could hear was the muffled roar of the Camaro's engine. "Okay," Georges went on, "if they stop there, take 'em when they get out away from the truck, it's good and private, and I don't see why they'd take guns out with them. You still got Moynihan's guys?"

Trumbill glanced at the rearview mirror. The florist's van was still there, a couple of cars behind him.

"Yes."

"Right, well, kill the mustache and dart Crane. But if they go on past there, toward the lake— Why would they be going to the lake? Rhetorical question, I don't need your guesses. I don't like it if that's where they're going." He sighed. "Catch them somewhere in the desert north of Henderson. Shoot a tire out or something and then just *confront* them."

"In the desert." Trumbill forced his mind away from the recollection of having only three days ago seen Death itself, the obscene skeleton under the skimpy dress of dried skin, capering in the desert south of town.

Confront them, he thought as he gunned the Camaro through the Desert Inn Road intersection and watched the dusty blue truck barrel steadily along on the bright highway ahead of him. I'm valuable to the old man, he thought, but when it gets down to the bone, I'm an expendable piece in his equation.

As I've always known I was.

He sighed heavily. "If they kill me out there," he said into the phone that was wedged under his pendulous jowl, "you won't forget your part of our old bargain."

He heard Georges sigh, too. "Packed tight in the center of a big cement cube within an hour of your death, Vaughan, don't worry. But I hardly think these guys will take you. Blood pressure, a sledge-hammer of a stroke, is what's going to take you out, my friend."

Trumbill smiled, his cold eyes still on the truck ahead. "Okay. I'll call you after."

He hung up the phone and returned his full attention to the blue truck.

CHAPTER 38

Not the Skinny Man

Neither Crane nor Mavranos spoke as the abandoned gas station swept past on their right.

That's where it all really started to go wrong, Crane thought. To think that we could have just killed Snayheever or broken his arms or something in Baker, if we'd known, if the goddamn cards had told Ozzie about it in the Los Angeles Poker casino. But instead here we are, Scat probably dead by now in the hospital, Oliver in some state home for orphans, Diana and Ozzie certainly dead, Arky and I not looking good at all—why couldn't Ozzie have seen it in the cards?

He hiked around in his seat and looked back. No Jaguar, he thought, but that green Camaro has been hanging around behind us for a while. Probably just tourists wanting to go see the dam—but if he doesn't pass us before long, I'll tell Arky to pull over and let him go on past.

Crane looked out at the scrubby, baking dirt receding away to the distant mountains under the cloudless sky, and he remembered driving along this highway on that early evening in '69, in a Cadillac convertible with—what had his name been? Newt—with Newt at the wheel, nervously explaining to Crane the rules of Assumption Poker. By that time Ozzie had probably already checked out of the Mint and had been gunning for home, to move Diana and all their stuff out of the house and tack the quit-claim up on the front door. It occurred to Crane now, for the first time, that Ozzie must have had the quit-claim ready in case the fact of Crane's terrible father ever became a threat to young Diana. Well, it hadn't *become* a threat, as it happened, Crane had *made* it a threat. Crane had almost certainly led the fat man to her.

He looked over his shoulder again. The Camaro was still several car lengths behind them, its chrome trim winking in the sun. And behind it was a van that, it seemed to him now, had been in *that* position for a while.

He popped open his seat belt and turned around, kneeling on the seat, to rummage in the back.

"Change your mind about the beer?" said Mavranos.

"I'm probably imagining things," said Crane as he found his .357 and Mavranos's .38 and wrapped them in a shirt, "but why don't you pull over and let that Camaro and that van pass us, if they want to." He sat back down in his seat and unwrapped the guns.

Mavranos's eyebrows went up when he looked at the items in Crane's lap. "Pull over where? This shoulder's just gravel. By the time I slowed up enough to pull off, they'd have either passed us already or come right up our tailpipe."

Crane was silent for a while, staring ahead; then he pointed. "There's a slant-in cutoff for a dirt road up there, see it? You could turn in to it without slowing down much, if we hang on. And then if they're bad guys, we should be able to leave them behind on the dirt road. Neither of them's sprung as high as this thing."

"Shit," said Mavranos, "I wish we'd sent Wendy another five grand." He reached over and picked up his revolver and tucked it into his belt.

The truck bucked when the big tires hit the unpaved track, and the jack and spare tire and toolbox all banged back down onto the bed after having been flung into the air, and Crane pitched forward against the dashboard, grabbing his bouncing .357 and squeezing the trigger nearly hard enough to fire it. The truck was shaking violently back and forth, and Mavranos was squinting furiously ahead and shouting curses.

Crane held on to the back of the seat and looked back at the whirling dust cloud the truck had kicked up, and for a moment he thought the two vehicles had gone on past down the highway, and he opened his mouth to tell Mavranos to slow down; then he saw the nose of the Camaro plunging along after them through the dust.

Again he almost spasmodically fired his revolver.

"They're after us!" He shouted to be heard over the cacophony of squeaking and banging. "Go!"

Mavranos nodded and held on tight to the steering wheel. They were onto the dirt road now, some surveyor's track, probably, and booming straight out into the desert at what seemed like breakneck speed.

Crane glanced back again. The Camaro was falling back a little, its suspension not made for this kind of hummocky road. The van had left the highway too, he noticed, and was wallowing along farther back. A tall, three-legged plume of dust was streaming away to the south.

A particularly rough bump threw Crane against the door, and he blinked ahead through the cracked windshield at the road. A gully paralleled the road on the left, with a low slope rising to the right. The road still stretched straight as a pencil line ahead, and he wondered if it could possibly go all the way to the I-15. He and Mavranos would certainly have left their pursuers behind long before that, assuming this truck didn't blow a tire or break an axle.

Even over the racket inside the truck, he heard the hard boom of a gunshot.

"Faster!" he yelled. He grabbed the window handle and started to crank it down, thinking to shoot back at the Camaro, but he could hardly brace himself well enough on the jumping seat to turn the handle, and it occurred to him that he would have little chance of hitting the car, shooting from such a shaky position, and he might need every bullet if the truck were to be stopped.

And the next *boom* was simultaneous with an echoing slam from the rear of the truck—and then the truck, still thundering forward, was sliding around to the left, kicking and jumping on the sandy road, and Crane grabbed the dashboard with his free hand and braced his feet against the floor, thinking the vehicle was going to roll over on his side. Mavranos was fighting the wheel, trying to wrestle it to the right and turn out of the skid.

"Shot out the left rear tire," Mavranos gasped as he finally got the back end in line and then stomped on the brake, bringing the truck to a clanging, thudding halt turned sideways across the road, pointed up the slope and away from the gully.

Mavranos threw the gearshift lever into park, and then he and Crane were out the doors.

Crane didn't know where Mavranos was, but he crouched up the slope by the front bumper, coughing in the stinging dust cloud, and squinted over the barrel of the cocked .357 as he swung it from side to side over the hot hood.

Instead of the two recent shots, it was a shotgun blast from three days ago that was echoing in his mind. Bring me the fat man, God, he prayed, and you can have me.

"Freeze!" came a harsh, choked shout from out of the dust fog. "Police, Lieutenant Frits! Crane and Mavranos, step away from the truck with your hands on your heads!"

The wind was thinning the dust, and Crane could see Mavranos now—he was plodding slowly toward the gully, away from the back bumper, his empty hands raised.

Crane had lowered his own gun and straightened.

A vague silhouette was visible ahead, against the bulk of the Camaro. "Crane!" came the voice again. "Away from the truck, now!"

Uncertainly Crane stepped around the front of the truck and took two steps along the slope. His gun was still in his hand, but by his side, pointed at the ground.

A gust of wind cleared the air. The fat man, Vaughan Trumbill, stood in front of the Camaro, both arms extended forward, his left hand pointing an automatic at Mavranos and his right pointing a rifle at Crane. A white bandage bobbed on his spherical bald head, but his hands were steady.

"*Not* really," said Trumbill. "Drop it, Crane."

The van was rocking up into position behind the Camaro. Its windshield was opaqued with dust, and Crane could only wonder how many guns might be leveled at himself and Mavranos behind it.

Right, Crane thought dully. Frits would have had sirens or a light, even in an unmarked car.

Crane looked across the road at Mavranos. Mavranos's eyes squinted at him almost humorously over the dusty mustache.

"I'm okay," Mavranos called. "I liked Ozzie too."

Trumbill was striding toward Mavranos, his tie and the tails of his suit coat flapping like banners on a ship. "Drop it or I kill your buddy, Crane," he shouted, his pouchy eyes staring hard into Crane's face.

"Hah!" yelled Mavranos, stomping one foot in the dust.

Trumbill's head whipped around toward him, his automatic up—

—And Crane, as aware of the imagined guns behind the van's windshield as he would have been of a scorpion on his face, was grateful to his friend for making this easy—

—as he snapped his revolver up into line and touched the cocked trigger.

The full-throated *bam* rocked his head back and he let the recoil spin him around to fall onto his knees with the gun aimed at the windshield of the van.

The van must already have been in reverse gear, for even as Crane was falling to his knees, its front end had dipped and it had begun to back away at full throttle, its front tires throwing up sand in two churning clouds.

Crane swiveled his gunsight toward the rear of the truck, but Mavranos was standing alone in the road, his back to Crane, looking away from the receding van now to peer down into the gully.

After one more tense, hard-breathing moment Crane raised the barrel and stood up.

The van, which Crane could now see had a florist's logo on its side, had reached a wide spot and backed around broadside; now it moved forward, turning back toward the highway, and drove away faster.

Crane plodded down the slope and across the road, and he stopped at the lip of the gully a few yards away from Mavranos.

Trumbill lay sprawled on his back in the sandy bed of the wash a few yards below them. His coat was open, and the white shirt over his belly was reddening fast. The rifle he had been carrying lay on the roadside near Mavranos, and the automatic rested upright against a stone halfway down the slope of the gully.

"Good shootin', Pogo," said Mavranos.

Crane looked at him. His friend hadn't been shot, but he was weaving on his feet and looked pale and sick.

"Thanks," said Crane. He supposed he must look the same way.

"Camaro," said Trumbill loudly. *"Take it to . . . telephone."* Speaking the words seemed to cost him a lot, but his voice was strong. *"Medevac."*

No, thought Crane. "No," he said.

I've got to kill him, he thought in sick amazement, finish him off. I can't take prisoners here. Would the police jail him? For what? Ozzie's body is gone, and even if the fat man left enough evidence to be charged with Diana's murder—which isn't likely—he would certainly be freed on bail. Of course he'd be in a hospital for a long time, but couldn't he work for my father from a hospital? He wouldn't let Scat and Oliver slip through his fingers, as he did with the infant Diana.

And I'd be in jail, at least for a while. Maybe a long time. What the hell kind of story could I tell the police?

I've got to kill him. Right here. Right now.

"Mavranos," Trumbill called now. *"I can cure your cancer. You can . . . go back to your family . . . a healthy man. Decades."* He inhaled loudly enough for the men up on the bank to hear. *"Trank darts—in rifle. Shoot Crane."*

Crane turned and looked at the rifle that lay a yard from Mavranos's feet, and then he looked up and met Mavranos's gaze.

Crane didn't think Mavranos could get the rifle up before he could raise the revolver and shoot him—but he realized that he was physically incapable of shooting Arky. He slowly opened his hand and let the revolver clank to the dirt.

"Do what you gotta do, Arky," he said.

Mavranos nodded slowly. "I'm thinking of Wendy, and the girls," he said.

Slowly he stepped over to where the rifle lay on the ground, and then he kicked it away, toward the truck's front tire.

"Wendy saved you."

Crane exhaled and nodded, then turned back to Trumbill and swallowed hard as he crouched down to retrieve the revolver.

"Okay," moaned Trumbill. His face was pale and gleaming with sweat in the harsh sunlight, and his pudgy hands

were fists. *"Last request! Call this number . . . tell him where my . . . body is. Three-eight-two—"*

"No," said Crane, shakily raising the mirror-bright gun. "I don't know what kind of magic he could do with your corpse." He blinked tears out of his eyes but spoke steadily. "Best you rot out here, feed the birds and the bugs."

"No-o-o-o-o!" Somehow in spite of his terrible wound, Trumbill was roaring down there, and the fearful, jarring noise seemed to fill the desert and shake the remote sky. *"Not the skinny man, not the skinny man, not the—"*

Crane thought of Ozzie and of Diana, both killed by this man.

And he pulled the trigger.

Bam.

"—Skinny ma-a-a-a-an—"

Bam. Bam. Bam. Bam.

Click.

The hot air of the flat desert gave back no echoes from the shots. Crane lowered the emptied gun and stared, astonished, at the red-spattered body sprawled motionless in the sand of the dry stream bed.

Then the dirt surface of the road was under Crane's face, between his spread hands, and he was spasmodically vomiting up the dregs of the Coke he'd had for breakfast.

When he was able to roll away to the side, spitting and gasping, he saw through his tears that Mavranos had opened the back of the truck and was lugging the jack to the flat tire.

"I can do this, Pogo," Mavranos called. "Why don't you see if you can't push that Camaro into the wash. I've got a couple of tarps we can throw over it and weight down with rocks. No harm if this goes *undetected* for a while, and I don't think the boys in that van are gonna make any calls."

Crane nodded and got wearily to his feet.

Fifteen minutes later they were driving slowly back along the dirt road toward the highway, Mavranos absently cursing the damage that he imagined had been done to the truck's suspension. Crane rocked in the passenger seat and stared out at the broken stones of the desert, trying to feel a grim satisfaction at having avenged Ozzie, or to feel pride in having competently shot the fat man, or to feel *anything* besides the remembered horror of pulling that sweat-slick trigger again and again and again.

After they had got back onto the highway and were again rolling south toward the lake, he looked at his right hand, and for a moment he hoped that his father would succeed in taking this body away from him.

CHAPTER 39

Combination of the Two

"This don't look much like Vegas," Mavranos said as he steered the shaky, dusty truck through the quiet streets of Boulder City. Somehow the radio was playing what Crane thought was the best rock song ever recorded, Big Brother and the Holding Company's "Combination of the Two."

Today Crane felt as though he'd lost the right, the *ability*, to participate in it.

He blinked and looked around at the complacent Spanish-style houses and the green lawns. "Hmm? Oh—no, it's not anything like it." His voice sounded oddly flat in his head. He was making an effort to talk normally, to talk as he would have if he had not just . . . *killed* a man. "This is the only place in Nevada where gambling's not legal," he went on doggedly. "In fact, hard liquor only became legal here in '69."

"No gambling at all?"

"Nope." He grinned stiffly and shook his head. " 'Cept for a—a certain Poker game on a houseboat once every twenty years or so."

And that starts up tomorrow night, he thought. And when this latest series of games is done, come Holy Saturday, he'll assume this old body of mine, unless I've stopped him somehow.

On the radio Janis Joplin was wailing, but not for him.

"Huh," said Mavranos. "Nothing to do me any good. Maybe I can get in a game of penny-lagging."

Crane glanced at Mavranos, feeling oppressed now about him, too. Mavranos was definitely thinner and paler than he had been when they'd driven out from Los Angeles, and now he was never without the bandanna tied up tight around his throat. I wonder, Crane thought, if Trumbill *could,* possibly, have cured Arky's cancer. Surely that was just a desperate bluff.

"Left up ahead there, on Lakeshore Road," Crane said.

"We're not going to the dam?"

"No. The nearest marinas and beaches are up the west shore of the lake. That's where we can rent scuba gear and a boat. At the dam all you can do is look."

"I wanted to see the dam."

"We'll go see it later, okay?" said Crane shortly. "Later in the week. You can buy a T-shirt and everything."

"It's one of the seven man-made wonders of the world."

"Yeah? What are the others?"

"I don't know. Montezooma's Revenge at Knott's Berry Farm's one, I think."

"We'll get you a T-shirt there, too, on the way home."

Their laughter was brief and tense. Mavranos finished his beer and popped another. Poor dead Janis Joplin howled on out of the speakers that were hung on adhesive tape from the roof struts behind the front seat.

At a dive shop near the Government Dock Crane rented a new outfit of U.S. Divers scuba gear and a full wet suit with hood and boots and a gear bag to carry it all in. They rented a speedboat at the Lake Mead Resort Circle, and by noon they were gunning out across the blue face of the lake under the empty blue sky.

After a few minutes they had left behind the water-skiers and had got out to where the wind was raising random choppy waves, and Crane pulled back on the Morris throttle, reversing the engine and bringing the boat to an uneven, rocking halt. Mavranos had been hanging on to the dashboard bar during the bouncy, spray-flinging ride, and now he took off his Greek fisherman's cap, whacked it against his knee, and put it on again.

"You through shakin' us up?" he asked in the sudden quiet.
"I'm gonna step back to the ice chest, but not if you're gonna
bounce me right out."

"Yeah, I'll take it easy."

They were alone out on the water under the arching, cloudless sky, but Crane had to focus his eye to stop seeing the fat
man's body jumping and bursting as the bullets hit, and he
yawned so that his ears would pop and he would blessedly
hear only the wind and the idling engine.

Well, he thought, here I am. What do I do now, just jump
in?

A little red fishing boat rocked on the water a hundred yards
away, and the man in it seemed to be looking at them. Crane
wondered if their crashing arrival out here had scared off all
the fish.

Mavranos came back and sat down in the bucket seat, a
fresh beer foaming in his fist. "Ride did the beer a lot of
good," he growled, wiping foam off his mustache. "Where's
the head?"

"You gotta just piss over the side, man," said Crane. "No,
I know what you meant." He brushed the wind-disordered
hair back from his forehead and looked around at the vast
face of the lake. "I, uh, don't know, exactly. It's probably
in this section of the lake, the Boulder Basin; there's also
the Overton Arm and the Temple Basin and Gregg Basin,
miles away over those mountains, but this is certainly the
most *accessible* part."

There should be a hand holding a sword, he thought helplessly, sticking up out of the water.

He unfolded the map the boat rental clerk had given him.
"Let's see what we got," he said, tracing his finger along the
outline of the Boulder Basin. "I don't know, here's Moon
Cove; that sounds possible. And Deadman's Island; I like
that."

Mavranos leaned over and breathed beer fumes at him.
"Roadrunner Cove," he read. "I like that. *Beep-beep*."

Crane looked back at the gear bag, wondering if he would
even get into the wet suit today.

"Let's just go," he said finally. "I'll take it slower, but
hang on."

He drove the boat along at a steady twenty miles an hour northward, paralleling the west coastline up toward Moon Cove.

Blank your mind, he told himself. Maybe the dead King is ready to guide you, but the static racket of your thoughts is keeping him from getting through.

He tried, but he wasn't able to make himself really relax into it. Blanking his mind in these circumstances seemed too much like leaving one's car running and unlocked in a bad neighborhood.

After only a few minutes they had rounded the cove's north point. Crane consulted the map and learned that the inlet ahead of them was called Pumphouse Cove. A houseboat with bright blue awnings was moored there, and he could see a family and a dog around a picnic table on the shore.

This didn't feel like the right place. The sun was hot on his head, and he envied Mavranos his cap and his beer.

He swung the boat around and headed back south, angling further out away from the shore, heading for the string of islands poking up above the water like a dead god's vertebrae in the southern reaches of the basin.

"What kind of fish they got in here?" Mavranos called over the burbling roar of the engine.

"Big catfish, I hear," said Crane loudly, squinting in the breeze. "And carp. Bass."

"Carp," repeated Mavranos. "That's goldfish grown up, you know; they don't die of natural causes, I heard. And they survive winters frozen solid in pond ice. The molecules in their cells just refuse to take the shape of crystallization."

Crane was glad that the breeze and the motor roar made it natural not to reply. His search for a sunken severed head almost seemed rational compared with Arky's notions about math and science: anti-carcinogenic beer, phase-changes in the sports betting at Caesars Palace, goldfish that couldn't be killed . . .

Deadman's Island, hardly more than a bumpy good-size boulder with a narrow beach around it, was the closest of the islands. He squinted at it, and then stared at the red fishing boat that stood on the water very close to the east shore of it.

Mavranos had brought his battered Tasco 8 x 40 binoculars

from the truck, and Crane let off on the gas and took them out of their box.

He stood up on the fiber glass floorboard and leaned on the top of the windshield to steady the binoculars, and then he got the fishing boat in his view and twisted the center focus wheel.

The little fishing boat sprang into clarity, seeming now to be only a dozen yards away. The fisherman was a slim man in his thirties with dark hair slickly combed back, and he was staring straight at Crane, smiling. He bobbed his fishing pole as if in greeting.

"Arky," said Crane slowly, "is that the same guy there, fishing, that we saw when we first stopped? 'Cause I don't see how he could have got here so fast from—"

"Fishing where?" Mavranos interrupted.

Still staring straight at the man through the lenses, Crane pointed out over the bow of the boat. "There, by the island."

"I don't see anybody. There's some water skiers way off."

Crane lowered the binoculars and glanced at Mavranos. Was he blind drunk?

"Arky," he said patiently, "right *there,* by the—"

He stopped talking. The fishing boat was no longer there. And it could not have moved around the island out of sight in less than several minutes—certainly not in the second and a half that he'd looked away.

He exclaimed, "It's gone!" even though it seemed like a stupid thing to say.

Mavranos was staring at him impassively. "Okay."

Crane exhaled, and realized that his heart was thudding in his chest and that his palms were damp.

"Well," he said, "I guess I know where to dive."

He sat back down and cautiously stepped on the gas pedal.

The level of the lake was down, and the lower stretch of the Deadman's Island shore was a morass of once-drowned and now reexposed manzanitas, their short branches hung with strings of algae—like, Crane thought, Spanish moss strung on cypresses in a bayou. Here and there, too, were algae-covered angularities that must have been long-lost fishing poles. The rocks were just slick-looking humps with no definition under the blanket of green algae, and the breeze near the island was tainted with the wet, fermenting smell of the stuff.

"It's a real soup you're gonna be divin' into," observed Mavranos as Crane sat on the gunwale and worked his arm through a wet suit sleeve.

"Cold, too," said Crane morosely. "And rented wet suits never fit snug. There's a special kind of headache I get when I'm under cold water for too long."

He had tugged and coaxed the wet suit on and had pulled the Buoyancy Control Device, looking like a deflated life preserver vest, over his head.

"Should have got a dry suit," said Mavranos helpfully. "Or a diving bell."

"Or scheduled this meeting somewhere else," Crane said. He adjusted the straps of the backpack harness and then had Mavranos hold up the tank while he snaked his arms through the straps. He bent forward with the weight on his back to adjust them, and he made sure that the waistband release was clear and that it opened to the left. In spite of his reluctance to enter the cold, murky water, he was pleased to see that he still remembered how to suit up.

He hoped he still remembered how to breathe through a regulator. His old diving instructor had always insisted that the most dangerous thing about diving was the way gases behaved under pressure.

Dressed at last, with his weight belt on over everything and its quick-release buckle situated well clear of the BCD, he stood up and stretched. The wet suit was tight enough that it took effort to straighten both arms, but he thought it could be snugger across the front.

Oh well, he thought. A long, hot shower at whatever motel we wind up at.

His mask was up on his forehead, and the regulator mouthpiece swung by his elbow, and he turned to Mavranos before fitting it all on.

"If . . . say, forty-five minutes goes by," he said, "and I'm not back here, go ahead and split. The money's in a sock in my pants there."

Mavranos nodded stolidly. " 'Kay."

Crane pulled the mask away from his forehead and set- tled it down over his face, and then he tucked the regulator mouthpiece between his teeth, breathed through it a few times

and pushed the purge button to check the lever spring, and
finally put one foot up on the gunwale.

Dimly under the mask strap and the foam neoprene of the
hood, he heard Mavranos say, "Hey, Pogo."

Crane turned. Mavranos was holding out his right hand, and
Crane clasped it with his own.

"Don't fuck up," said Mavranos.

Crane made a circle of his thumb and forefinger, then
stepped up over the gunwale and jumped into the water with
his feet together, his right hand behind his head holding the
tank down.

He splashed in, hearing the crackle of the bubbles muffled
through his wet suit hood.

The water was cold, about sixty degrees, and as always,
it invaded his crotch first. He hooted through the regulator,
blowing a cloud of bubbles up past the face plate.

He swallowed and wiggled his jaw, feeling his ears pop
as the pressure was equalized, and then he began breathing.
Slow and deep, he told himself as he stretched his feet out
through the bottomless water. Careful the cold doesn't get you
breathing fast and shallow.

He was sinking slowly, and he relaxed and let himself go
down. Visibility was terrible—a dust of brown-green algae
hung in suspension in the darkening water, and shreds like
puffy cornflakes swirled up around him.

About six feet down he passed through one of the planes
of temperature difference called thermoclines, and again he
hooted at the suddenly colder water. He spread his hands and
kicked, halting his descent.

Dimly he could see the slope of the island through the fog
of algae. The cobblestone-size rocks were all fuzzed with the
yellow-brown muck, and he wondered how he could identify
any of the shaggy lumps as a severed head.

But the fisherman had been a little further out anyway.
Crane began swimming away through the murk, kicking with
long strokes and feeling the pull in the tendons of his insteps.

Very soon his left leg began to ache where he had stabbed
it eight days ago.

The repetitive routines of breathing and kicking began almost
to hypnotize him. He was remembering dives off Catalina after
spring rains, when the visibility was a hundred feet of crystal

blue and the boundary plane between the fresher top layer and the saltier one below was a rippling refraction, like heat waves over a highway; and he remembered climbing deep down in tide pools off La Jolla, picking up tiny octopuses and touching twitchy rainbow-colored anemones, and having to patiently untangle himself from long rubbery strands of kelp, and one time accidentally elbowing the release buckle of his weight belt and watching it plummet away into oblivion through the glassy clear water.

All he could hear was the metallic echo of his breathing in the steel air tank, and the air that he sucked in long pulses through the regulator valve was cold and tasted of metal, and as always somehow had a *gritty* feel in his mouth.

Several times he had glanced at his watch and the pressure gauge, but he had not looked at either one for a while when he began to hear, faintly, something more than his own breathing.

It was a high and rhythmic sound, and scratchy, but too slow to be echoes of any boat engine. In the algae fog he couldn't tell if he was rising or descending, so he was careful to breathe continuously, remembering that holding one's breath in a scuba ascent of nearly any distance could rupture a lung with no warning at all.

It was music, the sound he was hearing. Some kind of old forties-style swing, with a lot of brass.

He arched his back up and spread his arms forward, stopping in the dim brown opaque water.

Was this it? Was something about to happen here? He had once seen a siren device that was supposed to be lowered into water to call divers back on charter boats, and he'd heard of terribly expensive underwater speakers, and he'd read about submarines being tracked by music played in bunk rooms. . . .

But he had not ever heard music underwater.

The sound was clearer now. The tune was "Begin the Beguine," and he could hear a background clatter that was unmistakably laughter and talking.

An old, dead King, he thought with a shiver that was not all dismay, and he kicked forward again.

A knobby, pyramidical stone pillar formed in silhouette in the smoky twilight ahead of him. He sat up in the water again, letting the half-inflated BCD hold him at neutral buoyancy, and he sculled with his hands to approach the submerged tower slowly.

The air that hissed into the regulator when he inhaled was warmer now, and carried the scents of cigarette smoke and gin and paper money.

As he got to within a yard of it, he could see that the lump at the top of the rough spire was a head, a skull draped with algae instead of flesh.

The cheekbones and sockets had turned into coral, and in the left socket gleamed a big pearl.

Crane understood that this sea change was a repairing of damage, a kind of posthumous healing, and he thought of the cherub head on the Two of Wands with the two metal rods transfixing the face.

The music was loud now, and he could almost make out words among the background voices and laughter. Very clearly he smelled charbroiled steak and Béarnaise sauce.

He reached out slowly through the dirty water, and with the tip of his bare forefinger he touched the pearl that was the head's eye.

CHAPTER 40

La Mosca

And he jumped violently, blowing out a burst of air in an involuntary shout of surprise.

He was sitting in a chair, across a table from the man he had seen fishing, and they were in a long, low-ceilinged room with a pair of broad windows behind the fisherman opening out onto a bright blue sky.

Crane held very still.

The regulator mouthpiece was still between his teeth, but he was no longer wearing a diving mask, yet he was able to see clearly; therefore he was out of the water.

Slowly he reached up and took the regulator out of his mouth.

His mouth instantly filled with lake water, and he put the regulator back in his mouth and blew the water out through the exhaust valve.

Okay, he thought, nodding to himself as he tried to hold back his ready panic, you're still underwater; this is a *vision*, a *hallucination*.

This man must be the famous *dead King*.

Not wanting to meet his host's gaze quite yet, Crane rocked his head around to look at the room. A broad cement beam ran down the center of the ceiling, with wooden beams crossing through it at right angles; pictures of landscapes were framed on the cream walls, and low couches and chairs and tables were arranged casually across the broad expanse of pale tan carpet. Through the open windows behind his host he could hear laughter and the splash of someone diving into a swimming pool.

That was disorienting.

The air in his mouth tasted faintly of chlorine, and more immediately of leather and after-shave lotion.

At last he looked at the man across the table.

Again the man seemed to be in his thirties, with slicked-back brown hair and heavy-lidded, long-lashed eyes that made his faint smile secretive. A tailored pinstripe suit jacket was open over a white silk shirt with six-inch collar points.

On the polished surface of the table between them rested a pair of wrapped sugar cubes, a can of Flit insecticide, a golden cup like a chalice, and a haftless, rusted blade six inches long.

Crane remembered that Cups was his own suit in the Tarot deck, and he reached out a hand—he noted with no particular surprise that he seemed to be wearing a silk shirt, too, with onyx cuff links—and pointed at the cup.

Apparently pleased, the man smiled and stood up. Crane now saw that he was wearing high-waisted pinstripe trousers to match the jacket, and expensive-looking leather shoes with pointed toes.

"You're you, still," the man said. Crane noticed that the voice was not perfectly synchronized with the movement of the lips. "I was afraid you might not be." From inside his jacket he pulled a shiny automatic pistol. Crane tensed, ready to jump at him, but the man took the gun by the barrel and laid it on the table in front of Crane. "Take it. Safety's off, and it's chambered. All you gotta do is pull back the hammer and pull the trigger."

Crane picked it up. It was heavy Springfield Arms .45 with wooden grips. He paused, wondering if the man wanted him to do anything with it; then his host turned away, and Crane shrugged and tucked the gun into the belt of the gray slacks that had replaced the black wet-suit pants.

The man walked to an open sliding glass door at one corner of the pool-facing side of the room, and looked back and beckoned with a manicured hand.

Crane got to his feet, noting that he was wearing shoes instead of rubber fins and that he didn't seem to have the weight or bulk of the scuba tank on his back, and he walked across the carpet and followed his host out onto a small square terrace.

Below them a green lawn dotted with palm trees stretched out to the concrete apron of the pool, and beyond the pool was the casino, painted pistachio green. On the far side of the casino, past the narrow highway, the desert stretched away to the horizon, and Crane had to lean over the terrace coping and look to his right to see the nearest building, a low, rambling structure on the highway's far side half a mile north.

He recognized it. He'd been there many times as a little boy.

That was the Last Frontier, a sort of dude ranch casino and motel with western decor and a short "street" of transplanted ghost town buildings behind it to entertain children.

It was later sold, reopened in 1955 as the New Frontier, and then was torn down in '65. The Frontier Casino in which he had been playing Poker last week was built in '67 on the same spot.

And of course he knew where he was. He looked down, and shivered to see the remembered rose garden.

He was on the penthouse terrace of the Flamingo Hotel as the place had been in early '47, before the murder of Benjamin Siegel—popularly known as "Bugsy," though the man had seldom been called that to his face. This was how the Flamingo had looked when it was still the only elegant casino-hotel in Las Vegas. With its fourth-floor penthouse, it was the tallest building within seven miles.

Crane straightened and looked at the flashily dressed man standing beside him. He tried to say, "Mr. Siegel," but only succeeded in blowing air out of the regulator.

"You know what place this is," said Siegel. Crane caught a trace of a New York accent, and he saw that the sound was now synchronized with the mouth.

Crane nodded.

"My castle," Siegel said as he turned and walked back into the long living room. "Your father probably took you here, after he shot me up."

He paused at a narrow bookcase that was built into the wall; the lower section was enclosed, and he winked at Crane and lifted away the knee-level bottom shelf, spilling books onto the floor. Under the shelf, instead of the narrow box of a cupboard, was a rectangular shaft that receded away into darkness below, with a wooden ladder mounted against the far wall of it.

"Bolt-hole and hidey-hole," Siegel said.

He tossed the shelf aside and strode back to the table and resumed his chair.

"Sit down," Siegel said.

Crane walked back across the carpet and perched himself on the edge of the opposite chair, aware of the hard bulk of the gun under his belt. He reminded himself to breathe steadily and not hold his breath; back in the real, 1990 world, he might be rising or sinking right now, or even floating on the surface.

"John Scarne showed me a gimmick for a proposition bet one time," said Siegel, peeling off the paper wrappers from the sugar cubes. He put the bared white cubes out on the table and then unscrewed the cap of the can of Flit. "It's called *la mosca*. That means 'the fly' in Spanish."

From below the table he lifted an intercom microphone. "Hey, chef?" he said into it. "This is Benny. Jack's here, and we need one live fly." He let go of the microphone, and it dissolved into smoke.

Siegel dipped a finger into the can and then lightly touched the top face of each sugar cube. "I won ten grand off Willie Moretti with this, once, right here in this room. The idea is, you bet on which sugar cube the fly will land on. It looks like

an even-up bet, right? But what you do, you turn the cubes so
the one your man picked has the DDT face up, and the other
is DDT down. The fly always goes for the unpoisoned face,
and you win your bet."

A quiet knock sounded on a hallway door behind Crane,
and Siegel called, "Come in!"

Crane heard a door open, and then a figure in a tuxedo had
walked up from behind and stopped beside his chair. Siegel
pointed at the tabletop.

Crane was able to keep from shouting through the regulator,
but he did twitch back in his seat when he saw the room service
waiter's hand.

It was the hand of a skeleton, the bones furred and strung
with wet brown algae. The long fingers daintily set down a
cardboard box with holes punched in the lid. A loud buzzing
sounded from inside it.

One of Siegel's eyes was blank white now, with the sheen
of pearl, but he smiled at Crane and turned one of the sugar
cubes upside down, and then he lifted the lid off the box.

The fly was a buzzing insect that seemed to be the size
of a plum, and it was up and out and flying around the
table in an instant, its jointed legs dangling loosely under
its swooping body.

Crane flinched away from it, but it was circling the sugar
cubes now.

"Say you'd bet five grand he'd land on that one," Siegel said
cheerfully, pointing at the one with the DDT face still up.

The fly landed on the other one, its long legs seeming to
hug the cube, its face working at the surface.

The light through the windows was dimming; Siegel waved
a brown hand, and several lamps came on, casting a yellow
glow over the table. The motion had startled the fly away
from the sugar, and while it was looping heavily through the
air again, he picked up the cube the insect had spurned and
tossed it over his shoulder, out the window.

"That was for betting," Siegel said. His voice was raspy
now, and Crane looked up at him. The tan skin of Siegel's
cheek was peeling, exposing rough blue coral. "This is for . . .
illustration."

Again the fly landed on the cube and began gnawing at it.
Crane could hear a tiny grinding.

"It knows there's a poison one," wheezed Siegel, "but it doesn't realize this is the one. It sees the sweet edible face and doesn't know it hides the same poison."

In the dimming light, dots seemed to be flickering on the cube, as if it were a white die; then the flickering marks seemed to be card suits. The fly was tossing aside fragments of sugar in its haste to devour the cube, and its bristly head was buried in a hole it had eaten into the thing.

Then the fly shuddered and tumbled off. It lay on its back, its long legs working in the air and a muddy liquid running out of its face.

"Too late," said Siegel huskily, "it realizes its mistake."

The windows behind him were closed now, and behind the glass rectangles, as if they were panels of an aquarium, churned the algae-fogged water of Lake Mead.

The walls and furniture were dissolving, and the light was going fast.

Siegel's head hung in the smoky dimness in front of Crane. The hair was gone, and the skin was a mossy smoothness except where the coral showed through. "*He killed me,*" grated the head, "*shot out my eye, cut off my head in the mortuary, and threw it in the lake! In memory of me, too, do this.*"

The rubber rim of the diving mask was suction-cupping Crane's face again, and its sides blocked his peripheral vision, and he could feel the slick layer of water between his skin and the neoprene wet suit. When he kicked himself away from the head that sat on top of the spire, his fins propelled him well back, so that the head was now just the bumpy top of the column in the murky water.

Breathing fast through the regulator, he thrashed spasmodically away through the dirty cold water.

Okay, he thought nervously, *think.* What did I get out of that? I learned that my father killed Bugsy Siegel, who was apparently King before him. But what do I do now? Am I supposed to . . . what, put poisoned sugar in my father's coffee or something?

Whatever had happened here today, it was clearly over, and he turned and started to swim back the way he'd come. His left leg was feeling tight-strung, and every time he breathed now he could hear a ringing metallic *broong* in the tank, a sure sign that he was low on air.

*   *   *

He arched his back upward, ready to ascend to the surface—and saw the silhouettes of two divers above him. Both carried spear guns.

And both had obviously just now become aware of him; they curled downward in the water, extending the guns at him.

Crane jerked in horrified surprise and started to thrash around, hoping to kick his way fast down to the deeper, darker water, but an instant later the spears punched him.

One wrenched his head around as it tore off his mask, and the other had hit the buckle and heavy web fabric of his weight belt; he could feel that that one had cut him.

Its barbs had caught in the skin of his torn wet suit, and he could feel it being tugged upward; if it tore free, the man would yank the tethered spear back, reload, and fire again. The other diver was probably already pulling in his own spear, perhaps had already retrieved it and reloaded.

Crane fumbled at his belt and the shaft of the snagged spear, and then he found the spear's tether and pulled at it, dragging himself up toward the diver.

Crane's eyes were open, but his mask was gone. He could see nothing in the murky water, and had to exhale through his nose like a novice. Over his panic he was peripherally aware of the music again, "Begin the Beguine," and of laughter and loud talking.

Then, even without a mask, Crane saw the blurry bulk of the diver above him, and at the same moment the tether went slack in his hands; the man had let go of the spear gun and would now probably come in close with a knife to finish Crane off.

The man was close—only a couple of yards away.

Without thinking, Crane dragged his hand back down through the water and grabbed again at his belt—and Siegel's .45 was there. He pulled it free, thumbing back the hammer as he thrust it up through the water and pointed it at the looming figure whose agitation of the water he could now feel, and he pulled the trigger.

The gun actually fired, though Crane saw no flash, and the underwater shot sounded like a loud, hoarse shout.

Blurrily he saw the body above him convulse in the water.

Christ, I've hurt him, maybe killed him, Crane thought dizzily. *How could I have known a .45 would shoot underwater?*

He heard a muted crack then, and the mask strap tugged at his throat—the other diver had fired his spear again, and had again hit Crane's mask, which was now broken and swinging loosely below his right ear.

With his free hand Crane reached up and gripped the shaft of the spear. With his other hand he raised the automatically recocked .45.

His eyes were straining through the cloudy water as the fast bubbles from his nose churned in front of his face— and all at once he was again seeing through his false right eye.

From against a black background that might have been the night sky, a whitely luminous figure was moving toward him. Like a double-exposure photograph, it was a scuba diver with mask and fins but was also a robed, bearded King, and the object it held out before itself was at once a spear gun and a scepter.

Crane raised his right arm, seeing it draped in a baggy sleeve as well as cased in black neoprene, and though he felt the grip of a .45 automatic, he seemed to be holding out a golden chalice.

His tank was ringing with each breath—*broong, broong*— and it was taking effort now to pull air into his lungs through the regulator.

You have to shoot, he told himself over the shrill, despairing wail in his head. You have to squeeze the trigger and kill another man—and maybe the gun won't shoot a second time underwater anyway.

The double-exposure figure was almost upon him. If the gun did fire, Crane could not possibly miss.

He pulled the trigger, and again the water shook to the short, hard shout of the report—and abruptly he could see only the blur of cloudy water in front of his left eye.

He kicked away, pulling the spear along with him; the only drag on the spear was the inertia of an unencumbered spear gun, and he felt safe in tucking the .45 back into his torn weight belt.

His air was just about entirely gone, and the rented tank had a simple K-valve, with no reserve-air mechanism. He needed to get up right now.

He looked up and extended the spear over his head and began to kick upward. Without the mask he couldn't see how fast his bubbles were rising, and he had no idea how deep he might be, so against the urgency of his laboring lungs he made himself kick slowly.

If there was any air at all left in the tank now, his lungs didn't have the strength to suck it out—but he kept the regulator clamped in his teeth to help resist the increasing spasmodic urge to inhale lake water.

He was exhaling steadily through his nose, but there wasn't much air left in his lungs. Surely I can hold my breath *now,* he thought desperately. If the goddamn tank's empty, there's no pressure to pop a lung!

But he remembered seeing a diver surface once with a ruptured lung, the face mask opaque with bloody froth, and he kept on exhaling.

I'm going downward, he thought in sudden, pure panic. I've been kicking myself straight down. It's the *bottom* I'm going to hit, not the surface.

He paused, his heart pounding, and he stared down past his fins to see if the water was brighter in that direction—and suddenly his ears were out of the water.

He yanked his head back, spat out the regulator mouthpiece, and for half a minute just hung at the surface and stared into the blue sky and gasped huge lungfuls of hot dry air. If there's bad guys on a boat nearby, he thought, let 'em shoot me. At least I'll die with oxygen in my blood.

Nobody shot at him. After a while he fished up the BCD mouthpiece and inflated the thing enough so that he could float without using his hands or feet to tread water.

When he reached up and peeled off the wet suit hood, he heard his name being shouted across the water. He turned around. There was Deadman's Island, and there, perhaps a hundred yards away, was the speedboat, with Mavranos standing up behind the windshield.

Crane waved his free hand. *"Arky!"* he yelled hoarsely.

The boat roared, turned its bow toward him, and began to increase in size, rising and falling and throwing spray out to the sides.

He hoped Mavranos could handle the boat well enough not to run him down—especially since Mavranos was looking off to the starboard and pointing at something.

Crane blinked water out of his eye and looked more closely. Mavranos was pointing his *revolver* at something.

Crane twisted his head around in that direction and saw another boat, further away, with a couple of figures standing up in it.

Then Mavranos had arrived and had spun the boat out in a spray-flinging halt, blocking Crane's view of the other boat.

"In, Pogo!"

Mavranos had flung an end of rope over the side, and Crane grabbed it and pulled and kicked, and at the expense of all his remaining strength he managed to clamber aboard even with his tank and weight belt still on.

"You take the gun," Mavranos said, shoving the revolver into Crane's shaking, dripping hand. "I'm getting us out of here."

Crane obediently tried to hold the gun up and aimed at the men in the distant boat. "Who," he gasped, "are they?"

"I don't know." Mavranos sat down in the pilot seat and shoved the throttle forward. "Their boss and another guy went in the water with spear guns a little after you went in," he shouted over the roar of the engine, "and I looked at them and they looked at me, but neither of us had any real excuse to mess with the other—but they got real agitated just now when one of them, their boss, I guess, came back up."

He took one hand off the wheel to point, and Crane let himself glance away from the other boat long enough to see the hooded and masked head bobbing inertly on the surface of the water behind them. Mavranos's wake rippled under the head just then, and it rocked as loosely as a floating basketball.

"They don't know if he's dead," called Mavranos. "We want to be well away before they make up their minds what to do."

The distant boat seemed to be moving now, but Mavranos had a good head start, and the men in the other boat would probably stop to pull the floating body aboard.

Crane let his quivering arm lower the gun, and after just sitting and panting for a dozen bouncing jumps over the waves, he got up on his knees and popped open the release buckle of

the weight belt . . . and then, though he could feel hot blood
leaking across his skin under the torn wet suit, he stared for
several seconds at the rough object the belt had been holding
against him.

It was recognizably a semiautomatic pistol, but the wooden
grips were gone, and the slide was rusted solid with the frame,
and crusty brown corrosion had narrowed the muzzle to a
rough-edged little bore that a .22 round wouldn't fit through.

He put it down carefully on the pebbled white plastic deck
and after a moment remembered his cut side and reached for
the backpack harness release buckle.

Under the neoprene skin, blood had blotted down his leg
nearly as far as the knee and had gorily soaked his crotch,
but the cut itself, though long and ragged, wasn't deep; when
he tied the sleeves of his shirt around his waist, balling up
the bulk of the shirt over the cut, the cloth didn't seem to be
absorbing much blood.

He picked up the decayed gun and then dizzily groped his
way forward and collapsed into the seat beside Mavranos. The
lake breeze was wonderfully cool on his sweaty chest and in
his wet hair.

"That's—that was their boss, all right," he said loudly,
"and I believe he is dead. The lake won't contain a dead
would-be King's head. If I'd died down there, *my* head'd be
poking out."

Mavranos glanced at him with one eyebrow raised over a
squint. "You kill the other guy, too?"

"I—yeah, I think so." Crane was shivering now.

"With what? Your knife?"

"Uh . . . with this."

Mavranos glanced down at the rusted chunk of metal on
Crane's lap, and his eyes widened. "That's a *gun*, isn't it?
What did you do, hit 'em with it?"

Crane was pressing his side above the bump of his pelvis.
His cut was starting to ache, and he wondered if Lake Mead
water was particularly infectious. "I ought to try to eat something," he said. "I'll tell you all about it, over dinner back in
Vegas. Right now let's return this boat and get the hell out of
these mountains. The wet suit's too full of blood to turn back
in to the shop, and the weight belt's got a spear tear in it—I'll

tie the whole lot of gear together and sink it before we get in. The dive shop can put it on my Visa."

Mavranos shook his head and spat over the side. "The way this goddamn royal family throws money around."

As Mavranos backed the Suburban out of the marina parking space and clanked it into drive, he paused, then pointed ahead through the cracked, dusty windshield.

"Look at that, Pogo," he said.

Crane shifted on the seat and stared at the opposite row of parked cars baking in the sun. Three were white El Camino pickups.

"You wanna go see if the *El C* is busted off their emblems?"

"No," Crane said, wearing a souvenir Lake Mead sweat shirt now but still feeling shaky. "No, let's just get out of here."

"I don't think we *need* to check, at that," said Mavranos. He drove forward and rocked the truck down the ramp to the road. A sign said that Lakeshore Road was to the right, and he spun the wheel that way. "I think you killed the King of the Amino Acids."

In the parking lot of the Fashion Show Mall across the Strip from the Desert Inn, the raggedy man watched the parked camper and tugged at the forefinger of his left hand and wondered when he would get something to eat today.

He couldn't get the free shrimp cocktails anymore at the Lady Luck up on Third Street by the Continental Trailways bus depot—a waiter there had given him five dollars and told him they'd call the cops if he ever showed up again, looking the way he did and smelling so bad—but Dondi Snayheever could still get plenty of free popcorn at the Slots of Fun on the Strip.

And at the many cheap buffets and breakfasts all over town he had run into specimens that looked far worse than he did.

He was good at begging, too, it turned out. The shadowy, mechanically moving people would often, if briefly, become real Persons when they approached him; and then it would be Strength with her humbled lion, or the Hermit, or the naked hermaphrodite that was the World, or the Lovers, if it was a couple, who dropped gold coins into the palm of his hot, lean right hand. The Persons quickly disappeared after that, leaving in their places the little shadow people, who even with their dim, papery faces managed to express vague puzzlement and distaste and surprise at what they'd done, and the gold coins turned into mere quarters and chips, but he could spend the stuff. Probably more easily than he could spend real gold coins.

He knew what cliff face it was that he was destined to dance on soon, on this coming Friday, Good Friday—he had seen a picture of it, a postcard in a rack in a souvenir store—but he still had to find his mother.

And kill his treacherous father.

That last was going to be hard, since his father could change bodies now. Snayheever had been watching the little figures on the trapezes in Circus Circus yesterday, and he had suddenly been talking to his father—*gumby gumby, pudding and pineal*—but the guards there had made him leave, and he hadn't stayed in contact long enough to work out where his father actually, physically *was*.

The fingers of his right hand were still in under the dirty bandage that wrapped his left hand, wiggling the cold left forefinger.

He had seen a man leave the camper this morning, and he was pretty sure that it was his father. The man had been dressed in a white leather jacket with sequins on it, and high white boots, and his hair had been shellacked into an impressive pompadour, but before Snayheever had been able to come shuffling across the parking lot to him, he had got into a cab and left. And now he must be aware of Snayheever's presence here, for he was staying away.

He won't come back until I leave, Snayheever reasoned. He thinks he can drive away then, and ditch me again. But I'll put a homing device on his truck, so I can always know where he is.

The finger popped free at last, with no pain at all but with a bit of a smell. He pulled it out of the bandage and looked at it, and saw that it was black. Perhaps I'm becoming a Negro, he thought.

He shuffled over to the truck, cleaving his way through the thick air by making swimming motions with his hands, and he crouched by the rear bumper and wedged the finger tightly in behind the license plate.

Free to leave now, he began swimming away across the parking lot in the direction of Slots of Fun.

CHAPTER 41

Bolt-Hole and Hidey-Hole

On Monday morning Crane sat in a motel room off Paradise and stared at the telephone. He shivered in the breeze from the rackety air conditioner, and he pressed the bandage over his hip-bone, wondering if he should change it again.

Nearly twenty-four hours had passed since the spear had cut his side, but the wound was still bleeding—not a lot, but every time he untucked his shirt and peeled back the bandage, he saw fresh red blood on the gauze.

And his scalp and his scarred ankle itched, and his right eye socket throbbed—but while the muscles of his arms and legs should have been aching from yesterday's exertions in the lake, instead he felt altogether stronger, springier, than he had in years.

Mavranos was sitting in a chair by the window, rubbing a finger over the flimsy paper one of the Sausage McMuffins with Eggs had been wrapped in, and then he licked the re-coagulating cheese off his finger. He swallowed, though he apparently had to rotate his head to do it.

"Back of my throat feels like it's dry, no matter how much I swallow," he said irritably. "Even drinking *water* doesn't help." He looked at Crane, who was still pressing his side. "Cut still bleeding?"

"Probably," Crane said.

"Well, it's right where Snayheever's bullet tore you. Place ain't gettin' a chance to heal."

Crane sipped his coffee. Mavranos of course had brought in the ice chest and was working on a beer. "The Fisher King's supposed to be wounded," Crane said. "Maybe this is a good sign."

"That's a healthy attitude. If it ever does heal up, you can

409

stab your leg again." Mavranos looked at the clock radio on the nightstand. "Your man probably just wanted to get rid of you."

Since midafternoon yesterday Crane had been calling local Tarot readers and New Age occultist shops, and finally this morning he had been referred to a bookseller in San Francisco who specialized in antique Tarot decks.

The man had at first tried to interest Crane in some of the decks that had been reprinted in Europe in 1977, which apparently had been declared the honorary six hundredth anniversary of playing cards, but when Crane repeated the name of the deck he was interested in, and told the man some of the things Spider Joe had said, the bookseller had paused for so long that Crane had wondered if he had hung up. He had then got Crane's phone number and promised to call him back.

"Maybe," Crane said now. "Hosin' me, maybe." He wondered if the man had given the motel room's phone number to some terrible Tarot Secret Police, and if shortly there would be a hard knock at the door.

The phone rang instead, and Crane picked it up.

"Is this," said the bookseller's voice, "the gentleman who was asking about an old Tarot deck?"

"Yes," Crane said.

"Very good. Sorry for the delay—I had to wait for one of the employees to get back from her break, and I didn't want to discuss this over the store phone. I'm in a phone booth right now. Uh—yes, I know what deck you're talking about. It didn't ring a bell at first because it's not sought by collectors and isn't even considered an antique deck. No versions of it that survive are older than the 1930s, though the designs do seem to go way back, possibly antedating, as the name would imply, the recently rediscovered twenty-three cards known as the Lombardy I cards, the owner of which chooses to remain anonymous. Mostly these cards are used now by a few avant-garde psychoanalysts, who don't wish that fact to be known. Not exactly sanctioned by the AMA, hmm?"

"Psychoanalysts?"

"So I am given to understand. Powerful symbols, you know, effective in reviving catatonics and so forth. Equivalent of electroshock therapy in some cases."

Over the phone Crane heard the booming rattle of a truck driving past the man's phone booth.

"Uh," the man said when he could again be heard, "I gather you are not yourself a psychoanalyst, but that you know something about this deck, these so-called Lombardy Zeroth cards. Did you know that there is no one, right now, painting them? At one time there was a sort of guild of a few men who . . . *could* paint them, but since the war it has been a capital crime in several European countries even to *own* a deck. Nothing on the law books, you understand, but a capital crime nonetheless. Yes indeed. But I do happen to know of a source. You realize this would involve . . . a good deal of money."

"Yes," Crane said.

"Of course, of course. Well, if you could bring a deposit of half what I estimate it will cost, I can approach the owner—an elderly widowed woman in Manhattan, who keeps the cards in a"—he chuckled uncomfortably—"a lead box in a safe-deposit vault. I'd need . . . say, two hundred and fifty thousand dollars, preferably in cash. She owns twenty cards, from a deck painted in Marseilles in 1933, and—"

"No," said Crane into the phone, "I need a full deck." And by this Wednesday, he thought.

"My dear sir, there simply *aren't* any. Even in the Visconti and Visconti-Sforza collections, for instance, there are no surviving examples of the Devil or the Tower cards. The . . . *shock treatment* was too severe, I suppose. I can say with confidence that if any complete Lombardy Zeroth decks are in existence anywhere, they would be in the hands of old families in Europe, and not for sale, or even acknowledgment, under any circumstances."

"Bullshit," said Crane, "I've *seen* two different complete decks, one in 1948 and one in 1969. And I've talked to the man who painted one of them."

There was a long silence from the other end of the line. Finally the man said, quietly, "Was he all right?"

"Well, he was blind." Crane was silent now for a few seconds. "He, uh, cut out his eyes twenty years ago."

"Did he indeed. And you've seen the cards, a full deck. Are *you* all right?"

Crane pressed his side and enviously watched Mavranos sip beer. "No."

"Trust me," said the voice on the telephone, "it won't help you to look at those things again. Absorb yourself with crossword puzzles and daytime soap operas. Actually, obtaining a lobotomy might be your wisest course."

The line clicked and went dead.

"No luck," Mavranos observed as Crane hung up the phone.

"No," Crane said. "He said he *might* be able to get me *part* of a deck for half a million *dollars*. And then he told me I should get a lobotomy."

Mavranos laughed and stood up, then braced himself on the wall and felt the bandanna around his throat. He looked angrily at his beer can. "These things just aren't working, Pogo."

"Maybe you're not drinking them quite fast enough."

"Possible." Mavranos tottered to the ice chest and crouched to lift out another. "Your dad's got a deck."

"Sure, but even if I could find them, he couldn't use them if I had them, could he?"

Mavranos blinked. "Guess not. Can't have archaic and eat it, too—har-har-har." He popped open the fresh beer. "But he had another deck once."

"The deck he cut out my eye with, yeah. He probably didn't use it again, not with my blood on it."

"You figure he threw it out?"

"Well, no. I wonder if you'd even dare *burn* a deck of those things. I suppose he . . ."

Crane stood up and crossed to the window. Outside, palm trees waved in the breeze over the morning traffic.

"I suppose he *hid* it," he said softly, "with the other things that might otherwise be used to hurt him."

"Yeah? Where would he hide such stuff?"

Crane remembered the last day he had spent with his father, in April of 1948. They had had breakfast at the Flamingo, but before they had gone inside, his father had put something into a hole he'd knocked into the stucco under the side of the casino's front steps. Crane could still remember the rayed suns and stick figures scratched into the stucco around the hole.

But that old casino wasn't there anymore. That whole building, and the Champagne Tower at its south end, had been knocked down sometime in the 60s. A big glass and steel high-rise stood there now, with the present-day casino, much bigger, as the ground floor.

Still, it was his father's place, the old man's castle in the wasteland—his tower.

Crane shrugged. "Let's go look around the Flamingo."

Al Funo tapped his finger against the cab windshield. "That blue truck," he told the driver. "Follow it—I'll make it worth your while, even if you've got to follow it back to L.A."

The Glock 9-millimeter, fully loaded with eighteen rounds of Remington 147-grain subsonics, hung in his shoulder holster, and the oblong jewelry box was in his jacket pocket. *Time to settle Scott Crane's hash*, he thought. *Give him the good news*—he patted his jacket pocket—*and the bad news*—and he touched the lump under his armpit.

"I can't go outside the city limits," said the cabdriver.

"Then you just better hope *they* don't go outside the city limits," Funo said in a hard voice.

"Shit," said the driver derisively.

Funo frowned, but forced himself to relax and watch the truck ahead. He would take a bus home to Los Angeles this afternoon. The Dodge he'd been sleeping in was no good.

Saturday morning, when he'd started the car in the Marie Callender's parking lot, the engine had made the most horrible clattering din he'd ever heard; it had quieted down, though, and he'd been able to drive it until last night—when he went over a speed bump in the parking lot of the Lucky supermarket on Flamingo Road, and the terrible noise chattered out from under the hood again, and the engine had simply stopped for all time. He had managed to push the old Dodge into a parking space, and he spent the night in it right there.

And then this morning, while he'd been away for breakfast, somebody had broken into the car, had popped the lock right out of the driver's side door! Nothing had proved to be missing. To judge from the scattering of dust bunnies, the intruders had groped around under the front seat, but Funo hadn't been keeping anything there.

Funo was bobbing slightly on the cab seat now, staring at the blue truck ahead. *Settle his hash*, he thought tensely, *pop a cap, drop the hammer, sell him the farm, hand him his ass, feed him his shorts.*

*   *   *

Mavranos parked the truck in the multi-story parking structure behind the old Flamingo buildings, and he and Crane got out and took the elevator down to street level and then walked around to the Strip side face of what was now the vast Flamingo Hilton Casino Hotel.

North of the wide casino doors a new front was being added onto the casino building, and a chain-link fence separated the Strip traffic from the dusty raw dirt under the new glass facade, over the top of which marched a procession of two-dimensional pink glass flamingos, some still with the manufacturer's stickers on them. Men in hard hats were hammering up wooden forms for concrete across the dirt, and Crane and Mavranos stood on the sidewalk outside the fence and leaned against the chain-link to let the streams of tourists walk past.

"Where was it your daddy hid his secrets?" Mavranos asked. A fat woman sweating in an orange sunsuit stared at him as she swung past.

"About where that guy's setting up rebar," said Crane. "But the ground's been planed off. There's nothing left from the old days."

Mavranos yawned a couple of times, frowning as if the yawns weren't catching. "Well, it ain't likely that any of the reconstruction would have caught him by surprise. Where would he have moved his hidey-hole to?"

Hidey-hole, Crane thought.

Bolt-hole and hidey-hole.

He stepped back from the fence. "To some place that hasn't changed since the old days. Let's go look at the original Flamingo building—what they call the Oregon Building now."

They retraced their steps to the front entrance and went inside and threaded their way through the cold, dark, clanging casino, between the banks of slot machines and the closely spaced tables—Mavranos craning his neck to see cards on the Blackjack layouts and no doubt wishing he'd brought along some kind of goldfish—and out the back doors into the hot glare of sun on splashing water and bone white deck and oiled, tanned bodies.

And there, across the glittering pool and framed by the curved trunks of palm trees, stood the long, low building that Crane viscerally remembered as the Flamingo.

It was painted pale tan now instead of pistachio green, and little wrought-iron false balconies had been bolted across the lower halves of the windows, and the narrow terrace on which he had seemed to stand with Benjamin Siegel yesterday was walled in now—though he thought he could still see its outline—and to the right the sky was blocked by another high-rise wing of the Flamingo Hilton, and to the left loomed a tall crane and beyond that the pagoda-roofed towers of the Imperial Palace; but this neglected building down here at the feet of the giants was the heart of the Flamingo, the heart of the Strip, the heart of Las Vegas.

"Your place, Dad," he said softly, stepping down to the concrete deck and starting around the right side of the pool.

He and Mavranos pushed open the narrow glass doors of the Oregon Building and wandered around in the quiet green-carpeted rotunda. Crane rapped on a wall, noting the cold silence of marble under the wallpaper. Siegel had built his castle solidly.

They took the elevator to the fourth floor, but one of the double doors to Siegel's penthouse suite had a brass plaque on it that read "Presidential Suite," and Crane decided that whatever high roller was renting the place wouldn't let a couple of bums come in and start prying shelves out of bookcases.

Back down the elevator they went, and out through the back doors to a sloping lawn with a pink metal flamingo standing on it. Crane remembered a parking lot back here, and a couple of bungalows with nothing but desert beyond, but now there was a driveway and the Arizona Building, with the new parking structure peeping up over its roof.

"Dig under that there flamingo?" suggested Mavranos.

Crane was looking back up at Siegel's penthouse. "In the . . . vision, or hallucination, he had a ladder hidden behind a book-case," he said thoughtfully, "leading down. That would wind up in the basement, I guess." He pointed at a driveway off to the left that led down to an underground delivery and service entrance. "Let's go in there."

"Hope they aren't rough on trespassers in this town," Mavranos growled as they trudged forward.

"Act drunk, and tell 'em you were looking for the men's room."

"I think I *am* drunk. And I wouldn't *mind* finding a men's room." Mavranos shook a Camel out of a pack and lit it, walking backward to shield the match flame. Then he waved the pack at Crane.

"No, thanks," Crane said.

"You haven't had a cigarette since you climbed out of the lake," Mavranos observed. "You on that wagon, too?"

Crane shrugged. "Just haven't wanted one. I'm getting healthy, I think."

The descending driveway ramp led them out of the sunlight to a dock area set back in under the building. A broad conveyor belt ran up to the surface of the dock, and big boxes of Soft Blend bathroom tissue were stacked on the extended forks of a little parked power-lift truck.

Up on the dock level a green wooden counter window opened in the far wall, with a NO SOLICITATION sign posted on the inner wall. No one was at the counter, so Crane stepped around a plastic mop bucket and hurried up the three steps. Mavranos was right behind him, cursing under his breath.

They were at the south end of a long corridor with a lot of wheeled blue bins parked along the wall. White-painted pipes were hung under the ceiling, making the corridor seem to Crane to be roofed with bamboo.

"The ladder would have come down . . . somewhere this way," he said, starting down the hall and trying to keep the shape and size of the building in his head.

Every door they passed had "NO EXIT" stenciled on it in red, but at one of them Crane paused, and then tried the knob. The door opened, and they stepped into a high-ceilinged room in which thrummed an enormous water heater. Pipes and gauges made it necessary to duck, in order to walk around, but Crane hunched and sidestepped his way to the very back of the room—and for several seconds he just stared at the wooden ladder that was bolted to the concrete wall and disappeared into a dark shaft above.

Crane was certain that it led all the way up to the bookshelf in Siegel's suite.

It genuinely wasn't a hallucination, he thought. I really did talk with the ghost of Bugsy Siegel yesterday.

At last he tore his gaze away from the ladder and looked around the room. "This here is all too new," he called quietly to Mavranos, who was still standing by the door. "But I swear we're on the right track."

Mavranos squinted at the plywood and concrete and throbbing machinery and sniffed the disinfectant-scented air. "If you say so. Let's get out of here, okay?"

Crane climbed out from behind all the machinery and pushed the door open and peeked around it, but there was no one in sight. He stepped out, followed by Mavranos, and they walked further down the corridor.

The hall was more blockily shadowed now and had narrowed almost to a tunnel, with pipes running along the walls as well as overhead, and the green linoleum floor was cracked and water-stained, but at the same time Crane sensed that these walls and ceiling were older and more solidly built. As if to confirm it, he noticed that the big dark green cans stacked on an ankle-high shelf along the western wall were labeled as Civil Defense-certified-safe drinking water. Apparently this older section was stout enough to have been designated an official bomb shelter.

He remembered the marble walls behind the wallpaper overhead.

"Siegel had this tunnel built," he said softly as he shuffled along, bracing himself against the pipes and watching by the broken light of occasional caged bulbs to avoid clanking his head against any of the down-hanging valves. "I believe we're in the onetime King's emergency escape route."

Bolt-hole and hidey-hole, he thought.

And then it was Mavranos who saw it.

A red jackknife handle stood out of the wall ahead of them, and Mavranos pointed at it. "I guess this is where he practiced knife throwing," he said.

The knife handle protruded from a foot-wide circular patch of newer cement, and Crane shivered when he saw the scratched figures in the old bricks around it: suns and crescent moons and stick figures carrying swords.

Mavranos had idly taken hold of the knife's handle and was pulling at it, but it didn't budge. He swore and tugged harder, even bracing his leg against the wall, and finally had to let go and wipe his hand on his jeans.

"That's in there solid," he said breathlessly.

Feeling as if he were taking part in an old, old ritual, Crane stepped forward and closed his right hand around the now-sweaty plastic handle. It seemed to be a Swiss army knife.

He tugged, and the jackknife came out of the cement patch so easily that he rang a water can against the far wall with the butt of the knife.

"I loosened it," said Mavranos.

Crane kept his right eye firmly closed. He didn't want to see the jackknife as some kind of medieval sword.

He was already hearing things.

With his good eye he looked up and down the hall, but there was no one in sight besides himself and Mavranos, so he ignored the sound of the Andrews Sisters singing "Rum and Coca-Cola," and the rattle of chips and laughter, that seemed to echo from just around some unimaginable corner.

He swung the knife back to the east wall and pressed the point against the newer cement. The blade cut through as easily as it would cut cardboard, and after a few moments of sawing—while Mavranos stared—Crane had cut the disk of cement free and pushed it inside.

"Do you happen to hear . . . music?" Crane asked.

"I hear nothin' but my heart, and I don't want to have to start worrying about *it*. Why? Do *you* hear music?"

Crane didn't answer but peered into the hole.

The space inside the wall was about a cubic yard in volume. Dimly he could see a very old and fragile-looking Tarot card, the Tower, tacked to the far wall of the little chamber. The card was upside down.

He closed the knife and put it into his pocket, smiled nervously at Mavranos, and then reached into the hole.

He groped around carefully in the cavity and found a little cloth bag that proved to be full of teeth and a small cracked mirror in a tortoiseshell frame—what must it one time have reflected, or failed to reflect?—and in a bottom corner there were three little hard lumps that might have been pomegranate seeds; and finally his groping fingers found, under everything, wedged flat against the floor of the space, the wooden box he remembered.

He pried it free, lifted it out of the hole, and opened it, and he shuddered to see again the innocent-looking plaid backs of the cards.

He turned over the first one. It was the Page of Cups, a

young man standing on a rippled cliff edge holding a cup, and the corner was lightly stained. Hesitantly Crane licked that corner of the card, and he thought he faintly tasted salt and iron.

The Andrews Sisters started on "Sonny Boy:"

> *"Whe-e-en there are gray skies*
> *I don't mind the gray skies. . . ."*

"We're out of here," Crane told Mavranos hoarsely. He left everything inside the hole but the wooden box, which he tucked inside his Levi's jacket.

A tall brown man wearing a Hawaiian shirt and a white pith helmet and Sony Walkman earphones was smiling broadly and sweeping the lens of a video camera across the back lawn of the Oregon Building. Gleaming sunglasses hid his eyes.

"The basement service entrance, under the building on the south side," he said, still grinning, into the video camera's microphone. "Now's the time."

"Gotcha," came a voice over the earphones.

The tall man swung the camera toward the dock area under the building, catching in its focus a young man in a dark suit who was standing uncertainly by the stack of bathroom tissue boxes. The young man held something dark and oblong in his right hand, and the man with the camera instinctively felt for the bulk of the automatic in its holster on his right hip, under the untucked shirttail. He was showing a lot of white teeth in his smile now.

"Now's the time," he repeated.

Two men in unspecific tan uniforms were pushing a Dumpster down the paved ramp, and a station wagon with Montana license plates was weaving along the driveway between the Oregon and Arizona buildings.

One of the men with the Dumpster let go of it to approach the young man in the suit. Their conversation was brief, and the smiling man with the camera heard none of it, but a moment later the man in the suit was doubled over, his chin by his knees, and the two uniformed men grabbed him, took a gun away from him, and tossed him into the Dumpster and began pushing it back up the ramp.

The station wagon had stopped. Its tailgate was down, and the man in the suit was quickly bundled out of the Dumpster and into the car. The uniformed men climbed into the back with him and pulled the tailgate shut.

The smiling man had tucked the video camera under his arm and strolled across the grass to the car. He took off his white pith helmet and got in on the passenger side, still smiling.

The station wagon started forward again, turned east past the parking structure and around west onto Flamingo Road, signaling for every turn and proceeding at an inconspicuous speed.

They had thrown a blanket over Al Funo's head, and he could feel the bite of a narrow nylon tie-wrap drawn tight around his wrists behind his back; his ankles were bound together, too, doubtless with another tie-wrap.

His heart was thumping, but he could breathe again, and he was grinning toughly against the scraped metal bed of the station wagon. You've always lived by your wits, old son, he told himself, and you'll find some way to talk or fight or run your way out of this. Who *are* these guys anyway? Friends of Reculver and the fat man? Damn, and I almost had Scott Crane at last. I wonder if these guys mean to keep Crane's gold chain. They've got another think coming, if they do.

One of his captors spoke. "We got time for lunch before Flores comes in from Salt Lake. I never got breakfast."

"Sure," said another one from the front seat. "Where do you figure?"

"Let's go to Margarita's," said the first speaker.

Funo didn't appreciate being ignored. "The Dumpster and the uniforms was good," he said from under the blanket, proud of the ironic humor in his voice. "Like having a pencil behind your ear and carrying a clipboard—hey-presto, you're invisible."

"Shut up, Fucko," said the man in the front seat. "That's in the Frontier," he went on.

"So?" said the man sitting over Funo. "It happens to have the best chimichangas in town."

"Bullshit," said somebody else.

"There's a guy back there in the Flamingo basement," said Funo with a chuckle, "who ought to buy you guys lunch. You saved his life. I was gonna give him that gold chain and then drop the hammer on his ass."

"Shut up, Fucko."

Funo was glad the blanket was over him, for suddenly he could feel his face reddening. Good God, he'd said he wanted to give Crane a gold chain, and then he'd said something about "the hammer," and "his ass." What if these men thought he wanted to *sodomize* Crane?

"I—I went to bed with the guy's wife—" Funo began desperately.

"Shut *up*, Fucko." Someone knocked him stingingly on the back of the head with a finger knuckle. "And they make their own tortillas right there, you can see the guy making them."

"I just want a burger somewhere," said the man in the front seat.

By the steady roar of the engine and the smoothness of the ride, Funo could tell that they were on a highway; he couldn't tell which one, but all highways in Las Vegas lead quickly out into desert.

One of these men *might* be the person who he had all along known was out there in the world somewhere, the person who would one day kill him, become the most important person in Al Funo's life.

And now—*now!*—they wouldn't even talk to him!

Every time he tried to initiate a dialogue, sincerely and with no judgmental attitude, they rapped him on the head and called him Fucko. It was a worse thing to be called than *fucker*. At least *fucker* implied that you had had sex. Fucko sounded like the name of a clown.

At last the car was slowing, and soon Funo heard gravel grinding under the tires.

He braced himself. When the car came to a stop, he would lash upward and back with his head, hoping to hit the face of the man over him; with the blanket off his head he might be able to grab the man's gun and then pull his bound hands far enough around one side of his body to be able to shoot.

The car rocked to a halt, and he used the rebound of the shock absorbers to get more force into his move—

But the man who had been above him had apparently shifted over against the back door since last speaking, and Funo's head just brushed the car's ceiling before he tumbled back down onto his face again.

The men might not even have noticed the action. Funo heard the tailgate swung down, and even under the blanket he smelled the spice of the dry desert air, as workmanlike hands took hold of his ankles and dragged him out; other hands gripped his upper arms, and then he was lowered onto the sand, and the blanket was snatched off his head.

He twisted his face up from the sand and blinked around in the sudden glare. The men had stepped back. One of the uniformed fellows was squinting away, apparently watching the road. The tall man in the Hawaiian shirt had his pith helmet on and was smiling with all his white teeth as he jacked a round into Funo's own gun.

"There's something you should probably know about me," Funo began in a confident tone, but the man in the pith helmet just kept smiling and aimed the muzzle into Funo's face, and Funo realized that the man was about to simply kill him, with no discussion at all.

"For what, f-f-for wh-what?" Funo choked, thrashing on the dry dirt. "My n-name's Alfred F-F-Funo, tell me your name at least, we're imp-p-p-portant to each other, *at least t-t-tell me your n-n-n-name!"*

The hard *boom* of the gunshot rolled away over the bright desert, startling tiny lizards into brief, short darts across the sand.

"Puddin' Tame," said the cocaine dealer, wiping off the gun with a handkerchief and then tossing it down beside the bound body. "Ask me again and I'll tell you the same."

CHAPTER 42

Beam Me Up, Scotty

On Tuesday morning Mavranos dropped Crane off in front of the liquor store on Flamingo Road and then drove around the block to park the truck in the back lot and just sit and watch.

Inside the liquor store Crane noticed that the clerk at the register wasn't the same one who had been working last Thursday, and anyway, Crane's black eye had by now faded to the faintest yellow tinge. He was able to buy two six-packs of Budweiser without getting a second glance.

The pay phone on the back wall rang as he reached out to push open the parking lot door, and it occurred to him that, for plausibility, he ought to be carrying an opened beer when he approached the Dumpster in the back lot.

He reached into the paper bag as he stepped out into the heat, and tugged a can free and popped it open. Chilly foam burst up around his forefinger.

His hand was halfway up to his mouth, the wet finger extended, before he remembered his new resolves, and remembered, too, the ringing pay phone—and he lowered his hand and wiped the beer foam off on his shirt.

The Lowballers were again hunkered down in a circle in front of the Dumpster, but Crane didn't see the very old man they had called Doctor Leaky.

He didn't recognize any of them as Wiz-Ding, the young man who had given him the black eye, either.

"It's just me, the beer man," he said with forced cheer when a couple of the ragged young men looked up at his approach.

" 'Bout time," commented one of the players, holding out his free hand without looking away from his cards.

Crane pulled another beer loose and put it in the hand, then set the bag down on the hot pavement. "Where's my old pal Wiz-Ding?" he asked.

The man who had spoken looked up at him now. "That's right, you're the guy he hit last week, aren't you? What'd you do, put a Gypsy curse on him?"

Again Crane thought about the ringing pay phone. "No, why?"

"He got the horrors real bad that night, ran out into traffic and dived under a bus."

"Jesus." Crane tipped his opened can up to his mouth, making certain to do no more than wet his lips. "Uh," he said as if it were an afterthought or a tactful change of subject, "how about that real old guy? Doctor Leaky?"

The player's attention had returned to his cards. "Hah. You're hoping to score a big pot of flat pennies, right? He ain't here today."

Crane didn't want his next question to seem important, so he sat down lithely, scratching his hot scalp and wishing he hadn't lost his Jughead cap. "Deal me in the next hand," he said. "Does old Doctor Leaky play here steady?"

"Most days, I s'pose. Buy-in's ten bucks."

Resigning himself—and Mavranos—to an hour of wasted time, Crane suppressed a sigh and dug in his pocket.

The full moon hung in the sky to the east like the print of an ash-dusted penny on indigo velvet.

Finally the full moon, thought Diana as she glanced at it through the windshield. And our monthly cycles are matched, for whatever archaic, repulsive value that might have. Hold my hand, Mother.

The blocks around Shadow Lane and Charleston Boulevard, north of the Strip and south of Fremont Street, all seemed to be taken up with hospitals, and Diana wasted ten minutes in circling before finding a parking space in the University Medical Center parking lot. She locked the rented Ford, pushed her sunglasses up on her nose, and walked swiftly toward the gray buildings on the far side of the lot. She was wearing a loose shirt—*not* linen—and jeans and sneakers, in case she might have to run, and she wondered why she had not borrowed a gun from Ozzie and Scott, or even Mike Stikeleather, when she had had the chance.

Her steps were light on the radiant asphalt in her new white Nikes, and she spread out her hands in front of herself, as if surrendering to something, and tossed aside the cloud of her blond hair to look at her knuckles and wrists.

All the old scars were gone: the crescent of a dog bite, the hard line where a jackknife had unexpectedly closed, all the tiny pale graffiti of the years. This morning, rousing from yet another motel pillow wrapped in the old yellow baby blanket, her forehead had been itching, and in the bathroom mirror she had seen smooth skin where the boy in fourth grade had hit her over the left eye with a rock.

And of course she had been dreaming, for the sixth night in a row, about her mother's island, where owls hooted in the tossing, bending trees and water clattered over rocks and dogs bayed out in the darkness.

Like her skin, her memory was growing younger. On Sunday she had decided to visit Hans's grave, but after getting into a taxi, she'd discovered that she couldn't remember where he had been buried, nor even what he had looked like; and as she had sheepishly improvised some destination for the driver to take her to, she had realized with no alarm that the faces of all her long-ago lovers were likewise gone; and yesterday, after she had felt the death of the man who had been called Alfred Funo, it had occurred to her that she no longer knew anything about her onetime husband except his last name, and knew that only because it was the name on her driver's license.

But her son Scat was somewhere inside this building ahead of her, pierced through with drains and hoses, and her son Oliver was at Helen Sully's place in Searchlight, and she could remember both of them perfectly, their faces and voices and personalities; and her abandonment of them, though she had had to do it to protect the boys, had bulked constantly in her consciousness like an infected splinter. She had talked to Oliver several times on the telephone, and though Scat hadn't regained consciousness, she had called the doctor every day and had sent a cashier's check to cover Scat's treatment.

And she could remember Scott Crane. He had been with her on her mother's island in several of the dreams.

She blushed now and frowned behind her sunglasses and quickened her steps.

*   *   *

Three agitated old men sat at a table in the hospital cafeteria. They had been sitting there for an hour. Two of them had had to go to the men's room, and the other was wearing diapers under his high-waisted polyester pants.

Through the merry eyes of the Benet body, Georges Leon squinted sideways at his companions. Newt looked nervous, and Doctor Leaky, with his jaw of course foolishly hanging open, looked as if he'd just heard of some appalling impending threat.

Dr. Bandholtz had called at dawn, his voice both resentful and scared, and told Leon that Diana Ryan had called the hospital once again and that this time she had asked what time today she could meet with Bandholtz and actually visit her son in person.

Bandholtz was to meet her in the lobby sometime between ten and noon and, after Leon had reasoned with him, had reluctantly agreed to stop in the cafeteria first and then bring one very old man along with him when he went to see her.

Leon stared at Doctor Leaky now and thought, *Vaughan, where are you when I need you?*

Vaughan Trumbill had simply never come back from his last trip to go fetch Scott Crane. Leon had called Moynihan late Sunday night, but the piping voice of the Benet body had not been authoritative enough to get any information out of that damned Irish hoodlum. Moynihan had denied even ever having spoken to Benet before, and had just laughed and hung up the telephone when asked about Trumbill's whereabouts. Subsequent calls to Moynihan had gone unanswered or unreturned.

If only that Funo person had not killed the Betsy Reculver body!

Leon lifted his styrofoam cup and puckered his lips at the coffee, but it was still too hot. He put it down and sucked in a deep breath through his tension-narrowed bronchial tubes. He tugged his inhaler out of his vest pocket and took two puffs of Ventolin. It seemed to help.

The time was nearly 11:00 A.M. by the cafeteria clock. Dr. Bandholtz should be arriving before too long.

Leon hoped the police would somehow kill Doctor Leaky when they arrested him. The old body had a lot of sorcerous protections, but a hot .38 round would probably get through them.

Newt had finished his own coffee and was shakily tearing shreds of styrofoam from the edge of the cup. "He won't be able to *do* it," he whispered, "any more than I can fly. I'll bet you he's forgotten again. And *I* ain't gonna do it, Beany."

"Call me Leon, damn you." Leon leaned toward the horrible old, emasculated body that was sitting and drooling next to him. "*What* is it that you're going to *do*?" he asked once again, speaking very quietly.

This time Doctor Leaky remembered. *"Kill her!"* he yelled shrilly, fumbling at the high waistband of his lime green pants for the little Walther .380 automatic.

Leon jabbed his elbow into the belly of the old body that had once been his own. "Shut up, you imbecile." Then, for the benefit of anyone who might have been looking over at them, he smiled and patted Doctor Leaky's bald head.

"It's them!" Doctor Leaky choked, blinking around tearfully at the nurses and visitors. "The people in Doom Town!"

Leon gave up any hope of being inconspicuous and began to play to the audience, shape what the eventual testimonies might be. "Stop it!" he said, speaking loudly. "Your wife shot you in 1948—it's all over, she's dead—you've got to stop brooding on it!"

"My—my *dingus*!" Doctor Leaky exclaimed. "She shot my *cock* off!"

From somewhere deep in Benet's brain, not from Leon's mind at all, came the thought that these people listening would assume she had shot some man of Scottish-Russian ancestry: Dingus McCockov.

"Yes, yes," Leon said, angrily suppressing the accompanying smile and hoping that his tone sounded soothing. "It was a long time ago."

"*That* was real enough," Doctor Leaky went on, finally speaking at just a conversational volume. "But the cards aren't fooled by any of the rest of it. The people in Doom Town, and all the human-sacrifice statues around town. All your Fijis that died, too, they haven't changed anything." He smiled sadly. "It's still just me."

Newt's wrinkled old eyes were closed. "Beam me up, Scotty," he said softly.

The innocent cliché angered Leon. *"Shut up,"* he said through clenched teeth. *"Just shut up."*

Ray-Joe Pogue carefully backed his camper-laden pickup truck into one of the spaces in the hospital parking lot, then shoved the gearshift into park, turned the engine off and tapped an inch of ash off his cigar.

The ash didn't hit the upholstery. As before, it shattered to dust in midair and swirled into the three-dimensional outline of a small fat person sitting on the passenger side of the seat.

Bloated and black and fermented, came the voice in Pogue's head, *ripped to bits by coyotes and covered with sand flies. What's left of my belly looks like cooked bacon. The tattoos are a wreck, like a vandalized painting.*

"You already told me your body's screwed up," said Pogue nervously.

He lied to me; he broke his promise.

"A real bastard," Pogue agreed.

He had first met the ghost this morning; it had taken the form of popcorn and cigarette butts on the asphalt outside his camper door at dawn, its voice haltingly sounding in his head, and later it had tried, unsuccessfully, to animate a sheet of the Las Vegas *Sun.* After about ten minutes they had settled on cigar ash as the easiest medium for its physical appearance.

I don't care if my mom's dead, said the voice in Ray-Joe Pogue's head now, *just so they don't call me Ollie like Hardy.*

Pogue held the door lever and stared uneasily at the churning fat person silhouette-in-ash. "I thought your name was Vaughan."

You can call me that. Or you can call me Bitin Dog. Our bodies were left in the desert. Our name is Legion.

"Like in the Bible, huh?" said Pogue. "But anyway the King *is* here, at this hospital?"

He is.

Pogue had a gun under his jacket, but he hoped he wouldn't need it. He took the brown plastic bottle out of the pocket of his white sequined denim jacket. "Inderal," he read off the label. "I've known musicians who take this stuff—athletes, too—to keep from getting the shakes and jitters when they have to perform. You sure it'll do, and not just mellow him out?"

He's asthmatic. It'll close his bronchial tubes.

"Asthmatic, right. Okay, you're the doctor."

Your camouflage.

"Don't worry, I didn't forget."

Before stepping out of the truck, Pogue obediently put on his Polaroid sunglasses and took off his shoes to tuck the newly bought water-filled plastic sole-liners inside.

"And I'll walk counterclockwise all the way to him," Pogue told the dim gray ghost as he put his unwieldy shoes back on, "like what you said, a windshield." Last he put on a baseball cap from the Tiara Casino, the logo of which was the best hand in Kansas City Lowball, 7–5–4–3–2 unsuited.

Inside him, said the voice in Pogue's head, *there's a—a skinny man waiting to get out.*

"Skinny man on deck," agreed Pogue nervously as he opened the truck door and felt the heat.

The ghost became just a pinch of grainy powder in his ear when he stepped through the doors of the hospital, and Pogue had to resist the impulse to scratch it. He hoped none of it had got into his long sideburns, where it would look like dandruff.

The ghost's voice was a buzz now, directing him down this hallway and that—and making him pause frequently to walk in a tight counterclockwise circle on the carpet—and when Pogue pushed open the cafeteria doors the ghost said, *There. The man on the left at that table over there.*

"Are you *sure*?" Pogue murmured.

The man on the left, repeated the voice.

Pogue sighed, with both tension and disappointment. He had known that the King might be in any sort of body, but it offended him that this body was so short and round and red-faced and jolly-looking. Damn me, he thought, with a beard he could pass for Santa Claus! And that's a cheap suit.

An abandoned newspaper lay on a table near the three old men, and Pogue sat down and began reading it. The cafeteria smelled like macaroni and cheese. He could simply wait until the King left and then shoot him in the parking lot, but he didn't know if he dared wait for that. The man hadn't glanced at him yet, but Pogue was afraid that if the King were to focus his eyes on him, he would *see* him, see *him*, in spite of the fact that Pogue was in effect standing on water, and had neutralized any electromagnetic emanations from his eyes behind the Polaroid lenses, and wore a disguising poker hand on his hat.

In his pocket he broke the cap off the medicine bottle and palmed one of the capsules.

Just shoot him, said the voice in his head.

Out of the corner of his eye Pogue saw the King look up, as though he'd heard the voice. Pogue's face went cold, and he felt a drop of sweat run down his ribs. He watched for any sudden movement at the King's table; if any of the three old men seemed to be going for a gun, Pogue would roll to the floor and draw his own gun. Come up shooting, and worry about getting away afterward.

"Shut—up," he murmured.

No. Shoot him now.

The King pushed back his plastic chair and stood up on ridiculous little bow-legs. He looked around the room, but his gaze swept over Pogue without stopping. Pogue's hand, still palming the capsule, was sweaty on the grip of his gun.

The King said something to his companions, and they got to their feet, too, and the three of them walked to the cafeteria doorway. They stood there, looking up and down the hall.

Pogue's back tingled with anticipation of a bullet as he stood up himself, still holding a section of the paper in his left hand, and strolled past the table the King had been sitting at.

As he passed it, his right hand broke the capsule like a little egg and shook the tiny grains into the King's coffee.

He kept walking. The only exit in front of him was the twin metal doors that led to the kitchen, so he pushed them open and walked into the steamy clatter beyond.

Go back and sit down, Your Majesty, he thought as he blundered between steam tables and people in white aprons, looking for another door out. *Nothing's wrong. Sit down and finish your coffee.*

Diana sat restlessly on the hospital lobby couch, and finally she put down the magazine she'd been trying to read.

Scat had been transferred to this hospital last Wednesday, and though this was the first time she had come here, she knew what room he was in. This was where she was supposed to meet Dr. Bandholtz . . . who was probably the only person who knew that she was alive.

Would he have sold that information? Or, more likely, would someone have learned from the police that only one person had died in the bombed apartment on Venus Avenue and then have exerted leverage on Bandholtz, who would be the likeliest to hear from her?

Her heart suddenly beating fast, she stood up and looked around the lobby. The receptionist was writing in a file, and a young couple was talking intently to a very old woman on another couch, and the young Asian woman by the door was probably just blinking at Diana because she had stood up so abruptly.

Still, she was not going to wait here obediently for Bandholtz and whatever companions he might arrive with.

She walked quickly to the elevator and tapped the up button.

Nardie Dinh waited until the elevator door had closed, then went to the one next to it and pushed its up button.

She was blinking back tears. I *can* do it, she told herself firmly, and I *will* do it. In a way it'll be self-defense, for if I'm not the Queen, I'm not anything at all. I wasn't born for it, but my damned half brother carved me into it. It'll be his fault, not mine.

In the last few days she had managed to eat several meals—mostly spinach and beans and rice, with olive oil—and had drunk several cartons of milk. She hoped she would have the strength for what she'd have to do here.

The doors slid open, and she patted the bulge under her jacket and stepped resolutely inside.

And someone was right behind her. She turned, and as the doors sighed closed she recognized Ray-Joe Pogue grinning down at her.

"I've got you!" he exclaimed joyfully. "You knew I was here? And I forgive you. Listen, Nardie, I just killed one of the King's bodies! I just heard a nurse say that an old guy who was drinking coffee in the cafeteria stopped breathing and then died of a big heart attack, ventricular fibrillation, before they could do anything with him!" He touched her shoulder. "I'm going to win, Nardie. Saturday you and I can get married."

The elevator had started moving up. She could feel her weight increase.

Nardie knew he had a gun. Well, so did she. But she doubted if either of them could draw a gun in here without being jumped by the other before the gun could be freed. And in a hand-to-hand fight he'd beat her.

He doesn't know why I'm here, she thought, where I'm going. Pretend to be giving in to him.

So she sighed and nodded, looking at his feet. "I had to fight," she said. "For my self-respect."

"And you fought well," he said, laughing. "Once or twice I thought you were going to evade me and ruin us both." He was brushing some kind of dust out of his ear.

The doors opened on the second floor, and an old woman pushing an aluminum walker hobbled in.

"I'm glad you found me," Nardie said in a small voice.

"I wasn't looking for *you*," the old woman snapped.

Nardie glanced up and caught her half brother's gaze. Both of them grinned—

And Nardie realized that they were sharing a joke, and that she *wanted* to kill Diana now, and then leave with this man, whom, after everything, she apparently still loved. She opened her mouth to tell him why she was here and ask for his help—

And only when her knuckles cracked hard into his nose and she fell back against the closing doors did she note that she did still have some willpower—in her spine, perhaps, if not in her brain.

The old woman was screaming shrilly. Pogue had tumbled into the corner, and bright red blood was spilling out from between the fingers of the hand that was clasped to his face. His eyes were still blank with pain and surprise, and Nardie turned around, forced the doors open and hurried away down the hall.

She would take the stairs up to the room where Diana Ryan's son was. She patted her hidden gun again and wondered if she had broken her knuckles. Even if she hadn't, the recoil was going to hurt. It was going to hurt badly.

She wondered if she would ever recover from it.

* * *

"You certainly don't *look* like you've been too sick to visit him," the nurse said coldly, standing in an almost protective posture beside Scat's bed. "You look like you've been at some kind of health resort." She looked Diana squarely in the eye then, and must have sensed her real agony, for after a moment her expression softened. "Well, he's better. You can see he's breathing on his own now. He's being fed through the nasal gastric tube; the IV is mainly just for hydrating and antibiotics and to keep a line open for anything we want to get into his veins fast." She waved toward the monitor over the bed. "His vital signs are stable. He's"—she shrugged—"just very deeply asleep."

Diana nodded. "Could I be alone with him?" she said softly.

"Sure."

The nurse had started toward the door, and Diana added, "I'm supposed to be meeting Dr. Bandholtz in the lobby in a few minutes. Could you not tell him I'm here yet? I'll be down soon."

"Okay."

Diana looked down at her son in the tilted-up hospital bed, and she bit her knuckle. The green nasal gastric tube dented his blond curls on the right side of his head; the left side was bandaged, but she could see that his scalp had been shaved on that side. His eyes and mouth were closed, but he was breathing gently, and the monitor over him beeped regularly and showed a regularly bouncing green line on its black screen.

Even if I'd been here every day, she told herself earnestly, he wouldn't have known. He's probably dreamed of me, and that's been more immediate than my physical presence would have been.

Until today. Today, with the full moon overhead, I might make a difference by being here.

She reached out toward the little limp hand that was bound to the rail of the bed by a strip of plastic.

And then she stopped, for she had heard the solid click-and-snap of an automatic pistol being chambered behind her.

For three heartbeats she just stood there with her arm extended; then she lowered her arm and turned around.

It was the young Asian woman she'd seen in the lobby downstairs. The barrel of the gun she held was lengthened with a fat metal cylinder—a silencer, Diana was sure.

"Do you mean to kill me?" Diana asked. Her voice was calm, though her heart thudded and her fingertips were tingling. "Or him? Or both of us?"

"You. My name is Bernardette Dinh."

"Diana Ryan. Uh—why?" Dinh was too far away across the carpet for Diana to be able to kick the gun, and there was nothing she could hope to grab and throw. She could dive behind the bed, but if Dinh shot at her the bullet would probably hit Scat.

"To be Queen. Do you have any change in your pockets? Bring it out slow, and if you throw it, I'll shoot."

Mystified but glad of any delay, Diana slid her hand into the pocket of her jeans, then took it out and held it forward in her palm.

The quarters and dimes still shone silver, but the pennies were all black.

With her free hand Dinh reached into her own pocket and took out a penny. It was shiny red-brown.

"See?" she said. "And if you've tried to wear linen during the last few days, you'll have noticed it goes black, too, just like the pennies." She was talking fast, licking her lips nervously between phrases. "And purple cloth bleaches if you touch it. And if you should happen to approach a beehive, the bees will all leave the hive. All this year those things have happened to *me* at my time, at the full moon."

"You want to become the Queen," said Diana. "Why?"

"I didn't really come here to talk. Why? To . . . for the power of it. For the family of it, to be a—a mother, in the profoundest way."

"I already am a mother."

Dinh glanced past Diana toward Scat. "Biologically, I guess. Maybe you sent a lot of get-well cards."

Diana felt her face reddening, but she made herself smile. "And you'd kill me to get that? You'd make a ten-year-old boy an orphan to get that?"

"I'll—I'll adopt him. I'm going to have a very big family."

"But *I'm* the Queen's *daughter*."

"Damn it, that's why I've *got* to. With you gone, I'm the

most natural successor." Dinh sighed unsteadily. "There's lots of deaths in this, you know that. Death waits in the desert and in the hot sky, for any of us. I don't know how many times I've thought of suicide."

"Is it important?"

"Suicide?"

"No, how many times you've thought about it. Is this gonna hold us up? Couldn't we say, like, a hundred, and be okay?"

Dinh blinked, and her mouth worked and then kinked in a narrow smile.

Diana reached slowly out to the side, bending her knees to lower herself, and touched Scat's hand. Dinh gasped, looking at the boy, so Diana felt safe in looking, too.

Scat's eyes were open.

His blue eyes swung blankly from his mother to Dinh and then back again, and then the irises shifted slightly as he focused.

His mouth opened, and he started to speak, then coughed hoarsely. *"Mom,"* he croaked finally.

"Hi, Scatto," said Diana. "I think you'll be coming home soon." She looked hard back at Dinh, trying to convey through her gaze, *Go ahead. Stake your claim to being the earthly Queen of the mother goddess by murdering a mother right in front of the eyes of her wounded son.*

Dinh's face was white, and she lowered the gun.

"But what can I do?" she whispered. She blinked at Diana. "Why am I asking you, eh?" Her gun arm bent up sharply at the elbow.

And Diana lunged forward and knocked the blunt silencer out from under Dinh's jaw in the instant before it jerked.

The shot sounded like a bed sheet being instantaneously ripped in half. Dinh fell to her hands and knees on the carpet, but her head was up, and Diana could see no blood in the black hair. Diana looked up and saw the neat hole punched in the acoustic tile of the ceiling.

Diana got down on her knees and lifted Dinh by the shoulders. "You're asking me because I can answer you," she said urgently. "I'm in danger, and I have two children who are in danger." Dinh was staring into her face, and Diana bared her teeth in a cold smile. "I'm going to need help."

Dinh tucked the gun away in her belt, wincing. "You expect
me to—"

"No. No, I *hope* you will. Will help me. Don't answer now,
I won't listen to you now with your ears still ringing. But if
you will help me, *help* the Queen instead of *be* the Queen, if
that's something you *can* do, then meet me tomorrow at dawn,
at the—at the Flamingo pool."

Dinh stood up. "I . . . won't kill you," she said quietly, "I
guess. It looks like. But I won't be there."

"I will," said Diana, still on her knees and looking up.

Dinh turned and strode out of the room. Diana got up and
walked back to her son's bed.

Scat was weakly flexing his bound hands, and his feet were
moving under the blanket. He was moaning weakly; the nasal
tube seemed to bother him.

Diana pushed the nurse-summon button and stepped toward
the door, but a doctor was just hurrying in. Obviously Dinh
had paused on the way out to tell the staff that the boy had
awakened.

CHAPTER 43

Pot's Not Right

The dew that was misted and beaded on the pink plastic chaise
lounges around the pool seemed brave and forlorn to Diana—
fugitive moisture, briefly condensed by the cool dawn air but
doomed to be evaporated again as soon as the morning sun
cleared the low bulk of the Oregon Building. In the seat
of the nearest recliner some of the drops had run down to
combine and form a little puddle, but she knew that wouldn't
help them.

The moon, hidden now behind the Flamingo's south high
rise, was already past full by the tiniest shaving, but her
near-clairvoyance would last, she knew, through Easter, four

days from now. She stared uneasily at the long, low bulk of the Oregon Building, aware that it was the Tower of the King, and that Scott Crane had been inside it recently.

Nobody was in the pool yet, but the casino doors on the opposite side of the pool were swung open every few minutes to let a burst of the clatter and clang of the perpetual games come shaking out into the quiet dawn air. Though she was still looking up at the dark penthouse of the Oregon Building, Diana knew it when the doors opened to let out Nardie Dinh.

Diana didn't turn around. She heard Nardie's footsteps scuff slowly down the steps and around the pool past the presently closed outdoor bar.

Nardie stopped behind her.

"You saved my life yesterday," Nardie said quietly, her voice not seeming even to reach the dark shrubbery around the building. "I'll try to see to it that it wasn't a big mistake."

Diana turned around. Nardie was wearing a cabdriver's uniform and cap. "How will you do that?"

"By leaving. I've got money—maybe I'll go back to Hanoi. If I stayed here, I'd probably try again to kill you, and that'd be lousy thanks."

"I want you to stay," Diana said. "I've got a lot to do before Easter, and I'm going to need help."

Nardie shook her head. "I might not kill you," she said, "I might let the—the queenhood go, but I'd never *help* you get it . . . for *yourself*."

Diana smiled. "Why not? You've worked hard in this. If you just take off, you're abandoning everything. You won't even know if there'll *be* a Queen this time; there hasn't been one since 1960—1947, really. At least if you work with me, you're still working with what you hold valuable. Is the Queen thing only good and worth working for if it's you that's being it?"

"You go be valuable without me."

"Huh." Diana walked to the coping of the glassy-smooth pool and back. "Did you ever hear of Nick the Greek?" she asked. "A Poker player, my father knew him. He was in the first heavy Poker game at Binion's, in 1949, and it was just him and Johnny Moss playing head-up, no limit. The game lasted five months, and the Greek lost about two million. Years later he was playing Five and Ten Draw in Gardena for a living, and somebody asked him if that wasn't a big step down, and he said, 'It's action, ain't it?'"

For a few moments the pool area was completely silent. The blue pagoda roofs of the Imperial Palace towers next door shone in the descending morning sunlight.

Then Nardie laughed harshly. "That's—that's the *incentive* you're offering?" Her voice, though still quiet, was shrill and incredulous. "I can be Nick the Greek to your Johnny Moss? Christ, girl, you make a lousy recruiter. I wouldn't—"

"You want the same thing I want," Diana overrode her. "To be a sister and daughter and mother, in a *real* family, not some fucked-up arrangement that looks like it was put together for . . . for cruel laughs. That family is still here, in potential at least, and wants you. Be a part of us."

Diana waited for an answer, wondering what her own answer would be if the situation were reversed.

Nardie looked sideways up at the sky and exhaled. Then she pushed her cap back and rubbed her eyes. "For now," she said, her voice muffled. "Provisionally." She lowered her hands and stared at Diana. "But if I wind up killing you—"

"Then I'll have misjudged you."

"Your judgment's been real good so far?"

Diana smiled, and the sun touched the highest mirrored windows of the Flamingo high rises. "I'm happy to say I can't remember."

This morning Crane saw the old man as soon as he carried his bagged six-packs out of the liquor store. Doctor Leaky was the only one of the players by the Dumpster who was wearing a hat—a wide straw thing with a yellow paper rose on it.

"Beer man," Crane said when he limped up to the ragged circle of players.

His left leg was stiff and his side ached under the perpetually wet bandage, but he felt young and strong. Today it required no willpower to only fake sipping the open beer can he held.

"All *right*," said one of the young men eagerly. "Sit thee doon, dude." He tugged one of the cans free of the top six-pack when Crane put the bag down. "What's your name, anyway?"

he asked after popping the can and taking a deep morning-restorative swig.

Crane sat down and looked over at Doctor Leaky. "Scotto," he said.

The very old man frowned at him in huge puzzlement, his mouth of course hanging open. "Scotto?" he said.

"Right. And I don't know about you guys, but I'm a little sick of Lowball, hmm? So I got a suggestion." Crane was talking fast and cheerful, like a proposition bet hustler. "I've got a new game we can play, and since it's my idea, I'll fund all of you for the first few hands, how's that? Here." He pulled five rubber-banded bundles of one-dollar bills out of his jacket pocket and gave one to each of the players except his father's body. "There's fifty bucks for each of you. I figure nobody'll mind if Doctor Leaky keeps on playing with trash."

As if choreographed, each of the ragged players tore the rubber band off his bundle and riffled incredulously through the bills.

"On this basis," said the young man who had spoken, "you can call any game at all, dude." He stuck out a grimy hand. "I'm Dopey."

Crane decided that the young man meant it was his nickname. He shook his hand. "Glad to meet you." Crane had kept one of the bundles for himself, and he now peeled off a dollar and tossed it onto the asphalt in the middle of the circle. "Everybody ante a buck."

Doctor Leaky was blinking and shaking his head. "No," he said, on a rising note almost as if it were a question. "I'm not going to play with you." His trembling right hand scratched aimlessly at the empty crotch of his lime green pants.

All the others had tossed in their antes.

"Pot's not right," said Crane softly, "Dad."

The last word visibly jarred Doctor Leaky. He gaped at the bills on the parking lot pavement, and then down at his pile of flattened pennies and holed chips. Then, slowly, he reached down and pushed one of the chips forward. "Pot's right," he muttered.

"Okay," said Crane. He was tense, but he put easy assurance into his voice. "This game is sort of Eight-Card Stud, but you gotta make your hand by buying someone else's."

And as he took the fixed-up deck of Bicycle cards out of his pocket and shuffled them, he began, carefully and clearly, to explain the rules of Assumption.

Tonight it starts.

Tall and muscular and still genuinely dark-haired at the age of seventy-five, and immaculate now in a suit, the Art Hanari body stood in the sun by the curb in front of La Maison Dieu's front doors, waiting impatiently for the ordered limousine.

From behind the blue eyes in the unlined, sunlamp-tanned face, Georges Leon watched the big camouflage-painted trucks trundle past along Craig Road. La Maison Dieu, at the north end of North Las Vegas, was a discreet complex of green-lawned condominiums and medical facilities tucked between the Craig Ranch Golf Course and the Nellis Air Force Base Pumping Station, and most of the traffic out here was military vehicles.

Tonight the game starts, he thought.

Getting out of this glorified old folks' home had proved to be more difficult than he had anticipated. When, as Betsy Reculver, he had put this perfect body away here for safekeeping, he had made sure that the contract stipulated that Hanari was free to leave at any time he might choose—but when he had tried to exercise that clause yesterday morning, the staff had tried to block him, had got the security men to tie him to his bed and refused to fetch his clothes.

In a way he couldn't blame them. After dying on the linoleum floor of the hospital cafeteria yesterday morning, strangling on his own closed bronchial tubes and then feeling his heart agonizingly seize up and stop in his chest, he had awakened in his bed here—in his only remaining body. When his heartbeat had slowed down and his breathing was under control, he had pushed the button that summoned his caretaker—but when the man had arrived, and Leon had opened the Hanari mouth to ask to be released, it had been the voice of a querulous old woman that had come out of him.

It had been the voice of Betsy Reculver, moaning about being abandoned in the desert and about to lose her body. And then he had heard Richard's voice resonating out past his helpless vocal cords and chattering teeth, droning on about sitting on a bungalow roof in the rain; and of course after that had come old Beany with Poker talk, chortling over rolled-up Trips that had become Aces-Full on Fifth Street.

When Leon had finally got control of the body and, in measured tones, asked to be released, the caretaker had at first dismissed the request entirely. When Leon had insisted, threatening legal action, they had tried to call Betsy Reculver or Vaughan Trumbill, and of course they had not succeeded.

Finally, this morning, they had decided to wash their hands of him, and had had him sign every sort of declaration and waiver. They had even videotaped him, to have evidence that he seemed to be in his right mind.

And at last they had let him get dressed and call a limousine and walk out. They'd been very friendly then, patting him on the back—something he hated—and telling him to be sure to come back for a visit sometime. His physical therapist had made some remark about finally getting some use out of the penile implant, and had winked, but Leon hadn't even wanted to stay long enough to file a complaint.

He had to find Doctor Leaky and then prepare for the game. He would have to call Newt and remind him to have thirteen players ready at the Lake Mead marina dock at sunset.

But he had to find Doctor Leaky first of all.

All day yesterday, when he was not arguing with the staff, Leon had been brooding, and then nearly panicking, about something old Doctor Leaky had said in the hospital cafeteria.

The cards aren't fooled by any of the rest of it, the wrecked old body had said at first. *The people in Doom Town, and all the human-sacrifice statues around town.*

Leon had suspected for years that the mannequins in the built-to-be-bombed houses out at Yucca Flats in the 1950s had been, unknown even to the technicians who had set them up, sacrifices to the gods of chaos that were about to be invoked by the detonation of the atomic bomb, and it had seemed to him, too, that the multitude of statues around Las Vegas, from the stone Arabs in front of the Sahara on the Strip to the towering figure of Vegas Vic over the Pioneer Club on Fremont Street, exposed constantly to the sun and the rain, were offerings to the random patterns of the weather, another manifestation of the chaos gods. Chaos and randomness, after all, in the form of gambling, were the patron saints of this city and had to be appeased.

If the cards, the personifications of randomness and chaos, weren't fooled by those tokens of human sacrifice, it didn't really bother Leon.

But the old body, *his* old body, had gone on to say, *All your Fijis that died, too, they haven't changed anything. It's still just me.*

Belatedly it had occurred to Leon that this might refer to the bodies he had inhabited that had died, Reculver and all the rest of them; perhaps Doctor Leaky had meant *effigies*, and that these token deaths that Leon had suffered were not fooling the cards.

It's still just me.

Maybe, in spite of all his body switching, Leon was still fated to die when the senile, emasculated Doctor Leaky body died.

The Hanari body shuddered, and Leon snapped its fingers in a passion of impatience.

He had taken such shabby, contemptuous care of the broken-brained old thing all these years! He had avoided death only by chance many times, if this guess was true. Yesterday he had even hoped that the police would kill it!

He had to assume that what it had said was true, and take measures. A week and a half ago, on the same night when he had sensed the big jack and the big fish crossing the Nevada border, a thought had come from nowhere into his head: the notion of a chicken heart, cut out of the chicken and kept artificially alive for many many times the normal lifetime of a chicken. Grown now to the size of a couch.

Right now, before starting the preparations for this new game on the lake, he had to find the Doctor Leaky body and put it somewhere safe. Afterward Leon would bribe or terrorize some doctor into cutting out the heart and keeping it pumping for decades, and then passing it on to other doctors so that it would keep beating for centuries, and grow no doubt to the size of a house.

The mind that was Georges Leon would still be immortal, still be King.

He could see the limousine sedately approaching up Craig Road now, moving past the grassy hills of the golf course.

Your next stop, Leon thought at the driver, who was invisible behind the tinted windshield, is that parking lot behind the liquor store where the old fool always plays cards with bums.

And you're going to move a good deal faster.

CHAPTER 44

The Hand Under the Gun

The sun was nearly overhead now, and Crane had twice had to give one of the players money to run back to the liquor store for more beer.

Now the deal had finally come back around to Crane—he was grateful that by common consent Doctor Leaky was not expected to deal—and he shuffled rapidly and thoroughly and spun the cards out to the players. Two each down, and then one up to bet on.

At first the players had objected to the four extra cards Crane had put into the deck, four Kings with the letters *KN* laundry-markered across the faces, but Crane had finally got them to agree to accept the cards as Knights, ranking between Jacks and Queens, and it had taken several hands before they caught on to the way the bidding worked and how a player could often make more money by selling the unconceived four-card hand than by buying somebody else's four and staying in for the showdown; but for the last several hands the game had gone smoothly. A couple of the players, including Dopey, had substantially increased their stacks, and Crane had had to give additional cash-rolls to two players and agree to do the same for the rest of them.

But Doctor Leaky had still not bought a hand, and seemed to be getting restless. He had wet his pants, and the smell of urine evaporating on the hot pavement seemed to bother him.

Crane had been hesitant to interfere with whatever natural processes might be at work here, but the game on the lake was supposed to start tonight, and Doctor Leaky looked as if he were ready to leave.

"You know," he said to the body of his father, "you *can* buy a hand from somebody."

From under the rose-decked straw hat Doctor Leaky gave him a glance behind which Crane almost imagined he could perceive a spark of intelligence. "You think I don't know the rules, Scotto?"

Staring into those well-remembered eyes, even though now they were pouched in dry, wrinkled skin, made Crane feel small and futile, and he found that his own gaze had dropped.

For relief he looked around the parking lot as the bet went around the circle. Mavranos's blue truck was parked at the far end of the lot, and a taxicab was idling not far away from it, and now a shiny black limousine was turning in from Flamingo Road.

"Your bet, Scotto," said one of the players.

Crane saw that Doctor Leaky had pushed three copper ovals into the pot, wincing as though they were painfully hot. Crane threw in three dollar bills and dealt everybody a second up card.

"Ace bets," he said, nodding to the player on his left.

Then he heard heavy tires grind to a halt close behind him, and he turned around in alarm.

The limousine had stopped a couple of yards away from where he sat, and a back door opened, and a man stepped out. He was tall and tanned and dark-haired—Crane had never seen him before, but he recognized the gold sun-disk on a chain around the man's neck. It was identical to the one Ricky Leroy had worn when he had hosted the game on the lake in '69.

This, Crane thought with a sudden hollowness in his chest, is *really* my father.

The front of the man's pants bulged, and Crane wondered bewilderedly what there might be about this scene to give him such a rampaging hardon.

Crane got slowly to his feet, aware of the stiffness in his leg and the pain in his side but aware, too, of the bulk of the revolver in his jacket pocket.

His fingertips were ringing like struck tuning forks. I could shoot him right now, he thought. But what good would that do if he's got another couple of bodies he can switch into? And look at all these witnesses; even that taxi is moving forward.

"We're in the middle of a hand right now," Crane said, trying with some success not to let tension drive his voice up into the falsetto range. "But we can deal you in on the next one."

The tall man turned his calm, unlined face on the cards that lay on the pavement. "It's Razz you're playing now, no doubt," he said. "Always low end for you people. Well, Doctor Leaky is going to have to forfeit his hand, I'm afraid. I'll fade his investment in the pot." He reached into his coat and pulled out a leather billfold.

"The doctor will finish playing the hand," Crane said.

The eyes in the smooth brown face focused on Crane. "You're Scott Crane, aren't you?" The face didn't smile. "You do get around. Go play high-end for big money somewhere; you'll do better, take my word for it." He looked down at the old man in the wet pants. "Come along, Doctor," he said, "we've got to get you cleaned up."

Crane put his left hand on Doctor Leaky's bony shoulder, holding the old man down. "He's going to finish the hand."

Crane heard Dopey's voice from behind him: "Jesus, who cares? Let the old man go."

"Why don't you wait for him over there?" Crane said to the tall stranger who was his father. "This should only last another couple of minutes."

The man's eyebrows rose just enough to express puzzlement. "I said I'd cover his bets with cash." He shook his head. "Oh, very well, I'll wait." He started to turn back toward the limousine.

But then one of the players said, "Good, I want to buy the old guy's King and Knight."

And when the tall man turned back from the limousine, there was a snub-nosed revolver in his hand. *"No,"* he shouted, *"he is not to play Assumption!"*

For a moment the man's eyes were on Doctor Leaky, and in one smooth motion Crane drew his own revolver and with all his strength cracked the butt of it into the tall man's face.

The tall body fell heavily against the side of the limousine and then clopped and thudded in a limp heap to the pavement, bright red blood already masking the face and spotting the gray asphalt.

Several of the players had started to get to their feet, but Crane turned the gun on them.

"Sit down. We're going to finish this hand."

The limousine was clanked into gear and drove away, the back door still open and swinging. Slowly and tensely the players sat back down.

"Ace bets," Crane said again. "Hurry." God, he thought, how long before the limo driver calls the police on the car phone he undoubtedly has?

The man with the Ace showing shakily put a dollar bill into the middle of the circle, staring at Crane's gun. All the players still in line to bet just folded except for Doctor Leaky, who smiled vacuously and rolled a punctured chip into the pot. Crane threw a dollar bill in.

He grinned with clenched teeth. "The hand, uh, *under the gun* is up for bid," he said.

Nobody moved or said anything.

Mavranos had the truck's engine running now. The taxi was still in the parking lot, stopped closer to the Flamingo Road entrance, its motor idling.

Crane could hear sirens—not out front yet, but not too many blocks away. He glanced at the body on the pavement. Dizzy with nausea, he wondered if it was dying, and what Lieutenant Frits would have to say to him about this.

"The hand is up for bid," he said, hearing the pleading tone in his voice.

Doctor Leaky blinked around. "I'll go two, Scotto," he said, laboriously pushing forward two flat pennies.

"And I don't bid," Crane yelled, "so it's yours!" He tucked the gun into his pocket and snatched up Doctor Leaky's hand and the four cards the old man had bought. Then he had scrambled to his feet, broad-jumped over the unconscious body, and was sprinting across the expanse of hot asphalt toward Mavranos's blue truck.

The police were right out front; he could hear the change in the echoes of the sirens and even the wheeze of the shock absorbers and thump of tires as they turned into the driveway.

The blue truck was rolling, turning to be able to leave through the side of the parking lot away from Flamingo Road, and Mavranos had opened the passenger side door.

Crane was running flat-out, his legs pumping furiously to stay under his full-tilt torso, but he knew the police cars would turn into the lot before he would reach the truck.

He heard a squeal of tires, and out of the corner of his eye he saw the taxi lunge forward and crash head-on into the first police car. He was aware that the taxi's doors were immediately flung open, but now he was level with the truck and had to scuff around, flailingly keeping his balance, to get to the open door.

He clawed his way in, crawling across the seat with his legs still kicking outside. *"Out the back!"* he yelled.

But Mavranos had pulled the steering wheel around the other way now, as if trying to make a figure–8. "Gotta pick up the girls," he said loudly over the battering racket of the engine.

Centrifugal force was pulling Crane out of the truck, and the playing cards crumpled in his hand as he dug his fingers into the upholstery. *"Girls?"* he shouted as his feet banged the swinging door, trying to get a purchase on anything.

Then, though the truck had not even slowed down, the back door was yanked open and a couple of people piled in back. Crane heard the gas pedal whomp down onto the floorboard, and the four-barrel carburetor kicked the truck hard forward.

As Crane's right foot finally found the door frame and pushed him inside, he was aware that Mavranos had made an abrupt U-turn into some kind of roofed entrance. When he sat up and pulled the door closed, he saw that they were in the Flamingo parking structure, driving slowly up the first ramp, hardly a hundred yards from where they had left the crashed police car.

"Oh, Arky," Crane whispered breathlessly, "this is a dangerous move."

Mavranos was frowning, and his face gleamed with sweat. "Shit, Pogo, tell me something I don't know. But if we tried to drive away on the Strip, they'd have radioed ahead and caught us within a block."

Mavranos swung the truck around the first bend, onto the second-floor ramp of the parking structure. Crane could hear sirens, but none of them were echoing as if they were in here too.

"Jesus, make it work," he whispered, clutching the dashboard with one sweaty hand. "Make them not think about looking in here."

"Turning in here was the best move," came a woman's voice from the back seat, and Crane turned around.

It was a young Asian woman in a cabdriver's uniform who had spoken; there was a branching pattern of blood running down her face from her forehead, but Crane was staring now at her companion.

And his heart was thumping harder now than it had when he'd been running. "Diana?"

Her nose was bleeding, and she was pinching it shut. "Yeah," she said thickly. "Hi, Scott. It's good to see you, Arky."

"Well, I'm lovin' life now," growled Mavranos.

To his own surprise, Crane felt even more frightened than he had a few moments ago. He had once played in a $500 buy-in Hold 'Em tournament—he had been too drunk to get all the rules straight before he started playing, and so he had not been expecting the option of being able to buy in again after going broke; and when he did go broke, and the re-buy was offered to him, he took it eagerly, happily paying out another $500. But the blinds and limits had been steadily increasing, and the minimum bet was now $150, and he realized belatedly that the expense of making the full investment again had only enabled him to play one more hand.

He couldn't remember now whether or not he had won that next hand.

"You two were in the cab that hit the cop car," Crane said.

"Right," said the Asian woman. "And I guess I'm surely committed to this," she said to Diana. "I left my cab there, and they saw us run. I can't claim you were holding a gun on me."

Mavranos had turned onto the third uphill ramp now. Still, there were no parking stalls empty, and the rumble of the exhaust filled the low-ceilinged space.

"Ozzie said you were dead," said Crane to Diana. "He said they blew you up."

"They nearly did. They *did* kill my poor boyfriend." Diana gave Crane a hard stare. "How is Ozzie?"

"I'm sorry. He's dead."

"Your fault?"

Crane thought about it bleakly. "Yes."

"Ah."

Her face was blank, but tears were running down her cheeks now to mix with the blood on her chin. Nobody spoke while Mavranos slowly turned the truck up onto the fourth level.

At last Crane recognized the young woman who had apparently been driving the cab. "I know you, don't I?" he said. "You drove me away from that shooting by Binion's. Your name was . . . ?"

"Nardie Dinh." She was blotting her forehead with a handkerchief. "Incidentally I take back my advice that you kill yourself. You're everybody's best hope now, such as you are, and I find myself on your side."

Crane looked around at the three people who were in the laboring truck with him. "We're a side?" His voice sounded brittle and hollowly cheerful in his ears. "And I'm the leader, am I? What's your opinion of your leader, Diana?"

Her face was still blank. "I'm in a state of suspended admiration."

Mavranos turned the wheel and swung the truck into an empty stall, the tires echoingly squeaking on the glossy cement floor. "We're gonna have to get some paint up here," he said, "and paint this thing some other color." He turned off the engine. "What you got there, Scott? Something worth all that . . . *furor?*"

"Yeah." Crane opened his fist and straightened out the eight crumpled cards. "My father's real body."

CHAPTER 45

No Use Taking Half a Dose

Crane paid for two adjoining rooms in the Flamingo, and he bought two souvenir decks of playing cards in the gift shop before leading the way upstairs.

On one of the beds in the room that was to be his and Mavranos's, Crane broke the seals on the decks and scattered the cards face up across the bedspread.

Mavranos had carried the ice chest up, and Dinh called room service for six Cokes.

"What are you doing?" she asked Crane when she had hung up.

Crane was tentatively arranging the cards. "Trying to figure out how to stack a cold deck for a very complicated Poker game." He had separated out the eight cards that had been Doctor Leaky's hand: the Six and Eight of Hearts, the Knight of Clubs, and the Seven, Eight, Nine, Ten, and King of Spades. "I wish my—my father's body had drawn a better hand. *Consisted* of a better hand. This has to win, and in thirteen-handed Assumption a King-high Flush isn't that great."

"Somebody's going to play with Flamingo cards?" Mavranos asked, sipping a Coors. Diana stood by the window, looking down at the pool.

"No," Crane said, "but I want to use these to set it up. Less wear and tear on my head. The actual game is going to be played with"—he sighed—"a Lombardy Zeroth deck."

Nardie glanced at him sharply. "My half-brother has a card from that deck," she said. "The Tower. He wants to use it to become King."

"Swell," said Crane. "I hope he looks at it cross-eyed and goes crazy."

450

"He already did," she said. "Are you . . . talking about the game on the lake?"

"Yes."

"You're not going to *play* in it, are you? Again?"

"Yes."

She shivered visibly. "You couldn't get me out on that boat."

Diana turned around. "When are you going to do this, Scott?"

He didn't look up from the cards. "The game's going to be played tonight and tomorrow night and during the day on Good Friday. I'll start tonight, and keep on playing until I get the trick done."

"Is that guy you conked gonna be there?" asked Mavranos.

"Yeah," said Crane. "In that body, if it's not dead or in a hospital. He's the host."

"He'll recognize you."

"He would, but I'll be disguised."

"How?"

There was a knock at the door then, and Diana walked across the room and let in the bellboy, who set the tray of Cokes on the table, and gave him some money.

"How are you going to disguise yourself?" Mavranos asked again when the bellboy had left.

Crane grinned worriedly at his friend and shook his head. "I don't know. Shave my head? Wear glasses? Dye my face and hands black?"

"None of those sound very good," said Diana.

"You could go in full clown makeup," Nardie said. "I think they do it for free at Circus Circus."

"Or you could go in an ape suit," said Mavranos. "There's gotta be a place in town that rents ape suits."

"'Each one volunteered his own suggestions,'" quoted Crane with a forced smile. "'His invaluable suggestions.'"

"That's Lewis Carroll," said Nardie.

Crane looked at her, and his smile became genuine. "Right." She and Diana had told him what her connection was to all this, but now he really paid attention to her for the first time, and he noticed her fine black hair and porcelain face. "I love that poem," he said. "'Neither did he leave them slowly, with the——'"

"A woman," Diana interrupted harshly.

Mavranos raised his beer as if in a toast. "A woman!"

Crane frowned at her. "What?"

"Go as a woman. It's the only disguise that will work."

Crane laughed shortly—but saw that Mavranos and Nardie had raised their eyebrows as if considering the idea.

"No," he said. "This is going to be tough enough without showing up in *drag,* for Christ's sake. I'll shave my head and wear glasses. That'll—"

"No," said Nardie thoughtfully, "your face is too distinctive. I haven't seen you very often, but I'd recognize you bald and with glasses. I think drag is it—lots of makeup, lipstick, a striking wig—"

"Makes *me* hot," allowed Mavranos.

"It wouldn't work," said Crane in a confident, dismissing tone. "What about my voice?" He pitched his voice falsetto and said, *"Do you want me to talk like this?"*

"Just talk normally," said Diana. "They'll all just write you off as a brassy transvestite."

"Nobody's gonna look hard at a queer," Mavranos agreed. "If anybody starts to, just wink at 'em."

Somehow, dwarfing his fear that he would fail, and that Diana would be killed, and that he himself would lose his body on Holy Saturday when his father assumed the bodies he had bought during the 1969 games, Crane felt light-headed with panic at this new suggestion. I will not do it, he assured himself. Don't *even* worry about it.

Nardie touched his shoulder. "What if it's the only way?" she asked softly. "Do you remember Sir Lancelot?" Crane shook his head stubbornly, and she went on. "He was riding to rescue the Queen, Guinevere, and on the way he had to ride in a cart. It was a horrible disgrace to ride in a cart in those days; criminals were paraded up and down the streets in them, so that people could jeer and throw things, okay? Lancelot hesitated for just a moment before climbing in, and afterward, when he had rescued her, she wouldn't speak to him because of his brief hesitation, because for a couple of seconds he had put his personal dignity ahead of his duty to her. And he agreed that she was right."

"God." Crane stared down at the cards.

It *would* be the best disguise, he admitted to himself. And what do you care, really, if a bunch of strangers—and your *father*—think you're a drag queen? They won't know who it is. Is Diana's life worth less than your—your raddled dignity? *Your* dignity, the dignity of a trembly old bum only six days on the wagon? Six days on the wagon and at most three days on the cart.

He looked at Diana, and she didn't look away. "Let the record show," he said hoarsely, "that I hesitated no longer than Lancelot did." He turned to Dinh. "Did Guinevere forgive him?"

"That was in Chrétien de Troyes's book, right?" said Mavranos. For a moment Dinh was clearly baffled by his barbarous pronunciation of the name, but then she blinked in comprehension and nodded, and Mavranos told Crane, "Yeah, she did eventually."

"Hear that, my lady?" Crane said to Diana.

As if to punish them all, he pulled his father's wooden box out of his pocket, opened it, and spilled the Lombardy Zeroth deck out on the bedspread. With a trembling hand he fanned them out.

"*Ah*," sighed Nardie, her voice suddenly wounded and sad.

Crane was staring at the horribly affecting, morbid old miniature paintings, but he was peripherally aware that Mavranos had stood up and Diana had stepped closer. Suddenly sorry, Crane reached out to hide the cards.

"No," whispered Diana, catching his hand tightly. "I need to . . . meet these things."

"It's done," said Mavranos gruffly. "No use taking half a dose." He bent down and spread the cards out more fully with steady, callused fingers.

The Fool and the Lovers and the Moon and the Star and the Emperor and the Empress stared back up at the four of them, and Crane found that he was holding Diana's hand on one side and had clasped Mavranos's on the other. Mavranos was also holding Nardie's hand.

Though the cards on the bed didn't move or change, in his head their patterns shifted like the scales on an uncoiling diamondback rattlesnake, and though the sun shone in brightly through the window, he fell away into the well in the bottom of his mind, down into the subterranean pool all such wells shared.

He didn't know how much time passed before he began to float back up into his own consciousness.

Crane found himself focusing on the World card, a hermaphroditic figure pictured dancing within a wreath that was an oval with pointed ends. Gotta be male *and* female for this, he thought dazedly.

He found that he could sense the minds of his companions— Mavranos's bluff front covering profound fear, Diana's anxiety for her children and suppressed love for Crane, Nardie's cocksure despair—and he knew that they could sense, too, whatever his own character was.

At last he released their hands and picked up the wakeful-seeming cards. "I've got to arrange these," he said awkwardly. "While I'm doing that, maybe you girls could go downstairs and buy me some clothes and stuff."

"I think you'd be a size twelve," said Diana, moving away from the bed.

At no time during the taxi ride south to Lake Mead did Crane manage to forget the weight of the foundation and blush and powder on his face and the hair spray that was holding his eyebrows down smooth. To his own humiliation he had tried to speak in a falsetto voice when he told the driver where he wanted to go. It had been a failure; the man had started violently and then mumbled obscenities for the first few minutes of the ride, relapsing finally into outraged silence.

Crane spent the half-hour drive trying to read the prop Dinh had found for him, a copy of *Poker for Women* by Mike Caro. The advice in the book struck him as sound, but of course there was no chapter on Assumption.

The stacked Lombardy Zeroth deck bulked in his white patent-leather purse like a chambered automatic with the safety off.

When at last the cab pulled into the marina parking lot, Crane looked at his new gold chain-link watch; it was only four-thirty. He hoped Leon was letting players come aboard this early, for he didn't want to have to wander around. He could sit in a bar, but he shuddered at the thought that someone might try to pick him up.

"Fifty dollars, dearie," said the driver. Crane paid him without speaking again and got out.

He walked past the grocery store and the bait shop toward the docks, resisting the impulse to hold his arms out from his sides for balance; walking in high heels on pebbly asphalt was as awkward as walking with ice skates on, and he could feel stage fright sweat rolling down his ribs under his cotton dress. Diana and Nardie had also had to buy a linen dress because Diana handled it, but he hadn't been able to wear it because of the black marks where she'd touched it.

The long white houseboat was moored at the same slip it had occupied twenty-one years ago. Crane stood and stared at it, breathing through his open mouth.

Full circle, he thought. Back again, goes around comes around, dog to its vomit, criminal to the scene of the crime.

He flexed his chilly hands and breathed deeply.

Three grizzled old fishermen were carrying rods and tackle boxes up from the docks, and they stared at Crane as they walked past him.

"There's your date, Joey!" one of them muttered.

"What's the matter, Ed," put in another, "don't you say hi to your mom no more?"

Crane could hear them snorting with suppressed laughter behind him, and he started tottering forward on the clumsy shoes, his face burning under the makeup.

A white El Camino was backed up to the slip, and two young men were unloading open-topped boxes of liquor and soft drinks. Crane looked at the pickup's flank as he approached and was not surprised to see that the *El* and the capital *C* had been pried off. Looks like the Amino Acids have found a new King to serve, he thought.

One of them looked up and saw Crane. "Jeezuss," he said, almost respectfully. "Can I help you, Sweet-cheeks?"

Crane had always been good at doing a Brooklyn accent, and he put it on now. "I come to play Poker," he said, waving the Caro book.

"That's what this is all about," said the young man, "and you're in plenty of time. There's only six aboard so far. Just step through the detector."

Crane noticed the two upright plastic poles set up on the dock. "Is that a metal detector?" he asked.

"Sho' nuff."

Oh well, Crane thought, I'm not here to make a big bankroll

that someone might want to hijack, and I can't let them go through my purse and find the Lombardy Zeroth deck. He reached into his purse and carefully pulled out his .357 by the barrel and held the Pachmayr grips toward the young man. "I suppose this would set it off."

"Goddamn." The Amino Acid took the gun from Crane. "Yeah, that would, sister. What were you planning to do, exactly?"

"Just self-protection," said Crane. "A girl can't be too careful in these parts."

"Well, you can have it back when you disembark. And if you come back again, leave it at home."

Crane stepped through the metal detector and set off no alarms, then crossed slowly to the edge of the dock and took hold of the boat rail—cringing at the sight of his red-painted nails—and managed to step across onto the stern deck.

Footsteps sounded to his right, and he looked up to see his host standing outside the lounge doorway. Both men flinched.

Georges Leon was still in the body Crane had hit this morning. A thick white bandage rode above the left eyebrow, disarranging the perfectly moussed brown hair, and the eye below it was a glittering sliver between swollen, pewter-colored lids. His slim, muscular-looking body was wearing a tailored white suit, and the gold sun disk still hung over his heart, and Crane could only imagine how much the man must resent the gross injury that ruined the elegant effect.

And he could only imagine what the man thought of this newly arrived player. Crane had resolutely looked at himself in the mirror after Diana and Nardie had got through with him, and he knew that the dress and makeup and socks-stuffed bra were an effective disguise but did not make him look much like a woman.

"My name is Art Hanari," said his host. His voice was a rich baritone.

Crane realized that he had not thought of a name for himself. "I'm Dichotomy Jones," he said at random.

Leon was nodding, not happily. "You've come to play?"

"Yessir! Something called Assumption, I heard?"

"Yes." Leon's distaste for the spectacle that was Crane was evident in the curl of his upper lip. "It's sort of Eight-Card Stud—"

"Somebody already explained it to me," interrupted Crane. "I'm ready to play."

"Go on in and sit down. Have a drink, if you like, and there'll be a buffet soon. We should have thirteen players before long, and then we'll get under way."

Crane got a glass of soda water and lime from the young man—no doubt another of the Amino Acids—who was tending the bar, and he took it to a chair in the corner away from the big round table.

Now that he was here, sober and prepared at least to the best of his abilities, he felt relaxed, almost contented. Some sleight of hand would be required when he got the deal and had to switch the cold deck in and do the pull-through shuffle and the table shift to negate the cut, and these cards were bigger than normal playing cards, but Ozzie had taught the young Scott how to do those moves smoothly before he was ten years old, and he had no doubt that his hands remembered the skills; Ozzie had never recommended cheating, but had believed that a good Poker player should know all the ways it's done.

The six other people in the lounge were younger than he was: a couple of out-of-town executive types in suits, several denim-clad men who might be professional players, and two young women sitting on a couch, watching the television set hung over the bar. Crane wondered what they thought of this battered old transvestite, and what they would think if they knew he was there, among other things, to save their lives.

He opened the Caro book and began absentmindedly reading about Five-Card Draw.

CHAPTER 46

We're Now Thirteen

Several more people arrived singly over the next hour, and then four came shuffling and mumbling aboard at once. Crane looked up, and recognized the one among the newcomers who was not young. The face was a hard couple of decades older, but was still recognizable . . . Newt, that was the name, the man he and Ozzie had played Five-Stud with at the Mint in 1969, the man who had then met Crane at the Horseshoe and driven him here on that terrible long-ago evening. Apparently Newt was a procurer for Leon.

Leon followed them in, and Crane heard the boat's engines start up.

"We're now thirteen," Leon said, sitting down at the table and reverently laying a wooden box down on it. "Let's play cards."

The boat surged as it moved out onto the face of the twi-lit lake.

The way Crane had stacked his Lombardy Zeroth deck required that he sit at Leon's right, and he got to that seat a second ahead of one of the young women. Leon gave Crane a cold look but let him sit there.

"Hundred-dollar ante," said Leon, "and then it's two hundred a bet, and then there's the mating, at which time you can bid for a hand or sell yours. After that there's another round of bets, still at two hundred."

Same stakes as twenty-one years ago, Crane thought as he pulled his roll of bills out of his purse, peeled off a hundred, and tossed it into the center of the table. Very damned high ante, so that you've got an investment before you even see your first card and then no sharp increases to chase anybody out.

His father opened the wooden box and fanned the Tarot cards out across the table's green felt surface.

Though they did still start up a ringing wail in his head, Crane was able to look at the cards without flinching now; it was as if the sight of them had broken his identity so many times that his identity had finally begun to conform to them. The Hanged Man and Death and the Two of Sticks now seemed to stare up at him as if at a peer.

Other players weren't so fortunate. One of the necktied executives bolted his drink and tremblingly crossed himself, and the two young women gagged, and no one at all looked happy. One man was suddenly crying, very softly. No one remarked on it.

Several people had cigarettes smoldering in ashtrays, and the smoke from all sides drifted in over the center of the table.

Leon separated out the twenty-two Major Arcana cards and put them aside. Then he flipped the remaining cards over, quickly shuffled them seven times, and began to deal out the first two face down cards.

Crane of course had to wait through twelve hands for the deal to come all the way around to him. During that time he never bought a hand, but managed five times to sell his own uncompleted four-card hands for a profit, and by the time it was his deal he had made a couple of hundred dollars. Several of the players seemed to be checking, and then either calling or folding, without subjecting themselves to the ordeal of actually looking at the cards they held.

When the deck was at last shoved across the green felt to Crane, he picked it up and said, with a little bit of urgency, "What time is it?"

During the moment when everybody was looking at a watch or craning to find a clock on the wall, under the cover of one spread hand he quickly spilled the deck into the open purse on his lap and flipped out the stacked deck.

"Eight and some change," called the Amino Acid bartender from the other end of the lounge.

"Thanks," said Crane. "I get luckier after eight." He split the switched-in deck and riffled the two blocks together, but then, while the interleaved blocks were still at right angles, he smoothly pulled them through each other as though he were separating two meshed combs; he did this rapidly several more times, seeming each time to shuffle the cards thoroughly but actually keeping them in the same order.

Finally he passed the deck to the man on his right for the cut. When the man had lifted off half of the deck and set it beside the remainder, Crane completed the cut but left a step in the two blocks of cards, Scarne's "infinitesimal terrace," so that when he lifted the deck in one hand, he was able to reverse the cut with his palm and the bases of his fingers.

Despite the apparent shufflings and cut, the cards were in the same order as they had been in his purse.

He was absorbed with the play now, and he had forgotten his ludicrous disguise. He spun the cards out across the green felt, two down and one up.

An Ace of Cups to the left of Leon brought in the bet for two hundred dollars, and it was called all the way around; the second up card paired one woman's Ten, and she bet two hundred, and again the bet was called by the whole table. Everybody was staying for the mating, as Crane had anticipated.

Crane had dealt himself half of the hand that Doctor Leaky had bought this morning, the Ten and Eight of Swords down and the Seven and Nine of Swords up; the other half of Doctor Leaky's hand was now Leon's hand, which was showing the Six and Eight of Cups, and since Leon was the play-er to Crane's left, his was the first hand to come up for bid.

"We got the Six and Eight of Cups for bid," said Crane lightly. "He's got five hundred in the pot."

At least one of the thirteen players would have to be frozen out when the mating cut the action down to six hands, and the man Crane had elected for that office, who was showing a Nine of Cups and a Two of Sticks, bid $550 for Leon's hand. Crane knew the man had the Two and Seven of Coins down and was hoping for a Straight.

Leon shook his head.

"Six hundred," said Crane.

Leon shrugged and nodded, and Crane looked to the other bidder to see if he would top that bid.

But the other bidder waved in defeat.

Leon flipped up his down cards and shoved all four across to Crane.

With a steady hand Crane slid them next to his own cards and separated out of his roll six hundred-dollar bills, tossing them onto the empty spot of green felt in front of Leon.

Crane was now holding the complete hand that Doctor Leaky had bought in the liquor store parking lot—a King-high Flush—and if the other players followed the courses he had prepared for them, he would win this hand at the showdown, and Leon could then exercise his Assumption option.

The Ace-King that had led off the premating betting was bought by one of the necktie-lads—to make, as Crane knew, an Ace-high Straight—and the next hand was reliably bought to make three Fours for one of the women.

But the next man, whose hand showed the Three of Cups and the Six of Coins, and who was supposed to sell his hand to the man showing the Nine and Five of Coins to make a Nine-high Flush, refused the expected bid.

Crane stared at the man with the Nine and Five. Offer him *more,* he thought, trying to project the order telepathically. You've got four of the Coins suit down, and he's showing one up; you'll have a Flush, you idiot! *Buy it!*

The man, though, shook his head; no one else bid on the hand, and the next hand in turn came up for auction.

Crane's carefully constructed sequence was broken.

He sat back and pressed his side, absently wondering if the steady bleeding would soak through the bandage and stain his dress. He tried to remember all the cards in all the hands, and to guess how the hand might turn out, now that it was out of his control. His King-high Flush might still win; he had been careful to give everybody cards that *looked* good but wouldn't add up to any killer hands.

But when the ninth hand, showing a Six and a Four, came up for bid, the man who had refused to sell the Three and the Six bought it.

You're one lucky moron, thought Crane bitterly as the cards and money were exchanged across the table. You paid for a low Straight, but I happen to know you bought a Full Boat, Threes over Sixes. Which beats me. And I can't hope to bluff you out at the showdown—my board doesn't even show a pair; I clearly can have nothing better than a Flush.

When the sixth hand was mated and conceived, and the raised bet came around to him, Crane smiled tightly and turned his cards face down.

"I'm out," he said.

The cigarette smoke just hung in flat layers under the paneled ceiling. Neither Crane nor Leon was involved in the hand any longer.

All Crane could do now was play for money and, of course, never buy a hand from Leon.

And twice he looked on, helplessly, as Leon became a parent of a winning hand, matched the pot, and lost the Assumption. Each time, the big brown man smiled under his bandage as he ran his fingers down the stack of cards, and his smile didn't falter when he failed to feel the crimped Two—he must have thought some player had straightened the card—and he picked the low card even without that help.

"You're taking money for the hand," Leon said each time as the player was happily raking in the enormous pot. "And I've bought it. I've *assumed* it."

Both players seemed puzzled by the ritual statement, but agreed. Neither one seemed to notice Leon's intense satisfaction.

Dawn had paled the sky behind the jagged mountains when the houseboat chugged back to its slip, and the twelve guests shambled out onto the deck, blinking and breathing deeply in the fresh and still-cool air as the Amino Acids tied up the lines.

Now that they were all fellow veterans of the long night's play, several of them tried to make small-talk with Crane where he stood at the rail, but he was already thinking about how he would stack the deck in his purse for tonight's game, and they drifted away to find somebody less taciturn.

A couple of them decided to get beds at the Lakeview Lodge, and Crane was able to catch a ride back to town in Newt's Cadillac; one of the players fell asleep in the back seat, and nobody talked much during the drive.

When Crane unlocked his hotel-room door and stepped into the air-conditioned chilliness, the connecting door was open, and Diana was sitting on one of the beds. The faded yellow baby blanket was spread out over one of the pillows, as if she'd been napping with her head on it.

"Are you up," he asked, "or *still* up?"

"Up," she said. "Everybody crashed out after an early dinner, and four A.M. seemed like morning."

Crane took off his wig and tossed it onto a chair. "Where are the kids?"

"Across the street at Caesars, checking the sports book for a cancer cure." She stood up and stretched, and in spite of his exhaustion, Crane found himself noticing her legs in the tight jeans and the way her breasts pressed out against the fabric of her white shirt.

"You didn't sell it to him, did you?" she said.

"No." Crane kicked off the high heels and padded into the bathroom. "Some guy bought the wrong hand," he called, "and now I've got to cook up another thirteen hands for tonight and try to make sure *they'll* link up right." He soaped and rinsed his face but saw smudges of tan makeup on the towel after he dried himself. "How the hell do you get this stuff off?"

He heard Diana giggle, and then she was in the bathroom with him. "Cold cream," she told him. "Here." She unscrewed the cap from a plastic jar and then massaged his face with the cold, slick stuff. He closed his eyes, and after a moment put his hands on her waist as if to steady himself. She didn't flinch or say anything and her fingers kept pressing smoothly across his face. "You'll want to shave," she said as she picked up the towel and rubbed it down his forehead and nose and chin. "You must have looked like what-was-her-name, Rosa Klebb in *From Russia with Love*—'the oldest and ugliest whore in the world.'"

"That's what I need to hear right now," he said, nodding.

His hands were still on her waist, and now he unhurriedly leaned down and kissed her on the mouth. Her lips opened, and in the moment before she stepped away from him he tasted the faint scent of recent minty mouthwash on her tongue.

"I'm sorry," he said, lowering his empty, trembling hands. "I shouldn't—"

She took his left hand in both of hers. "Shut up," she said quickly. "We were all in each other's minds yesterday, and

I know you know how I feel about you. I . . . love you. But there's a bed in there, and a chain on the door, and we wouldn't stop after a good kiss, would we?"

He grinned at her ruefully. "*Su-ure* we would," he said. "*Trust* me."

"On Saturday," she said, "after this is all done, if we win—we'll get married. At one of these screwy chapels in town. You should hear Nardie's stories about the people she drives to them." Suddenly she gave him a stricken look. "My God! That is, if you *want* to marry me."

He squeezed her fingers. "You saw into my mind. You know I do." He was still leadenly tired, but excited, too, and embarrassed; he freed his hand and turned around. "Could you unzip me?"

He heard the buzz of the zipper being pulled down. "No funny business, now."

He turned back to face her again. "I'll be good. You know, it's a good thing we do want to get married. I don't think we would really have *won*, if we didn't do that."

"The King and Queen have got to be married," she agreed, "and have children." She touched his hair. "That's not Grecian Formula, is it?"

"No. I'm ungraying." He kissed her forehead. "And you've lost that scar. Blessings from the old killed King and Queen. I wonder how young we'll get."

She winked at him. "Not pre-puberty, I hope." Then she was out of the bathroom. "Shower and get some sleep," she called from the other room. "When do you want to be waked up?"

Waked up, he thought. Never. "Make it two, I guess."

"Okay."

He heard the connecting door close, and, his mind turbulent with joy and fear, he began to work on getting out of his dress.

Mavranos reached up in the dimness of the wide hall and patted Cleopatra's right breast.

The carved and painted female body he had touched was the figurehead of the big, mechanically rocking boat by the steps up to Cleopatra's Barge, one of the bars in Caesars Palace.

"Sure," he said with a weary smile to Diana and Dinh, "you girls go ahead and blow some chips. I've got to medicate my beer deficiency, and I'll be fine with Cleo here."

Diana took Nardie's elbow, and the two of them walked back down the carpeted hallway toward the playing floor. Diana's purse, bulky with the folded-up old baby blanket, swung between them.

"I gather," said Nardie, a little stiffly, "that he didn't sell the King the senile hand, and that you two are planning to get married on Saturday."

Diana glanced at her, concealing her surprise. "Right both ways. Okay with you, I hope."

"Failing with the King—no, that's not *okay with me*. I don't want to have hitched my cart to a horse that's a loser. *My* half-brother is a pretty good candidate, too, you know. I could have put my money on him. As to who you marry—that's none of my business."

"It is your business," said Diana, "if you're with us. I know you tried to seduce Scott yourself a week ago."

Nardie grimaced and seemed about to spit. "S*educe* him? I ran from him. I told him he should go kill himself." She yanked her arm free from Diana's grasp. "I don't *need* you people, you know; I'm still a contender. Just because you—"

"Are you very tempted to go back to him? To your brother?"

Nardie's lips pulled back from her teeth, and she inhaled—and then her narrow shoulders slumped, and she just sighed. "Hell, yes. If I was with him, I wouldn't have to think all the time, be alert. Every time I'm near a pay phone that rings, I think it might be him, and I want to pick it up. Wouldn't you?"

They were among the banks of chugging and clanging slot machines; young men in the armor and helmets and skirts of Roman soldiers stood as still as statues on raised stone altars behind the slot machines, and a man dressed as Julius Caesar and a woman dressed as Cleopatra moved through the crowd, graciously welcoming everyone to Caesars Palace and urging people to have a good time. Doric pillars, and marble, and heavy purple curtains framed all the electrically flashing action, and Diana wondered what a genuine classical Roman, time-traveled to now and dropped here, would think of the place.

"Arky should have come with us," whispered Nardie, nudging Diana and tangling her hand in her purse strap. "I think we're about to get an audience with Cleopatra."

Sure enough, the woman in the gold-belted white skirt and Nefertiti hat was striding across the figured carpet toward them.

"She's going to ask us how come we're not playing," said Diana.

They both were touching the baby blanket that was stuffed into the purse, and it was warm, even hot.

Then Diana felt something shift, in the space around her and in the depths of her mind.

All at once most of the lights were snuffed out, and the laughter and ringing bells stopped, and the floor was tilted. Diana gasped and took a balance-catching step backward, and she could feel that she had stepped onto springy grass.

The cool breeze smelled of trees and the sea instead of paper money and new shoes, and the woman walking toward them was taller, incalculably tall, and wore a crown with a silver crescent moon over her high, pale forehead. Her eyes glowed in the shifting white light.

Nardie was still standing beside Diana and had tightly grasped her hand; but when the goddess stepped closer, she let go and hurried back, into the shadows under the tossing moonlit trees.

Diana strained her eyes, trying to keep the approaching woman in focus. The cold and inhumanly beautiful face was above Diana now, and seemed to be a feature of the night sky. Dogs or perhaps wolves were howling somewhere, and surf crashed on rocks. Fine salt spray dewed Diana's parted lips.

Her knees were suddenly cold, and she realized she had knelt on the wet grass.

When the goddess spoke, her voice was literally musical—like notes stroked from inorganic strings and ringing silver. *This is my daughter,* spoke the voice, *who pleases me.*

But Diana heard suddenly the rapid-fire *clank-clank-clank* of coins spat into the payout well of a slot machine, and for a moment it was the sound of spent shells, ejected from the hot, fast-jacking slide of a semi-automatic pistol, hitting the sidewalk pavement as a woman fell away with three holes punched through her head, and Diana turned and began frantically crawling across the dewy grass toward the trees in whose shadows Dinh was already hiding.

This is my death, Diana thought. I'm being invited to die.

Sometimes one risks death, spoke the goddess behind her, *to save one's children.*

Still facing the trees, Diana stopped; and she thought about the night when her mother had been killed, and she herself had survived and been found by Ozzie and Scott.

And she thought once again about Oliver and Scat.

She forced herself to breathe deeply and stop panting. "Did you do that?" she asked quietly. "Could you have . . . got away from that death, if you hadn't paused to put me somewhere safe, where I'd be found by strangers?"

There was no answer, and finally Diana turned around, still kneeling, and looked up.

She was shaking but didn't look away from the goddess's gaze.

Stand up, daughter, said the voice, *and take my blessing.*

Diana got to her feet, leaning a little against the strengthening offshore wind. Owls swept past overhead.

"My . . . friend," Diana ventured to say. "Can she be blessed too, Mother?"

I see no friend.

Diana pulled her attention from the face that was bending down over her in the sky and blinked into the waving shadows under the trees behind her.

"Nardie," she called. "Come out."

"I'll die."

Diana smiled tiredly. "Not right away."

"I'm not," sobbed Nardie from among the shadows, "in any way . . . *dressed* for this!"

"Nobody is. She'll overlook it. Come out—if you're not too afraid. I'll understand, if you are."

Nardie stepped hesitantly out onto the moonlit grass and then with visible effort walked up to stand beside Diana.

"I *am* too afraid," she said, looking down. "But I'm more afraid of what I'll be if I don't do this." She took a deep breath. "Okay?"

"Look up," said Diana.

Nardie obeyed, and in the moment before she, too, raised her eyes to the inhuman gaze overhead, Diana saw her friend's face glow with reflected light.

Be a true friend to my daughter, Bernadette Dinh.

"Yes," whispered Nardie. "I will."

An idea was conveyed then, something like *bathe* or *cleanse* or *be baptized,* and in Diana's head appeared a clear picture of a vast lake behind an enormous man-made dam.

The face leaned down closer and breathed on them, and the warm wind of it swept them off the ground. The dark island was gone, and they spun through vast golden halls whose pillars resonated to a triumphant chorus of deep, inhuman chords, as if the sea and all the mountains of the world had found voices to raise in a song that was older than mankind.

And the two of them were noticed, and remotely greeted.

Then they were ascending through darkness, and Diana's only anchor was Nardie's hand clasped tightly in her own. Lights began to wink at some indeterminate distance, and a choppy murmur grew in volume.

A whiff of cigarette smoke tickled Diana's nostrils—and a moment later the racket of chattering human voices and clicking chips crashed in on her ears, and she could see again.

She and Nardie were sitting on stools at another of the dim bars in Caesars Palace, and they released their hands and blinked dazedly at each other.

"How are you girls doing?" asked the bartender.

Diana picked up the glass in front of her and sniffed the inch of clear liquid in it; she could detect no smell at all. She cleared her throat. "Uh—what are we drinking?"

The bartender didn't quite roll his eyes. "Quinine water."

"Yeah, give us another round."

Diana's heart was still pounding, and she had no peripheral vision; to meet Nardie's gaze again, she had to look directly at her. The ashes in a nearby ashtray weren't shifting at all, but Diana thought she could still feel the hot wind of her mother's breath in her hair.

Nardie was clutching the edge of the bar. "Are we," she whispered, "going to *stay* here, do you think?"

"Yeah," said Diana, "I think we're in a landing pattern."

*   *   *

Somehow a live turtle, its shell as big as a dinner plate, was walking along the top of the bar toward them, pushing glasses out of its way with stumpy, leathery feet.

In its beak-like mouth was a Poker chip. Perhaps because of the artificial light, the turtle's shell and skin appeared to be gilded. Nobody else seemed to see the creature.

Diana forced herself not to close her eyes. "Um—turtle," she said levelly. "Coming up behind you."

Nardie pursed her lips and nodded, then sighed and turned to look.

The turtle was beside her drink now. It lowered its head and opened its jaws, and the chip clicked to the polished surface of the bar. Nardie slowly reached out and picked up the chip, and the turtle bowed again and and—was gone.

Both women jumped at the abrupt, noiseless disappearance, and the bartender, stepping up with their drinks, spilled a splash of quinine water out of one of the glasses. "What?" he demanded irritably, looking around.

"Nothing," said Nardie. "Sorry."

When he turned away, shaking his head, she held the chip out toward Diana on her open palm.

The center of the clay disk was a grinning harlequin face, like that of the Joker in a deck of cards. Around the rim were imprinted the words "MOULIN ROUGE, LAS VEGAS."

"I thought that was in Paris," said Nardie.

"It was the name of a place here, too," said Diana. She picked up her drink. "I think it burned down in the 60s. It was the first casino to let blacks in. See the harlequin pattern, checkerboard black and white diamonds?"

"'*Ebony and i-vory*,'" sang Nardie in a frail voice. "I get it." The rim of her glass chattered against her teeth. "Guess who the turtle was."

"Touché Turtle. I give up, who was he?"

"Well, I don't know. But I grew up in Hanoi, okay? And there's a lake in town there, where the post office is, called the Lake of the Restored Sword. In the fifteenth century a guy called Le Loi is supposed to have been out on it in a boat, and a golden turtle swam up and took back from him a sword that he'd been given to drive out Chinese invaders. Hey, excuse me," she said more loudly.

The bartender strode up to them again. "Can I help you, miss?"

"Can I get a hamburger here? Fried, rare?"

"Sure, if you like. Everything on that?"

"Doesn't matter. And a—a Budweiser, please." She turned back to Diana. "I can feel the air conditioning now, and see things to the side of me."

Diana darted her eyes around and shivered. "Me too. I guess we're all the way back." She could smell the quinine water in her glass.

"But when we were still circling in, the turtle gave me this." She rolled the chip end over end across the backs of her fingers and then tucked it into her shirt pocket. "I guess I'd better hang on to it."

"You might have to call a bet," Diana agreed.

Within a couple of minutes Diana was comfortable in the gin-scented coolness, but Nardie was still shaking. Diana asked her if anything in particular was wrong and if she wanted to leave, but each time Nardie just shook her head.

At last the bartender set the steaming hamburger and the frosty beer in front of Nardie, and she picked up the hamburger and took a bite of it. Diana looked away from the red-stained bun around the rare ground beef.

"There," said Dinh a few moments later, after taking a deep sip of the beer and clanking the glass back down on the bar. She was smiling, but tears shone in her eyes.

Diana stared at her. "There?" she said, mystified.

"You . . . raised me up, to your mother, to the goddess. You asked her to bless me, too, and she told us *both* to get cleansed in the lake. You're not the first person to make me more than I was, okay? But you're the first person to do it without standing to benefit from it—in fact, risking your own safety. I think I could have displaced you, after receiving that blessing."

"Okay," said Diana cautiously.

"But . . . damn, don't you see?" The tears overflowed her eyelids and ran down Nardie's cheeks. "I just now ate red meat, probably cooked on an iron grill, and I drank alcohol! I've unfitted myself for the queenhood! I've totally pledged my allegiance to you now; I'm of no use to my half brother anymore."

Then Diana did understand, and she leaned forward and hugged her friend, ignoring someone behind her who whispered, "Jeez, check out the dykes!"

"Thank you, Nardie," Diana said quietly. "And I swear, by our mother, that I won't leave you behind. I'll take you with me."

Nardie patted Diana's shoulder and then they both sat back, a little self-consciously. Nardie took another sip of her beer and sniffed. "Well, you'd better," she said. "Right now I'm an orphan, in a tiny boat, on a goddamn big ocean."

After they had walked back to the Flamingo and Diana had shaken Crane awake, he wearily got dressed and made coffee.

Then, in the afternoon sunlight that slanted in through the unopenable hotel window, he sat down on the carpet and began laying out face up the cards of his father's Lombardy Zeroth deck. Leon had taken out the twenty-two Major Arcana cards yesterday, and Crane tentatively began moving the remaining fifty-six cards around into four-card combinations.

It was like slowly turning a kaleidoscope in which living faces fell into new patterns and alignments in the barrel instead of colored glass chips, and he passively let the razory identities resonate through his mind.

Again he tried to arrange the cards so that he could plausibly buy his father's hand and so that, after all the purchases and sales of hands, his King-high Flush would win at the eventual showdown. Twice he sat back and sipped his lukewarm coffee, confident that he had a lock on the hand, only to notice a rogue buy that would give one of the other players a Full Boat or Four of a Kind, and he had to break it all up and start again.

In his mind, crystalline lattices of alien hatreds and fears and joys grew and were broken, over and over again, like ocean waves rising and then falling and shattering into spray.

At last he was satisfied with the layout, and he carefully picked up the cards in the order in which they would be dealt.

"Front!" he called as he tucked the stacked deck into his purse.

It was Nardie Dinh who appeared in the connecting doorway. "What am I," she asked, "a bellboy?"

"It was a joke," he said, standing up and running his fingers through his hair. "Sorry. Listen, could you do my makeup? Getting the dress on I think I can do by myself now."

"Sure, come in the bathroom," said Nardie, leading the way; then she stopped and turned around, smiling. "Hey, Scott, congratulations on your upcoming wedding! Diana told me about it."

"Thanks." His good eye was burning with fatigue already. "I hope we all live to be there. But right now I've got to get ready for . . . my bachelor party." He waved her on ahead. "I suppose most guys don't have their fathers along at their bachelor parties."

"Well," said Dinh judiciously, "most guys don't go in drag."

CHAPTER 47

The Flying Nun

An hour later Crane stood in his high-heeled shoes in front of the million-dollar display in Binion's Horseshoe Casino. Behind bullet-proof glass, a hundred ten-thousand-dollar bills were ranked together in five columns of twenty, framed inside the doorway-size arch of an enormous brass horseshoe. A pair of stout security guards were staring at Crane in sour disapproval.

"Must be rough," said someone by Crane's elbow. He looked down and saw old Newt, looking withered and old and jug-eared in a wide-lapel plaid suit.

Here the two of us are again, Crane thought, twenty-one years older and both looking pretty bad.

"Hi," he said to Newt. "Can I get a ride out with you?"

"Looks like," said the old man. "My other three haven't shown—down with the nightmarey shakes, I bet. That happens. Let's give 'em a few minutes for courtesy." He looked at Crane's purse. "No gun today, I hope. Throw it in the lake this time, and maybe you, too."

"No, not today. It looks like a peaceful bunch of players anyway." He looked down from the height of his heels into Newt's empty, bird-bright eyes. "What was it that you said 'must be rough'?"

"Shaving, with all that fruitcake makeup—sorry, *pan*cake makeup. Jams up a blade, I bet, or the holes in an electric shaver."

"Well, I suppose it would, but I shave before I put the stuff on." Crane was tired, and forlornly wished for a beer, the way beer used to be for him, and a cigarette, the way they used to taste. And he was thinking of the ghost of Ben Siegel, who had gone to some trouble to let him know that a fly might be tricked into eating a poisoned sugar cube if the poison face was concealed and the fly saw only the harmless face. "It's a hassle," he said absently, "but I do it for the Lord."

The little old man's bushy white eyebrows were halfway up to where his hairline must once have been. "For the Lord, hey?"

"Sure." Crane blinked and made himself remember what he had been saying. "You don't think I *choose* to dress this way, do you? I'm a member of a religious order, is what this actually is all about. Lots of religious orders have to dress weird."

"Huh. They ain't gonna show, I guess. My other players, not your religious orders. Let's blow." Instantly he held up one wrinkled hand. "By which I don't mean—"

"Jeez," said Crane, following the little man through the casino dimness toward the bright patch that was the open door onto Fremont Street, "you're safe from me, Newt, honest."

"And no funny business in the car."

Everybody's cautioning me against funny business, Crane thought. "You have my word of honor."

They were in the noise of the slot machines, and Newt mumbled something that sounded like *Like applying none*.

Crane frowned. Applying none of what? Honor? Could this strange little man possibly have some intuition about Crane's plan to dethrone his own father? And he leaned down as they zigzagged their way through the crowd. "What did you say?"

"I said, 'Like the Flying Nun.' Religious order where you gotta dress weird. She could fly, remember?"

Crane was oddly relieved; apparently they weren't talking about honor after all. They were outside now, on the baking, sunlit sidewalk, and he had to shout, "Yeah, I remember!" to be heard over the droning of the picketer with the megaphone.

"I guess that made up for it," yelled Newt, "for having to wear that stuff all the time. At least she could fly."

"I guess."

Crane followed the little man across Fremont and down First Street toward the pay parking lot at the end of the block. This was where he had been shot at eight days ago and saved by a couple of shots from the gun of the fat man—whom he himself had killed four days later. He scuffed the toe of his ridiculous left shoe across the chipped curb, and rasped the painted nails of his right hand over the pockmark in the brick wall.

Crane would have the deal next.

The sky was dark behind the open ports, and the still-warm wind, smelling of distant cooling stone and sage, had raised the lake surface into choppy waves; the levels of the drinks on the green felt table were all rolling and uneven. The cigarette smoke was a mushroom cloud over the pot's scattered bills.

Newt sat to Crane's right and was flipping out the last of the second face-up cards. ". . . and a Duck to the Seven," Newt was chanting, "no apparent help, Seven gets a Seven, Sevens are cheap, the Flying Nun gets an Ace and a possible Flush draw, another Ten to the Ten of Sticks, pair looks good, and the Nine gets . . . an Eight toward a Straight." He sat back. "Tens are the power."

Not wanting to consistently sit next to Leon, Crane had this time stacked the deck with the requirement that he sit two places to his father's right, and he had succeeded in getting that seat. The man between Crane and his father held the pair of Tens, and he rapped the table to check. Leon bet two hundred, and everybody called it, and then the man with the Tens raised it another two hundred. All the other players called the sandbag raise.

Crane's hand was up for bid now, and he managed to sell it for the seven hundred he had in the pot. The man with the Tens refused a $700-bid for his own hand and then bought Leon's hand in turn for $750.

"All *right*," the man said as he gathered Leon's cards face up into his own board, now showing a Tens Up Two Pair, "I wanted that, thank you, Mr. Hanari. I figured I could buy it; I notice you always sell your hand, never wait and buy one."

Crane saw the Art Hanari face frown slightly under the bandage, and he realized that his father wasn't pleased to have his Assumption strategy noticed. Leon made the Hanari lips smile. "I'll have to start mixing up my play," he said.

Not quite yet, thought Crane, please.

The betting went around again, and at the showdown the man who had bought Leon's hand had a Full Boat, Tens Over, which lost to an Aces Over Boat.

The deal was now Crane's.

He gathered in the cards, and then, as he tossed into the center of the table the hundred-dollar bill that was his ante, he hit the edge of his glass of soda water and sent it rolling across the table, spilling the water out in a series of pulses like a sine wave.

It was a fine distraction, and Crane had the cards dumped into his open purse, and the stacked deck flipped up onto the table, while everybody was still in the first syllable of a surprised curse.

"Sorry, sorry," Crane muttered, reaching out to dab ineffectively at the stain with a paper napkin.

"Stevie!" called the Hanari body to the Amino Acid bartender, "a towel here, quick!" Crane's father gave him a wrathful glance out of his unswollen eye. "The Flying Nun doesn't seem to appreciate the fact that these are hand-painted cards and must not get wet!"

"I said I was sorry," said Crane.

The green felt in front of him was dry, and he began smoothly riffling the cards and doing the pull-through shuffle. The deck that was in his purse now was the one with the Jack of Cups card that had split his eye forty-two years earlier, and he wished for luck's sake that were the deck he would deal from tonight.

After seven riffles and false shuffles he passed the deck to Newt for the cut, and easily negated it when he recombined the cards under his fast-outswept hand. Everyone's attention was still on the mopping-up of the spilled water.

When the green felt had been blotted with a towel and then

been painstakingly blown dry with a hair-dryer that one of the Amino Acids had had to fetch from the bathroom, and the game was finally allowed to proceed, Crane spun out the first three cards to each player, two down and one up.

The first round of betting added fifty-two hundred dollars to the pot, and then Crane dealt out the second up cards.

This time his father held the Ten and Eight of Swords down and the Knight of Clubs and the Six of Cups showing. Crane's cards were the remainder of the hand Doctor Leaky had bought in the parking lot game the day before, the Nine and King of Swords down and the Seven of Swords and the Eight of Cups showing. Crane could plausibly buy the "Art Hanari" hand now, seeming to be trying for the Six-Seven-Eight three-Straight.

"And," said Crane after the last bet had been called, "Mr. Hanari's hand is up for the mating. What is he bid?"

One man bid $500, and a woman raised it to $550, but Hanari just kept shaking his head.

"I'll go six hundred," said Crane. And, he thought, if the rest of you bastards will just have the simple card sense to buy the hands I've laid out for you, I'll win this with the King-high Swords Flush.

"Uh," said Leon through the lips of the Hanari body, "no."

"Six-fifty," said Crane, concealing his impatience. He could feel sweat starting out under the makeup on his forehead; it would begin to look odd if he had to bid too much more for an apparent middle-size three-Straight.

"No," said Leon, "I think *I'll* buy one this time."

He's chosen this hand to *vary his play,* thought Crane, because of what that son of a bitch said in the last hand.

"Seven hundred," said Crane, trying to conceal his desperation.

"No," said Leon, swallowing the word so that it sounded almost like the French *non.* "The bidding is closed on these cards."

Crane's heart was pounding, and he kept his chin lowered so that the pulse in his throat wouldn't be visible. "Okay," he said. "Then the next hand is up for auction." He allowed himself a slow sigh. "What is *he* bid?"

Crane had again lost the chance to buy Doctor Leaky's hand and then let Leon buy it from him at the Assumption.

*   *   *

Leon eventually bought the hand of a young man who had been playing very loose. Crane had to admire the tactic; if the conceived hand should happen to win, this was the one player aside from Leon himself who might choose to match the pot for the Assumption option.

But Leon's Two Pair lost to a Flush, and the cards were gathered and stacked and passed to the man on Crane's left to shuffle and deal out another hand.

Again Crane was left with nothing to do but play for mere money until dawn.

To his intense annoyance, his Flying Nun nickname was picked up by everyone else at the table. At one point the announcement of "A pair of Queens to the Flying Nun!" drew such laughter that the betting was delayed for a full minute.

When the sky had lightened, and everybody had stood up and put on his or her coat and the engines were gunning in reverse as the boat surged in toward the docks of the marina, Leon rang an empty glass with one long, manicured fingernail.

"Attention, gamesters," he said. He was smiling under the bandage, but there was a harshness in his voice that silenced all the idle, tired chat. "Tomorrow is Good Friday, and out of respect this game will end at three in the afternoon. Therefore, to get in at least a little bit of decent play, this boat will . . . set sail at noon. That's only about six hours from now, so you might want to get rooms at the Lakeview Lodge here, and arrange for wake-up calls."

Fatigue coursed through Crane's arteries like a powerful drug, but it struck him as odd that the game should *end* at three. When businesses had acknowledged Good Friday, he recalled, they were *closed* from noon until three.

If this was a gesture of respect, it was a strangely *inverted* one.

Dancing on the edge of the cliff.

Shuffling dizzily through the still-cool air along the Fremont Street sidewalk, Dondi Snayheever was momentarily eclipsed in the shadow of the towering steel and neon tubing cowboy over the Pioneer Casino. He paused to squint up at the slowly waving figure, and he wondered what personage it might be nearly the shape of.

His maimed hand jerked him forward, and he resumed pushing himself forward through the resistance of the morning air.

Shapes waiting, he thought, like the implicit whirlpool in a bathtub just waiting to come into existence when someone would pull the plug. As if when a cloud formation came to look very damn like some certain enormous bird that was waiting in potential, it would actually *become* that bird.

Birds. Eye of the crow was right last week, but Isis's temple was blown up now. Another bird now, according to the dreams, a pink one.

In a dream Snayheever had seen the fat man blow up the temple. The fat man had achieved a shape, too—had become the giant that had got stunted and round and lost his green color, had become the warty black ball in the math field, containing all the points that would never become infinite.

The fat man wasn't that anymore. He was dead, his boundary broken, and the points would soon be scattered across the desert, free to become infinite or not, as they pleased. Snayheever wondered how long he himself would continue to be the thing he had come authoritatively to resemble.

Dancing on the cliff edge, the dog snapping at his heels.

He could sense his missing finger; it was far away to the south, up high, ringing with the vibrations of tremendous hydroelectric power.

He had no choice but to go there; the personage whom he had become was going to be there, and of course would need its shape.

But first there was someone to say good-bye to, and someone to forgive.

CHAPTER 48

Last Call

When Crane unlocked the hotel room door and pushed it open, he smelled hot coffee. Diana and Dinh were standing by the window with cups in their hands, and they looked over at him anxiously.

"No," said Crane. He took off his wig and watched, to his own mild surprise, as his arm drew back and flung the cap of auburn hair against the mirror. "No, he didn't buy it. I've got to be back there before noon, and I've got to stack the deck again in the meantime. I won't have time to get any sleep."

Diana hurried over to him and touched his arm. He forced himself not to pull away. "Would you like some coffee?" she asked.

"'Wood eye, wood eye?'" said Crane absently, quoting the next-to-last line of an old joke Susan had liked.

Diana gave him her cup, which was nearly full and still steaming. "Here," she said. "I'll make me another one."

Crane put it down on the bedside table. "I don't want any." The smell of coffee hung in the air like smoke, and he couldn't get out of his mind the image of a coffee cup on a stove set on low.

And paramedics, and an ambulance, and after that a bottle to keep him from remembering his dreams.

"That was a line from a joke," he said irritably. "'Wood eye, wood eye.'" Diana stared at him blankly, apparently never having heard the joke herself. How could she not ever have heard it? "'Hunchback, hunchback' is the last line," he snapped. "I've also heard it as 'Harelip, harelip.'"

Mavranos had walked in from the next room, and Crane saw him exchange a look with Dinh. That's right, Arky, he thought, I'm going crazy—talking about hunchbacks and harelips. Damn my soul, I would move heaven and earth for a—

The telephone rang on the bedside table, and everyone except Crane jumped. Dinh started toward it, but Crane was closer and snatched it up.

"Hello?" he said.

"*Whom wilt thou find to love ignoble thee,*'" crooned the voice on the telephone, "'*Save Me, save only Me?*'"

Crane recognized the lines. They were from Susan's favorite poem, Thompson's "The Hound of Heaven."

And of course he recognized the voice.

It's my wife, he thought.

I shouldn't talk to her.

Why not?

Because it's *not* my wife, he told himself. Remember? It's drink, or Death, or something that's both of those things. So I can't even talk to her. But what if it's her, a bit of the real Susan, *too*? Maybe it really is her ghost, and the bad stuff has been laminated onto her.

And even if it's *not* her at all, what if drink can do a convincing imitation of her? I'm probably going to die tomorrow, after I've failed to do this stupid card trick for the third time, after my father kicks me out of my body. Can't I at least *talk* to this thing for a couple of minutes, over the *phone*? What's the harm of just listening to what it has to say? And it might have some information we need. And it sounds so much like Susan, and I'm so tired, that I know I can make myself believe that it *is* Susan. If everyone would just leave me alone.

Finally he spoke. "Just a sec," he said into the phone, then put his palm over the mouthpiece. "This is private," he told the other three, "do you mind?"

"Jesus, Scott," said Mavranos, "that's not—"

"*Do* you mind?" Crane repeated.

"*I* mind," said Diana, her voice breaking. "Scott, for God's sake—"

"Well, if I can't even—all I'm—" He shook his head as if to clear it. "Damn it, go mind in the other room, would you?"

For several seconds Mavranos and Diana and Dinh stared at him; then Mavranos jerked his head toward the connecting doorway, and the three of them silently filed through it and closed the door.

"We're alone," Crane said into the mouthpiece.

"What do they say," Susan's voice asked, *"in a bar, at ten to two, when it's your last chance to get a drink?"*

"They say 'last call.'" Crane was trying to be calm, but his voice was shaky.

"This is last call," said Susan. *"This is the last time I'll call you. After you hang up, I'm either gone forever or with you forever."*

"You're—um, you're a ghost," said Crane. He wished he could think clearly. His false eye stung—he hadn't washed it or irrigated the cavity since Wednesday; he knew he was just asking for meningitis—and his leg ached and he could feel blood leaking out of the bandage below his right ribs. A wave of exhaustion made him close his eyes.

"So would you be, a ghost, if you'd come with me. Forever, whole again. Go to the card game, why not? Pretend you turned me down—go ahead and stack the deck again, if you want, but leave it in your purse. Who cares what hands go where? And have a drink. . . . "

"'And when you're mine,'" he said, quoting another poem Susan had liked, "'I'll kiss you in my glass, fair goddess Wine.'"

"I'll kiss you back. 'It's even better when you help.'" Now she was quoting Lauren Bacall from *To Have and Have Not.* *"'Oh, whistle and I'll come to you, my lad.'"* That was from a ghost story. Well, this was a ghost story.

"I know how to whistle," he said dreamily. "Just put your lips to the bottle and suck." It warmed him to know that all this was making sense to her, as it would not to anyone outside the once-cozy bounds of their marriage. This *had* to be Susan's genuine ghost.

"And you can sled all the way down the hill, right out of the sunlight—on good old Rosebud," said Susan's voice. Susan had always loved *Citizen Kane.* "This Bud's for you."

The cup of coffee still steamed on the table. Crane touched it. The handle was as hot as if it had been sitting in an oven, but an instant later it was damply cold, and the cup had become a bottle of Budweiser.

He picked it up curiously. It seemed to be a real beer.

"It's the only way you can reach me now."

One sip never hurt anybody, he thought. He tipped up the bottle, but paused with it still short of his lips.

"Go ahead," said the voice in the telephone. *"They'll see only a coffee cup. Diana won't know about us. Who cares what hands go where?"*

A drink, he thought, and sleep, and Susan in my dreams.

"You'll have two eyes again," she said. *"Your father won't have hurt you, won't have left you. I won't have left you."*

Crane could remember how he had worshiped his father when he was five years old, and how he had loved Susan. Those had been good things; nobody could claim they had not.

There was a knock at the hallway door, and Crane jumped, splashing cold beer out onto his wrist.

"Quick," said Susan.

Whoever it was out in the hall was calling, "Heidi, Heidi."

"It's just one of my drunks," said Susan urgently. *"I'll send him away. Drink me!"*

The wetness of the beer was cold on Crane's wrist. He remembered old Ozzie fixing bottles of formula for the infant Diana. Crane's foster father had heated the bottles in a pan of hot water and tested the temperature by shaking out drops onto his wrist. He wouldn't have let her have it as cold as this.

I can't let her have it as cold as this, he thought. My love for my father, my love for Susan were good things, but Diana loves me *now*. I love her now.

He wondered if, in the next room, Diana was sensing his temptation to embrace the dead.

"No," he said, all at once shivering in his flimsy cotton dress in the chill of the air conditioning, his voice finally breaking. "No, I—I won't, not—not me, not your husband. If you are any part of—my real wife, then you can't want me to, at this cost." He put the beer down.

"You think you can help your sister?" asked Susan, her voice shrill over the phone. *"You can't help her. Oh, please, Scott, it's your wife you can help, and yourself! And your real father, whose feelings you haven't thought of once."*

"Heidi, Heidi!" came the call again from the hallway.

"Oh, go and die!" wailed Susan. Crane thought she was probably talking to the man in the hall, but he chose, despairingly, to take it as addressed to himself.

"I'll go," said Crane, "and if I die, at least I'll—" What, he thought. Be aware of it. Still be the man Diana loves. He took the receiver away from his ear and swept it toward the phone cradle—and his fingers went numb and dropped it.

He reached for the receiver on the floor with his other hand, and it, too, went numb; he was only able to brush the plastic crescent with limp fingers.

"You love me!" cried the voice out of the receiver.

Gasping for breath, almost sobbing, Crane got down on his hands and knees and picked the thing up in his teeth. Susan's pleading voice was a buzzing in his jaw-muscles now, vibrating through his head. His vision blurred, and he felt his very consciousness fading, but he bit down harder and got up on his knees.

Tears and saliva were beaded on the receiver when he had dropped it at last into the cradle, silencing the voice, and his teeth had cut dents into the plastic.

He flopped back against the side of the bed and blurrily saw that the connecting door was open again; Diana and Dinh were staring at him in uncomprehending alarm, and Mavranos crossed to the hallway door and pulled it open.

Dondi Snayheever walked in on tiptoes, jerking his filthy bandaged hand up and down and smiling crazily with all his teeth. "Heidi Heidi ho," he said.

Mavranos had moved quickly back to the bed and slipped his hand into the canvas bag in which he kept his .38.

Crane wiped his face on the bedspread and stood up. "What do you want?" he asked Snayheever unsteadily; though he was still panting, he wearily tried to put authority into his voice.

Snayheever had lost weight; his skull shone through his feverish skin, and Crane could faintly see a red aura flickering around the young man's angular body. The wounded arm was still twitching. Then Snayheever's bright eyes lit on Diana, and he grunted as though he'd been hit and fell to his knees. "Eye of the flamingo," he said, "not the crow. I've found you at last, Mother."

After a moment Diana walked over to him, ignoring Mavranos's bark of warning, and touched Snayheever's greasy hair. "Stand up," she said.

Snayheever got to his feet—awkwardly, for his left leg had started jerking. "The other one will find you and kill you," he said, "if I don't stop him. But I will. It's what I have left to do." He tugged at the lapels of his corduroy coat. "A coat I borrowed from James Dean, and I'll sing there for the two of you, like a bird, like a lovely little stork that wheels in circling flight, right? Hemingway said that. Flight makes right and he'll bite. You could say that. I've got my finger on the pulse, jammed behind the license plate, and it's at the penstocks and spillways and floodgates. And he wants to let the spinning wheel go circling around another twenty years, since he's got a busted nose now—a tweaked beak—and no Queen. He's gonna squawk on the wave band so nobody can hear anything until it's too late, and he'll dirty up the bath water so it's too screwed up for anyone else to use at all. Ray-Joe, it's a sad salvation."

"He's talking about my brother," said Nardie, "and it makes sense."

"Sure, he's got *my* vote," growled Mavranos, his hand obviously tight on the grip of the gun in the bag. "Diana, will you get *away* from him?"

Diana stepped back and stood beside Crane.

"He means that my brother is at Hoover Dam," said Nardie tensely, "and that Ray-Joe is going to try to postpone the succession, the coronation, the King's resurrection in the new bodies—let the cycle go around again, with no issue this time. It's what Ray-Joe *would* do; if I did break his nose, he can't become the King this time around. You've got to be physically perfect to do that, and he'll still have a couple of black eyes and be all puffy, okay? So he's going to . . . generate some kind of damping psychic noise, to drown out the King's signal, and then I think spiritually pollute the water, and everybody will have to wait another twenty years for all this to be ripe again. By then the old King will probably be dead, not having been able to get into any new bodies, and Ray-Joe will have had time to groom another Queen, probably right from birth—and he'll be able to just step right up to the throne and . . . sit right down."

"God," said Crane, trying to keep the eager relief out of his voice, "is that so bad? If your brother screws it up so that my father can't do his tricks this year, then I won't lose my body.

And we can all just go home, can't we? And I'll have twenty years to think up what to do when finally his . . . hour comes round at last."

Nardie stared at him. "Yes, that's right," she said. "But you won't have a wife. Ray-Joe will have found Diana and killed her, like this guy says. Ray-Joe would never want somebody like *her* for his Queen, and just by being alive, she'd be a big problem, okay?"

"The phone is for calling room service," said Snayheever, pointing at the bitten telephone on the bedside table. "You order . . . foods, your various items from a menu, and you eat *them*. What you *don't* do is eat the *telephone*." He nodded emphatically. "*He'll* try to eat *me*, I shouldn't wonder. I always have a dog. For now he barks all night long at the end of his tether."

He looked up at Diana. "This son came here to, as you would say, because he wanted to say good-bye to his mother," he said softly. "We won't meet again."

Diana's eyes were wet as she again ignored Mavranos's shout and crossed to Snayheever and hugged him, and Crane knew she was thinking about Scat and Oliver.

"Good-bye," she said a moment later as she released him and stepped back.

"It's not an easy thing," Snayheever said, "being a son." He turned his hot gaze on Crane. "I forgive you, Dad."

Crane looked at the grimy, stained bandage at the end of the shaking arm, and he nodded, acknowledging that he was grateful to have the forgiveness.

Then Snayheever had turned and limped out into the hall.

Mavranos, his hand still in the canvas bag, crossed to the door and closed it. "Lotta fucked-up people wandering around," he said quietly. He turned to Nardie. "Your brother's at the dam, right? And if he disarms the old man's clock, he's gonna come looking for Diana."

"That's it."

Mavranos sighed and touched the bandanna around his neck. "One more day," he said. "I guess I'm going to the dam. Anybody need a ride south?"

Diana looked at him solemnly. "Thank you, Arky. I wish—"

Mavranos gave her a dismissing wave. "None of us exactly like doing what we're doing. I'll stop at a pet store on the way and get me a goldfish, just for luck. How about the ride?"

"Yes," said Diana. "Nardie and I have to go get baptized."

Crane plodded around the bed and picked up his purse. "Give me half an hour to stack my deck, and I'll go, too."

Nardie and Diana had bought a couple of big cans of red paint and some brushes the day before and had painted Mavranos's Suburban.

As he jiggled on the front seat of the barreling truck now, Crane tried to hold his head in a position at which the cracks in the windshield would not pick up the garish red of the hood. He didn't like to see what seemed to be a metallic red spider flickering on the horizon.

"Visions and dreams and a crazy man's talk," Mavranos said resentfully, squinting ahead and steering with the fingers of one hand. "We're probably all crazy, too—look what they've done to my truck, Ma." With his free hand he lifted his can of beer and took a foamy sip. "I knew a guy once who claimed he was a Martian. His TV set had told him he was. Makes just as much sense as any of this. Poor old Joe Serrano, I should apologize to him."

Diana stirred on the back seat. "That's not a Martian name," she said, "that's a Mexican name. Who was he trying to fool?"

Crane started laughing, and soon they all were, and Mavranos put his beer between his thighs to grip the wheel with both hands.

CHAPTER 49

Ahoy, Cinderella!

At Boulder Beach, still short of the marina, Mavranos pulled over and stopped on the shoulder to let Diana and Nardie climb out. The beach was only a hundred yards away, beyond the ranks of colorful campers and RVs with their awnings flapping, and the lake was blue against the distant jagged brown mountains of the far shore.

"By afternoon everything should be over," Diana said, standing on the roadside gravel and leaning in through Crane's rolled-down window. "Us girls will walk up to the marina after we've had our dip. There's a hotel there, Scott says, the Lakeview Lodge. Let's meet at the bar." She kissed Crane, and he curled his fingers in her blond hair and kissed her fiercely.

"And tomorrow," he said when he had finally let go of her, "we'll get married." His voice was hoarse.

"That's what we'll do," she said. "Arky, Scott—both of you watch it, hear? And we'll be careful, too. We need to have a bride and groom and maid of honor and best man. All four."

Mavranos nodded, then took his foot off the brake and gave the engine gas and in seconds had swung back onto the highway.

"Drop you off at the marina?" he said, loudly over the wind in the open windows.

"Sure, that's close enough. I'm getting better at walking in these shoes."

"Couldn't tell to watch you do it."

"I'd like to see *you* try it."

"I bet you would, Pogo." Mavranos took another sip of his beer. "On the phone—she tried to talk you into ditching Diana and going with her instead?"

"Yeah." Crane shivered in his dress. "I talked myself out of it."

"Jawed from the snatch of defeat."

"Yeah, right." He shifted around on the seat. "Arky, I—"

"Don't say it. You may be wearing a dress, but that don't mean you can kiss me, too."

Crane smiled, feeling the makeup in the creases of his face. "Okay. Be there this afternoon."

Mavranos made a right turn, toward the marina, and at a red light Crane climbed out of the truck and straightened his dress. He rapped on the red hood the way a Craps shooter might blow on dice, and then the light had changed and the blotchy truck boomed on across the intersection.

Crane walked slowly down the slope toward the gleaming white boats moored at the docks and slips, and he was not even aware now of derisive hoots from a passing car. He walked in the sunlight and the cool breeze and the smells of lake water and gasoline and sage, and he thought of all the people who were dead: Susan, and Ozzie, and the fat man, and probably Al Funo, too, considering the way Diana had said she'd set *him* up. And tomorrow night Crane and Arky and Diana and Nardie might be down in the black water themselves, down where the Archetypes lived. He wondered if in some dim way ghosts were able to talk among themselves, and, if so, what they would all talk about.

"Ahoy, Cinderella!" came a call from ahead of him. He looked up, and saw one of the Amino Acids waving at him from the deck of the houseboat. Crane quickened his pace.

"You wait till high noon," the young man said, "and you'll turn into a pumpkin left on the dock here. Skate your weird ass over, girl, and step into my metal detector, as the spider said to the fly. There're a dozen aboard now already, and you're number thirteen."

Diana stood in the hot sand in her Nikes and looked up and down the beach at the broad towels and beer coolers and scampering children.

"I guess it would be a mistake to go to jail over this," she muttered to Nardie.

"I think they're pretty conservative around here," agreed

Nardie with a nervous giggle. "Even in our underwear we'd probably get arrested. Fully clothed it is."

"I'll ditch this, at least," Diana said, unbuttoning her denim jacket and tossing it onto the sand. "The walk back might not dry us out, and the bar's likely to be air-conditioned."

Dinh just hugged herself and shook her head. "I'm an as-is package."

Several tanned little boys were splashing each other in the shallows ahead of them, and after a few steps down the slope Diana stopped, staring at them.

The boys' faces were stiff, almost painted-looking, and their arms seemed to Diana to move as if they were hinged.

Dinh was ahead of her, looking back. "Hmm?"

"Let's . . . go farther down the beach," Diana said.

The first thing Crane noticed was that old Doctor Leaky was aboard the houseboat, sitting in a wheelchair in the corner under the television set. There didn't seem to be anything wrong with him, aside from the fact that he had wet the pants of his sky blue leisure suit, and he kept fumbling ineffectually at the belt that kept him in the chair.

"Pay no attention to the old man in the corner," said Leon in his booming baritone. Crane looked across the red-carpeted lounge to where the host was already seated at his place at the green table—and Crane made himself just smile and nod.

The Art Hanari body was looking bad. Red lines, apparently inflamed veins, curled and branched down the bad side of his face, and the high cheekbones and decisive shelf of the jaw were lost under puffy swelling. Crane imagined that Leon was yearning to flee into a new body as desperately as he himself had ever yearned for the escape of drink.

The engines shifted out of neutral, and the carpeted deck shifted as the boat got under way.

"Sit down, everyone," said Leon. "We've only got three hours, and we want to get as many hands bought and sold as we can, right?"

Right, Crane thought desperately. One hand in particular.

He squeezed his purse, feeling the bulk of the once again agonizingly stacked Lombardy Zeroth deck, as he hurried to the seat he had selected for himself, the first position to Leon's left this time.

He had thought about buying a pack of cigarettes so that he could at least have one smoldering beside him, even if he couldn't bear to puff on it; he'd forgotten to, but it didn't matter—Old Newt was tremblingly stubbing out a Pall Mall in an ashtray already crowded with butts, having just lit a fresh one.

Leon opened the wooden box and spread the terrible cards out across the green felt. A couple of yesterday's players had not returned and had been replaced by newcomers, and these now shivered and looked ill.

Leon turned the cards face down and began shuffling them. The cigarette smoke curled over the table, and it seemed to Crane that two almost inaudible sounds vibrated the levels of the drinks and made his teeth itch—one sound too low to hear and one too high—and he thought that the interference between them must be about to form words that would resonate unrecoverably deep in the minds of all present.

The brown Art Hanari hands were steady as Leon passed the deck to the man on his right for the cut.

Crane's bad eye stung, and he wiped at it with the lace-edged handkerchief the women had bought for him.

The children had walked with mechanical stiffness out of the lake shallows and onto the hot sand. Beyond them their parents waved and nodded, slowly, like the grasshopper heads of pumping oil wells.

Nardie and Diana hurried away, carrying their shoes now, toward the empty stretch of beach to their right. Diana tried to slant toward the water, but through some trick of perspective, every sliding footstep through the shifting sand took them further away from the lake.

It was in the bending of Nardie's knees that Diana first saw the stiffness start to appear here; then her belly went cold as she noticed that her own arms were swinging metronomically, and that the very birds and waves and stalks of shore grasses were all shifting their positions with angular rigidity.

"What's—exactly—happening," said Nardie, obviously struggling to make her voice come out as something besides a monotone quacking.

Mother, thought Diana in panic, *what's happening here?*

A concept appeared in her head, and the image of a sword.

Diana tried to put words to it. "Crystallization," she droned, unable to put a questioning lift at the end of the word. "Like—" She searched her mind for an image that would fit the idea. "Like pure silicon crystals—no good for—information transfer. Need—mix—doping of boron or—something. If it's just one pure thing, it's just a crystal—what this is." She inhaled and exhaled jerkily.

The image of a sword: Nardie had said that the turtle in the myth had taken back a sword. "Get out—your sword, your chip."

"Chip," intoned Nardie. "Dip, slip, crip. Chip like in—silicon." She reached up like a saluting robot, and her rigid hand hit her forehead. "Cannot—get it out."

"No," said Diana, wondering how much longer she would even be able to speak. The air was so still it seemed almost to have jelled. "Poker—Poker chip." Repeating the word was the only way she could convey emphasis. "Moulin Rouge."

Nardie nodded and then kept on nodding, but her spread fingers found the pocket of her jeans, and after some ungraceful wrenching she held out her hand.

On her palm was the black and white chip, with its androgynous jester face grinning under the diamond checkerboard pattern of the fool's cap.

The air rippled over it, and Nardie seemed to encounter resistance when she moved her hand—she had to cup her palm around the chip and push it through the air.

Diana sensed cracks spreading invisibly out from the space around Nardie; the field of rigidity was being broken up.

Then the air shifted and seemed to spring apart, and Diana nearly fell as her joints suddenly loosened.

"*God*," said Nardie, wobbling sinuously and twisting her feet in the rounded sand, her freed voice running up and down the scale, "what in *hell* was *that*?"

Diana sighed. "Opposition," she said. "Let's get into the water."

They turned toward the now-wide stretch of sand that separated them from the blue waves, then froze.

The air over the sand was no longer glassy clear.

A crowd of translucent figures and tall structures like oil wells wavered, insubstantial as heat waves over highway pavement, on the expanse of sand between them and the water.

Diana looked closer, trying to see the misty forms in the glare of the sunlight, and she saw without comprehension that they were not living figures but were nearly-transparent moving statues, perhaps not standing at various distances but built to different scales. She strained her eyes to focus on the things and saw that several were dressed in Arab robes and headdresses, some in Roman togas, and a couple as cowboys or prospectors. One was a giant ape, though no more lifelike in its motions than the others.

Then she looked up, and saw that the two tall structures were the clown from the front of the Circus Circus and Vegas Vic, the cowboy who perpetually waved over the Pioneer Casino on Fremont Street.

For a long, stretched-out second she simply stared, her belly cold and her mind blank.

Then she choked off a despairing wail and tried to think above the thudding of her heart. "It's all the figures," she said unsteadily, "from town. Or their spirits, I guess."

"Their *shapes*." Nardie shook her head, now holding the chip tightly in her fist. "What do *they* care?"

"I guess Scott's father cares."

"Can they," asked Nardie shakily, "*hurt* us?"

"I doubt they're here to escort us to the water." The two women had stepped back. "This is his magic, the King's. Male only—he doesn't want a Queen." Diana put one hand on Nardie's narrow shoulder, and they stopped retreating across the loose sand. "My mother gave us the chip. It's yin *and* yang," said Diana tensely. "Mixed, linked opposites—the face on it is both male and female. His . . . *things* might not like it."

Nardie had been squeezing the chip, and now she gasped and opened her hand. There was blood on her palm.

"It's got an edge," she said wonderingly.

"It'd better have." Diana held out her own hand. "Cut me, too, and then see if it will cut them."

Five miles to the southeast, the canyon-spanning concrete shoulders of Hoover Dam held back the lake.

After Mavranos had parked his truck in the broad lot by the snack stand on the Arizona side of the dam, and begun the long walk through the heat back toward the arc of the dam where the tourists had been milling with their cameras when he had driven by, the first thing he became aware of over his own exhaustion was the crying children.

The Arizona Spillway was a vast, smoothly curving abyss to his right, big enough, he thought dizzily, for God to take a roomy bath in or for ten million skateboarders to fly away down to their doom; but it was the agitated line of humanity, dwarfed to insect scale by the immensity of the dam, that commanded his attention.

Everyone was hurrying past him, back toward the parking lot. Children wailed, and the wheels of rental baby carriages being pushed too fast rattled shrilly on the concrete, and the adults all seemed to be in shock; their faces were blank-eyed and twisted with rage and horror and idiot mirth. Their bright holiday clothes seemed to have been put on them by attendants who didn't care, and Mavranos wished he had seen ranks of buses back in the lot, ready to take all these people home to some unimaginable asylum. Nut day at the dam, he thought, trying to smile and not be afraid, half price if you can bibble-bibble your lips and cross your eyes.

He tried to walk toward the dam quickly, but he was soon sweating and panting, and he had to lean on one of the concrete stanchions of the rail.

He peered ahead, at the curve of the dam. It seemed too imposingly *big* to be so far away. He could see cars moving slowly along the highway that was its crest, and he could make out figures moving along the sidewalks and the bridges that led out to the intake towers on the water. From this distance, at least, he could see nothing to have caused all the panic.

But fear was in the wind like the smell of hot metal, like a vibration in the air, like a rat gnawing underground.

He wanted to get back in the truck and drive away on the Arizona side, keep driving until he ran out of gas and then walk further.

Instead he pushed away from the stanchion and walked on down the broad sidewalk, toward the cathedral arch of the dam.

Crane sold his first four-card hand to a middle-aged man in a necktie and sport coat and then watched as the bidding started up for the next hand. It didn't hold his attention; he

was still a parent of the hand that would include the four cards
he had sold, and thus he might still win a tenth of the pot, but
he certainly wouldn't be matching the total and claiming the
Assumption.

He glanced out one of the ports at the lake, dotted with
scooting water-skiers, and he concentrated on breathing deeply. He had sat on Leon's left this time, and the next deal would
be his.

The inaudible high and low vibration had receded away
in both directions, and he couldn't sense it anymore, but he
thought that some of the others still could. Leon shook his head
sharply a couple of times, and Newt had fumbled his first hand
and exposed one of his down cards, and the Amino Acid at the
bar had broken a glass while getting one of the new players a
third martini.

The loud crack of the glass had so enormously startled
Doctor Leaky that the smell in the lounge shortly went from
smelling faintly of urine to smelling a good deal worse.

A Straight Flush wound up beating a set of Trips. Neither
Leon nor Crane was a parent of the winning hand, and after
the winner had swept in the money with a nervous smile, Leon
pushed the nearest folded hands to Crane.

"Your deal," growled the Hanari baritone. "Let's snap it
up here."

"Uh," said the Amino Acid at the bar, "you want me to take
the cap'n out on the deck, Mr. Hanari, and get his pants off
him and hose him down?"

"*He's* not the captain," said Leon loudly. "*I'm* the captain.
No, he's got an appointment with a surgeon on Sunday; this
won't kill him before then." He waved irritably. "Open the
ports, if you like—the breeze will be fresh, if not cool."

Crane thought that ordinarily most of the players would
have objected to the smell and demanded that the bartender's
suggestion be followed, but today even the toughest of them
seemed cowed and uncertain.

The last of the cards were gingerly pushed across the green
felt to Crane, who carefully stacked them and patted them
square.

Everybody's looking at me, he thought, looking right at the
cards. I can't switch in the cold deck right now.

He cut the deck that was in front of him and gave it a

genuine riffle-shuffle. "Must be some nice-guy surgeon," he said, smiling at Leon, "to see a patient on a Sunday." With luck someone would agree, or disagree, and draw away the attention of the table.

"S'pose so," said Leon, staring at the cards. Nobody else spoke.

"Say, sonny," Crane called to the bartender as he gave the cards another shuffle, "what time you got?"

"Twelve-fifteen."

Nobody had looked away.

Crane shuffled the cards again. At the average rate of fifteen minutes per hand, the deal might not have time to come around to him again before the game was ended at three. He could wait, and hope, and try to hurry the game along, but at that rate he might well have to go meet his friends and tell them that he had not even got the stacked deck out of his purse.

And then, he thought helplessly, what? Kill myself, I suppose, to keep Leon from taking me?

"Let's go," said Newt.

Crane felt a drop of sweat run down from his armpit and soak into his bra.

Gotta just jump, he thought, and hope there's deep water.

He passed the shuffled deck to his father for the cut, and as soon as the Hanari body had taken off the top of the deck and laid the stack beside the bottom, Crane leaned back lazily and sang, *"Whe-e-en there are gray skies . . ."*

"'What don't you mind in the least?'" screamed Doctor Leaky in a grating falsetto.

Crane almost whipped his head around himself, along with everyone else at the table, so abrupt and loud was the interruption—but he kept his concentration and dumped the cut cards into his purse and flipped the stacked deck up onto the table.

"Damn," he said, not having to fake a nervous tone in his voice, "what's the *matter* with him?"

The Hanari head was twisted around to look hard at Crane through the unswollen eye. "Why did you start to sing that song?"

"I don't know," Crane said. "Is that what set him off? I've got a tape I was playing in the car—Al Jolson, you know? White guy that always wore blackface? It's a song he used to sing."

Leon seemed jarred, and shook his head. "Deal the cards," he muttered. "Get this over with."

Crane willed his hands to be steady as he skimmed the first cards across the table. Don't want to screw up here, he thought, and have them declare a misdeal.

Nobody really looked likely to, though. *Get this over with* was clearly the mood of the table.

The animated, nearly invisible statues on the lakeshore seemed to be angular ectoplasmic balloons—when Nardie swiped at them with the edge of the chip, they tore and blew away like cellophane dandelion seeds, releasing hot, dry air and a smell of long-desiccated organic stuff.

And though the nearly invisible substance of the things warped the glaring sunlight like rippling lenses when they all crowded in around the two women, forcing Diana to squint and bob her head to guess exactly in which direction the water lay, she was able to push the things aside as easily as if they had been big soft-skinned helium balloons.

Their yielding skins were cold to the touch, and Diana's hands were becoming achingly numb even as the sun beat down on her head and face.

At one point the giant transparency that was the Circus Circus clown dropped one ludicrously big foot right over her, and she had a moment of fishbowl vision and felt as though she had been bathed in a shower of menthol.

"Straight ahead, I think," she gasped when it had lifted and freed her. "This isn't so bad, you know?"

Dinh had been keeping the things away from herself with the sweeping edge of the chip. "They're getting tougher to cut, though," she gasped. A moment later she added, "Especially the ones you've touched."

Diana realized that she was tired—sweating and breathing through her slackly open mouth—even though she was hardly doing anything more strenuous than walking slowly across the hot sand; and when she glanced around her at the crystal shapes she had pushed out of her way, it seemed to her that those ones were more substantial and were visibly tinted pink, faintly filtering the colors of the sand and the distant water.

Every one of the figures, in fact, looked solider.

Suddenly she was cold all over again, but from fear now,

and she crowded in close to Nardie's back. "God, Nardie," she said tightly, "I think they've been *draining* me here, somehow, when I was pushing them out of the way, like *eating* me. Keep 'em off with the chip; I'm not touching them anymore."

"We got to get to the water."

Diana ducked and scampered away from a dwarfish crystal cowboy with long, flailing arms. "Soon," she panted in agreement. The air was sour with a smell like broken old bones.

"How come they would"—Nardie swiped at a grinning transparent Arab—"want to eat you, eat us?"

"Maybe so we'd—take their shapes. Absorb us before we get to the water, while we're still not—unpalatable, inedible."

Diana was sure she could see some of her own lost substance in the phantoms; their arms *whistled* through the air now, and their feet made indentations in the sand.

They had weight now.

Twice the giant Circus Circus clown had nearly stomped them before Nardie had danced in and cut its ankle; one towering leg was now emptied and gone, but the clown was hopping from one dune to another on its remaining leg, substantial enough to kick up real, stinging clouds of sand, and it seemed more likely than before to land a Volkswagen-size foot on them. And it looked as if it would be a pile driver blow now, not a menthol shower.

The glassy pink figures were crowding up from the lakeside. Diana and Nardie were being slowly driven back, toward the highway.

And now suddenly the figures had something like fingernails; twice Diana had narrowly ducked away from one of them, and her upflung arm had been raked by something that stung and raised blisters.

Worse even than the very real possibility of physical death was Diana's conviction that the things were capable of more, that they could somehow *consume* her and Nardie, render the two of them down into some basic psychic stuff that would fill their multitudinous, presently empty shapes.

And then Nardie and Diana would be no more than unaware ghosts in the mannequins and effigies scattered all over the city, no longer any kind of threat to the King—just semi-sentient sacrifices to unknowable chaotic gods.

Diana kept one hand on Dinh's shoulder, and together they

darted and retreated and advanced, step by step diagonally closer to the water, moving toward it in a slant to keep the two giants hedged back by the more normal-size figures.

Nardie's hand snaked out again, and a grinning two-dimensional figure in the apron of a dealer tore apart silently into translucent splinters.

"Good," said Diana tensely, "we're nearly there."

"But it's using up our chip," panted Nardie as she cut one of the Caesars Palace Romans. "Look." In the instant before Dinh swung the edge again toward one of the legs of the giant clown, making the shimmering figure hop mindlessly back, Diana had seen that the Moulin Rouge chip was thinned down to no more than coin-thickness now and was white as a bone.

"The sword the turtle gave us," Nardie said through clenched teeth, "is wearing out."

The wind was strong on the highway on top of the dam. Mavranos thought he could hear weeping and laughter on the wind but then realized that the sounds were in his head, resonating from the minds of the tourists who were rushing in all directions to get away from the induced madness.

A man in a white leather jacket was leaning over the lakeside rail not far from Mavranos, waving one hand out over the long drop to the water. Mavranos saw blood on the man's hand and realized that this must be Ray-Joe Pogue.

Security guards were out on the highway directing traffic, having to shout over the wind at the drivers, who were simply intent on getting away. Even as Mavranos watched, one of the guards tossed his hat away and began running down the middle of the highway toward the distant Nevada side of the dam.

Mavranos wanted to get back down out of these mountains to the plains. This was much too high up—the sun, which was glinting so blindingly in the chrome of the rushing cars, seemed too close overhead, and the gunning of the engines didn't seem as loud as it should have, as if the air up here were less able to carry sound.

Pogue is doing this, he told himself, having to think loudly over the shouting and weeping in his head. He's shaking his blood into the lake, and somehow he's got a psychic chain reaction going here—all the minds of these people are echoing and reechoing insanity.

If I can knock him out . . .

He could feel a whimper starting up in his throat, and he wondered how long he could hold on to his purpose in the battering of the induced passions.

Or kill him, he thought.

Veils of pink fog spun in the wind. Mavranos stepped to the rail and looked down toward the water, and he saw that the wisps of fog were bursting into existence in the air below where Pogue leaned out over the parapet. The drops of his blood were apparently exploding into steam before they reached the water.

He hadn't yet succeeded in poisoning the lake.

Mavranos summoned all his remaining strength in order to take the last few strides along the walk and approach Pogue. He tried to smile like someone about to ask for directions or a match, and he shoved one hand in his jeans pocket to keep his untucked shirttail from flipping up in the breeze and exposing the walnut grip of the .38 tucked into his belt.

Pogue's jacket was blindingly white, and glittering rhinestones on the high collar sent needles of rainbow light into Mavranos's squinting eyes. Pogue was wearing a red baseball cap on the sculptured perfection of his pompadour, and when he turned toward Mavranos, glaring out of two blackened eyes past the white bandage on his nose, Mavranos saw the oversize card tucked into the band.

It was the Tower card from a Lombardy Zeroth Tarot deck, and the picture of the lightning striking the Babel-like tower and the two men falling struck Mavranos's mind like a blow.

He staggered back and looked away, forcing himself not to simply surrender to the violation of his mind by the potent symbol. This must have been what was causing the mental racket—every tourist who had looked squarely at the card, breathing the steam of Pogue's blood, would have got the psychic equivalent of a shock treatment, and even the ones who couldn't have seen it were nevertheless in the fog and picking up the signal and stepping it up and re-broadcasting it.

He clenched his fist and turned back to where Pogue stood—but the man wasn't there anymore. He was farther away, though he hadn't changed his rail-clutching posture. Mavranos wondered if his apparent nearness a moment before had been some kind of optical illusion in this thin, treacherous air.

Mavranos locked the fingers of his right hand on the grips of the .38 and started forward. But even as he watched, Pogue became, without moving, farther away.

It's some kind of magic he's doing, thought Mavranos. Playing with space and distance and scale. What the hell can I do against that? It doesn't look like I can get to him, and I don't dare shoot at him, not knowing where he really is. I might hit anything, anybody.

A lean hand grabbed his shoulder and shoved him aside, and Mavranos saw the twitching figure of Dondi Snayheever limp past him and out onto the surface of the highway.

Snayheever rocked free on the windy pavement, then raised his skinny arms, too long for his tattered corduroy coat, and opened his mouth. "*I'm blind!*" he roared up into the sky. "*Blind as a bat!*"

Mavranos felt an echo of the words in his own chest and realized that his vocal cords were helplessly working in sync with Snayheever's; and he'd heard Pogue barking out the words, too; and Mavranos's vision darkened as if at the suggestion of the words.

"*Blind as a bat!*" Snayheever boomed again. "*Can't fly with no hat, simple as that!*"—and the chorusing volume of his voice was for Mavranos the worst thing about this whole-top-of-the-world scene, as his own lungs ached with the stress of matching Snayheever's bellowing.

Mavranos found that he had sat down on the curb, the cold gun butt jabbing into his ribs. People were getting out of their cars now, not even bothering to turn off the engines or put the gearshifts into park, to flee this terribly amplified voice that had burst out of their own throats; abandoned cars rolled forward into the bumpers of others and, to judge by the screams, crushed the legs of a few suggestion-blinded pedestrians.

. Pogue was yelling now, though his voice sounded squeaky and shallow after Snayheever's. "I've got to get my head into the water," Pogue screamed. "An imperfect King's head! I've got to stop the action!" He seemed to be addressing no one but himself, trying to order Snayheever's forcefully obscuring nonsense out of his head. "As soon as the fucking blood stops boiling away!" He was shaking his hand furiously, and gusts of steam whirled up around him.

Snayheever led Mavranos and Pogue in a dizzying hum.

"*How you say*," Snayheever went on, "*feet like Antaeus can't get off the pavement no way you can climb over and fly down to the water.*"

Mavranos remembered how Snayheever's voice had come booming out of blind Spider Joe in the living room of that dusty trailer, and how compelling the imposed madness had been, and he realized that Snayheever was keeping Pogue from jumping.

Good, Mavranos thought. Better you than me, Dondi. He sighed deeply against the jabbing resistance of the revolver and dared hope that he might not have to use it.

He looked up when he heard a clatter and scuffling. Pogue had reeled away from the coping and stumbled off the curb, apparently blind but lurching toward Snayheever's voice.

And behind and above him the vault of the blue sky was stippled with fluttering spots of darkness.

Noon was not far gone, but the sky was full of bats.

The houseboat seemed to be listing, and the tired players leaned more often counterclockwise than not in their chairs, as though the boat were spinning in some unphysical clockwise whirlpool.

So far the pattern of cards that lay on the table had not yet deviated from the one that Crane had set up.

All the hands except for Crane's and Leon's and one other man's had been mated, had been conceived, and now Leon's hand was finally up for auction.

"Mr. Hanari's hand is up for bid," Crane said hoarsely, "and the dealer will presume to make the first bid of five hundred and fifty dollars." It was how much Leon had put into this pot so far.

"I'll go six," said the pale young man whose hand was the other still-unmated one, but he seemed to be speaking automatically, with no eagerness. Since the incomprehensible syllables of the great voice had come booming across the lake like some lament from distantly shifting rock strata, the boat had seemed smaller, and the players had been stating their checks and calls and raises and passes more often with gestures than with statements, as if fearful of being overheard by something in the lake or in the sky.

Leon was pale. His hands were trembling, but he gripped the cards as if they were a lifeline and he were drowning.

The hot breeze through the ports was cold on Crane's sweaty forehead, and he remotely wondered what his mascara must look like. "Seven," he said stolidly.

Doctor Leaky was not speaking anymore, but shifted furiously in his fouled clothes against the restraint of the safety belt.

"Yours," said the pale young man, pushing his chair back from the table and getting up to go to the bar.

Leon flipped up the Six and Eight of Cups next to his showing Knight of Sticks and Seven of Swords and pushed the four cards over to Crane.

"Deliver our child healthy, Mother," said Leon as he, too, stood up and reeled away across the tilted red carpet, toward the wheelchair-bound figure of Doctor Leaky. Leon could be heard muttering in an urgently soothing tone to the very old man.

Crane hoped he would be able to deliver the healthy child in question. Two of the players had bought the wrong hands, and now one of them, Crane knew, held an Ace-high Flush in Coins, which would beat Crane's own King-high Flush in Swords if they both stayed in to the showdown.

Crane pointed at that player, who was showing two Aces. "Aces are the power," Crane said flatly.

The player, a haggard young man with a two-day beard, blinked when Crane spoke to him and then fumbled in his stack of bills.

"Aces are worth two," he said, tossing out two hundred-dollar bills.

Diana hopped back away from a pair of life-size faceless mannequins, and she lost her footing in the loose sand and sat down heavily; before she could scramble back up to her feet and limp to where Nardie was slashing right and left with the chip, the two figures had managed to burningly claw her shoulder and side.

The pair of mannequins were moving awkwardly, like newborn mechanical colts, and the eyeless fronts of their heads swept back and forth metronomically.

Diana clutched the back of Nardie's shirt and tried to take

deep breaths of the stale, hot air and hold back the glittery haze of unconsciousness.

There was no way she and Nardie were going to be able to fight their way through these things down to the lake.

She wondered if they could even make it back to the highway now—the increasingly solid angular transparencies were crowding around on that side, too, so that the passing cars on the far side were just flickering blobs of refracted color in the incalculable distance—and she wondered bleakly if getting all the way back to that solid asphalt pavement would, in fact, help at all. What if the drivers of the cars proved to be just more hinged zombies?

From the corner of her eye she glimpsed a couple of figures.

"Behind you!" Diana yelled as the same two faceless mannequins came scissor-stepping across the sand.

But they *weren't* faceless anymore; their faces, though expressionless, were solid, and they were recognizably the faces of Nardie and Diana themselves.

Nardie flinched back from the things, and Diana had to skip aside to keep from being knocked down.

And Nardie hopped forward in a spasmodic lunge, sweeping the edge of the diminishing chip across the space where the mimic faces had been an instant before.

The Diana-thing and the Nardie-thing had gone flailing and scuffling away backward.

Then Nardie had turned her back on them and was slashing madly, gasping, and cutting a path through the phantasms as if the Moulin Rouge chip were a machete. She was crowding up, sliding her feet forward through the sand to claim every slack yard or foot or inch, away from the two figures and perhaps toward the water, and Diana limped along after her.

"They've started to . . . *digest* us," panted Diana.

An idea intruded itself into her mind, and she moaned hopelessly.

"We've got to do more," she said in a voice that shook with exhaustion.

"Like what?" panted Nardie.

"The goddamn *chip* is what they can't digest, what repels them," Diana called. "We've got to do more than just *cut* ourselves with it." She had to lash out and hit one of the

Huck Finn boys from the riverboat facade of the Holiday
Casino, and she shouted in pain as the grinning boy's teeth
scored her wrist, but the figure did fall back. "Cutting our
hands with the chip was a token, a gesture," she sobbed,
shaking her burned hand. "This isn't about tokens. Look at
the chip now."

Nardie feinted furiously, and then, in the bought second of
the figures' retreat, she held up what was left of the Moulin
Rouge chip. It was a flimsy white disk now, seeming as thin
as paper.

"Break it," said Diana, "and we'll eat it." The gummy air
whistled in her throat as she tried to take a vivifying breath.
"Then, when the chip is part of each of us, it'll be *us* that they
can't digest."

The giant ape, transparent as cellophane, made a rush at
them across the sand and Diana and Nardie scrambled several
yards back before a swipe of the disk drove the thing back.
"It will kill us," Nardie said.

Nardie's words hung in the heat that surrounded them.

Will it kill us, Mother? thought Diana. *Is it your will that
your daughter, and her friend that you blessed, die by their
own hands rather than at the hands of these things?*

She sensed no answer.

"Give me half," she said despairingly.

"Christ." After a moment of hesitation Nardie broke the chip
and reached over to hand half of it to Diana.

Again the big voice from across the lake boomed a couple
of incomprehensible syllables.

The towering Vegas Vic cowboy from the roof of the Pioneer Casino, grinning with a mouth made of ghostly neon tubes
under his giant phantasmagorical cowboy hat, bent down and
swatted Diana with his open palm.

She tumbled away across the hot sand, but she held on to
the half of the chip, and when she rolled to a stop, she put
it into her mouth. It had sharp edges and cut her tongue
and the roof of her mouth as she made her throat work and
swallow it.

But suddenly she sensed something in her that partook of
Scott and Oliver and Scat and Ozzie, and of something in the
lake itself, and even of poor Hans, and she was sure that she
was not too exhausted to stand up again.

* * *

Mavranos was certain he was going to have a stroke and cheat cancer.

He was tasting blood as he limped across the street, not knowing if the blood was his own or Pogue's, and his throat burned from having shouted, *Eat me!* in helpless tandem with Snayheever's ground-shaking voice a few moments ago.

And now, in a fast halo of swirling, fluttering bats, Snayheever had climbed up and was dancing on the coping of the far wall.

—The wall that fell away at a very steep slope for six hundred feet of empty air to the cement roof of the power plant on the downstream side of the dam.

Pogue was in the street, blundering among the stopped cars, and at one moment he seemed to be close enough for Mavranos to lunge to him and at the next seemed hundreds of feet away.

Mavranos was afraid that Pogue would knock Snayheever down into those yawning half-natural and half-engineered canyon depths and then, freed from Snayheever's induced insanity and blindness, make his way back across the street and dive into the lake, stopping the clock and ruining the water. If Pogue tried to do that, Mavranos probably would have to try shooting at him.

The air was hard to breathe—it was suddenly cloudy with hot, steamy, sticky mist, but it didn't seem to be Pogue's blood anymore; when Mavranos brushed his hand across his mouth, he felt his mustache slicked with something that smelled like algae. He tugged the .38 free of his belt and held it out in front of him as he bumped and stumbled among the cars after Pogue.

And though he was still half blinded by Snayheever's demanding pronouncements, he was sure that some of the things that he saw darting in circles around Snayheever's capering form were fish: bass, and carp, and catfish with sweeping tentacles. Some of the finny shapes seemed to be so tiny as to be circling in front of Mavranos's face, and others seemed to be huge, and moving around with astronomic speed somewhere as far away as the orbit of the moon.

The pavement under his boots was shifting, and when he looked down, he saw cracks in the concrete rapidly expanding and narrowing like pulsing arteries—was the dam breaking up?—and then he seemed to be hanging far above the earth, himself way out there in the moon's orbit, and what had seemed to be cracks or arteries below him were great river deltas changing in the violet-shifted radiation of unnaturally quick-passing centuries.

He made himself look up, and he saw the bats scatter away from Snayheever in ribby, fluttering clouds, for the crazy man had started roaring again: *"King and Queen of Caledon, how many miles to Babylon?"*

Snayheever was prancing along on the precipitous edge of the chest-high coping, kicking up his feet and tossing his arms, the tails of his threadbare coat flying in the wet wind. He seemed to Mavranos to be taller; in fact, it seemed for a moment that he towered over the mountains on either side of the dam, his joyfully upturned idiot face the closest thing to the sky.

"Threescore miles and ten," he sang harshly, his voice mirrored in the quaking of the bats and the flying fish. *"Can I get there by moonlight? Yes, and back again."*

The sky was dark, as if with a sudden overcast, but the full moon shone clearly over the mountains. The dam shook with turbulence and disorder in the penstocks and turbines that were its heart.

"I guess I make it more," said Crane as he tossed another couple of bills into the pot, trying to put a faint tone of theatrical reluctance in the statement, as would someone who holds a cinch hand and is trying to look weak to get a call.

Crane had promptly raised the original two-hundred-dollar bet, but the young man, after some thought, had raised it back to Crane.

He felt as though this hand had been in play for at least an hour.

The houseboat seemed to be turning in the water, and Crane had to force himself not to grip the edges of the table as several of the other players were doing.

Now the young man was facing another two-hundred-dollar raise, and he rubbed his stubbly chin dazedly and stared at Crane's six showing cards: the Six and Eight of Cups, the Knight of Clubs, and the Seven, Eight, and Nine of Swords.

Crane knew that his opponent held an Ace-high Flush in Coins; the young man was clearly wondering whether or not Crane's Seven, Eight, and Nine of Swords could possibly be part of a Straight Flush, which would beat him.

Crane saw the young man's pupils dilate and knew that his opponent was about to call the raise and end the betting for the showdown.

Crane was about to lose. And he had one urgent thought: *Ozzie, what can I do here?*

Got it.

"What's your name, boy?" Crane said abruptly, flashing a wide and no doubt lipstick-stained toothy grin, and he prayed that his opponent had a one-syllable name.

"Uh," the young man muttered distractedly, moving his hand toward his stack of bills, "Bob."

"He called!" Crane shouted instantly, flipping over his two hole cards, which were the Ten and the King of Swords, but keeping his palm over the name printed at the bottom of the King, so that only the end of a sword could be seen on the card. "And I've got a Jack-high Straight Flush!"

"I didn't call!" yelled young Bob. "I just said 'Bob'! You all heard me!"

Crane instantly flipped the King back over, and then intentionally fumbled in turning over the Ten so that everyone could see it before it was again hidden.

Crane looked up then, trying to put a look of tight outrage on his made-up face. "I say he said, 'Call.'"

"You freak," said Newt, wiping his sweating old face. "He said, 'Bob.'"

The other players all nodded and mumbled assent.

Leon was staring at Crane. "You're awfully eager to get one more bet," he said, frowning in puzzlement. "But the boy said, clearly, 'Bob.'" Leon turned his unswollen eye on Crane's young opponent. "Do you *want* to call?"

"Against a Straight Flush? *No,* thank you." Young Bob turned his cards over and tossed them aside. "The Flying Nun can take a flying leap."

Crane shrugged in faked chagrin and reached out to rake in the pile of bills. Thank you, Ozzie, he thought.

"Ah ah!" said Leon, holding up one smooth brown hand. "I am a parent of that hand, remember." He turned on Crane a

smile that was terrible under the bandage and behind the gray
and purple swelling and the inflamed veins. "I'm claiming the
Assumption." He pulled a billfold out of his white jacket and
began fanning out hundred-dollar bills. "Newt, count the pot,
would you?" Leon smiled at Crane again. "*I'll* make the last
call—for *everything*."

Crane spread his hands and kept his head down to conceal
the fast pulse in his throat. It was dark outside, and Crane was
afraid to look out the ports; he thought he'd see solid brown
lake water at each one, as if the boat had turned upside down
and it were only some kind of centrifugal force that held the
players in their chairs.

"Okay," Crane whispered, "though you—you *know* you've
got a little bit of me *anyway*."

"*If your heels be nimble and light*," roared Snayheever, his
voice shaking dust down from the mountainous slopes, "*you
may get there by candlelight!*"

Ray-Joe Pogue was still trying to cross the street; one old
woman had seen his hat and begun screaming, and he was
blindly trying to grope his way around her. There were only
a few other people, apparently injured, still visible along the
top of the dam—everyone else seemed to have fled away
on foot.

Mavranos had zig-zagged through the stalled and crashed
cars, up over the curb to the sidewalk on the afterbay side
of the highway, and he flung his arms over the coping a few
yards from where Snayheever danced and for a breath-catching
moment stared down past his .38, through the volumes of
foggy air at the galleries of the power station far below, with
the churning water of the disordered spillway overflow dimly
visible below and beyond that—and then he straightened up
hastily and stared at the cement coping he was leaning on and
ran the callused palm of his free hand along the edge of it.

It was as wavy and rippled as if a jigsaw had been working
on it, as if it were meant to be a theatrical exaggeration of
an eroded cliff face, and he remembered the Fool card in the
Lombardy Zeroth deck: The Fool had been dancing on a cliff
edge that had been scalloped like this.

And when he looked up again at Snayheever, Mavranos
saw that the mad young man's coat was longer and looser, and

belted with a rope, and that he wore a headdress of feathers.

He was terribly tall.

Pogue finally stepped up to the curb now, seeming to be only a few yards from Mavranos. The card was still in his hat-band like a lamp on a miner's helmet, and he blindly raised a little automatic pistol through the wet wind toward Snayheever.

Still leaning on the coping, Mavranos swung the barrel of his .38 into line, aimed at Pogue's chest, feeling the brass shells of the plastic-tipped Glaser rounds click back in the cylinder— and with his finger on the grooved metal of the trigger he froze, suddenly certain that he could not kill anyone.

Pogue's gun banged, jerking his hand up, but Snayheever's mad dancing didn't falter. Pogue's first shot had flown wide in the shattered, rainy air.

I'm still a damn good shot, though, thought Mavranos, sighting instead on the shimmering target of Pogue's out-stretched gun hand. Maybe I won't *have* to kill him.

He pulled the trigger through the double-action cycle with-out the sights wavering at all, and when the hard *bang* punched his eardrums and the barrel flew up in recoil, he saw Pogue go spinning away.

But he had seen dust spring away from the wall and the sidewalk, and he wondered if the Glaser round had come apart, like a shot shell, before hitting Pogue's hand. If so, he *might* have killed Pogue, in spite of his careful aim.

Pogue was getting back up on his feet, though, and his hand was a splintered white and red ruin, jetting arterial blood; clearly Mavranos's shot had gone as aimed. The sight of the ruined hand drove a column of hot vomit up Mavranos's throat, and he resolutely clenched his jaw and swallowed . . . but for a moment he wondered if his gun had somehow shot *several* bullets, or rather several *likelihoods* of bullets.

Pogue was howling now in the green seaweed-tasting rain, and he lunged at Snayheever's ankles.

Mavranos raised his .38 again, but the two figures were together, and the pavement was shaking over the laboring heart of the dam, and he didn't dare shoot. Pogue had climbed up on the coping and was sitting straddling it beside Snayheever, and he had clasped his one good arm around Snayheever's legs. His hat had come off and gone spinning away down the afterbay wall, and his pompadour was broken into wet strands plastered across his forehead.

Snayheever was just standing there on the coping surface now, but still smiling into the dark sky and waving his arms. "*Blind as a bat!*" he roared, with Pogue and Mavranos moaning it in synchronization.

"Is there anyone that can hear me?" Pogue shouted over the hiss of the hot rain. His darkly swollen eyes were screwed shut, and the bandage taped over his nose was blotting with blood.

Mavranos waved his gun helplessly. "I can hear you, man," he called.

"Help me, please," Pogue sobbed. "I'm turned around, and I'm blind, but I've got to sink my head right now. I can't wait for the blood to behave! Am I on the *lake* side of the highway? Is it the *lake* below us here?"

If I say yes, Mavranos thought, he'll let go of Snayheever and jump, and I can yank Snayheever down from there.

But I'll be killing Pogue, as surely as if I'd shot him through the face.

If I say *no*, he'll throw Snayheever off and then cross the highway unimpeded. I won't be able to reach him, stop him, with his optical illusion magic going full strength again. He'll jump off the lake-side edge, and Diana will be doomed.

And if I say nothing at all . . . ?

Okay then, he thought despairingly, I'll *go* to hell.

"That's the lake below you," he said loudly, feeling the words brand burns into his soul. "You're on the railing at the north side."

Pogue's lean face split into a white grin under the straggling wet hair and the bandage—

—And he snapped his head forward, buried his teeth in Snayheever's calf and swung his highway-side leg up and kicked Snayheever's knee.

Then Snayheever had tipped, and Mavranos swore and started forward in horror. He couldn't tell whether the flailing of Snayheever's arms was a useless attempt to keep his balance or still part of the crazy dance; Snayheever disappeared over the side, and Pogue, his arm still around his legs and his teeth still in his flesh, rolled off the coping after him.

Mavranos slammed into the cement wall and peered over the edge.

For several seconds the locked-together figure that was Snayheever and Pogue spun free in the mist above the dizzying abyss, rapidly diminishing in apparent size. Then they touched the steep slope and bounced and tumbled away apart, arms and legs flailing horribly loose, and they cartwheeled and sprang all the way down to the cement power station roof, where they briefly shook in what must have been prodigious bounces, and were two tiny, still forms.

Then the resounding air was stilled, like a struck piano wire when the foot pedal is tromped on, and the dam under Mavranos's feet became again as solid as the mountains, and the flow of water through the mighty penstocks and giant turbines must abruptly have been restored to a full, even flow, for the face of the river below the dam quickly became as smooth as a plate of glass.

The rain of lake water stopped, and the wind was steady, and the bats and fish were gone. Clouds blocked the sun intermittently, and the edges of cloud shadow on the pavement were as sharp as if they had been razored out of black cardboard.

And Mavranos stood away from the gradual geometric curve of the coping, which stretched in an unrippled arc from one mountain to the other. He uncocked his revolver and put it back in his belt and pulled his shirttail over it. He took a deep breath, then swallowed, and swallowed again.

He tapped his jacket pocket, then fished out the Baggie. It had burst at some point during the last several minutes, but the little goldfish was still flopping in the wet plastic bag.

He walked quickly out onto the highway, between the cars and across to the lake-facing railing. He held the Baggie out over the abyss and the lake water below, and he shook the fish out, then leaned over and watched it tumble away until he couldn't see it anymore.

His exhaustion was gone. He sprinted away over the drying pavement, down the center of the long, curving highway, running with his knees well up, swerving effortlessly around the abandoned cars, toward the parking lot where he had left the truck.

And twenty-five miles away to the northwest in Las Vegas, every pair of dice on every Craps table had come up snake-eyes in the instant of Snayheever's death, and every roulette ball rocked to a solid halt in the 00 slot, and every car in town that had its key turned in the ignition at that moment started up instantly.

The sky over the west shore of the lake was still almost as dark as night, and though the moon should have been three days past its full phase, it hung overhead as perfectly round as the worn white disk Diana and Nardie had shared.

The two of them were alone on their section of beach; Nardie, empty-handed now, was still in a defensive crouch, and Diana was swaying on her feet and clutching her throat. A hundred yards away to their left, the children and parents were hesitantly but at least loose-jointedly wandering back up the beach toward their towels and umbrellas, clearly puzzled and ill at ease and wondering about imminent rain.

Shapes seemed to rush through the sky on the rising wind, fluttering and sighing, but Diana sensed no threat in whatever the things might be; and the waves were high, as if giants under the water were shifting uneasily in sleep, but she thought that any such giants would not harm her.

She spat on the sand. "I'm bleeding." The inside of her mouth was cut, but the half disk had apparently broken up before reaching her throat. She spat again. "Kind of a lot."

Nardie straightened up lithely and laughed, coughing in the midst of it. "Me too. But I guess we won't die of it after all."

Diana took a step toward the water, hitching and wincing and wondering how many of her ribs might be cracked. "Let's get in the water."

CHAPTER 50

Raising Blind

Crane allowed himself to hang on to the edge of the table for a moment. The sky was brightening again outside the ports, and the yellow light cast by the lamps on the paneled walls began to look sickly.

"Dizzy," he said as Newt finished counting the bills in the middle of the table.

The Amino Acid bartender had pulled the ports closed again shortly after the huge voice had begun to roll its syllables across the lake from the direction of the Black Mountains and the dam, and the air in the cabin was stifling with the smell of Doctor Leaky and cigarette smoke. Crane thought his dizziness now might be as much from nausea as from the illusion of spinning . . . spinning *diesel*, as Ozzie would have said.

"Seventy-nine hundred," croaked Newt finally.

Leon separated out of his billfold a thick bundle of thousands and hundreds, and his good eye burned into Crane's good eye as he tossed the bills onto the stack Newt had counted.

The socket of Crane's false eye throbbed, and he wasn't quite able to close the eyelid. Good joke, he thought, if I succeed here but die later of meningitis. Gingerly he touched the corner of his eye. It hurt, and his fingertip was smudged with mascara.

"Cut for high card," said Leon.

Crane looked across the room at Doctor Leaky. Once again alertness seemed to glitter in the old man's gaze, and Crane looked away in case his father's body might guess something, say something that would warn Leon.

But the senile old body couldn't have been alert and guessed Crane's purpose, for it didn't say anything at all.

Crane flexed his right hand, noticing for the first time that he had chewed the painted nails down to the quicks, and he lowered his fingers over the deck and lifted half of it off.

He showed the card to the other players, then looked at it himself.

The Page of Cups. His card, Ozzie had said; soon to be replaced by the King? He quickly lowered the cards back down onto the deck, fearing that Leon might notice the card's faintly stained corner.

Leon was smiling, and panting. "A tough one to beat!" he said.

Newt leaned forward, slid the deck to himself, and shuffled it again, then pushed it to a spot in front of the shivering Hanari body.

With a trembling hand Georges Leon lifted off the top half of the deck, and he hesitated even as he raised the cards.

Crane's heart seemed to have stopped. *He missed the crimped card,* Crane thought. *He's going to come up with an Ace—*

But the card Leon showed was the Ten of Swords. Crane's heart was beating again, and he laughed weakly and rapped the table with a fist. *"Yes!"* he said, letting his hot burst of triumph show, for everyone would assume he was just pleased at having won the doubled pot. "Gotcha!"

"Aw, bad beat," said one of the other players to Leon.

Leon grimaced and shrugged. "You win," he told Crane. "I don't know when I'm going to learn that that's not a smart bet."

"Thanks," said Crane hoarsely.

"You're taking the money," said Leon.

Crane thought of Ozzie, and stared coldly into the unswollen eye. "Looks like it."

"You're selling the hand. I've bought it, I'm *assuming* it."

"It's all yours, believe me."

Crane tamped the stacks of bills and slid them in between his spread elbows, leaving one hundred out on the table as his ante for the next hand.

He had done it.

He had sold Leon the hand that Doctor Leaky had conceived in the informal Assumption game by the Dumpster behind the liquor store on Wednesday.

Crane had no idea what might happen now. This scheme might not work, and he might lose his body tomorrow, but he had done all he could.

"That's two hundred to you."

Crane looked up from his gnawed fingernails. Leon had been speaking to him.

"Oh," said Crane. "Sorry." He lifted four hundreds from one of his stacks and tossed them into the pot. "I make it four," he said.

"You haven't looked at your down cards!" said Newt petulantly. "You're raising blind?"

"Raising blind," Crane agreed.

Station wagons with luggage belted onto the rooftop racks jammed the marina streets on this Friday afternoon, and tanned young men and women in scanty swimsuits thronged the sidewalks and drank beer from dewy cans or drove puttering scooters between the slow, smoky lanes of traffic.

Easter break, thought Crane as he walked slowly up the street, carrying his high-heeled shoes under his arm and feeling the hot pavement abrade the soles of his nylons. We could all do with an Easter break.

"Ahoy, Pogo!" came a shout from among the horns-and-laughter-and-chatter background noise.

Crane smiled tiredly as he looked back and shaded his eyes.

Arky Mavranos was striding toward him at his old gangly pace, and though he was pale, he seemed solemnly happy, too.

"You look like a real piece of the old shit today," said Mavranos quietly when he reached Crane. They began walking on toward the Lakeview Lodge, Mavranos ostentatiously walking a yard or two to the side of Crane and letting an occasional pedestrian pass between them.

"You did it," said Mavranos.

"Sold it to him," Crane agreed, "bought and paid for."

"Good."

"How did it go with you?" asked Crane, in a moment when they were alone in a sunny crosswalk.

"They're both dead," Mavranos said softly. "Snayheever and Pogue. Pogue didn't get to screw things up. I'll . . . tell you about it, tell all three of you . . . sometime later." He coughed and spat. "Maybe not today, all right?"

Crane could see that whatever had happened had cost Mavranos. "Okay, Arky." He reached out and squeezed Mavranos's elbow.

Mavranos stepped away from him. "None of your fag tricks."

"Seriously, Arky, thank you."

"Don't . . . *thank* me." Mavranos unknotted his bandanna and tossed it into a planter they were walking past. "Pogue's magic was a—a randomness thing, disorder, chaos—and when he . . . died, the dam snapped back into order. It was a phase-change like what would have set Winfree's mosquitoes all doing the chorale from Beethoven's Ninth, with Busby Berkeley dance steps."

Crane blinked at his friend and wondered if he was too tired to be understanding what Mavranos was saying. "You mean you think . . . ?"

Mavranos touched the lump under his ear. "I swear it's smaller already, perceptibly smaller, than it was on the drive down here."

Crane was laughing and blinking rapidly and shaking Mavranos's hand. "That's terrific, man! Goddamn, I can't tell you—"

And then they were hugging in the middle of the sidewalk, and even Mavranos ignored the hoots and catcalls.

With their arms around each other's shoulders they stepped up to the lobby doors of the Lakeview Lodge and shoved through and hurried breathlessly into the dark bar.

Diana and Nardie pushed away from the table at which they'd been waiting, and though they winced and limped like people who have recently had too much exercise, they were laughing when they hobbled over and hugged Crane and Mavranos.

They all sat down, and Mavranos ordered a Coors—and then made that two, one for Nardie. Crane and Diana both ordered soda water.

"You sold it to him," Diana said to Crane when the cocktail waitress had walked off toward the bar.

"Yes, finally." Crane rubbed his hands down his face, not caring what his makeup looked like. His right eye socket stung. "And I think my arachnoid is infected."

"Spider," said Mavranos, translating the word. "Spiderlike. What, something about Spider Joe?"

"It's a part of the brain," said Crane through his hands. "It gets infected when you've got, uh, meningitis. The socket of my missing eye is just . . . on fire." He lowered his hands and leaned back in the booth. "I've got the saline solution and rubber bulb in my purse. As soon as we trade news, I'll go to the head and rinse out the socket."

Diana has seized his shoulder. *"No,"* she said now, urgently, "you're going to a doctor, are you crazy? My God, *meningitis?* I'm going to drive out to Searchlight in a couple of minutes to finally get poor Oliver. I can drop you off at a hospital—"

"Tomorrow," he said, "I'll see a doctor. I've got to be back here at the lake at dawn. My father will want to start assuming bodies as soon as the sun's up, and I've got to see the end. And I want to disarm and ditch the two decks of cards, if I can, if the . . . poisoned sugar cube gets him." He blinked at her through his good eye. "Tomorrow," he repeated. "Not before."

The drinks arrived then, and Crane took a deep gulp of the cold but comfortless soda water. He inhaled. "So," he said, "did you ladies get your bath?"

Diana let go of Crane's shoulder and sat back, still frowning.

Nardie drank a third of her beer. "Eventually," she said with a shiver.

She described the phantom statues that had tried to stop them and how she and Diana had fought them and then finally dispelled them by actually *eating* the yin-yang Moulin Rouge chip.

Mavranos brushed beer out of his mustache and smiled crookedly at Crane. "Weird sort of sacrament."

Nardie picked up Diana's glass of soda water. "And then when we finally got into the lake," she said softly, "before we got out to where we could duck under, the water was fizzing around Diana's feet, like this!" She swirled Diana's glass, and bubbles whirled up in it, hissing. "And for just a second, before the wind blew it out, there were—you could hardly see it in the sunlight, okay?—*flames* around her ankles!"

"Sounds like *electrolysis*," said Mavranos. He was looking into his beer, and Crane guessed that he had somehow been directly responsible for the death of Nardie's half brother out there at the dam and now didn't want to look her in the eye.

"You were busting apart the H_2 and the O, Diana. I remember ol' Ozzie saying Lake Mead was tamed water; maybe you untamed it."

"I did," Diana said. "With help from all of you. The bubbling kept up nearly the whole time I was in the water, and I could . . . feel, or hear or see, *ride* the whole wild extent of it. I could feel the houseboat spinning north of me, and I felt the shaking at the dam."

Nardie had drained her beer and waved the empty glass at the bartender. "So," she said to Mavranos in a conversational tone, "did you kill my brother?"

Mavranos let go of his beer glass, and Crane thought it was because he was afraid he might crush it in his fist. Mavranos's eyes were closed, and he nodded. "I did," he said. "I—in effect I pushed him off the downstream wall of the dam. Snayheever, too—I killed both of them."

Crane was looking at Nardie now, and for an instant had seen her eyes widen and her mouth sag. Then she put on a battered smile, and she tapped the back of one of Mavranos's scarred hands.

"Each of us has killed someone," she said, a little huskily, "in this. Why'd you ever think you'd be special?"

Crane realized that was true: himself, Vaughan Trumbill; Nardie, that woman in the whorehouse outside Tonopah; Diana, probably Al Funo. And now Mavranos had broken a part of himself in the same way.

"Doctor, my *eye*," Crane sang softly, pushing his chair back and standing up. "I've got to go irrigate the cavity."

Mavranos got up, too, awkwardly. "I gotta call Wendy," he said. "Home tomorrow?"

"You'll probably be home by lunchtime," said Crane.

Nardie reached out and caught Mavranos's flannel sleeve. "Arky," she said, "I'd have had to do it myself, if you hadn't. And it would have hurt me more than it's hurting you. Thank you."

Mavranos nodded and patted her hand, still not looking at her. "I appreciate that, Nardie," he said gruffly, "but don't *thank* me."

He and Crane walked away toward the rest rooms and the telephones, and Nardie and Diana silently sipped their different drinks.

EPILOGUE

I'LL STILL HAVE YOU

> MOSCA: Are not you he that have to-day in court
> Profess'd the disinheriting of your son?
> Perjured yourself? Go home, and die, and stink.
> —BEN JONSON, *Volpone*

> But were I joined with her,
> Then might we live together as one life,
> And reigning with one will in everything
> Have power on this dark land to lighten it,
> And power on this dead world to make it live.
> —ALFRED, LORD TENNYSON, *Idylls of the King*

Dawn would be soon, and had already paled the blue sky behind the mountains ahead of them, but out the back windows of the roaring and rattling truck the sky was still a dark purple.

Nardie was in the front seat next to Mavranos, and Diana and young Oliver were in the back seat, and Crane, once again wearing his beat Adidas and a pair of jeans and a long-sleeve shirt, was half lying down in the truck bed among the scattered books and empty beer cans and crescent-wrench sets. His eye hurt. The truck smelled as though Mavranos used old french-fry grease in the engine.

Oliver sat close to his mother. She had talked to him on the telephone several times since he had seen their house blow up and thought that she was in it, but it seemed he hadn't *really* believed she was alive until she had hugged him in Helen Sully's yard in Searchlight yesterday afternoon, and even now he had to keep checking.

Mavranos made the left turn off Highway 93 onto the

narrower Lake Shore Road, past the still-dark Visitor Center
building.

He lit a cigarette, and Nardie rolled down her window. The
morning air was chilly and fresh. "Maybe he'll have taken the
cards and just gone off somewhere," said Mavranos, sounding
almost hopeful.

"No," Nardie told him. "To take the bodies, to in effect
give multiple birth to himself, he needs a token mother, and
the lake's that. He'll still be on the boat."

"I don't think the lake's just a token anymore," Mavranos
said.

Crane shuddered, dreading confronting his father. He could
feel the bulk of the Lombardy Zeroth deck in the inside pocket
of his Levi's jacket.

Diana hiked around on the seat and looked back at him.
"How's the eye?" she asked softly.

"Won't be any different an hour from now, when I can be
in an emergency room." He didn't tell her that when he had
squirted the saline solution into the socket yesterday he had
felt the painful bulge of some sort of tumor in there.

He clutched his elbows to stop shaking. Diana looked twenty
years old now, and almost inhumanly beautiful with the blond
hair blowing around the smooth lines of her jaw and throat. It
would be too horrible to win her and then have some doctor
give him a death sentence. For the first time he thought he
understood what Mavranos must have been feeling during
these past months.

"I can see the lake," said Oliver softly, pointing.

Mavranos stopped the truck in the parking lot of an all-night
Denny's restaurant by the marina, and everyone climbed out to
stretch in the chilly predawn air.

"Nardie and Diana and Oliver can wait inside the restaurant
here while Scott and I go to the boat," Mavranos said quietly
as he walked around to the back of the truck and unlocked the
lift-gate and swung it up; the ratchety *click-click-click* of the
struts was loud in the empty parking lot. "If we're not back
in—what do you think?"

Crane shrugged, still shivering. "An hour," he said.

"Call it an hour and a half," said Mavranos. "If we're
not back by then, just go away. Leave a message for us at

the Circus Circus desk." He looked around the nearly empty parking lot. "And if Crane comes back alone . . ."

"Call the police or something," Crane bleakly finished for him. He touched his still-bleeding side. "My father might have assumed this body after all, and it'd be him, not me."

"And Oliver," Mavranos went on sternly, "no funny phone calls, right?"

Oliver pressed his lips together and shook his head and mumbled something.

Mavranos leaned toward him. "What?"

Nardie shrugged at him. "He, uh, says he isn't going to steal any more of your beers, either."

"Huh. Well—okay." Standing so as to block the view from the yellow-lit restaurant windows, Mavranos passed Crane the .357. Then he wrapped the short-barrel pistol-grip shotgun in a nylon windbreaker and laid it on the asphalt.

He pushed the lift-gate up and let it slam shut, then turned the key in its lock and opened his mouth as if to say something—

—But Crane had gasped involuntarily and pressed the fingers of one hand against his right cheek and forehead. The pain in the eye socket had suddenly become a bright, razoring heat, and he hastily pried out the hemisphere of intrusive plastic and let it fall to the asphalt.

"He's being assumed!" yelled Oliver fearfully, scrambling back away from the truck.

Diana caught Crane by his free elbow, and over the pain in his head he realized she must think he was about to fall.

Embolism, Crane thought in fright as the expanding, bulging pressure in the socket drove a shrill moan up against his clenched teeth. *A stroke, I'm having a stroke.*

"Scott," Diana yelled, catching his other arm, too, and shaking him, "you're in no shape to do this!"

He was hunched over, his chin on his chest and his knees shaking.

Then, abruptly, the pain backed off. Tears, and perhaps blood, were running out of the eye, but he blinked in sudden astonishment down at his knees and his shoes and the pavement.

. He was seeing them as three dimensional.

He blinked both his eyes and realized, too numbed with shock even to be glad, that he *had* two eyes.

The new eye stung, and was involuntarily blinking in the unaccustomed light, but the savage pain had evaporated.

"What did you say?" he asked hoarsely.

Diana was still holding his arms tightly. "I said you're in no shape for this!"

He took a deep breath, then straightened up and squinted at her. "Actually . . . I think I . . . finally *am* in shape for this."

All four of his companions stared at him in uncomprehending alarm.

"You . . . put the fake eye back in?" faltered Diana, glancing down at the pavement. "I thought you—shouldn't you—"

"He grew a new one," said Nardie flatly. "You and Scott are both now . . . what, at your physical peaks, okay?—except for the wound in the side that the King always has."

"Jesus," said Mavranos softly.

Diana was still clutching Crane's elbow, and now she tugged at him. "Come over here, Scott." Crane and Diana walked a dozen steps away and stood by the coping of a dusty redwood planter.

"You grew a new goddamn *eye*?" she said. "Is that *true*?"

"Yes." Crane was breathing rapidly. *I'm not dying,* he thought tentatively.

"Scott," she said with quiet urgency, *"what's happening here?"*

"I think—I think it's going to happen," he said unsteadily; his throat was quivering with imminent laughter or sobbing. "I think you and I are about to . . . become the Queen and the King."

Both of them were breathing fast.

"What—*today*? What does it mean? What will we do?"

Crane spread his hands helplessly. "I don't know. Get married, be fertile, have children, work, plant gardens—"

Diana almost seemed angry. "—get special T-shirts, print up some letterhead . . ."

Crane grinned at her, but took a deep breath and went on seriously. "If we're healthy and productive, you and I, so will the land be. The land, and us, are going to be sort of

voodoo dolls of each other." He thought of the dull, constant pain in his wounded side. "Warning lights for each
other."

His fingers brushed her blond hair. "We may lose this
honorary youthfulness in the winters, but I'll bet we'll get
at least most of it back each spring. I hope it'll be a good
long time before those winters start to get too harsh."

"You don't figure this is . . . immortality."

"No. I'm sure part of our job is to one day die, so another
King and Queen can take over. Maybe kids of ours. In twenty
years or so there'll be jacks to watch for, and there'll still
always be disease, and eventually old age. The only way to
get *immortality* out of this is to—well, become Saturn, eat your
children."

"I haven't been a great mother so far," Diana said shakily,
"but I'd pass on that."

"And I think we'll—in visions and dreams or hallucinations—I think we'll deal with the things the cards are pictures
of, the Archetypes that subterraneanly drive people. We might
even be able to . . . be *diplomats*, somehow induce the things
to assume patterns for less terrible crap in the world. My father
didn't dare deal with the Archetypes face-to-face, so he went
through the formal channel of the cards and used people
like matches to light the things up. There's power here—
my father's been using it just in a crippled way, like having
a great car but only running the engine so you can cook on
the hood." He gave her a frightened smile. "I think we've got
to learn how to drive it."

"God," she said quietly. "I guess we can *try*."

They walked back to the others.

"Let's hurry," Crane called to Mavranos. "The sun's going
to be up soon, and he's going to start."

Mavranos picked up his bundled windbreaker, and he and
Crane walked away down the street toward the dark boats.

They were challenged when they stepped onto the dock.

"Whoa, boys," said a young man on the deck of Leon's
houseboat. Crane recognized him—it was Stevie, the Amino
Acid who had been tending bar. "If you're looking to play
Poker, you missed it—and if you're looking to steal cameras
or fishing gear"—he stepped out of the shadows and let them

see the revolver he was casually pointing at them—"you've come to the wrong boat."

"I've come to talk to the owner," said Crane. "I believe he'll be awake already."

"Jesus!" Stevie's eyes suddenly widened and he held his gun up at arm's length. "You're the two guys that were in that boat on Lake Mead Sunday. You killed our King!"

Mavranos quickly stepped to the side, raising the wrapped shotgun, and Crane darted his hand up toward the revolver under his shirt.

But at that moment a deep voice shouted, *"Freeze!"* from the shadows behind Stevie, and everyone tensely held still. "Drop your gun over the side, Stevie," Leon's Hanari voice went on. "Do it!"

For a moment Stevie's gun hand just shook, still extended, and Crane expected Leon to shoot the young man in the back. Then with a shaky curse Stevie tossed the gun over the rail.

Mavranos lowered the shotgun and exhaled harshly through his fluttering mustache.

Leon stepped forward into the brightening light, and he was smiling under the bandage on his forehead. Again Crane noticed the bulge in the tailored slacks, and he guessed that his father had had some kind of artificial implant put into the body. His notion of physical perfection? Crane wondered. A perpetual boner?

"You're Scott Crane," said Leon in a tone of cold satisfaction. He was holding a big-caliber automatic down by his thigh. "You seem to know something about all this, about what you and I did in the '69 game. And you went and killed *this* guy's candidate for King?" He was laughing now. "Well, thanks for saving me the trouble. Why have you . . . *come* here?"

Crane was glad nobody recognized him as the poor Flying Nun. He glanced past Leon at the lake, where he had killed the Amino Acids' King with a magical .45, and he remembered the place that was the physical totem of the King.

"I'm going to assume the Flamingo," Crane said.

Now Leon was laughing harshly. "Oh, really. You're a fish, sonny, not a jack." Abruptly his inflamed face went blank, and he glanced to the still-dark west; then his pistol was up and pointed squarely at the middle of Crane's torso. "Stevie!" Leon barked. "Go up to him and look at his eyes!"

Stevie hesitated, then shambled across the deck to Crane and peered into his face. "Uh," he said, "they're blue . . . his *eyes*, right? . . . They're bloodshot—"

"Bloodshot's good," said Leon cautiously. "Hold a lighter flame up to each of them—*don't* burn him—and tell me what his pupils do."

Crane's new eye was dazzled by the flame when Stevie held it up in front of him, but he managed to keep both eyes at least squintingly open.

"Pupils both went narrow fast," Stevie said.

Leon relaxed and started laughing again, clearly with relief. "Sorry, Mr. Crane," he said, "it's just that I once . . . knew someone else with your first name. An old friend of mine named Betsy used to worry about it, but she was getting paranoid." He waved his pistol at Mavranos. "That guy's got a rifle or something in the cloth there, Stevie. Would you take it from him?"

Mavranos looked at Crane, who nodded, and he let Stevie take the shotgun.

"Now," said Leon, "Crane, you come aboard, you can be the first—you wrecked my beautiful Hanari. Your friend can wait out here on the dock. You'll probably have some things to talk to him about when you leave."

Crane walked up the dock to the section of the deck where the rail had been folded back on a hinge, and he stepped across the gap easily now that he was wearing sneakers.

The cards were spread out face up on the otherwise-empty green felt table, and in spite of the dawn light outside, the wall lamps threw a late-evening glow across the long room. Doctor Leaky was belted into his wheelchair again, but he was mercifully wearing a different leisure suit. Another armed Amino Acid stood alertly in front of the bar, puffing a cigarette.

The air conditioner hummed, and there were no smells in the cool air.

The Art Hanari body was still carrying the gun, and Leon faced Crane from the other side of the room, glaring out of the inflamed Hanari eyes. "Why did you *come* here? I really don't think you know what happens now," he said.

You take what you bought, Crane thought. May it please be the right one. "I assume the Flamingo."

Again the declaration seemed to jar his father. "You *sold the hand*," Leon said, his voice flat but louder, "you'll become the King the way . . . the way his *food* does! I don't have time for—"

"Why do you keep a wrecked old clown like that around?" Crane interrupted, nodding toward Doctor Leaky and blinking tears out of his new eye. "Hey, Doctor," he called, "how's your love life these days?"

Doctor Leaky began giggling and making fart sounds with his mouth. "Beam me up, Scotty!" he said.

The Amino Acid tossed his cigarette toward an ashtray and started forward.

Leon's already purpled face went darker, and he stared hard into Crane's eyes—lifted one hand—and then closed his eyes and inhaled.

And Crane was falling away into the darkness of his own mind, aware of the ancient, shifting gods so far below.

His last articulated thought was: *It didn't work. He won.*

Like galaxies, the things turned beneath him, and though there was no light, he could see them by the images they rang into vibrant compulsion in his mind.

There was the Fool, dancing on the precipice, and the sphinxes that pulled the splendid Chariot, and Judgment calling human forms out of opening graves, and the Moon, with luminous rain falling into a pool, and, somehow closer, the hermaphroditic figure that was the World; and then he was able to look at himself.

His own form was the robed and powerful body of the Emperor, and he held in his right hand the looped Egyptian cross, the ankh.

He rose, and the other entities seemed to bow in repectful greeting, and he heard a chorus of singing and weeping and shouting that evoked, for all the bass roars of horror and rage that abraded the pure high voices, triumph and hope.

He continued to rise, up through the ringing, glittering blackness.

* * *

And vision came back to his eyes, and he was standing on the red carpet in the lounge of his father's houseboat.

The Amino Acid's cigarette hit the ashtray, and he took another step forward.

The Hanari body, suddenly expressionless, took a step backward to catch its balance.

"*No!*" screamed Doctor Leaky in sudden panic, "not this, I love life, my love life? Love wife? Burned up my Chevrolet, took my boy away from me, my wife did." He was breathing deeply, with his eyes closed, and Crane could see that the old man had wet his pants again. "I *won't* sink in this," shouted the Doctor Leaky body, "I can gather my thoughts." Again he was silent, and Crane was afraid Leon might actually be able to exert the broken, senile brain and jump back into the now blank-eyed Hanari. "I will gather the—the—I know what—the *cards,* I spilled them. Well, really I threw them."

The Amino Acid was gaping around, his hand on the butt of his holstered revolver.

"Go sit down," Crane told him. The young man nodded and went back to the bar and sat on one of the stools.

"You—I've got it, I've got it," shouted Doctor Leaky, his eyes still screwed shut. "I can . . . *push*—" He grinned suddenly and blinked around, until he saw the Hanari body still standing across the room from him. "*No, goddamn son of a bitch* charged me, what was it? Two hundred dollars! For a used engine, in '45, or wait, no, that's right, '45. I—I made my—my *displeasure* clear, I assure you. Of that."

Crane stared at the frantic wheelchair-bound body, and he realized that this was the first time in more than twenty years that his father's mind had been in his father's body. This thrashing old man was his complete father, whole again.

Crane clenched his fists and forced himself not to run over to the wheelchair and hug the man. Remember Ozzie, he told himself. Ozzie was your true father. This man you still love so much killed Ozzie.

Doctor Leaky was subsiding into giggles again. "Do you think that boy cried?" He frowned suddenly and looked around, as if at a crowd of debaters. "Never! I cut the hook out of his finger and he never cried. . . ."

Crane pushed past the blinking, mindless Art Hanari and crossed to the big round card table. Bending down, he reached out with both hands and swept the Tarot cards into one stack and turned the stack face down on the green felt.

"You're not to touch those cards!" shouted the Amino Acid.

Crane looked over his shoulder. The young man had drawn his revolver and was pointing it at him. "Why not?" He smiled and jerked a thumb at the Hanari. "*He* doesn't have any objections. Ask him."

"I'm going to have to ask you to step away from the table," he told Crane. "Mr. Hanari has told us to kill anyone who tries to take the cards."

Crane hadn't anticipated this problem. He thought of the chilly gun in his belt, under the untucked shirt, and knew he wouldn't be able to drag it free before the Amino Acid had time for at least two shots. And the young man was already aiming at him.

Crane sighed. "Why Amino Acids?" he asked lightly.

"How do you know that name?" The young man seemed grudgingly pleased that Crane did know of it, like a writer meeting a stranger who has read one of his stories.

"Bitin Dog told me."

"Hah." The young man waved the gun barrel. "Step away from the table." Crane walked over and stood beside the Hanari.

"Our leader came up with the name," the young man said. "We're—we *were* a—a men's club, all pretty hip to the New Age wisdom . . . though our leader got killed last week, and now most of the guys have split. Amino comes from the Greek Ammon, the name of the Egyptian sun-god, for your information—and there are twenty amino acids that are the basis of all proteins, such as DNA, which is the currency of sexual reproduction, which we were against." He shrugged. "There were twenty of us. There are twenty cards in the Major Arcana if you throw away the Moon and the Lovers. We figured to be the psychic pool's DNA and immaculately conceive ourselves a real Fisher King, no woman needed, in the person of our leader. And after our leader was murdered, Stevie and I found Mr. Hanari, who's *already* that kind of King."

He blinked and frowned. "And would you step away from Mr. Hanari, too, please. Further than that. Sit down in the far chair. I'm perfectly willing to kill you, sir. Mr. Hanari has given us specific instructions." As Crane sat down in one of the farther chairs, the Amino Acid glanced at the slack-jawed, dully staring Hanari body. "I'm sure he'll have instructions for me in just a moment, when he's done . . . thinking."

He's empty, boy, thought Crane. He won't be speaking ever again—unless my father can throw his mind clear of his old body with his broken old brain, which he hasn't managed to do yet.

Crane glanced at Doctor Leaky, who was alternately frowning and chortling. But he *might*, Crane thought nervously, if we let him have enough time to try.

He remembered having once, while drunk, sunk in a vision down to the Archetype level below his mind and then come up through the wrong personality well and found himself in a woman's body. Maybe he could do that *intentionally* now, and come up in the Hanari body, and order this young man to throw his gun into the lake and leave. Crane closed his eyes and let his mind descend deeply, beginning to lose the mental outriggers and nets and emblems of his own individuality as he sank toward the level everyone shared.

But he found himself instead in a vivid hypnagogic dream, in which he was sunk in the darkness of the lake's deep water. He knew he was still sitting at the card table aboard his father's houseboat, he could see the paneled walls and the glowing lamps and the Hanari body standing and rocking on the carpet, but he could also see now, dimly, the walls of Siegel's Flamingo penthouse, and dark lake water beyond the aquarium-like windows, and the cupboard behind which had been concealed the shaft that led down to the basement tunnel.

Now, in the dream, the shaft led away upward instead. And a voice in his head, so faint that he couldn't be sure he wasn't imagining it, said, *You're too big now to fit. There's only a little bit of me left. I'll go.*

Thank you for helping me, Crane thought, and a moment later he was afraid the deteriorated personality out there might have caught the feelings behind the consciously projected thought: doubt, and embarrassment, and repugnance.

But the voice seemed wryly jocular: *Happy to. Be a good one, now, and one day help someone else.*

I'm grateful to you, thought Crane, more sincerely. Thank you for my family.

There was a faint flicker of associations in Crane's head: a slight bow, a touched hat, a smile.

Crane sensed the remains of the Siegel identity climbing or swimming away up the narrow shaft.

And the dream dissolved, and Crane was wholly sitting in the chair and staring at the Hanari—

—Which blinked and opened its mouth.

Crane darted a glance at Doctor Leaky, but the old man in the wheelchair was just staring at the blank television and drooling.

"Outside," said the Hanari body slowly. "Both of you."

Crane stood up and led the way out onto the breezy deck, closely followed by the Amino Acid. The sun was not yet visible over the Black Mountains, but a dazzling corona shone over the distant peaks.

Crane looked away from the brightness and saw Mavranos and Stevie sitting stiffly in deck chairs on the dock. Stevie was holding the shotgun across his knees.

"Scott Crane," said Hanari, "slowly, with your left hand, take the gun out of your belt, and drop it over the side."

At the mention of a gun, Stevie stood up and raised the shotgun and the other Amino Acid stepped back to have a clear field of fire.

Crane dragged his left palm up the tail of his shirt and tugged at the Pachmayr grips of the gun. When he had got it free of his belt, he paused.

If it's my father in the Hanari body, he thought, I should just spin and try to shoot him, and both of the Amino Acids, too.

He was cold with sweat, but he began to bend his knees in a slight crouch, and he tried to think about how he'd hike the gun to slap well back into his palm and where he'd fall after the first shot.

"Bolt-hole and hidey-hole," said Hanari softly.

That was what Siegel had said to him in the vision under the lake.

I've got to trust in somebody, Crane thought, blinking against the sting of sweat in his eyes. Shall I trust in . . . *Bugsy Siegel*?

He straightened and tossed the gun out over the rail, and it splashed into the water. He took a deep breath and let it out.

"Now you, Frank," said Hanari, "into the lake with it."

After a moment's hesitation a revolver flew past Crane's shoulder and into the water.

"Stevie," said Hanari, "bring me the shotgun."

Crane turned to the dock and saw Stevie scramble onto the deck and hand the shotgun to the purple-faced Hanari body, then step respectfully back.

Hanari hefted it and racked the slide, chambering a shell.

He pointed the gun at Frank.

"Stand over with Stevie, boy," said the baritone voice wearily. "On the dock. There's a new King, and you two have nothing to do with him."

Frank and Stevie scrambled off the boat, and the two Amino Acids stood together fearfully on the planks of the dock.

White light touched the street, and Crane looked back and was dazzled by the first sliver of the new sun over the peaks of the Black Mountains.

"Go far away," called the ghost of Benjamin Siegel through the mouth of the Art Hanari body. "Forget all these ambitions. Go!" He walked toward the two Amino Acids, and they retreated up the dock toward the parking lot.

The Hanari body followed them to the driveway and then just stood there holding the gun, staring after them as they hurried across the early-morning pavement toward the two white El Caminos parked side by side in the lot.

Still sitting in the deck chair, Mavranos stared after them, then looked around at Crane.

Crane jerked a hand at him. "Come on aboard, Arky," he called softly.

Mavranos paused in the lounge doorway and looked around the big room, from the wide green felt table to the twitching figure of Doctor Leaky in the wheelchair. The old man was asking over and over again whether anyone else smelled roses.

The table was empty. The Lombardy Zeroth cards were scattered all over the red carpet.

Crane exhaled a hoarse moan. "Help me gather 'em up," he said.

Mavranos walked over by the bar and then crouched to gather cards, and Crane got down on his hands and knees by the table and began scooping up the ones that were scattered there.

Doctor Leaky stirred in his wheelchair. "Climb up on my knee, Sonny Boy," he said.

Crane ignored him. *Two of Swords,* he thought as he picked up that card, *and here's the Ten of Cups . . .*

"'*When . . . there are gray skies . . .*'" sang Doctor Leaky.

Crane had gathered a good handful of cards, and he shoved them carelessly into his pocket to keep them from getting away, and then scrambled to another spot and started picking up more.

Finally he couldn't stand the uncompleted lyric hanging in the cool air. "'What don't you mind in the least?'" he recited, through clenched teeth.

"'*I don't mind the gray skies . . .*'" Leaky sang.

Crane crumpled more cards into his pocket and hunched his way over to another cluster of them on the carpet. The painted faces stared up at him idiotically as he scuffled them together and balled them up in his fists.

"'What do I do to them?'" he said, furious that he remembered the old routine. *Six of Cups, Ace of Sticks, the Fool . . .*

"'*You make them blue . . .*'"

Christ, Crane thought, feeling tears welling up in his eyes. "'What's my name?'" he said dutifully, his voice catching.

"'*Sonny Boy.*'"

"I've got 'em all over here," said Mavranos, standing up with two fistfuls of cards. He wasn't looking at Crane or the old man.

"Okay," Crane said, getting to his feet. He spoke levelly. "Bring them to the table here. I'll nail down the ones we've got, and then we can search for any others."

He pulled from his jeans pocket the jackknife he'd taken out of the wall of the tunnel under the Flamingo, and after Mavranos had crossed to the table and laid his cards on the green felt, and Crane had dug out of his jacket pocket the cards he had picked up, he opened the blade and pressed the point against the back of the top card. Then, reminded of the night when he had stabbed his own leg, he brought his other fist down hard onto the butt of the knife, spearing the cards.

The boat didn't shift, no rain pattered against the ports, and no voices spoke out over the lake.

The knife stood upright, its point buried in the wood under the green felt.

"There's more here and there," Mavranos said quietly, "in the corners."

"Let's get 'em." Crane crouched by a half dozen cards against the starboard molding—and he could feel Doctor Leaky's eyes on him, his father's eyes.

He looked across the room and saw the old man in the wheelchair staring at him imploringly.

"'What will friends do to you?'" asked Crane softly.

His father smiled and opened his mouth. "'*Friends may forsake me . . .*'"

"That's it for over here," said Mavranos, walking back toward the table with another handful.

"And with these," said Crane, straightening up, "I think that's the lot. Here, count 'em all, would you, Arky?" A sob was building in his throat, and he waited until he knew he could speak steadily. "I don't think I can."

"Sure."

Mavranos took Crane's cards from him, and Crane looked angrily over at his father. "'What will you let them do to you?'" he said.

"'*Let them all forsake me . . .*'"

"Seventy-eight," said Mavranos, his own voice sounding a little unsteady.

"That's it," said Crane. From his inside jacket pocket he took the second deck and laid it next to the first. He tugged the knife out of the table and began cutting all the cards up, sawing and hacking at them.

He thought he felt shiftings and resistances under the blade, muscular flexings of protest and outrage as the steel edge violated the cardboard surfaces and forcibly scraped and scored the paint, but after a couple of minutes the cards were a pile of irregular fragments.

He stood back from the table. "'What will you still have?'" he said absently.

"'*I'll still have you . . .*'" sang his father.

I suppose you will, thought Crane with bitter helplessness—the piece of me that's still a five-year-old boy, at least.

Crane gathered up the pieces. "Let's go out to the bow," he said to Mavranos. "I'll scatter them in the lake, like somebody's ashes."

"And let's be quick," Mavranos said. "I'd really like to be away from here, you know?"

Crane paused before stepping out onto the deck, for the lyric hung uncompleted in the face of all the years to come.

"'What's my name?'" he whispered.

"'Sonny Boy.'"

Half an hour later the old truck was rattling along north on Highway 95, through the desert toward the McCullough Range and Las Vegas beyond.

"And when we came back inside," said Crane, finishing the story for Nardie and Diana, "he was dead." Crane's arm was around Diana, and Oliver was squeezed against the window on Diana's left. "And even though he——" Crane sighed deeply and squeezed Diana's shoulder. "Even though he couldn't have been dead more than a minute, he was as cold as the lake water when I touched him. I cut the seat belt on the wheelchair, and then we went outside again and I threw the knife into the water. When it——"

"I'm sorry about your father," Diana said.

"I don't think you should be, at all," Crane said. "I don't think I should be, at all."

Oliver shifted, and Crane thought he was going to say something, but the boy just stared out the window.

"And," Crane went on, "when the knife was about to hit the water—you couldn't really see, with the sun glittering on the waves—I swear a *hand* stuck up out of the water and caught the knife! And then just sank back down under with hardly a ripple."

That caught Oliver's attention. He whipped his head around. "A *hand*?" he squeaked. "Like someone *alive* under the water caught it?"

"I don't know about alive," Crane told him.

"*I* still say it was a turtle," commented Mavranos from the front seat. He took a sip from his can of Coors without taking his eyes off the road. "*I* saw a *turtle* stick its neck up and catch the knife, in its mouth."

"I like Arky's version," put in Nardie.

"What about . . . Siegel?" asked Diana.

Crane shook his head. "He was still standing there when we left the boat. Didn't even look at us. And then you all heard that boom."

"I guess the verdict will be that Art Hanari, whoever he once was, committed suicide in the parking lot," said Mavranos.

"The last of the deaths," said Diana, and Crane knew she was thinking of Scat, who was expected to be released from the hospital in the next week or two.

"For a long while, at least, let's hope," Crane said. He thought about crossing his fingers, but clasped her hand instead.

And the old truck sped on up the highway in the morning sun. And in the desert all around, the Joshua trees were heavy with cream-colored blossoms, and the glowing cholla branches shaded the flowering lupine and sundrops, and in the mountains the desert bighorn sheep leaped agilely down to the fresh streams to drink.